THE KING'S BROTHER

THE KING'S BROTHER

The Second Volume of the Last Book of the Kings

H. M. Snow

iUniverse, Inc.
New York Lincoln Shanghai

The King's Brother
The Second Volume of the Last Book of the Kings

iUniverse books may be ordered through booksellers or by contacting:

iUniverse
2021 Pine Lake Road, Suite 100
Lincoln, NE 68512
www.iuniverse.com
1-800-Authors (1-800-288-4677)

ISBN-13: 978-0-595-36252-3 (pbk)
ISBN-13: 978-0-595-80697-3 (ebk)
ISBN-10: 0-595-36252-4 (pbk)
ISBN-10: 0-595-80697-X (ebk)

Printed in the United States of America

YESTERDAY: WEEPING SKIES

Through a rumble of thunder, the voice of Denei Mata-son rang out in staccato syllables: "Jarod! Jarod, come inside *now*."

"I know he's here." Young Colin sounded so helpful that anyone could tell he didn't know he was betraying his brother. "I saw him come out a little bit after supper."

Denei was losing patience. "Jarod, your father must see you. *Now!*"

That was Uncle Denei's guaranteed lure and he knew it. Jarod would never disregard his father's command, no matter how inconveniently timed. Tucked away among the thick arms of the Prince's Tree, Jarod gave another fleeting glance at the darkening ceiling of clouds that hung so close to earth that he could see them regardless of night. A spatter of rain touched his nose; almost at once it increased to a shower that saturated his clothes. In the distance, troubled voices rose and fell underneath the patter of rain. "I'm coming." Jarod climbed down to the ground.

Uncle Denei exhaled loudly. "There you are. Come along."

His absence of scolding disturbed Jarod. "What's wrong?"

"We've wasted the better part of an hour searching the house for you, an hour we can ill afford to spare. Hold your tongue until we get to the War Room. Your father will answer you as he sees fit."

Now Jarod was frightened in earnest, though he hardly showed it. His fears deepened when he met Uncle Owen in the corridor. Owen looked from Jarod to Colin and back again. "Good. They're waiting inside. Go on in."

Now that he was out of his safe tree, he heard the nasty voice in his ear again. *Perhaps you've done something terrible.* Jarod didn't question the remark consciously. Somehow he just knew he was too small to cause the kind of catastrophe that could make Uncle Owen stop smiling. He followed Denei into the War Room in silent contrition.

Kohanan relaxed when he saw them. "Sit by me, boys. We have little time."

"I'm sorry, Father," Jarod said without prompting. "I hid. I didn't know it was serious."

"We'll discuss it later, Jarod. Right now, I need you to listen." Kohanan addressed his sons as if they were already men. "The river is already to flooding-point. We have to leave this place before the waters come and wash us away."

"But Father," young Colin protested, "won't we be safer inside the walls?"

Jarod nearly batted him across the head. *Don't argue, Colin.*

Kohanan was more patient. "No, Colin. The extra water is changing the river's course. You remember the dry riverbed outside the north wall, out where we hunt sometimes? It's already full. The tunnel has flooded. We don't have any choice but to leave."

"What do you need us to do and how much time do we have?"

Every man in the room stared at Jarod. Even Denei blinked in surprise. Kohanan, once he recovered, said, "You must go to your suite and load one pack apiece. Stay close to your mother and be ready to move when we give the word. You have half an hour."

Say goodbye to your sire, the mean voice told Jarod. *You will not see him again.*

Jarod asked carefully, "When are you coming to say goodbye, Father?"

"What do you mean, Jarod?"

"You're evacuating the people. You'll be last to leave, if you still *can* leave by then."

"Don't say that," protested Colin. "He *will* come away safe."

Kohanan looked sad. "I'll come see you off. Just don't give me up for lost yet, Jarod."

"No, sir. May we be excused?" Once in his room, Jarod packed a light knapsack. Mostly, he took sturdy clothes. He also included the compass Owen had given him for his birthday and the old tin-boxed flint set that had been Denei's gift to him for no particular occasion. When he knew that no one would see him, Jarod also stuffed into his sack two of Kohanan's handkerchiefs. They still held the scent from being carried in his father's breast pocket a few days earlier. Jarod had sneaked them from his father's wardrobe.

"Mama, is it time yet?"

Jarod's ears perked at the voice. It belonged to Perrin, one of Denei's stepchildren. But it was Colin who made it out of the suite first to greet the other the children with a quiet, chastened voice. Listening, Jarod could tell that Colin was afraid. Colin hated to have his routine broken by anything, let alone a natural disaster. He liked his predictable books. Jarod knew this as only one exact twin could know another: without needing to understand it.

"Colin," their mother Camille was saying as Jarod stepped into the hall, "I don't know. Are you sure you can carry all that?"

Jarod looked at his brother's knapsack. It strained its seams to hold everything Colin had put inside it. The corner of a book poked out from under the flap. Jarod shook his head.

"Of course I can," Colin was protesting.

"No, you can't. Give it here." Jarod reached out a hand.

"No. You'll toss it all out."

"I promise I won't." He pulled his brother's overloaded pack to the floor. "Watch." Jarod reached inside and started shifting the contents without looking. Little by little, the bag's shape started to relax until the flap lay neatly shut with no corners protruding. "See?"

"But it still might be too heavy," their mother pointed out.

"I'll help him."

In the hush that followed, a little hand tugged at Jarod's sleeve. "Help me, too, please."

Only then did Jarod look around to the faces that surrounded them. There was Aunt Sylva, carrying her baby Lyndall on one hip and holding her daughter Phoebe by the hand. Behind her stood Riana, Denei's wife, surrounded by her three children as she held Denei's son Nässey in her arms. The request had come from Ivy, Riana's younger daughter. She was a year older than Jarod, but shorter by a handsbreadth. Jarod could have shrugged her off, but everyone was watching. "All right. Give me your pack."

This one was almost as unwieldy as Colin's, but the contents were more pliable. Jarod dumped the lot onto the floor and started to roll all the garments into tight logs of fabric. The soft toys were stacked neatly, with their heads alternating left and right, and tamped down. He squeezed the flap shut. "That's the best I can do. Your stuff is too fluffy to pack nice."

"Thank you, Jarod." She did not take his gruffness amiss, at least. Jarod hated it when girls started crying over nothing.

Kohanan approached soon after that. He wore his casual training-field garb as if he were on his way to drills. Only the creases around his mouth and the compression of his lips signaled otherwise. He scanned the group, letting his gaze linger longest on Colin. "Are we ready?" Kohanan asked in an almost normal voice. He let a little smile play around his mouth. Jarod saw it almost reach his eyes—enough to convince Colin, but not quite easy enough to be genuine.

Camille answered in a matching tone, "As ready as can be."

Finally, after half an eternity, Jarod saw his father's eyes turn in his direction. Instead of speaking, Kohanan motioned for the bunch to proceed toward the courtyard. He trailed behind, falling into step with Jarod. One long arm slipped around the boy's shoulders; even at eight years old, Jarod was tall enough that Kohanan hardly had to bend down to squeeze him. "Jarod," his father began, "I need you to do something for me."

By then, they had fallen far enough behind the rest for Jarod to respond aloud. "Anything I can, Father."

"You know the wilds better than the other younglings do, Jarod. That means you're the responsible one, and that means you can look out for them and show them how things work out there. Understand? I'm giving you an important job here, since I can't be there to do it myself."

"Aye, sir."

"Good. I'll rest easier knowing that you're looking out for the family." And Kohanan sounded as though he meant it, to Jarod's surprise.

*   *   *   *

"Don't!" Jarod doled out his words of warning with miserly care.

"What am I doing this time?" His brother was eager to know what he had done to cause Jarod's scowl. He had begun taking Jarod's every admonition as seriously as if it came from their father's mouth, much to the adults' bemusement.

Instead of a reply, Jarod gave his brother a long stick. Colin stood there with the stick in hand, doing nothing, so Jarod added, "Prod the leaves. Vipers like such places."

Behind him, Camille and Sylva walked together in companionable silence. One nudged the other as the little girl Ivy hunted around and claimed a long, willowy stick. The two women watched her prod every leaf-filled hollow she passed.

Then they started when the girl shrieked in alarm. One of her proddings had produced results. A striped green and blue serpent raised its head, baring four curved fangs at the girl in a silent grimace. Amber liquid dripped from the upper fangs. Riana, the girl's mother, cried out softly and started forward. A loud "Stop!" from Jarod brought her up short. Faster than any of them could follow, Jarod lashed out with his walking-stick. Instead of striking the serpent, the stick hovered just in front of its mouth, parallel like a fence rail. The serpent clamped its jaws around the stick, and in one smooth gesture, Jarod flicked the stick into the air to fling the creature far into the undergrowth. The frozen watchers breathed again. Ivy's brother Perrin spoke first. "Jarod, Jarod, why didn't you kill the creature?"

Jarod gave him a pitying glance. "It's good for catching vermin." Then he walked onward as if nothing had happened.

*   *   *   *

They had hoped to find shelter on the king's nearest estate, a small country manor named Takra House. Much farther north and a little westward across the plains, the first low mountains darkened the horizon. Jarod knew that the sea lay somewhere beyond. He was disappointed that he could not see it, but that was to be expected. They were too far from Takra House to see *it*, either. "One more night in the tent," Jarod's mother said, trying to be cheerful for the children's sake. "We'll see Takra tomorrow."

Camp was a dismal place made even more so because of the eternal dampness and the invisible biting insects that plagued the refugees. Camille and Sylva assigned Jarod the task of settling their own families while they mingled among the rest of the people to see that everything was all right. For a time, Jarod focused on setting up his and his brother's tent in the hopes of boring the small, hateful voice to silence. Audune, the shepherd-giant who owned the voice, began to pinch him cruelly, trying to make him react so that others took notice of how unnatural Jarod was. Jarod knew the motive behind this torment, so he kept a stoic countenance. In time, Audune gave up his game and waited for a more opportune moment.

The last company from Halimeda did not catch up with them until late the next day. Camille had received word of the king's approach and had chosen to linger on the way, with Takra House tantalizingly visible in the distance. While they waited, Jarod could no longer sustain the pretense of normalcy. He retreated to the edge of the firelight to hide himself. The dim music of horns roused him from the invective that Audune poured into his thoughts. Moments later, a distant voice alerted the rest of the people. "They've come!" Everyone but Jarod scrambled up to meet the last group from the beleaguered city. Jarod stayed where he was, suddenly weakened with relief. Before long, he saw the face he had been watching for all along: his father was safe. Jarod edged up to the circle of firelight. *If I can get close enough, Audune will have to leave me alone.*

Subtle though his entrance was, it did not go unnoticed. Kohanan spotted him at once. "Jarod, come closer." The king's face was worn under the grime that covered him, but his eyes remained as sharp as ever. When his son stood at attention before him, Kohanan smiled. "Well done. How did it go?"

Jarod swept a gesture over the assembly, as if to say, *All accounted for.* What he said was, "Here they are, like I promised."

"And here I am, like I promised." Kohanan searched his son's face.

In the stillness, Uncle Owen asked, "So, did I miss any good stories?"

All the children except for Jarod clamored for his attention. Young Ivy won out with the story of her rescue from the serpent, a tale aided and elaborated upon by the other children. Throughout the recounting, Jarod stayed quiet. "That was good work there, Jarod," his father said softly, for Jarod's ears alone. "Quick thinking, quick acting."

Surprised, Jarod said, "It was my job. You told me so." But the praise warmed his face with a light blush of gratification. For an instant, he nearly was able to forget the small voice and simply be eight years old, like his brother.

KOHANAN

Halimeda never recovered. What little could be salvaged from the flooding had to be removed by boat from the ruins and transferred to the country house called Takra. Takra was considered by everyone a pretty house, but far too small and inconvenient for permanent residence. It sat surrounded by Pamirsi and Nandevi farmland, with scarcely acreage enough to support its own needs, let alone the needs of the settlement that must inevitably spring up to create a new crown city. It was the dearest wish of Berhus son of Carthus, the new young Pamirsi patriarch, to welcome the king and his family into suitable quarters in Chliaros, his own seat of power. There the royal family would have every luxury, ample room and company—but, as other clans' leaders pointed out in remarks of varying subtlety, no freedom. Promises of diplomatic immunity withered in the face of a shockingly hierarchical Pamirsi society, so none of the other clans agreed to Berhus Pamirsi's offer.

The king listened patiently to every argument, but when all had been said, he chose to remain in little Takra House. When the surrounding Pamirsi landowners refused to surrender any part of their land, calling it their ancestral birthright and setting a higher price on this legacy than on their vows to crown and Tree, Kohanan sacrificed his own lands immediately around the house in order that representatives from the other clans could take up residence near him without having to submit to Pamirsi rule. In response to this, Berhus immediately began construction of a sister city not two leagues west-southwestward. He named it Carthae after his father and made it bigger, grander, and more prosperous than the new settlement, which was called simply King's City, could hope to become.

Kohanan seemed not to notice Carthae at all. He built his walls and organized the new King's City with a practicality born of his humble upbringing. There were no wide, gracious boulevards or monuments. The only park lay within the new wall that encircled Takra House proper. The city lanes were laid out economically; the houses were built tall and narrow for the most part. To fit his life to these more restricted conditions, Kohanan reduced his household staff, dispersing the extra servants to other properties around the kingdom.

Appalled by what they saw as a deliberate attempt to disgrace the king, the other clans united for once. As a result, the small gates of King's City saw far more tithe-traffic than Halimeda's many splendid gates had ever witnessed. Many speculated over Kohanan's reasons for staying on in such cramped quarters, suffering such indignities, but he himself seemed unaware that he had lost or suffered anything by the move. Eventually, the kingdom accustomed itself to these circumstances and ceased to wonder. There were other matters of more concern: natural disasters of various kinds abounded in the years after the flood, claiming one of the king's twin sons as their victim; and once the natural disasters had finished battering them, a stretch of plague years robbed the kingdom of more than twelve thousand souls. Among the fallen were the kingdom's two most beloved ladies, Lady Sakiry and the queen, who had labored tirelessly among the sick, only to succumb to the illness themselves one right after the other. Immediately afterward, the greatest blow fell: without warning, Kohanan abdicated and forsook the kingdom altogether, taking with him only Byram son of Solam as a companion.

After this, it was no longer any wonder that the crown stayed in Takra House. The young new king, Colin son of Kohanan, had grown to manhood in King's City and knew no other home. At once he proved himself a good king, winning widespread affection for the decisive and compassionate way he led the kingdom after the plague passed. Colin was a likable young man; he had married a demure Massifi lass named Selena. They produced a fine daughter, Maia. The kingdom had its royal family again and believed it could afford to let the past tragedies fade into their rightful place—the past. The present, after all, held more than its share of troubles.

One night, in the dark corridors of Takra House, a clock had just finished chiming twice when heavy booted feet thudded across the carpets, announcing the unexpected arrival of the general. Denei Mata-son strode past the pair of dozing guards, waking them on his way to the royal suites. He rapped sharply on the king's door. "Colin. Get dressed and come, now."

In moments, the king emerged and followed Denei without a word.

They met up with Owen at the gate of the monument grove. He stood much like a pale marble sculpture himself, with the firelight flickering against his skin. He didn't move, not even when Colin spoke his name. Following the older man's stricken gaze, Colin stared into the blaze that lit the grove. It was a huge fire, dazzlingly bright but in no danger of spreading. At first, he didn't comprehend the meaning behind it. Then his eyes adjusted to the dancing glare. Something was different about the grove. The fire must have been deliberately set among the monuments dedicated to the Keeper kings. A pungent, exotic odor of incense wafted from it. The fire had been blazing for some time, judging by the extent of the ashes. The pop of embers rang out harshly in the night. Colin, moving forward with difficulty, stumbled once on the dark lawn before coming at last to the object that had so engrossed Owen. A small stone statue threw its shadow towards them. It was new to the grove, not carved from native stone but from hematite polished to an exquisite sheen. The statue, a piece of excellent workmanship, depicted a tree encircled by a crown. Its squared base wore a single word: *Kohanan*.

"How did this get here? Who did all of this?" Colin demanded hoarsely.

Owen couldn't respond, so Denei said, "We don't know yet. I came to you at once."

Eerily, one of the dogs kenneled beyond the orchard howled. The mournful sound sent a shiver through all three men as they returned their gaze to the fire.

*   *   *   *

Dew still sparkled on the awnings when Owen entered the market sector the following morning. He took his time. Nothing pressed him for his urgent attentions, and he had long since learned that at such a time, he had to make the most of the chance. Even the spring air smelled cleaner than usual. No one else was out yet that morning, save an occasional shop assistant out sweeping. The sun had yet to top the city walls and give the signal for the workday to begin.

Something about Doran and Phoebe's cottage attracted Owen, more than simply its dear occupants. Many folk would probably have laughed to hear that the wealthy, influential Lord Sakiry, who had the ancient royal blood in his veins, wished he could live in such a house. It was not a very charming cottage, neither pretty nor whimsical. It was just a cottage, plain and small. It had a commonplace slat fence around an unremarkable lawn with a straight gravel path to the front door. There was nothing about the cottage that would draw anyone, let alone royalty. And yet Owen found it irresistible, and only he knew why. It reminded him of Sylva. She had been much like that little cottage—plain compared to other women he had known, never showy, always hating undue attention, always ranking herself as lowly even after years of marriage to a prince. But it was exactly that which had always drawn Owen to her. Sylva's humility still challenged him, even years after her death. Her gentleness haunted him all the more as news of Kohanan's death bore down so heavily upon him. For that reason he had left his rooms at Takra House early in the day and walked rather than rode across the city. He felt the need to go humbly, as if the manner of his going drew him close to her.

Rather than approach the front door at once, Owen let himself in through the wooden gate—never locked—and circled around the cottage to the backyard. He found a trio of cenotaphs there in a corner, half-hidden by shrubs and flowers. Only the one farthest on the left interested him. It was Sylva's. Owen knelt down in the damp grass, heedless of his clean trousers. His fingers touched the cenotaph's face, traced its stone cheek, and lingered against its cold lips. Stricken mute just as he opened his mouth to speak, Owen merely leaned his head against the chilly statue and breathed. He fought for control. One shuddery sob escaped despite his efforts. Then a pair of hands took him by the shoulders. Owen swallowed. "Morning, Doran."

"Come inside with me." Doran Clary-son nearly had to lift his father-in-law in order for the older man to gain his feet. The healer was always gentle, but his brow creased now with concern at the sight of Owen's face. He said nothing more, but slung Owen's arm over his shoulders as they walked to the cottage door.

Owen looked up from the ground to find his daughter Phoebe watching him with unusually grave eyes. He was especially thankful for these two today because they asked no questions. He let Doran seat him in the parlor, but when the younger man tried to take his pulse, Owen waved him off. "Never mind that." He was recovering his poise already. "I'm all right."

"What's wrong, Father?"

He blinked away the rush of tears that moistened his eyes just when he thought he had mastered the impulse to cry. "We got word last night at the palace. Kohanan is dead."

They said nothing at first. Phoebe leaned her head against her father's shoulder, gave him a firm hug and whispered, "I'm sorry, Father." Over her head, Doran took a deep breath, not entirely steady. His eyes met Owen's for a searching moment. "What happened?"

"We don't know." Slowly, Owen described the scene in the monument grove. "I don't know what to do about Colin. I've been up with him all night. He wouldn't sleep after we found…. He didn't break down, either, not once. It changed him. He has such a grim look about him now. I think he…he's been working all these years with the notion at the back of his mind that Kohanan would come back and take over again." Owen gave a hard, humorless laugh. "I always knew it was a fool's hope—that Kohanan would come back and rescue us again, just like he did at the first. But what can I say? 'I told you so'? It wouldn't help." *What a waste. What an utter waste.* Owen forced his mind away from that thought. "I wish he'd never left."

Doran's eyes lit with understanding. "I think I understand Colin's position, though. All my life, I thought of Kohanan like that—after what he did for me, I mean."

Owen paused. Phoebe's husband Doran had been born in the outland village where immortals had hidden Kohanan as a child to save him from the false seer Phelan. When the village had relocated under threat of Kavahri attack, Kohanan had saved the toddler Doran from certain death, and from that moment Doran's parents became Kohanan's most devoted subjects. They had moved to the Second Kingdom when Kohanan was revealed as the rightful king. Years later, Doran had won his place as Sylva's apprentice and married Owen's daughter. "I owe him for that," Owen said. "I don't know what we would do without you."

The sudden compliment made Doran smile. "Is there any way to find out what happened to him? It doesn't seem right, not knowing. There must be some way to learn how he died."

"Find whoever put up the monument," Phoebe said patiently—then ruined the illusion by adding, "*Obviously.* Even *I* knew that much, dearling. You must be slow in waking up this morning. Here, take some tea."

"It doesn't look like that person is in any great hurry to make himself known," replied Owen. "But I'll ask around, all the same. Colin needs to know, if only to enable him to let go of his father finally." He sat back with his eyes closed, listening to the comforting sounds of the cottage and his children. He could almost hear Sylva walking among them.

Phoebe was nothing like her mother. She had Owen's coloring, his poise, and a bubbly, empty-headed manner to cover over the same keen mind. In all things, she was her father's daughter, and yet she never failed to make him think of Sylva. They had been inseparable. Doran had brought them closest together, and he reminded Owen of Sylva even more than Phoebe did. It was Sylva who had made Doran what he was; no one else would have ever entertained the notion that a man, no matter how gifted, should become a fully trained *practicing* public healer. He had been first Sylva's shadow, then her assistant, then her partner and, at her death, her successor as chief healer. It was Sylva too who had gently nudged her young apprentice toward Phoebe, knowing how Phoebe had been crazy for Doran from childhood. On her deathbed, Sylva had gazed at Owen's face for a long time, and then turned her dulled green eyes to Doran and charged him with the task of watching over her grief-shattered husband.

Owen sighed deeply, without opening his eyes. "Doran, you'll be late."

The younger man's voice answered him evenly, "They can wait." By this time, Phoebe had wandered to another part of the cottage, leaving the two men facing each other. "You lost your friend and kinsman today. That's hard for any man to bear. I made the promise, Father. I mean to keep it."

"I've never been able to talk you out of anything yet, but that doesn't mean I can't try."

After a companionable silence, Doran asked, "How did the general take it?"

"He went home to his wife." *As I wished I could have done,* he added privately. "But I saw his face before he went. It crushed him, Doran, and not just hearing of Kohanan. I can't believe he still hoped so strongly that Kohanan and Jarod would be restored to us. He really believed." Owen shook his head. "But as soon as he realized that Kohanan wouldn't be returning, he looked so devastated."

"I wouldn't have guessed." Doran paused. "Why?"

"Jarod was always his favorite, I suppose, and not just for Ivy's sake. He favored the boy, though I never understood why. Perhaps that *is* why. Both of them had that same disconcerting, inscrutable nature. As for Kohanan—Denei made it his personal duty to protect him always, for his father's sake and then for Kohanan's own sake. They were closer friends than most people guessed." Owen stood. "I'm going to see him. He ought to be up and dressed by now."

"Are you sure?"

Owen smiled wearily. "I'm well enough, Doran. Don't worry about me. We have to stick together, Denei and me. We're the only ones left out of the old crowd." But a stray thought arrested him even as he spoke: *What about Byram? What became of him?*

✻   ✻   ✻   ✻

Echoes from the open door warned Owen that he should head to the war room, but he stalled at his desk a few minutes longer. Before him lay the most recent copy of the Book of the Kings, open to almost its last page. "What would you say to me?" he murmured, speaking not to the book itself but to the one whose hand last wrote in it more than seven years ago—to Kohanan. "He asks for counsel, but what do I tell him? If you were here…" Owen stopped himself short. "But you aren't. We're lost, Kohanan, and have been since you left us in favor of that…that pointless quest…" Again, he shut his mouth tightly. "Maybe *you* knew what you were doing, but I don't." After another moment, his frustrated musings came to an abrupt end when Denei's voice addressed him from the open doorway, saying, "Are you coming, or do I tell them you're indisposed?" Owen thought he saw disapproval flickering deep in his elder brother's eyes.

They were the last to arrive at the New Chamber of Warriors. The marshals had gathered and divided into their habitual factions already. To the king's left, Third Marshal Simon Miklei-son listened with polite interest to the rambling discourse of Owen's son Lyndall, who served as Senior Counsel. Lyndall had few areas of expertise, so when he found someone who would sit still long enough to listen to him ramble on about the import market for rare books or armor, he gladly expounded at length. Across from them, Second Marshal Jonas Denei-son, commonly dubbed Nässey, rifled through a stack of documents as if oblivious to the others' presence. Doran, now in his role as first marshal, engaged in sympathetic conversation with the king. Owen was almost sorry to take his place between the two men. He gave his son-in-law a nod of gratitude when the king was not looking.

Colin Kohanan-son cleared his throat to interrupt the various activities around the table. Once he had the attention of all, he spoke. "First item for consideration, gentlemen, is our recent run-in with the marauders. I think we would do best to begin with our esteemed third marshal. I myself have only one question: what went wrong?"

This was the only part of the meeting that had intrigued Owen. He watched as the youngest of the marshals stood in acknowledgement of the question. "My lord, there is no simple answer to that question. I wish there were. Part of the fault lay in the intelligence received. We anticipated an attack, but not in such numbers, and we were ill-equipped to meet it, let alone defeat it. Since the previous encounter with them, they have built up their numbers—something we failed to do. That, perhaps, is the most sizable failure on our part. Your armies are weak, my lord. I don't fault my colleague," Simon bowed toward Denei's son Nässey, "for any fault in his Academy programs. We have skilled warriors; we simply don't have enough of them."

"I believe we discussed this before, Marshal, to no avail. There is no need for any expansion of Academy programs. Those who pass through Nässey's schools are meant to be officers and advisors, not common soldiers. But enough about that for now, since it's unlikely we'll come to an agreement on it. You mentioned faulty intelligence. Who is at fault there? How can we remedy the lack?"

"That, my lord, is not wholly my province." Simon bowed courteously to the general.

Denei stood, leaning on the table, but he made no sign that he noticed the third marshal's implied derision. "My lord, I can answer your question, but I take no pleasure in the answer. We have a spy, perhaps more than one, within the ranks of our reconnaissance. I knew of one. I am not yet sure if he acted alone."

With grim amusement, Owen noticed that he was not the only one to hear Denei's odd use of past tense. The young third marshal, though he made little outward indication, stiffened in his chair. His brown eyes sharpened, but apart from a lightning glance to the king, Simon kept his attention fixed on Denei, who had not paused in his report.

At its end, Colin said, "Fine, fine. Thank you. The question remains, gentlemen: how will we prevent this kind of debacle from happening again? You've had four days to consider. You must have come up with some inkling of a plan, amongst the six of you."

No one made a sound. Owen drew his conclusions from the others' expressions. *Simon has only one horse to run and he knows that he has run it almost to death. Denei is in almost the same position on the other side of the issue. Lyndall— bless him—hasn't anything useful to say, as usual, and Nässey wants to stay out of it altogether. As for Doran...*Owen smiled a little at the younger man, who watched him with concern. *No, my headache isn't back, Doran. I'm fine.* Sitting at the king's right hand, Owen had only Colin's profile to gauge. His heart sank at the bitterness he saw in the downturn of Colin's mouth. *Ah, Kohanan, why did you leave him?*

"In that case, this meeting is useless. We'll reconvene in two days. I hope by that time someone has come up with an idea."

The Cabinet stood in unison as the king trudged out of the war room. Owen met Denei's eyes. The general tipped his head slightly toward the east wing hallway, where Colin had just disappeared. Owen nodded once. As the others scattered, the two brothers conferred in lowered voices. "But do you think I'd make it worse?" Denei asked. "You know we haven't been on the best of terms lately. Maybe you ought to go by yourself."

"So long as you don't start harping on his choice of third marshal again, we'll do fine. He needs you to stand with him right now."

"It *was* a terrible choice, and you know it."

"I know it, Colin knows it, we all know it *now*—but what's done is done. Leave it alone for now."

They found the king in his office, his elbows scrunching the papers on his desk into disarray as he hunched forward with his head in his hands. At their entrance, he dropped his hands and started sorting and straightening the rumpled documents with an air of nonchalance that fooled no one. He refused to look up until they had both settled into the chairs in front of the desk. Then he grew defensive. "Well...I'm just guessing here, but I suppose Denei came to find fault with my third marshal again?"

Denei did not hesitate. "Stating the obvious is Owen's specialty, not mine."

"Careful," Owen retorted. "Your sense of humor is showing." A glance at Colin stilled Owen's mirth and triggered pity in him instead. "Listen, Colin, no matter what we differ on...no matter how we've disagreed, we're still family. When you need us, we're at your disposal."

"I know I haven't served you as well as I should, Colin," Denei chimed.

The king's face softened into a reluctant smile. "It's not your fault, Uncle. If there were any candidates truly fit to choose, you would have made your choice. I'm glad you're holding on in spite of it all."

"If Denei retired, he would drive Riana mad within a month," Owen quipped.

Out of habit, Denei ignored his brother's remark. "I'm not in my prime. That hurts more than just my reputation. It's causing you unneeded grief, and for that I apologize. Twenty years ago, I could've pulled a victory even out of the wretched circumstances I faced last week."

"You have a high regard for your prime," his brother countered. "No one could have pulled a victory out of that fiasco. You were set up. Something about it smells in the highest. What did you mean when you said you 'knew' of a spy, while we're on the subject? What shouldn't we know about that?"

Denei made little of it. "I may not be in my prime, Owen, but when a man chooses to stand and fight to the death rather than give himself up, I can still make an adequate showing."

"What happened?" Colin demanded, more than half in admiration.

"He thought that only an old man stood between him and his freedom...and he was right, after a fashion. No, Owen, I didn't have any of the guards with me. Truth be told, I didn't know which to take with me. Whatever is going on, it runs a good deal deeper than we thought. Who knows what other quarters it has infected? I wouldn't be surprised...I would hate to think it, but I have no choice...it's possible, Colin, though I have no proof..." Denei sighed. "Some of your own guards are involved."

Owen stiffened. He knew without asking that Denei was in earnest. "How do you know?"

"I said already, I have no proof. Perhaps I'm growing too easily alarmed in my old age."

"If you're uneasy," said Colin, "there must be a cause. Go on. What has alarmed you?"

"I have nothing better to go on than feelings. At times, something in a look or a motion makes me think that, had I only been a little quicker, I might have seen something important. But I'm never quick enough. I've thought of drawing one of them aside for...for a talk."

"Like you did with the spy?"

Denei acknowledged his brother's question-cum-rebuke with a pensive shake of his head. "Not like that, no. I thought of approaching Rowan first, but then I feared that I might put him at risk if they knew that he suspected anything. If he did suspect one of them, he would have said something by now. Then I thought of questioning one of the lieutenants; they're closer to the rest than a commander or a captain would be. If they're that close, I reckoned they might well be involved too—and I'd never before noticed how hard it is to find any of the lieutenants alone."

The silence that filled the king's private office was morose. Owen looked from his brother to his liege. Both wore strangely identical expressions of melancholy and reminiscence. He thought he knew why. "No new information on the bonfire?"

"Nothing, but if Denei is right, I can't trust the men investigating it. I'll never learn anything about...about Father's death, not at this rate."

"Then we need to consult an outsider." Then Owen had a spark of an idea. "I think I know a fellow to try."

"Another of your collection? You certainly do collect strange friends, Uncle."

"I think Denei and I should call on him this afternoon, before the wake tonight." Hearing a cue in those words, Denei got up and stood over Owen, impatient to be on his way. Owen rose also, but hesitated long enough to reach a hand toward Colin. "Listen...once, when your father and I were in trouble, it really looked as if we wouldn't see the other side of it. The thought that kept me going was that, in seven hundred years, our line has never failed. Not once. I told him that, and it turned out to be true. Somehow, we will overcome this. Try to remember that."

"I've read my own history, Owen. The line continues, but that's no guarantee that you or I will. Jarod didn't; Father didn't. Why should I hope to succeed where they failed?"

Once they were outside, Denei nudged his brother with an elbow, meaning to reassure. "Nothing you could have said would have improved him. He's turned moody these days."

"I'm glad they're going on with Maia's masquerade ball all the same. Maybe it'll help Colin throw off his gloom." Owen sighed. "I can't help thinking that he has been working all these years on the assumption that Kohanan was coming back. I miss the old cheerful Colin. The truth of it is…he reminds me somewhat of Jarod these days."

"He's nothing like Jarod was."

Owen glanced at him, surprised at the force behind the remark. "You say that with certainty…and not a little vehemence. I meant no aspersion."

"I apologize."

"No, you don't," Owen retorted. "You never apologize. You're just trying to avoid the subject by heading me off. It won't work."

"I'm too old to bicker with you, Owen."

"Then don't. Why did it bother you—my remark, that is?"

Denei didn't reply until the end of the block. When he did, he said nothing about the subject at hand. "Are we walking all the way?"

"I'll call for a carriage if you like, but it isn't far. We'll go slowly."

"I'm not sunk that far into decay. This friend of yours—you never gave his name."

"Just as you never answered my question."

"The difference is," Denei pointed out, "the longer we keep walking, the nearer I get to finding out what I want to know."

"Another instance of the world's injustice. All right. I know an immigrant fellow who owns the most successful curiosity shop in the kingdom. I happen to be one of his most devoted patrons. Besides possessing a shrewd eye for quality, he also has connections not usually found within our borders. I've never asked for details." Owen pointed. "That's the place."

Denei cast a dubious look over the building. "The most successful?"

Like the rest of King's City, it lacked the patina one could have found in the lowest cottage of old Halimeda. Owen suffered a twinge of regret for the ruined city and all the history layered into its streets. King's City was still brash and new after more than twenty-five years' worth of wear. "It may not look like much," he admitted, "but wait until you're inside. Tyrell imports from everywhere." He crossed the street a step or so ahead of his brother so that he could have the pleasure of seeing the look on Denei's face upon entering the cool dimness of the shop.

As it was, Owen was crestfallen at the reaction Denei produced. He strode into the midst of the shop with his hands clasped loosely behind his back and surveyed the merchandise with a dispassionate, appraising eye. Before either could make an attempt at conversation, they were interrupted by a smooth, accented voice that addressed them from nearby. "You honor my poor shop once again, Lord Sakiry. Yet I think—yes, I believe that you would take more pleasure in a simple conversation than in any of my wares this day. Will you follow me? We shall be far more comfortable upstairs."

As they climbed a dark, tightly twisting stair behind the silhouette of Tyrell the curiosity merchant, Owen risked a backward glance to ask his brother something. A flood of light drove all questions from his thoughts as it lit Denei in time to capture his face as it was transfigured by a look of awe. Owen turned.

"Welcome to my meager dwelling." The shop owner, a smallish brown-skinned man with slender hands, stood as if deliberately posed under an exquisite chandelier wrought in the form of a cascade of cut-glass vines. Clusters of small round candles served as its fruit. Tyrell swept his hand toward the room and its contents as if they were of little worth. "Please, treat my home as if it were your own. May I provide you with anything? My cupboard is small but well-stocked."

"Nothing at the moment," Owen replied, seeing that Denei was in no state to respond. Owen himself could hardly take his eyes from the room's furnishings. "Why have I never been invited up here before? You, my friend, have been taking the cream and leaving the rest of us with…with little better than water!" He held out his hand for the merchant to grip. "How do you do these days, Tyrell?"

"I do well, my lord. Please, sit here, General. Your visit is an unexpected honor."

Denei wrenched his gaze away from the furnishings. His scrutiny of the man Tyrell was acute. "Unexpected? If you looked for nothing more than a usual shop visit, why invite us up?"

"I only said that *your* presence was unexpected. I have been waiting for Lord Sakiry for some time now…shall we say, for two days? Yours was not the only house to receive a strange visitor that night. Now I must insist. Please, take your seats. Our conference may be of some duration, and it will be better endured in physical comfort. Yes, my lord, I anticipate discomfort to come from this meeting. Such is the nature of truth—would you not say as much, General? It did not please you to learn that you may have misplaced your trust in those nearest to the king."

"How did you—"

Tyrell held up a slender hand to hush Denei. "Ah! But we must begin in the proper place, would you not agree? The proper beginning, in this instance, lies several years in the past. How many years, I do not know precisely. I had not the pleasure of claiming citizenship at that time. Perhaps you may correct me in this. If I tell you that the departure of the king's father is our proper beginning, you may disagree, yet so it must be. Then again, perhaps the beginning came further back than that. After all, had the king's brother never disappeared under such clouded circumstances, the king's father would have never chosen to take his fateful journey."

This time, it was Owen who interrupted. "Why do you call it fateful?"

"As a master storyteller, my lord, you should know the proper way to unfold the events of a tale. Please." Tyrell gave him a gently reproachful look. "I continue. Had the king's father never journeyed in search of his lost son, he would have never met a certain person. So much turns on the loss of a son! Both of you owe much to that loss. You may not know your debt, but it is both real and considerable. One may say without embellishment that lords and common men in every land owe much to that loss. I have been empowered to tell you as much as I know.

"The beginnings, you yourselves know best: how the floods begat drought and the drought begat the great fires and the great fires swept away the king's twin brother. He was given up as forever lost in the thoughts of all but two men. One of those was his father. Upon the untimely death of his queen, King Kohanan declared his intention of forsaking both crown and country in search of his lost son. My lord, you quarreled with your cousin when he made this decision. You saw no purpose in his journey. You called it—what is the phrase? Ah, yes—a *pointless gesture*. Still he pursued his course. You saw him go and knew that he meant to not return, be his journey successful or unsuccessful. The report of his death did not distress you as greatly as it did the king. You had resigned yourself to it from the beginning.

"Your response, General, was quite opposed to your brother's. You approved the king's journey. Moreover, it is reported in certain circles that were so sure of the success of his venture that you wrote a letter for King Kohanan to give to his lost son. I find it curious that you have shown far more interest in the messenger who brought you the report of Kohanan's death, instead of seeking clarification of the message itself."

"The message was clear enough," Denei answered austerely. "The messenger was not."

Tyrell permitted himself a smile to match Denei's dry tone. "You speak as an astute and experienced campaigner, General. The reproach has found its target. I shall return to my tale at once. It may be that this journey is our proper beginning, but only its end concerns me now. He may not have found precisely what he sought, yet he found something. In his last days, Kohanan met a man. Does the name Orlan hold any meaning for you?"

Owen shook his head, but Denei looked uncertain. "I have heard it. I don't recall where."

"It is a curious name, Orlan—always simply Orlan, without patronymic, without epithet of any kind. One need only say 'Orlan,' and see what results! In years past, that word was sufficient cause for dread. Villages have been emptied merely by the sound of that name. Yes, it is a curious name. It has grown all the more curious, for now it is a name without an owner. I know not how Kohanan worked this miracle. It has been said that he was a man of powers beyond the mere mortal. Who knows? What is known is this: in his final days, Kohanan met the man named Orlan, and from that fateful meeting onward, this violent man of intrigue, this infamous warrior, he abjured his curious name and swore an oath of enduring loyalty to the Second Kingdom. It was he who brought you word of Kohanan's death two nights ago, without revealing his presence to you. It is he who has spared you the full strength of the marauder prince these three years following the death of the king's father."

"What do you mean by that?" Denei demanded, at the same moment that Owen asked, "Yes, but who is he?"

"Worthy queries, both of them, but I may answer only the general's with any accuracy. The other would be composed of rumor and speculation, I fear. No one knows the man. He owns neither to ancestry nor to heritage. When he yet wore the name Orlan, he was an intimate of the marauder prince Malin Fohral'aku, Lightning-vengeance as he has been dubbed in his own tongue—this same Malin who has plagued your borders. Some have said that he who was Orlan is Malin's son. Some have said that he was a fallen spirit made flesh, for his prowess and his ruthlessness were beyond measure. It is said that he sees all that happens in the world, and if he does not know of it, then it is not worth knowing. But none of this is known with certainty. What is known about him, I will divulge: it was he who led the Thousand Companies of Fohral'aku during the height of their power and built up the raiders' territory to its present extent, and now it is he who has taken steps to destroy the very dominion he won for his former liege. Fohral'aku commands thousands upon thousands of rogue warriors. He holds many lesser warlords in thrall as well. Had he descended upon you in the fullness of his strength, none of your warriors would have returned to tell of their failure, but he will never attack you in such numbers while your champion keeps vigil at your gates. This answers your question, General."

With the cessation of Tyrell's voice, a hush entered the sumptuous chamber. Owen gazed at his brother, unwilling to speak before Denei had considered the information and given his opinion. At length, Denei did so. "You call him our champion and say he swears loyalty. Why does he not come forward to speak for himself? You said it yourself—you expected Owen to come. *He* must have told you of our need for this information. Why not tell us himself?"

"Who has fathomed the workings of his mind? What you say is true. He forewarned me of your questions and gave me leave to tell you what little I know. Why he does not approach you himself, I do not know. He has chosen to conduct his business in this way. That is all that matters. When he wishes to contact either of you in person, he will. I believe," Tyrell mused, half to himself, "if he does, he will approach you, General. You are of his own breed, in one sense."

"If I had to contact him, how would I go about it?"

"You may send any messages to me, General. I will direct them onward as needed."

"Do you have writing materials here?" Denei insisted. "I'll leave a letter before I go."

"As you will, General. I do not know when I may offer it to him, or when he may answer it. He has many concerns to occupy his thoughts, your own not least among them. It may be that he will choose to answer through a different courier, for I know very well that I am not his only contact in the kingdom. You must be alert for his answer. However it may come, you may be sure that it will come in a way or at a time least expected."

KING'S WAKE

Simon Miklei-son, a product of generations of illiterate Nandevi farmers, gazed around in satisfaction at his luxurious library. Rich leather bindings faced outward from the shelves on three sides of the high-ceilinged room, casting back the light from the tall windows in a muted gleam. This was, to Simon's knowledge, the most comprehensive collection of scholarly and arcane works assembled within the bounds of the entire kingdom. He had money enough to indulge his passion by ordering codices, manuscripts, and monographs sent to him from every center of knowledge in the mapped world. More gratifying still was the collection of earnest young soldiers sitting in a loose half-circle between Simon and the books. Each was a would-be statesman and leader of men. They looked at Simon as if in his counsel was wealth greater than the treasures of the fabled foundation-city Leimma. He waved them off. "That will be enough for today. I have errands to run before the king's wake." Even though he knew that, in this company at least, he need not remind them of this mark of his importance, he said the words all the same. Not every man received an invitation to such a prestigious political gathering, and Simon savored every new mark of privilege.

The youths scattered obediently. Simon got up from his comfortable tapestry-upholstered chair and went to his private chambers. Along the way, his housekeeper fell into step beside him. "What am I wearing to the wake tonight?" he demanded of her.

"I ordered a new suit of clothes in dark green. I thought that highly appropriate. Green looks well on you, somber but not excessively dark. It is laid out ready for your return."

"My return?" Simon questioned.

"Yes, sir, from the monument groves. I have ordered the horse and gig prepared for you."

Inwardly, Simon cursed this impediment heartily. He had forgotten that he was expected to visit the pair of forgotten cenotaphs dedicated to his father and mother. Everyone would be out on similar errands in obedience to that hide-bound old custom of visiting one's own dead when a king died. It would be just as well to be seen doing the expected, Simon knew, so he made no outward grumble against it. "Very well, Ilsa. No, nothing for the noontide. I'm not hungry."

As he had foreseen, Simon encountered a number of significant people either en route to the public monument grove or circulating in the vicinity. They greeted him with sober, dreary platitudes about the sadness of the occasion, and Simon disciplined himself to respond in kind, although he failed to see anything in the occasion that called for grief. The late king had disappeared so many years ago that it seemed unwarranted to now hold a wake in his honor. What the occasion did offer was an opportunity to mix with the significant people, a thing Simon loathed but pursued all the same for the sake of improving his position in life.

Greeting by greeting, Simon worked his way nearer to his professed goal. In an obscure corner of the grove, surrounded by a patch of weed-choked lawn, were the two familial monuments he had raised (admittedly under duress) once he had purchased his property in Carthae. Too many people knew his roots and insisted on his adherence to outdated traditions. They wanted to see the proper respect offered his dead parents—*after all they've done for your advancement,* as more than one busybody had informed him in an acidic tone. Simon had bowed to public criticism, had raised two especially fine monuments, and then had forgotten all about them until now. Conscious that others might be watching, Simon knelt down stiffly in front of the pair of cenotaphs and spoke softly enough that no one could overhear. "I have no reason for being here, apart from the appearance of the thing," he began. "People think you had worth when you were alive, so they expect me to pay respects now that you're dead. For that alone, I am here. If I had any cause to be *grateful*—" Simon ejected the word with a twisted grin "—it was for the one useful inquiry you helped me perform, and of that we need not speak at length. Suffice it to say that further inquiries into this manner have been successful." This he said as if expecting the stone figures to applaud.

Distracted by his new line of thought, Simon lapsed into an easy, comfortable reverie in the heat of the late afternoon sunshine. He remembered himself as a

young boy, out in his father's farmhouse in the middle of the most prosaic countryside imaginable. His father had owned a meager library of six books, half of
them agricultural treatises, all of which Simon had mastered before his eighth
birthday. Knowledge was a mysterious, tantalizing thing in those days—always
just beyond his grasp, unless one counted farmers' lore. Simon had been more
fortunate than most: his talents were so great that they could not be ignored. The
Pamirsi landowner whose land Miklei tenanted had come around one day to ask
questions, which led to a welcome change in Simon's life. Upon the satisfaction
of the landowner's curiosity, Simon had packed his small trunk and moved to
King's City. He was then twelve years old, the youngest student admitted to the
crown city's prestigious Academy. By fifteen, he completed his theory studies and
was declared strong enough to begin practical lessons in swordplay and hand
fighting, but his thirst for knowledge was too great to pack away with his theoret-
ical studies.

Simon gave the cenotaphs one last glance. It struck him that perhaps he had
not been accurate in his previous statement. His parents *had* served one other
purpose, unintentional though it was. They had showed him the need for caution. If he admitted any weakness in himself, it was merely a weakness inherent in
his hunger for learning, manifested in a certain amount of heedlessness. When he
was still a boy, he had often rushed into hazards that a far stupider child would
have anticipated and avoided. As a young man, even now he had to remind himself to make a cautious approach when there was risk ahead. *Like now,* he
thought, getting up to depart the groves. Simon knew full well that he courted
danger in his present venture. He set his hand almost affectionately on the nearest
cenotaph in passing. He still heard their dying screams in the recesses of memory,
warning him: *Keep an independent judgment.*

The gig ride back to his modest house was much occupied by other memories.
Simon counted back the years to the day when his extracurricular readings had
shown him a new avenue of inquiry. Back then…back then, he was the protégé
of Nässey Denei-son, back when Denei-son was the third marshal and Simon a
student at the Academy. Back then, he had read everything he could lay hands
on, everything his mentor suggested in the realms of astronomy, the sciences, his-
tories, and essays. In a venerable historical diary Simon had discovered the insolu-
ble problem of humankind waiting for him to solve. Simon recalled perfectly
those first stirrings of awareness that as much as said, *This has waited all these years
for me. Only I can find the solution to this matter.* His first tentative questions to his
mentor had been swiftly, ruthlessly suppressed. Denei-son had not been discour-
teous, but he had been firm. "Listen to my counsel," he said with condescension

wholly unsuited to advice offered from a lesser intellect to a greater. "Your aim is noble, but it is false. The only answer for the Gardens of the Forbidden is to keep well away from them."

Such short-sighted advice could have only come from a man who had reached his apex and could no longer help one still in ascension. Once Simon had come to see the truth of this, he had felt the manacles drop from him. Denei-son had no more influence over him after that—quite the reverse, in fact. Simon, just coming to the end of his formal schooling at the age of eighteen, had requested a month's leave to visit his parents. From their doting ignorance, he need hide nothing. He left them after scarcely twelve hours, telling them only that he had decided to take a walking tour. He headed directly for the nearest crossing, which took him into the outlands on a straight path toward Durward. The only Garden of the Forbidden that he knew of was off west of that great city-state, tucked away in a desolation of stunted oaks and brambles. It was worth the trouble, however, if only because at the end of the journey waited the wisdom of the mystic seer Nekhral.

The old man had met him on the edge of the barren rock garden to warn him away, as he would any hapless traveler who wandered too close to the Forbidden. When Simon began to question him about the nature of the garden, however, the seer seemed to warm to him. "You hold great ambitions," was what Nekhral had said first. "Few have the wisdom to look beyond the apparent into the sublime. It is a dangerous venture, certainly, but with a few precautions, you need fear little by way of adverse consequences."

"Precautions?"

"First and most important, for no reason should you ever touch a piece of rock from within the Garden," the seer had warned him soberly. "That is the downfall of every victim: to be tricked into touching. There is a great power at work within those fragments. That power can be very persuasive. Never forget that."

Together, Simon and his new mentor had begun their lessons. Simon learned to wear thick leather gauntlets when handling the stones; thanks to this precaution, he never felt the least danger to himself. He examined the stones very closely, but this yielded no real revelations. Nekhral always warned him to err on caution's side. "It may take years, but the man who can search out and reconcile the secrets of a Garden of the Forbidden could one day unite the five kingdoms and the masterless realms into one empire again. Patience!" Then, one day—an epiphany. A wounded crow had fallen to the ground within a few paces of the garden's edge. Simon had seen it lurch to its feet, trembling. It cocked its head to one side and aimed a longing glance to the sky, but one attempt was enough to see that flight was impossible. Then, only then, the bird began to stare fixedly at the massive crumbling stones ahead of it. It hopped one hop forward, stopped, and then with inexplicable purpose the crow hopped until it ran headlong into the nearest stone. In another moment, the crow was no more than a feathered carcass on the ground at the stone's foot.

While this memory traversed through Simon's mind, the gig came to a halt at home. Simon roused himself to climb down and head inside to his private chambers. Before he entered his bedchamber, he paused to make sure that the door to the left of his bedroom door was securely locked. There was no use in taking unnecessary chances, after all. That first crow had taught him as much. In the days that had followed, Simon had kept close watch over any animal that ventured near the Garden of the Forbidden. When such animals proved scarce, he trapped beasts alive and brought them to the garden, to release them in the midst of the mazelike tangle of boulders and observe their actions. Every conclusion pointed in the same direction: the Garden sought to devour, always to devour, regardless of the victim, be it hatchling chick or lizard or dog or man. This last conclusion—man—had to be taken on faith at first, because Simon kept taking every precaution suggested by his new mentor. His month's leave went swiftly, until it was necessary to curtail his inquiry. Simon was understandably disappointed. He had felt so close to really useful knowledge that it grated to leave it all behind. Then a compromise had suggested itself to him: Why not bring back a sample to study? But where to keep it? Simon at eighteen had no house of his own, only a set of rooms in a stuffy boarding house and a makeshift study in Denei-son's house. Neither of these places suited his purposes. Simon had decided to return to his parents' farmhouse for one last break in his upward journey.

Still occupied in thought, Simon found the dark green suit of clothes just as his housekeeper had promised. He dressed rapidly, without attention to detail. That was a valet's job, but Simon's was not allowed into the private rooms. Simon allowed none but the housekeeper to trespass beyond the outer salon. The housekeeper was a woman of rare judgment and discretion. She could be trusted not to meddle with anything she found there. Simon removed himself from his bedchamber to the salon that separated his personal chambers from the rest of the house. His valet sprang forward to attend him. To this assiduous service Simon paid no attention either.

Simon appreciated his house and servants more than most people realized, however. The house was on the smallish side, only three bedrooms and two salons, but he could overlook its inconveniences because it sat in a thriving, politically vital quarter of Carthae. The Pamirsi patriarch's mansion roof rose just above the trees across from Simon's front door. The Nandevi clan compound blocked one end of the street, and the Alti clansmen kept property two blocks behind Simon's house. He was perfectly situated to keep company with the social and political elite. That was all he needed—at the moment. When the time came, he would have a far more impressive house, but his father had not been very well-off. Simon had had to strike a shrewd bargain to get even this small house with his inheritance money. Property in Carthae was and always had been expensive. Whenever the old busybodies chided him about gratitude toward his parents, Simon only remembered the trouble he had gone through to stretch his measly legacy. *Yes, many thanks to you, Father, for having so little ambition of your own that you had nothing to leave but a pittance. Many thanks, indeed.* All that kept him from speaking his mind to the old busybodies was the memory of his father's death.

Sometimes when he slept, he could still hear the scream. Just one scream, the overflow of a lifetime of untidy, ignorant emotions, but it had power enough to return in the night. Simon tried to ignore those times. Sitting upright in his tangled sheets at night, he calmed himself with this: *If a man is to become unsettled by every adverse result to an inquiry, then he may as well give up pursuing knowledge altogether.* He had been warned. The important thing was to keep an independent judgment about the matter.

The valet finished preparing Simon for the king's wake and stepped back respectfully. "All finished, sir."

"Very well. That's all." Simon descended to find the gig waiting for him again at the front door. The street outside was full of traffic as the elite headed toward Takra House. Simon's vehicle took its place in the slow procession. He had plenty of time to finish his thoughts while he waited for his turn at the front door of the palace, plenty of time to tidy away the disturbance of his father's dying scream—or his mother's helpless sobs, for that matter—into the corners of his mind where they could do no harm. *One would think,* he often thought, *that five years would be more than enough time to forget such things.* His parents had not only given him the chance to move up in life, but they also had served their purpose in uncovering a new facet of knowledge. Simon no longer had to take it on faith that the Forbidden would devour a man or a woman as eagerly as it would a mere beast.

In the years that had passed since that major discovery, Simon had felt occasional qualms about his research. From time to time, he fancied he felt a slight weakness in his body upon waking after a night's inquiries. Simon paid these fancies no mind because nothing ever came of them, but he still reminded himself to take care. He began bringing in more subjects for his experiments—animals for the most part, but once in a great while he sought out one of the ragtag beggars, the dregs of the city, and watched the stone devour them. There was a pattern to it. Simon could vaguely see it already: the animals were taken as if in a gulp, without hesitation, but the humans varied according to some as-yet undefined quality. Some went as quickly as the beasts, but others remained, shrieking for some time. Simon had yet to discover what variable distinguished some from others, but he felt certain that the knowledge could not be far off.

The first person he met upon crossing the threshold of Takra House was the elderly general, who hated Simon. He and his lady had just emerged from the private suites and were poised at the top of the stairs in preparation for descending to the ballroom. General Mata-son paused and looked down upon Simon with no expression at all. His wife turned to see what had arrested his attention. When she saw the young man at the bottom of the stairs, she grew solemn and tugged gently at her husband's arm to urge him onward.

Simon mounted the stairs as if he had noticed nothing. He saw the general's back ahead of him, descending into an already crowded ballroom. Simon paused at the top of the stairs to scan the faces below. Then he took the straightest path to the royal family. Simon thought the king had definitely seen better days, judging by his hard eyes and tight-lipped expression. The man almost looked like a man. Simon bowed. "My lord king," he said dutifully. "Please accept my condolences for your loss." With a glance, he stretched the words to cover the queen as well, but he doubted that it had any effect. She was busy watching her husband covertly, her forehead creasing in a worried frown as she held tightly to the king's arm. *Something is wrong with him,* Simon realized. *Something serious.*

He looked around for the princess, but in the press of bodies he could see no sign of her. He began to push through the crowd. Before long, he passed the chief healer and his silly wife; Lord Sakiry's tedious son Lyndall was not far away, relegated to an obscure table full of obscure people. Simon bumped against Lord Pamirsi's spinster sister and apologized. A sudden distaste for this overwhelming crush of humanity washed over Simon. People, everywhere he looked, more and more people, all talking too loudly of petty things that mattered to no one but them…ignorant people, dull-witted people. Simon had to force himself to smile in response to a random greeting, but inside he wanted nothing to do with any of these idiots. He shouldered his way to the corner of the ballroom in search of space. What he found instead was the princess. She stood with her back against the wall, leaning, arms folded around her lithe body. Drawn up short by the surprise, Simon lost hold of every facile witticism that he had ever planned to use in case of such a meeting. He gazed at her blankly at first. Then he leaned against the wall beside her. "Good evening to you, your highness."

"Not really a *good* evening, is it?" Her voice was smooth and surprisingly low for such a young woman. It sent a shiver through Simon. She kept her large, dark eyes fixed upon her father with a look almost as troubled as her mother's. "It was so long ago, I don't really remember him anymore. I wish I could remember him better. Everybody says he was a really remarkable sort of man, a great seer and king. I was too little when he left. I don't remember him."

Something strange happened to Simon as he listened to her. He felt…*regret.* Even though he cared nothing for the old king or his death, he felt sorry that this beautiful girl should have missed knowing him. He almost wished that he had known the old king himself. "That is what a wake is for," he said awkwardly. "They'll tell stories, those who knew him, so those who didn't can learn. That's what a wake is for." An impulse moved him to reach out and set a hesitant hand on her shoulder. "They can tell you what you want to know."

She smiled a teary little smile. "It isn't the same. I don't want to know *about* him." Something caught her attention from across the way. The girl pushed herself away from the wall and said, "Good day all the same." She might have said the same to anybody.

She doesn't know who I am. This gave Simon a genuine sense of loss.

SOCIETY

Shears in hand, two ladies knelt amid a riot of verdure that went by the dubious title of garden. Servants went about their quiet tasks at a distance, leaving the pair of ladies sufficiently alone for discussion.

The taller of the two ladies was the less important, socially speaking. It was the shorter lady who owned the garden, just as her husband Berhus Pamirsi owned the sprawling mansion that still shadowed them against the morning sun. Lady Russa Pamirsi wielded her shears with a haphazard air. She nearly severed a beautiful chrysanthemum blossom instead of the weed beside it, so intent was she upon her speech. "You really must speak with your father, dear Ivy. For the good of the kingdom, dear, if not for his personal welfare—the time has long since come! Surely you've had your own little private concerns over his health, haven't you? He's reached a hale old age, to be sure, which is more than most of his peers could say for themselves, if they were alive still. And it isn't as if he had a dearth of candidates."

"That's true," Ivy admitted gently. "He has a good deal too many. There are so many considerations to make. If he takes his time, it's only so that he can satisfy himself that he truly has chosen the best of them. He takes his charge very seriously. It's no use asking me, either," she said with a hint of mischief behind the words. "He won't talk about it with any of us. As I understand it, he hasn't even talked with Colin about it, or Uncle Owen either. He's so infuriatingly secretive sometimes, isn't he?" Secretly, Ivy wished she could yawn. She knew perfectly well that the Pamirsi woman had only invited her for this morning's visit because she hoped Ivy would give her a clue about the succession. That clue would then travel directly to the office of Berhus, Lord Pamirsi, to be used against someone for some reason. Ivy knew also that Russa would prefer to hear that one of the two Pamirsi candidates was in favor. It would even suffice if the sole Nandevi candidate, Simon Miklei-son, led the pack. With the Nandevi clan in every respect subject to the larger, wealthier Pamirsi clan, it would amount to the same thing.

Knowing all these things, Ivy deliberately kept her distance from the entire subject. She had no wish to get involved. None of the candidates appealed to her personally. She had met them all repeatedly, in various circumstances and for various reasons, and her conclusion was simple, if not entirely rational: *If only Jarod had never died! He would have made a far superior general than any of these.* Since her favored candidate was long dead and thus completely out of the running, Ivy took little interest and even less pleasure in the contest.

"I fear the hour is rather early," Russa said stiffly, catching Ivy's moment of inattention.

"No, no, not at all. I was just considering the succession, that's all. It's a complicated matter. I confess it's beyond me." Then, to keep the other woman from feeling utterly cheated, she offered a bit of news that Russa wouldn't have heard yet. "I've had all I can manage with the princess' masquerade ball. There are so many last-minute arrangements, and wouldn't you know, my musicians only just agreed to the wages I offered them!"

Russa gave her a startled look. "They're going on with it, then? How unaccountable!"

"Not really," Ivy answered calmly. "I can't say it better than Colin did. He said he's been mourning his father for the past seven years. If you look at it like that, the masquerade ball comes a full five years after even the strictest mourning periods ought to last."

"Is it true, then, that nobody knows who brought the news home?"

"It is indeed true, Lady Pamirsi. The messenger is unknown. They say it might have been a foreigner that the late king befriended in his travels, but he seems very shy of attention. He delivered his message and hasn't been heard from again." Ivy gathered her basket of gardening tools. As she folded her gloves neatly, she said, "I've enjoyed your company, Lady Pamirsi, as always, but I'm afraid if I don't start now, I'll be terribly late to Takra House, and then Lady Caretaker will never forgive me. There are so many last-minute details yet to be arranged. Do give my fondest greetings to your husband and the rest of the family. I look forward to seeing you at the ball tomorrow night."

"Certainly." Russa stood up and offered her hand to Ivy in a limp clasp that lasted scarcely a second. "Do take care of yourself, Ivy, and offer your parents our greetings in return."

"I will certainly do that. Good day, Russa." Ivy breathed her sigh only after she was well outside the gates that screened the drive from unwanted visitors. "That's done," she said to herself. With her basket dangling from her elbow and a sense of accomplishment warming her spirits, she set off on the road back to King's City. It had always struck her as a peculiarity, the way King's City and its sister city Carthae sat facing each other with such a short distance separating them. It was highly inconvenient to those who had business with both the king's household and that of Lord Pamirsi in the same day and had no carriage to bear them from one city to the other and back. With the sun growing hotter and hotter against her brunette head, Ivy struck up a brisk pace amid the traffic of the day. She had made this journey so often that she knew almost to the minute how long it would take her to reach Takra House. To alleviate the boredom of the walk, she watched the carriages and wagons pass her. Often, she had to cover her face with a handkerchief to keep from breathing the dust they kicked up as they rattled past. *It had better rain soon,* she thought, *or else the gardens will all wither up and die by midsummer.*

She reached the gates of King's City without incident. The guards at the gates nodded to her courteously. They all knew who she was, and she could name more than a few of them without pausing for thought. Ivy had grown up surrounded by soldiers. She addressed the gatekeepers by name and inquired after their families before continuing on her way.

Now that she was home, she found her progress slowed by the number of acquaintances she met. To save time, she took a shortcut that led her through the rougher East District. In distance, it was not a shorter route, but it was far less likely to attract anyone Ivy knew and therefore presented fewer hindrances. It had been some time since Ivy herself had taken this route—several years, in fact. Little had changed. The houses still were shoved against one another in tenements, leaving hardly a crack for the sun to seep down through them to touch the barren soil where grass might have grown. The smell, compounded of unwashed bodies and spilled alcohol, lingered just as persistently as ever. Children still roamed unchecked through every alleyway and in the gutters, hunting vermin or playing with rubbish discarded by those residents who operated only in the night.

A slight tickle of a thought arose: *Visit Eva.* Ivy recoiled from the idea, conditioned by long years of experience to respond, *What if someone finds out?* The East District as a whole, and this one street in particular, was so disreputable that the mere rumor of a visit would endanger her reputation and could very easily, by association, stir up rumors against her nearest acquaintances as well. But the day was early and the sun shone bright on the nearly deserted street, and Ivy found just enough courage within herself to hasten along to the house of her former friend Eva.

I wonder how she's been all this time. Goodness, Ivy realized with surprise, *she'll be past forty now, and little Alanah will be older than I was when I last saw Eva. How time passes!* Excitement stirred at the thought of reviving a dormant friend-ship, even if only for an hour. Ivy didn't dare trespass on the tenuous patience of the Caretaker matriarch for longer than that.

At the corner, she stopped with a sickly lump of dread weighting her stomach. Eva had formerly made her home in a pair of rooms above the tailor shop where she had worked as an assistant on alternate days. That same tailor shop stood vacant now, its once respectable front badly weathered through neglect. The win-dows of the room above it were boarded shut. Ivy climbed the external stairs with trepidation at their dilapidated condition. She tapped meekly at the door.

"Who's that?" a wary young woman's voice responded through a crack.

"My name…my name is Ivy, and I'm looking for a woman who lived here before. Her name is Eva."

"She's dead. Whatever it is you wanted, you're too late. Years too late. From the looks of you, you don't belong around here. You'd best take yourself off before you come to trouble." Floorboards creaked at the other side of the door, as if the speaker had withdrawn from her post to end the conversation.

Stunned, Ivy descended to the street again. She put a hand to her mouth, but she could not stop the warm tears from coursing down her cheeks. *Eva, dead.* Ivy hurried away. Before long, she had returned to the main thoroughfare. Instead of going straight on to Takra House, Ivy went home to her father's house. Neither her father nor her mother was at home, so there was no one to question her about the tear-streaked dust on her face. She took a moment to calm herself while sponging her skin with a damp cloth.

From her father's house, it was a quick few minutes' walk to Takra. Ivy arrived to find the Caretaker matriarch ill-tempered. "I'm sorry for being tardy, Lucinda," Ivy said, briefly taking the elderly woman's pudgy hand. "I had an early visit with Russa, and you know how long a walk it is from Carthae once the roads fill up." Ivy had a fair idea of how little Lucinda knew about the time it would take to walk anywhere beyond the walls of Takra House. The Caretaker matriarch had not walked any distance for many years. "Have the costumes come?"

"Oh, yes, those came at dawn, but we haven't done any fittings yet because her highness the princess has taken a notion to sulk in the park and won't set foot indoors. Her ladyship is out there now, trying to reason with the child."

Ivy wanted desperately to rebuke the Caretaker woman for her tone. Instead, she said, "I will find them and see if I can be of any help, then." She barely kept her countenance until she was out of Lucinda's sight. "Spiteful old beast. She's a great one to talk about moods and getting nothing done because of them," she muttered to herself. "Half the work wouldn't get done at all without poor Ardith to do it, I'm sure." Then, as she set foot in the ornamental garden, Ivy saw her best friend Selena reclining between two thick roots of the Prince's Tree. Selena's daughter Maia sat with her arms folded over her knees. It took only a glance to tell Ivy that Lucinda had been correct in one item, at least: Maia was extraordinarily downcast. Ivy took a few steps closer and called out, "Is it a private talk, or may I join you?"

Selena checked with her daughter first before saying, "Come sit with us, Ivy. You're always welcome."

Ivy sat on the lush carpet of grass with her feet tucked neatly beneath her. "Are you upset over something, Maia? You don't look yourself today." She reached out to brush her fingertips against the cheek of her honorary niece. Again she marveled at the girl's beauty. Selena was a handsome woman in an austere fashion, with her spare build and almost gaunt features. Her daughter would exceed her in beauty before long. The girl stood nearly as tall as her father, with long, dark braids and a smooth, tawny complexion. Today, her black eyes were damp with tears. "Do you mind?" Ivy added in a belated aside.

The girl shrugged casually. She moved her feet aside to make more room for Ivy. "I don't mind. Doesn't mean I can answer it any better for you than for Mother, though. I don't really know what's wrong."

"How did you describe it for your mother?"

Maia gestured for Selena to answer that question. Selena said, "Well, we were talking about marriage. Maia isn't exactly looking forward to the masquerade ball. She said…" A look of reflected distress crossed her thin features. She reached out to take her daughter's hand. "Just before you came, Ivy, she asked me a difficult question. She asked if I would be unhappy with her if she never married."

"What did you answer?"

Selena's grip on Maia's hand constricted noticeably before the queen addressed her daughter. "I didn't, but I will now. I may never understand why, dear, but if your heart leads you in that path, I will honor your choice. Have you absolutely set your will against marrying?"

"No, Mother. It's nothing that simple." Maia glanced at Ivy.

"No one says you have to decide by the end of the ball, my girl," Ivy tried to encourage her. "Or even by a year after it, for that matter—you could delay as long as it took to find the man who suited you, you know. The ball is just symbolic." That made no impression on the girl, so Ivy gave Selena a helpless glance. Something more compelling was required. Ivy decided to speak plainly. "When I was sixteen and had to declare myself eligible, I didn't want a party of any sort." At a loss for the proper approach, she began again. "Haven't you ever wondered why they call me your aunt when I'm nothing of the kind?"

That caught the girl's attention. "No, not really. I always thought, well, you and Mother were always so much like sisters, it was natural to call you Aunt."

"That's true, but I knew your father a long time before I knew Selie. This isn't the easiest thing for me to talk about, so you'll have to be patient with me. You must understand, Maia, the only reason I didn't want a party was because…I didn't want to be declared eligible, Maia. Not because I didn't want to marry, but because I had already chosen my husband and my parents forbade it." She saw a spark of interest and pushed onward. "I was in love with Colin's brother."

Maia was openly amazed. "Father has a brother?"

"He *had* a twin brother. He's dead now. They said there was something wrong with him, so they wouldn't even go talk with Jarod's parents about the possibility." Ivy waved a hand vaguely. "I knew he was troubled. He had moods where he spoke harshly to everyone, even to me. There was a story that went around once, something about him running away and nearly getting eaten by a mad wolf. I never knew what he would do next. He was brilliant, though. He could figure just about anything out, and so quick, too! I never knew anyone like him." Ivy caught herself on the verge of becoming emotional. She had to take several slow breaths to distance herself from the memories. "When he died, I felt as if my life was ended before I had a chance to start it. I never found anyone to take his place, so I never married."

To her surprise, Maia brushed tears from her eyes and straightened eagerly. "But, Aunt Ivy, that's just like what I was trying to explain to Mother, but I couldn't say it right. It's just like what you said, like my life was ended before it started. I wake up some nights, crying…because I know something's wrong. I just don't know what."

"Darling, why did you never say anything of this?"

"I didn't want to worry you, Mother, since you can't do anything to fix it. Nobody can."

Selena rocked her daughter gently. "Ah, dear heart, I wish I could make every-thing perfect for you."

Left out for the moment, Ivy felt a twinge of envy and pushed it aside. *Selie is such a wonderful mother. She reminds me a little of my own momma.* She refused to compare what might have been, had she had the chance to bear children of her own to rear alongside Selena's girl. Ivy waited until Maia pulled away, embar-rassed at having shed her tomboy exterior. "Are you ready to see your costume yet, Maia? It might cheer you up."

"Not likely," was the girl's tart response. She wiped her eyes fiercely. "It's probably a full gown, all over lace and bows."

"Not likely," Ivy retorted. "You'd ruin the lace. It would be a waste. No, my girl, it's trousers for you, but I got my revenge all the same." She wrinkled her nose comically.

With one last sniffle to interrupt her laughter, Maia said, "I'm frightened now, Mother. Maybe I should s-suddenly fall ill and call off the masquerade." She climbed to her feet and helped her mother to stand. The three women returned to the house and ascended to the family quarters. There they found Lucinda's daughter-in-law Ardith busy among the servants, giving orders and answering questions. As soon as she saw them, Ardith grew even more animated. "Oh, there you are! I couldn't resist a peek at the costumes. Oh, Miss Ivy, they're a marvel!"

Ivy led Selena and Maia to the wardrobe in Maia's suite, only releasing them to fling open the wardrobe doors. "This is for you, Maia."

"Is this it?" the girl said with ill grace, holding the deep crimson costume out as if it might bite her. "Is all of the costume here?"

"Yes, it is," Ivy answered, "and coming from *you*, my dear girl, that was an outburst of sheer delight. I hadn't expected half as much enthusiasm from you. Oh, and Selena, this one's yours. Oh, I can't wait to see you try it on! Liande, Rhendi, help the queen. That is a difficult dress to manage." Ivy hovered nearby as the two twittering young chamber maids proceeded to assist Selena in dressing.

"I can't wear this!"

The two older women turned to find Maia already mostly in her costume, looking outraged. She gestured emphatically at her bare midriff, which showed slightly through the long, sweeping jacket of translucent red that she clutched around herself as a defense against onlookers. "I can't go out like this! I'm nearly *naked*!"

"I wouldn't call it naked," Ivy protested. "You can hardly see anything."

"Can I have part of Mother's costume to wrap around me?"

"Don't be silly, Maia. They don't match. Anyway, you look lovely. Some young man is going to be completely swept away with a single glimpse."

Steering away from that hazardous topic, Selena asked, "What sort of material is that jacket made of, Ivy? It's so delicate! No wonder Maia feels only partly clothed—I daresay she can hardly feel the weight of it."

"Isn't it marvelous? There's a woman named Beth in the weaver's quarter who's responsible for that. She has very clever fingers. I met her when her boy got into mischief at school. Nässey heard about the boy, who by all accounts is big for his age and very clever too, in his own way, and since there wasn't much to be done with his case as far as the public schools…" Ivy stopped to draw her own blue costume over her head and resumed talking as soon as her face emerged, "…are concerned, he recommended the boy to me. I found out his main trouble was fighting in the school yard, so I told Nässey he needed to enroll the boy in his classes, teach him how and when to fight, you know. The boy is doing well now, and Beth was very thankful. She wanted to do me a favor, and there you hold the results. It just warms the heart to finally come to the problem and see a way to mend it, don't you agree?"

Selena nodded. She intercepted a laughing glance that passed between Rhendi and Liande as the two maids smoothed out the unwieldy folds of her garment. Both young women lowered their eyes when Selena shook her head ever so slightly at them.

Ivy guessed the direction of their thoughts. It was no secret to her that other women believed she meddled in others' family troubles merely because she had no family of her own. As Ivy's best friend, Selena felt compelled to curb the ignorant in their laughter, no matter how benign it was. Once Selena had her costume on, she dismissed the maids and offered Ivy an apologetic glance. Ivy smiled ruefully. "It's all right, Selie—really, it is. You don't need to stand up for me all the time."

"Aunt Ivy, what will Father's costume be?" Maia asked as she sat on the backless bench before a floor-length mirror. Her maid Kenda, armed with a wide black ribbon, deftly arranged the princess' multitude of slender beaded braids into a tame knot high on the back of Maia's head to keep them out of the way for the fitting. A cascade of the braids hung down from the knot, beads hissing gently like rainfall whenever Maia moved.

"You'll have to wait until tomorrow to see. Put on the mask so we can see the whole effect before we change anything."

The girl obeyed without enthusiasm. Ivy was taken aback. With her face covered, Maia was no longer the tomboyish child, but an alluring young woman, tall and lithe. The mask was of a large-eared fox. Maia's smoky eyes stared through the slanted apertures. "Well?"

Selena gave her daughter an approving smile. "You look perfect. I don't think yours will need much adjustment." She turned from Maia to watch Ivy. "Ivy, what is that? I've never seen fabric to match it for shine. It's lovely."

"Isn't it? I was so pleased. It does make you think of the sea, doesn't it?"

"What sort of sea creature are you going to be? Where's your mask?"

Ivy picked up a flat lacquered box from the dressing table. "In here. Wait 'til you see. I have enough to practice it this once. I had the idea when I was at the market, buying fish."

Even Maia couldn't help but watch the transformation. First the maid finished fastening Ivy into the smooth, clingy, glistening blue gown. Selena reflected aloud, "Those ruffles—I don't know how they made that crepe look like silver; are they your fins? It's a good thing you have those. Someone might mistake your dress for a second skin, otherwise. Think of poor Russa's sensibilities!" The prospect of shocking the Pamirsi patriarch's wife did not appear to greatly dismay the queen, certainly not enough to keep her from laughing aloud at the possibility.

Ivy covered her brown hair with a flowing wimple of the same crepe. With deft hands, the maid took up the lacquered box and drew out—of all things—a tiny paintbrush. She began to paint Ivy's face using tones of silver, blue and green matching the gown, but leaving enough skin bare to suggest that the transformation was still incomplete. "What do you think?"

Selena gave her best friend an admiring inspection. "I think it's the cleverest costume I've ever seen. You'll put the rest of us to shame."

Ivy joined Kenda beside the queen. "I had my fitting when I went to check on the costumes last week. I think maybe we should take yours in a little there," she pinched the bodice fabric just above Selena's waist, "so it drapes properly." When she turned, she caught sight of Maia examining herself pensively in the mirror. The girl was so preoccupied that she jumped when Ivy put a hand on her shoulder. "You are the prettiest girl I know, Maia—whether you like it or not," she added wryly. "I'm sure that you'll find your way. You shouldn't give up hope. You never know what might happen tomorrow, or the next day."

YESTERDAY: DESTINED

The schoolroom of Takra House was empty except for the tall, lean boy in the corner. He held a thick book on his knees and would have appeared the picture of a studious young man if not for the exhausted nodding of his head. His forelock nearly brushed the open pages of the book as his head sank lower. The dark half-moons under his eyes bespoke many nights without rest. "Leave me alone," he muttered, his own voice startling him from his uneasy doze.

The giant only laughed. *I said nothing. Your own dreams accuse you…small wonder, given what you are. Go ahead, mortal child. Fight me. Give me cause to hurt you. You deserve no better, freakish mortal child.*

Jarod turned the page back to the last words he remembered reading. Doggedly, he stared at the words until they stood out in his thoughts when he closed his eyes. Three pages of material he absorbed in this painstaking manner before the schoolroom door opened with a slow groan of hinges. He looked up to see who had found him.

"There you are." It was the girl Ivy. "Nobody knew where you'd gone."

He avoided her eyes by lowering his head. "I was reading."

Do you suppose me ignorant of mortal ways? the voice sneered. *Just because you look at anything but her, do not suppose you have tricked me. I know your thoughts toward this foolish girl. I know what it is you want, even if you are too great a coward to confess it to yourself.*

When an obscene picture intruded upon Jarod's thoughts, he shoved it down. "What do you want?" he asked snappishly, annoyed that the voice could needle him so easily.

His tone of voice made Ivy hesitate. "I wanted help...help with my studies."

"What kind of help?"

The girl brought forward a thin book of figures. "I can't make any of these come out right. I think I'm doing it the way the teacher said, but if it isn't coming out right...I must not be doing it right, right? And I thought, since you're so smart, maybe you could show me where I'm going wrong."

He took the book from her. After a rapid scan, he said, "You aren't working them in the right order. The braces come first. That's your problem."

"Oh." Ivy settled against the wall beside him and looked at the book without taking it from him. "Oh! I see what you mean!" She smiled up at him. "You're smart."

"Not really."

"Yes, really," she replied earnestly. "You're smarter than anyone else I know."

"I just learned to figure things out faster. That's all." *Audune, be silent!* He surprised himself with the ferocity of the command. It seemed to surprise Audune as well. The shepherd-giant ceased whispering its coarse suggestions into his mind—for a time. "That's all," Jarod repeated. "You should go now and finish your work. It'll be dinner soon."

"I almost wish we weren't in our own house now," she admitted. "It was more fun to have all our families eat together."

"It was too crowded."

"Maybe so, but I—I miss sitting with you," the girl said in a bold rush.

"You're here every day."

"It isn't the same."

"Did you..." Jarod stopped sharply, changing his mind at the last moment.

"What? What were you going to say?"

"I heard you got in trouble with your folks."

Ivy blushed. "Brigid told on me. I didn't know what sort of girls they were. They were poor. They didn't have hardly anything to call theirs. They said they were tavern workers. I didn't know what they really did—I *didn't*," she stressed, suddenly intense, "but I'm going back anyway. It doesn't matter. They're my friends now."

Jarod almost smiled at her defiance. "Good for you, Ivy. They could use a friend like you, I bet." He hesitated, hardly daring to speak his next thought. "Does that mean you won't get to watch the reception ball next week?"

"I don't suppose Momma will want me to. I'll ask Poppa. Maybe if I ask nice, he'll let me come along. He wasn't as upset about me visiting the—the prostitute girls," she stammered with another blush. "I think maybe he understood. Brigid and Perrin will get to go to the dance. I hate being left behind to sit with Nässey, like I'm still a little girl. I'm thirteen, for goodness' sake. Are you going to watch, or are you going to shut yourself away in your room like always? You act like you don't like to be seen."

Jarod could feel the mocking laughter in the back of his head. He summoned his courage to speak anyway. "I'll…I'll watch part of it."

The girl smiled her approval and tipped up her innocent face like a blossom to the sun.

Why don't you kiss her, boy? She wants you to—

Suddenly scowling, Jarod blurted, "I have to go now." He scrambled up from the floor and sped out of the schoolroom, away from the girl, but he could not outpace the small voice.

MASQUERADE

Takra House's courtyard clattered with the constant passage of carriages in orderly procession. One carriage in the line differed from the others. Its curtains were drawn shut except for one, which had one corner pulled back. Inside, the air was thick and silent. When the carriage wheels bumped across the gate's threshold, the oldest of the three men inside spoke up. "I still can't figure why you want to avoid the king's eye, Ammun, but as you like. The least likely door is the one in the armory, if you want to sneak in."

"I know."

The clockmaker continued, "They'll wonder why we had to take our own carriage. I can always say I needed a private word with my reprobate son."

"Hey, now," drawled the son. "I haven't the time to be reprobate, Ta. He'll be my witness to that—he keeps me busy enough, as you well know."

"That's true. Especially tonight. Damon has work ahead of him."

"Work?" Kyte Noah-son hooted softly, amused. "At a masquerade ball? With that many women around, Ammun, you'll be lucky if he can remember his own name."

"The women are his work tonight, Master Clockmaker."

That answer only made the craftsman laugh harder. "Sunk to a new low, Damon!"

"No, Ta," Damon protested fervently, exasperated. "It isn't what you think!"

"As for you, Clockmaker, since you're a lifelong, honored family friend, you may stay near the king's table without arousing suspicion." Though no one said it, they all knew now that instructions were being given. "Many will come to greet the king and his daughter. It may be that the queen will wish to converse about matters close to her heart. Light matters, perhaps, but…matters of her choosing."

The one they called Ammun leaned back against the carriage seat, well out of the line of sight, when the door opened to let his two companions descend at the palace steps. The carriage swayed without the extra weight. As it clattered around the curve, he let the curtain corner drop down again. He had seen already what he needed to see. The carriage circled around, heading for a space at the wall. The hired boys were more interested in their amusements than their charges. The boy in charge of his carriage ran off to the stables almost before the tethering knots were tightened. Ammun waited only a few moments, and then descended from the carriage.

The windows of Takra House blazed in the main section, where the guests were arriving steadily, but the western wing of the house was dark and silent. He gazed around. Since every other guest was masked, for once his own hangman's mask drew no attention as he strode toward the orchard that peeped around the west end of the mansion. He met more than a dozen young folk on his way through the fruit orchard, but the young folk only nodded to him at most and went on with their gaiety as if he weren't there. His goal was nearer the house, and he took his time reaching it. By the time he stood under the shadow of the Prince's Tree, he had taken note of everyone who passed him in the darkening orchard. None of the voices were familiar to him. He leaned against the trunk as if catching his breath while he surveyed the flowerbeds and the row of bright windows. Then the moment came. No one was looking. He reached up to grasp the lowest branch and swung himself up in a single graceful arc. From there, he climbed until he found a sturdy branch that afforded him the most complete view through the ballroom windows.

The king and his family were easy to pick out from amongst the crowd. Clad in brown and green to mimic a tree, the Keeper sat at a small table at the eastern end of the spacious chamber, his wife seated at one side and his daughter at the other. A steady parade of guests passed by the table, presumably for the purpose of congratulating the family on this happy occasion. Through the open door, voices tumbled out like a cataract, a constant rush of indistinguishable sound. The watcher focused on faces. He saw Lord Sakiry and the general seated at another table next to the king's. Neither of the two older men wore masks, though Lord Sakiry wore a costume of black-upon-black and held a raven mask in both hands, toying with it now and again. Lord Sakiry spoke often, but the general stirred himself only to look uneasily around the hall at faces. The watcher asked, *What disturbs the general, Chike?*

You and I. His shepherd Taio senses us, but does not know us for ourselves yet. Taio stays very close to his charge tonight. You may not have much time to contact the general as he asked of you.

The watcher stared solemnly at the distant figure of the general. "Not tonight, not until I have the information he needs. Otherwise, there is nothing I can do for him. I will be useless to him if I reveal my involvement too soon."

You know best, little brother.

With a small, crooked smile at the remark, the watcher shifted his attention to other faces. The masks made recognition virtually impossible. He had to pick them out by association. Damon and his father Kyte Clockmaker were easy enough to recognize when they made their way through the parade of guests stopping at the king's table. The king greeted Kyte with a strong handclasp as befit a friend of the family. As the master clockmaker gestured toward Damon in what must have been an introduction, the watcher outside noticed a guest in a yellow hawk mask and golden-brown garb wading through the crowd from the wrong direction. This one addressed the princess first. She gave him scant attention, snubbing him for his interruption, but the hawk continued to hover close at hand despite this reception. Behind him, Lord Sakiry and the general leaned close together in conference. Neither man looked pleased to see the hawk. After a moment of almost furtive discussion, Lord Sakiry nodded with no great enthusiasm and rose to address the hawk.

The watcher kept the ballroom under relaxed surveillance. He saw the conversation between Lord Sakiry and the hawk end with little regret on either man's part, but it had served its purpose: the musicians in the loft above had struck up, and the king had claimed his daughter's hand for the first dance, brushing easily past the guests who wandered away from the center of the floor. Ammun watched the hawk retreat to the wall, brooding, his head never turning except to follow the progress of king and princess around the circle of dancers.

Then that dance ended. The hawk pushed violently away from the wall to almost snatch the princess from her father for the next dance. The princess danced stiffly all while she was partnered with the hawk. Outside, the watcher smiled slightly to see her reach down and deliberately shift the hawk's hand from its grasp on her waist to a more appropriate position at the crook of her outstretched arm. The way she did it was as much a rebuke as any words could have been. *She has spirit enough. One might make something of such a girl, if she were taken in hand now while she's still young enough to learn—and if her teacher had a deft enough hand.*

She belongs to a special line of females. What plans do you have for her, little brother?

The watcher shook his head. *None yet, Chike, but it's a thought to keep in consideration. I suspect she will make a good ally.* His eyes shifted again and caught on the curvilinear figure of a woman dressed in sleek, shimmering blue. The sight of her jarred him.

What plans do you have for her, *little brother?*

Don't mock what you cannot comprehend. He moved his gaze deliberately, but his attention was slow to follow suit. Many faces passed under his surveillance until he finally began seeing them again. While he tried to set himself to his task, he couldn't completely ignore the unseen presence that leaned on his consciousness. *She is innocent. Let her stay that way.*

Little brother, I may not quarrel with you, but—

But neither can you resist a quarrel, so you'll phrase it as advice? I know you too well.

I cannot advise when you never stop to listen. You were given over to my keeping for good reason when you threw off your former shepherd's influence. If you do not release this burden of self-reproach—

It will destroy me? Can anything destroy me now? Be at peace, Chike—I am well. Let me keep watch for now. We'll discuss it more afterward, if you like. The watcher nestled back against the tree's bulk, well aware that the matter was anything but settled. He found that, while his attention had wandered away in those few moments of debate, the arrangement of the room had changed. The king and his wife were out on the floor among the dancers, as was the princess. It was a refinement of a more popular folk dance and didn't involve partners as such, but the hawk still persisted in his pursuit of the princess. The lady in blue—he couldn't help but make sure of her whereabouts—stood in close conference with an older Caretaker woman. They gestured toward the buffet tables in such a way as to let the watcher infer that the two were discussing the arcane details of entertaining.

After a time, the younger guests began to filter out by twos and threes into the garden. This distracted the watcher for a few moments until he satisfied himself that no one would come near his perch. Once he was assured of this, he returned his attention to the ballroom. King and queen had seated themselves, and their daughter followed them to rid herself of the hawk. Then Lord Sakiry joined the social skirmish on the princess' behalf, scooting his chair adroitly into the vacant place beside the princess' seat of honor and striking up a conversation with her.

Thus blocked, the hawk retreated a few steps away, watchful for the least opening.

Behind the princess, the king and queen sat together yet strangely separate. The watcher, after gauging their silence, determined that it originated with the king. The queen tried several times to draw him into conversation, and each time she succeeded only for a few minutes before the king sank back into his cheerless musings. His shoulders slumped as if he had forgotten how to straighten them. Soon the queen stopped trying and turned slightly away from him in order to listen to Kyte's conversation. Then the blue-clad lady came to stand behind the queen, put a hand on her shoulder, and bent down to speak in her ear. The queen's mouth curved upward, and some animation returned to her bearing as she replied. Both women glanced at the princess as their exchange became more secretive. The woman in blue nodded decisively. Her hand tightened briefly on her friend's shoulder before she crossed between the royal tables and the hawk's station against the wall.

The watcher traced her leisurely progress to the near side of the ballroom. There, a trio of women sat around one small table, while a young man in an innocent white mask tipped his chair back against the window as if to distance himself from them. The lady greeted one of the women and conversed for a few minutes as if she had no other purpose. The woman whom she had addressed gestured to the two other women, and the blue-clad lady spoke graciously to both in turn. Offhandedly she turned to the youth, who sat with his profile to the watcher. Her face was suddenly full of mischief, as if she were teasing the boy. He responded with broad, expressive hand movements. Then he bounded to his feet and left his table with a hasty nod to the women.

When this youth in the guileless cherub mask arrived at the king's table, he remembered to address himself first to the parents of the princess before he applied for her hand as his partner in the reel that the musicians had just commenced. Before the hawk could interfere, the princess stood and followed this new acquaintance onto the floor with an eagerness that betrayed her awareness of the hawk's vigilance. If that had not given her away, she then accepted a second dance with the cherub-masked boy. While they whirled around the dance floor, the lady in blue returned to her friend the queen for a moment's discourse. The two women watched as their conspiracy flourished into yet a third dance. Lord Sakiry pulled his chair closer in order to converse with the king, and the clockmaker's son Damon came to stand by the blue-clad lady. All the while, the hawk stalked the perimeter of the ballroom as if drawn in the princess' train.

The crisis came at the end of that third dance. From his vantage point, the watcher saw the musicians rise from their booth on the second floor of the ballroom. It was respite time for them. Below, the dancers dispersed into the rest of the crowd of guests, creating a minute of chaos. The princess' head bobbed above the other heads, looking swiftly over her shoulder toward the hawk's last known position. Her mouth below the fox mask moved slightly. Then she surged through the crowd with the white-masked youth in tow, emerging in the doorway to the garden. A stream of other young people accompanied them with great laughter. "Let's play seek!" someone shouted. The young people scattered out into the darkness of the orchard.

Servants came after them to light the paper lanterns festooning the lesser trees. Soon the grounds of Takra House echoed with youthful laughter. The hawk stood just outside the ballroom door. He did not attempt to follow the princess any farther than that. Instead, he wandered among the ornamental trees on the other side of the garden, well within the hedges that divided the flower beds from the rest of the palace grounds. A man joined him surreptitiously after a few minutes more. "What news, Marshal?"

"News means change, and of that we have none. The old man still withholds his choice."

"He must make a decision soon, though. Who else is as eligible as you? No one claims as many honors. You need not fear that he'll choose one of the others."

"No? If only to bar me from my destiny, he would choose any fool with a uniform. Don't delude yourself, Hobe. The general hates me. He didn't want me to take the marshal's badge this winter, and he certainly won't give me the general's crest now."

"But the king…the king supported you for marshal."

"The king? The king is a useless, soft-hearted fool, easily manipulated. Let us focus on the old man first. He has to be made to see the advantages that I would bring to the generalship. One outstanding victory might tip matters my way, if I could only devise a way."

"What of your alliance—"

The hawk hushed him, listening. He pushed the other man into the shadows and arranged himself on one of the benches in time for a pair of guests to walk past. They greeted him loudly: "Good evening, Marshal Miklei-son! Fine evening!" He nodded politely to them and, when asked to join them in their promenade, got up from the bench as if he had done nothing but sit there alone until their interruption.

Chike? Does the king's shepherd stay close to him as well?

Close, but not inordinately so. He offers sympathy, where Taio shows only concern. I do not think that there is danger for the king.

Not yet. What is his name? The watcher nodded as the identity of the king's shepherd-giant was impressed upon his thought. He knew better than to speak the name and risk drawing the shepherd's attention to him so soon. *Thank you. I may need to speak to him myself, judging by the hawk's words.*

There is a taint on that one.

I know. I felt it myself. Who should know that feeling better than I? Ammun shuddered in revulsion. *Trouble comes to this house.*

The musicians returned to the loft. When they struck up the next tune, they drew some of the youths from their orchard romps. The princess was not among them, not until the next dance. Then she and her companion in his cherub mask returned to the royal table briefly. There, Lord Sakiry claimed the princess for a dance, leaving the boy to converse awkwardly with the general and his wife. They seemed to know the boy, if the general's half-pleased, half-skeptical expression was a reliable indication. In a lull between songs, the babble of voices lessened enough for the watcher outside to hear the boy laugh, "Unfair, Grandfather!" to the general. Then the watcher knew him for who he was: Giles, the only son of Denei's stepson Perrin.

Nothing of note happened during the rest of the dance. The hawk seemed to have given up the field altogether. He did not appear in the ballroom at all for the remainder of the night. During the respite, the king had drawn to himself several acquaintances—Damon among them—and seemed in better spirits than before. The general and his wife retired early, causing a temporary stir by their exit. The watcher guessed at the topic of this renewed buzz of gossip. *They know he feels his age, yet he refuses to make his choice. Why is that, Chike?*

I cannot speak for the general's decisions. You must speak with him yourself, or permit me to reveal my identity to Taio if you are unready to speak with the general yourself.

The watcher let that suggestion pass without comment. He kept watch for only a little while longer before withdrawing slowly along the same path back to the carriage. No one was in sight. Laughter echoed from the guardhouse, where it appeared that all the hired hands were making merry themselves. This made it a simple matter for the dark-cloaked watcher to conceal himself in the clock-maker's carriage without being seen. He settled into the corner, drew his cloak around his body, and drifted into a light doze while he waited.

When the carriage shook under the weight of the driver, its sole occupant came alert at once. He heard the voices of guests in the distance before the carriage lurched into motion and drowned out other sounds. The cessation of movement made him shrink back as far from the carriage door as a man of his size could manage. In climbed the clockmaker and his son. Damon was in mid-sentence: "—said it lightly, but he doesn't strike me as merely a fellow who speaks to hear his own voice."

"No," his father agreed, "he hasn't that sort of reputation about him." Then the door shut, and Kyte Clockmaker lowered his voice. "Had a good evening, Ammun?"

"Yes. And you?"

"Fair. The king asked us to join his table—I thought it a good sign. He seemed in low spirits at first, but he cheered after a while. Very affable, just like Kohanan." Seeming to sense a misstep in that remark, the clockmaker hastened on to say, "There was quite the to-do about his daughter, though. Seems the third marshal wouldn't let her out of his sight, and she wasn't having any of it. Made the king uneasy, I thought. I didn't speak with the marshal myself."

"I did, in passing," Damon chimed. "Nasty little creature. He thinks highly of himself."

"He has good reason."

"Aye, maybe, Ammun, but others have better reason and never flaunted it."

The watcher brushed the topic aside. "What of the queen? What did you make of her?"

"Pleasant lady," the clockmaker asserted. "She's devoted to her husband, that's clear. I thought she looked a bit washed out, to tell the truth. When I saw her at the wake at the top of the week, she didn't look near as downhearted as she did tonight."

"I like the girl better. She has fire to spare," said Damon.

Kyte sighed. "Why am I not surprised that that's what caught your eye, my boy?"

"How did you find her otherwise, Damon?"

"I got the feeling she wanted to be anywhere else. She took no pleasure in this party, and the third marshal didn't help matters any. I wonder about that boy she seized upon. Poor lad. Looked as if she made a conquest there, the way he let her lead him like one of the family paldin dogs. Anyone would have suited her, the mood she was in, and he just happened to come at the right time. Poor fellow."

Relaxing in the corner, the watcher considered what he had been told and what he had seen for himself. *We shall see. First, I need to know more of Simon. Then I can plan my approach. I think the general comes first.*

INTERVIEW

Having entered through the main doors only once before, and that only after dark, Giles paused on the intricate tiles to marvel at his surroundings. Beneath his feet, the beautiful tiling depicted a dark, slender tree trunk pointing forward toward the stairs; its mosaic canopy, picked out in myriad shades of green, stretched to either side as if to guide the newcomer to the cloakrooms situated on either side of the hall. The crown that encircled the tree trunk glittered in the afternoon light. Bending low, Giles suppressed an exclamation of wonder: the crown was wrought, not of precious metal as expected, but of pale white stone flecked with amber. A single, small leaf was suspended inside the stone.

Someone in the lofty hall cleared his throat. Giles looked up to find one of the pale servants gazing down at him from the top of the stairs. "Can I help you, young sir?"

"I hope so," Giles answered, straightening hastily. He held out his invitation. "I'm due to meet with Princess Maia here today. Can you tell me where I might find her?" He identified himself and was promptly abandoned as the manservant disappeared down the stairs in the opposite direction. Giles raked his fingers through his hair in anticipation. The footsteps of the returning manservant startled him into an almost military stance, poised and eager for action.

"Her ladyship asks that you join her in the park. Follow me, sir."

Mounting the stairs, Giles fell into step behind the servant, down the other side, through the dim and silent ballroom, and out through the doors into a luxurious pleasure-garden of flowering shrubs and shadowy trees. Giles had little attention for the details of the place. The cool shadows touched his hot face as he entered the heart of the garden, a compact quadrangle of benches with a fountain splashing in its center. There, standing as if she had just risen from one of the benches, the princess waited to greet him. He was struck again with the sense that she stood above him in ways less tangible than her stature. As he bowed and spoke pleasantries, Giles did his best to restrain the expression of his admiration to a few carefully chosen, glib phrases that the girl could easily dismiss. Her amusement at his gallantries helped him to steady himself. "It was good of you, your highness, to invite me here to laugh at me in person."

"And what else was I to do? I get bored, too, you know. You don't live in King's City?"

"Not I. My father's house is outside, though nearly in the walls' shadow."

"That's odd. I thought all of Uncle Denei's kin lived inside."

"Indeed not. My other aunt, the woodsy one, lives at a Sakiry crossing in the southern lake country. I've been there once. Rude sort of a place. Too many gnats for my tastes...not that I eat them."

Maia laughed again. "I should hope not. Do you want to sit, or walk around the park awhile? It's all the same to me."

"I'd love a tour."

They strolled around the pleasure garden, and then out into the orchard, which the princess called "the park," talking of inconsequential matters for some time. When Maia asked him what school he attended, Giles dipped his head apologetically. "Alas, your highness, I'm not the bookish kind. Once the public schoolhouse gave me up for lost at thirteen, I pursued the lighter things of life. There are so many people to meet, you know. I hear you've chosen the Academy. Do you mean to be a warrior-queen when you're done? Thrash me if you think I'm cheeky. I don't doubt you'd do a proper job of it."

"Thrashing you, or the warrior-queen business?" she retorted.

"Of both."

"Thanks, I'm sure. I can't really say what I mean to do yet. I enjoy the Academy. Have you ever thought of trying it yourself?"

"Now that I know I'd see you there," said Giles smoothly, "but they'd never have me."

"I doubt that. Not with the relations you have."

"My relations are partly the problem, your highness. My father would foam at the mouth if I suggested the notion. It's his pet hobby-horse, you know—soldiers are parasites and troublemakers, and no good ever came of dabbling among them. I never quarreled with him on that before, seeing as how the only soldiers I'd ever dabbled amongst were those who came to collect me for my, ahem, visits with the local elders. For that matter, dear Father doesn't know I came calling today. He doesn't appreciate these great cities or their entertainments, not as I do."

"You know," said the girl with a sidelong glance, "if you sampled fewer entertainments, you wouldn't get collected so often by the soldiers."

"Ouch, your highness. Ouch, indeed!"

"How old are you? You know my age—everybody does—but I hardly know a thing about you."

"Seventeen, your highness, leaning toward eighteen. I have two elder sisters, one nineteen and the other one-and-twenty."

"I have no sisters or brothers at all. I've always been sorry about that."

"I don't know why. They're overvalued, siblings are. Especially elder ones. They have a way of pecking at a fellow, as if they were birds and he a poor worm."

"Poor worm. It must be a dreadful life, to be sure."

Poor worm, Giles echoed in thought. His eyes had lifted to examine the magnificent façade of Takra House, noticing for the first time the many windows that overlooked the park. He could easily imagine the eyes behind them. The more he considered the windows, the more unnerving he found them.

"You've gone awfully silent. What are you thinking about?"

"Do you ever find it strange, always to be watched like this?" Giles gave an explanatory nod toward the windows. "Any of a hundred people might be watching you down here."

"I don't really think of it much. It's just how things are. We can go inside if you like." Maia led him back in through a different door that took them through a sunroom into the Great Hall where the Caretakers congregated in their habitual hum of activity.

A number of them observed the pair as they passed, but no one made audible remarks. Giles felt their attention on his back as he followed Maia into the corridor, and was glad to shut the door behind himself. Then they ascended a small, winding stair to the next floor up. This floor, Giles found, was more graciously spread. His first view was of a series of arched doorways framing a distant set of high, sunny windows at the far end of the wing. Charmed, he followed Maia through the path of archways, looking into the small, open salons to either side. He didn't realize how perfect the silence was until he found himself whispering. He cleared his throat self-consciously. "You have a pretty house here, your highness. Very pretty."

Maia replied only after they had reached the end of the row of arches. She settled herself in a comfortable chair in the private salon that occupied the main part of the end of the building. "Do you like it? Nana Lucinda is forever grumbling that it's shamefully cramped, but I've never felt cramped. The doorways are a little low upstairs, at least for Father and me. Dara, stop a moment! The boys are all out on errands, I suppose. Be a good girl and tell the kitchen we want drinks, would you? Thank you." With a smile, she sent the child scampering. "There. You should stay to supper. Father tends to be gloomy these days. You might cheer him up."

Abandoning his plans for the evening, Giles replied helplessly, "Glad to, your highness."

"Good!" She had an emphatic way of expressing herself that daunted and beguiled him all at once, though she seemed not to notice his tongue-tied state.

The salon windows, which faced east, turned dark gradually. Servants came with drinks, and sometime later came with lights to fend off sunset. When they came to set up a table in the center of the room still later in the evening, Giles swallowed his discomfort. So far, he had only been introduced to the king and queen in passing during the ball. He had an idea that the king knew some little information about him, most likely through Owen or Denei, but this was no comfort. Quite the reverse: if the king knew anything of Giles' legal experiences, he would be extremely unlikely to desire Maia's further acquaintance with a young man of Giles' sort. As the minutes ticked loudly from the clock, he began to squirm inside. *Poor worm,* he mocked. *Why take fright when you've little enough to expect?* Giles couldn't stop watching the doorway surreptitiously to time. He leaped up when he recognized the towering form of the king.

Colin entered with his arm around his wife Selena. Between them they shared the look of two people whose secret conversation has been cut short by the appearance of its subject. The king was kind but still slightly reserved when he extended a hand to Giles. "Young Giles Perrin-son! Welcome to our table." Then he drew out a chair for Selena.

Turning to do the same for Maia, Giles discovered that the girl had already seated herself. He had nothing to do but take his own seat feeling even more like a boor.

"How did you like the masquerade?" the queen was asking him. "I heard some say there were too many people. It wasn't to my tastes, to be honest, but I thought most people enjoyed it."

"I don't know when I've had such fun," Giles replied with more fervor than he intended.

"It was too bad that your father couldn't come. Did your mother and sisters enjoy it?"

"I'm sure Mother found it very useful."

"Useful?" the queen echoed curiously.

"It's her highest hope to marry my sisters off well. The more chances she gets to start them among important people, the happier she is. Last night she was so happy, I walked home."

The king smiled a little. "That must have taken a while."

"I never noticed if it did. It was a fine night." *If that doesn't give the game away, I don't know what will,* Giles said to himself in disgust. "Anything but listen to who wore what dress and who danced with which sister more than any other girl. It's all fine for them, but where do I come into it? I say, let them have their fun. I'll amuse myself."

"From all reports, you amuse yourself in some interesting ways."

Giles felt his skin turning a rosy shade. "Yes, sir. I suppose I do."

"Doesn't Perrin have any employment for you?"

"I don't suppose that thought ever crossed his mind, sir. If the work he did was his own, maybe he'd be eyeing me as a replacement down the road, but as it stands, I don't suppose he has the time to find use for me. His master would never take me on. Says I can't stick to a job long enough for blisters to form. If I wanted blisters, I'd join an Alti work crew. When I told him that, he didn't take it in the proper spirit."

"What do you want to do?"

Since the question was Maia's, Giles found it hard to answer. "I don't rightly know," was the best he could manage.

To his surprise, the king smiled gently. "Were I you, I'd ask Owen's advice on that."

"Uncle Owen is a busy man, my lord."

"True. So am I, but here I sit. I don't know you, Giles—apart from what I've heard," he added with a wry smile, "but I've noticed your taste in society improving lately. I insist. Owen's busyness is no excuse. Kenda!" the king called, beckoning. When a maid came to the door, Colin said, "Go speak with your grandfather. Find out from him when Owen has an hour free in the next few days, and make an appointment in the name of Giles son of Perrin." The gaze he turned on Giles then was half challenging, half laughing. "There you go. Problem solved."

"Thank you, my lord." Giles was never much for weighing his thoughts, but he found a childish measure of comfort in the idea of sitting at his great-uncle's desk for a chat—and maybe sweet biscuits and chilled lemon tea, too, if he had any luck. The prospect moved him to repeat himself: "Thank you."

*   *   *   *

"What's this?" His father dropped a letter on the table. The seal had been broken.

Giles knew the handwriting after one glance. He left the letter where it lay and squared off against his father instead. "Letters are sealed for good reason. That was private, meant for me, not for you. What'd you go doing that for? Wasn't your business."

Perrin sat down. "I've turned my back rather than say anything, but you've been spending too much time in King's City. You aren't keeping that appointment. If you want to talk with Lord Sakiry, then invite him to come here for once. Sit down and eat your supper, Giles. I won't argue with you about this."

"Sure." Giles remained standing. "Invite Uncle Owen here? I'm sure he'd be glad to take an extra hour from his day just to call on the house of a man who can't figure out where his loyalties lie. I'm keeping the appointment. I won't argue with you about this."

If Perrin noticed the mockery in Giles' last statement, he gave no sign. "You are not going back into King's City until this trouble dies down. That's an order. If you don't obey me in this, I will have you picked up and held for a week, no surety offered the jailer on your behalf." With that, he picked up a spoon and began on his soup as if there were nothing more to be said on the matter. He only looked up when Giles refused to sit down. "Sit down. I am your father."

And what does that have to do with anything? Giles picked up the letter, smoothed its creases, and slipped it into the cuff of his sleeve. "Good day, *Father.*" He went down the hall to his bed chamber. With the door shut against the rest of the household, he sank down onto the edge of his bed to read Owen's letter.

To my great-nephew Giles Perrin-son,
From Owen, Lord Sakiry:
Greetings.

First, let me say it's high time I heard from you. That said, let me apologize. It has been too long, and the fault of that I take entirely on myself.

You're young and forgetful—what cause could you have for giving thought to an old great-uncle? But I assure you, though I have not acted upon it, I have thought of you often. You must imagine how glad a surprise it was for me to discover your name on my appointment schedule. I have cancelled everything else from that hour onward. Once you come, you may have as much of my time as you wish, until you choose to quit my company. I assure you, I look forward to renewing our friendship. Until tomorrow!

Giles searched his pockets without coming up with anything useful, not even so much as a stub of pencil. He worried the edge of the table with his fingers out of habit while he thought about the problem, until at length he accidentally worried off a large splinter, startling himself with the resounding crack. A smile slowly overtook his face. *It's the right shape, if small. But ink? Stupid, stupid,* he castigated himself. *What's ink made of?* He went to the lamp that sat unlit and cold on its pedestal high on the wall.

The lamp had not been cleaned for several weeks, so there was more soot than oil left in it. Giles discovered that the mixture, though a bit thick, was good enough to allow him to scratch out a few words for his great uncle: *P forbids Ill find a way G.* He blew on it lightly to help the ink dry more quickly, but the mixture was stubbornly moist. Returning to the floor, Giles used both hands to sweep up some dust. His bed chamber had last been cleaned around the same time as the lamp, a state of affairs that worked in his favor for once. He sprinkled the sweepings over the ink. Then he gingerly pressed down on the message with his sleeve to make sure that all was dry and permanent. It pleased him to note that very little of the improvised ink came off onto the fabric. He closed the letter and examined it to see if any bleed-through might betray that its contents had changed, but found nothing to give alarm.

With the creases renewed, the letter sat closed, as if it had never been opened. Giles nodded in satisfaction. "And now...the excuse." He returned to the lamp. For a few minutes, he dabbled in the soot and ink mixture, smearing it liberally on the sleeve he had used for blotting the letter. He even put a few smudges on his face. Once his hands were thoroughly grubby and any telltale marks on his garments were covered over by new stains, he took up all the parts of the lamp and carried them down to the kitchen where his mother and sisters were tidying up after the noontide meal.

His oldest sister saw him first. "Giles! What have you done?"

He set down the lamp on the worktable. "My lamp won't work. I was trying to clean it, but nothing helps."

"Well, no wonder!" his mother exclaimed. "If you took better care of your things, they wouldn't come to this! I can't see why you'd make such a mess. It's the middle of the day."

"Late to be repairing the lamp once it's already dark out," was Giles' retort. "Anyway, I don't need light. I need to heat the seal on my letter. If I'm not keeping my appointment, then I have to send the invitation back unopened or he'll suspect things. We wouldn't want him to know my good father doesn't want me to have anything to do with the king or his family, right?"

"You know that's not how things are," chided his mother mildly. She was already well into the process of setting the lamp to rights. "Your father is simply looking after you. You're no soldier, Giles, and the less you meddle with them, the safer you are."

"Certainly." Giles wiped his blackened hands on a kitchen towel, drawing another scolding cry from his sisters. He made a face. "That's what towels are for, isn't it?" To humor them, he went to the sink and washed with soap to remove as much soot as he could.

Always efficient, his mother reassembled the lamp and was polishing the glass chimney clean before he could finish drying his hands. "Leave the soot alone next time, Giles; it's there for a reason. Tsarai, bring me the kitchen lamp, please." She tipped Giles' little lamp toward the flame of the large kitchen lamp until the wick caught flame; then she capped it with the chimney and handed it to her son. "There. On your way, now. The kitchen is no place for a boy your age."

That's what I love about you, Mother, Giles quipped. *You never ask questions.* He closed himself in his room to finish the task, hoping Owen was still as clever as he remembered.

NAMELESS ONE

Dew still hung on the shrubs when a carriage arrived at the house of Denei Mata-son. After a few moments, the housekeeper hardly finished announcing the arrival of Owen, Lord Sakiry before Owen breezed into the dining room. "Good morning to you, Riana," he said, bending to kiss his sister-in-law's cheek. "Is there any for me?"

Denei motioned for him to sit. "Ivy isn't up yet. Take her chair. You're out early."

"I have a problem that can only be solved—" Owen paused to thank the cook for setting a plate in front of him. "—by someone in this house. Did you know Giles made an appointment to see me today?"

"No, did he?" Riana said, a smile brightening her face. "That's good."

"Yesterday I sent him a note just to say how pleased I was, but the note came back to me later that same day, apparently unopened. At first I thought it had just gone astray, but of course it had been opened; the boy faked the seal to make it look like it hadn't—an artful little counterfeit it was, too—but inside he'd scribbled a few words to say that his father forbids the visit. He still means to find a way, but this is unacceptable. One of you has to go have a long talk with Perrin."

Denei exchanged a look with his wife. "It may be that the time for talking is past."

"We've...lately..." Riana drew a deep breath, forcing herself to continue. "We've seen that something must be done about Giles. His mother...well, she doesn't hesitate to make it known that she thinks young men raise themselves.

She insists that his father knows the right way with Giles, if only Giles weren't so disobedient, she says. Perrin, well, he sees things only one way. He never did have much in the way of a sympathetic imagination. He doesn't…doesn't *try*. If Giles doesn't accept the plans he makes for him, then he washes his hands of the boy. He left the poor child in jail for three days last month before he would go and offer surety for him."

"Ivy is of a mind that Giles' only hope is his upcoming birthday," Denei added.

"Ah…when he'll be declared a man and can leave his father's house?"

"Exactly, Owen! But we've talked about this before, and three months more of this might be too much. I for one am sure that the boy's disciplinary troubles wouldn't have grown so pronounced if he'd had someone to look after him properly. And if Perrin has gone as far as to forbid him to see you…" Riana shook her head angrily. "That's the end of it. The boy has to come and stay here with us. Don't you think so, Denei?"

"If you lend us your carriage, Owen, we'll pick him up today. When is his appointment?"

"Two this afternoon."

"Take Ivy with you," Denei said to his wife. "Go collect the boy and his things as soon as the carriage is free. If you go before the noontide, Perrin won't be home. You know that wife of his is easier to manage when she doesn't have him to hide behind. Ivy can help smooth things over with her. Have her bring a…a dress pattern or some such thing. The less said about your real reasons, the better, I think."

Owen grinned. "A dress pattern? Can it be—my brother has learned to be subtle?"

Denei gave a smile in response, but it was half-hearted and tinged with frustration. "Not subtle enough, and least of all when it matters the most. Have you seen or heard anything more inside the palace, now that you know to look for it? I can't grip my hands around it. There's something afoot. I know that much, but what it is, I can't pin down." He pushed a sausage around with his fork, scowling at his thoughts. No one responded, so he spoke the thought that had weighed most heavily upon him. "Owen? Do you know of anyone who has the Sight?"

"A seer?" Owen raised his eyebrows. "No. I don't know of any."

"We need one. If we haven't found one…perhaps we must make one."

Owen looked at him sideways. "What are you tiptoeing around, Den? Speak your mind."

"I've thought about this ever since...ever since the bonfire last week. The only person I know of who has the qualities needed to become a seer...it's you. I've never had the aptitude, you know, but you, Owen, you're of Kohanan's blood. You can read the old tongue. You know the lore. Why not?"

"Why not you?" Owen challenged, reddening as he grew more flustered. "You say you haven't the aptitude, but no one else could withstand Kohanan's power better than you could when it took him."

"I saw his master once. I couldn't bear it. I begged him to leave me. He said..." Denei shivered as if chilled, despite the room's warmth. "He told me that when I saw him again, I would be glad, but others would grieve. It doesn't take much insight to understand what he meant, Owen. The day I gain the Sight is the day of my death."

An uneasy lull filled the room until Ivy, Denei's second stepdaughter, came down to breakfast. Blithely, she kissed her mother's face and the top of Denei's head before dragging an extra chair to the table beside Owen. "Good morning, Uncle Owen. You're out early today. I hope nothing's wrong."

Owen stirred himself to respond in a natural voice, but Denei saw the sobered glance that Owen kept giving him. Denei bent over his plate as if it occupied his attention while his brother explained the predicament concerning young Giles. Ivy responded with an appropriate level of dismay and promised her uncle to do whatever it took to see that Giles kept his appointment. Then Riana entered the conversation. "While he's with Owen at the palace, dear, we'll need to ready Perrin's old room for him. He's coming to stay with us for the time being."

"I think it'll be wonderful, having him here," Ivy replied. "He's a good fellow, Giles is. He just needs a little reforming, that's all. I'm sure Poppa Denei can take him in hand in no time—can't you, Poppa? He'll be much better off here. At the very least, he'll be closer to young Maia, and that's bound to cheer him up no end."

"Whether it'll do *her* any good," Denei said dryly, "remains to be seen."

"He's not so bad!"

"He's not so good either, Ivy. You haven't heard half the tales I've heard."

Owen intervened. "Colin and I talked of that last night, too. Giles stayed to dine with them night before last, and Colin says the boy acts in the proper ways when he wants to. I haven't had as much chance to observe the two of them myself, but it seems as if she has a good effect on the boy. Maybe nothing will come of it. Maybe something will. All the same, what could it hurt to work with him now, while he's willing—whatever the reason?"

"You'll have to find a way to work with him when Maia's around, then." Having had the last word, Ivy turned the subject. "Uncle Owen, while we have the use of your carriage, would you mind terribly if I used it a little longer and went to run a few errands? It'll go so much quicker if I don't have to walk everywhere, and I have such a lot of places to go. Please?"

"Of course. I don't mean to go anywhere once Giles comes. Use it as long as you need. Speaking of going anywhere, Den, are you finished? We ought to get going ourselves. I have a petition hearing to attend. How early is Colin expecting you?"

"We never set a time. I want to go over the papers once more for myself before I meet with him." Denei set down his napkin beside his empty plate. He kissed his wife farewell, received Ivy's kiss on his cheek, and went in search of his boots. He felt Owen's attention on his back all while he attended to the minutia of departure.

All during the brief ride to the palace, neither one spoke. Owen had sunk into his ruminations so deeply that, when the carriage stopped at the door to Takra House, Denei had to nudge him with a foot to rouse him back to the moment. The only insight Owen gave Denei regarding his state of mind came as they parted ways to each enter his own office. Then, Owen said only, "I just don't know if that's how it works." Then Denei understood. He made no reply, knowing that Owen would be deaf to it.

Troubling himself over what I said—as if he could think it through. Denei laughed softly to himself. *I hope he finds his way soon.* He went to his desk and pulled out a rumpled file of papers bound together with string. Spreading the sheets evenly across the desk, he gazed at each one in turn. Each sheet represented a viable succession candidate, with a list of his merits and detractions occupying most of the document. Because he did not want to, Denei forced himself to consider the third marshal's document first. *Merits: has shown superior tactical abilities. Has shown ability to negotiate effectively with other clansmen. Has shown ability to lead warriors effectively.* Denei shook his head. *Demerits: has displayed lack of respect for law. Has not created rapport with Colin. Has shown tendency to pursue Maia regardless of her preference. May hold ambitions that endanger the royal house.* The last, supplied out of his own head rather than seen on the paper, made Denei draw in a deep breath and lean back with his eyes shut. *Cannot be dismissed, will not be ignored, ought not to be trusted—but I have no proof!*

He sat with his documents in the oppressive silence, always coming back to that one troublesome paper, like a grain of sand that he could not flush out of his eye. In the end, he found nothing to do but bundle the lists up again and shut them away in a drawer. Even then, with that decision made, he sat back in his chair, doing nothing. He could hear the passage of men going back and forth outside his door—Owen's voice rang out clearly for a moment, saying goodbye to someone quieter—two pair of booted feet strode past, out of sync—the monotonous voice of Owen's dozy son Lyndall discoursing to some hapless listener—several young men, debating loudly. Still, Denei sat immobile. He felt the frustration of his limitations like a physical weight. On a whim, he lifted a hand and flexed it, just to see if it still obeyed his will. The inertia held until he finally set his mind to get up. "No use putting it off." He rose with a groan and had to steady himself against the edge of the desk for an instant.

Outside in the corridor, he was slightly disconcerted to find the third marshal facing him. The young soldier had apparently just emerged from his own office at the other end of the intersecting hallway. He too stopped short. "General." He made his bow stiffly.

"Marshal." Denei nodded and went on his way down the corridor toward the private east wing. There, he found the king standing in the corridor with a startled, almost guilty look. "Headed out? Don't worry, Colin. I only need a few words. I won't keep you long." He escorted the king back inside the office. "I only came to cancel our meeting today. There's no use in it. I can't settle my mind to any of them. I'm sorry."

"Do you think it would help if we sat down and talked through the difficulties? I'm due at a welcome for the Sea Folk heir and his wife presently, but maybe this afternoon?"

Denei shook his head. "I can sum up the difficulties for you while we stand here: five candidates, none outstanding enough to make up for his shortcomings. You have Miklei-son, obviously, who may be most able but certainly is least worthy of trust. Your Alti candidate, that youngling Raddlai-son, who we all know is most trustworthy, is the least qualified for this level of command. Nobody will countenance a Pamirsi general except Berhus Pamirsi, not with the crown city standing in Pamirsi territory as it does, so that washes out two more candidates, leaving us with the Sea Folk fellow, Dermot-son, the mediocre one nobody can abide. Those are my difficulties. I've weighed them time and again."

"I see." Colin was silent and thoughtful for a short while. Then he said, "It's hard to know which way to turn, when you put it like that. I know you said that your successor has to be someone I can get along with, but if the only objection to Dermot-son is his personality, you can pass over my preferences, if that helps you. Perhaps it's time to narrow your qualifications to trustworthiness and ability, and find the one that best balances the two. I can put up with quite a lot, you know. It's all right."

"That's generous of you, Colin. I'll take it into consideration. Go on. You have somewhere to go, and I have thinking to do." Instead of returning to his office, however, Denei wandered through the private wing, down the stairs, and eventually out into the courtyard on his way home.

He had not gone far before he felt the old heaviness in his chest again. His tired heart gave two or three odd beats before it returned to its rhythm. Denei slowed his pace in hopes of preventing a recurrence. In the hazy sunlight, heat rolled off the street to fill his lungs. He stopped after a few more steps, too aware of passersby to show his discomfort and his weakness. There was some sort of flower bed near the street, so Denei gazed at it with dimmed eyes, seeing nothing as the irregularity in his pulse returned. Dizzied, he lost count of the odd beats. Slowly, however, the attack passed. Denei turned from the little garden box and continued on his way, but he knew that he would not make it far afoot before the fit took him again.

"Good day to you, General!"

Roused from his weariness by the stranger's voice addressing him, Denei looked up to find a young man smiling down at him from the seat of a large closed carriage not half a dozen paces ahead. The face stirred a memory, though it took a few moments for Denei to attach a name to it. "Ah. You're Kyte's boy, aren't you? The roving one."

"Damon to my friends, General."

"Yes…Damon. I remember seeing you at the masquerade." Grateful for the excuse to rest, Denei leaned on the hitching post. "Your father must be glad to have you back from your wandering at last."

"So he says, but I'm in town for business only, not to stay. It's promising to be a hot day, General. Can I persuade you to accept a ride to wherever you're going? It'll save you time, something I have an abundance of at the moment." The young man hopped down lightly to the pavement and went to open the carriage door to bolster his offer.

"I appreciate the offer." Denei climbed inside, aware of the subtle hand at his elbow giving him assistance. He settled into the forward-facing seat, only to realize with a faint tingle of alarm that the carriage was already occupied. Then the door shut, leaving them in shadow.

"Good day, General. I hope you don't mind. It may be a less than conventional meeting place, but it is at least secure from listening ears," said a low, rasping voice.

Denei's eyes began to adjust. He saw the outline of a man, a veritable giant, stretched out lazily in the opposite corner. Two large boots extended across the floor, crossed tidily at the ankles, the essence of ease. The man's face was too shadowed to be discerned. Denei cleared his throat. "I believe I know who you are. Tyrell warned me of you."

"Warned? That's a curious choice of words."

"He said that you'd show yourself when I didn't look for you."

A deep, appealing chuckle filled the carriage. "In one village, that is how I am known—their name for me translates as *the Unforeseen Guest*. There are many things we must discuss. Your enemies approach even now, General Mata-son. My men have been harrying them for miles. I rode ahead to meet with you. Your third marshal: how well do you know him?"

"Well enough to cause misgivings."

"Only misgivings, say you? Then you certainly do not know enough. Some time ago, before he came to his present office, your third marshal disappeared for several weeks. I have intelligence of where he went, and how he spent those weeks: dabbling in a Garden of the Forbidden. He has kept this secret even from those who know him best, but a man does not emerge alive from such a place without making certain choices, and he has brought those choices with him here. It is imperative that this man be removed from the king's service. I understand that such a course of action is politically unrealistic for now, so I present you with an alternative. You must choose your successor from among the other candidates. It no longer matters which is most suitable. Any of them will do, so long as you make it known to all that you have finally chosen one."

"Which would you have me choose?"

"I have no advice to offer. You know them best. As I told you, the man himself doesn't matter. I will provide whatever is lacking. I am your ally. There are other steps you must take, however. You must see to it that the princess is removed from her classes at the Academy and begins at once her apprenticeship under her father. She must begin to learn her future role immediately. Above all, keep her close to the king. Choose for her a new half-set of guards, proven warriors in their early prime whose honor is unassailable. She has come of age; now she must begin to take up some of the responsibility of her birth."

Two forces warred inside Denei's mind as he weighed the demands. One side of him welcomed the prospect of positive action—any action—to take against the third marshal's ambitions. It was this side that impulsively favored the stranger. The other side, however, was not so easily persuaded. "What pledge do you offer that I should do as you demand?"

The ring of steel answered him. There, in the dim, stuffy carriage, a gleam: the muted reflections of a polished, engraved blade balanced on the man's fingertips. Denei reached forward to take the blade, recognizing it immediately. "You bear my lord the king's sword."

"A gift given by a dying man to seal a pact. That, General, is the only pledge I bring."

Denei offered back the sword. "It's enough. I will see that your requirements are met."

"Good." The shadow moved, knocked sharply on the carriage wall, and opened the grate to let in a blinding shaft of late spring sun. He gave orders in a tongue that Denei did not recognize. In response, the carriage turned and picked up speed. Then the grate shut, leaving the carriage darker than before. "You should receive information about the raiders' next attack soon. Miklei-son will bring the news, expecting it to come as a surprise. What he cannot tell you is the strength of the force that you must face. I can. By the time they reach you, the raiders will number no more than six thousand."

"You're very sure of that," Denei remarked.

"My men are accustomed to rendering strict obedience. Before I rode ahead to warn you, I set them the task of reducing your enemies to that number or fewer. I have every reason to believe that they will fulfill their duty. They are not many, but their quality is unsurpassed."

Denei felt his approval of the man rise. "I look forward to meeting them one day."

"I hope that day comes. You seem not to realize your peril. Do you not see that you are the first obstacle in Miklei-son's way? As long as you stand between him and his ambition, you walk under a shadow. My hope is only that I have come to give you the warning in time." The shadow shifted and drew back the edge of a curtain to look out at the street.

Squinting, Denei caught the briefest image of a dark cloth mask, fashioned after the style of a public executioner's, covering from the nape of the neck in back to the jaw in front. Dark, piercing eyes stared through the window for only a moment before the curtain dropped again.

"We have arrived. I hope I need not warn you to keep this meeting a secret. Good day, General. The next time we meet, I hope to have more information to offer you. If you wish to contact me, do as you did the last time, and I will hear of it."

As if those words were a cue, the carriage came to a halt. It swayed as the young man hopped down from his driver's box. Then Damon opened the door, blinding Denei for a moment. Denei descended from the carriage and gazed up at the city infirmary. "Why here?" he asked the young man, who had only just shut the carriage door.

"I only did as told, General. I hope you had a profitable ride. Good day." He climbed up, took up the reins, and left Denei staring pensively after the carriage.

Inside the infirmary, Denei went to the first orderly he saw. "Is Chief Healer Clary-son in today? I wish to speak with him."

"Certainly, General. Come with me." The orderly led Denei up a flight of steps to the office of Owen's son-in-law. "Chief, the general is here to see you."

"Come in!" Doran stood to greet Denei. "What brings you, sir?"

"I need your advice as a healer."

Doran's expression grew more solemn the longer he listened to Denei's description of the fit that had befallen him on the way from Takra House. At the end of the account, he drew a long breath. "How long has this been happening, and you haven't said anything?"

"It never was this bad before."

"Well, first off, I have to insist that you don't travel on foot any longer. Your heart is weakening. The more work you force it to do, the more these episodes will multiply."

"Is there any action to be taken? Any at all?"

"Less worry. More rest." Doran had a knowing look in his eye. "It's the succession. It caused the fit to worsen. It's not good for you."

While the healer spoke, Denei began to grasp the vague shape of an idea triggered by Doran's remark about the succession. *Wait…he said he'd fill in the lack, but what if…why not? He's qualified. It would be unconventional. So what if it is? Conventional answers have gotten me nowhere. There are details to be crafted, to be sure…must consult Riana. She's sensible and won't carry the tale anywhere.* Then he heard the healer call him sharply by name. "Pardon?"

"Are you feeling ill? Has it started again?"

Denei was too caught up in his new line of reasoning to feel abashed at having his inattention exposed. "No, no, I'm well. There's another thing I wish to…once I've sorted it out, naturally—you and Phoebe should come to dinner soon. Then we can talk at leisure." He recalled himself with an effort. "I've taken up enough of your time today."

"And where would you be going?" the healer asked with a hint of shrewdness. "Afoot, no less? No, sir, I'm afraid I have to ask you to stay here until someone fetches you. You can rest here undisturbed for as long as need be. Truth be told, I'd like to keep an eye on you for a few hours. It strikes me that you don't take this episode of yours as seriously as you should. I insist. There's a comfortable chair by the window if you like."

Denei shrugged. *This is as good a place as any, since what I need most of all is time to think. No one will disturb me here.* He took the chair by the window and looked out onto the street for a while, letting his mind grow calm under the muted rhythm of the carriage traffic below. Then, as if unpacking a knapsack, he began laying out his argument. *This foreign warrior has proven himself as a leader of men. Battlefield experience far beyond anything a native-born candidate could boast...even Miklei-son. He swore loyalty. Kohanan himself took his oath. That's greatly in his favor. He shows judgment. True, I don't know him past the short time we met today. I can't say why I trust him, but I do. If I know anything, I know warriors, and this is one to be respected. He knows how to maneuver. He seems like the sort that seizes the chances as they come, and he succeeds at it. The Unforeseen Guest, truly.*

Then, just as methodically, he marshaled the most obvious objections. *He's foreign. I could hear it in his voice, that bit of accent. Where does he come from? He doesn't acknowledge his name any longer. That name...what little I've heard of Orlan's past has all been alarming. Who knows if he holds ambitions of his own, like Miklei-son? He knows how to give orders, yes, but he seems to feel no need to explain them. That will hit the Council the wrong way. Also, Colin hasn't met him. Who's to know if they'd get along? Given all that...why choose him?*

The answer rose spontaneously from somewhere deep within: *Because we need him.*

"Who would be the most likely person to come fetch you?" Doran asked suddenly from across the room. "Does Father have time to bring his carriage?"

"What? No, no, he let Ivy use it for her errands."

"How did you get here?"

Denei hesitated. "I met a young fellow on the way. From boyhood, his father was a friend to Kohanan, and the young fellow offered me a ride. But he's gone about his business already. Have you been thinking again of resigning as marshal?"

The healer's straw-colored eyebrows rose at the unexpected question. "I had thought to let it rest until the greater matters were settled. Is someone mentioning it again?"

'Someone' being Miklei-son, Denei understood without being told in so many words. "No. It was a thought that crossed my mind. I still hold to my position. I only wondered. It has to be hard on you, but I need someone like you in the first marshal's office. No. I merely wondered because I have, as you said, been trou-

bling myself day and night over my own replacement, but I may have struck on something today. I'm not ready yet to open it for discussion, that's all."

"Ah! Dinner makes more sense now. I won't pry much, but have you decided?"

Denei nodded. "I believe so. There are negotiations to be made...witnessed..." He returned his gaze to the window. This time, he surveyed the array of tall houses, all nestled so close together that the grass could not flourish at their bases. He saw women leaning out of windows to shake rugs or to call to children running in the streets below. The sight of those few busy housewives gave rise to a question: *Is he a man with family? Wife, children? How does he live? I feel that he's worthy of trust, but what manner of man is he?* In his mind's eye, Denei saw again the mask that he had glimpsed on the way to the infirmary. Then, without any preparatory thought, an idea sprang fully formed into his mind: his stepdaughter Ivy beside the stranger in the midst of an elegant crowd, making introductions.

Before Denei had a moment to process such a shocking idea, someone discreetly knocked at the office door. "Chief? Here's a man to see the general."

Doran seemed only mildly surprised at the announcement. "Go on, Tavi, show him in."

To Denei's astonishment, it was the curiosity merchant, Tyrell, as elegant and courteous as ever. "General." He bowed. "Chief Healer." He bowed in the other direction. "I happened to be nearby when I was told that you had come to visit this good healer. If I may have the honor of offering you my carriage once you have completed your visit...?"

Denei wiped all surprise from his face and voice. "Doran, you haven't met Tyrell. He's a recent acquaintance. Owen introduced us." He watched their greeting. "Well, Doran? May I?"

The healer gave a rueful smile in response to the question's irony. "I'll expect to see you here again in a few days, sir. Otherwise, I'd say we're done today. Remember what I told you."

"Of course."

Once they were comfortably ensconced in Tyrell's single-horse gig, Denei said, "I hope he didn't take you away from important business to make you cart me home like this."

Tyrell smiled. "I am always glad to be of service, General."

"You were right to say I wouldn't expect him. Are you sure you've told all you know?"

"I have told you everything that I have been empowered to tell you. It only happens to be true that the same information is all the information that I possess.

May I ask the good general why he asks this of me? I hope that I have not given the impression of deceit."

"Is it strange to think I'd want to know more of this man?"

"To me, it *is* strange. For much of my life, among my people, it was considered deadly to know much of him. Only recently have I found it more profitable than perilous."

"Where do you come from?"

"I was born in the principality of Sulvisin, eastward beyond the Minghar peaks."

"I have heard something of it," Denei remarked. "His reach stretched so far? I had thought that the raiders' territory was northerly."

"It was, and it now is again. Only under Orlan's domination did we learn to fear the northerners even more than the Kavahri, our natural threat. I left Sulvisin before Orlan became an ally. There was opportunity here that one such as I could never find at home. My mother's people are herders; my father's people miners. Neither suited my likings, so I joined a merchant caravan as an apprentice. At the time, Orlan was in his ascendance. He had not yet reached the height of his power, yet we feared him." Tyrell glanced out the window. "Ah! Your home lies ahead of us, General. As for telling tales, I fear I would only be able to offer hearsay, and what is a tale told second-hand? I speak only what I know. I have found this the only sensible way."

"Highly sensible. I have one question more before I take my leave: when you were told to come pick me up from the infirmary, did you happen to see the young man driving his carriage?"

"There was a young man, yes—fair-haired and light of heart? Yes. I do not know him myself. I told you, General, that your ally has other contacts, of which I know nothing at all."

"I remember." Denei drew a breath. While the merchant was talking, the general had made up his mind without pausing to think the matter through. "Will you do something for me?"

"Anything that lies within my abilities, sir."

"Find me an apartment somewhere near the palace. I don't care how much it costs."

"What sort of rooms do you require? Are they for your personal use, for entertaining? Or perhaps—for your younger daughter?"

Denei glanced sharply at the thin-faced merchant. "Why do you say that?"

"I have heard rumors about your daughter, General. She has drawn his interest, shall we say? Property within the walls is an excellent addition to any woman's dowry."

"I'm relieved to hear that, if you mean what I think you mean. I take that to mean that he isn't already married? If other—rumors—happen your way from the same source, make free to share my drift with him. That reminds me: if my wife and I were to hold a small, private dinner after a few days, would you come? I'll send word around of the details."

"Certainly. Good day, General Mata-son."

Denei's wife was glad to see him when he found her in the kitchen. When she came to kiss his cheek, Riana asked, "How was your meeting with Colin? I've thought of it all morning. You're home early…does that mean you came to an answer at last?"

"Something else happened." He told her briefly of his encounters that morning, withholding only his outrageous notion about the succession. "I'm myself again," he assured her when she reacted to the news of his attack of illness. "It was too much exertion in this heat, nothing more. I only needed rest. There's more I need to tell you, but not here. Let's go to the sitting room where we can shut ourselves in. This needs privacy." For once, he had great difficulty maintaining his impervious expression when he saw his wife's curiosity.

The sitting room was shady and cool on the north side of the house. Through the half-open window, a breath of air stirred the curtains. Denei shut the window and, for good measure, pulled the drapes shut as well. Then he returned to Riana's side and sat down with his arm around her. He let his pulse slow rather than launching immediately into his revelation. "I believe I have found my answer."

"But you said—"

When she didn't continue, Denei nodded. "Yes. I told Colin I couldn't choose between any of the candidates I had, but then…this meeting with the outlander…as unlikely as it sounds, he is the one. In a certain light, Kohanan himself chose him. I have never been so certain of anything: this is the man to follow after me. There *are* problems," he allowed.

"Aren't there? An outlander! But I've always known you to be a man of sense. If you say he's the one, then what are a few problems? Naturally, you'll be slighting the majority of the patriarchs, and they'll none of them be overjoyed to have a foreign general. They'll call him a mercenary. Does he have the proper sort of courage to walk into the Grand Council and convince them, given that? I know he's a warrior, but there's courage and courage, you know."

"I would never dare put anything beyond the reach of this one. He speaks with hardly any accent to note. Perhaps he doesn't know the names and personalities, but that can be learned."

"I hope he learns quickly, then. A lot of damage can be done while he's learning."

"This one is a man full grown, a seasoned leader of men, a—a—I'm not sure what to call him, in fact, but I'd wager any amount of money on it: he can meet the patriarchs on their own ground. In his own lands, I'm sure he's looked upon as some sort of prince, if not more. He does not strike me as a learned man, but a knowledgeable one, yes. And let's not forget that he has his own connections in a number of quarters." Denei paused for a moment of quiet reflection. In his mind's eye, he saw the hangman's mask again. "Some changes will be needed. He does bring with him a reputation…and though it may not be commonly known among the plains folk, the Pamirsi especially, I cannot expect everyone else to be oblivious."

Riana mused aloud, "There's respectability in a man with family, whatever else is known of him. Does he have a wife and children?"

"Tyrell says not." He struggled to speak the thought that had come to him earlier in the day. Then he looked to his wife, only to find a startled epiphany in her eyes. He ventured, "Ivy?"

Riana seemed afraid of the sound of her own voice. "What greater testimony? Son by marriage? For once, your partiality for Ivy will serve an impartial purpose. No one could doubt that he has your trust and your approval. He gains by it, too. She knows the patriarchs' families intimately. She grew up among them and…and her intimacy with the royal family. How many have said it? 'She would make the perfect diplomat's wife.'" Her fists clenched on his chest.

"But do you think she would? After all this time, she still holds to Jarod's memory."

"Would she? *Should* she? Denei—you must find out what manner of man he is. Not even for the sake of the kingdom's safety would I force her into…oh, Denei. How can we?"

YESTERDAY: NOTHING TO LIVE FOR

Jarod's opportune moment came when his mother sent him out into the orchard "to get some air," all because he was too pale for her liking. He obeyed as if it meant nothing to him. In the orchard, he wandered toward the dog kennels and called for his favorite paldin dog, Vailla. "Good girl," he muttered, stroking her silky ears. Although the small voice of Audune was still for the moment, Jarod felt the immortal shepherd-giant's attention. Dark thoughts rose from Jarod's mind to overwhelm him. No one took note of him as he walked with the dog at his side. When he came to the servants' gate, however, he found that he would have to pass under the gaze of the dog master, Dante. The immigrant skewered him with a shrewd look, but made no effort to stop him. *Maybe he didn't really guess. He won't say anything.* All the same, Jarod forced himself to walk at a nonchalant pace.

King's City was quiet. Because the king and his heir were out of the city on a tour of the Massifi territory, most of the political residents of the crown city had taken the opportunity for a holiday of their own. King's City being primarily political in nature, it was almost made a ghost town by this exodus. Jarod was glad for the absence of watching eyes as he made his way northward out of the city. He wanted no witnesses who might tell his family that they had seen him at all, let alone in which direction he had traveled.

He could not endure himself any longer. That was the conclusion that he had reached in the darkness of his sleepless nights. If he could not free himself—and no one in all the course of history had ever broken free of an immortal shepherd—then he would renounce his life. Anything rather than let this misery hurt his family.

The nearest wilderness lay to the eastward, beyond the Great River. Jarod made short work of it on his long legs, the dog trotting beside him in casual obedience to his will. He avoided the Sakiry crossing, choosing instead to swim the river. When it paused for him, he took it as a favorable sign. *I have not been utterly rejected,* he pointed out to the small voice goading him onward. *The river still stopped for me.*

If its master cared for you, came the acerbic reply, *he would make his river sweep you to sea and be done with you. You are beneath his notice, just as you are beneath the notice of everyone who matters in this mortal realm.*

On the other side of the river, Jarod reached the foothills of the Minghar Range just before true dark set in. He had brought nothing, not even a bedroll or a flint for starting a campfire, but the night was summery. He lay under the star-sprinkled dome of sky, feeling the dog's warmth beside him.

A stranger's voice, not the voice of his malicious shepherd Audune, addressed him. *This is what you call a fine night, is it not?*

Startled, Jarod asked, "Who spoke?"

I beg your pardon. I heard you speak to your own giant, and I thought that perhaps I might make free to speak to you also.

"Sure, but who are you?"

I am called Gia. You call my charge Vailla. Your dog.

"Vailla has a giant, too?"

As do all mortal creatures.

"Why did you never speak to me before?"

Silence! Audune cut in sharply, frightening the other shepherd Gia into obedience. *Who are you to speak with a human, beast-shepherd? Learn your place!*

Vailla the dog raised her head with a yelp of alarm, skittering a few paces away from Jarod as her immortal shepherd cried out as well. For a moment, the dog would not respond to any of Jarod's persuasions. Jarod crawled closer slowly, holding out his hand. "Easy, girl. Easy. It's all right." His heart ached over the beast's distress. "It's all right," he crooned to the dog. "Don't be afraid...I won't make you stay with me. Home, Vailla. Home."

The dog wouldn't budge. It wouldn't come nearer, but neither would it leave him.

"Go home, Vailla. Gia, take Vailla home. This is no place for her. I command it!"

Down on her belly now, the dog crept backward, keeping Jarod in sight until they were too far apart in the darkness. Then Jarod heard the dog's loping footfalls head off on the path homeward. He stretched out on his back and stared up at the sky with dull eyes.

Morning found him half awake already. The ground was hard, and his dreams had served only to deter him from sleep. Stiffly, Jarod rose. The wooded foothills lay before him, and he plunged into their depths with determination. Now he began to hear the calls of wild beasts, some of them alarmingly near. Jarod kept onward, knowing that Audune meant for something dreadful to happen to him. *Do whatever you like. However it ends is fine by me.*

In the forest, day looked much like dusk, with the gaps in the canopy serving as stars above to light his path. The deeper he roamed, the thicker the canopy grew. Soon, it was like midnight. Insects swarmed in the heavy, still air. Jarod plodded onward, wiping away the sweat that streamed into his eyes. Then, poised on the edge of a dimly-lit clearing, Jarod halted.

A slavering wolf leaped to its feet, disturbed by Jarod's arrival. Strings of saliva ran from its jaws. Jarod backed away, holding his hands carefully still as he edged backward. "So sorry," he murmured gently. "Didn't mean to intrude." He noticed signs of illness in the beast. His heart sank. He was entirely unarmed, and the wolf was sick enough to attack him despite his conciliatory attempts. "Easy…easy…" Jarod watched it crouch, but before it could spring, he jumped for the nearest tree trunk and shinnied up far enough to evade the first lunge.

That's it, boy—run away. It is no more than I expected from a coward like you.

"What else am I supposed to do?" Frustration welled up inside of Jarod. "I'm unarmed, and anyway, the wolf is mad. If it bites me once, I'm finished." He listened to his own reasoning with surprise. *I want to live.* A new calm settled over him. He looked down at the wolf, which kept lunging and snarling at the base of the tree. A series of ideas passed through his head swiftly; Jarod knew that he didn't have time to consider them. The wolf was only the most immediate of his problems. He had to outwit Audune as well if he wanted to live. Jarod reached up and scraped at the tree trunk above his head until he had a fistful of bark. He cast it toward the wolf's hindquarters as a distraction.

The wolf took this strange bait, snarling and twisting to bite at itself for a moment until it realized that nothing threatened from the bark's fall. By then, Jarod had jumped to the ground several paces away. He poured all his will into the command: *Shepherd of this wolf, obey me! Drive your charge away from me! Whatever it takes!*

For an instant, it seemed as if time stopped. Even the insects ceased their buzz. The wolf froze as it crouched for another lunge at Jarod. A weak, gentle voice spoke into Jarod's thoughts: *How is this? You speak…to me? Ah!* The voice seemed grateful. *You are he of whom I have heard. Please, little brother, I beg this boon of you. Bring death to my charge. She suffers greatly, and there is no hope of healing for her. Please! End her suffering, little brother!* As the voice pled, the wolf backed away on its belly as Vailla had done, confused but submitting.

"I don't know how I—" Jarod cast about for answers and found a dead tree leaning heavily to one side. The storm that had severed it near the ground must have been a powerful one; the splinters of its demise stood upright, spear-like, from the ruins of its stump. Taking care to make no startling motions, Jarod went to this tree and wrenched loose the thickest of the sliver-spears with a resounding crack.

The wolf snarled, backing away a few more steps.

Jarod hefted his makeshift spear to see if it was solid enough. It felt good in his hand, so he began his approach. As he stalked forward, the wolf backed away, eyes rolling. "Be still," Jarod murmured. "I'll try to make it quick."

Quick? mocked Audune. *By all means, let it end swiftly. I will help hasten matters.*

Jarod couldn't see what his shepherd did, but the wolf's shepherd cried out a warning as something stung the wolf into attacking. It lunged forward, snapping its jaws, and would have bit Jarod if he hadn't taken the warning in time. He thrust out his spear blindly and knocked the wolf tumbling away. When it sprang to its feet, it limped from a deep gash across its chest. Its eyes had rolled so far back that only the whites showed. It snarled and tried to lunge again, clumsily this time. Jarod heard its shepherd weeping. He heaved his spear at the wolf with all his strength, but the wolf proved itself wilier than that and dodged to one side. Unarmed again, Jarod had to sprint after his spear and hope that the wolf's shepherd would warn him in time. He imagined the wolf's noisome breath on his back. *It can't be far behind*—Jarod tripped and hit the ground hard enough to skid. Audune's malicious snigger rang in his ears. *Why do you want me to fail?*

Fail? I will make a warrior of you. I will present you as a gift to my master the mighty one. There is only one like you. With your help, the mighty one will return to his seat of power.

Jarod rolled onto his back, expecting the wolf to be upon him any moment. At the same time, he heard the approach of a horse ridden hard. The yowling wolf spun around after its own tail in a mad fury. *I cannot hold her back—it hurts me to violate the command—please,* begged the beast-shepherd's weeping voice. She must have released her hold upon her charge, because the wolf staggered to one side in surprise. Jarod stretched out his hand for his spear, which had lodged upright in the soil.

"Jarod!" The horseman burst into the clearing, hurling a javelin through the wolf before the horse had come to a halt. Owen swung down from his horse and threw himself between Jarod and the impaled wolf. "Get on the horse, Jarod. Now!" As he spoke, he drew his sword.

Please, little brother, do as your friend asks, the wolf's shepherd said. *Flee.*

Jarod scrambled to his feet. He hesitated. "No, Uncle Owen." Crossing the distance between them, he reached around Owen and wrenched the knife from his hand. "Stay back. It's still dangerous." He gripped the blade in a surprisingly steady hand. As the wolf used its teeth to tear at the javelin shaft that protruded from its flesh, Jarod knelt near the beast's head. His free hand darted out to seize the wolf by the scruff of its neck. Lifting it upright to keep it from biting him, Jarod took the knife and held it against the wolf's throat. *Whatever your name is, I do this for your sake.* He slashed the wolf's throat open. *You are free.*

"What were you thinking? If anything happened to you, I don't know what we'd tell Kohanan," Owen shouted. "Do you know how badly you frightened your mother? Sending one of her paldins back without an owner? I don't understand how you could be so thoughtless!"

But Jarod was too busy with his own thoughts to justify himself to Owen. *'Make a warrior of me,' Audune? I won't be the kind of warrior you'd make. I won't do it. I'd rather die.*

We shall see. One day, you will do what I require of you. One day, your hands will be covered in the blood of innocents—of humans, not of an ailing, mad beast.

I will fight you!

We shall see.

FIRST ENCOUNTER

Ivy sat before her mirror, opened her cosmetics jars, and arrayed them with the ease of practice. Then she paused, gazing at her reflection. Two candelabra bracketed her mirror to aid the dying sunlight that filtered through her window. With the aid of the extra light, Ivy stared hard at the bruises on her face. Had her cheekbones been fashioned more severely, like Selena's, the natural shadows would have helped conceal the bruises, but Ivy's face had been a plain oval all of her life. The light showed each bruise without flattery. Ivy reached for the first jar and a brush to begin applying the feminine equivalent to camouflage.

I would sooner see her die by my own hand… Though her memory supplied the sound of the rough voice, Ivy still shivered as if the man himself were present. Two days weren't enough to soften the recollection. The only way she could continue was to suppress memory, paint it over and conceal it. After the work of a few moments, Ivy set down her brush and leaned closer to the mirror. "Drat!" The first layer of cosmetic paint was not sufficient. Hints of purple still showed through.

The day before last had begun as a simple errand-day. In addition to her regular errands, her father had given her three invitations to deliver. As a result, the sky was already darkening by the time Ivy delivered the last invitation to one Tyrell, a merchant in imported trinkets. Being accustomed to walking alone, Ivy had set off home again with only the occasional streetlamp to light her way. The curiosity merchant's elegant bachelor apartment was near her father's house, and Ivy had particularly wanted to be home in time to catch a private moment with her nephew Giles, whose turbulent spirits had not escaped anyone's notice.

There was no longer any traffic on the streets when she had alighted on the pavement before the curiosity shop. Everyone had gone home by then, even the lamplighters. Ivy set out at a brisk pace. Soon, despite the hot weather, she was shivering without cause. Ivy folded her arms across her bosom. It did little good. The sky had begun to cloud over so that the emerging stars were all swallowed in thick darkness above. Ivy shivered harder. "It would have to rain," she grumbled. "I wish I had taken the merchant up on his offer now."

"You no more than I," said a low, rough voice from a nearby alley. "Come here at once."

Stopping, she said, "Who are you?"

"I told you to come over here, Miss Ivy." He stepped out of the shadows, looking left and right along the street uneasily. He came to her, seized her by the arms and dragged her into the alley. "You should not be out here. It is unsafe."

"Who are you?"

He hushed her. In the dark alley, Ivy shifted uneasily from foot to foot. He was without question the most enormous man she had ever met, and he was standing much closer than was socially proper. Moreover, his manner of speaking was entirely too high-handed for someone who had only just approached her as a stranger in the street. "I don't know who you—"

He covered her mouth with a hard hand. "If you love your life," he hissed, "quiet!"

Frightened and hurt, Ivy pried at his hand, only to have both arms pinned against her sides by one of his encircling arms. She squirmed, but without effect. Then it came to her: she could still make sound, even with her mouth blocked.

In uncanny anticipation, the stranger shifted his hand so that it covered both her mouth and nostrils, trapping the breath inside of her and denying her fresh air. Now Ivy panicked in earnest as she began to suffocate. She put her hands up as high as she could reach and clawed at the hand, but he was impervious to the pain. Her chest hurt with the effort to draw breath through the solid flesh of his hand. Soon she could not even struggle. Tears welled up in her eyes and pooled against his index finger. Not even they could slip underneath his hold. *Why does he want to hurt me?* Ivy's mind drifted as she lost consciousness. Random, fantastical sensations swirled around inside her head. She even imagined she heard a timorous, pained voice saying, "Please, little brother—no more, please. She will be quiet now."

Ivy stared down a sheet of darkness into the most absolute nothing she had ever known. Something evil lurked in that nothing. She felt as if she lay draped over a tree limb, gazing down into the nothingness in search of that horrific evil.

The limb gave a terrible shake, as if it might drop her into the darkness. Terrified and helpless, Ivy waited to be swallowed by the thing that waited in the nothing, but it did not happen. Light returned to the world suddenly—bright light, and with it, human voices.

"What happened, keiri? Is the lady hurt?"

"I told you to keep her here while I made sure the road was safe. Did I not say that?"

"She would not listen to me, keiri. Would you have me hold her prisoner here?"

"Yes," said the harsh voice flatly. "That would have been preferable to letting her wander into the grasp of the Unclean."

"My lord?"

"It would have been preferable to finding myself in the position of having to smother her to keep her silent until the danger passed by," continued the wrathful voice. "Yes, Tyrell, you should have kept her prisoner here, if necessary. Better to be held against her will for a time than to meet up with an evil that she is not able to face. I would sooner see her die at my own hand—the voice broke in fervency, "—than to stand by and watch her fall victim to that fate."

That was the harsh voice that now resonated within her thoughts. Remembering herself, Ivy squeezed her eyes shut to forestall another fit of tears. *Do not think of it. You will not think of it! Finish getting ready for dinner. Your guests will be coming soon. They will expect to see you as you always are. Poppa Denei and Momma will expect to see you being brave. Remember why you're doing this.* She breathed deeply, willing herself to stop wanting to cry. *You're a grown woman, not a child. There is no reason for you to keep bawling like a calf. Many women have found themselves in far worse circumstances. Just remember why you're doing this.*

Having mastered herself enough to go on applying the cosmetics, she made short work of her face. She could still see the ghost of one bruise by the time she finished, but she was confident that no one else would notice. No one else would be expecting to see any such mark on her. With only that to comfort her, she tidied away her tools and materials.

Her parents were waiting when she arrived in the front parlor. Denei stood up to greet her with an awkward squeeze of the hand. "Are you still resolved?"

She replied with a quick nod, unable to trust her voice.

"Good girl. I've heard nothing from Tyrell or young Kyte-son to say otherwise on his end. We'll get this business moved along tonight, before I have to leave."

"Leave?"

"It is settled. I lead the army out in seven days' time. This time, we will not be caught unawares. We know their path of approach, and we have our new allies with us. The marauders will lament the day of our next meeting—those who survive, that is."

If Ivy had harbored any thought of speaking her fears, the new optimism in her stepfather's tone made it utterly impossible. She had not heard him so animated for a long time. She bit her tongue and then turned to admire her mother's shawl. Then the door opened to admit her elder sister Brigid. Ivy had worried over this moment. Her sister, a widow twice over, was notoriously difficult to deceive. Perhaps it was all the time she spent in contemplation beside the Great River, or perhaps it was just the innate sharpness of her perception that made Brigid see details that others missed. Ivy tried to keep Brigid from approaching her on the side where the bruises were. "Are you recovered yet from your journey?"

"Tolerably," Brigid replied. "I'm glad I left the choosing of my clothes to you this time. I do like this shade of green. I think it suits me."

"Of course it does, or I wouldn't have chosen it for you."

The housemaid came in. "Chief Healer Clary-son and Lady Phoebe," she announced, bobbing a quick curtsey as the first guests entered.

Ivy turned to greet her cousin Phoebe, a vivacious little dark-haired woman. Doran had bypassed Ivy altogether—not meaning to be rude, she realized, but so intent upon speaking with Denei that he had no thought for niceties of protocol. Ivy focused on Phoebe instead. "Welcome, cousin, I'm so glad you could come." Ivy nearly faltered when she saw little Phoebe's wide blue eyes fix upon the concealed bruises as if by some instinct borrowed from her healer-husband.

"Oh, no more glad than we were to come, surely! You look charming, as always! And Brigid! How long it has been, to be sure! You look the same as ever. Years don't touch you, do they? Only just yesterday, I found three gray hairs on the side of Doran's head, the poor dear. Ah, Aunt Riana! How lovely! It's a little reminder of the old family dinners, isn't it? I do wish we could all get together once, though I daresay half of us couldn't abide the other half after an hour of it. Isn't that just like people? Funny how one can't always appreciate kin. Isn't Giles here? I looked forward to seeing the boy. Speaking of gray hairs, I imagine his father will have something to say, given all the time that the boy stays up at the palace, according to my Doran."

Gladly, Ivy handed off the responsibility for Phoebe to Riana, because the next guest had just been announced through the little woman's chatter. Ivy drew her sister forward with her to greet Tyrell. "Master Merchant," she began, holding out a hand. Then she paused with her hand in his, unable to speak in the face of his enigmatic gaze. It brought back memory of a prior conversation that had taken place two evenings ago:

"You are very welcome in my home, Miss Ivy. I trust your father is doing well?"

"Oh, yes. He's doing very well, thank you, Master Merchant. I have come on his behalf, in fact, to issue an invitation to dine at our house on the evening after next. Please say you'll be able to come. My sister will be joining us, so you need not worry about bringing a dinner partner with you." Ivy held out the written invitation.

Tyrell smiled with his eyes more than with his mouth. "Miss Ivy, it does me great honor. You may inform your father that I will not fail him."

"Splendid! Then I shall see you the day after tomorrow."

"Miss Ivy—you came just as I was sitting down to my own humble supper this evening. Please, will you stay and share it with me? There is more than enough for two. It would be my great pleasure to offer my hospitality, such as it is, and then to escort you to your father's house in my carriage afterward." Tyrell smiled again. "Let me have the honor of your good company for an hour or so. It will save you the trouble of walking home in the dark. I am certain that your day has been long enough. Please rest awhile and keep me company."

"It is kind of you to offer, but it isn't so far to walk, and I wouldn't want to alarm my family by staying out any later than I already have. Thank you all the same, Master Merchant."

"But it grows dark," he persisted. "I cannot in good conscience allow you to walk home."

"It is no trouble to me to walk. Besides, it isn't so far from here. Please, you mustn't trouble yourself. I'm sorry I interrupted your dinner."

"Stay for a few minutes and drink a cup of bladebriar nectar before you go. It is a rare delicacy, and not to be missed."

"Your offer is very kind, but I'm sorry to say I can't. Perhaps on another visit. I'm late enough as it stands. It's very kind of you to offer. I mean no offense by refusing."

Tyrell bowed with an air of surrender. "Far be it from me to deny a lady her will. Until dinner two days hence, then?"

"Certainly. Good evening, Master Tyrell."

Although that encounter had not been the last time she had seen Tyrell, it carried so much weight in light of subsequent events that she found it difficult to bypass. Tyrell spoke now, his words an unintended echo of her thoughts: "Let me wish you a good evening, Miss Ivy." The merchant bowed as the sound of his voice forced her to the present. "I trust I find you in health?"

"I'm in good health, yes, thank you, Master Merchant. May I introduce my sister Brigid? Brigid, this is Master Curiosity Merchant Tyrell of Sulvisin. He's a friend of Uncle Owen."

Instead of holding out a hand, Brigid pressed her palms together and touched her fingertips first to her lips and then to her forehead before extending both hands to the merchant.

Ivy saw that Tyrell was impressed. "You have spent time beyond your borders, miss."

"No," Brigid replied, "only at the border. I have met many strangers from other lands who come to the crossing where I live." She led the merchant toward the others, leaving Ivy to her own devices.

Since the moment was free, Ivy slipped from the room to check with the cook, Arlys. "Is everything ready?"

He replaced the lid on a pot of soup. "Just a few minutes more and we'll be ready, Miss Ivy. I hope you're in good appetite tonight. I say, I outdone myself this time. Won't give the general's guests any cause to complain."

"When have you ever given cause for complaint?" Ivy teased the ex-warrior. "Judging by the smells alone, not even your dear mother Shae could have done it better."

"I bet she could've, but there! Shouldn't you be in the parlor, Miss Ivy?"

"Yes, I suppose I should. I have one more guest to greet before we can come to the table." Ivy returned to the parlor, hearing the rattle of a coach stopping in front of the house even as she crossed through the entry hall.

After a few moments, there came the housemaid to proclaim, "Damon Kyte-son." Ivy had been surprised by Damon from the first, but in a good way. She approved of the spark of wit in his eyes. "Miss Ivy!" He took her hand and bowed so low over it that his forehead touched her knuckles lightly. "You can't imagine how glad I am to be here."

"You are most welcome, Damon." She took his arm and led him farther into the room to introduce him to the rest of the party. Then each dinner pair proceeded to the table, with Denei and Phoebe leading.

To her relief, Denei said nothing about business during the entire meal. The conversation was light and aimless. It almost lulled Ivy into forgetfulness. Then the last plate was cleared from the table. Her father stood up. "Let's retire to the sitting room, and then down to our business."

Once they had arrived in the sitting room, Ivy could not abide the expectant silence. "Can I get drinks for anyone?" She felt she would have said or done nearly anything to stave off the inevitable. Once she had seen a glass in each guest's hand, however, she had no other excuses. She had to sit down and let the current of events sweep her away.

Denei spoke quietly. "Doran, remember what I spoke of two days ago? You're here tonight to serve as my witness, should anyone question my actions later on." Then he turned to the other two men. "I am glad to call the two of you allies. You know why I have invited you here. I sent you each a separate message in your invitations. What have you to say in response?"

The two men exchanged that same portentous glance again. Damon spoke. "Tyrell may as well serve as a second witness, for I'm the only one with authority to speak on that matter, or any other concerning my master. I have shared your proposal with my master. He sends this in response." Damon took from a sack at his waist a small, velvet-wrapped bundle. Unwinding the cloth, he revealed a small lacquered box and, to Ivy's surprise, offered it to her. "This, Miss Ivy, is for you. My master offers this gift as a token of his sincere admiration."

Ivy hesitated. Another memory rose to press down upon her spirits. The same day when her father had suffered his fit of illness, when Ivy had returned home her parents had taken her aside. "Ivy," her stepfather said, "I have to speak with you on a very important matter." The gravity of his manner impressed her with his urgency. Ivy had listened carefully to his account of the intrigues that were plaguing the royal house and the army. "It has come to the point where we must take actions that we would not have considered in less perilous times," said Poppa Denei.

"It sounds terrible. What can I do?"

"I have found a powerful ally, Ivy. I intend to name him as my successor. He is a great warrior but foreign to us. The Council, especially the patriarchs, will certainly oppose him. For all that, I believe that he is the only hope we have for saving Colin and Selena and Maia." Poppa Denei's hesitance did not make sense until he had spoken his next sentence: "There is a way for you to ease my successor's path, Ivy, if you'll agree to make him my son by marriage. You can help him find his place among the counselors and prove to them that he has my trust."

Remember why you're doing this. Ivy took a deep breath and, after a hasty glance at the young man Damon, accepted the ornamented case. It rested cool against her palm. She stroked the catch to open it. Inside the case, on a bed of patterned silk rested an exquisite set of delicate, shimmering white bracelets, each slightly larger than the last. Unable to contain her amazement, she lifted her eyes to Damon once more. "They're so beautiful! What are they made of?"

"These are fashioned out of a single giant pearl." He took the box from her and set it on the arm of a nearby settee. Then he girded the bracelets on her. One he slid over her right hand to dangle at her wrist; two others he slipped likewise over her left hand. The last and largest he slid his fingers over to open a clasp that split the bracelet into two half-circles. He put this one around Ivy's right arm above the elbow.

Charmed by the beauty of the gift, she ran a finger over one bracelet, feeling its polish and admiring its shine. "It's a lovely gift." She thought back to the harsh voice, the merciless hand over her mouth, and the chilling statement: *I would sooner see her die at my own hand.* She shivered, unable to reconcile these gifts and that voice. Looking up, she found an expression in Damon's eye that hinted of sympathy. She glanced away again.

The sitting room was rapidly growing stuffy with the windows shut. Riana unthinkingly rose and approached the nearest window, but Denei stopped her. "Close the door as well." He motioned for Damon to take the seat beside him, exchanged a significant look with Doran across the room, and began. "So you speak as proxy for the nameless one?"

"Yes, sir. I'm the only man so authorized."

"Yet you still claim citizenship in this kingdom, do you not? Then you know that your loyalty to the king must surpass any personal loyalties."

Damon gave him an astute look. "It does, sir. So does my master's. In my opinion as a subject of the crown, I think this alliance is the best thing that could have happened to any of us, my master included, sir."

"Does your master object to living among us?"

"Not at all, sir. He owns a few properties in the kingdom already, including a very fine horse ranch just south of Palas. We often winter there."

Denei nodded thoughtfully. "Good. One other thing—just to be certain we leave nothing assumed. Those baubles you delivered to my daughter. Here, such a gift would signal...certain intentions. What does it mean to your master?"

"Quite the same thing, sir." A mischievous smile tipped Damon's lips upwards. "He understood your message perfectly and was very clear on that count. He had an eye for this match already. High time, too, I say. He needs a wife. I promise you, he's well able to provide for her. I can vouch for his temper. Since he renounced his name, I've never had cause to complain of my treatment, and I've seen him through every possible mood. Such a match would benefit both sides, as I'm sure you can see for yourself easily. He understands that he is unknown among your people, and what little is known doesn't reflect well on him. Welcomed by your family, he would have a more secure standing among the people…a fine excuse to do what he already had in his heart to do."

Ivy kept herself still and quiet, knowing that Damon had his eye on her for her reaction. *Let Poppa Denei handle it.* Divided within herself as she was, she knew better than to let it show. She traced the shimmering surface of a bracelet again. *Remember why you're doing this.*

"That's good to hear," Denei said. "Ivy?" His eyes flickered toward the sideboard across the room, giving her an unmistakable directive.

She obeyed, covering her fear under a mask of proper gravity. In the sideboard, in the top drawer on the right, rested a narrow roll of blue matte silk. Ivy had placed it there herself that morning. She retrieved it now, feeling the tempered steel blade within the gentle silk. A few steps brought her from the sideboard back to Damon's chair. "Here. My groom's gift." Without anything to anchor her hands, Ivy felt as if the faintest breath could send her drifting, feather-like, into the air. She went back to her seat, folded her hands, and withdrew inside the numbness while her father disposed of her future with a few last negotiations.

Afterwards, when the guests had left, Ivy headed for her room quietly, hoping to avoid meeting any of her family members. She made it only to the top of the stairs. There she met her older sister Brigid, who said, "Ivy, I want to talk with you."

Ivy brushed off her sister's hand and shut the door in her face.

STORM

"You what?"

"I want you to keep Maia home instead of sending her to Academy."

"No wonder you're here so early. Why?"

"Will you tell her first? Call her in. It concerns you both."

Colin gazed at his general with an inquisitive air, but he didn't argue. "Certainly." He gave Denei one last long, amazed look before he went to the door of his office. "Boy!" He leaned out into the corridor. "There you are, Oliver. Fetch my daughter—that's a good lad." He waited at the door for the girl to come along. While he waited, he diverted himself by guessing what fancy had seized Denei. "Good morning, dear," he said, kissing his daughter's forehead as she arrived at the door. "Denei wants a word with you."

"Now what have I done?" she teased Denei. "It's nothing to do with Giles, is it?"

"I should hope not. He may be my grandson, after a fashion, but I still don't think it a good idea."

"Then I shall cancel the wedding plans. What did you want to tell me, Uncle Denei?"

Denei leaned back in his chair; Colin thought he looked smug, if anything. "It isn't only for you, little one. Your father needs to hear this as well. Do you recall our last meeting, Colin? Something happened on my way home. The upshot of it all is this: I've found my successor."

"Have you?" Surprised, Colin leaned against the front of his desk. "I confess I hadn't expected that. Which did you settle on in the end? Dermot-son?"

"No. I settled on a man you've never met. You recall our meeting with the curiosity merchant, surely. I met the man he spoke of. He's the one I want for my successor."

Colin knew that his jaw had dropped open. He couldn't help it. "You can't be serious."

"I'm in earnest, Colin. Just ask Owen."

"I think I will. Oliver! Oh, it's you, Tolliver," Colin said as a different boy came to the door, "you'll do just as well. Fetch Lord Sakiry. It's important. Tell him I need to speak with him immediately. What do you mean by—?"

Denei hushed him. "Shut the door first, if you please, Colin."

The king obeyed instinctively, but was not distracted. "What do you mean by settling on a man no one but yourself has ever met—and an outlander to boot? Does that not strike you as a little rash? Because that's how the Council will see it. I promise you they'll scream."

"Let them. Good morning, Owen. I see I'm not the only one getting an early start today."

"What's going on? I was meeting with my clan elders when the boy came and said you needed me to come *right away*. What's wrong?"

"You tell him, Denei. I still don't know what to say."

Denei spoke slowly and simply. While he listened, Colin watched Owen's face for a reaction. The surprise of Denei's revelation quickly took second place to Owen's response. Denei hadn't finished speaking before Owen burst out, "You met him, and you waited all this time to tell me? Unkind, Denei! There's no other word for it."

"It wasn't intentional. I wanted to be sure, so I had in Kyte's boy Damon and your friend Tyrell for a private dinner. Doran is my witness. This is the one."

"Well, if you say so. When are you bringing him by so that Colin and I can meet him?"

"I have no idea. I must see to the marauders first. Six thousand of them, he says, but no more than that. In return I've promised I'll see to certain changes he deems necessary. The first is yours, Maia. You aren't to attend Academy anymore. You have to start apprenticing with your father. I've begun assembling a list of guards for you—fifteen, since you're only apprenticing."

Colin sank slowly into his desk chair, struggling to absorb everything he had heard. "He presumes to dictate how I'm to train my daughter? I can't express how surprised I am over you, Denei. How could you agree to such terms? You didn't think I might have some opinion on it?"

"I'm sorry you took it that way. I thought it only made sense to remove Maia as far from Simon as possible. She's safer close to home. I don't think she'll object…?"

All three men looked at Maia, whom Colin saw was trying to hide something by keeping her eyes directed toward her feet. Suddenly she realized that they were waiting for her and glanced at her father first. "I'd like to work with you, Father. I'd like that a lot."

"Has he been bothering you, dearest?"

"Not really, not anything I can point out. He doesn't do anything. I'm only getting tired of him watching me." She seemed to realize that that hadn't helped matters any. "Father, please don't upset yourself. I hardly ever see him. I'll see him more working with you than I ever did the Academy." Then she put her hands over her mouth. "I'm sorry. I'll be quiet now."

"I'm going to see to that—that—"

"Colin, I don't think that's wise. I hadn't finished. During the interview, he told me that he knew that Miklei-son had gone into a Garden of the Forbidden and come out again."

"That's impossible," Owen exclaimed. "No man escapes once he's entered such a place!"

"Miklei-son did. Only yesterday, young Damon informed me in private that it would be unwise to let any of my household go out after dark. You may draw your own conclusions from that. If my candidate is correctly informed," Denei persevered, ignoring his brother, "then we have no choice but to treat Miklei-son as an outright danger and not merely an ambitious pest. My candidate said that a man doesn't emerge from the Gardens without making certain choices, and now Miklei-son has brought the results here among us. My man didn't say anything further, except to note that it is politically unrealistic to think of removing Miklei-son from his post at this time. He *knows*, Colin. He may be a foreigner, but he's well-informed."

"Where does he get his information?"

"I don't know," Denei admitted. "No one seems to know. If they do, they won't say so."

"This secrecy doesn't sit well with me. What sort of man is he? Why does he need to hide himself away like this? If he *is* our ally, he has no need to hide himself away. If he has any need to hide himself, then we need to know those reasons *before* we welcome him freely into our confidence. Qualified he may be, but his circumstances are such that the burden of proof is his to bear. He must prove himself…to *me*."

"I know that it will become necessary to arrange a meeting between the two of you, and soon, Colin, but I can't guarantee that I can make it happen in the next few days. The best thing I can do is direct you to Damon Kyte-son. As proxy to my candidate, he is the only man who can legitimately speak for the northerner and the only man who can answer your questions…if he will. I cannot guarantee that he will choose to do so. He keeps his master's secrets with great loyalty. You've never put much stock in my judgment of character, I know, but I can prove it when I say this man has my full confidence. I have negotiated a marriage between him and Ivy."

"But…" A profound stillness encompassed Colin. He didn't say the first words that came to him, or the second. He knew better. "That…that puts this on another footing, certainly."

Denei gazed at him with an expression unlike any Colin had ever seen before. "They've exchanged the gifts. You know my mind on this, Colin. It'll have to be enough for now. Let it rest. We have enough to worry us right now. Let it rest." The general got up from his chair. A bluish tinge around his lips gave Colin misgivings. When Denei started for the door, Colin followed.

They walked together in silence. "You have duties to occupy you," Denei finally said.

"Let *them* rest. I'd rather talk with you, Uncle. You know." When a pair of Caretaker servants passed them, Colin nodded to acknowledge their greetings. He kept from pursuing the conversation until they had reached the general's office, where they could closet themselves in reasonable privacy. "Ivy is to marry this stranger? She agrees to this plan?"

"I suspect she agrees for my sake, not because of her own likings."

"Ivy's practically my own sister. I hate to see her put in such a position."

"What would you have me do, Colin? I don't expect to see another year. Before I die, I want to see my family provided for. The bulk of my estate goes to Nässey. Ivy…she deserves better than an empty house and a pension. I know you don't like it. The fact remains that she was never wed to your brother, Colin. She shouldn't have to live as his widow."

Abashed, Colin went on the offensive. "Weren't they wed? You know what they say of exact twins, Uncle. Nobody told me anything, but he couldn't hide much from me. The only thing they lacked was your blessing and Father's; I know that much. According to law, Uncle, that's still marriage after a fashion. But it isn't the idea of her remarriage that troubles me, so much as the idea that you're disposing of her for politics' sake. As you said…she would do anything to help you out of difficulty."

"Speak plainly, Colin, if you *will* speak." In a softer voice, Denei added, "This isn't about Ivy. Tyrell once said something that wasn't true. He said only two men believed your brother might still live: your father and me—but that isn't true."

Colin swallowed with effort. "You know what they say about exact twins. If he's d-dead...I'm truly alone."

"You have Selena. She's very worried about you."

"I know, Denei. She's put up with more than any woman should have to bear, but it isn't the same. He's my brother...and, in a way, myself, but different. As long as *you* believed, I believed it too...and now...you're pushing Ivy into this as if he's d—as if he's never coming back. I know; I'm making no sense. Sorry." Colin got up to leave the conversation. His last glimpse of Denei showed him an elderly warrior with eyes that mourned.

*   *   *   *

"I don't know what to do about it." Colin urged his horse over a low fence and heard his companion's steed follow suit. "Selena's worried enough already. I hardly want to tell her about this newest turn involving Ivy."

"If you don't, Miss Ivy will. Wouldn't Selena wonder why *you* hadn't said anything?"

"There's my problem, Lane. It can't be kept a secret."

The two horsemen slowed to a walk, and the second drew up alongside Colin. He was named Virlane, second son of the Pamirsi patriarch Berhus. Colin considered him his best of friends. They were alike in temperament, save Virlane's ambivalence to the company of others. It was to Virlane that Colin had taken his most recent conversation with Denei. "Is it possible," the Pamirsi lore master said, "that you're anticipating more of a reaction on your wife's part? Given what I know of Selena, I imagine she'll be pleased about this. She hasn't your delicacy of feelings on it."

Colin gave his friend a sour look. "My delicacy of feelings?"

"I only mean that she never knew your brother. I also imagine that that's why you won't discuss it with her. It would distress you, I think, to see her exulting over something that grieves you. It really is a common practice, historically speaking. In some lands, a woman is kept a widow because her husband's kinfolk think to preserve his memory through her celibacy."

"I wouldn't wish that for Ivy!"

"Wouldn't you?" Virlane nudged his horse to a quicker pace, leaving him that thought to worry at his conscience.

＊   ＊   ＊   ＊

The weather turned sullen and oppressive late in the afternoon. Not a leaf stirred in the palace orchard. Clothes stuck to bodies and breath was hard-bought as the hot, humid air grew increasingly thick. The servants went about with slower steps and lower voices, fanning themselves as they tendered their duties. If at all possible, everyone was outside in hopes of catching an elusive breeze.

Colin sat in the heavy stone seat beneath the Prince's Tree. His daughter knelt before him. "Whatever the reason," he said, "I am glad to finally begin this. My own father sat here in this very seat, and I knelt where you are now. One day, you will be where I am now, and your own child will kneel before you. This is how the generations have passed, one after another. Thirty generations, to our knowledge, Maia! And who knows how many went before them? Every Keeper has had this task of handing down the charge to his heir."

"Do you suppose every heir knelt down like this and hadn't any idea how she'd ever manage it all?"

That brought a wistful smile to Colin's face. "I don't know about every one, but I know I certainly did. I knelt there feeling like…" His smile faded as he remembered.

"What's wrong, Father?"

"Nothing. I was just thinking about when I was…when I was in your place." *Keeping his memory alive…*Colin straightened with sudden purpose. "Did you know that I had a brother?"

"I heard about him once, just a while ago. From Ivy."

Colin didn't dare to dwell on this information. "Your mother and I, we've never talked of him to you, I know. Lately it has occurred to me that I was wrong in keeping silent. Yes. I had a twin brother named Jarod."

"What happened to him?"

"When we were just finished building this city, we went through a year of terrible wildfires. Everything was so dry that something caught fire almost every day. One day, the fires came close to this city. My father called out every able man to dig a fire trench around the walls, and Jarod and I weren't exempt. We took our shift early…before the heat of the day. I went back afterward and washed up. Next thing I heard, the alarm went out that the trench wasn't finished but the fires were closing in on us. We thought we'd lost Denei that day. He had third shift and got trapped away from the walls when the fire came. They found him in a pond, saying that Jarod had been out with him on the line. Jarod...never came through." Colin sighed heavily. "Seeing you kneeling there, I couldn't help remembering. I began my training after we gave up searching for him. I always suspected that Jarod would have made a better king. He was smarter, more resolute. I was the elder, but I always felt inferior to him."

"He must have been a real marvel, Father, if he could have been better than you."

"He was, dearest." *Was. Was?*

"Do you think I'll do well, Father?"

That question jarred Colin from his doldrums. "If I do my part well, you'll have every reason to do well. You've got a good head, dearest. That's the best way to begin."

YESTERDAY:
REMOVAL

The earliest age at which boys could begin training in the army was thirteen, and that only held true among the Alti. The Alti clansmen believed that manhood was less a matter of age than a matter of physical and mental readiness. To determine this, they tested their youth yearly through two weeks' worth of ordeals. Each year, Kohanan took his sons to witness this testing time. This was the first year they entered it themselves. They were fourteen years old.

Kohanan had a quiet, private conversation with the Alti patriarch, Greynán. They were still in view of the pack of boys who waited together under the Prince's Tree in the middle of the village of Nisi. A circle of snow-topped peaks walled Nisi in from the rest of the world. While they waited, Jarod heard the raucous scream of a crag eagle. Its massive shadow blotted the ground in a sweeping path that crossed the shadow cast by the tree's verdant canopy. He breathed the soft, thin air and felt as if he might have come home. Some of the boys were already shifting from the discomfort of the stony ground beneath them. Jarod pressed his palms flat against the rock. The tree whispered to him, but he could not understand what it said. To keep from seeing the words that shaped his father's lips, Jarod inched toward one of the tree's roots just where it disappeared into apparently solid rock. *Tree,* he said in his mind, *how do you live? There's no soil to feed you here. It's dry rock. How do you live?* The tree sang a few indecipherable notes to him in response. A vague image rose with the notes: subterranean water rushing through its deep, hidden courses, caressing the tips of tree roots as it passed.

"Pre-*sent!*"

The boys scrambled up from the ground to line themselves in uneven ranks before the sergeant-at-arms. One by one, they trotted either left or right as the sergeant assigned them to their cohorts. Jarod found himself in the same cohort with Greynán's second son Greysin. Across the way, Colin stood in friendly conversation with Ronán, Heir Alti. Although he refused to consider the reasons behind it, Jarod appreciated the symmetry of the arrangement. *Heir with heir, second-born with second-born.*

Now that they were no longer in the shadow of the Prince's Tree, the biting voice of Audune revived. *Your father knows better than to trust you in violent sport beside your brother. Perhaps he has seen your future and knows you are destined to kill your weak brother.*

I am not! Jarod protested, but without conviction. He knew well enough that no man knew the future except perhaps seers, and his father was a seer of great power. Perhaps he *had* seen—but Jarod refused the thought. He focused his attention intently on the sergeant-at-arms and his shouted instructions. The boys around him made an unnecessary amount of noise, rustling and shuffling their feet nervously as they learned what would be expected of them. "First two days," the sergeant called out, "foot races to prove your speed. That shouldn't be too hard on you." His chuckle was rather on the dark side, Jarod thought as he saw the smiles that the grown warriors tried to conceal. *This isn't what they want us to think it is.*

The air is too thin. These children do not know what it means to run at this height.

Quit it, Audune. Let me figure it out myself.

Do you wish to succeed? The giant's voice was mild for a change. *You wish to stay here, do you not? You wish to stay because you know your brother will not succeed at these rigors and you wish to be far from him. You believe it will save him if you stay away. I can help you succeed. I can tell you things you do not know yet.*

Jarod tried to block the voice. He knew why Audune wanted him to succeed at this. He had not yet forgotten the giant's dark promise to make a warrior of him. What frightened him was not the promise itself; it was that he recognized the potential in himself for becoming the warrior that Audune wished him to be. He must take Denei's place one day, just as Colin was to take their father's place. It was expected. Jarod knew he could do it, and do it well. He was less certain that he *should.* The prospect of taking all that power with Audune always there at the back of it—Jarod could not reconcile himself to this image of his future. He did not trust his strength of will as far as that.

The foot races were scheduled for after noontide. The boys separated into smaller groups as they waited for their turn at the trestle tables. Jarod sat by himself at first, alone in the curve of a great tree root. From there, he commanded the best view of the green where the rest of the boys milled around impatiently. He saw Colin in the largest clique, chatting animatedly with several peers. Colin could get along with anyone, and everyone instinctively gravitated to Colin's sunny good cheer. Jarod read the words on his lips: *Hope I can keep up with the rest of you.* That was Colin all over, never sure of himself. Jarod sometimes thought that the division that produced two of them in the womb instead of one had given him all the confidence and Colin none of it. One of the other boys said something to Colin that made him laugh. Again, Jarod read his lips: *We'll all be watching his back the whole way.* Everyone turned to look at Jarod. That, ironically, was Colin's one fixed assurance. He seemed to believe Jarod capable of boundless proficiency.

Kohanan rounded the tree from the other side. "Mind if I sit with you?"

Wordlessly, Jarod made room.

"Here." Kohanan held out his heaping bowl. "To carry you over 'til it's your turn."

"I can wait. Thanks anyway," Jarod added belatedly, trying not to sound like an ingrate. He settled his shoulders back into the curved root and stretched out his legs, noting idly that they were already as long as his father's. "Why is it hard to run at this height?"

His father swallowed his mouthful of food before answering, "Thin air. Makes breathing a lot harder, especially for those unaccustomed to it. You can make yourself properly sick if you don't take care. Some pass out altogether."

"So the trick is a steady pace, not a quick dash," Jarod said, mostly to himself.

"That's a good thought." His father's tone was noncommittal, but his glance was bright with approval. He leaned his head toward the feast. "Looks like a good time to join the line."

Jarod obeyed without speaking. In the line, the Alti patriarch's second son nudged him. "Why're you sittin' all the way over there, hey?" He was a small boy for his age, hardly as tall as Jarod's elbow. His bowl was already mostly full, although they had not yet traversed half the length of the table. Greysin caught Jarod looking askance at his bowl and said laughingly, "Hey, I gotta eat if I'm gonna grow up proper, hey?"

"You'll drop halfway through the race with all that inside you," Jarod answered flatly. His own bowl was half full and held mainly vegetables. At the end of the table, he was offered a flagon of ale, which he refused. He took the second bowl from underneath his food bowl and dipped water into it instead. Out of the corner of his eye, he saw the diminutive Alti boy hesitate at the ale. Jarod watched him covertly and saw him run back to the other end of the table, retrieve a bowl, and fill it with water. Jarod returned to the tree to find his father had gathered around himself a few of the Alti warriors. Their company interested Jarod more than that of his peers, but he would not make himself pathetic by fawning. He removed himself slightly, just far enough around the tree's thick bole to remain unseen, but near enough to listen while he ate his frugal meal.

"Which is your pick this year, Morio?" the king asked lightly. "Who will take the prize?"

Morio, a young Alti warrior, was rumored to have a place reserved for him in the royal guard corps as soon as he completed his present year of duty. Everyone spoke of him as the most promising of his year, if not of his entire clan. He replied good-humoredly, "With all due respect, my lord, I wonder that you ask. *You* brought the young pardelé with you, after all."

"It doesn't become a father to boast too loud," Kohanan replied with a laugh. "Leaving him out of it—who do you favor?"

Morio paused for a lengthy perusal of the boys before him. "Well then, my lord, as long as I can split my bets equally, I'll name three for you: Josu son of Nikodim, there; Kibbe's son Kibo; and for my third, my young kinsman Kintaro. If those three don't follow along behind me soon enough, I'll forever doubt my reason."

"I'll remember that."

Jarod was not sure how he knew that his father wanted him to come around the tree and join the company, but he knew it. He edged into view without looking at any of them.

"Jarod, did you hear Morio's predictions? What do you think?"

"I don't know them," he demurred. "Which are they?" Once the three favorites were pointed out to him, he stared hard at them. He felt the silent expectation of the men around him. It made concentration difficult. Jarod willed himself to block it out. He stared at the favorites and saw nothing in their demeanor to gainsay Morio's prediction. "They look promising enough." His gaze encompassed the rest of the group and came to rest on the runty boy he had met in line. "I can predict next year's prize, though."

"Who's that?" Kohanan asked to encourage him.

"Greysin."

Before he could stop himself, Morio gave a sharp snort of laughter. "The little fellow? Why him?"

Jarod slewed around to stare at the warrior. "He wants it most. That's what'll count." He saw Morio shrink back slightly from his stare. "I say Greysin will win it next year. What kind of bet do you want to make on it? I'll wager you anything."

Kohanan's gentle voice intervened. "I wouldn't recommend it, Morio. Not at these odds."

"I think you're right, my lord. I think you're right." Morio spoke it on a breath of respect.

*   *   *   *

By the end of the race, Jarod's chest strained against the dearth of air, but Jarod would not relent. He concentrated on the rhythm of his feet, *one-two, one-two, one-two,* in their steady lope. He could see the rally point ahead. *Only have to keep going a little farther.*

Do not collapse at the rally point, Audune said sharply, *or you'll regret it. Walk a little. Drink water. Once you have walked, lean against something if you must—do not sit.*

Leave me alone, Audune.

You will not regret listening to me today. Keep my advice in mind. By it you may spare yourself great distress.

Jarod stumbled into the circle of men well ahead of his nearest competitor. He doggedly planted foot in front of foot in a staggering walk as he gasped for air. He shook off anyone who tried to hinder him with their congratulations. His father met him on his circuit and pushed a cup of water into his hands. "Drink slowly. It'll help." Then he fell back to let Jarod work off the exertion on his own.

The next few runners came lurching to the rally point, Colin last among them. He wobbled into Kohanan's arms with a shaky laugh. "I made it," he gasped, sounding surprised that it was true.

"Try to walk a little," his father suggested. "As much as you can. I'll bring you water."

"Can't walk...any more," Colin said. His knees sagged.

Kohanan caught him again. With one of Colin's arms over his shoulders, he walked his heir around until the boy's strength revived a little. When the king began to say, "If you're all right, I'll go get you a cup of water—" Jarod was there, handing him his own cup, refilled. "Thank you, Jarod." Kohanan put the cup against Colin's mouth. "Drink slow—don't gulp it, boy—that's right. Easy as it goes. Drink it all. All right now? See if your own legs will hold you now. Good."

With slowly brightening eyes, Colin grinned wearily at his brother. "I kept you in view the whole time. That's as much as any of us could say."

Shut up, *Audune!* Jarod commanded as the guardian spirit again tried to taunt him about how easy it would be to kill Colin. Jarod averted his eyes to keep his brother from sensing any traces of the fear that washed over him. In averting his eyes, however, he caught sight of little Greysin, who came staggering to the rally point that moment in the next wave of runners. Jarod took three long strides and grabbed the boy by the collar to keep him on his feet. "Don't collapse now. You're walking, like it or not."

"Walking?" The boy coughed. "Not I." When he tried to fall, he gagged against the edge of his collar drawn tight across his throat.

"Come on." Jarod felt the attention given him and the small Alti candidate. He lowered his voice. "Come to the stream. You'll want water to freshen you up. Keep walking! I won't drag you all the way. You have to keep moving, or you'll smart for it later." He escorted Greysin to a spot upstream that was reasonably free from company. He dropped the boy on the bank beside a natural dam where the water tumbled merry and clear. "Drink. Drink slow, but keep drinking. A mouthful at a time, so it doesn't make you sick."

Greysin lapped at the water on all fours, only pausing to draw breath at intervals. "Why?" he asked. "Why help me?" The boy wiped his hand across his dripping mouth. "Sorry for me?"

"Why should I feel sorry for you?"

Greysin blushed furiously. "Everybody does, 'cause I'm a runt."

"That's no good reason to feel sorry for you. Listen. You aren't going to qualify this year. Stop it," Jarod cut the boy off before he had the chance to launch his next fiery protest. "You need to use what you learn this year, and next year you'll come out first of them all. You know about the run now. Practice it. Take to the high hills as often as you can and build up your stamina that way. Learn to go without water, without rest."

"Without rest?"

"You weren't listening to the sergeant-at-arms. Today's run was just the start. Tomorrow, the real trials begin. Stay close to me. Watch what I do. Remember *everything*. If I need to, I'll explain myself, but you need to figure as much of it out for yourself as you can. That way it's yours through and through, not something I gave you. Understand?"

Greysin nodded and held out a hand for Jarod to grip. "Deal."

✳   ✳   ✳   ✳

The trials ended with celebration. To the surprise of no one, Jarod had emerged the dominant candidate in every trial. He was the talk of the assembly. His brother had acquitted himself well, but it was tacitly acknowledged that he would not begin his training with the Alti warriors just yet. Colin was unfazed by this. He celebrated his twin's triumph as enthusiastically as anyone.

Jarod took his habitual place in the shelter of the Prince's Tree. A great weight should have lifted from his shoulders at this achievement. He had never faced such strenuous physical and mental challenges before. Despite his overwhelming relief at having accomplished what he set out to do—to remove himself from his family—he was not comforted. On the following day, his father would return home with Colin, taking with him the only real relief Jarod had from Audune's malice. He felt the giant's anticipation. Once Kohanan left, Jarod had only this strange, hardly intelligible tree for his comfort and protection against Audune. He leaned his head against the heavily scarred tree bark and listened for the song deep inside the trunk. All around him, the festivities slowly died down. Eventually the daystar appeared in the cleft of two mountains.

He thought he was alone at last once the bonfires burned low. No one had spoken for so long that Jarod twitched at the sound of his father's voice. "Well," Kohanan said lightly as he knelt down beside his second-born son. "You proved yourself above and beyond expectations. Lord Alti will see to it you get every chance to grow in your training." When his son did not look at him, he said, "Maybe you'll find your peace here, Jarod. That's my greatest hope for you. I hope this will help you, since…since I can't."

Jarod swallowed hard. "Maybe." *I doubt it,* he added in thought.

"I'll come back in a couple of months to see how you're getting along."

To that, Jarod could only nod fervently.

"Oh, my boy," Kohanan whispered. He slapped a hand down on Jarod's shoulder. His grip was painfully tight. "I wish I knew the right way to help you." Disregarding Jarod's lack of response, Kohanan pulled his son close and held him in his arms like a child. "I will not say goodbye to you, Jarod. We will meet again soon."

APPRENTICE

Although it was night, Maia could not sleep. She lay on her bed with a head full of buzzing thoughts that upset her stomach. *Go or don't go?* She lay with a scrap of paper in her hand, reading, *If you are still afraid, meet me in the armory at two.* It was unsigned. *Who knew I was scared? I never told anybody. I thought nobody noticed. If they noticed, why not speak to me? Why not ask, instead of sending this…this…* She put the unsigned note where she had found it: on her pillow. *But who would write this?*

The great clock downstairs struck one, startling her. *Go or don't? If I'm going, I need to dress.* As if she had already made up her mind, Maia rolled off the mattress. She slid into a soft shirt and a pair of trousers, stomped her feet into the boots she used to wear to Academy, and tied her dark braids back into a tail at the nape of her neck. Her hair was the one aspect of her appearance that Maia took pride in; she called it her one vanity, and that was nearly true. It made her feel like a warrior. She glanced once in the mirror, almost negligently. A pair of dark eyes looked back for that instant before Maia turned away from the questions in them. "This is silly," she muttered to herself. Her brain retorted, *Silly that you're going, or silly that you're so anxious about going? You have an hour to walk down two flights of stairs and across to the other wing, which ought to take you hardly any time. Yet there you stand, ready to go to a meeting you never decided to attend.* Maia shook her head and sat down to wait.

After half an hour of sitting on the edge of her bed, Maia stood up again. "Whoever it is, they won't care if I come early." Her boot soles made hardly a whisper on the polished wood floor of the sitting room that divided her bedroom from her parents'. She crept through the sitting room to the central corridor that led her to the private stairs. Downstairs, Maia followed this hallway until it branched off into a wide, silent portrait gallery. At the end of the gallery, she arrived at the armory.

She was intimate with every room of the palace, and in her confidence she had not carried a lamp with her. She could have found the armory without opening her eyes. Inside, she felt only marginal surprise when she found a single lamp burning in one of the wall niches near the door. At that hour, a deserted room would have been totally dark. The lamp made Maia glance around, but she saw no one present and no voice greeted her. The young princess sat down beside the door to wait in the semi-darkness. Then the lamp's flame guttered low. "You are Princess Maia," a gruff voice said to her.

Maia sprang to her feet at once. "Who's there?"

"Softly, Princess, softly." The speaker continued at his original level, just above a whisper. "You must not raise your voice." Then one of the shadows neared. As it separated from the rest, it distinguished itself as a colossus in dark clothes.

A shock of fear ran up Maia's back. She whispered, "Who are you?"

He now stood close enough that she saw the glitter of eyes. "I came to offer you my help, so that you need not fear anymore."

"Not fear? How do you know anything about what I'm afraid of? And who are you?"

"I am your teacher, if you agree. I am a friend, regardless. I can teach you how to deal with the trouble that is coming. I can help you."

Maia shook her head to clear it. Her heart thudded in her ears. "If trouble is coming, you should speak first to my father," she said, but stopped when the stranger shook his head.

"Your father cannot know about me. I offer you the guidance that you will need to face the coming trouble. Without my help, you risk the downfall of your family and the whole kingdom with it. I have few requirements."

"Name them," Maia said.

"One: that you obey me without question. Anything that you need to know, I will tell you. For the rest, you must simply trust me. Two: that you tell no one about your lessons or me."

"And if I do tell?"

"Then I will go away. That is all."

This…this must be the man Uncle Denei spoke of. Maia studied what she could see of the man. He was a head taller than she, which awed her. He seemed unnaturally broad, but that was partly a trick of the darkness and the cloak that hung from his shoulders. He wafted a light scent of outdoors, a mix of trees and grass and clean night air. But even at closer range, Maia could discern nothing about his face. It might as well have not been there. All she could see were the glitter of his eyes and the movement of his lips and bearded chin when he spoke. Then it dawned on her, with a tingle of horror—he wore a hooded mask, like a hangman would. "What's your name?" she said, each word clearly formed and separate.

"I have none."

"None? You mean you have no name at all?"

"I have outlived every name given to me."

Shaken but determined not to show it, Maia said, "Then what am I supposed to call you?"

"How did you address your teachers at Academy?" he returned.

"I called them Teacher."

"You may call me the same, then."

The interview was sweeping Maia along much more quickly than she could comprehend, and without any intention of doing so, she held out a hand. "I...I accept, Teacher." She watched in a numb fog as a gloved hand swallowed her own in a firm, cool grasp. She looked up to catch a smile on his lips.

"We begin tonight. There is little time." He continued to hold her hand and look into her eyes, probing. "I know this is strange to you. All the same, you must hold to my terms. Obey me without question, without hesitation. And no matter what happens, you must not tell anyone about me." Then he made an abrupt transition. "Take a sword from the cabinet. No, leave only the one lamp burning. We need no more light than that." The stranger went to shut the door.

Maia was slowly fighting her way out of the shock that gripped her. *I must have fallen asleep and this is a dream.* But her feet moved to obey the order, carrying Maia across the room to the sword cabinet. She selected a blunted wooden blade first, but her teacher interrupted.

"No. Take a real blade."

"But Teacher, I've never—" But she had no sooner spoken than he interrupted again.

"I know. Just do as I say."

"Yes, Teacher." Maia put the sword back and reached for another. She slid it from its sheath and watched the burnished blade emerge stark and cold in the faint light. Hilt gripped in a sweating hand, she met her teacher in the center of the room.

For the first half-hour, they worked at stance and basic moves. The stranger never once spoke above a whisper, and Maia found herself doing the same. Then, he attacked. Before she had any inkling of his intention, Maia felt the edge of cold steel against her throat. She spoke out of reflex: "That wasn't fair! You never told me—"

"You expected, what? 'Get set, I'm going to attack'?" To Maia's surprise, the man chuckled warmly, provoking her into an uncertain smile. "A man stands in front of you with a drawn sword. What else are you to expect from him? I'll expect better than that from you in the future, Princess. I gave you more warning than you have a right to expect. Your enemies won't offer you as much. Tell me," he said, "what is it that you fear?"

Maia blinked as the sword lowered from her throat. She watched him sheathe his blade and then awkwardly followed his example. "I...I'm not sure."

"Princess. Don't tell me that."

"But I don't know, truly."

"Think hard."

The princess bit the inside of her lip, trying to think of a reasonable explanation. "Ever since I started Academy, I've been hearing talk among the soldiers. Harsh talk. They don't respect Father, some of them, because—oh, I don't know why. A few of them think we ought to be conquering more land, expanding the kingdom or something. They want the army to be bigger than it is. They say we aren't as great as we ought to be, and they're angry at Father for holding them back."

"Which of them think that?"

Maia hesitated to say. "I don't know them personally."

"No," her teacher corrected patiently, "I meant, what sort of soldier thinks that? Do they have anything in common? Clan, city, teacher, company?"

"Oh. Well, I think most of them...*oh*," she repeated, this time in true comprehension. "The ones I've seen and heard of most are all Miklei-son's students or friends. He's the one behind the gossip, isn't he? But—"

"Continue," said her teacher.

"It doesn't make sense," Maia admitted with embarrassment, "because why would he try to denounce my father if he...if he has interest in *me*? That's what they're all saying, and that's what I've started noticing. But he ought to know I'd want nothing to do with him if I knew he was slandering my father."

"Have you spoken with the third marshal at all?"

Maia shrugged. "Not much. They try to keep him away from me, so I've never really had to talk to him. He was a real nuisance at my birthday masquerade."

Her teacher sat down against the wall and motioned for her to sit beside him. For the first time, he seemed uncertain of himself. "Princess, there are things that I will need to teach you that will be difficult for you to learn. If I knew of another who could teach you these things, someone you knew and trusted, I would send you to that person, but there has not been a seer in this city for many years. I am the only one who knows." With this as his only preface, he began on a wholly different tack. "You have not put a name to your distress, but I think I can guess when it began. You spoke to the third marshal on the night of your grandfather's wake, did you not?"

"Well, yes," she admitted, "in passing. It was hardly anything at all, though."

"But from that moment, you began to find it difficult to sleep at night, did you not?"

She gazed at him in astonishment, but found nothing in his words that was inaccurate. "How did you know?"

This her teacher did not answer. He continued, "You dread your dreams now. They scare you, but when you awake, you cannot remember them beyond a vague sense that you have lost something." Then he paused and looked closely at her for confirmation. At her nod, he said, "In all of this, you do not know what distresses you. I do. Your intuition is a gift in its own right; your ancestry has formed you to match one man in particular, to balance out his weaknesses. The man you should have taken as your husband is a man of formidable knowledge but no insight—the sort of man who would undercut the very ground beneath his feet in pursuit of a goal, knowing what he must do to succeed but heedless of the implications beneath his methods. Do you know of such a man, Princess? I think you do. Had circumstances arranged themselves differently, the two of you could have come to an agreement. Your intuition would have softened his impracticality, and his knowledge would have helped you make better use of your intuition."

Slowly, unwillingly, Maia said, "I'm supposed to marry Simon Miklei-son?"

"*Were* supposed to, Princess. That is the source of your distress. That match can no longer take place. You still contain the promise of greatness, but now you must continue without the wherewithal to attain full capability…and we are hindered as a kingdom because of it."

✳   ✳   ✳   ✳

The next morning, Maia could scarcely open her eyes when her maid came in to awaken her. "What's the hour, Kenda?"

"All of half-past seven. Are you unwell? You're never this late abed."

"No, not at all," Maia protested hastily, sitting upright in spite of her aching arms and back. "I'm fine. I overslept." The pain convinced her when she might have been tempted to consider the night's work a dream. When Kenda turned away to prepare the wash water, Maia stretched her arms forward, fingers laced together, in an attempt to loosen her sore muscles. She smothered a groan.

She arrived at the breakfast table after both her parents had begun to eat. Her father looked up in concern. "I'd begun wondering, dearest. Is everything all right?"

"Just tired, I expect." Mindful of her teacher's instructions, she sought a harmless excuse. "I've had so much to take in, you see."

"It isn't too much for you, is it? We could take it at a slower pace if you like."

"Oh, no, Father. It's not too much at all. It's just different. I'll get used to it." She slid into her place to avoid further conversation on that subject. "What's our schedule today?"

"Today is a presentation day. Your mother and I will both be there, so we can spend the morning all together."

Maia had never attended one of the presentation days before. As a child, she had always been too restless to keep silent. Once she was old enough for school, she had been too occupied with her studies. She couldn't summon much enthusiasm over the duty now. "What am I to do?"

"Nothing complicated. Your mother and I will handle most of them. After the first few, if you're comfortable, you can step in if you like. It's likely that you'll recognize a number of these young people. Many of them have only just finished Academy. Ah! Here's Mattieu with the lists. It's a ghastly long list today, isn't it?"

"The general has added to it only this morning, my lord. A whole page."

"I see." Maia's father glanced at her briefly. "That explains much. Well! How long before you're done, Maia?"

"Only another few minutes."

However, Maia finished eating long before the stately figure of Mattieu, a grandson of Nana Lucinda, returned to announce that "the screens are in place, my lord." Maia followed her parents from the private family quarters, through the deserted second floor of the ballroom, past Uncle Owen's and Denei's offices, all the way to the smaller stairs of the western wing. At the bottom of the stairs, Maia understood Mattieu's announcement. A row of patterned silk screens created a corridor for the king and his family to pass unseen through the gallery. Maia heard the murmurings of many voices on the other side of the silk. Then she entered the petitioners' hall itself. The noise in the hall was equal to that in the gallery outside, but everyone hushed and stood up when the royal family entered. Three seats stood in front of four tapestries. The king took the central place, Selena the place on his left, and Maia the remaining seat.

"Begin at the beginning, Mattieu," said the king. "Who's first?"

The Caretaker opened the gallery door and called out in a resonant bass voice, "Henrietta, daughter of Sally, of the clan Pamirsi." A young woman of no more than fourteen years entered confidently, clothed in a fashionable, close-fitting robe of blue. She curtseyed low before the king and then reached out to take the queen's offered hand. "Thank you for your kindness in welcoming me, your majesties." A moment's uncertainty crossed the girl's face as she tried to figure out how to properly greet the princess. She settled for another, smaller curtsey.

"Very good, Henrietta. Give my regards to your mother," Selena said warmly.

That was the pattern for the majority of the presentations. Maia wanted desperately to yawn after the first half-dozen. Then she saw Owen sidle into the room and take his place in the corner just inside the door. He winked at Maia when he found her eyes upon him. She barely had time enough to wonder about his impish smile before Mattieu announced, "Giles, son of Perrin, of the clan Sakiry." Maia felt her father's eyes upon her briefly.

Then Giles entered. His hair had been trimmed short in the approved fashion of the day, and his stubble was shaved clean away. He wore a finer suit of clothes than Maia had ever seen on him before. The roguish lilt in his stride, however, was the same. He bowed to the king and queen. "Good morning, your majesties. Fine day, is it not?" Then, without missing a beat, he shifted himself to stand before Maia. "Your highness."

She held out her hand as she had seen her mother do. It flustered her a little when Giles took hold of her hand and kissed it. Trying not to laugh, she said, "Very good, Giles. That will do." As Giles strolled away to sit beside Owen, Maia saw the assembly whispering. *Gossips.*

Near the end of the presentations, Mattieu announced a young man in uniform. Maia recognized him at once with a burst of excitement. "Hollister, son of Yuri, of the clan Nandevi." The young soldier came and bowed before the king and Maia. Maia, since she knew him, made the greeting herself. "Well, Hollister! You're looking well."

"Thank you, Princess. So are you." Rather than retreating as the others had, Hollister took a step back and stood at attention.

Only then did Maia notice Denei's presence beside Owen and Giles. A succession of young soldiers came forward one by one to be presented, and each went to stand alongside Hollister. When they were all assembled, they numbered fifteen.

Then Denei came forward. He made a slight bow that encompassed king, queen and princess. "I have the honor of presenting Princess Maia's new personal guards. With your permission, my lord, I will take their oaths now, with this honorable assembly to stand as witness." He turned to the soldiers. "Warriors tried and tested, state the ancient oath."

In unison, the fifteen solemnly intoned, "Until I meet my honest and just end, my life for hers. May shame ever haunt me, should I break faith with my lady. May death come swift and cruel to claim me, should I recant this path or shrink from any duty it brings me."

"May it be so," Denei replied. "You are dismissed to the king's office to await orders."

The dismissal of the new guards served as the signal for the others assembled there to disperse as well. They stood respectfully as Colin, Selena and Maia left the room. Maia followed her parents back along the same path that had brought them to the petitioners' hall. Her head still buzzed with the idea of having her own guards. *Why do I need guards? What sort of danger*—Before this thought completed its circuit, she reached the top of the smaller stair and found the third marshal waiting. Maia averted her eyes from his eager face and hurried after her parents.

Her mother continued onward with a short farewell, leaving Maia to accompany her father into his book-lined office. For once, it felt crowded. Maia smiled at Hollister. "I was never so surprised! But I'm glad to have you here. And you as well, Isaac. In your father's steps already!"

"You'll find many second-generation guards here," Denei said as he closed the door. "At ease! Isaac, have you worked out the duty roster yet?"

Isaac Rowan-son stepped forward. "Yes, sir. Meg and her squad have the first shift."

Maia smiled. Meghala was Kenda's elder sister. As she gazed around at the circle, Maia counted many faces she knew. Hollister she knew because his late father Yuri once belonged to her grandfather's royal guard corps and his mother Berdina was head of the Caretaker kitchen staff of Takra House. Hollister was the last of six brothers to have passed through Academy and the only one to have been chosen for the corps. Isaac was the eldest son of Owen's brother-in-law Rowan, who commanded the king's corps. Isaac had seniority over the entire group—at the age of thirty, he was also the oldest of them.

"Where will they bunk?" Colin asked. "We'll have a time of it, housing them alongside my guards and Owen's."

"There's plenty of room upstairs in the guest quarters for now. I'll work on it when I get a moment. I have already asked Lucinda to see to the rooms." Denei bowed stiffly. To the guards he said, "Dismissed." Once the guards had filed from the room, Denei finally sat down in one of the chairs. "Well, Colin. Do we have anything to discuss, or shall I go to my office at once?"

"What do you mean?"

Maia thought her father sounded wary, not inquisitive. She saw the wry twist of Denei's mouth and knew that he thought the same.

"Very well. If you won't speak of it, I cannot force you. Good day."

Once Denei had gone, Colin turned to Maia. "Why don't you take the rest of the day for yourself, dearest? You'll want to get acquainted with your guards. They look like a fine lot."

"Yes, Father, they do. I'll go, then." She could tell that he was not attending to anything she said. He was so distracted that he hardly seemed able to hear his own words. Getting up quietly, she went first and kissed the top of his head. "I love you, Father. I wish I was more help to you." It encouraged her somewhat to see him lift his head and give her a dispirited, wistful smile. She smiled back. "It'll be all right." *I wish I could tell him about my new teacher. If he could only meet Teacher, he'd feel better.*

When she was halfway through the waiting room outside her father's office, a pleasant male voice startled her. "You're looking glum, Princess. Can I cheer you at all?" Giles sprang up from one of the benches that sat along the wall. "It'd be my pleasure to serve, lady."

"Hello! Don't frighten me like that," she scolded without anger. "Pouncing up out of nowhere like that—how did you come to be here?"

"A long time ago, my mother and my father met and—"

Maia laughed. "Don't be an idiot, Giles. What did you want?"

"Are you terribly busy? I can wait longer if you are."

"Not at all! My father gave me the afternoon for my very own, to do whatever I please. What were you being introduced as this morning? I can't see you as a courtier."

"I'll have you know that I'm now Lord Sakiry's personal companion. I fetch and carry for him, send messages and bring back responses—all that nobody-work. It means that I might turn up on your doorstep at any moment of the day…bringing a message, waiting for you to respond…or just hanging about, waiting for nothing at all."

"I get the feeling the last takes place before the rest."

Giles shrugged. "I dare not contradict a lady of the blood." But he failed to smile quite as brightly as before. "Are you sure you're not busy? I've found something."

"What do you mean, 'found something'?"

"Upstairs. In the attic. Come on, quick, before someone comes to hand me more chores."

To make up for offending him, Maia took his hand and ran along with him as if they were two younglings. They ascended the stairs to the attic, a long, dim chamber with a peaked ceiling and dormer windows sending in dusty shafts of light at long intervals. Tall stacks of crates stood like pillars among a jumble of bare furniture. Maia followed as Giles picked a cautious path through the jumble. "What are we looking for?"

"Wait. Wait 'til you see it. Does anybody ever come here?"

"I doubt it. *I* never knew anything was up here. There's so much dust! Be careful."

"That makes it stranger still. Over this way." Giles steadied her with a hand at her elbow as she climbed over a box. "I was bored yesterday and thought I'd get away from everything and explore. Here we go. Just as I...no, not just as I left it," Giles exclaimed in surprise. "Someone else has been here! I never touched the bed."

Maia stooped under the low slope of the rafters until she caught up with Giles in the light of the dormer window. There she saw what he meant: within the makeshift walls formed by crates and stacks of furniture, one of the bed frames had been set up, mattress and all like a proper bed chamber. The covers were dusty and faded from the sunlight, but there was a definite mark in the dust, as if the bed had been occupied recently. "This is peculiar. I wonder what it means. What are you doing now? If you pull at that—have a care! You'll bring the whole pile down on us!"

"I'm not as stupid as that, my lady. See? It comes out easy enough. It's meant to come out. See? Slides out beautiful. Somebody's used this before as a sort of hidden treasure cache, from the looks of it. I don't think anybody's been into it, not like with the bed. Look at this." He reached inside until his arm disappeared up to the shoulder. After a moment's blind rummaging, he extracted a book. "See here!" he objected when Maia snatched it away. "I found it first!"

She already had it open. A gasp escaped her throat as she saw a name on the first page: Jarod Kohanan-son. "Oh! This belonged to my father's brother." She flipped to the next page. "It's an old exercise book. Look at it, how the pages are yellow and rumpled. It's…I think it's some sort of strategy exercise book. Peculiar. Look at the margins."

Giles took the book back and read the margins as commanded. "What tongue is that?"

"Goodness, I don't know. I'm no scholar. He couldn't have been more than fifteen when he wrote that. He died soon afterward. So Ivy and my father told me. I wonder what it says." A shiver went up her back. "Put it back, Giles. I don't think we should disturb this box."

"What's the matter?"

"I don't know, but it doesn't feel right. It's like trespassing. Put it all back as it was."

"As you wish, my lady." Giles replaced the little book and pushed the box into place. "It's a nice, quiet spot. Not somewhere anybody would come looking. I doubt anybody else will find this. The view's nice, too. Take a look." He swung his legs over to the other side of the bed and unlatched the window. When it slid noiselessly up in its track, Giles looked to Maia with raised eyebrows. "Somebody *has* been here. That's a well-used window."

"You would know," she teased. "Move over so I can see." It wasn't such a big window, but it was more than big enough for her to lean her head and shoulders out into the hot midday sunshine. She saw Caretaker gardeners below, hard at work in the orchard. No one looked up to see her. When she pulled her upper body back into the attic, she thought Giles looked daft. "What's wrong with you?"

"I think I need air. My turn at the window." He leaned on the sill, drawing deep breaths of the air outside. He stayed out longer than Maia thought necessary; she got bored waiting for him to come back in, but though she prodded his hip with a finger, he acted as if he didn't notice.

"Oh, come on, surely you've had enough air by now?"

Giles gave up his windowsill perch and sat beside her. His face was pink in the hazy sunlight. "Sorry, sorry. I just…needed some air."

"So you said. Are you all right?"

"No," he said plaintively, "no, I'm not all right, and I don't suppose I'll be all right ever again." His blush darkened. "Come on, my lady, we'd best go back downstairs."

When he started to turn away, Maia caught his arm. "Wait a minute. What's wrong?"

He dropped his head. "It's nothing you need to trouble yourself over. Best let go of me."

"Answer the question and I will."

At that, Giles grinned crookedly. "No doubt you will—let me go, that is, once I answer that question. The truth of it is that I'm no fellow to be trusted to keep company with a girl as pretty as you. If I didn't still have a smidge of conscience left, I'd have kissed you by now. Believe me, it's hard work, keeping that smidge of conscience alive. You don't make it easy."

Taken aback, Maia let go of his sleeve and folded her hands together. "Oh."

They were silent after that, awkwardly silent. "I'll go now," Giles finally said. "Good day to you, Princess."

"Oh, don't be stupid! Let's go down to the sitting room. It's dusty up here."

"And better populated down there," he quipped. He offered her a hand to help her out of the makeshift chamber. "Uncle Owen will scold me for mussing the new clothes he gave me."

"I thought you looked more civilized than usual. New haircut, too? Was it all for your presentation this morning? And I thought you didn't care what folk thought of you. Owen has his work cut out for him, making a courtier out of you!" Maia spoke as lightly as she could, keeping away from the other subject while they picked their way through the shadowy clutter to the steps. "Have you heard from your father or mother yet? I would've thought they might have something to say—why, they must've started to miss you by now!"

"Miss me? Not until the sun burns cold."

"That's an awful thing to say about your family."

"It's an awful family to say things about. They care nothing for me, my lady. Your family has treated me more like kin than mine ever has. I'm having a fine time with Uncle Owen all the same. Interesting man, Uncle Owen. Hmm...I think these belong to you, lady." Giles gestured through the open door of a portrait gallery. "If I'm not mistaken."

Maia stopped short. A dozen new guards gazed at her blankly. Hollister had his mouth halfway open, as if he had been interrupted. "Hello," Maia said.

"Where have you been? Meg has been all over the place, trying to find you, ranting on and on about losing you before she'd had charge of you for five minutes together. You'd best stay here until she comes 'round again. Do I know you, my good fellow?" Hollister asked Giles.

"Giles Perrin-son," said the other, stiffly offering his hand. "You?"

"Captain Hollister Yuri-son, of the princess' guard corps. What's your business around here...that is, when you have any business being around here?"

"I am Lord Sakiry's companion. The general is my grandfather."

"Leave him be, Hollister. He's my friend." Maia did not look at Giles when she said it. "It's odd to have my own guards, you know. Especially one who used to be my big brother."

"What do you mean, 'used to be'?"

"I haven't seen you in so long; naturally, I assumed you'd given up the job."

"I've been out on patrol, earning my way back here to where I am now, thank you."

"Out on patrol? Where? Did you fight the marauders?"

Hollister nodded with sleek satisfaction. "These last three campaigns, I did."

"Come with me to the salon downstairs. I want to—" She stopped, looking around for Giles, but he was nowhere to be seen. She finished, "I want to talk about things." Glancing around once more in search of Giles, Maia didn't know whether to be troubled or relieved at his sudden voluntary absence. *I'll work it out later.*

IDENTIFICATION

When she was troubled in spirit, Selena had the habit of going out to the small monument grove in the shadow of the southern wall of Takra House. It didn't matter what time of day or night it was. She found comfort in the silent presence of the cenotaphs. Those with imagination might have felt the presence of the dead in such a place, but Selena had not been formed with any such faculty. It was the silence that comforted her. The monument grove was the only silent place to be found on the palace grounds. Its walls were high and thick. One of the orchard trees peeped over the westernmost wall; otherwise, no one visited the grove. After supper one night, Selena paced her thoughtful, distracted way in that direction, the better to order her thoughts.

Something was wrong with Maia. Selena saw the changes in her and could not account for them. The girl seemed to welcome her new duties—though Selena felt that Maia was gladder for the company of her father than anything else. No, she reasoned, it could not be that specific change that had altered the girl so. Perhaps it was the boy. Perhaps. Selena had wondered at his absence. Following the day of his presentation at court, Giles had vanished without cause. Owen showed no concern, so Selena knew that the boy couldn't have been in any great trouble, but still she thought it strange. The boy had been so attentive in his manner toward Maia...

She set her hand on the curved handle of the monument grove gate and stood, like one of the cenotaphs inside, for several moments. She was unexpectedly reminded of her father-in-law Kohanan and his last instructions to her: *Poor Colin. He has lost mother and father in the same day. He will need you now, Selie.*

Stand with him. He does depend on you, you know. I can't help him myself, but if I last long enough, I'll send help for him…if I'm successful in my quest. Be strong, Selie. Be strong for him. She couldn't think why this lost wisp of conversation had suddenly come back to her after such a long time—years and years.

Selena opened the gate silently. The sun was so far gone that the cenotaphs showed only as pale, insubstantial blurs in the twilight. The lights of the house behind her, on the other hand, cast a strong gleam that outlined the top of the north wall of the grove in buttery gold. As Selena found her way to her favorite bench, she stopped short to see her Colin kneeling in front of the monument that honored his mother Camille. She realized in the next moment that it was *not* her Colin. She had left Colin in his office, surrounded by Maia's new guards, and anyway, this man had a long, thick warrior's queue hanging down his back and was notably larger even than her Colin. The sight of him stirred in her mind a word that she had heard her Colin speak often in his nightmares of late: *Jarod.* She spoke it aloud.

Startled by her voice, the man lifted his head with quick wariness, like a wild creature. His face was invisible save for his bearded chin and his eyes that glittered as they darted toward her. Then, he rose from his knees as if preparing to leave.

"I'm afraid I interrupted your meditations," Selena said hurriedly. "We have not yet been introduced. I'm Selena—your brother's wife. Welcome back! How did you come here? Have you been waiting long? Have you been to the house and seen Colin yet?"

"You are very certain that I am someone in particular, my lady. We have never met."

"After nineteen years of marriage, it would be strange if I couldn't recognize my own husband's twin when I saw him. I thought you were him when I first entered, but of course you aren't. Who else would you be, then?" Selena took another few steps forward. "What do you have covering your face? Isn't it rather warm weather for that? You can't be comfortable."

"That," he said in a peculiar voice, "is an unarguable fact. I believe we must talk."

"Have you not been to see Colin yet? He'll be so relieved to see you after all this time."

"He cannot know of me, for good reason. I came this night to meet with your daughter, not your husband. For the time being, he must remain ignorant of my existence and I must demand your silence on this matter. Tell no one who I am. Do you understand?"

Selena paused, unwilling to be rushed into anything. She was by now close enough to reach out a hand to him, so she did, startling him again. Selena held it out until he accepted it, bowed over it, and kissed it formally. Then, without speaking, she took his arm and walked with him to the bench where she often sat to think about important matters. Even when they were seated side by side, Selena would not hurry. "Why must he not know? It would encourage him so much. His spirits have been so low these past months—but especially since he learned of his father's death. He was always so cheerful before. If he knew you had come home, it would encourage him."

"I cannot help the state of his spirits, low or high, at present. I'm too busy trying to make sure he stays alive."

"Stays alive?" Selena's heart gave a horrified lurch. "Is he in danger?"

"Grave danger. You must trust that I know what I'm doing. Will you do that?"

She nodded. "Yes. Please, don't let anything happen to him. I couldn't bear to lose him." She paused at another thought, which she spoke after a moment's reflection. "I couldn't bear to go through what Ivy has gone through these twenty years. Will you tell *her* that you've come home? You've come just in time. Her father has arranged that she marry a foreign ally. Ivy never forgot you. You must go to Denei and explain that he can't go through with his plans—"

The man held out a hand to hush her. "I have already spoken to Denei. Have no fear." A wry smile twisted his lips. "She may be marrying a stranger, but I will not remain so for long."

That was the impetus needed to string the thoughts together in Selena's head. She drew in a sharp breath. "You're the—"

"Yes. As you can see, I have not forgotten her either."

Selena bowed her head. "Very well. I will do as you ask of me. It will be hard. I can't bear to see him so low-spirited without reason."

"I understand. Thank you."

They stood. As she sought some adequate way to express her gladness at his return, Selena found the moment taken entirely out of her control. Jarod took her hands in his and pressed them firmly. "In the days to come, I may have to ask you to do a very difficult thing, and to do it without question. Only bear in mind that I will not ask it of you unless it is the only way. Remember that." He released her hands. "Now, if you would be so kind, please take your daughter aside for a private word and ask her to meet her teacher for tonight's lessons after the household has gone to sleep. Only say that. She will understand."

Selena nodded. "Certainly." She took a last, lingering stare at him before she left the grove to return to the house. If her steps were slower than usual, it was for the best, because she could not see the path ahead of her. She was too deeply buried in her thoughts. Before she was aware of entering the house, she had arrived at the door to Colin's office. The noise of the gathering inside made it impossible for her to continue thinking. She slipped in unnoticed and worked her way around to her daughter's side. "Maia, come outside for a moment, please."

"Certainly, Mother." The girl didn't remark upon such a request; she knew of Selena's aversion to the din of crowded rooms. She got up and followed Selena into the waiting room.

Selena shut the double doors for privacy. "How does it go? They seem a cheerful lot."

"It's going well. Father seems to be in a better mood."

"That's good to hear, dearest. I hope these new faces help him." Then she paused, finding no adroit way to change the subject. "I was given a message for you. Your teacher expects you tonight, as soon as the household has gone to sleep."

The effect of her words surprised Selena. The girl stood still for several breaths after the initial gasp of surprise. Her lips moved, trying to frame words that would not come. "M-Mother, I…How do you know? Did he…speak to you? Himself? Tonight?"

"Yes."

Maia looked enormously relieved. "You've met him, then. Well…what do you think?"

"About what, dearest?"

"About *him*. Now that you know."

Selena weighed her reply cautiously. "I believe we're lucky to have him with us."

"Mother—I'm glad you know. I didn't feel right about keeping it secret from everyone."

"Keeping what secret?" Denei's mild voice asked from the outer door.

Selena was lost for a safe response. To her relief, her daughter came forward and shut the hallway door behind the general. "I shouldn't have been so careless," the girl said in chagrin. "Not that I mind *you* hearing, Uncle, but I should know better. You're here awfully late. Why?"

"I found I had business. Yours first, little one. What sort of secret could you have?"

"It's safe to tell *you*, Uncle, since you brought him in to begin with." She leaned closer to him despite the closed doors. "I've met him. Your candidate."

Denei's heavy eyebrows rose. "Have you, now? Both of you?"

"Mother only met him today—that's right, isn't it?"

Selena nodded. "Not a quarter of an hour ago. In the monument grove."

Maia went on, "He came to me a few days ago, the day I got my new guards, and he said he wanted to…to teach me. Swordplay, he said, but he's teaching me other things at the same time. Strange things—" Something troubled the girl; the shadow of it dimmed her enthusiasm. "He won't let me tell Father about him. He's adamant about it."

"He said the same to me," Selena added. "Colin must not know."

"That's strange indeed. He never said I wasn't to mention him. Why is that, I wonder?"

Hesitating, Selena offered, "He told me that Colin is in danger, and that's why he mustn't know of his work. He said…" Here she paused, wondering if she ought to tell them. *Why not this? I don't have an idea what he meant by it, anyway.* "He said that it might come to the point where he'll have to ask me to do something that's difficult for me, if it means that Colin will be safe. I don't know what he meant."

Denei frowned over that. "I see my news in a new light now. I received a messenger tonight at my home, sent by the northerner. He says that the marauders are making their approach even now. He was insistent that Colin must remain here, no matter what men may say of his courage. Those were his exact words. I had wondered what he meant, but now…"

"If you're going," Maia began slowly, "what cause would Father have for going, too?"

Selena and Denei exchanged a glance, but it was Denei who answered. "When this first began, your father put forth the suggestion in private conversation, and Owen and I found ways of squashing it without insulting him. Our main argument was distance—and that held, so long as the marauders never came nearer than Adeelah. Now they're practically in the courtyard. Colin has greater cause to want to go along now. He knows that the soldiers have little respect for him. I fear he'll want to prove them wrong in what they say about him. If we cannot trust his guards, there is no way that we can let him go into battle."

Maia's young face tightened into a frown of determination. "I'll settle that. Come on." She bounded to the office door, throwing the doors open wide as Denei followed sedately.

The chatter stilled at once. Colin stood. "Denei! What's wrong?"

"I've heard from my—my friend," Denei began with care. "The marauders are on their way even now and are expected to reach the river in three days or so."

"Whereabouts on the river?"

"Not five leagues northward from Eleusia."

Colin sank into his chair abruptly, his hands gripping the edge of the desk. "So near?" His manner changed again, mirroring the determination that Selena had seen in her daughter's face only moments before. "Very well. How soon will we be ready to head out? If we leave by noon tomorrow, we ought to get there in plenty of time—"

A sharp gesture from Isaac Rowan-son distracted him. Isaac had motioned for one of the guards to shut the doors again. He would not speak until they were closed. "My lord, it'll sound like impertinence, but I can't help that. I have to say it. Please forgive me. You cannot go with the army." A murmur of assent from his companions braced him to continue. "It would be folly, nothing less, if you set foot outside this city as matters stand now."

"It doesn't *sound* like impertinence," Colin retorted. "It *is* impertinence, Captain."

"Father," said Maia, "if you go, I'll go." When he tried to speak against that idea, she circled around the desk, put her arms around his neck, and whispered a few words in his ear. The longer she spoke, the more conflicted Colin's expression became. She tightened her hold to keep him in his chair and said something more.

Colin drew a deep breath. Before he said a word, Selena knew that Maia's counsel—whatever it was—had reached, convinced, and displeased him. That was made obvious by the mulish set of his jaw. "Very well. Off with you. Take your entourage with you."

Without argument, Maia kissed the top of his head. "Good night, Father."

Slowly, the room emptied. Denei and Maia were the last to exit, except for Selena. She could see that Colin wanted to be quiet for a while, so she followed the other two out. Her heart bowed a little lower when she heard the heaviness of her daughter's sigh.

"You convinced him," Denei said encouragingly. "That's the main thing."

"I hate this," Maia hissed, kicking a nearby chair. "Why shouldn't he be free to do as he pleases? Why do we have to creep around like mice for fear of our own servants? It isn't right!"

"We don't creep for fear, little one. We move forward with caution. It wouldn't do to risk condemning an innocent man along with the guilty ones. I'm not resting idle. There is such a thing as moving slowly so as not to startle your prey."

Maia's anger eased a little. "I guess. Uncle Denei, before you go, where has Giles been? I haven't seen him these two days together."

Denei appeared startled. Then he frowned. "But he said you didn't want to see him. Three days ago, he was waylaid by a couple of men he said were royal guards. They said he was to stop bothering you and left some marks on him to prove they were in earnest. He thought they were *your* guards."

"Couldn't be," Maia asserted. "I told mine to go easy on him. He wasn't bothering me."

"I'll be sure to tell him so. He's done nothing but mope ever since. Riana was troubled to think that he'd offended you somehow."

"He hasn't. Just to prove it, I'm sending someone to escort him here tomorrow."

Selena comprehended perfectly the anxiety in Maia's eyes. Something of the same kind moved her to return to her husband's office silently, not to disturb him, but to be near if he should need someone.

Colin seemed not to have noticed her entrance. He sat as had become his wont: head between his hands, shoulders bowed with troubles. Selena meant to find an unobtrusive place to sit and wait, but before she had the chance, Colin spoke. "I can't believe it's come to this. Lectured on prudence by my own daughter, as if I hadn't sense enough to look after myself! That was an unfair trick on Denei's part. I couldn't very well argue with her, not when she uses my own counsel against me! It doesn't matter to *them* if every man in my kingdom is convinced I'm a coward because I don't face the marauders. No! Keep my precious skin whole—that's all they want. It would be better to lose limb or even life than to walk around with this burden of...of *scorn* heaped upon me!" All the while, he sat with his head clasped in both hands. Selena caught a glimpse of one drop of moisture falling onto the papers on his desk. "Better to lose everything than turn into an empty puppet! Little by little, I lose it all: the regard of my people, my child's obedience, any worth I still own—"

Selena circled around the desk to put her hands on his shoulders.

He covered her hands with his, but didn't raise his face to her until he had salvaged his self-discipline. Then, briefly, he tipped his head back against her and gazed up with damp black eyes. They still held deep pools of misery that she felt helpless to banish.

"Come to bed," she urged. "There's nothing more to be done tonight. It's late."

"There's nothing to be done by me, certainly. I might as well go to bed. Let me get a book to read. I'm not sleepy yet."

Maia was lingering in the salon when they reached their suite. As soon as she saw them, she started up from her chair and merely gazed a plea with wretched eyes.

Colin paused for a moment. Then he held out an arm toward her. When she ran to him and embraced him, he rubbed her back. "You were only doing as you were told, no doubt. It's all right, dearest." With his free hand, he tipped her face upward. "It isn't your fault."

Selena tried to take comfort in this little reconciliation. She was unable to forget that Maia was due to meet with Jarod that night, and that Jarod said her Colin was in mortal danger. As she followed Colin into the bed chamber, she turned to give Maia a last look, but the girl had already retreated to her own bedroom door on the other side of the salon. There was nothing left for Selena to do but lie awake pretending to sleep while she waited for her husband to finally grow sleepy enough to put his book aside and extinguish the light.

YESTERDAY: FATHERS

"General Mata-son?"

When his wife spoke with such exaggerated formality before breakfast, Denei knew that she meant to lighten his mood before breaking bad news to him. His mind leaped to the same conclusion that had kept him awake all night—or what remained of the night, after such a disturbing scene. But Denei kept silent.

"The king is in our garden, dear. He regrets to disturb you so early."

Denei nodded. When he found Kohanan, he was not surprised that the king stood gazing up at one window in particular. Denei waited for his king to speak first.

"I spoke to him. He was forthright, at least. The one thing he didn't tell me, I'd already guessed. Why that window? Why last night? You were right, Denei. He wanted to be caught." Kohanan gazed at the side of the house. "You're keeping her confined to the house?"

"Yes."

"Good. I'd do the same with him, but what good would it do? It can't mend what's troubling him. I've never seen him show his heart as openly as this. I hoped that a year of training might give him the time to face what plagues him. I didn't think—I *should* have thought of it. He's a man now in all but name. I should have given him proper occupation when he came back. We should have spoken with him about marriage. Ah, but it's so easy to say 'should have,' isn't it? He worries me more than ever. Her affection helped him where none of ours could, but now he won't let her near him. His old trouble weighs on him all the more, but he won't tell me about it. The older he gets, the worse it grows, but he still won't say a word to me about it. He tried to provoke me last night. I sensed it in him. He wanted me to lose my temper."

"Was it a challenge to your authority?"

Kohanan shook his head in mute frustration. He began again. "I've pondered it so often, from before he was born to today, without finding an answer. Especially after it turned out that he...he isn't affected by my anger. I thought at first it meant he was another like me, but he isn't. Then I thought maybe he was like Camille, but he isn't that either. He's unique. Last night only proved it again. Last night, he spoke almost plainly to me for once. He wanted me to lose my temper so I'd punish him. He wanted to be confined to house, without visitors. Maybe he wanted a beating—I can't say. When he saw that I wouldn't do any of that, he...he asked that Ivy be confined instead. He said to keep her away from him."

"That makes no sense...unless he...does he blame her, then?"

"I can only answer that with his words. He said to keep her away because he was too weak to do it himself. He said she would only come to harm if they persisted. I asked him the same—did he only take advantage of her, then? Did he not match her feelings? I would have been truly ashamed of him then, but he said it was nothing at all to do with feelings. It was her safety that troubled him. He thinks he's a danger to her. That's why he wanted to be caught."

"It seems unlikely," Denei said slowly, thinking as he spoke, "attributing such subtlety to so young a boy."

"With Jarod, I think the danger lies in attributing too little subtlety to him. He's not as young as folk believe him to be. There's nothing I consider wholly out of his reach, even now. I wonder what he'll be like when he comes to full manhood."

"What would you have me do?"

"Say nothing," the king said after a while. "Not to her, anyway. I...I can't fault the boy's logic, wherever else he may have fallen short. If he says he's a danger to her..." He shut his eyes, but not before Denei saw them begin to pale from black to silver. With his eyes closed, he said, "My boy has a long road ahead of him. I cannot see more than the first few steps, but as far as I do see, he takes those steps alone." A tremor shook him. He opened his eyes as their color began to fade into black again. "Not even I can help him. If he lives, I believe that he will become greater than I am."

"May I try to speak with him all the same?"

Kohanan gazed at him with unsettling concentration for a minute. After he had had time to weigh both the request and the petitioner, he nodded. "He has always loved you as a second father. If you can't reach him, no one else will." The king let escape a gentle breath. "When you come, look for him in his room. He may not want to see you, but you have a right to demand an accounting from him. She *is* your daughter."

So it was that Denei made his way to Takra House later that afternoon, after he had seen to all his mundane property concerns. In the corridor, he passed young Colin, who flushed deep red at the sight of him and then looked away as if he too bore a measure of his twin's guilt. The house seemed otherwise deserted. Denei met no one else until he came within view of the royal suites. Then, to his alarm, his son Nässey hurtled headlong through the air to land with a thud against the wall. Jarod's flat voice followed him, saying, "Keep silent if you don't know what you're saying." The door slammed. Twelve-year-old Nässey picked himself up from the floor, all a-tremble until he caught sight of his father's approach. Denei asked, "What happened?"

"He wouldn't say he was sorry," the boy said in a voice low with outrage.

"Go home now, Nässey. Let me deal with this. Good lad." Denei watched until the boy was out of sight. Then he turned to the door that had slammed shut. He laid a tentative hand against the wood to listen, but no sound issued from within. After another moment, he entered.

There were two beds in the room. Only the one beneath the window was occupied. Jarod lay on his back, staring out the window at the sky with no expression visible on his face. At the sound of Denei's entrance, the young man cast a rapid look, expecting Nässey. He saw Denei instead and thrust himself to his feet in surprise.

Denei drew near until he stood an arm's-length from Jarod. Although he had to tip his head back to do it, he stared into Jarod's eyes, trying to find some sign of the young man's heart.

After submitting to this examination for only a little while, Jarod crumbled. His head bowed as his eyes sought the floor, unable to bear looking at Denei any longer. The rest of his body didn't take long to follow. In another few seconds, the young man knelt down with his head hanging between his arms. Shudders ran up and down his back, so great was the effort it cost him to keep from weeping.

Compassion drove Denei to kneel as well. He took Jarod in his arms as a man might comfort his friend in profound grief. It comforted him likewise when he felt Jarod willingly rest on his shoulder, unresisting. He wished the boy would speak, if only to release the tension that held him so rigid, but Jarod seemed beyond words. When Jarod pushed away a few minutes later, Denei let go of him reluctantly. Whatever moved Jarod had passed already. Denei's throat constricted with pity as the young man retreated to the window and refused to look at him again.

AMBITION

It was surprisingly difficult to return to an idle life. Giles had grown accustomed to waiting in attendance upon Lord Sakiry; the job had not been strenuous by any means, but he had known where he was expected to be and what he was expected to do. Now that he had to avoid the palace, Giles began to drift again. For two days, he loitered around his grandfather's house in discontented idleness, trying not to admit to himself that the princess' message of dismissal had meant anything to him. Had he not tried to warn himself that honesty would only get him booted out the door? His grandmother's pitying glances were too much of a reminder. Giles took to the streets again in an attempt to salvage his spirits.

The markets of King's City were crowded compared to those of Carthae, where he was more accustomed to waste daylight. There were even more shop-keepers to cultivate here, more grocers to wheedle treats from—and they were far more generous than their counterparts in Carthae, much to Giles' satisfaction. By this method he managed to avoid returning to his grandfather's house even for meals. He had struck up two dozen promising acquaintances by the end of his first day. Shopkeepers fell into two camps, as he had discovered early on in life: the busy and the busybodies. The first camp he avoided, because they tended to deal sharply with loiterers. Those in the second camp were his entertainment and main source of employment. Long before this, Giles had learned how to humor them profitably. He listened with gratifying interest to their gossip and either argued the point (if the gossip was argumentative) or held himself temptingly neutral so that the gossip had hopes of converting him to the point of view under discussion. Either way, he usually got free handouts from the encounters, and that was all he really wanted.

Carthae gossip had centered on the Pamirsi patriarch's family, as befit a town dependent on that worthy's patronage. In King's City, Giles found a more egalitarian vein predominating. Any patriarch or eminent public figure was declared fit for their active tongues. News of the royal family was met with special curiosity, but Giles noticed a greater restraint evidenced in this arena of discussion. It did not surprise him much to find that the civilians held the king in affectionate regard; he had taken good care of them through plague and plenty, as they liked to say, and none could ask for more. As for the king's daughter, shopkeepers of all breeds professed only the highest admiration for her burgeoning beauty and her down-to-earth gentility. Giles made no effort to budge them from this subject, though he knew he probably should change topics for his own peace of mind.

It was in the midst of one of these spontaneous tributes to the princess that Giles happened to look up and see two young men in uniform at the top of the street. One of them made a gesture toward Giles. Then they started toward him with a determined air that he had seen often. Giles made a quick excuse to his new acquaintance and slipped around behind the booth, settling on a left-hand course that would take him down a short alley and into one of the most thickly populated sections of the market district. He was well aware that these guards probably knew King's City better than he did, but he had spent so many hours already in the markets that he felt sure he had a sporting chance. If they were set on finding him, he stood no real chance of escaping them, but he could delay his arrest long enough to have a little fun at their expense. It was an old game for him. The city guards of Carthae had learned it from him; now he could teach it to the king's guards as well.

The first lesson was the hardest to teach guards: *look up*. Giles picked a likely booth, one that had a sturdy roof and not much traffic around it. Grasping the roof's edge, he clambered up to lie flat against the slippery thatching, catch his breath, and wait. He heard the firm footfalls beneath him a few minutes later. Gingerly he slid forward to peer over the edge of the roof. It was just as he thought. The guards had passed his hiding place and were standing at the intersection of the two streets, looking both ways for him. He heard the one say, "Take the left, Will. If you don't spot him within a block or two, come back here, and I'll do the same." Giles watched the two young men part company. From his high perch, he could see their progress in either direction and noted that the one called Will was a quicker walker than his assertive companion. He reached the end of his assigned path first and paused at the end of the block to survey the next street. Seeing that Will was about to turn back, Giles checked the other guard's position to make sure neither was close at hand. Then he slid down the thatching to land in the midst of the lane. He heard a sharp outcry from Will, but Giles was already backtracking at a healthy jog, just fast enough to keep out of reach. He knew better than to elude them altogether. A guard on duty might forgive a challenging game of seek, but he did not like to look a complete fool. Giles glanced back over his shoulder to make sure they were still after him.

From their exclamations, he soon learned the second one's name: Jules. Will and Jules were younger and fitter than most guards Giles had known. Twice they nearly laid hands on him, but Giles was wily enough to hide when he couldn't run and run when they weren't looking. They had a glorious chase around and around the bell tower, until Jules got a notion to double back and cut off Giles' escape route. This too was an old dodge to Giles, who had expected them to think of it much sooner. He heard the subtraction of one set of running footsteps behind him and knew that he had to veer off at the next corner or be intercepted. He vaulted a passing coal cart, much to the admiration of the crowd that had gathered to watch the fun. Concealed by the cart, he detoured down another alley and ducked into a crowded public house to sit by the windows. He judged that he had made them exert themselves for long enough; any more and they might grow really cross with him. Giles used some of the pocket money given him by his great-uncle, bought a pint of ale, and sat down by the window to await the inevitable.

He grew uneasy when the inevitable failed to transpire. A steady traffic of laborers came and went. Giles bought another pint and returned to his table. Still, neither Will nor Jules entered the tavern. One hour passed. Giles finally went out to see if they were waiting for him in the street—most guards didn't trouble themselves about arresting a wayward youth in someone's place of business, but it was possible that a king's guard might be reluctant to do so. Stranger things had happened to Giles, in his experience with soldiers. No one awaited him outside, though. Puzzled, Giles returned to the bell tower. The two guards were nowhere in view. A little tactful questioning unearthed no useful information. Giles glanced at the late afternoon sky, wondering what to do next. He hardly dared venture outside in the streets now that he had been so careless as to shake loose of those two guards. *Who knows? Maybe they went to get reinforcements.* Giles returned to the tavern. The fun of the chase was now replaced by a combination of glum expectancy, irritable nerves, and listlessness. Instead of ale, he purchased a bottle of wine and retreated to a corner to wait. *That was careless,* he berated himself. *I can just see Grandfather's face now when they add 'resisting arrest' to the charges.* It had never mattered before, not when it was just his father haranguing him about the shame he brought upon the family. The same scenario became truly shameful when he anticipated Denei's silent disappointment. Leaning back into the corner, Giles poured another cupful of wine and mulled over the many possible responses his grandfather might make.

*   *   *   *

In the morning, Giles was late to rise. He had no idea how or when he had gotten back to his grandfather's house, nor how he had avoided detection by the rest of the house's inmates. He vaguely recalled hearing Ivy call to him once or twice within the last hour, but his hangover had made any response difficult at best. Even when he did rise, he moved with a cautious tread to avoid jarring his head any more than need be. He put on his old clothes, brushed ineffectually at the traces of dirt on them, and descended to find the rest of the house deserted. With effort, he dredged up the memory of Ivy's voice saying, "Hurry, Giles, if you want to see your grandfather off to war!" Giles groaned. Despite himself, he had desired to see his grandfather go riding out at the head of the column. His grandfather had been the one soldier for whom Giles felt no smidgen of envy or resentment. He hardly dared admit that he might admire the old man, but the thought was there all the same. After drawing himself a cup of water in the kitchen, Giles resolved to go out and see if he was too late.

The street outside the house was eerily empty. Through the sultry air, a distant ringing of cheers drew Giles forward to the main thoroughfare, into the painful din of the crowd. He winced at their noise more than once. Squirming between the crush of bodies, he made his way down the avenue in an attempt to reach the street.

It was a colorful procession, unusually so when one considered it signified neither a wedding nor a birth, but a march to battle. Giles never understood the eagerness some young men felt at going to war. The notion of killing another human never triggered any interest in him whatsoever. Giles much preferred to live and let live in perfect indifference to his fellow man. He elbowed through to the street front just in time to see the first riders come around the corner down the block. His heart constricted. He had not thought of the possibility that the royal family might accompany his grandfather at least to the gates of the city, so he was unprepared to see the princess in the company. A mass of guards surrounded the riders and obscured them from time to time, but Giles watched for any sign that he had been noticed.

Just before the company drew abreast of Giles' post, his grandfather made eye contact. The old man smiled, clearly pleased to find that his grandson had some remnant of family feeling left in him. More than that, however, he turned to Maia and drew her attention to Giles as well. Giles could no more suppress his blush than he could look away from the girl once she had run him through with that direct gaze. She waved to him, smiling. Giles hardly believed the witness of his own eyes. *She isn't mad at me?*

Soldiers blocked his view in another moment. He shook himself mentally, trying to tell himself that it did not matter, since she was still unreachable for someone like himself. Then he made eye contact of a far less pleasing sort. The dagger-like stare of the third marshal caught him as through the joints of his armor, in the moment when his defenses had fallen before Maia's smile. Giles shivered. He glanced away from Miklei-son and pretended that he had noticed nothing untoward in the marshal's glare.

What pleasures the procession afforded were completely stolen from him now, so Giles pushed his way back through the crowd. If he had bothered to look behind him, he might have made it home. At the least, he would have gone more warily, or changed his course, or done something to evade the soldiers who trailed him as far as the first empty street. Giles only discovered their presence when one clubbed him over the head—and then he knew nothing but confused intimations of movement, light and shadow passing, then stifling, musty darkness. He tried to open his eyes. "Wha—?"

"He'll likely give you grief," a voice said calmly. "He's a troublesome one."

"I know how to keep 'em quiet."

The second blow to the head knocked Giles unconscious for several hours.

DEATH AND BATTLE

At the hollow tramp of the drums, two heads turned in eerie resemblance of manner: one was human, the other feline. The man was massive, but next to the gigantic cat, his size was negated until he looked almost like a normal human being. "Here come my new friends, Bela. What do you think?"

The gigantic pardelé yawned.

"True, they may not be as impressive as your children will be when they take the field, but I have claimed them. They are my tribe." The man scratched his feline companion's ears politely. "I thank you for your willingness to aid us." When the great cat gave a luxurious purr, the man grinned. "Yes. That is true. You will get as much out of it as I will—perhaps more. Just take care that you do not round up any of my horses by accident. I have taken a great deal of care and spent a good deal of time over them."

"Ahem."

"Go ahead, Damon. If you feel like shouting, you may report from all the way over there. Otherwise, feel free to join us. Bela says you are too scrawny to make a decent meal."

The younger man came a few steps nearer. "I can never tell if the two of you are kidding me," he complained. "We're ready. Are you coming down?"

"No. Rafe knows what to do. The general knows your face, Damon. Warn him to pay no heed to our pardeléi allies. If we do not warn him, it may disrupt discipline among his men."

"Aye, my lord. As you will. Before I go, here—" Damon tossed a small, jingling object to his master. "Tyrell the merchant sends you that with his best wishes for your happiness. I understand that one is a duplicate for his own apartments, should you need them; the smaller is for your lady's new rooms."

When the younger man had departed on his new errand, Jarod turned his attention to the vista below. His own men, he knew, were concealed around the base of the high hill upon which he sat. He did not attempt to look for them. Instead, he studied the movements of the Keeper army as it set up camp at the far side of the valley clearing. His keen gaze took in all that could be seen from the hill, including the solitary figure of Damon riding lazily toward the command pavilion. Damon was stopped by guards twice before he reached his goal. When Damon reached the pavilion, the general emerged to greet him. Jarod watched as the two spoke. Then Damon gestured toward the hilltop. "That is our cue, Bela. Time to show ourselves." Jarod stood up so that anyone below could see him. He set a hand on the pardelé's head and saw how the heads of Denei's soldiers began to turn toward him. He raised his other hand in greeting.

Far below, the general did likewise for a moment. Then he spoke again to Damon, who shook his head and replied briefly. The general reached up to shake Damon's hand before Damon took his leave.

Shifting his gaze northward, Jarod shaded his eyes against the high sun. *Chike? How many are they?*

They number no more than five and a half thousand, just as you commanded, little brother. Many were forced to turn back.

Good. Jarod took up his battle horn in readiness. *Denei came later than I had hoped. He is barely ready.*

Are you ready?

I know what I face, Chike. I can feel his presence. Why has he not confronted me yet?

Suddenly, despite the summer heat, an overpowering presence chilled Jarod and sent him to one knee. Bent double, he hung his head until his chin rested against his raised knee. "Keiri Emunya," he whispered. "You have come?" Breath was an effort for him, even with Chike's encompassing wings shielding him from the full presence.

I have come, came the faint whisper. *I have come so that you may stand strong. Take heart, Jarod. This day will be hard for you. I know that he is your other father.*

"Then…then today is…his last?"

Yes. You will carry him through the strong currents yourself. I have decreed it, that you may take comfort rather than grief from this day.

Then the immortal withdrew. Jarod stood and collected himself. He now could hear the din of voices approaching—although the marauders chose stealth, their shepherd-giants were voluble. *Chike, watch the general always. Tell me as soon as anything happens to him.*

What of the battle?

Since when have you been unable to look in more than one direction at a time? Jarod retorted. *You are not a mortal, bound by flesh.*

I only wanted to know if you wished me to watch for possible allies.

As always. Jarod sounded his battle horn. To the cat, he said, "Call out your tribe, Bela. Let the battle begin."

The pardelé screamed. In response, dozens of her kinfolk loped down from the wooded cover on the opposite slope just in time. To the north, Malin's raiders were charging. Bela's kinfolk broke upon that charge from the west, terrifying what horses they didn't take down in the first clash. At the far end of the valley, Denei's forces hurried to get into place, many of them shouting and pointing at the great cats.

Jarod paid little attention to most of the battle. He had enough to keep him occupied. Chike kept directing his attention to individual soldiers and raiders: *That one does not bear the taint, nor does his shepherd.* In one instance, when he found the man in question, he cast about for a nearby ally and settled upon a gold-spotted black pardelé. "Bela—call to Diggen. Tell him to imprison that man there, in the plumed helmet. He must not harm him." Jarod grinned to himself as Bela bent her thought upon the young male cat Diggen, who obeyed his matriarch and pounced gleefully on the hapless marauder, dragging him from the field as if he were prey.

The battle stretched on as the sun drifted westward. Chieftains' colorful banners drifted too, caught up in the tide of men. Jarod followed the movements automatically, noting with approval that his men held the base of his hill without much trouble. He had instructed them to hold back from the main fray and to harass the raiders from that hill, limiting his enemy's range of movement in that direction. With his own men on the east and the pardeléi on the west, Jarod meant to keep the raiders funneled down the center of the valley, where the Keeper army could fight them on a single front. So far, that plan had succeeded, but the raiders fought with boldness and practiced skill. They were pressing the Keepers back little by little, until the battle line reached the general's command pavilion. Jarod saw the general fighting just as fiercely as any of his younger soldiers. The sight amazed him. He had to ask, *Chike, what news of the general? How is he able to carry on the fight in his weakened state?*

Taio pours all of his might into his charge to sustain him. It cannot be long now; either Taio will exhaust himself, or the general's body will suffer a mortal wound. Ah!

Before Jarod could ask for explanation, Chike snatched him away from the hilltop so suddenly that Bela snarled in alarm at the disappearance. She cast about for sight of him. When she located him, she bounded down from the hilltop to his assistance.

*   *   *   *

As soon as he saw the general fall, First Marshal Doran Clary-son ran to help instead of sending one of his field healers to the general's aid. Regardless of the battle that surged around him, Doran sprinted to the last place he had seen the general, only to stumble to a halt in amazement. Every soldier, friend and foe alike, had deserted an area several paces in diameter, leaving Denei sprawled on the bloody ground. One man held Denei up in his arms while one of the snarling great cats kept all comers at bay—including Doran. The chief healer could only watch helplessly from a distance, hearing snatches of words.

"You will see to her?" Denei was saying.

"I will, with all…if she is willing…" The other man was a giant of a warrior clad in a blood-red outer tunic and a hooded mask. Because he spoke more softly than the general, it was harder for Doran to catch his responses.

"Pay no attention to Colin's moods. He may fuss, but he cannot argue against law. The papers have been written up. Maia has them. Please—do not let any harm come to him."

"As far…lies within my…I will not."

"Swear it to me. Swear on Kohanan's sword."

"I can do better than that." The stranger, whose back was to Doran, briefly pulled the mask up to expose his face before he bent down to place a filial kiss on Denei's brow. His voice dropped lower. "…my father…I swear it by…of my blood…"

Denei set a trembling hand on the stranger's shoulder. Neither spoke a word, though the general had a peculiar smile on his bloodied lips. Then Denei broke the silence. "It is time now. Now I can die in peace."

"I will go with you part of the way." The stranger made a swift slashing gesture in the air over the fallen general, lifted Denei in his arms, and vanished in the midst of a forward step, only to reappear empty-handed a few steps farther. He turned his masked face toward Doran and fixed upon the healer a commanding stare. "First Marshal." His voice was cold and calm.

"Who are you?"

"I am a friend of the crown. The general is dead. You must now see this battle through to its end and lead the king's army back to him."

"Wait!" Doran called as the stranger turned to go. "Where are you going?"

"I must carry the news back to the king. He must be prepared for what lies ahead. Bela!" he called, summoning the pardelé to his side. Slinging a leg across the cat as if she were a horse, the stranger departed at a startling speed. Doran stared after him, mouth agape.

✳   ✳   ✳   ✳

Jarod dismissed Bela outside of King's City, touching his nose to hers in a gesture of thanks before he sent her away. The sun had just dipped beneath the horizon across the plains. Jarod stood quietly, gazing up at the city wall. *Chike. Say something.*

What do you wish me to say, little brother?

"Never mind," he sighed. "Take me to Takra."

Four strong limbs encircled him. As Chike lifted him, Jarod willed himself to be still. His vision went dark as he slipped across the threshold into the world of the immortals for that fleeting journey to Takra House. Time meant nothing on that side of creation. Between two beats of his heart, he traversed the distance between the outer wall and the top of the stairs above Takra's entrance hall. He strode purposefully through the stuffy hall on the second floor.

"Who goes—? Hoy, you, where do you think you're—stop when I speak to you!"

Jarod turned his head without relenting in his pace. "Come with me, Captain Rowan-son. Your presence will be required." He felt the presence of the younger man at his heels all the way down the hallway, but the captain said nothing more. Jarod nodded his approval. "You know when to speak and when not to speak, Captain. That reassures me."

A few more steps carried the two men into the private salon at the end of the corridor. Jarod glanced left, but his feet carried him to the right, where a young guard sprang upright to bar his way.

"Sir?" she asked, glancing at the senior officer behind him for direction.

"Stand down, Meg," Isaac said mildly. "This gentleman has come to speak with her highness. Let's hear what he has to say."

Jarod rapped sharply on the door to the princess' chambers. When a slender Caretaker girl answered his knock, Jarod spoke in his gentlest voice. "I must speak with the princess, Kenda. Please let me in."

From inside the room, he heard Maia exclaim, "Teacher?" Then, suddenly, she appeared behind her maid, pulling the girl to one side to clear the doorway. "Why have you come?"

"Something belonging to me was left in your care, Princess. I have need of it now." Jarod saw that he had not overestimated her intelligence: the girl's eyes welled over with tears as comprehension dawned.

"He's dead, isn't he? Uncle Denei is dead."

Jarod bowed his head. "Yes, Princess. I am sorry. May I have what he left with you?"

"Oh, yes, of course." Maia rubbed the back of her hand against her eyes. With the other hand, she fumbled for the pouch at her belt. "I've been carrying it since he left. I didn't dare lose sight of it for an instant. Here. Take it. I'll sleep better without it."

Taking it as if it had no value, Jarod broke open the document and read it. Inwardly, he groaned. *Not unexpected, Chike, but I wish he hadn't. Perhaps there is a way out of it even now.*

Do you refuse this burden of service toward your people?

No, but I might serve better elsewhere right now. This is a singularly bad time to be pinned to this city. Jarod took a breath. "Thank you, Princess. Now, it is necessary that I meet with your father and with Lord Sakiry also, immediately if possible. Where may I find them?"

"I haven't seen them since early this morning. Isaac?"

"The king and Lord Sakiry are closeted in Lord Sakiry's office for a private discussion. The king gave instructions, my lady. He insisted that they were not to be disturbed."

Jarod nodded. "They will agree to meet with me. Please come, Princess."

"I wouldn't miss it."

With the princess on his arm and the two captains following close behind, Jarod retraced his path through the family quarters and across to the offices. Jarod had not taken three steps across the threshold of the western wing of Takra House when he caught a familiar, foul stench. *He is here, then? In this very house, Chike?*

This very house, the great warrior-shepherd confirmed. *Perhaps this city is where you are needed most after all.*

His knock may have been more forceful than necessary, and that may have accounted for the rapidity with which the door of Lord Sakiry's office sprang open. His lordship himself stood framed in the doorway. His hair was pure, soft gray, but his eyes were the same brilliant blue as they had been years before.

"Yes?" he snapped, irritated by the interruption. Then he saw the man who confronted him. His mouth opened without words for an instant before his poise reasserted itself. "You are he?" The question, though brief, sounded brittle.

"I am." Jarod handed him the succession document.

Sakiry was, if anything, quicker to draw the inference than Maia had been. His eyes closed briefly in pain, and he backed up to make way for Jarod. "We really must talk."

When it became clear that Owen meant to bar the princess, Jarod gripped the older man by the shoulder. "This concerns her also." He drew upon the accumulated authority of his experience, matching it against that of the august patriarch of the Sakiry clan as the two men swapped a long stare. "She must hear what I have to say." Then Jarod bent his will against the shepherd-giant that he knew must be somewhere near. He could feel its presence. *I command you to keep silence. You must give me your aid. You are obligated.*

As you will, little brother. Welcome home.

"Very well," Owen sighed. "I daresay you're right. Come, Maia—but I draw the line there," he insisted. "You may stand outside if you like, Isaac, Meg."

"Yes, of course, Lord Owen."

The door to the office had closed before Jarod turned to face the other man in the room. Again, he imposed his will—only this time, he broadened the command to include every giant in the room. *No one speak unless by my will!* His eyes stared coldly into those of his twin brother as if he had never met him before. Stiffly, he bowed. "Your majesty."

Passing Jarod, Owen tossed the succession document onto the desk, circled around, and resumed his seat behind the desk. "Formalities have their place," he said in a thick voice, "but not now. Sit down, Colin. Denei is dead. We must come to terms before Miklei-son returns. Look, you—whoever you are—this is an official, legal document. According to our law, you have no choice but to accept the rank and the responsibilities."

"Unless the king countermands the succession," Jarod said quietly. Once again, he turned his gaze to Colin. "Do you accept the general's choice? He seemed to believe that you did not."

The king sank back into the deep leather chair. "When did he tell you this?"

"As he lay dying in my arms." Jarod scraped dried blood from the front of his crimson tabard. "I wear this color for two reasons, your majesty. All of my warriors know the sight of it. In battle, they will rally to this color as to a standard. You may say that I *am* their standard."

"The second reason?" Colin asked in a tight voice.

"If I bleed, no one knows it. Do you accept the succession, or will you contest it?"

Tenting his fingertips together before his lips, Colin stared at the opposite wall without replying. Maia lifted a hand as if about to speak, but Jarod caught her eye and pressed his lips tightly shut until she subsided. As he transferred his gaze from her to her father, he was intercepted halfway by the blue eyes of the patriarch. Jarod returned the gaze evenly. "What do you wish to add, Lord Sakiry?"

"Nothing at all. You are right. He must make this choice himself."

Jarod bowed a fraction. "As your kinsman has said," he told Colin, "you alone may make this decision. What is your choice?"

"I disregarded Denei's judgment of character once before, to my cost." The king heaved a profound breath. "I dare not do it again. The succession stands."

Silence fell. Jarod picked up the document, rolled it between his hands, and meditated on his alternatives. *This cannot be borne. I cannot be both here and there.* "Very well, your majesty. On my oath to your father, I must accept this commission and fulfill it to the best of my ability. By your own choice, however, you have obligated yourself to a certain course of action as well."

"What do you mean by that?"

"In my commission, as you will see written here—" Jarod unrolled the document to point to a line of script "—I am from this day forth charged with your safety, and that of your family. If I am to carry out this duty, I must be given a measure of freedom to act and to advise you."

"Certainly," Colin said, perplexed. "You have a wide range of powers in that capacity."

"Under normal circumstances, perhaps, but these are not normal circumstances. For one thing, you seem unconcerned that the Unclean has taken up residence here within these walls." He looked from face to face, marveling at their naiveté. They sat frozen, taken off balance by his declaration. The words spilled out of him in wonder. "I can understand, after a fashion, how the king might forget what his father taught him, but you, Lord Sakiry, you were a witness to the past. How could *you* not know?"

"How do *you* know?" Owen demanded, reddening defensively at the tone of the question.

"I have smelled the stench of him. I know that he is here among you, brought by your third marshal as part of the bargain by which that young man escaped a Garden of the Forbidden east of Durward a little more than three years ago. Your house is no longer safe. Your guards' loyalty is suspect. Until I have had time to weigh them individually, this is what you must do: Princess, you must stay at your father's side at all times. If you are not with him, you must make certain that your mother is. If *he* is not with *you*, then you must find someone trustworthy to keep at your side. It is imperative that neither of you allow yourselves to be isolated."

"How long are we supposed to do this?" Colin demanded.

"Until I say otherwise."

Owen cleared his throat. "What do you recommend that I should do?"

They stared at each other in silence. Jarod forced himself to smile slightly. "You, Lord Sakiry, must go to your family and stay there. Do not set foot outside until you hear from me. I think you will find enough to occupy your mind for the time being."

To the amazement of them all, Owen bowed his head. "I will indeed. Colin, Maia—if you need me, I will be with Doran and Phoebe—but—" He looked to Jarod again. "I must first go to Riana. Someone must...*I* must break the news to her. I prefer that it come from me. She will take it hard. I could not pardon myself if I left it to another."

"Yes. I will escort you there myself once we have completed our business here."

"There's more?" Colin narrowed his eyes in suspicion.

"Yes. I must speak with Maia's captains. By now, they will have sent for young Hollister. I have instructions for them as well. But first—your majesty?" Jarod held out his hand. "Your ring, please." He saw that he had surprised the king with that knowledge, but he refused to let it show in his manner. "I have business to conduct in the city, where you will not be present to endorse me as your general. Only your ring will open those doors to me."

Colin pulled the ring from his forefinger and surrendered it. "All right. What else?"

Opening the office door, Jarod startled the three captains away from the wall. "In." They filed past him, and he shut the door behind them. "At ease. Rowan-son, from this moment henceforth, you are in command of Takra House. You are head of royal security in my absence. Every royal guard who remains in this building falls under your authority, as do the Caretaker servants. Yuri-son, Alene-daughter, you will serve as his captains. Between the three of you, you must guarantee the safety of the king and princess. You answer only to me." Before any of them could register disbelief, he showed them the royal seal on Colin's ring. "From now on, soldiers and servants patrol in pairs. Avoid being alone while you are in this place. No one goes out into the park or the monument grove at night. I will return when I finish my business."

"When will that be?" Colin asked in a subdued tone.

"I do not know. As soon as may be. Lord Sakiry? I am at your service."

They left the office in silence. As they came to the entry hall, Owen summoned one of the servants. "Pack one trunk for a week's casual visit and send Chessy to me here." He sank down onto a bench, stretched out his feet, and folded his hands while he waited. "You were with him? Tell me what happened at the end. I need to know."

"The battle overtook his pavilion. He was fighting as if in the strength of his youth when he was struck down from behind." When the older man choked on tears, Jarod continued as if he had heard nothing. "He lingered long enough to speak with me. I have a message for you. He bid me tell you that you are wrong *and* you are right. I did not ask him what he meant."

"That's all right. I know what he meant." Owen cleared his throat of tears. "That's just one of the things I'll be pondering in retirement, no doubt. Chessy!" He raised a hand to welcome the Caretaker elder. "I shall be spending time with my daughter and her husband. While I am gone, I will need you to direct my appointments for me." Then he glanced up at Jarod. "How shall we arrange this?"

"I suggest you continue to receive appointments. You will know how best to arrange the details. Once you have found your way, it will become increasingly necessary."

"You speak in riddles, General."

"I said I did not ask him what it meant. It does not follow that I do not know."

"You seem to know many things." Owen raised an eyebrow inquisitively. "There is limited space at Doran's house, Chessy. I must settle my arrangements with the children before we discuss this further. Give me a few days before you come to me. I have...I have much to think over." He drew an uneven breath. "General? I am ready, if you are."

They said nothing to one another in the carriage. When they drew up in front of Denei's house, Owen asked, "Do you mean to leave this entirely to me, or would you be willing to speak to them yourself?"

"I will leave the matter to your discretion, Lord Sakiry. If you wish me to speak, I am willing to do so." But Jarod held the older man back and descended from the carriage first. He took a moment to survey the area.

"What's wrong?"

"I would think that question easy enough to answer, even for a man of peace such as yourself. Your brother was the first obstacle. He has been murdered. You stand next in line, and after you, the king. I only take risks if it cannot be helped, Lord Sakiry. I suggest you adopt the same policy." When Jarod was satisfied that no danger lingered, they approached the house, were admitted, and in the entry hall were met by Ivy. Jarod saw the flash of fright in her eyes when she recognized him, but she subdued herself admirably to the necessities of courtesy.

"Uncle," she said carefully, greeting Owen with a kiss on the cheek. "We hadn't thought to see you today. Have the advance riders come yet?"

"Not to my knowledge." Owen waited through that awkward moment when Ivy forced herself to let Jarod kiss her hand. In his distraction, Owen seemed not to notice any peculiarity of manner between the two. "Is your mother at home? We wish to speak with her."

In the dim parlor, Jarod chose a seat in the corner, away from windows, where he could watch the door unobstructed. He heard the sound of not two, but three women approaching the salon. Then he stood along with Owen as Riana entered. Along with her came Ivy and her elder sister Brigid also. Riana was gracious. "Owen, how pleasant to see you, as always. And you, sir—" She gave a helpless little laugh. "I'm not sure how to address you, sir, but you are very welcome here. I'm only sorry Denei isn't back yet. Surely you knew he wouldn't be here?"

Owen cleared his throat uncomfortably. "I knew. It was you we came to see."

Before Lord Sakiry could continue, Riana gave an uneasy glance toward her younger daughter. "Ah. That is only to be expected, now that the arrangements have all been finalized. Naturally, sir, you have your rights. I do wonder, though, if you could be persuaded to wait until Denei is here—"

"Madam," Jarod interrupted, keeping his voice soft. "Please. I do not mean to show any lack of courtesy, but I ask that you first listen to what Lord Sakiry has come here to say."

Riana turned round eyes to her brother-in-law. "Of course." She sat down. "I apologize, Owen. I interrupted you. Do go on."

"This is the first time I have ever found it difficult to enter this house, Riana. I wish I had come under any circumstances but these…but it cannot be put off. Our first news from the battle is not good. Denei was struck down, Riana. Mortally. He is gone."

Riana gave two rapid breaths before she broke into deep sobs and fell to her knees. At once, Brigid was at her side, encircling her with both arms to keep her from falling over. From the other side of the salon, Ivy met Jarod's even gaze with a wild, horrified glance. Then she darted from the room.

Jarod followed. Out in the enclosed rear porch, he found her leaning into the corner, weeping. She shied from him when he touched her shoulder. He clasped his hands behind his back. "Before he died, your father entrusted me with a message for you." This failed to induce her to lower her hands from her face, but Jarod was undeterred. "He bid me assure you that he loves you, no matter how it may appear to you at present. He said that he only acted for your benefit. To this, I can only add that good intentions can at times wear various…masks," he added with a pained smile. "They can be difficult to recognize."

Ivy wiped her eyes with the back of her hands. As she crossed to a chair, she avoided his gaze. "Is that really…really what he said?"

"The day will come when you will not doubt my word, Ivy. Until then, I will bide my time. I can wait. I have learned how to wait." Slowly, while he spoke, he made his approach and sank down into a crouch by her chair. "When the incentive is so great, I can be patient indeed."

A blush heated her face. "I don't know how I feel about that."

"In time, you will know. In the meanwhile…" Jarod stroked a finger down the side of her face where the cosmetic powders had been washed away by her tears. He let his fingertips linger over the fading yellow bruises. "I have enough effrontery to ask that you give me your trust."

She turned her face sharply to avoid his touch, affecting to hunt for a handkerchief as she did so. With the bit of linen to hide behind, she replied, "I don't know if I can."

Jarod had the sense that his words carried no weight, so he refrained from cluttering the air with any more of them. He merely knelt beside the woman without complaint, waiting for her to choose a direction for their conversation. It soon grew apparent that, although she was unsettled by the silence, she would not break it to converse with him. He both regretted being the cause for it and was amused at her pretense. *She does not stop, even now. Go on pretending, Ivy. Go on. I will find a way through that façade sooner or later. If it comforts you, go on pretending.*

"Ivy?" Brigid startled them both. She exuded a sense of sober, earnest determination, from her steady gaze to the pair of beckoning hands that she extended to her sister. "I put Mother to bed. What she needs now is rest and quiet. What you need," she continued more quickly, as if to forestall any protest, "is to look after your husband now. Sir, I imagine you're eager to see Owen on his way—he mentioned the chief healer's house—but if you will bear with us a few minutes more, I'll help my sister pack her trunk."

"If she agrees," he replied. Then he looked to Ivy.

She had gathered her dignity around her. There was something passing between the two sisters, something in their gaze that Jarod only noticed because of the change it effected in Ivy. Her tears disappeared for the time being, and she drew herself erect with her shoulders back in resolution. "Thank you, Biddy. I could use help. Thank you." Only her backward glance when she was in the doorway told Jarod that her poise was a well-crafted deceit. She still feared him.

MARRIAGE

Ivy might be excused for feeling numb. She had just learned of her father's death. She had been forced to summon all her self-control in order to leave her family in the company of a man who had once threatened to kill her. Moreover, she was married to this man, whom she had never met apart from the night when he had threatened to kill her. All of this accumulated strain would have overwhelmed any right-minded woman. Ivy, however, far from being numb, felt an incredible sense of peace settle upon her mind. Perhaps at first she had been overwhelmed. Anyone would have, if put in her situation. That initial shock had worn off thanks to a few well-chosen, unwelcome words thrust upon her by her sister Brigid: *A promise made must be kept, Ivy, even if your first reason for making the promise is gone. Denei still needs you now; maybe more than if he were still alive.* Though Ivy had bridled at the words, they had given her purpose and direction where she had otherwise floundered in denial, unwilling to believe the terrible news of her father's death: *Poppa Denei wanted me to help this man. This I can do.*

The ride from her childhood home to Cousin Phoebe's house passed in silence. Uncle Owen withdrew into his own thoughts and said nothing, not even as he climbed from the carriage. Ivy could see that he had taken the death of his elder brother very much to heart. She wished she could say something to share his grief, but he would not speak and she hadn't the heart to break into his silence. The other man—her husband, the foreigner—sat beside her on the bench. He too kept his thoughts to himself, only in his case Ivy had no desire to pry into them. When he did speak, he spoke to command: "Stay here while I help Lord Sakiry with his belongings."

The carriage soon grew uncomfortably stuffy. Ivy gazed out at the familiar little building and fanned herself, trying to avoid thought. Before she was quite prepared, she saw her husband emerge on his way to rejoin her. *Now that Uncle Owen is out of the way,* she thought with some dread, *he will say something.* She heard the rasp of his voice outside, directed to the driver. When the door opened, Ivy braced herself to encounter him.

The carriage swayed under his weight. Again Ivy observed his unusual height as he took the seat opposite her and extended his legs out before him, knees loosely bent. His near leg brushed Ivy's whenever the carriage jostled. To her surprise, he was as silent now as he had been before. As far as he was concerned, she might not have been present at all. He gazed out the window with impassive dark green eyes. If she had the words to describe his demeanor, she might have called it dispirited. Certainly he seemed to entertain thoughts that displeased him. Ivy tried to pay the same amount of attention to him as he gave to her. She had enough to occupy her as she anticipated their arrival at the new apartment that she had hardly begun to make into a home. Mundane domestic arrangements were a blessed release from the other anticipations that lurked behind Ivy's thoughts.

Before long, however, they had arrived. He was courteous enough when he lent her his hand to help her from the carriage. His gaze hardly lingered on her for a moment before the man turned away again, this time to retrieve her luggage from the boot of the carriage. Ivy hurried to the door, sought her key in the wallet that hung at her belt, and scurried inside the apartment just as she heard her husband's feet behind her on the steps. She drew back and let him pass.

As lodgings went, this apartment was of respectable size. It sat above another in a building three stories high, and it looked across a pleasant little cul-de-sac courtyard to another building. A large well stood in the center of the courtyard. Ivy closed the door on this view and turned to face her husband, who had deposited her trunk and bags in the middle of the floor.

"Where do you want to keep your belongings?" he asked quietly.

Thankful for a question that lay within her abilities to answer, Ivy circled around him to the door on the near right. "I would like to put them in here. Thank you." The last two words slipped out as if he were a hired porter. Ivy blushed slightly, but could not retrieve them. She hastened on. "I'll deal with them later. Would you like something to eat?"

"Yes, please. I have not eaten since sunrise."

They stood close enough together that she saw the outline of light armor under his shockingly scarlet tabard. Ivy realized that he must have come directly from the battlefield with his news. She forced herself to walk calmly before him, all the while wondering why he chose to follow her to the small kitchen rather than wait in the sitting room. She could feel his gaze on her back at every step. *I hope he won't…impose himself…*

To Ivy's relief, as soon as they reached the kitchen, the foreigner headed for the two heavy ceramic water jars that sat in the corner. He glanced into each of them, found them empty, and said, "No water. If you will excuse me…?" There might have been a trace of sarcasm in the unfinished question. He hefted a jar under each arm and left Ivy alone in the kitchen.

After taking a little time to start a small fire on the hearth, Ivy rummaged through the half-stocked pantry. A tiny thought niggled at the back of her mind: *He knows that I don't like him.* She tried to ignore the thought. It was just as well if he did know. They ought to begin this awkward partnership with a right understanding of each one's role and duties. If he understood that she simply could not bring herself to do certain things, and if he could be brought to accept what she did offer, then perhaps this wouldn't be unbearable. Ivy nearly dropped a jar of preserved plums. Her hands were suddenly untrustworthy, so she clasped them together until they stopped trembling. *Be strong,* she urged herself. *This is your duty now.* Taking up the preserves, she moved them to another shelf and reached for the wax-sealed packet of flatbread at the back of the shelf. She carried this and a jar of preserved meats to the kitchen table. There was no butter, but a flask of oil served the same purpose.

The foreigner returned in the midst of her preparations. Startled, Ivy looked up to see him depositing both jars in the corner again. Part of her mind was impressed at his strength; normally, it took one strong man to carry each of those jars when they were full of water. This man carried both with little visible effort. No sooner had this notion crossed Ivy's mind than another came up to rival it. She could almost feel the foreigner's inexorable grip suffocating her. Ivy shuddered. To cover the moment, she turned to place her meat pasties on a rack over the fire. "I'll have dinner ready for you in a little bit."

The foreigner nodded. His hangman's mask concealed any expression that might have given Ivy a hint as to his mood. With no more response than that, he left the kitchen, only to return a few moments later with the pitcher from the bedroom. He filled it and left again, this time for quite a while. Ivy grew so jumpy awaiting his reappearance that the slightest noise made her pivot to look at the kitchen door. Then, when she turned around in the midst of her work and found him not three paces behind her, she dropped the pan on the table. "Oh!"

The foreigner bent to return the pasties from the table, where they had scattered upon impact, back to their baking pan. He had removed both the scarlet outer tunic and the armor. Now he wore simple trousers and a worn cambric shirt that stuck to his body with sweat. His long, dark warrior's queue stood out sharply against the fine white linen, drawing a line down the center of his back all the way down to his belt. Ivy detected a faint aroma of her chamomile soap wafting from him. Then, collecting herself with a start, she realized that he was watching her with an inquisitive tilt of the head. She blurted, "If you're ready, I have dinner for you. Would you prefer to eat here? I can set a place at the table in the dining room if you'd rather."

"Which do you prefer?"

"Me?" Ivy averted her eyes. "I'm not hungry."

"Then the kitchen will suit me adequately—that is, if you will consent to sit with me?"

"Certainly." As she retrieved a plate from the other side of the pantry, Ivy knew that her voice had lacked any enthusiasm. She couldn't help it. She was already queasy enough that the thought of eating was quite impossible. The notion of sitting across the small worktable from that foreigner was nearly as bad. Ivy wished for a moment that he had chosen to sit at the larger dining table after all. Pushing these thoughts from her mind, Ivy occupied herself with the table setting. Perhaps she took too much trouble over such a simple dinner, but she reasoned that a foreigner would hardly know the difference. He may very well be watching her to see what sort of wife she would make. Ivy did want him to see that she was an excellent hostess. He would have no complaints to make on that end of the bargain.

Then there was nothing left to be done but sit down. She folded her hands on the edge of the table and tried to compose herself. *I should know something about him. He is my…my husband, for goodness' sake.* Ivy mustered the calmest voice she possessed. "I understand that you are from the north?"

"I have made my home there for most of my life." His eyes watched her.

"Do you have family there?"

He answered with a flat voice, "I have no family but my son."

That thought unsettled her. "Then…you have been married before?"

"No. I have never legally married."

Ivy blushed at the tone more than at the words. He said it as if challenging her to remark. That alone ought to have put her on her guard against what he said next.

"What of you? Have you had lovers of your own, aside from the one?"

She felt that her face could not possibly glow any hotter. "Pardon?" That served more to gain time than as a credible request for clarification. Ivy knew what he meant, and that he had meant it to provoke her. His taunting half-smile told her as much.

"Come, now. You cannot deny it. What use is there in pretense between us? You have never married, but you have had one lover. I only wish to know if there have been others."

Angered, Ivy retorted, "No!" She felt the tears swiftly welling up behind her anger.

"That is unfortunate." The foreigner went on with his dinner serenely for a few moments. When he looked up and found her gaze still fixed on him, he explained, "If there has only been one, then it must mean that you loved him. That makes my position all the more difficult, since I must take his place. Had there been others, you might have been more willing to accept me. What was his name?"

"I don't want to discuss this with you."

"Then how are we to get acquainted?"

"We can discuss other things."

"But none that hold the same weight as this. What was his name?"

"What is *your* name?" Ivy returned. "Don't you think we should start with something simple like that? I don't know who you are!"

The foreigner shook his head. "If you truly want to know who I am, then you must find a better question to ask than that. My name, if I had one, would tell you nothing about who I am."

"What do you mean, *if you had one*? Everyone has a name."

"I have had many. For that matter, one waits for me even now, but I do not own it yet."

Ivy felt her consternation die. "That doesn't make any sense whatsoever."

"Believe it or not, that means we have made progress." He finished his dinner and pushed back his chair. "You are an excellent hostess…but I do not need a hostess at the moment. I was hoping for a wife. Which do you prefer: shall we clear away the dishes first, or shall we continue our conversation in the sitting room?" The taunt had returned to his smile. In anticipation of her reply, he began to gather his dishes himself.

It felt surreal to Ivy, washing dishes and handing them to the foreigner so he could dry and stack them on the table. Such a homelike tableau had no place in her conception of him. Always she was aware of his presence beside her, although he said nothing. Once they had finished tidying, there was nothing left but to follow him to the sitting room.

He opened the conversation with one word: "So." Then he tilted his head and gazed at her, patiently waiting.

"I believe we were talking about your name," Ivy began weakly.

"Why? I said already that a name tells nothing of a man. Ask me something else."

"Why do you wear that mask?"

"Because I have so chosen."

"But why?"

"It serves my purpose. Do not think me ignorant of your reasons behind this, Ivy. My face would tell you little more than my name would. My face would serve only to confirm what you know already—namely, that I have lived a violent life. If you mean to follow that by asking about my lineage..." He smiled with unnerving directness. "I will not answer that question, on the same grounds as the previous two questions. Try again."

"Then what am I to ask?" she returned, irritated at the ease with which he seemed to predict her thoughts. "You've forbidden me from all the significant questions."

The foreigner refused to stop staring. "Then you must ask insignificant ones."

Ivy cast about for the most trivial thing she could ask him. Finally, she lit upon a little thing: "Why do you keep your hair so long?"

He leaned forward to pull the queue over his shoulder. "Three reasons. First, it is the custom of warriors in many lands. It marks me for what I am—not unlike the way a skunk's stripe warns other creatures away from it," he said with a sudden, wry grin. "Second, it is useful. In battle, a warrior wraps his queue around his neck. Stretch out your hand." He held out the end of the long braid. After she had taken it briefly in her hand, he continued, "Did you feel something in its center? That is a strip of cured leather. It runs the length of my hair. Wrapped around the neck, this offers protection from attack."

"A hair scarf? It can't be comfortable."

The foreigner laughed softly. "When it comes to the choice between life and comfort, comfort matters little. The third reason is, I think, unique to me. My hair grows very rapidly. If I were to wear it short, in the style of so-called civilized men, I would need to have it cut weekly in order to maintain it. This is a matter of convenience." Unexpectedly, he winked at her. "Do you see? This question that seemed so little in your eyes has taught you something about who I am. Do you care to hazard another insignificant question, or may I have my turn?"

For an instant, Ivy considered asking something else just to keep him from the question she knew he meant to ask again. His stare, those shadowed eyes, seemed to pierce through flesh and bone. Ivy surrendered. "His name was Jarod. He was the king's brother. Yes, I loved him, but he died years ago. I can't see how it could possibly be important to *you.*"

Her husband regarded her with a reserved air. "No? You have lived as his widow, refusing all others. When I first saw you, I knew that I could never be content unless I made the attempt to win you over. I must know the obstacles I face." More softly, he added, "Even if I myself am the chief one."

His words took her aback. Ivy was lost for an appropriate response. She lowered her eyes to her clasped hands.

This impasse didn't last more than a few minutes. Then her husband rose swiftly and crossed to the windows that looked down into the front street. At first, Ivy had the unlikely thought that he wished to hide an emotion. When she heard the sound of horses' hooves outside, she knew better. "The army is back?"

He turned his head to look at her. "Yes." Then, with no explanation, he withdrew into the bedroom and left her there by herself.

Ivy got up as soon as the door closed behind him. She went to the window herself and looked at the infantry that passed below. Tears sprang to her eyes as she checked herself from seeking Denei among the soldiers. Since she was alone for the moment, she let herself cry a little to relieve the knot in her throat. *Oh, Poppa.* She felt adrift and dazed, like a child faced with knowledge beyond its ability to comprehend. More than anything, she wished she could be truly alone so that she could give full rein to her grief. *You'll never come back again.*

Someone beat a quick, rhythmic tattoo on the front door. Obeying this summons by instinct rather than intent, Ivy went to answer it, only to be brought up short halfway to the door. "*I* will answer the door," her husband said, loosening his grip on her arm before he hurt her. "You must learn to be more cautious about such things, Ivy."

She sank into her chair again. Her newest impulse was to hide from the visitor, whoever it was, rather than face the inevitable reaction. To her knowledge, only her family and nearest friends knew of the arranged marriage. Anyone else would require explanation, and for this Ivy was not ready. However, she stayed where she was. She had doubts as to her legs' ability to carry her after the way she had been startled by the foreigner's intervention.

A kindly touch on her shoulder brought her head upright. Damon Kyte-son stood beside her chair with the light of sympathy in his gaze. "I'm sorry if I alarmed you, Lady Ivy. I only wanted to say how sorry I am for your father's death."

"Thank you," Ivy managed. She remembered the tears on her face and made a desultory pass at drying them with her hand. "You don't know how much I appreciate that."

He sat down on a footstool and leaned close, keeping his voice soft. "If the world were as it should be, such a thing would never have happened. At least you can take some comfort in knowing that your husband will see him avenged. The man who murdered the general will suffer for it." A quizzical, reluctant expression entered his face. "I probably ought to not say any such thing—I know it's improper, and he'd probably box my ears for interfering, but…how do you like him, now that you've met?"

"I don't quite know." She gave a furtive glance toward the foreigner, who was in conference with a small, wiry man near the front door. The snatches of words that she heard were not in a language she knew. "There's much about him that's…strange."

"You know, I thought you might say that. I got the feeling that your father arranged the match mainly so that you could keep Ammun from putting his foot in it, socially speaking." Damon smiled. "Silly, really, if you knew him. He's not foreign except by experience, and if he were to commit some sort of social lunacy, you can be sure he would only do it for a reason. Still, he himself admitted to me once that he had need of you." Damon's bronzed face turned a shade of red as he finished, "I do hope you'll give him a chance. You'll find it worth your while and then some."

His irrepressible, sheepish laugh drew a smile from Ivy. "You're fond of him, I think."

"Best of friends, my lady. It comes with the job. I'll be seeing you another time," he said, catching his companion's eye as the conversation on the other side of the room ended. "It looks as if Rafe is done with his report. Until next time…" Damon took her hand and bowed over it.

Ivy couldn't see what passed between Damon and her husband when their paths crossed near the door, but the foreigner's mouth twisted in a wry smile. Damon ducked, but not before Ivy's husband cuffed him lightly over the back of the head in passing. Damon laughed. The foreigner said something to him that was unintelligible to Ivy. Damon responded in kind while the third man, Rafe, watched from the door. Then the two men were gone, leaving Ivy alone with her husband once more. She felt the air grow heavier upon their exit.

"Damon has brought me a change of clothes," the foreigner said. "If you will excuse me, I will take the opportunity to bathe." He didn't wait for her to respond, but disappeared through the doorway to the kitchen with a knapsack over his shoulder.

Ivy heard the splash of water almost immediately. Rather than think about him, she went to the bedroom and began to unpack her luggage. She had never had a personal maid. Her father had always said that wealth didn't matter as much as how you used it, so even though they had had more than enough money, he had insisted that his children learn to do for themselves. Ivy hung her dresses carefully in the armoire, one by one, just as they had been in her old closet. Once she had disposed of her clothes, she began to put the room in order. When she had come a few days earlier to humor the curiosity merchant, she had done little with this room compared to the rest of the apartment. The rugs were still rolled and tipped upright in one corner. The bed was bare mattress, with all of the new sets of bedding still piled on the chest in their coarse paper wrappings. Ivy shoved the enormous bedstead with all her power until she had it aligned in the center of the spacious chamber. Next, she spread the rugs. The corners all curled slightly, which frustrated her a little, but she gave after a few attempts to straighten them.

Finally, all that remained was to make the bed. Suddenly apprehensive, Ivy tiptoed to the door and listened, but heard no stirring from the kitchen. She shut the door just in case. For a few moments, she stood beside the empty mattress and stared blindly through it. Then, with unsteady hands Ivy opened and shook out the linens. She folded the brown paper to store in the kitchen for reuse. Better for the activity (though still unable to face the meaning behind it), Ivy made the bed up as best she could. She folded the quilt over the foot of the bed, since the weather was hot enough to make any thought of a blanket insupportable. She plumped the pillows, arranging and rearranging them without finding a satisfying composition for them. Her continued solitude began to feel unnatural. Ivy couldn't tell which caused more anxiety: wondering where he was or expecting him to seek her out. She made herself walk coolly to the sitting room, only to find it empty. *Surely he isn't still in the kitchen?*

He was, but Ivy had to come all the way into the darkened kitchen before she found him. The sun had set while she busied herself in the bedchamber. Apparently the foreigner hadn't thought to light a lamp when night overtook him. There was one window at the end of the long, narrow kitchen. The foreigner was sitting on the floor beneath the window, his head and one arm silhouetted in repose on the window sill. Most surprisingly of all, he seemed to be singing to himself. His low, rough voice hardly carried as far as the doorway where Ivy stood, mesmerized by it. Tears sprang to her eyes. The song, if that was what it was, had a forlorn sound. Ivy couldn't distinguish any words, though some of the notes spoke almost as clearly as words. They spoke of bereavement, and of hope not yet grasped.

When he realized that she had discovered him, he turned his head and asked with imperturbable calm, "What can I do for you?"

"I—I wondered where you'd gone."

"Nowhere." He rose up to block the light with his body. His silhouette bent. When he straightened, he brought the tub up and heaved the water out the window in one smooth movement. The foreigner brushed past Ivy on his way to put the tub away at the back of the pantry, ignoring the shout of surprised outrage that rose up from the pavement below.

Ivy stifled a giggle behind her hand. "We don't throw wash water out the window here."

"He should not be abroad after dark. Perhaps it will persuade him to go home. Either way, it did no harm. On so warm an evening, a downpour of cold water could be welcome."

"You didn't heat your bath?"

This time, the smile in his voice was unmistakable. "I have bathed in mountain streams that make the well-water of King's City feel warm in comparison." He left the kitchen.

Ivy lingered, caught up in a series of new impressions. She had known that he was foreign, but until that moment, foreignness was disagreeable. Now she saw him as one who had traveled to exotic places that she had probably never heard named. *And he…sings to himself?* Ivy found herself missing the sound of his voice. She turned to follow him.

It was unnerving to walk into the sitting room, straight into that dark, unwavering gaze. The hour was late. Ivy knew that she was running out of ways to cling to the daytime, but for the first time, she wondered if she still wanted to put off the night. It no longer seemed like such a fearsome prospect. Something about this man had begun to awaken a part of Ivy that had gone untouched since she had lost Jarod. One foot in front of the other, slowly Ivy crossed the room until she stood in front of him. One more step and her knee would touch his. Then she floundered in a final surge of doubt, torn between her newly-stirred interest and her lingering distaste for the foreigner's abrasive ways.

What made it so much more difficult was that he did nothing to help her make the choice. He sat immobile, leaving her impaled on his gaze without a word of encouragement. Not a hand raised toward her, not a breath changed its speed as he stared into her face.

A promise made must be kept, Ivy. She gathered all the bravery she had and stretched out a hand to him.

He took it and turned it over so that his breath brushed against her palm. He kissed her wrist gently. "I dare to make a guess: you will need time to prepare yourself for the night. Take what time you need. Call for me when you are ready."

Ivy swallowed with some effort. She even managed a tiny smile. "I won't take long."

SHORT SHRIFT

Simon moved with a display of ready efficiency that should not have surprised Colin, but it did. Alone in his office, the king waited for his messenger to return from Doran's cottage with Owen's advice, since the older man had suddenly refused to set foot outside. Colin said to himself, "Clever of him to hold off until this morning, until Council convened. After what they went through against the marauders, he knew it would take the Massifi and Sea Folk a few days to rest up and resume their normal program. He knew he would have a willing audience. Pamirsi and Nandevi—they're his people. Of course, they had to back him. But a Grand Council? I don't remember when the last Grand Council met—the reign of Abida II, maybe? He thinks he has a strong enough standing to get what he wants. Why, why, *why* didn't I listen to Denei?"

The shelves of leather-bound books didn't answer him back. Colin studied the rows of abbreviated titles with scant attention. None of them held any advice for him, and now he was bereft of his two eldest and most trustworthy advisors. *Denei is dead. Owen is...* He put his head in his hands. *Owen is locked inside his son-in-law's house, and he won't come out for any inducement.* Colin had a fair idea why. Anyone who had been escorted off in such a way by such a colossal, unreadable, relentless...Shaking himself from that train of thought, Colin tried another tack. "The fellow does have Denei's succession papers to show them. I don't care if Miklei-son says *he* has the real thing instead. Nobody in his right senses can say that Denei ever favored him in any way. They have to hear me on that point."

"So you mean to reason your way through this?"

Colin jerked violently upright, staring at the intruder. "What?" He drew a breath to steady himself. With the nameless one present, Colin found himself growing strangely passive and quiet. The fears that had spent the night inflating memory out of proportion suddenly fled. He saw him as a man again, rather than as an inhuman monster. "These are civilized men, most of them. They should hear reason."

A wry smile appeared on the nameless one's lips. "You know best your own friends; as for me, I would rather know my enemies. It is a well-worn proverb among my people, one that I think you ought to have learned for yourself long since."

"What sort of riddle is that?"

"You are an educated man. Figure it out yourself. What has he done?"

"Miklei-son? He's only called for a Grand Council, which hasn't been heard of in a century. He's that sure of himself."

"Of course he is. Did you expect less? What does this Grand Council do?"

"They'll hear his grievance and my answer. Once both sides have spoken, the Grand Council holds a debate."

"And the end of all this is…?"

Colin reddened, sensing the drift of the questions. "They advise the king on the best way to resolve the dispute." The nameless one's silence was anything but innocuous. Colin grew irritable. "I suppose things work differently where you come from, but in this kingdom, we too have our old proverbs, and one of them says, 'The king belongs to the people.' We don't rule by force of arms or coercion, but rather by the grace of the people. A Grand Council is all the more important in that light. It consists of everyone from patriarchs to village elders, whoever answers the call. It is supposed to be the true voice of the people."

"Can you anticipate the 'true voice of the people,' your majesty? What will they say?"

"No," Colin snapped, "I can't anticipate. I can only marshal my argument and let the process run its appointed course. There is something *you* can do, though. They're skittish enough as it is. They may be apprehensive of you at first, but if you made an effort to prove to them that you aren't—"

"Mercenary? Savage? Violent?" The nameless one's voice ran deep with sarcasm. "If you want me to pat their heads and assure them I am not dangerous, then you have taken leave of all good sense. I *am* dangerous. I cannot help that. If you want diplomacy, I cannot offer it. If I were diplomatic, I would have no need of a proxy."

Colin grasped at the idea thankfully. "Is Kyte-son nearby? Perhaps you can make good use of him. The Sea Folk patriarchy knows his family well. They'll listen to him."

"He is here. I will speak through him if that is your wish."

Someone tapped on the door. Colin stood. "They came sooner than expected, but it's no real surprise. This is a matter of great significance. No one wants to put it off." He stopped babbling by force of will. Though his nerves had every reason for fraying, he recalled himself to a semblance of sangfroid and left with the nameless one close at his heels.

The guard corps, clad in ceremonial blue and silver, fell into step around Colin. Many of them looked askance at the gigantic stranger. Maia and her guards were present also. She took her place naturally at Colin's side after offering a polite nod to the nameless one. They traversed the central block of the palace in relative silence, apart from the clatter of boots. At the door to the western wing, Colin saw his first marshal, Doran, still looking haggard and harassed from the battle. Young Kyte-son wasn't far away. When the chief healer joined Colin's procession, Damon too slipped into place beside the nameless one. Colin heard them conversing in low tones, speaking a tongue full of aspirants and dropped vowels. Their conference held Colin's taut attention even as he climbed the smaller stairs up to the third floor. Suddenly, Colin felt his innards twist unpleasantly. He wished he could understand them, because he had a sinking premonition that the nameless one had made plans that did not suit his own.

The Council Chamber was packed beyond its capacity. There were even a couple dozen of the lesser village elders shoved into the promenade, able to listen to the deliberations but unable to see anything that passed within the chamber. Colin saw them crowding around the doorways as he ascended the dais. His guards took up their places along the wall, shoulder to shoulder in the crowd. Maia's warm hand gave his clammy one a brief, encouraging squeeze. He had no time to even glance at her, because the third marshal had already stood to be recognized. Colin nodded shortly to him. "The crown acknowledges Simon son of Miklei, Third Marshal of King's City." Then he sat down by Maia.

The young marshal's voice rang out over the sea of heads. "I do not wish to offer my lord the king any discourtesy, but he has been deceived! I cannot attach blame; he has been bereaved of one—no, two—of his most trusted and august counselors now. Although his grief is understandable, even admirable, it comes at a perilous time to unseat his judgment! We dare not let this mercenary insinuate himself into our liege lord's confidence with a forged document of succession and a fireside myth of the late general's confidence! It dishonors the memory of a man who spent his entire life establishing the security of this kingdom. Who honestly believes that General Mata-son would cast to the wind his life's work by naming a foreigner, a mercenary, as his successor? I challenge this preposterous claim. Surely no member of this Grand Council can fail to support me in my dispute."

Colin looked to Doran, who nodded and stood to take up the defense. "I have no idea why you claim such confidence, Third Marshal, since you had to know I would—how did you say it? 'Fail to support you in your dispute'? Well, I fail to support you in your dispute. In fact, I dispute your dispute most sincerely. Would you like to call me a liar or a fool now, or will you wait until I've finished speaking?" he said dryly. "I stand as witness to the treaty that General Mata-son negotiated with his successor. It did happen. It was the result of neither madness nor treason, but the act of a man who knew he could no longer trust those around him."

Berhus Pamirsi lifted a hand, was acknowledged, and stood up. "The first marshal has made an interesting statement. I would be interested in hearing him explain it." His voice had a chilly bite to it.

"I don't know all the details of his reasoning. I only know that General Mata-son became very guarded during his last days. Perhaps my lord the king can cast more light on this."

Suddenly caught in a difficult position, Colin knew he could not reveal Denei's real concerns, or the Grand Council would certainly dismiss his decisions out of hand as mere senile paranoia. He cleared his throat. "General Mata-son had uncovered certain elements within the kingdom, certain elements that were tending toward rebellion, in his opinion. That much he shared with me. He had taken steps to deal with these elements. That was how he came to contact our newest ally in the first place."

Eyes turned toward the nameless one in expectation. Colin could not have given him a more blatant cue to speak. The man murmured to his proxy for a few hushed moments. Damon stood. "My master wishes to say that General Mata-son approached him in good faith in order to gather news about the rogue prince Malin Fohral'aku, with whom my master has been in conflict for some years now. It was only later when the good general brought up the notion of succession."

"You claim that he and the raider prince are enemies," Simon exclaimed, "but is it not more truthful to say that they are rivals? This mercenary is known the world over as the raider prince's protégé, or he *was* until he became too ambitious and challenged his master."

Damon turned as if relaying the accusation to his master. Puzzled, Colin felt his uneasy premonition rising again. *What is this act he's putting on?* He could hear the two men speaking in the same foreign dialect as before. Then Damon faced the assembly. "My master wishes to say that his connection to Malin was severed by his own discontentment with the life of a raider, not by any sense of frustrated ambition. He wishes to assure the assembly that, had he desired to take the raider chieftain's place in the world, it would have been a much simpler matter to kill him rather than waste time and effort in contention with a man so notably unequal to him."

If the nameless one had meant to reassure the Grand Council by that pronouncement, the results fell dismally short of that goal. Colin sensed that such had been the man's intention. He tried to catch the nameless one's eye, but failed. That dark, alert gaze covered the counselors unceasingly; it had no time for the king. Colin tried not to let his uneasiness show.

"Notably unequal?" This came from an Alti man. "Fohral'aku is said to be the most dangerous man alive in the world today!"

Damon smiled almost pityingly. "Not the most dangerous, sir. Perhaps second...although I have my doubts on that count, too. Malin grows old and arrogant. He takes risks he should not take. A force of no more than eight hundred can corner him with ease."

"Do you mean to insult your own countrymen?" a Sea Folk elder demanded. "You know very well that we have been defeated by this marauder time and again, Kyte-son."

"I have great respect for the armies of the Second Kingdom, Aidren. Led by the right man, they would soon be rid of the marauder threat."

"So you insult our late general instead?"

"I spoke with General Mata-son only four times, but that was enough for me to weigh his character. He was highly able, but highly conventional. He was not the least bit versed in plots or devices. I say that as a tribute to his character, not as an insult!" Damon exclaimed, raising his hands in self-defense. "He was above all an honorable man. The only tricky thing he ever did was to name my master as his successor, and he probably did that because he didn't know where else to turn. As my father is fond of saying, if you want a clock made, you don't hire a tailor."

The nameless one stood forward unexpectedly and spoke to the third marshal, but he spoke in a foreign tongue. Simon didn't turn a hair. With plausible confusion, he replied, "I have no idea what the fellow is trying to say. Are you going to translate?"

Damon glanced at his master. "I don't think that's necessary. It wasn't meant for the entire assembly—only for you, Third Marshal."

Once again, the nameless one addressed Simon. This time, Colin was sure he had seen the young man's face tighten, although Simon protested his confusion again. The nameless one made one last remark, a string of three syllables whose tone was indubitably meant to sting. A mocking smile followed as Simon drew in an audible breath.

The young marshal's voice had an underpinning of vibrato caused by the strain of holding his composure. "I do not know what he just said, but I am more than willing to see any insult paid back in blood. I will not suffer the impertinence of murderers and thieves."

The meeting adjourned in a state of chaos. Colin returned to his office before anyone had the chance to intercept him. Even Maia had difficulty keeping up with him. The nameless one managed to not only pass Colin in the corridor, but opened the door for him to sweep through in high dudgeon. Maia and Damon made it through the door before the nameless one slammed it shut in the guards' faces.

Colin trembled with anger. "I know I was making sound when I spoke to you. I heard my own words. Somehow—don't ask me how—you managed to miss every single word. Explain!"

"No."

Colin's much-tried temper went up in a flare of wrath. His vision went gray for a moment. He felt himself striding across the room, but until his fist connected to the side of the nameless one's head, he did not know what he was doing. Damon's sharply-drawn breath rang out in the silent office. Startled by his own rash action, Colin stared into the northerner's eyes.

"Did that ease your fears at all?" the man asked mildly.

Wanting nothing more than to rub his bruised fist, Colin retreated behind his desk and sat down. His legs trembled beneath him. "No." The full import of what he had done was driven home when he glimpsed Damon's pallor. Colin had to force himself to look at the nameless one directly. He found him unaffected, even...pitying.

"You need not make an enemy of me," the rough voice continued as if nothing had just happened. "You have enough among your own people. You seem unaware of your danger."

"What danger?"

The nameless one shook his head, disbelieving. "Still you cannot see it! I have never met a man of your rank and your innocence. One or the other, yes, but not both together. Not in a man of more than thirty years," he amended dryly. "They normally do not live so long. Mata-son did his work well, keeping you alive thus far. So. I will teach you about your enemy, if you will hear me. What is Miklei-son's ambition? You agree that he possesses it in great amounts, but you do not know the end to which he directs it. What does he desire?"

"Power."

"No. To him, power is a tool, just as it is to every intelligent mind. What does he hope to gain from the power he seeks? You do not know? Perhaps you should ask your daughter. She has spent more time in thought on the subject."

"Maia?" Colin saw his daughter suddenly as a slender, attractive young woman of reliable judgment. The insight shook him. "Maia, what is he talking about?"

"Miklei-son hasn't been exactly secretive about what he wants, Father. It's been floating around the Academy for a long time now. You know how Cousin Nässey began the new studies in order to make a new sort of warrior? Miklei-son wants to expand that to the whole kingdom. He wants the Academy system to take over the public institution so that everyone is trained for the army, whether they choose or not. He talks of some kind of rebirth of learning and of progress coming out of this plan of his."

Colin frowned over the words, weighed them, and then protested, "But even supposing we could persuade the Council to make that great a change, it won't stop people from refusing to attend, just as they do now. It wouldn't work."

"You have not traced his thought to its fullness yet," the nameless one said in a voice oddly gentled from its usual hard rasp. "He wants the expansion of the Academy programs. What would that gain him? At the present moment, as things stand, it would gain him nothing. A man of your type might come up with such mislaid idealisms out of your concern for the people, but Miklei-son knows no such sentiments. He is a visionary, a misanthropic visionary. He does not do this for the good of the people, but for dominion over them, so that he might enact his new policies among them. He would force them into an education of his choosing, according to what he thought it best for them to know. Given his alliance with the Unclean, you can see how perilous that would be. He does not desire the generalship for idle reasons. The man who serves as general has more functional power than anyone in the kingdom, save the one who wears the crown. How much more power does a general gain if every citizen is compelled to take Academy vows and all come under his command?"

"Yes…I can see that," Colin replied pensively. A chill raced up his back. "From there, he is a short step from being the one who wears the crown…is that what you mean?"

"Not as you mean it. You said before that the king belongs to the people. Miklei-son knows well enough that he stands no chance of imposing so radical a change. The people have been ruled by Keepers for seven centuries; one lifetime cannot hope to undo that tradition." The nameless one fixed a steady gaze on Maia. "How does one change the characteristics of any breed? By grafting onto it, crossing two strains to produce the desired new traits. Do you see your danger now?" he asked Colin sharply. "Miklei-son despises you. He has no use for you, except to gain from you the legitimacy that you currently deny him."

Hopelessness clutched at Colin like a weight in his flesh. "How is such a plan to be countered, or even exposed? With Pamirsi's backing and the admiration of the army, he carries public opinion away with him wherever he goes."

"That is why Mata-son sent for me. That is why you must give me the freedom to act as I see fit." The nameless one's voice was lazy, but with a menacing edge beneath it. "When I have finished with them, your Council will be glad to submit once again to your innocence."

*   *   *   *

The next day was, if anything, harder on Colin's nerves than the previous one. The stranger never showed up in the morning. When it became clear that he had to choose between waiting for the nameless one and being on time to the Grand Council, Colin turned to his daughter. "You," he demanded as if she were a stranger herself, "you talked with him more than any of us. Where is he?"

She quailed a little before the question. "He said last night that he had family business to tend. He said he would come back today. I don't know why he hasn't come yet."

"We don't have time for this. Come along."

Of course, that was the first question asked once the Grand Council came to order: "My lord king, where is the marauder?" Simon asked. "We cannot be so fortunate as to hope that he has thought better of his scheme, alas. So where has he gone?"

Colin gave the young marshal a hard stare. He knew he was about to offer more insult than was sensible, but his head was still full of the previous day's revelations. "The general had family concerns that demanded his attention. He will join us when he is able." He saw the flash of hatred before the marshal could conceal it. *The nameless one spoke truly on that item, at least.* "We will proceed in his absence. His proxy stands by to speak for him, if it comes to that point."

Nothing extraordinary occurred until the northerner arrived. His arrival was in itself only mildly remarkable, although Colin was already sure that remarkable behavior was an everyday phenomenon around this man. The Grand Council had not been convened more than three quarters of an hour when the new general shouldered his way through the doorway nearest to the dais. Those who realized who he was drew aside to let him pass. First, he went to his proxy and asked an unintelligible question, which was answered succinctly in kind. This didn't cause as much murmuring as his next action did. Once he had taken Damon's report, he presented himself before Colin and bowed crisply. Without a trace of accent, he announced, "I have finished my business, my lord king. Forgive my tardiness." He handed Colin the royal seal ring that he had been carrying since their first meeting.

The commotion was considerable and took time in calming. With the nameless one at his side again, Colin found it impossible to relax. As preposterous as it seemed to Colin, he felt as if the man were somehow anxious. That in turn communicated itself to Colin. He felt the rhythm of his heart changing—slowing— even as his breaths deepened. For once, Colin felt ready to pick a fight. "I disagree," he suddenly interrupted the flow of discussion. "You haven't listened to a word I said, have you? I have already told you that my own father took this man's vow of loyalty. He accepted this man as genuine and gave him a commission to fulfill. If I had no other proof in his favor, that fact would be enough for me, but that isn't all. I have great faith in the character judgment of my late general. I have found it invariably accurate and ignored it only to my cost. He repeatedly spoke in favor of this man. Denei's choice of successor was known to me well before his death. I won't say it didn't surprise me. It did, and it took me a shamefully long time to accept it." He felt a twinge of conscience in saying those words, since he wasn't remotely certain that he *had* accepted it yet. He knew perfectly well that it was his obligation to Denei, weighted with additional consequence now that Denei was dead, that pushed him to stand in support of this odd, impolitic stranger. Now he had committed himself to a course of action; now he had to follow it through to its inevitable end. *Do it. Do it now, while you have the nerve.* He pushed on with his speech. "But accept it I did. I have confirmed the succession document. Naturally, that means there is no more need for the Grand Council to advise me on this matter. My mind is made up. I apologize to those of you who have traveled distances in order to be here. Please stay in the city for a few days at least and take your ease. There are many of you to be introduced to my new general. See Chessy or one of his sons for appointments. Good day."

He exited the Council Chamber before the stunned silence wore off.

YESTERDAY: LOST

It was a taciturn, almost gloomy pair that climbed the palace stairs; Denei never took his hand from the back of the young man beside him. Under other circumstances, it would have seemed a gesture of affection, but not this time. This time, the pair looked like prisoner and warden on their way to the execution dock. Denei spoke first. "You know you need your rest. I'm going to make sure you get it."

"How would that be?"

Denei wondered at the soft, lifeless voice, and not for the first time, either. He knew this youth well enough to realize that the voice did not match the mind. "Your father has put you under my authority, so you will be staying with me."

"At your house?" For the first time in a long while, Jarod's voice held inflection.

Denei shook his head. "No. I'm taking up quarters here in the palace. I ordered a cot to be sent to my room, and that's where you'll sleep. Be warned, Jarod. I sleep very, very lightly."

"Me, too."

They said little else to each other. At the head of the stairs, Jarod perked up when he heard a cheery whistle floating down from the third floor stairway. He whistled back a quick burst of song and listened for the reply.

The whistler paused, improvised a little song of his own, and ended with a playful slide that matched the lithe body skimming down the banister. Owen hopped off the railing with a grin. "Hey, you two. What's news?"

"It's what you hear when you stop babbling and get to work instead of trifling about," Denei countered, deadpan, before he smiled reluctantly. "What have you been doing?"

"*Trifling* with a few maps. Where do you think is the best place for a fire trench?"

Jarod interrupted. "Around the city? That'll take weeks."

Snatching the opportunity, Owen said, "One man is said to be able to turn over four feet an hour—two, if the ground is especially rocky. How many men would it take to finish five leagues in an eighteen-hour day?"

The youth paused. "That's a rotten trick, Uncle. School is over for me." He thought for a few seconds, made a series of strange sketches in the air and answered, "Six thousand, six hundred, fifteen."

"And you would get that by doing…?" Owen asked, narrowing his eyes. "That wasn't the number Kohanan and I came up with."

When Jarod replied, his voice held a peculiar note of triumph. "You came up with about three thousand, didn't you?"

"We did," Owen exclaimed. "Now you have to explain yourself."

"You said an eighteen hour day. Even if you split that in half, not a man in a thousand can dig nine hours straight without rest. I used two feet instead of three or four and divided the day into three shifts. That way, each works six hours. Morale stays higher, the off-duty diggers still have the strength to go on fire watch, and it leaves the door open to finish early. You never know, maybe some can dig four, five feet an hour. Overachievers, you know." Jarod gave the two men a rare, cheeky grin.

"Get upstairs, you impudent young rogue," Denei said, swatting him on the shoulder. "Tell your father to come and we'll begin mobilizing the men…all six thousand, six hundred and fifteen of them."

*　　*　　*　　*

"Lie down here, Colin," Jarod ordered.

His brother eyed the drought-hardened ground at his feet. "What for?"

"You'll see."

Colin complied meekly, settling flat on his back amongst the stunted grass. "Here?"

"That's fine." Suddenly, the younger twin stabbed his shovel into the ground just over his brother's head. "Don't squirm." He waited for his twin to compose himself again before he pulled up the shovel and drove it into the ground below

Colin's feet. Working the shovel free again, he took one stride backwards and struck the ground with the blade of the shovel twice, parallel with each of his first two marks. "All right."

Colin accepted a hand up, brushed himself off, and stared at the four marks. "What was that for?"

"You'll see." Jarod glanced at the egg-shaped pocket watch he had filched from his father's wardrobe years ago. "I'll start here. You go on and find your own area." That being said, Jarod plunged his shovel into the ground. He appeared to have already forgotten Colin.

Colin didn't give it much thought; his twin was always doing odd things, and he had long since stopped trying to make sense of them. He went down the line to find his own spot and began turning the rocky soil over. His grip grew stiff and sore on the wood handle, but Colin was nothing if not determined.

At the end of the first hour, sixteen-year-old Ivy came by with a bucket of cool water. "Say, Colin, want a drink? You look thirsty." A dark, damp crescent marked her dress where she balanced the bucket at her hip; a drop of condensation plopped from the bucket's rim to the crusted dirt at her feet.

Colin swallowed, feeling his tongue scrape against the roof of his mouth. "And dirty and tired and sweaty..." he laughed. "Sure, Ivy. That sounds good." He drove the shovel deep into the hard ground and left it standing there, its handle quivering briefly.

"How far have you gotten? Most I've talked to have only gotten about a couple feet down their section. They say the digging is hard. Looks like you're doing all right."

"Don't know." Colin stared at the ground, now his enemy as well as his workplace. "I'd say about three. Not bad for an hour." He glanced down the line. "It's more than I'd expected to get done. The gloves help some. I wonder how Jarod's doing."

Ivy dropped her hazel eyes. A wisp of sticky brown hair clung to her damp forehead, drawing a line across her brow. "He's probably doing fine. He usually does."

"Yeah." Colin studied her face curiously, wondering if she would refuse to carry water to his brother. "You'll have to go see for me. I've got to get back to work here."

She laughed—a nervous, tremulous sound. Not resentful. Ivy never held grudges. "I'm headed over that way anyhow. I'll see you in an hour." She turned away and headed on down the line to where the other brother was doggedly turning over the soil. It unnerved her to see how he stopped working even before she called to him, as if he knew she was near before he saw her. "Hello, Jarod. Would you like some water?"

His dark head rose, but he only met Ivy's eyes briefly, in passing. "Thanks." He accepted the cup and sipped the water with maddening slowness.

"Why do you do that?" Ivy asked. "Most of the diggers gulp the water down like there's no more to be found anywhere, but you drink it like it's the worst tasting thing you've ever had. Why do you do that?"

At first, he didn't say a word. Then, Jarod spoke. He eked out his words with a hesitant, almost miserly care. "It's…a reward. I finish a certain distance; then I can have some water. But I don't want to get too used to not being thirsty, because it'll be a while before I get any more. Besides, I hold more if I just sip it."

"How far have you dug so far?"

Jarod straightened proudly. "Close onto six feet. I had Colin lie down so I could mark down his height before we started." A thought struck him. "How tall are you?"

Ivy caught onto his reasoning. "Want to mark down my height for another goal?"

"Sure." He grinned at her. "You're smarter than they give you credit for. Lie here." As soon as the girl was in place, Jarod repeated what he had done to Colin, only this time he marked the ground several inches above Ivy's head. "Thanks." He reached down and gripped her arms above the elbows, raising her back to her feet. They stood close for a minute, but then Jarod stepped away. "You'd better get going. Lots of diggers still need water." He turned his head to look at the plow team that passed several yards off, creating a wider ring of firebreak. "Go on."

*   *   *   *

A late-day shadow fell across Denei's shovel. He drove it into the ground and leaned back, wiping his forehead with a dirt-crusted hand. The digging sounds had so ingrained themselves in his consciousness that he had paid no attention to the sound until it seemed almost on top of him. "What the—Jarod! What are you doing out here?"

A thin layer of sweat-slimed dirt covered the towering young man from his hairline to the soles of his boots. He shrugged, and his teeth glistened white amid the mud-darkened tan of his lean face as he spoke. "I'm digging, sir. What else would I do with a shovel?"

"You took one shift already," Denei protested. *And dug more than two men combined,* he said inwardly. "What are you doing out here again?" *Why are you pushing yourself so hard, boy? What do you have to prove?*

Jarod lifted both hands. The blisters on his palms burned a fiery red against his tawny skin, but he seemed not to notice the pain as he added, "I'll sleep that much better tonight, won't I?" Jarod thrust the shovel into the ground. "Anyway, we're almost done here. I paced off about fifteen large strides from us to the other end of the line."

Denei would have pursued the matter, but a shrill trumpet-call interrupted from high on the City wall. He glanced up, worried. "Fire sighting. I wonder where it might be." As human forms trickled out of the nearest gate to line up at the trench, he groaned. "It's coming here."

The young man merely yanked his shovel free and started turning over the dirt furiously.

Denei took up a position facing Jarod, and the two dug together down the line as fast as they could. Soon, Jarod had passed the older man, stretching his side of the fire line ahead of Denei's for two, three, six, eight feet. Sweat poured from both of them, but neither relented. Their digging took on a swift rhythm, with Jarod setting the pace. The older man felt like his legs were mired down into the dirt and he started to pant heavily. He would have paused, but the threat of flame kept him struggling to keep up.

The smoke drifted to surround them. "It's no good! You're slowing me down," Jarod shouted to him between strokes. "The wall is too far away. I know a place—"

"No! We have to get back to the city."

"Would you listen? I'm telling you, there's no time to get there," Jarod bellowed. "I know a place, a safe place where you'll get away from the fire. I'll finish up here." He told Denei the location of a deep pond not too far from the walls. "Hurry up and I'll catch you up when I'm done. Get going!" Denei must have hesitated for a moment too long, because Jarod lashed out at him with the flat of his blistered hand. "Move!" He shoved the old soldier in the right direction.

*   *   *   *

"And that's the last I saw of him." Denei, still damp from his long wait in the pond, shivered uncontrollably.

They were still tallying up the losses. The fire had leaped over the line in places, and some of the defenders had died trying to fend it off from the city walls. It had been a violent sight, with withered trees exploding from the heat and flinging their hot cinders high in the air. Somehow, those cinders had landed in the East District of the new King's City and set a number of buildings ablaze. In the chaos, nobody had had time to find Jarod. It was only afterwards, when they were sorting through the debris, that they realized neither Denei nor the young prince had appeared. After Denei recounted his tale, the search for the prince began in earnest.

Kohanan sat beside Denei quietly. He had not made a sound to condemn or console the older man, and his silence drew Denei's attention.

"I'm sorry," he whispered.

Kohanan shook his head. "You don't know it all, Denei. It wasn't your fault."

"What do you mean?"

"Jarod came back home after his first shift. He...argued with his mother. She asked him again about the old incident between him and Owen and the wolf, and he wouldn't say anything. They both have such tempers..." Kohanan sighed. "She said something, and even she doesn't remember what it was, but it provoked him. He...He knocked her down, and then he ran out. I think he meant to die. We knew the fire was coming by then, so there was no way for him to miss knowing. We could see the smoke on the horizon." The king was unable to continue.

In the days that followed, the king's search parties roamed in ever-widening circles as far as the river, but slowly, hampered as they were by the fire's continuing devastation. In the end, Kohanan recalled the searchers himself. "The danger is too high," he said privately to Owen. "I can't risk these people any longer." But his eyes still strayed eastward.

"If he could come back, he would have by now," Owen said.

There was a spark of doubt in Kohanan's eyes, but he didn't argue. Instead, he looked across the courtyard at his remaining son. Colin without his brother looked lost and alone.

"You tried. We all tried. There was nothing we could do for Jarod. I'm sorry, but Colin is the one who needs you now," Owen said, following his cousin's gaze. "You can't abandon him."

"I know."

POLITICS

"As I see it," said Ivy, "there's just one path for us now. Where has Hoyberd gone? He must carry word to Phoebe that she must come here directly. Selie, you go to your grandfather in person. He won't very well deny a direct request from you—otherwise, what's the use of being an only granddaughter? Maia is the only one to send to Ronán. Tell her exactly what to say—something not too different from what I explained to you—and have her take along Kintaro. Let them see that one of their own supports her in this. Let's see…I'll begin here myself so that, if anyone should ask, I'm too busy to talk. I don't suppose Colin is feeling up to this, is he?"

Selena raised her head sharply. "I don't think we should bother him right now, Ivy."

"I'll just talk to him a little, Selie, don't worry. I won't bother him. I'll just ask him if he minds too much. We have to set the example, or the rest won't fall into place. Well," she said with as sprightly a tone as she could muster, "let's begin. The sooner, the better." She watched her best friend get up and leave. The queen's lagging steps gave Ivy a stab of concern. *Poor Selie. With Colin so upset, I wonder she can manage as well as she does.* She decided that Colin and Selena should not be troubled with anything but the minimum in this plan. With that in mind, Ivy got up in search of someone she knew would not be far off. She found him at one of the trestle tables in the dining hall, seemingly asleep. "Damon?"

"Aye, my lady?" he replied, springing upright with clear, attentive eyes.

"I need to speak with your father. Can you bring him to me here at once?"

"If I have to drag him behind my horse, Lady Ivy, he'll be here within the hour." Damon gave her a quick, conspiratorial wink and took off immediately on his assignment.

Having seen to this last message, Ivy steeled herself for a far less pleasant encounter. She ascended one floor to the king's office. The door was shut. Hobe, a captain of the king's guard, stood idly outside. "Good day to you, Miss Ivy," he said with a circumspect nod. "How can I be of help to you?"

"I have to see the king on a matter of some urgency."

"He didn't say anything about turning folk away," said the guard slowly, "but I know he doesn't much want to see anyone. Not after yesterday."

"I understand. I wouldn't ask if it weren't important." Ivy smiled to encourage him. "Just ask him if he'll see me. If he doesn't, then I suppose my business will just have to wait." She watched Hobe disappear inside the office, where he remained for an excruciating stretch of time. While she waited, she made a superficial examination of the pictures around her. She only felt spontaneous interest in one of them: a portrait of Colin and Jarod's parents. Ivy came to stand in front of this painting. It made her uneasy, as if she had to explain herself to its subjects. "I'm doing this for Colin's good, too," she whispered. "I'm trying to help him. *I haven't forgot.*" She sighed. The guilty feeling would not leave her that easily. As she turned from the portrait, she caught a glimpse of motion outside in the corridor but was too late to see what it was. Ivy had an uncomfortable hunch that someone had been outside listening to her impromptu admission.

"Miss Ivy? The king said you could have a few minutes."

She thanked Hobe despite his chilly manner. Inside the office, with the door closed upon her and Colin, she saw a trace of the same distance in Colin's greeting. Ivy put a brave face on it. "I'm sorry I disturbed you, Colin. I won't take very long."

"That's all right," he said, warming slightly to her. "What was it you wanted?"

Hastily, she laid out her plans for his inspection. When she finished, she could not make anything of his expression. "I only thought," she said timidly, "that it would help support your decision publicly. Since he's to stay on in...in Poppa's place, it's best we get the first round of social engagements out of the way as soon as may be. You needn't stay for more than a few minutes, if you don't want to," she added. "Just enough to make your appearance. I'm sure I can get Phoebe and Doran to preside jointly with Maia."

"Go ahead. Get it over with. As long as you've offered me the choice, I *will* only stay for a minute or two. I really don't feel adequate to such things at the moment."

Ivy reached out to him on impulse and seized his hand. "I know, Colin. I know it's hard."

"It doesn't seem very hard for *you*," he replied rather acidly.

Because she knew what he really meant, Ivy blushed for them both. "I'm sorry it looks like that to you."

Colin breathed deeply. "No, Ivy, I'm the one who should be sorry. You have a right to your own life, free and clear of any…past considerations." He squeezed her hand to reassure her. "I shouldn't have said what I did. Please, forgive me."

"What did you say that I haven't already said to myself?" Ivy stood up. "It's all right, Colin. And if it isn't all right now, it will be. Maybe he *is* contrary and willful and difficult most of the time. I think…maybe…he's just doing it because he hasn't had a chance to get to know us very well yet. If you can get past the abrupt way he does things, he's actually…rather nice. Well, maybe 'nice' isn't the word I want. He isn't very *nice*, but he seems *good*. I think, if you could get to know him, you might be inclined to make a friend of him. The trouble is," she said with a sigh, "he doesn't seem very anxious to be known better. I know *I've* had the hardest time talking to him. Some things he won't answer at all, and the tiniest things he treats as if they mattered. I don't really know what to make of him myself."

"You're going to a good deal of trouble for him."

"I have to," Ivy said simply, unwilling to risk further explanation when it appeared that Colin might relent in his mood. "Well, I have entirely too many things to do, Colin, so I'll have to thank you and scurry off again, I'm afraid. Try not to worry too much." She smiled at him and was pleased to see him smile a little in return.

Poor Colin. Ivy hurried back down to the dining hall, where she found Phoebe just taking off a hat with a broad, sweeping brim. "Thank you for coming so quickly, cousin."

"You're quite welcome, but I always thought directly meant directly, and you did say 'directly,' did you not? What is it that needed such directness?"

"I need a favor from you."

As soon as Ivy had finished explaining her thoughts, Phoebe laughed and clapped her hands with childlike delight. "What a good joke! I'll do it. When do I begin?"

"Wait until I've heard back from the others. It shouldn't take long."

"So," Phoebe asked in the interim, "how do you like married life so far?"

Ivy gave the smaller woman a look. After a thoughtful pause, she said, "So far? So far, it seems good enough. If I saw him more than once every couple of days, it might seem better."

"I'd say that's as good a sign as any. If you disliked him, you'd be glad you never saw him more often than that. So you're getting along with him, then? Father will want to know, or else I'm sure I wouldn't pry."

"I'm sure," Ivy echoed dryly.

"All right, so I would anyway, dear Ivy, but only because I care. I saw your sister the other day. She was walking that curiosity merchant to the front gate. I wonder what he was doing, calling at your father's house like that."

"Helping settle the estate matters, I expect." Ivy was proud; she had said it without tears.

"I daresay you're right."

Ivy was glad that the conversation did not drag out any longer than it did. Before too many more words passed between her and Phoebe, Selena returned from her own mission with a favorable reply. While they were discussing that matter, Maia came in to report that she too had met with success, though somewhat more limited in scope than her mother's. Maia's news led to more discussion while they waited for Damon to bring his father Kyte. That did not happen until nearly the end of the promised hour. Both men entered at a brisk pace. Ivy addressed Damon first. "You almost didn't make it within the hour like you said you would."

"I did my best," Damon protested. "It wasn't my fault!"

"For once, that's true," his father teased. "May I make a prediction, Lady Ivy? I predict you're about to ask me to make good use of my connection to the Sea Folk patriarch's family and persuade them to host a reception for your husband. Am I right?"

For a moment, Ivy only gazed open-mouthed at him. She nodded. "How did you—?"

"Don't let Ta trick you, Lady Ivy. When I found him, he was in conference with Ammun, who anticipated you. That's what took so long. We've already been to the compound and back again. The gist of our message is this: Dimona, Heir Sea Folk, will be pleased to host a small official reception on her father's behalf in honor of your husband's succession to the generalship. In fact, she had already got the menu halfway planned out by the time *we* got there, so it's not even our doing, when you come right down to it."

Kyte gave his son a sad shake of the head. "I don't know how you expect to win renown if you're going to be that modest all the time. Honestly—didn't I teach you anything?"

"Whoever is responsible for it," Ivy said with a pleased smile, "thank you for bringing that bit of good news. Phoebe, I think it's time you looked after your own little errand now. Let me know what happens. I'll be here until late, I expect."

"Aye, General," the little woman replied with a crisp salute. She swept her hat back onto her head and tied the ribbons securely. "As you command."

Later, Ivy couldn't help reflecting on Phoebe's nonsense. *I suppose I am waging a little war here. Except all of our skirmishes involve fancy pastries and half-veiled wit.* She chuckled at herself as she beckoned to the runner. "Hoyberd, take this menu to Ardith with my compliments. Tell her that it must stay simple and modest. She knows what I mean."

"Yes, ma'am. I'm to tell you the second marshal wants to see you in his office."

"Certainly, and thank you," Ivy said. "If he hadn't sent you, I think I would have had to go looking for him myself. I'll go straightaway." She sent the young Caretaker boy running on his errand. She began talking to herself as she tidied away her work. "It's been too long since I've seen Nässey. I wonder what he's been doing to keep him so busy." Her face fell. "Too busy to spend any time with his mother, not to mention sisters. Well! Now we can have a nice heart-to-heart, and maybe I can persuade him to come to dinner at home—with Momma, that is to say," she corrected herself.

Nässey had an office not far from her father's office; only Doran's office and the narrow corridor to the lesser stairs separated them. Ivy couldn't help it. Passing so close to her father's old haunts, she had to reach out and touch the door handle. Her fingers closed on the smooth metal. Ivy swallowed past the tightening of her throat. When she tried to open the door, it would not budge.

"It's always kept locked these days."

Ivy turned to find her brother standing in the doorway of his office, watching her. Her heart went out to him. "Oh, Nässey, you startled me! Are you all right?" The nearer she came, the worse he looked. "Truly, you don't look well."

He ushered her into his office and closed the door. "I'm...well enough, Ivy. Considering the circumstances, I'm well enough." He rubbed his shadowed eyes. "These are difficult times."

"I haven't seen you these past few days, since...since Poppa died. I missed talking with you. Momma asks about you sometimes."

"How is she?"

"Getting a little better as the days pass. Now she's able to talk about him a little."

"Good." Nässey sifted through the contents of his desk restlessly, looking for nothing. "Listen, Ivy, I asked if you would meet me here because I need to talk to you. Is it true, Ivy? Have you really agreed to marry this...this stranger?"

"I am married to him," Ivy answered cautiously.

For a moment, Nässey bowed his head and muttered to himself. His next audible words came with effort. "That's what I wanted to discuss with you. Do you have *any* idea who he is?"

"Not really. He's sort of *peculiar* that way. I don't know his name. He won't let me see his face. I know hardly anything at all…" Ivy faltered. She searched for something more to say about him. "I'm getting used to him a little, I think. I think I'm starting to like him. He's strange, true, but there's something endearing about him all the same. I only wish I had a name to call him by! It does get a little awkward, never knowing what to call him."

Her attempt to lighten Nässey's mood failed. He stared resolutely at his folded hands. "Ivy, I've been worried about you. I don't know what Father was thinking when he arranged your marriage, but I'm sure he couldn't have known what sort of man this stranger is. I've heard a good many things about his history…"

When he could not continue, Ivy leaned forward and covered his hands with her own. "I know that he's a warrior, Nässey. I'm sure, if he's as great a warrior as Poppa Denei said, he must have had to fight a good many people in his life. I understand that he…he has lived a violent life. He said as much himself. You mustn't let it bother you. I'm used to soldiers, remember? I've grown up around them."

"You aren't hearing me, Ivy. Please, just let me say what I need to say. This man is more than a mere warrior. I know for a fact that he has killed fighting men and civilians, the women and children alongside the warriors. Whole villages have died at his hands or by his command. He's ruthless, Ivy. His reputation in the outlands is terrifying. I've heard reports of brutality that would give you nightmares for the rest of your life." Nässey's voice trembled. "Can't you see why I might be worried for you? I love you, Ivy. I don't want you to come to harm. This man is dangerous. He doesn't have our sense of honor and fairness, Ivy. He does what he pleases, no matter who stands against him. What that proxy of his said before the Grand Council was true—this fellow is the most dangerous of his breed alive today. He's a greater rogue than Fohral'aku ever was, and he'll only involve you in that sort of life, too."

She sank back into her chair, stunned. "I don't believe you. Poppa Denei—"

"Father was losing his grip toward the end, Ivy. He took a foolish chance with your life, and now you're the one left with the risk." His voice was heavy with bitterness. "*He's* beyond all that now." He lifted his eyes to Ivy's face just as she began to cry. "Oh, Ivy, please don't—I didn't mean that he didn't care about you, or that he didn't think it the right thing. He couldn't have known what this stranger was like."

"But are you sure?" she implored. "Are you sure he's so…" She couldn't finish.

Something changed in his face as he gazed helplessly at her. "Ivy, sometimes I'm not sure of anything these days. I only know what I've been told. I didn't know that you felt—" He stood up abruptly. "I'm sorry, Ivy. Really. You have to believe that."

By now, Ivy was weeping in earnest. Nässey left her there alone, not bothering to shut the door in his haste. Ivy put her head in her hands. Through her tears, Ivy did not hear the shuffling approach. Only when the elderly man spoke did she realize that she was no longer alone. "Dear lady, what is wrong?" he asked her softly. "Why do you weep thus, all by yourself?"

Sniffling, she raised her face. "Oh. I'm sorry. I didn't see you there."

"You are greatly troubled, dear lady. Please," he protested as she began to rise, "do not disturb yourself for my sake."

"Have you come to visit Nässey?"

"I had an appointment with the marshal, yes, but it was not urgent. May I ask you the cause of your tears? Perhaps by telling a sympathetic ear, you may ease whatever grieves you. What troubles you?"

"It's just that I've heard something very distressing. I'm so confused. My brother…Marshal Denei-son, he is my brother. I've always thought highly of his opinions because he's so clever and knows so much, but he says that my husband is…" Ivy breathed deep to steady herself. "He says terrible things about my husband. I don't know what to think. Nässey is always right. If he says it…but I can't believe that my husband is as evil as that."

"You must know your own husband better than anyone, dear lady."

Ivy blushed. "That's just the trouble: I hardly know him at all yet. I haven't been married to him for very long, and I hardly ever see him."

"What is his name? Perhaps I've heard of the gentleman."

"I don't know his name. He says he has none."

The old man's expression changed. "I see. Is he a warrior? A great warrior of remarkable size and cunning? This is most troublesome news. Your husband is legendary. I fear your brother was right in warning you. You have married a fell warrior of no good repute. I am sorry for you."

"What do you know of him?" Ivy demanded. "Prove what you say, or take it back."

He paused. One withered, pale hand crept toward the bosom of his shirt and clutched at some concealed item that hung around his neck. "I am torn. You have a great need, that much is clear, but I would not put you at any more risk. If you remain in ignorance, he will have no cause to harm you. He has entered into this venture without revealing his true nature. Clearly his plans demand secrecy. If I reveal the truth to you, you must never reveal to him that you have spoken to me. Promise me." His voice trembled with fervor. "Or I dare not say a word."

Without a thought, Ivy answered, "I promise. What can you tell me?"

Instead of speaking at once, he withdrew the hidden pendant. "I am a seer of some power, dear lady. It is within my abilities to show you what I know of your husband, he who in days past was named Orlan. Look closely." He held out his hand to show her a smooth stone disc.

At first, the disc had a faint golden shimmer. The light rose to make a sphere of the disc, and inside the sphere, a picture of mountains sprang into being. Ivy gasped. In wonder, she stretched out a hand to touch the glowing disc.

"No, lady, you must not do that," the old man warned her. "Do not touch it."

She tucked her hands together behind her back, unable to take her eyes from the sight. The mountains grew until she could no longer see them for what they are. Soon she was so close she could see each stalk of the tall grasses in the fertile cleft valley. A road wound through fallen boulders, leading her to a village. Strangely enough, no one traversed the dirt streets of this little mountain village. The houses were boarded shut. Mounds of dust leaned against every wall. "What is this place? What does it have to do with my husband?"

"I do not control the images, dear lady. Have patience. All will become clear in time."

The high mountain walls cast a shadow over the street as the image drew Ivy onward. Soon she came to an open space, a little village square. In the center of the square stood a rough wooden sign. To Ivy's horror, she realized that the large white knob ornamenting the top of the sign post was a human head stripped bare by the elements. The lettering of the sign was foreign to her, but as she watched, the words were translated for her: *So end all who set their wills against Orlan. Take heed.* Ivy's breath caught in her throat. She could not pull herself away from the grisly sight, and the stone seemed to linger on that picture long after the image had burned itself into Ivy's mind. Then it turned from the sign. Ivy cried aloud, because all around her stood translucent human figures where she had thought there was no one. Women, children, elderly folk and warriors stared at her with hollow misery stamped into their features. A few of them pointed to the sign as if to say, *Here is the cause of our grief.*

Fresh tears rolled down Ivy's face. The mystical stone offered her only a moment's respite as it erased the village from sight. Soon it showed Ivy a crowd of warriors clustered together. They milled around without purpose, murmuring to one another. One of them raised his voice slightly, only to be hushed by the rest. They seemed to be looking toward one specific tent. Then they all bowed like the grass before a strong wind. A familiar form emerged from that tent—it was her husband, masked as always, with Damon following a few steps behind. Damon's voice was too distant to be clearly understood, but at one point Ivy heard him say, "Please, my lord, don't kill him. He's too good a man to waste like this! Give him a chance to atone for it, at least!" These pleas had no effect. Ivy watched as her husband strode forcefully through the assembled warriors until he reached one man. This one was half the height of Ivy's husband and less than half his weight. He had no chance at all. To Ivy's incomprehension, this smaller warrior only bowed his head as her husband began to thrash him without remorse. Ivy shrank from the violence of the beating, wishing she could cover her eyes. Before long, she was sobbing in earnest. When the smaller warrior lay prone in his own blood, Ivy's husband seized him by the collar and dragged him from sight. Damon sank to his knees and covered his face with his hands while the other warriors retreated to their tents to hide from their master's wrath.

Scenes crossed the surface of the glowing stone, too quick for Ivy to fully comprehend them. All she knew for certain was that they sprang from a long history of cruelty that she couldn't fathom. The last one was too much. She saw her father as he had looked when she had watched him ride forth to his death. Beyond horror now, all Ivy could do was stare dully at his image and watch as her husband approached him from behind amid the press of battle. At last, she found the strength to wrench her gaze away from the stone before she was forced to watch the killing blow.

The office had fallen into utter silence. Then the old man spoke. "If it were not for your great danger, dear lady, I would not have let you see these things. You see now the proof. He is able to harm even those who swear loyalty to him. You are fortunate, perhaps. He has found a use for you. As long as you serve his purposes, he will not reveal his cruelty to you…but disobey him, and I fear for your safety. Have you never sensed this in him?"

In Ivy's head, a memory surfaced: *If you love your life, quiet!* She felt the bruising pressure of his hand over her mouth again. Trembling, Ivy said, "There was one time, but…"

"If he dared lay violent hands on you once," the old man warned, "he will do it again."

"What should I do?"

"For the moment, I fear that you can do nothing but return to him. He must not find that you have spoken with me, or even that you have perceived the truth of his nature. You must be strong and behave as if nothing has happened. This is for your protection. It may be that you will learn something of use to those who would stop him from committing any further acts of cruelty. You have friends, dear lady. He may be powerful, but he has weaknesses like any man. Once we find them, we can see to it that he does not harm anyone else ever again. But above all, do not let him suspect you. Be obedient to him. Be a good wife. He must not suspect anything."

Ivy nodded. She rose from her chair. "I'll try. It won't be easy…not after seeing such things…but I'll try." She wanted to thank him for his kindness, but found that she didn't know his name. "Who are you?"

"I am a humble seer called Nekhral." The old man bowed. "If you need me, I will not be far away. You need only think of me."

Nodding again, Ivy wandered from the office. She felt a sudden desire for warmth, even though the day was oppressively hot. Her legs carried her through the palace to the kitchen. The next thing she knew, she stood just inside the doorway. Echoing voices drew her attention back from the things she had seen. There stood Phoebe, looking at her with uncomfortably shrewd blue eyes. "You've been away somewhere," she said quickly, taking Ivy by the arm. She led Ivy to the table and fetched a small cup half full of brandy. "Drink that. You look as if you could use a little reviving. What's the matter?"

"Nothing…nothing," Ivy gasped, her throat still stinging from the liquor. She pushed away the remainder. "How did your…your visit go?"

"Quite well. You were perfectly right in thinking the Massifi approach the right one. No sooner did Russa hear the words than she had to do one better than Lady Massifi. Berhus was no better when he heard of it. Not happy, perhaps, but content to think he would at least be doing them out of the honor of throwing the most notable reception. They've planned theirs for the evening, at eight or so. Do you need to talk to Doran?"

Taken aback, Ivy asked, "Why should I need to do that?"

"Oh, you can have your choice of reasons. He's awfully handy, my Doran."

Ivy thanked her uncertainly and sent her home again. With this last piece of the plan settled firmly into place, she realized that the old man was right. She had to pretend as if she was still ignorant. If she could keep the man appeased, then he might be content to serve as her father had served, to protect the royal family—to settle for the generalship and leave it at that. It was a terrible position to be in, but

Ivy knew she must somehow keep him happy. Too much depended on his cooperation.

*   *   *   *

The Sea Folk, inveterate northerners that they were, scheduled their reception earliest, in the late afternoon. This helped Ivy, because it meant she had Damon and his father at hand to carry the burden of conversation and to help the introductions along. Not even they could bridge the most awkward of moments, however. A man came to plant himself squarely before Ivy and her husband. His pugnacious jaw jutted out at them in a most intractable way. "So," the fellow barked, giving Ivy's husband a hard stare. "You're the one."

Her husband bowed. "Good evening to you, Durrant son of Dermot."

"So you know my name? Know who I am?"

"Yes, I know who you are. I had hoped to meet you here tonight. You have been spoken of as a man whose honesty is unswerving. I have need of such men."

"Do you, now?" Some of the bite had gone out of Dermot-son's tone. He clasped his hands behind his back and rocked a little on his heels. After a noise of surprised gratification, he asked, "How so?"

"Presently, I am dividing my attention along too many fronts. Would it be too much to ask you to meet with me sometime tomorrow in the early morning?" He named some obscure tavern in Carthae as the objective and added, "There I can speak my mind more plainly to you than I can now. Will you meet me?"

The small, truculent Sea Folk clansman thrust out a hand to the general in a gesture of acceptance. "Be most interested, sir. Most interested."

Once Dermot-son had left, Kyte and Damon exchanged a laughing glance. "Wasted no time getting around the right side of that one, Ammun," Damon said admiringly. "Not too many could have done it."

"I understand men like him. We share a common interest."

Ivy saw her husband give her a peculiar look, as if he wanted to say more but was reluctant to do so. When she met that look, she had to avert her eyes. The rest of the reception crawled past in agony for her. She was visited time and again by the disturbing intuition that he guessed something of her new knowledge. The proof was in his empty gaze during moments of repose, in his detached way of offering her his arm—in the very rigidity of his stance and the tension of his every movement. With sinking heart, Ivy sensed the futility of keeping secrets from him. Somehow, he always knew. *What will he do about it?* she kept wondering. He kept up a courteous façade during the reception, while the public eye was upon him. In the carriage, Ivy hid behind conversation with Damon, buoying her leaden heart with the hope that her husband would find distraction enough that he would forget, or that he would conclude that his suspicions were unfounded. Ivy certainly had made no sign to betray her new knowledge. She had been careful to obey the old seer's advice to the exact letter, but to no avail. Somehow he still knew.

At the Alti reception, there was an even more awkward incident to overcome. Without the same connections as they enjoyed with the Sea Folk through Kyte, they entered the reception rooms to a deeply disconcerting silence and a wall of stares. The patriarch's heir Ronán came forward first with no warmth in his greeting, but politely asked if he could show them to the refreshments. Ivy tried to respond as if she did not notice the cool atmosphere. She struggled in conversation with Ronán. "It was good of you to invite us to your house, Heir Alti. We certainly appreciate your hospitality."

Stiffly, Ronán answered, "We never fail to do our duty to the crown, Miss Ivy."

"Your duty—but nothing more," was the general's laconic response.

At once, the Alti heir bristled with stung pride. "Repeat that again, sir, if you dare!"

"Certainly. You do your duty, but you stop there. What praise is there for you in that? You kept your word! Yes, I congratulate you. You have done no more than what you were obligated to do. You deserve no commendation for merely doing your duty. Any man might do as much. You have kept the bare bones of your vows to Tree and crown—nothing more. Would you like me to continue, or do you understand me yet?"

"I would have taken the head of any lesser man who said that to me," Ronán said. "I would have *yours* now, were you not shielded by the presence of this lady and the memory of her father the general."

"I can send the lady on to the next reception," retorted her husband, "and as for the memory of her father, I dare claim to honor it better than you have. You have given up nothing either for his sake or for the cause of your king. If you wish to fight me over my claim, I am more than willing to oblige you. It will do nothing to redeem your honor...if indeed you have any left to your credit."

Ronán lunged, heedless of the spillage as his glass traversed a high arc to smash against the floor several paces away. Ivy screamed, but before the enraged clansman could do more than make his initial rush forward, the general stiff-armed him in the center of the chest and knocked him sprawling on his back. Ronán gasped fruitlessly as his lungs struggled to refill with air. All at once, Ivy and her husband were surrounded by the fierce Alti warriors. Her husband seemed not to notice this threat. His eyes were still fixed on Ronán. "I would give you the chance to prove me wrong, if I thought you cared enough for your vows to make the effort. For myself, I take no pleasure in recreant warriors."

"You—you are—*nobody,*" the Alti heir gasped. He used a companion's assistance to climb to his feet. "Outlander! What do my—my people have to prove to one such as you? We owe our allegiance to royal blood only."

"I am well acquainted with the Alti vows of allegiance. You have sworn yourselves eternally to the service of royal blood. So what if it has nothing to do with me? There is a vow to be kept, and your honor to be cleared. I bid you do both of those. Consider it a warning. As yet, you have not backslidden, only lost your forward momentum. I can offer you a chance to restore meaning to your vows, if you choose to take the chance."

Ronán glared at him. "I will do my whole duty to the crown."

To Ivy's bewilderment, her husband only smiled. "I am glad to hear it. You have not disappointed me, Heir Alti. You have matched Greysin's description in every respect. He will be pleased to hear that you have not changed...heartily pleased, and probably amused as well."

"Greysin? What do you know of my brother?"

"What do I know of your brother?" Ivy's husband repeated. He smiled again, but did not answer the question. "I thank you for your gracious hospitality, Heir Alti. I confess myself genuinely entertained. Good day."

Ivy found herself whisked from the Alti compound with such efficiency that she hardly had time to catch her breath before she was in the carriage with her husband and Damon once again. "That...that was no way to behave to a patriarch's son," she exclaimed before the shock wore off and she remembered herself again.

"I am sorry to contradict you," her husband said flatly, "but that was the only way to behave toward him." He turned to the window as if she were no longer present.

A glance at Damon offered her no comfort. He seemed very uneasy and kept looking between the two of them as if he expected an explosion of some sort. Ivy withdrew into her corner of the carriage. She did not have courage enough to speak again until she was forced to make introductions for him at the next reception, hosted by the Massifi clansmen—Selena's kin.

Ivy couldn't have drawn a greater contrast if she had planned it. Unlike the suspicious silence of the Alti reception, the Massifi met Ivy and her husband with gregarious affability that spilled over into an hour of introductions and conversations, all of which demanded Ivy's attention. It helped to have Dai Leith-son, Selena's uncle and a retired royal guard, always near at hand. Ivy gladly availed herself of Dai's conversation; anything was preferable to noticing her husband's increasing chill towards her. When they finally extracted themselves from the festivities, the sun rested lightly on the western horizon. "How many more of these do we have left?" Damon asked.

Ivy answered under the weight of her husband's silence. "There's one more here—back at Takra House—and then one more in Carthae at the house of Lord Pamirsi."

"Oh, that's not so bad. I tell you, though, I may bow out of the Pamirsi business. They won't need or want me there."

"You have other business to occupy your time anyway," said Ivy's husband.

"Oh…that's tonight, isn't it? I nearly forgot myself."

They returned to Takra House. Ivy had arranged for this reception to take place in the garden, in hopes of taking advantage of the cooler evening air. When they arrived, the paper lanterns had all been lit and looked very festive. Colin was there at the start, but after the formal introductions had been accomplished, he disappeared into the house. The rest of the guests were a mixed group. Most were genuinely interested in making her husband's acquaintance: Chessy and his wife, for example, had seen him in passing but had never been introduced, while their sons Gian and Mattieu were both present to see him for the first time. Alone among the royal guards, Maia's three officers offered pleasant, respectful greetings to the new general. Isaac made gracious apology for his father Rowan, who had meant to attend. Illness, Isaac explained, precluded both the execution of his duties and the satisfaction of meeting the new general.

Ivy felt her husband's forearm tense under her hand. "I hope it is nothing severe."

"We've had the healer in, and she says not. He may have eaten something that had turned bad. Knowing my father, that's more than likely. He'll eat anything that's put in front of him."

"I once saw him pick mold off a piece of dried fish and eat the fish without a thought," contributed one of the king's off-duty guards. "A day or two will set him right. Rowan's a tough old campaigner."

"That's what he says himself, when he isn't—" and here, Isaac gave Ivy a contrite look, "—isn't actively being sick, that is. I *am* sorry he missed this, though. He's been anxious to make your acquaintance, sir. I took a few liberties in telling him a little about you."

"Another day," said the general, relaxing. "Convey my greetings and my sympathy for his ill health."

"I will, sir."

Before long, Ivy heard Damon say his farewells and excuse himself from his master's company. The glow of dusk still lingered as she accompanied her husband to the carriage again, this time alone. Ivy admired the remnants of a sunset that must have been glorious; her husband brooded in the other corner of the carriage. They maintained this mutual silence all the way to the Pamirsi mansion in Carthae. Just before they descended from the carriage, however, Ivy made the mistake of meeting her husband's gaze. He looked away so quickly that Ivy doubted she had seen the unhappiness in his dark eyes. As for herself, she felt astoundingly little. There was no time for feeling. Already her husband waited for her outside the carriage, unreadable again. He held out his hand to assist her to the ground.

Ivy remembered little of the Pamirsi reception afterward. It was not an experience she would care to remember, all in all. It seemed that the Pamirsi and their neighboring clansmen the Nandevi had conspired to make the new general feel as unwelcome as a man could possibly feel. Ivy did her best to alleviate some of the tension. She introduced him to all as her husband first, and as the new general only as if by an afterthought. She had enough personal acquaintances among the clan patriarch's most intimate circle that she could scrape together a conversation that was at least civil, as long as she diligently kept the conversation moving among innocuous topics. It helped her forget the earlier portions of the day for a time, at least, and assured her that later she would sleep soundly enough to avoid the worst of her nightmares.

When that last reception was finally over, she let her husband hand her into the carriage. She was too worn out by the strain of the reception to even flinch from his touch. His rasp of a voice sounded briefly in a command to the driver before he climbed in to sit opposite her. One small lantern shed its light on the carriage's interior. Ivy let her head rest against the cushions and shut her eyes. The jostle of the vehicle's motion was gentle enough to lull her into a half-wakeful reverie that was only dispelled by the unexpected sound of her husband's voice.

"I thank you for the pains you went to tonight in introducing me. It was not easy for you."

She opened her eyes to find him still in his corner, his gaze resolutely directed at the impenetrable night sky outside. Ivy cleared her throat. "That was my part of the bargain, wasn't it? It was my—" She stopped herself short of the word 'duty.'

"Others have found reason to break their bargains. Again, I thank you."

Ivy found it hard to hear those words, but she had no way to dismiss them. Since he refused to look at her, she found no compelling reason to avoid looking at him. The mask, to which she had almost become inured by now, covered so much of his face that it left little for her to examine. Staring at the curve of his lower lip, Ivy marveled at how docile this man seemed in repose. Now, without the tension that had tightened his jaw for the duration of the evening, he bore little resemblance to the old seer's description of him. Then she froze as he swept his gaze from the window unerringly to her face.

"Is there something you wished to say?" he asked mildly. "A question, perhaps?"

Something in his gaze compelled her to speak, and with a good deal more candor than she had intended, too. "When was the last time you killed someone?" In her mind's eye Ivy saw the final scene of the magic pendant's revelations—her father's murder.

Her husband held her gaze without wavering. "Four months, fifteen days, twelve hours ago—approximately. His name was Prisha. We lived in the same longhouse during my first years with the Thousand Companies. Four and a half months ago, I intercepted him and his company of warriors on their way to attack your people near Adeelah. I offered him the choice to turn back peaceably. He chose to fight."

"Oh." Ivy could not break the stare that he held on her. She spoke impetuously again. "How did he die?"

"Do you really want to know?"

Ivy shook her head.

"I'm glad to hear it. There are some things you will be happier not knowing."

He does know. This time, Ivy was too wearied to care. All she wanted was time alone to cry, and then time enough to sleep and forget. *Let him know. Let him know everything, if that's what he wants. I'm too tired to be frightened anymore tonight.* Aloud, however, she only said, "We're taking a longer road back to King's City than usual, aren't we?"

"We aren't going back to King's City tonight."

"Why not?"

"Because the hour is late. They must have closed the gates against us already. I know of an inn not far away. We can take a room there and come back in the morning."

Discouraged, Ivy squeezed her eyes shut to forestall the tears. She was even too tired to question this line of reasoning. Although she could see nothing in the dark outside, she leaned her head back again and gazed blindly out the carriage window. Only gradually did she become aware of an approaching glow. She stirred herself enough to lean her forehead against the window. A lamp post stood lonesome in the middle of a yard off to one side of the road. It lit the face of a modest inn, where the windows of the ground floor still offered their own light. As soon as the carriage rolled to a halt before the front doors, Ivy's husband descended and offered her his hand in assistance once again. He kept his arm around her on the way inside. The night air moved more freely out in the country, but the oppressive humidity was just as hard to breathe. Ivy heard a dog's bark echo in the distance. Casting her eyes upward briefly, Ivy thought the inn looked respectable enough. Her husband ushered her down two steps into the inn.

The innkeeper met them just inside the door with an elaborate obeisance and utterances of welcome, all of which washed over Ivy's dulled mind like the tide over the sand, leaving only an indistinct impression upon her that her husband was known there. She allowed him to escort her up a broad staircase to the upper floor and a chamber there. Once inside, she fumbled out of her gracious reception robe, hardly aware that her husband caught it as she let it fall and hung it over the back of a chair for her. She climbed into the high bed and, in another minute, fell asleep.

Ivy woke once during the night, confused. Her surroundings were completely unfamiliar, and she was alone in the room. Hardly awake, she pushed herself up onto one elbow to look out the window over the headboard, hoping to learn where she was. Instead, she saw a distinctively tall figure on horseback in the yard below. As she watched groggily, she saw two others mount up to either side of him. One was lean, almost stringy in build, and he sat his horse clumsily. The other was compactly built and confident. The waning yard lamp shone momentarily bright on this one's blond head as he rode away. Ivy sank back into her pillows and fell asleep again.

When she woke in the morning, her husband lay sleeping on the pillow beside hers as if he had been there all night. She had a sudden temptation to pull the mask from his face while he slept, but even as she considered it, some movement of hers woke him. His dark green eyes opened wide. "Good morning. Did you sleep well?"

She nodded mutely.

"We'd best start back, then, if you're ready to begin the day."

Ivy dressed in the previous day's clothes again. Her husband sat on the edge of the bed and was drawing on his shirt when she next looked around. His shirt bore a fresh slash down the back. "You've torn your shirt," Ivy said as artlessly as she knew how.

"So I have, or someone behind me," her husband replied in much the same tone. "I'll need that mended once we get home."

Taking her cue from him, Ivy said nothing more on the subject.

OWEN'S VISION

Owen withdrew to the attic of Doran's cottage and asked that no one disturb him until he came down of his own will. He took with him only a roughly-bound copy of the latest Book of the Kings and an oil lamp. The attic had no windows to reveal the time. Owen read by lamplight until his eyes grew dry and heavy-lidded. He closed the book and used it for his pillow as he sank into a restless, confused sleep. When he woke, he suffered one wild moment in which he had no memory of his surroundings. The air was hot and still, but Owen took no note of it. He sat up, loath to take his hand from the cover of the book. The residual images in his head made no sense and fled as soon as he tried to examine them, so he opened the book and resumed reading.

Sweat ran in his eyes. The air was so close, it pressed him downward. His head sagged. When he found himself rereading the same page for the fifth time, Owen reluctantly put the book aside. "I don't know what I'm doing here," he said aloud. "I don't know. There's nothing here to guide me. A man can't demand the Sight." He leaned his aching head back against the wall. A yawn took him by surprise. He sank back down onto the Book of the Kings for another nap.

A rough hand shook him awake some time later. Owen was disoriented enough by the shift from deep sleep to wakefulness that he did not scold the intruder at first. Then, when he opened his eyes, the shock of seeing his brother standing over him was enough to drive all conscious thought to the far corners of his mind. "Den? But you—"

"I have something to show you. You must be very still and say nothing until we return."

"Wait…" A moment of suspicion made Owen pause. "Wait—the dead don't speak."

"The dead, as you call them, do not speak," Denei agreed, "but their master may speak through them. You listened to your brother once. Are you ready to see what I wish to show?"

After the first shock, Owen felt numb. "You came."

"Certainly. I came before, but you could not hear me. That is why I chose this form."

"Wha…what do you want to…to show me?"

The immortal shushed him. "Remember: you must keep still. Say nothing, do nothing, and you will learn much." He took Owen's hand and pulled him to his feet. The attic disappeared around them, leaving Owen blind and deaf.

Owen's heart thumped with a stronger, more youthful rhythm. For a space, it was the only sound resounding in the void around him. When the world reappeared, it inclined at a disorienting angle, as if Owen lay flat on his back. He was startled by a familiar tenor voice: "Hoy, you, how much longer do I have to stay here?" It was Giles, and he sounded upset.

"You got someplace to be?" The response came from a scruffy, undersized fellow who wore a ring of keys on his belt.

"Now that you mention it, I do have someplace to be—my grandfather's wake."

"He isn't going to miss you much. Sit back and shut your mouth."

"Listen," Giles tried again, clearly straining for a more conciliatory tone. "At least tell me what charges you're holding me on. If it's one of my father's, then let me write him a note at least! How am I to make amends if I don't know what I did? You have to let me contact him!"

"I don't have to let you do anything, boy. Sit back and shut your mouth."

The world righted itself violently. A row of bars rushed toward Owen before he realized what was happening. He saw two lean hands take a white-knuckled grip on two of the bars. "I've been through this enough to know what you have to let me do. It's the king's law!" After a horrified moment, Giles added, "What's the charge, jailer?" Owen felt the boy's heartbeat quicken. "What charge?"

"Sit back and shut your mouth." Unmoved, the jailer reached for a narrow club.

Giles retreated to the far side of the cell and threw himself down on the pallet before the jailer could beat him off the bars. Owen stared through Giles' eyes at the ceiling; he felt the tears gather in Giles' eyes. The boy's whisper hardly carried farther than his lips, but Owen heard it plainly. "I'm really in trouble this time."

It was hard to see what time of day it was. The cell had no windows. Neither did the outer chamber where the jailer sat. The hour could have been morning, noon, or evening. For that matter, Owen realized, Giles had no idea what day it was. No one had come to offer surety for him. The only news he had recently received was the blunt statement of his grandfather's death in battle. He did not know the reason for his arrest. His jailer only seemed to know one reply, and it was certainly not calculated to reassure. Now, as he lay quietly, the boy kept thinking the same idea: *What if nobody remembers to come for me?*

Owen wished he could say something to comfort the boy. He wanted to promise him that he himself would come for the boy as soon as he was able, but he did not dare trespass against the immortal's requirements. He had to wait and keep watch with the boy for what felt like hours, unable to speak or intervene in any way.

The dullness of the wait had so deeply permeated the boy that, when the jail door clicked open, he started half upright in hope. The boy turned to look, saw only that it was a stranger, and sank down in dejection. But not Owen. He knew the figure and wanted to urge the boy to look again, because without the boy's eyes to watch, he couldn't see what was going on. He could do nothing but listen, and what he heard fascinated him.

"What's your business?" The jailer took a far more polite stance with Denei's successor than he had toward Giles, Owen noticed.

"The boy."

That brought Giles up and around quickly enough. Owen found the scene growing dim, but he struggled to keep hold of it, to see what happened next.

"Sorry. He's here for the duration."

"On whose order?"

"I don't know, but it's backed by the patriarch's seal. I see the seal, I don't argue."

"What is his charge?"

"He threatened a person of rank." The jailer blenched under the stare that settled on him. "Look, now, I didn't write the charge. I just watch the cells."

"I want to see the arrest papers. Now."

The jailer produced a document after a brief search.

"You were not truthful with me. The charge says something else." The new general rolled the document and tucked it into his wallet despite the jailer's objection. "I advise you to leave. You look like a man who might benefit from travel. I advise you to take advantage of this chance and spare yourself a goodly amount of trouble." He set down a stack of coins on the table.

Giles, confused, watched as the jailer surrendered the keys and took the money. The new general stood motionless and seemed not to notice as the jailer collected a bag and walking stick from the corner. The jailer hesitated on the threshold, opened his mouth to speak, but stopped cold under the new general's stare.

"A wise man knows when to stay silent," the stranger said quietly.

Owen had forgotten that Giles didn't know who this man was. The boy said, "Why are you doing this? Who are you?"

"Your grandfather chose me as his successor. Your aunt Ivy is now my wife. In that sense, we are kinsmen. Come with me."

Owen was unsurprised by Giles' next question: "Did Aunt Ivy send you to find me?"

"No. I have use for you."

"Use? For me?" Giles echoed dubiously. A stray thought tiptoed through his mind: *No one has ever said that before.*

"Can you pay back the money I gave your jailer? I suspect you cannot."

They left the jail together. Judging by the stars, Owen reckoned the hour somewhere in the early morning, not long before sunrise. No one was about in the streets. He felt his grip on the vision loosening. He was too weak. He had to let go.

The deepest of slumbers engulfed Owen. When he awoke, he was aware only of a maddening thirst. "What happened?" He waited, but no voice came in response. That was when he knew he was genuinely awake. His chest hurt. For that matter, most of his body hurt. Owen had always been blessed with strong health, but now he felt the weakness of age. Lying back with his head upon the Book of the Kings, Owen closed his eyes but did not sleep. He sorted through the memories of his dreams. Before he knew it, the weariness of his body leeched into his mind. Lethargy won out. Owen sank into a deeper sleep.

✳   ✳   ✳   ✳

"He's been too quiet up there," Doran said, looking again at the trap door leading into the attic. "I don't like this."

"If you're going to fret," his wife answered, "be a lamb and do it over there by the table? You're muddling up my pastries. He'll be all right. Father knows what he's doing." She went back to her baking, to all appearances paying no attention to her husband. When Doran stood up, however, Phoebe remarked, "Be sure to take him some water. I'm sure he's all right, but I'm also sure he's terribly thirsty. He's been up there a long time."

Doran took a pitcher from the wash stand in the bedroom, filled it, and climbed the ladder to the attic. His healing instincts revolted at the darkness and heat of the attic air. "Father?" Guided only by the light that rose up from the kitchen below, Doran picked his way through the darkness. "Father?"

A groan led him to his wife's father. Doran had never understood how the instincts worked, but they told him that his father-in-law was not well. He felt weariness rolling off the older man like waves of the sea—weariness and pain. Something was wrong. Doran set down the pitcher and felt for the lamp. Its chimney was cool, proving that it had burned itself out long ago. "I know you said you weren't to be disturbed, but you can't stay up here like this. No, don't try to move. I'll see to you. Just take it easy." He left Owen in order to seek out the vent at one end of the low-peaked roof. It opened to admit a fresh, warm breeze that stirred the attic air and brought welcome relief from the stifling heat. It also let in some of the mid-morning sun.

"Doran?"

Thankful that Owen was able to speak, Doran returned to his side. "Easy, Father, don't try too much yet. Drink first." He supported the older man's head and held the pitcher to Owen's lips. "There. No, lie still. Let me see to you." Doran let the instincts take charge as he held his hands outstretched over Owen, searching for the cause of Owen's pain. When he opened his eyes again, he found both hands pressed flat over Owen's chest. "Does it hurt to breathe?"

"No. I feel as if I'd dived too deep. Nothing more." Already, bolstered by Doran's touch, Owen grew stronger. The older man heaved a deep breath. "I'll be all right, Doran. Just help me downstairs to the sitting room."

Doran had to lift Owen to his feet. The Sakiry patriarch was not a small man by anyone's standards, but age had reduced him enough that, with a little leverage, Doran had no trouble supporting the taller man for the few steps between them and the ladder. The tremors that chased themselves through Owen's body were more of a concern to the healer, who still felt something was amiss with his father-in-law. "Father, I don't often say this, but I insist this time. I want to examine you. You aren't well."

"I'm not well?" Owen's laugh was unsteady, bordering on scared. "I'm not well? You have no idea, none at all. Talk to Colin."

The trap door lay open at their feet, but Doran felt that Owen was unable to navigate the ladder. "Here, Father, put your arms around my shoulders. Can you hold on? I just want to get set on the ladder before you start." Owen's mute obedience worried Doran more than the tremors did. Owen never let his son-in-law fuss over him, not even when he felt so ill he had to take to his bed. Doran had always understood: after the death of Lady Sakiry, a change had overtaken Owen, and part of that change entailed a subtle but persistent refusal of all healing attentions. Doran had the advantage on him in this, and he had used that advantage several times when he had most feared for Owen's survival. As he used his body as a brace to keep Owen steady on the way down the ladder, he began the process again.

It was not difficult, requiring only that he let the warmth build deep inside him. He concentrated on his footing and on his father-in-law's progress. If he left the process alone, he knew it would soon build until it seeped out of him and into Owen, mending any hurt that Owen suffered. It had worked every other time before. This time, however, as soon as the warmth spilled over, a devastating chill surged into Doran's body, making him gasp. It was over in the next instant, but it shook Doran. His attention shifted to what was happening inside of him, and he misplaced his foot. Instead of placing it on the bottom rung, he thrust it between the rungs, scraping his shin and bruising his heel. He smothered his exclamation of pain. "Another step and we're on the floor," he reassured Owen. "You just take it easy."

Phoebe lingered near the chair. "What's the matter?"

Before Doran could begin, Owen burst out, "What news have you heard, Doran? When did you visit Takra last? I need to know."

"I've heard no news. There's been no business to take me there today. Two days ago, the Grand Council was dismissed, and yesterday was mainly a round of formal receptions for the new general."

"Dismissed? What do you mean by *dismissed*?"

"Colin sent them away. He said that he had been advised already, and he didn't need any more advice to know what needed to be done. The new general stays. They weren't happy about that, but he is the king. There wasn't much they could say but good day."

"The new general…the new general," Owen groaned, rubbing his hands over his face. "I can't remember. Something about the new general…and Colin, treason, murder…oh, I wish I could remember! Something is wrong at Takra." He lowered his hands to reveal a drawn, haunted face. "Are you sure there's been no news?"

"Nothing." Doran looked to Phoebe for support.

"I've heard nothing, either, except the odd spate of grumbling about being dismissed and the gossip about the receptions. The biggest news was that the new general started a brawl with Ronán Alti and won. If anything had happened to Colin, I'm sure we would have been the first to hear of it. Especially with *you* staying here, Father. He kept sending messengers while you were up in the attic, asking your views on what he ought to do with the Grand Council, but I kept sending them back because you didn't want to be disturbed. What were you doing up there all that time, Father?"

Owen filled his lungs in a visible effort to calm himself. His hands still shook. "Denei was right after all. He said I had the necessary qualifications to become a seer—and I have seen, children, oh, I have seen so many...I saw Giles...but Colin! I saw him. I saw...I wish I could remember. Colin at his desk...Head in his hands, bowed down, like he always does when he's worried...he dismissed the Grand Council? He wouldn't do such a thing. It isn't like him. He must have been pushed to do it. The foreigner, he must have pushed Colin to do it—why? Colin at his desk, and a flash of light...light on a blade...Oh!" Frustrated, Owen gripped his head with both hands. "I wish I remembered it better!"

"Father," Doran said calmly, reassuringly, "I will go to the palace and see the king myself, but you have to sit back and rest. You're in no state to upset yourself like this." He had deliberately chosen a calm tone of voice because he was beginning to fear for the older man. Owen's pulse was still too quick, even though he had been seated and at rest for several minutes. Such agitation did not match his usual demeanor.

"Yes, Doran, do. Check on Colin. I know that something isn't right."

Since nothing else would calm Owen, Doran left at once on the straightest route to Takra House. It would have only made the older man's condition worse to have admitted that now he, Doran, was also growing worried about the king. He kept thinking of what had happened when he surreptitiously tried to heal his father-in-law, about how the healing had failed. Doran had only ever experienced that sort of bitter cold once before, back when he attended at the deathbed of the late queen Camille. At the queen's death, her husband the king had collapsed onto his knees on the floor and Doran had run to him, thinking at first that the king too had fallen ill. He had put his arms around the king's shoulders to steady him, only to find that the man he held had grown so cold that Doran could not bear to touch him. Ever since, that peculiar brand of chill had come to represent for Doran the touch of the Upper World. He could not question now that Owen had experienced the Sight.

The courtyard of Takra House lay nearly deserted under the midday sun. Doran passed unhindered through the front doors. His business at the palace almost never took him to the private quarters, so he had only a vague idea of where to begin. He caught the eye of a young guard in passing. "Excuse me," he began.

"Yes, First Marshal?"

"What's your name? I don't know that we've met."

"Najhid, sir. I guard the princess."

"Ah. I've just come with a message from Lord Sakiry for the king. Where is he?"

"The king?" Young Najhid looked uncertain. "He's not seeing anyone today, Marshal. If you'd like to see the princess…?"

"That's a start, at least," Doran replied. "Why is the king not seeing anyone?"

"I don't know, Marshal. I just do as I'm bid. Come with me." The young guard led Doran down the second-floor corridor to the family salon. "My lady, the first marshal is here with a message from Lord Sakiry."

"Thank you, Najhid. Come in, Doran. Is everything all right?"

Doran gazed blankly at the girl for a moment. Maia seemed calm enough. The queen sat quietly nearby. He glanced at her and saw that she looked rather downcast, but still tranquil. "I came because Owen wouldn't rest unless I did. He's in a state of high agitation following a…a dream of some sort that he had. He's very worried about the king and wants to know if there's anything wrong with him."

"Oh." The princess gave her mother a questioning look. "How was Father when you last saw him, Mother?"

"He was perfectly well. A bit troubled, of course, but otherwise, nothing was wrong."

"If you're sure…" Doran couldn't give a reason for his certainty, but he now was sure that Owen had just cause for his worry. The two ladies seemed to be telling the truth, but perhaps not the truth in its entirety. Something in their manner told him that what they knew and what they were saying did not match. "Maybe the king would make an exception in this case. Owen has had a vision concerning him. He ought to know about this."

"What sort of vision?" Maia asked.

"He says that the king is in great danger. He didn't tell me the whole of it. It had something to do with the king in his office. Something about an assassin." Doran's years as a healer had sharpened his instincts about human nature. He could usually tell when he had touched a painful spot—and that was the sense that he now got from the princess. "Princess Maia, I really need to speak to your father."

"You can't. Not today. He's resting."

"Why? Is he unwell?"

"No. He just doesn't want to see anyone."

Doran knew that he could press the matter no farther. "All right. That's what I'll have to tell Owen, then. Good day." He sighed to himself as he left. *Something is wrong here.* The walk home was nothing more than a blur to him. He arrived to find both Phoebe and her father seated on the front steps. Phoebe's expressions rarely changed, no matter what she felt, but Owen was on his feet before Doran reached them. "What news?"

"I couldn't see Colin himself. They say he's seeing no one today. I saw Selena, and I spoke with Maia. They say he's fine, just a little disheartened, but I know there's something else they wouldn't say. When I told them about your dream, Maia looked almost frightened."

"To hear her father might be assassinated? Imagine that," Phoebe remarked.

"No. Not frightened of an assassination. She looked more as if she had been caught at something. She wasn't surprised to hear about the possibility. I don't know what to think."

"Come with me," said Owen grimly. "Maybe you couldn't get past them, but I will. I need to get to the root of this." He strode through the little gate so quickly that Doran had to hurry to catch up with him. *Well,* Doran thought, *at least he's feeling better.*

Back at Takra House, in the private quarters, Owen drew up short in front of Maia and her mother. "What is going on?" he demanded. "I will see your father or know the precise reason why I cannot. No more of this 'he isn't seeing anyone' foolishness. Where is he?" When Maia's glance accidentally strayed toward her parents' bedroom door, Owen pivoted and headed in that direction immediately, in spite of the girl's protest.

Maia ran to block his way. "He isn't in here, Uncle Owen. He isn't."

"If no one is in that room, then why do you wish to keep me from it? Where is your father? Either answer my question or step out of my way, child."

The door behind Maia opened to show that the bedroom was completely dark. Out of this darkness, a low voice rumbled like the warning growl of a pardelé. "She cannot answer a question when she does not know the answer to it, Lord Sakiry." Then the new general emerged, ducking under the lintel and straightening to his full height before Owen. "I must speak to Lord Sakiry privately, please," he said, his voice hardly more than a whisper.

Maia nodded and retreated to her own room, taking her mother with her. Doran edged backward, reluctant to leave his father-in-law alone to face the undercurrent of displeasure in the general's voice. The general's dark gaze struck him. Doran knew that the man would prefer that he leave, but he drew a deep breath and stood his ground, saying nothing. Then, to his surprise, he saw the man nod to him. The dark eyes swung to Owen and held firm. "You have broken our agreement, Lord Sakiry. You have emerged from your retirement before I summoned you. I will not ask for any explanation from you. I have heard what you told the princess, and there is nothing that can be added to that. The damage cannot be repaired."

"What do you mean? Where is Colin?"

"Clearly, he is not here. The king has departed Takra House for his own safety. Count yourself fortunate that Colin left in good time. In any event, he has a head start on any pursuit…no thanks to you. I must now demand that the chief healer return you to his house. I will soon assign guards to that house. From this day onward, you must not leave the healer's house, no matter what happens to frighten you into rash action." Contempt turned his voice into a finely edged weapon. "You have proven yourself unequal to the gift you sought. Despite your years, you know less of immortal things than that half-trained princess—and after all your education and experience! This too disappoints me. I had hoped to have the advantage of a seer in the city, but an immortal gift, once misused, does not return swiftly to the one who has made damaging use of it. I suggest you use the remainder of your retirement to ponder this day's work. Perhaps, if you are granted time enough, you may find some way to make amends. I doubt that you can. By your disobedience, much has been betrayed prematurely. You should hope that Colin survives in spite of you."

Owen turned silently from the general's scathing gaze. The old patriarch never lifted his eyes from the floor, not even when he stretched out his hand for Doran to lead him. Doran was shocked to see the tracks of teardrops on his father-in-law's face. He offered Owen his arm to lean upon, and together they made their way slowly back to the cottage. Phoebe met them at the door with the offer of a noontide meal, but Owen had hardly any appetite. Doran watched over him while he toyed with his food. When Phoebe tried to start a conversation, Doran caught her eye and shook his head ever so gently. Owen got up from the table before long, having barely touched his plate, and withdrew into the sitting room.

In his absence, Phoebe circled around the table and wrapped her arms around Doran's neck. "What happened, dearling?"

"He was wrong. I don't understand it all, but that much was clear. Oh, Colin was in danger, but not from this new fellow. Owen didn't even accuse him. He just seemed to know that Owen had assumed…but Owen was wrong. You can't look at the man and believe that he would ever lift a hand against Colin. Whatever else he's capable of, I'll never believe that of him, and neither can your father now. But I don't think anyone has ever spoken to your father in that tone. It wasn't even the words that hurt him; it was the...the scorn that truly beat him down."

"So? What do you recommend for treatment, chief healer?"

"Leave him alone for a little while. Give him time to recuperate from the harshest tongue-lashing he's probably ever had. Then try to cheer him up. He'll need it. He's confined to quarters indefinitely now."

But later, when Phoebe brought Owen the Book of the Kings from the attic in an attempt to cheer him, she came running to Doran in the kitchen a moment later in alarm. "I don't know what happened," she said, hauling Doran by the hand. "He just opened it to the back, read a couple of paragraphs, and then he turned so white I thought he might faint."

They found Owen bowed over the book, shoulders trembling with the force of his weeping. Doran took the book away and examined the open pages. "Oh, Phoebe," he said in dismay, "come and look."

Together, they read the newest entry, written in Owen's own elegant script.

＊　　　＊　　　＊　　　＊

I, Owen son of Joced, father of the Sakiry clan, here write my first entry as seer of the court of Colin son of Kohanan, gentle sovereign of the Second Kingdom. Would that I had better tidings to bear! For the king is betrayed, almost to his death if not for his great nameless champion. As soon as the king dismissed the Grand Council without waiting for its decision, a thing unheard-of in the history of our kingdom, the forces that work against our king took action. I will say it again: if not for the intervention of the king's protector, he who once bore the name Orlan, the king would surely have perished.

For a night and a day, the king kept mainly to his office to avoid confrontation with those who disagreed with his dismissal of the Grand Council. He gave orders that when he entered that sanctuary, he should rest there undisturbed until he chose to emerge. One guard stood watch outside his office door most often: Hobe son of Merrick, of the clan Pamirsi. Alone in his office, the king meditated upon the events that surrounded him. Even at this juncture, after he had boldly spoken forth in favor of his new general, he still doubted the man. He tried for hours to find peace within his soul. Night had taken firm hold of the sky before the king realized it. Then, as if summoned by the king's thoughts, his protector appeared beside him in the room.

"The hour of your worst danger has approached," said he. "If you will trust in me, I will meet that hour in your stead." Like Clemens of old, he demanded the king's ornaments and his seal ring. The king made no protest, but surrendered his possessions to the nameless warrior. He then took the place assigned to him, a dark corner behind a silk screen.

Clad in royal finery, the king's protector extinguished every light but one that hung on the far side of the room. He sat down in the king's chair, bowed low as if by many cares, and placed his face in his hands, the very image of the king himself. The nameless warrior sat like this for many long, silent minutes while the king waited, watched, and wondered at it all behind the concealing screen. The king did not have long to wonder, for soon the click of the door latch rising caught his ear. Had he been lost in his thoughts, as the nameless warrior appeared to be, he would never have heard such a tiny sound. From his corner, he also heard stealthy feet treading along the carpet. The king's heart froze in his chest. In that moment, when the assassin stood with knife raised over the nameless warrior, the king knew beyond doubt that his protector was genuine. He had placed himself in mortal danger, risking his life for his king's. The king almost cried out to warn him. He did not understand why the nameless warrior did not lift his head to prevent the strike. Fear gripped the king: perhaps he had not heard the sounds that had warned the king. Perhaps he did not know that the moment of mortal peril had come even now.

In the seconds occupied by these thoughts, the assassin struck. His knife plummeted toward the nameless warrior's bowed back, seeking his heart—but the blade glanced aside on impact. The armor concealed beneath the warrior's clothing had done its work. Swiftly, like a hunting pardelé, the nameless warrior seized the assassin by the throat. "You may come forth again, my lord," he said to the king. "Come and look your would-be murderer in the eye before I render judgment upon his worthless body."

The king emerged from concealment only to find that he knew his assassin. It was Hobe son of Merrick, of the clan Pamirsi, a captain of his own royal guards under oath to protect him. The king spoke to his true protector. "Forgive my doubt, General."

"You will have ample opportunity to make amends. As for you, traitor, there is only one path laid out before you. Tell your master that I will not be defeated by the likes of you." The nameless warrior raised his hand in a sweeping gesture. Although the king's eyes could not see the truth, I by the grace of my master saw the abyss that had opened in midair. It was darker than even the most beclouded night, save for a single pulse of yellow that beat slowly in the distance. Without the aid of one of the dread Lethek, the nameless warrior cast the traitor Hobe into this abyss and sealed it with his own hand.

Shaken, the king asked, "What manner of man are you?"

"I cannot answer that question now. Your time is short here. Come." Rather than move to the door, the nameless warrior embraced the king. I saw a magnificent creature appear in the form of a great winged deer. It enfolded both the king and his protector in its four limbs and bore the men aloft. By the grace of my master I followed them as the creature bore them through every tangible obstacle, depositing them at last in the royal chambers. The creature vanished, and the nameless warrior deposited the king trembling in a chair. The nameless warrior summoned the king's daughter. "Your father must leave. You will take his place."

"I—but, Teacher—" Maia protested.

The nameless warrior was adamant. "Remember our bargain, Princess."

Despite his debt to the warrior, the king rose up. "What bargain is this? How do you two know each other? What did you call him, Maia?"

"She called me 'teacher,' and that is what I am. You will leave this place. She will stay. She is far better able to face the threat posed by the third marshal than you are. She is his equal and opposite. Once you are no longer here creating another opportunity for him to threaten her, she will deal with him as she must. You are a distraction and a liability. You must leave King's City until I see fit to bring you home again."

"Where do you mean to send me?"

The nameless warrior did not answer the king. He spoke to Maia instead. "I will stay at hand to help you. Now go and bring your mother." As soon as the girl had left, the nameless warrior turned to the king. "You asked me what manner of man I am. Do you intend to have your answer the hard way?"

The king drew back. "No. You win. I'll turn recreant, abandon my duties, run like a coward." In bitterness of spirit, he almost hated the man who had saved his life. When the queen came, the king learned that she, too, had submitted to the nameless warrior's authority without her husband's knowledge. This provoked the king. I will not record what he said; such things are best forgotten, if possible. Suffice it to say that their farewell was miserable on both sides. Now the king is gone, and we are in the hands of his uncanny protector. I hope good fortune finds each of these great men on his respective quest. Our fate as a kingdom depends upon it.

YESTERDAY: THE CONTEST

Confused. Agony, agony, until mind and flesh rebelled against each other. Then darkness came, dissipating just long enough to teach the youth to dread consciousness' return. His drifting mind blessed the darkness and cursed the light. Pain came with the light. The dreams that visited him in the dark were no less disturbing, but they didn't hurt. He heard voices that sang to each other over his helpless body. Their words made no sense.

He was given to me!

He does not belong to any of us. We will not let you harm him.

The law favors me. He was given to me.

No! We will not let you harm him.

If you hinder me, I will destroy you.

Of all these voices, he recognized only the one: Audune, his ever-present tormenter. He had fought Audune through the wildfires until he had lost all sense of direction. The depraved spirit kept driving him into traps and dead ends where fire would soon destroy him, but Jarod began to hear other voices telling him how to escape. The voices that led him through the fires were smaller, weaker, and hardly intelligible by themselves, but now that they joined together in opposition to Audune, they bore a greater force than he could muster: *We will not let you harm our brother.*

Brother? Jarod didn't understand. He had one brother. These childlike strangers, whoever or whatever they were, couldn't be his brothers. Couldn't be.

Through the haze of fire and anguish, his body smoldering from the proximity of the flames, he raised his body up on his forearms to look around. He saw nothing. For a moment, he heard nothing and wondered if the voices were merely the invention of his abnormal mind. Then he saw a tiny whirlwind of fire dancing in a hollow of the rock. It swerved closer, searing the side of Jarod's face and one of his arms as he tried to shield himself. In another instant, it was gone.

Heed me, servant of the Unclean. The sizzling voice seemed to come from the heart of the flames. *You are of a higher order than I, but that does not give you the right to use my element for your wicked ends. He will not burn.*

He will not burn, the chorusing voices agreed. *Come, rain, and rescue our little brother.*

A great hiss rose as the clouds above deluged Jarod. Soon he was shivering in a puddle, soaked to his skin. The water continued to gather in the concavity of rock that served as Jarod's bed. He felt a touch on the back of his head. Something was pushing him down in an effort to submerge his face in the puddle.

Rise, freakish mortal boy, if you still want to live. Rise. We will leave this place.

No, the others protested, *no, you will not leave. Not with our little brother.*

I am his guardian, not you. You cannot take him from me.

Perhaps not, but we can keep you here. We cannot keep you forever, but we can hold you long enough. He will learn.

Shivering violently now from the chill that the rain meted out to his blistered flesh, Jarod turned over onto his back and gasped at the contact between his raw back and the coarse rock shelf. Tears ran down his face involuntarily and blended with the rain. "Please help me," he whispered. "Please." Every time his body quaked, the rock beneath him abraded his wounds, but he could not stop shivering.

Then, with no prelude but a pause in the rain to herald it, an unbearable weight pressed down upon him. He would have cried out, but the weight squeezed the breath from his lungs. His wounds burned as the rock dug into them cruelly. Within the weight, a voice silenced every other sound. "Enough. Audune has charge of him. He will leave this place with him. Although you do not obey law any longer, recreant giant, because you have invoked the law of shepherds, that law will bind you whether you will or no. You are forbidden to harm his flesh. If you transgress this rule, you forfeit your trust irrevocably. This also I decree: you will have your chance to shape him according to your will. When he learns his strength, however, you will abide by his choice."

Let none of my brothers teach him this. Let him learn it alone.

"You yourself shall lead him to it, though you try to hide it from him."

Unable to endure the agony any longer, Jarod lost consciousness. He felt nothing when Audune lifted him up and bore him far away.

*   *   *   *

When he knew himself again, he was dry. The air around him was stale with the odor of other bodies as well as his own. He tried to open his swollen, gritty eyes. For the first attempt, he managed to squint in the darkened room. The walls were formed of rough-hewed timber and mud daubing. He raised his heavy arm to find it wrapped thickly in bandages plastered over with a pungent ointment. With clumsy fingers, he pried at the bandages. They stank, so he dropped them as far from him as he could. As stuffy as the air was, it felt blessedly cool on his half-healed skin. He rotated his hand, flexed his fingers tentatively, and measured the pain. Just by the feel, he knew the burns were well on the way to healing. He knew too that they had only marked him; he would wear the scars forever, but the use would return to that limb soon enough.

What he didn't know yet was the use that he would find for it. He could hear voices coming from the adjoining room—not voices like the last he had heard, but voices belonging to bodies, men's voices. They spoke in a tongue he didn't recognize.

I can tell you what they say.

I can't trust you.

You have no choice. I am your only hope now.

Jarod pulled himself up from his pallet, but Audune was not finished.

You are so far from home, there can be no return. No one will search for a creature like you. You are lost. What hope do you have but me?

"Leave me alone," he said, resisting. "Liar."

You will learn to know me better. You have no hope but me.

Anything was better than listening to that horrid smug tone in the giant's voice, so Jarod got to his feet and went in search of human company. However, before he stepped fully into the lit room adjoining the sickroom, he peered around the corner to see what he might expect.

The adjoining room was a long, low hall, lit by a row of braziers down the center. Smoke hung in the air, blurring the figures of more than thirty men who ate, rested, drank, and talked in a deep rumble of ease. These were warriors, all of them, and they kept their weapons stacked against the outer walls; Jarod looked at the weapons rather than at the men. He saw swords of many lengths and blade shapes. He saw gnarled quarterstaffs, some embedded with spikes. Longbows sat unstrung, crossbows lay at rest, every object well-used and well-maintained.

A murmur ran from the near end of the hall to the farthest corner. Then silence came as one of the warriors stood to meet Jarod. He was a large man, but fifteen-year-old Jarod was taller. Even so, Jarod knew to keep quiet and watch the older man closely. The stranger addressed him in a foreign tongue for a moment, but upon seeing the incomprehension in Jarod's face, beckoned for a scrawny, withered man to come forward. The little man began testing different languages on Jarod. When he hit on Kavahran, Jarod blessed the days he had spent with the dog master, learning to speak the tongue of the enemies of his house. He answered, "I do not come from here."

The first man broke in, "Kavahri, boy? What rahg ruled you?"

Jarod stared hard at the man. He couldn't tell if his accent was natural enough to pass as native, or if the man believed him at all. "No rahg rules me."

With a short bark of a laugh, the man replied, "Good enough. What's your name?"

"Orhlahn," he replied—the word meant 'spear of rock' in Kavahran, and all Jarod could think of was his last clear memory, that of waking on a pointed shelf of rock to the sound of many voices. "That is what you will call me."

"What was your father's name?"

"Orlan is enough," Jarod said firmly.

"What are you good for, Orlan? We don't keep useless hands about."

"Test me and learn for yourself." With that, Jarod knew that in at least one thing Audune had spoken truly: there was no returning from this. The faces turned toward him told him as much. They were hard faces belonging to hard men who watched him now only to see if he would provide sport for their amusement.

I will teach you the warrior's way, boy. Listen to me, and you will make these warriors respect you. You will rule them. If you do not subdue them, they will kill you.

I don't know where you've taken me, but you know my father will come. He'll find me. He can do anything. When he comes, I'll tell him everything. He can find a way to be rid of you!

Your father, come for you? Audune laughed. *Your father has a son and heir to train. Do you think he will abandon kingdom and kin to hunt for you? And if he should find you out, will he be pleased with you—you, who struck your own mother to the floor in a fit of rage? When have you ever been the son he wanted you to be? Do you see this man before you? He is called Malin. He is a more suitable father for someone like you. He will be able to understand you as your own father never could.*

Jarod caught the plain quarterstaff that Malin had thrown to him. He stared warily at the man, hearing two voices almost overlapping.

"Show your worth, then," Malin commanded.

You can never go home, gloated Audune.

Fist tightening around the smooth wooden staff, Jarod took a deep breath. He gazed warily at the warrior that Malin had summoned forward to fight him. *No going back.*

MANEUVERS

Night's all-encompassing veil swathed the entire street in darkness until a door opened. One, two, three, four men stepped into the night. The door shut behind them, taking with it the light, but they paid no mind to the dark. They were silent enough that only their footfalls told of their passage: one, two, three, four…five sets of feet? Taking counsel inaudibly amongst themselves, the men dispersed. Only one of them remained on their original course, and he slowed his steps in order to let the lagging fifth set of footsteps catch up to him.

"Alwen?"

"Good evening to you, Meir," said Alwen son of Dellim. "What brings you out so late?"

Drawing abreast of Alwen, the younger man retorted, "I was just about to ask the same of you. I *saw* you leaving Miklei-son's house. You, Uriel, Arald, and Darvon. It makes a man wonder what business four of the king's guards could have with a man at odds with the crown."

Alwen's hand moved to the knife at his belt. Had the moon shone, young Meir would have seen the gesture and taken warning, but the stygian night concealed it from him. Casually, Alwen said, "Our visit was purely business, my lad. The king is missing, and that foreigner had a hand in his disappearance. We went to ask the third marshal a few questions. That's all."

"Does Commander Solam-son know that you went?"

"We didn't like to disturb the commander while he's not feeling his best."

Meir laughed shortly. "I don't believe you. I'm reporting you to the captain when we get back. You don't have the authority to approach the marshal."

"Norrie knows," lied Alwen easily. "We had to sign out in order to come, didn't we?" While the young guard was pondering this, Alwen stabbed him under the ribs. He opened his mouth to mock the dying man for his naïveté. Before he could speak, two large hands cut off his air and wrenched him to the ground beside his former comrade with astonishing strength. Before his daze lifted, Alwen found himself bound and immobile on his face, with someone's knee planted in the middle of his back. The weight that bore down upon him made his ribs creak. Then a voice spoke sharply in some foreign tongue. A thrill of fear ran along Alwen's nerves. The weight rose from Alwen's spine without warning as the foreigner shifted to kneel beside Meir.

"I came too late," rumbled the foreigner. "Forgive me."

Meir coughed weakly; Alwen knew the blade had gone into his lung, so the young guard would not be able to talk well, if at all. The lad struggled for breath. "No…not your fault." He gasped, this time in fear.

The foreigner lifted him up. Alwen didn't know if it was a hallucination or not, but he saw the foreigner begin to glow gently, illuminating the dying man and the ground all around them. The foreigner spoke in that unknown tongue again, but not to Meir. Then he said in a gentled tone, "Let go. You have fulfilled your oath. Depart in peace. Death holds no sting for the one who has remained true."

Out of the corner of his eye, Alwen saw the dying guard vanish from the world of flesh, snatched from the foreigner's arms. The foreigner didn't twitch. He bowed his head respectfully for a moment. Then he turned his head. His ethereal light burned hotter, like a flame doused with oil. "But for the oath breaker, the traitor, no such promise exists. You have broken faith with your liege. You have murdered your brother in arms. There is one fate for men of your breed, Alwen son of Dellim."

Terrified, Alwen protested, "You can't harm me! Only the king can condemn to death."

"There is a type of justice that transcends kings," replied the inexorable foreigner. "That justice lies in *my* hands. Have you seen the fire that burns but yields no light?" He dragged Alwen to his feet and stepped back. "Mortals cannot see it, except those whose lives are at an end. It burns in an abyss deeper than thought can reach, and in its depths lives one so cruel, so rapacious, that the blood of every traitor, every malefactor on this earth is insufficient to quench his thirst." The foreigner made a strange gesture, as if drawing a curtain.

Alwen gaped. The air split before him to reveal darkness more impenetrable than the night around him, just as the foreigner had described. Deep within the dark, a jaundiced light pulsed and writhed and reached for him. His heart hammered until it was fit to burst, but there was no escape for him. He felt himself leaning closer to the abyss, obeying the summons that emanated from that horrible yellow light.

"Greet him for me," mocked the foreigner. "Tell him he has failed again."

Those were the last words in Alwen's ears before the world vanished and the agony seized him.

*   *   *   *

Maia started awake with a soft cry. Her heart slowed as she realized where she was: safe in her bed at home. She lay still for a while, trying to grab the fleeting tail of her dream.

"Are you all right?" her mother's gentle voice asked.

"Yes." Maia got out of bed and smoothed the covers into place before she joined her mother beside the window. "Didn't you sleep, Mother?"

"A little. It's nearly dawn anyway. Did you have a nightmare?"

Nodding, Maia leaned against the window frame. "I can't remember what it was, though. I can't ever seem to remember them anymore."

"Ask your teacher. I'm sure he can tell you."

"Father...he was so angry. I don't understand, Mother. Why was he so angry?"

Selena breathed a gentle sigh. "Dearest, your father is the gentlest of men, but even he has his pride, and that's taken such a trouncing these past months. He spoke in anger. He didn't mean what he said. Once he's had time to reflect, I'm sure he'll realize that your teacher only acted in his best interests."

"He isn't angry at us, too, is he?"

"No, dearest. Of course not." Selena took Maia's hand. "Put on your dressing gown and let's go downstairs for breakfast."

Berdina, Hollister's mother, already had the kitchen bustling by the time they arrived. She greeted them warmly and made sure they were comfortably settled at the table. "You don't mind sharing the table with us, do you, ma'am?" the plump Caretaker matron asked. "I thought, just as well to get most of the work done in the cool of the morning. Does fruit sound good to you this morning, or should we stir up some porridge for you?"

"Fruit will be excellent, thank you, Berdina." Selena nodded to dismiss the woman.

While Maia and her mother breakfasted on fresh fruit salad, the new general entered the kitchen, followed respectfully by Commander Rowan Solam-son and a trio of guards: Rowan's son Isaac to represent the princess' guards, Temora daughter of Kalanna on behalf of Owen's guards, and Morio son of Jubilee, a massive Alti lieutenant attached to the king's corps. These five sat down around the table after suitable greetings had been offered to Maia and her mother. The new general spoke first. "Apart from the three I named to you, I know of no one who should be excluded from service. Solam-son, you and your son must divide them between yourselves as best you can. I have business in the city, so I will not have time to do this myself. You," he said with a pointed look at Morio, "will accompany me."

Rowan had a meek, chastened look. "I cannot complain over my lot, sir, but you must realize that sixteen guards won't be nearly enough to secure such an open target."

"You must recruit reinforcements according to your best judgment. The one thing you must avoid is the appearance of military force. As long as there are only sixteen guards, no one will be any wiser about your true aims. Lord Sakiry is still receiving visitors; a few more old friends hanging around the house will not draw undue attention. Work on it from that angle."

"Yes, sir."

As intrigued as she was by this conversation, Maia could not help but be distracted by the antics of one of the young Caretaker maids. Liande did not normally work in the kitchen, as far as Maia knew, but then, Liande rarely kept one set of responsibilities for very long. Maia tried to focus on what her teacher was discussing with the guards. It was difficult, however, because Liande kept darting to the table, putting things in the wrong places. She set a huge bowl of cut fruit in front of Isaac Rowan-son instead of putting the bowl on the counter nearby; Berdina had to come fetch it herself. Then, because the over-full bowl had slopped sticky juice onto the table, Liande had to wipe it up, leaning so far in front of Isaac that her head must have obscured everything else for him. It apparently came as a surprise to Liande that the dry dishcloth stuck to the table instead of blotting the spill. She pressed down harder, only to find the cloth practically fused to the wood. In jerking the cloth free, she spattered a few drops of coagulating fruit syrup onto Isaac's shoulder. One would have thought the syrup was blood, judging by the way Liande blanched with horror; she ran to the sink, soaked the cloth in soapy water, and thoroughly dampened the entire left side of Isaac's uniform jacket with her attempts to clean away the traces of syrup. Berdina, squeezing the bridge of her nose as if to ward off a headache, chose that moment to intervene. She seized the maid by an ear and dragged her out of the kitchen.

Upon returning, Berdina came directly to the table. "I'm very sorry for the disruption," she said to the new general tiredly. "It won't happen again." She took up the cloth, went to wring it out in the sink, and tidied up the tabletop. Then she gave Isaac a towel to dry himself.

The gathering dispersed not long after this. When Maia's teacher stood, he asked, "Have you finished your breakfast yet, Princess? There are matters that we must discuss."

"Yes, certainly. Please excuse me, Mother." Maia got up, glad to leave the kitchen. "What is it, Teacher? What were you all talking about?"

"It has become necessary to reorganize the royal guard corps. This is not altogether bad," her teacher assured her. "It means we have uncovered the traitors and removed them, and we can now change our tactics without fear of word reaching our enemies. Isaac Rowan-son is now the commander of the corps and will oversee the guards who remain here. His father will take charge of security for Lord Sakiry. Temora is a capable woman, but under these special conditions, it is best to have someone of broader field experience to handle this more sensitive outpost."

"What do you mean?"

"If you were the third marshal," said her teacher shrewdly, "consider it: what could be more sensible than to gain the upper hand over the royal family? And how better to do this than by seizing or killing the clan patriarch?"

If nothing else had convinced Maia of the seriousness of this matter, her teacher's rhetorical question succeeded. "He really would try to kill Uncle Owen, wouldn't he? Because if he just seized him to hold as a prisoner, sooner or later someone would demand to talk with him, or at least see him, and Uncle Owen would make it clear that he was being held against his will. He couldn't leave him alive to do that."

"I cannot argue with your logic, but take heart. Nothing has yet been attempted, and we have all day to arrange our defenses. By nightfall, Owen will be safer in that cottage than you will be in Takra House."

*   *   *   *

As the sun set, an unobtrusive manservant came and drew the curtains shut in Tyrell's elegant parlor, where Jarod and the curiosity merchant both sat, enjoying a moment's peace over fine chilled wine. A half-heard sound roused Jarod. *Chike? What do I sense? Who's coming?*

Your enemies are almost upon you.

How did they learn that I was here?

The answer to this question was slower in coming, but Chike could not be less than honest. *Your wife. She has been to Takra House again, but not to see her friend. It was she who spoke of your connection to Tyrell.*

Tyrell noticed Jarod's tension. "What is it, my lord?"

"I must leave immediately. When they come, you will be checking your books. You did not see or converse with me at all today. If pressed, you think I had a meeting in Carthae that kept me longer than I expected. Can you remember all of that?"

The merchant glanced toward the windows involuntarily. "When who comes, my lord?"

Jarod drew on his light cloak. With scarcely a backwards look, he removed himself to the bedroom, reached up and opened the trap door leading to the attic. "The third marshal's allies. Make no mistake: they mean to find me. By now, it is known that you are connected to me. They may not yet know the nature of our connection, however, and you must use that any way you can. Good evening to you, Tyrell." He pulled himself up into the attic and shut the trap door behind him. In the dark, he reached overhead once again to feel for the latch that would open the second trap door. This led out onto the shallow slope of Tyrell's rooftop. There Jarod perched like a bird of prey, motionless, watching the shadows of the street below.

Before long, his expectations were richly rewarded by the sight of half a dozen armed men approaching from the direction of the Academy. Two of them stationed themselves on the ground, one at the door to the closed shop and one at the foot of the alley stairs, while the other four climbed the stairs to hammer at Tyrell's door. "Open your door in the king's name," one of them shouted through the door.

Tyrell spoke with admirable composure. "What is your business with my house?"

"We are under orders to search your property for signs of the outland mercenary."

"Under *whose* orders?"

"We come under order from the rightful general, Simon Miklei-son. The Council chose him over the foreigner from the first; now the king's missing, they have granted Simon son of Miklei both the rank and the powers rightfully attached to it."

"Indeed?" Tyrell sounded suitably surprised, as if this was news to him. "I had not heard of a new assembly of the Council. Very well; my home is open to your inspection. I assure you, you will find no outland mercenary within my walls. Please refrain from damaging my goods. Some are rare and delicate. I would hate to present your new commander with such an expensive claim of recompense on his first day in office. That would be very inauspicious for him."

The trammeling of feet soon faded as the door closed them in. Jarod had heard what he wanted to know. *Take me to Lord Sakiry, Chike.* For a heartbeat, he was both blind and deaf. When the mortal world returned his senses to him, he found that the giant had not taken him directly to the cottage where Owen stayed in retirement. Rather, Chike had deposited Jarod nearly a block away. *What is this?* He saw the cottage with its windows lit peacefully. One guard leaned against the front door, while another paced idly at the fence. All seemed well, but Jarod had instinct enough to mistrust the appearance of peace.

Then one of the shadows rose up to disclose itself as an archer with his bow in hand, an arrow nocked and ready to fire. He took aim at the guard by the fence. Jarod bent and scooped up a large pebble from the gutter. This he whipped at the archer just before the arrow flew. Jarod's pebble smacked against the archer's hand and foiled his aim just enough to send the arrow into the fence rather than into the guard. The guard stiffened, alerted by the noise but still unsure of its meaning. Jarod heard him call to his partner, "Did you hear that?" Jarod already had selected another pebble of suitable size. This he hurled at the archer's head. From his hiding place, he heard a sudden rush of booted feet and a startled outcry from both of the guards as the assailants mobbed them. Jarod sprinted toward the fray.

He and one of the guards recognized each other almost in the same instant. "At my back," he commanded the guard. Back to back, they beat off their foes with fists and knives; there was no room for any other weapon. The other guard had already raised the cry for reinforcements. All that came in response was the sound of a skirmish at the rear of the house. Jarod knew there were two guards stationed there as well, and two inside the house. Despite his preoccupation with the fight at hand, he was relieved to note that the two guards inside the cottage did not come out to aid their fellows. Instead, a group of six or seven from down the street came running in response to the call. By that time, the fight had turned in Jarod's favor. Whoever had sent this assault had not anticipated Jarod's intervention; if he had, he doubtless would have sent soldiers of higher quality. As it was, four of them already lay sprawled on the ground. The remainder saw the reinforcements and dispersed back into the darkness beyond the fence.

"What happened, sir?" Rowan Solam-son was foremost among the reinforcements and reached Jarod's side first.

"Take your squad around the back and make sure no one broke through there." Wiping his hands against his trouser legs, Jarod turned to the guard who had stood by him. "Hail and well met, Narayn Kivva," he said.

"'Well met,' indeed, keiri," was Narayn's response, accompanied by a stiff bow.

"What damage did you suffer?"

"Nothing much. My side." The immigrant peeled his uniform jacket away to show a dark blotch. "You spared me worse, keiri."

Jarod set a hand on the man's shoulder. "Go in to the healer and he will see to it. I will wait here." He settled himself there to await Rowan's report. All around, guards gathered up the fallen assailants. When one guard asked him how they were to dispose of the riffraff, Jarod answered, "Lock them with the other traitors in the jail. The king will dispose of them in due time, once he has returned." He flexed his bruised and scuffed hands to keep them from stiffening while he waited.

After several minutes, Rowan came back to report. "All secure, sir. Seems the attack force at the rear wasn't expecting to move so soon. We caught one, and he's still alert enough to talk. You...you did a rather too-thorough job on these here," he said in a tentative jest. "We won't get much out of them for a few hours, I'd wager. Our captive says there was supposed to be a signal, but they never got it. When they heard the sound of fighting, they reckoned they'd best forget about the signal and get down to business, which they did until they saw us round the corner. Most of them scattered pretty quick, except our captive and two others hurt too bad to run. Do you want to see him, sir?"

"Not tonight. I trust you recovered sufficiently from your illness, Captain?"

"That?" Rowan nodded. "It passed just as the healer said it would."

"You don't think it was somewhat suspiciously timed? It was convenient to have the commander of the royal guard suddenly taken ill at that particular juncture."

Rowan was not surprised. "Glad I wasn't the only one to think that."

"Good enough. That will be all. Good night, Captain."

He had not taken half a dozen strides before a guard called to him from the house. "Sir! General, sir, begging your pardon, but the chief healer wants a word before you go."

The chief healer? Jarod paused. *What might he want, Chike?*

You know how to answer that for yourself, little brother: go to the man and hear him.

He returned to the cottage and entered. The entry hall was so tiny that he had to tip his head to one side to keep it from bumping the ceiling. There was no room left for the guard, who had pressed himself against the wall in order to make room. "They're in there, sir."

They. By that word alone, Jarod knew that his suspicions were accurate. *The chief healer wants a word, does he? Somehow I doubt it.* He ducked under the lintel of the doorway that connected the sitting room with the front entry. Sure enough, he spotted Lord Sakiry slouched in a chair in the corner. Jarod gave him a look, but did not address him.

The chief healer was busy stitching Narayn's wound, but he glanced at Jarod with undisguised curiosity for a second. "Please, make yourself comfortable, General," he said as he snipped the catgut at the end of a row of stitches. "There you go, Sergeant. That will hold you together. Get yourself something from the kitchen before you go." Doran collected his tools. As he rewound the coarse thread between his fingers, he said, "Who were they?"

"No friends of yours," Jarod replied. "I suspect they came to call on his lordship."

"Me?"

Jarod gave the older man another look. What he saw surprised him mildly.

Owen sat up straighter in his chair with a look of sudden comprehension in his eyes. Respect followed almost immediately thereafter, culminating in Owen's remark, "You expected them to come." Then he frowned. "But why?"

"Surely you must be familiar with the concept of leverage, Lord Sakiry."

This stilted exchange was interrupted by Doran, who exclaimed, "General, you're bleeding. I can smell it." The healer interposed himself between Jarod and Owen as he sought the source of bleeding. His gaze roamed up and down Jarod's torso. Doran grabbed Jarod by the wrist, examined the abraded knuckles of the right hand and then the left, but still was not satisfied with what he found. He began prodding Jarod wherever a bloodstain showed on his garments. This ended when his finger sank into the stain that began two finger-widths below Jarod's collarbone. "Ah!" With a deft and gentle hand, he peeled back the shirt to find a gash as long as his thumb. His eyes rose in some amazement. "Doesn't it hurt you?"

Jarod stared back without response.

"Sit and let me throw a bandage over it, at least."

Jarod obeyed. He felt Owen still watching him as he shrugged out of his jacket and pulled his shirt over his head. Once Doran had cleaned the gash, Jarod stopped him. "No bandage, please, Chief Healer. If you have any gilsim sap handy, that will suffice."

"Gilsim? What does that have to do with anything?"

"A simple remedy I learned from my own healers. Let me demonstrate." He took the oilskin pouch that the healer gave him, uncorked it, and thrust his forefinger deep into the sap inside. "If you will please hold the edges of the wound together for me?" Then, with the healer offering him this small assistance, he spread sap over the gash and blew on it gently. In a matter of moments, the clear sap had set up enough that he told Doran, "There. You may let go. It will not reopen. Within the hour, the sap will harden enough to function as well as any bandage, with the added advantage that I may wash without fear of ruining or replacing it."

Doran sat back, fascinated. "How do you remove it without reopening the wound?"

"A little watered arboccol will dissolve the sap when it is no longer needed."

"I have never seen that done before."

"That is probably because you have worked primarily in civilized conditions."

"You did that as if you'd had a lot of practice at it. Have you trained at all?"

"Yes. I am a fully qualified field healer. I learned long ago the value of being able to tend my wounds or those of my allies. There is not always someone else to depend on."

Softly, Owen remarked, "From the looks of it, you've taken injuries enough to train anyone in the healing arts." The older man examined the assortment of scars on Jarod's torso and arms. His gaze caught on Jarod's left shoulder and side. "What sort of injury was that?"

Jarod answered flatly, "That was a burn, Lord Sakiry, a severe burn. What was it you wished to say to me? I have business elsewhere."

"I *was* the one who wanted to speak to you," Owen admitted. "I didn't know if you would come if you knew."

"I knew. What did you want?"

"My daughter brought me back news from the assembly halls. She said that you and Ronán fought at the reception the Alti clansmen hosted for you. I wanted to know if there is anything I can do to intercede on your behalf."

"I thank you for your concern, Lord Sakiry, but there is no need. I have met with the man himself this morning and enlisted him to provide extra guards for the neighborhood around this house. He and Dermot-son have assumed joint command of the force I am building. Your third marshal is giving it out that the Council has acted in the king's absence to name him general. They are using this ploy to search private residences for me and for my allies. Unfortunately for him, the Sea Folk clansmen are of a perverse and uncooperative nature. They do not recognize his authority. Kyte tells me that they have refused to contribute men and arms to his cause, so he has focused his attention at their properties in the city. Others who have spoken on my behalf have suffered indignities as well. This very night, he sent a squad to the home of the curiosity merchant in search of me."

"He can't expect to get by with this," Doran protested. "There's been no such decision made by the Council!"

"Not by the Council itself, but by a private meeting involving Berhus Pamirsi, the Nandevi patriarch Omatu, and a scattering of other local counselors. Your city sits in the midst of Pamirsi land. He is accustomed to setting laws according to his own notions of how things ought to be. Take this for an example." Loosening the drawstring of the pouch at his belt, Jarod took out the arrest document that he had confiscated from Giles' jailer.

Owen took it and read it in burgeoning disbelief. "So that's what you meant. 'Laid hands on a person of rank,' indeed," the older man snorted. "This goes as far beyond that as Miklei-son himself has gone beyond his authority. And sealed with Berhus' own seal, no less! What does he mean by this—'violently assaulted a person of noble birth'? 'Dishonorable liberties against a lady's will'?" He handed the document back in disgust. "I knew those new regulations of his would lead to no good. Now he's using them to help Simon. I assume this 'person of noble birth' refers to Maia. What a pile of rubbish. Giles never 'violently assaulted' anybody in the course of his life." With that, Owen dropped back into his chair and seemed to deflate. "Is he all right?"

"Yes. He has gone with Colin. I thought it best to remove him from the reach of Miklei-son's jealousy as soon as possible." Jarod pulled his soiled shirt back over his head. "He should do well in his new surroundings."

Doran leaned his elbows on his knees and held his head between his hands like a man with a headache. "How can we fight this?"

Little brother, Chike said gently, *strengthen your friend. He is weary of the discord.*

You must help me. My strength is insufficient. "You are a man of peace, Chief Healer. You must let me worry about the fight." Standing, Jarod placed his hands on Doran's head and felt Chike's touch overlap his own. As the giant's strength seeped into him, so also he let his own strength overflow into the healer. He went on, "As long as you stand your ground, I ask nothing more of you. You must not let the conflict dispirit you. That is his aim."

As soon as Jarod withdrew his hands, Doran sat up straighter, his eyes clearer and more serene. "What did you just do?"

"We each strengthen one another, some in one way and some in another." Jarod sensed that Owen's curiosity had intensified, so he withdrew. "Now, if neither of you have further need of my presence, I will bid you good night." He left without giving them a chance to speak up one way or the other. Outside, he lingered only long enough to see that the grounds were secure. Then he strode purposefully into the night. *Chike, take me to the apartment, please.*

To your wife?

I must, Jarod admitted, *whether she will hear me or not. I must try.* In a blink, he stood outside the bedroom that, until only a few days before, he had shared with Ivy. Before he set hand to the doorknob, he heard weeping, but it was not Ivy's voice that cried. Silently he entered the room.

Ivy sat on the bed with her face toward the door, obviously awaiting his entrance. Her features quickly arranged themselves into a smile as her hands compulsively smoothed the fabric of her nightdress. "Good evening," she said. "I thought you would never come." Then, too casually to be accidental, she added, "I suppose you've been busy?" Jarod's prolonged silence made the smile on her lips waver. Her eyes told the truth as they roamed over the bloodstains on his clothing. She loathed him. The air felt heavy with her resentment and disgust. All the while, Ivy's shepherd continued to weep bitterly over her protégé.

Chike, Jarod said, *speak to Ianthe. See how far Ivy has fallen. I dare not.* By force of will, he stopped himself from trembling with the emotions that pulled at him. He knew the smell of the Unclean's taint too well to believe that Ivy had not critically compromised herself. Beyond that dire truth, he had no desire to know more. "Yes," he finally responded to Ivy's clumsy attempt at prying into his plans. "Yes, I have been very much occupied. I came only to inform you that my business will keep me much later than I expected. I will not return again tonight." He bowed politely, turned his back on her, and shut the bedroom door between them. *Refuge, Chike. Take me to my refuge. I cannot bear this anymore.*

DEPOSED

Utterly ignored, Colin slumped in his saddle and let the horse choose its own path. It seemed to know where it was going, which was more than Colin could say for himself. Nothing had ever prepared him for such a day. In his worst nightmares, he had never imagined himself deposed, exiled from home and family without so much as a whimper of protest from anyone—not even his wife! The look in Selena's eyes dogged him through the wilderness. Her allegiance had shifted, just like Maia's had, to that man—if he was indeed a man, which Colin doubted. No man could do what that man had done. A cold shiver raced up his body. *Why spare my life only to get rid of me?* Colin could make no sense of any of it.

"Sitting up there all day?" a mild voice inquired.

Colin looked up from his horse's mane to find his guide, young Kyte-son, watching him with an inquisitive tilt to his head. They had come to a halt and the younger two men had dismounted already. Colin did likewise. "Why are we stopping?"

"Noontide."

"Let's get it over with," Giles sighed.

"Ah, don't tell me you're tired of my excellent provisions already! At least put a brave face on it, little man. You don't see Colin making such a fuss, do you?" Damon Kyte-son winked at Colin when Giles wasn't looking. "We've got to put some starch in you. You're not living in your grandmomma's house anymore. Got to learn to look after yourself."

"If you 'little man' me once more," Giles growled, "I'll—"

"You'll what? Listen, boy, if you want to fight me, I'm at your service, but I don't recommend it. I've been at it longer, and I've had the best of teachers. Keep your temper in hand. Where you're going, not everybody's as understanding as I am."

"Where *are* we going?" Colin asked as he built a fire. "Or am I not allowed to ask?"

"You can ask any question you like. I'm not obliged to answer any of them," Kyte admitted ruefully, "but that doesn't stop you from asking. This one's not a problem. We're going home to the village."

"The village?"

"It's more of a town, really. Started as just a little village. Ammun owns it. It's named Chamika. I've called it home for…what has it been now, eight years? Since its inception."

"Chamika," Colin repeated. "All right. Why send me there?"

"Good question." Damon busied himself with a copper cooking pot. He measured three handfuls of a peculiar grain meal out of a canvas sack, and then he began to dribble water into the pot of meal, stirring the concoction with a peeled stick. When he was satisfied with the results, he pushed the coals into a heap under the pot and let the mixture cook. "Mind you, I can't answer it with any better than guesses. He doesn't tell me everything. The village is neutral territory. The only allegiance we swear is to him as our lord. No outsiders enter save by appointment, and none of the villagers leave save on business for Ammun. I don't know that I've ever seen a more secure place. That's why, if you really wish to know. There's nowhere safer to keep you, outside of his presence. It's a good place to live. He makes sure of that."

Colin got out his bowl and held it out so that Damon could pour the cooked gruel into it. Without waiting for Giles to be served, Colin poured a little water into his bowl to cool his portion. Four days' travel had taught him the only way to swallow this concoction—straight down, without pausing to let the taste linger. He tipped his head back and poured the contents of the bowl down his throat. Even with practice, he couldn't avoid a quick shudder as he finished.

The boy Giles hadn't yet gotten the knack of eating Damon's gruel. He took a mouthful, gagged, and swallowed with visible effort. "Ugh," he gasped. "Disgusting."

"It'll keep you alive," Damon said laconically, "and that's the main thing. Once, I had to live on this and boiled marsh water for two weeks. Nothing'll give you a better appreciation for food than two weeks of sour gruel and stagnant water. We were keeping watch over a little country manor house, waiting for the opportune moment. I drew the short straw and ended up watching on the low-land side."

"What do you mean, 'opportune moment'?" Giles asked.

Damon's response was philosophical. "You can't just break into a heavily-guarded house when you feel like it. You wait for your moment."

"Breaking in? As in, 'stealing'?"

"Recovering something that had already been stolen, but otherwise, yes."

"What got stolen?"

"Rafe's little cousin. They thought they could use her to force him to betray Ammun. They didn't know Rafe as well as they thought. Nor Ammun. He'd never leave one of his own as a prisoner, and Rafe knew it. They put their heads together and came up with a way to get Evany back and make old Malin sorry he'd ever tried. It was a beautiful coup. Malin didn't even know the girl was gone until we were two days away."

Colin took no part in the conversation. He had found at once that his own reservations about this fellow whom Damon called Ammun were the exception. Giles' enthusiasm for the fellow was unmistakable. He had retold the tale of his rescue from a Pamirsi jail until Colin had irritably hushed him. That had only driven the boy to wheedle stories from Damon, and if Damon had an excess of anything, it was stories about his master. He relished the opportunity to tell the most lurid tales of intrigues, battles, duels, and plots. Half of them Colin was unwilling to believe, at least until he thought back to the night of the attempted assassination. Then he didn't know what to believe.

On the night of the attempted assassination, the three of them had crossed the river, riding full out under the cover of darkness as if they were pursued. Damon had done all the necessary talking so that no one should recognize Colin. Since crossing the river four days ago, they had followed a steady northeastern route. The king was not as sure of his landmarks here as he was in his own lands, but he was almost certain that he could see the bulk of Cloudveil looming farther east. The day he recognized that great mountain, they began to veer more toward the north until they buried themselves in a maze of canyons. Now, by noontide on the fifth day of their travels, Colin was thoroughly lost. He would never find his way home even if an opportunity came.

"Shouldn't we be pushing forward?" he said abruptly.

Damon began gathering up his utensils, bestowing a patient look on Colin. "It's not far now. I thought maybe we could spare the horses and take it easy for a day. They've been ridden harder than I like."

"Nairne seems to be holding up well." Colin went to his horse and stroked its powerful neck so that he would not have to look at Damon for a time.

"They're bred for it, but I have to answer for their wellbeing, so I'd rather not risk it. Besides, we've no reason for haste. No one is going to be following us out here. If they do…well, let's say I wouldn't like to trade places with them."

"What do you mean by that?"

"Watch the trees when we're on the move again. Maybe you'll see one."

Intrigued by that cryptic suggestion, Colin obeyed. As he rode up the steeply climbing thread of a path, he craned his neck from side to side in an effort to catch sight of whatever it was that made Damon so confident. He saw a flicker of something on a course parallel to theirs. Then Damon slowed them to navigate a stone bridge just wide enough for one horse at a time to traverse its length; it had no railings to block the horsemen's view of the rapids below. As Colin reached the apex of the bridge, he noted another flicker of movement from the corner of his eye. He lifted his eyes from their morbid preoccupation with the turbulent water and caught sight of the largest feline he'd ever seen. It leaped the stream; another followed after it, landing with a gentle thump in the tall grass on the other bank. This one paused to return Colin's stare. Its tail twitched along the ground.

"They've been following us these last two days," Damon said calmly. "As a favor to Ammun, I figure."

Colin nudged his horse onward. When he looked again, the pardeléi were gone.

*   *   *   *

The next morning, after they had saddled up the horses and were ready to mount up and start, Damon stopped with boyish diffidence. "We're near enough," he began, drawing each word out, "that I have to ask something of both of you."

"Sure, Damon," Giles said blithely. "What is it?"

Damon dug two heavy pieces of canvas out of his saddlebag. When he held one out to Colin, the king saw that it was a small sack. "What's this for?"

Rather than answer, the younger man pulled the sack over Giles' head. "Every stranger has to go through this. It's nothing personal. Only residents are allowed to see the approach. Once you've been there a while, this won't be necessary."

"Sure, Damon," Colin muttered. "Sure, Damon. Be glad to. Perfectly happy to oblige." He pulled the sack over his head and groped for the stirrup. In a moment, Damon was there, helping him into the saddle.

"Sorry about this, sir. Really, if there were any other way—there you go."

Riding blindfold was a novel experience. He felt the undulating movements of the horse much more keenly. Giles rode so close at his side that Colin felt the boy's knee prodding him. After a time, the horses began a swift, lurching climb up a grade so steep that Colin grabbed at the saddle in a momentary panic. Colin swayed wildly as the horses rounded a sharp corner with no warning. "Are you trying to shake us off?" he shouted, hoping that the canvas did not muffle his voice too much. "If you are, then you're doing a fine job of it!"

Damon's voice drifted back cheerfully. "Sorry! Turning back the other way now—it's a switchback road. Hang on."

The first intimation that they had reached the village came in the form of a strange, melodic buzzing sound. Colin turned his head back and forth, trying without success to locate its source. Then, at his feet, someone stifled an involuntary exclamation. Colin jumped. That one exclamation was followed by a brief silence. Damon called out to someone in a language that Colin only recognized as the one that his new general had used when he wanted to conceal his intentions. Damon's tone had grown more assured, and the man who responded to him had the sound of a soldier under orders. *He's a young lord here,* Colin thought, *while I am nobody at all. I suppose I'll take orders from him, just like everyone else. And why not? I've been found wanting as a king; what else is left but to serve and obey like a commoner? There are worse fates, I suppose...if only I could have my Selena beside me.* He flinched at the thought of her face as he remembered it last. Smarting under the lash of his bitterness, somehow she had still found a tremulous, encouraging smile to give him. *Oh, my dear Selena, I'm sorry. I wish I hadn't parted from you like that. Who knows when we'll meet again—if ever?*

It took a moment before Colin realized that he sat astride a motionless horse. Then a hand grasped his foot. "We're here. Let me help you down." Damon took his elbow and guided him down to a pavement of stone. When the canvas sack was whipped off his head, Colin blinked in the thin, clear sunshine. Before him stood a modest house, a hunting lodge by the looks of it. Small-paned windows looked out of two stories, but of more interest to Colin was the massive wooden door. It wore the scars of several axe-cuts, especially around the handle and hinges. He climbed three shallow steps in pursuit of Damon, who had already gone inside.

"Welcome," the young proxy said over his shoulder. "Why don't I first show you where you'll be sleeping? Follow me!" In his exuberance, Damon took the gracious stairs three at a time to the upper floor. His voice echoed down. "Are you coming?"

Colin shook off his melancholy. "Presently," he replied. When he reached the top, he found not just Damon but a small crowd waiting for him. His eyes lit upon an unexpectedly familiar face. Colin could only gape in astonishment for several seconds.

"Well, Colin," said Byram Solam-son with a smile. "It has been too long."

Gladly, Colin embraced his father's last companion and nearly lifted him from his feet before releasing him. "Byram! By all that's still good, I didn't imagine I'd be seeing you!"

"I'd say the same, but we received advance warning of your visit. How was the journey?"

Damon interrupted, "I'd like you to meet my wife Aurelia, sir." He pulled forward a lovely blonde girl. "And this fellow here is Laszlo. He serves as Ammun's steward here in Chamika. By him is his wife Arrosa, assistant healer. Manon, just beyond her, is the woman to see if you need anything here in this house. Aurelia," he said, looking around, "where's Luck?"

"Visitin' Ferris. I don't know when he means to come back."

"Ah. I'll fetch him. Byram, do you mind? Thanks."

Byram took charge of Colin. "I'll show you your rooms while we wait." He paused, looking at Giles. "Why do I know your face, boy?"

"Depends. Did you ever know my father?"

"He's Perrin's boy—Denei's grandson," Colin added for clarification.

"Ah! I knew I'd run across you somewhere. You've grown somewhat, I'll say. Well, well. Ah, we've readied rooms for you both. Small, but comfortable enough, and right next door to each other. Here you are, Colin. Yours is there, my boy. Hector will bring your luggage up presently. Let me, ah, show you the rest of the house. Then you can wash off the travel dust. Everything up here is a bedroom, save for the room next to yours, Colin, and that's the library."

Colin followed the man down the staircase. Downstairs, he saw the great room at the front of the house, a room called the evening room, the dining room, and the kitchen. They had just passed a row of servants' chambers and emerged briefly in the entry hall on their way to the morning room when Byram stopped short. "There you are, Master Lucky. Look who's here!"

An undersized, wiry boy stood with one foot on the bottom step. Colin caught just a glimpse of round sapphire eyes before the boy bowed low. "Your majesty!" said the boy in a light, clear voice. "I bid you welcome!" With conscious dignity, he crossed the distance between them and said to Colin, "May I join you?"

The incongruity of such fully-fledged manners in a child so young made Colin smile. "Yes. Thank you...Lucky, did he say?"

"That's what everybody calls me, sir. Properly, I'm Lucien."

"Where has Damon gone off to?" Byram asked.

"He called the chieftains to meet before he has to go."

Colin frowned. "Go?"

"Yes, sir. He said he'd come back to take his leave of you before he went."

Colin looked to Byram for confirmation. The older man shrugged. "He's a man in great demand these days. You'll have to get used to a great deal of upheaval around here. Ammun has a hand in everything, it seems. People are forever coming and going on his business. It's been awkward, him not being here for so long. Your business has come to the fore at a highly inopportune time, but that can't be helped. Well, well. Come along to the kitchen and we'll all have a good sit-down and some food."

They had no further chance to talk until after Damon came back. With him came another man, lean and weathered to the point where his age was lost somewhere between his forties and his sixties. Colin stood at their approach. "This is Rafe," Damon began without ceremony. "For the time being, he's charged with the governing of Chamika." He paused as Rafe bowed. "He'll look after you until Ammun or I should come back. I'm sorry to be dodging off like this, but I have other orders to follow."

Nodding in acknowledgement of the apology, Colin said, "I understand. What orders did he give you regarding me? What am I to do with myself?"

"I wouldn't call them orders," the younger man demurred. "You're free to occupy yourself however you see fit. The only thing you aren't to do is stay indoors, awake, for longer than two hours at a time. Rafe will see that you never lack reason to break that one rule."

Colin raised an eyebrow. "Indoors, awake."

"That's what he said. Now, I ought to pack up and head out if I'm to make any distance before sundown. I hope you're all settled in here?"

"I'm situated well. Don't let me detain you." Colin offered a bow to the young proxy.

The gesture flustered Damon. The young man bowed in return and left Colin to face his first village chieftain.

"I beg pardon for my ignorance, sir, but what am I to call you?"

Rafe shot an inscrutable look to Byram. In the moment it took Colin to turn also and look at the older man, whatever had passed between them was over. Byram said, "I'm afraid we're all at a loss today. Before we can proceed, I think it would be helpful if we established your role here. This is above all a political village, Colin, as you'll quickly find. We're used to hosting men of high rank from time to time."

"And men of low rank, too?"

"Ah, well, yes, certainly. We're far more accustomed to those, as you can imagine."

"Then we have no problems at all." Colin tried to divide his gaze between the two men. "I am nobody. Treat me accordingly. No, Byram. I have been deposed and put here to keep me out of the way. I'm still getting accustomed to the truth, but I will not lie to anyone about this."

Byram surrendered reluctantly. "The appropriate title for a man of Rafe's position is 'natai.' All the village chieftains answer to that title."

"Thank you. Please tell me, *natai*, what duties you have for me? I wish to be useful."

"Duties? Fain y'duties sammas ivver'un—gunda try-al, lak ivver'un. Ken ye th' blai?"

Bewildered, Colin said, "Sorry—what was that again?"

Byram took up the thread of conversation: "He says you'll find out your duties through trial. He wants to know what experience you've had in swordsmanship."

"Ah. I have trained with the blade, but not for many years, since my early manhood."

The chieftain appeared to be a man of little speech. He received his answer with a grunt and gestured for Colin to sit. "Rest up a'day. Sunup, y'go t' try-al."

Courtesy seemed to dictate that Colin and Byram share a drink with Rafe and then accompany him to the door. When Manon the housekeeper brought the three cups, she handed one to Rafe and let Byram and Colin choose between the two that remained. Colin only caught a glimpse of the contents of all three, but he noticed that Rafe's drink was a different color than the other two. He made no comment on this, but drank his wine along with the others. All this they did with scarcely two words exchanged between them. Once they arrived at the door, they found another warrior squatting on his haunches, waiting patiently for something to happen. He sprang up as soon as he saw them. Colin stopped so abruptly that he nearly stumbled. "Greysin Alti," he said in disbelief. "I thought you were dead."

The slender Alti warrior grinned at that. "No, my lord. Not last I checked. The instant I heard of your arrival, I could find no peace until I saw you for myself. You are most welcome to Chamika, my lord, most welcome."

"But Denei…he said you fell in battle."

Greysin's face darkened. "I fell, true enough, but not into death. I was a captive, my lord. For more than a month I lived in a cage at the raider's camp. It isn't a memory I like to recall, but here I am, at your service." He executed a crisp bow. "I still hold true to my vows, my lord."

Colin shook his head gently. "Enough of the 'lord' business. Here, I'm no more than any other man. Perhaps you and I will get a chance to spar again, just as we did in our early days."

The Alti warrior shot a questioning look at Byram, who raised his hands in disavowal of the entire subject. "I do not understand, my lord. What do you mean, 'here'? Why should the place make any difference in your rank or blood? You are here just as you were at home, my lord. You are my lord the king. Nothing can change that." Gazing intently into Colin's face, the small warrior clearly did not see the expression he wished to see. "Do you suppose he would do you such a disservice? If you were removed from the realm of your authority, my lord, it was for your momentary protection."

"You seem sure of that."

"I seem sure because I *am* sure, my lord. He has told me of the snares set around you. As far as that goes, there is little he has not told me about what is going on. You may think," Greysin said with rising agitation, "that because I live here, I do not hold true to the vows I made as a member of your guard. That is not true. I swore to remain loyal to Tree and crown, to serve the royal house until the day I die. I would have returned to you as soon as he set me free from the raiders' prison, but I learned that I could serve as well here—" He shut his mouth with a sharp click of his teeth, as if he had spoken out of turn. Once he had regained his composure, he finished, "I have fulfilled my vows at a distance, my lord. It is my pleasure to fulfill them now by asking that you set aside this foolish idea that you have become less than what you are."

The man's fervor was unmistakable. Colin regarded him in mild curiosity before saying, "But it pleases me to become common for a time, Greysin, according to the standards of some who think it degrading to mingle with rougher men."

"That," Greysin said with a bow, "is not common, my lord. That is kingly indeed. If I may dare to say, it is Ammun's way as well. If that is your choice, far be it from me to protest it. I have long missed your company and the company of your family. I know Byram agrees with me in that. We have spoken of it many times."

"Come in now and talk a while, if you like," Colin offered.

"I would be honored to do it, but I have duties that will not wait any man's pleasure, my lord. I apologize. Perhaps tomorrow."

Colin and Byram returned to the evening room to watch the retreating sun set the western peaks alight. The boy Lucien went to bed soon after the supper hour, and Giles asked permission to explore the village. The servants had all but disappeared. After a long stretch of silence, Colin said, "Byram?"

The older man stirred himself. "Yes? What is it?"

"How is it you came to live here?"

"Do you mean, how did I come here? Or do you mean, why did I stay?"

"If you will," Colin said simply, "please answer both. I'd like to know."

"It's a tale that deserves a master's telling. Someday, if I'm spared so long, I want to hear Owen tell it." Byram cleared his throat and folded his hands. "When your father and I had traveled a week, I knew he had spoken the truth about his fate. Without your mother, he was a doomed man, and nothing could anchor him to this world for long. He walked with his eyes burning silver, always facing straight ahead. By the third week, I didn't hear him speak more than a word or two every few days, and almost none of them were for my ears. Still he walked, on and on, leading me through all manner of wilderness. It would take more than one night to tell you all that befell us on that journey, all of the people we befriended along the way. We mainly lived by the kindness of those we met. Imagine it—the two of us, mendicant wanderers at the mercy of beasts and weather and the goodwill of mankind for four long years! For me, it was the loneliest four years that any man could endure. I had no companion save a man who could neither see nor hear me, let alone speak to me in the manner he once had. At times, when that great power took hold of him, he seemed almost ready to walk through the barrier they say holds Hepuran separate from us. I feared he would leave me alone in the wilderness. The prospect of wandering with a man in a trance was, after all, preferable to the prospect of wandering alone. I'm no great traveler, Colin. I never was. All I ever asked was a quiet home, well-defined duties, a life of peace among my kith and kin." Brooding, the older man lapsed into a brief silence. "I wanted it more and more the farther we roamed. I wanted to turn back. I was even tempted to leave him to himself, though it shames me to recall it. Some days I stayed only because I knew I would never find my way back alone.

"Then, one day, I awoke to bitter frost. We had strayed into the regions that locals call the Deep Cold. The ice never melts there. There was no village to shelter us, no road of any kind to follow, and still Kohanan went onward as if he knew where he wanted to go. He was weakening. After a few days of the harsh north winds, he collapsed. His eyes were clear when he looked at me. For the first time in months, he looked at me and knew me. I begged him not to abandon me in that forsaken place. 'Someone's coming,' he said, and he was right. Someone came."

"The nameless one," Colin supplied when it seemed that Byram had run out of words. "The one they call Ammun. He came for you?"

Byram gave him a peculiar look. "Yes. Almost the next moment, he came out of nowhere and frightened years off my life by setting his hand on my shoulder. He picked up your father—it didn't bother him to touch Kohanan, not even with the power coming upon him again. He had a little hut there in the middle of the wasteland. That's where he took us. He tended your father for three days. I swear, somehow, though I don't know how, he was able to communicate with your father through the trance. I heard neither of them speak, yet still I know that they spoke together somehow. Then, after three days, Kohanan started upright on his bed. I heard him speak in some strange language, more like a song than speech, and he threw his arms around Ammun and called him by his rightful name. With that, he was gone, vanished from the world of men—this time, forever." Byram sighed. "That is how I came to be where I am today. I don't know that I can as easily explain how I came to stay here these three years. In part, it has not entirely been my choice. I have seen his face and heard his true name, Colin. As much as it pains me to admit it, I believe he does not trust me to keep such secrets, were I to return home again. On the other hand, I elected to stay because…because I felt that he needed me. He has been through many hardships. When he found us, he was nearer to death than most people realize. The scars that he carries in his flesh are paltry indeed compared to those he hides within, yet he tries valiantly to overcome these and embrace life again. The companionship of a man from…of a man such as myself…was highly beneficial to his recovery, or so he says. Then there's Lucky to consider, too. I tutor him in history and law, and I honestly can't imagine a more pleasant occupation."

"I wanted to ask about that as well. Who is the boy? I feel as if I should know him."

With a look of mild surprise, Byram replied, "I thought you knew. He's Ammun's son."

$*$ $*$ $*$ $*$

It took Colin hours to fall asleep that night. Every noise was strange and unsettling, every scent foreign. The texture of his blankets and the plump pillow under his head, comfortable as they were, made him constantly aware that he was far from home. The last impression to flit across the nebulous surface of his thoughts that night was simply that of the wind breathing his name against the window pane. When he awoke the next morning, it was raining. He felt groggy. His slumbers, once begun, must have been profound, because the morning was already advanced by the time he climbed from his bed and washed his face at the basin that stood on a table under the window. Colin dressed. Stepping out into the hallway, he paused at the sound of voices murmuring down on the ground floor. Colin didn't examine the impulse he felt at that moment, but rather obeyed it and kept out of sight. Instead of heading for the dining room and his breakfast, he took a nearer doorway and entered the room Byram had pointed out to him as the nameless one's office. It was a windowless room with double doors, one of which was latched shut and the other ajar to let in the light as Colin crossed to the table. It was a table and not a desk that dominated the room. All along the table's length, maps curled their edges slightly. Some he didn't recognize. The names and contours depicted on them were unfamiliar to him, but there were others he knew as well as his own name, maps of his homeland. These were all recent and detailed. As he looked closer, he saw snippets of fabric tacked to the locations where the raiders had attacked along the kingdom borders. Everything was documented, even the most recent attack that had claimed Denei as its victim. *How did he know? He was with us at the time…he could not have been here to mark that off.*

To pursue that line of reasoning would have been to dredge up thoughts Colin wished to put to rest, so he left the maps and explored the rest of the room. He examined the small writing desk in the corner. Unlike the table, this desk was piled high with documents, stained with ink, and scarred with much use. The chair was far too small for the nameless one's use, but Colin could imagine Damon seated there, writing his master's correspondence much like Chessy's son Gian had always done for Colin. Colin's delicacy of feeling would not stretch far enough to let him peruse the documents. He scanned the walls once without much attention, and then turned back for a second, more intense scrutiny. The room was like a small armory, or a museum of weaponry. To this point, Colin could not think of a single room in the house in which he had not seen a weapon on display or in ready storage. This room topped them all. Spears, swords, axes, and other weapons Colin could not name were all on display along the walls of the office. After a while, he saw that no two were the same and that all were of superb craftsmanship, but none were solely ornamental. Every bladed weapon was sharp. Every handle or hilt showed wear.

"There isn't one he hasn't mastered," said Greysin behind him. "I've seen him prove it."

"What sort of man is he?"

Greysin didn't answer immediately. Instead, he stood beside Colin and studied the collection of weapons. "I owe him my life, so you may well say I cannot speak of him without partiality, but I tell you, I would sooner owe him such a debt than own the world's wealth. Even so, I scarcely know him. He is a man who guards himself well—if necessary, with weapons."

"Is he a hand-fighter?"

"Yes, but that is not my meaning. I have spent many hours in his company and known him but little better for it. I think this would hold true for anyone else…except perhaps you."

"I do not know him at all," Colin returned sharply. "At times, I don't want to know him."

After another slight hesitation, Greysin said, "That grieves me, my lord. I don't know how else to say it."

"You say you owe him your life? So too do I, but I cannot love him for that reason alone. Until I know why he has done all this, I must guard myself as much as he does. He bears the burden of proof. He must prove himself to me."

"And what must he do, beyond what he already has done?"

When Colin glanced at his companion, he saw that he had nettled the smaller man. The Alti warrior's defensive anger made him hear his own words as if for the first time, and he was ashamed of them. "If he would only condescend to speak with me face to face for an hour together, it might help. I don't mean to offend you, Greysin. After all, I forget that you've known him longer than I." Curiosity piqued, he blurted, "Have you seen his face?"

"Yes, my lord." Greysin's composure had returned, and with it a sense of distance sprang up between them that had not existed before. "My lord, I was instructed to convey to you the compliments of *natai* Farris, who asks if you would join him this afternoon at his longhouse so that he may become acquainted with you."

Colin felt duly rebuked. "Yes, of course." He left the office with Greysin. It did not escape his notice when Greysin locked the door to Ammun's private office behind them.

SIMON

Third Marshal. Third Marshal. If I hear that empty title once more today, I'll kill the idiot who speaks it. The day had not gone well for Simon Miklei-son, but the day suited the week perfectly. Since the night of the king's disappearance, nothing had gone as planned. Simon picked up the latest communication and held the top of it to his candle. As the paper burned, he read it one last time. *Commander Rowan-son has replaced the gate guards with men of his own choosing. If you wish us to continue, say so, but I will make bold to predict that we stand even less of a chance now with the gates unbarred.* "There must be a way to be rid of that foreign pestilence," Simon murmured. "I simply haven't thought of it yet."

Direct force had failed. For six days, he had ordered the gates barred at night. He had flooded the streets with his allies in order to trap and kill the foreigner, but the foreigner had proven devilishly elusive. They had kept watch over all his known haunts: his new wife's apartments, the curiosity merchant's home, the chief healer's cottage—all for nothing. The foreigner had taunted them with measly glimpses, mere flickers in the shadows. If he did show himself, it was in combat. Because of him, fifteen good men lay badly injured and twice as many more were jailed. *He toys with us, but I will find a way to ensnare him in the end.*

Very well—direct force had failed. So be it. Simon would use indirect means. He rose from his desk and locked the door of his office first. Next, he blocked the windows with a blanket hung on nails. When the room was entirely dark save for the candle and the note's smoldering ashes, Simon drew on his leather gloves and opened a plain cabinet that sat in the corner. From its innards, he lifted a bundle of cloth that he began to unwind with slow, reverent hands until he had revealed the stone hidden within. His fingers offered the stone a brief caress, awakening the soft throb of yellow in the stone's center.

"What do you desire?" The voice of an elderly man whispered from the stone, fatherly, almost affectionate. "Or perhaps I would do better to restrict my question, for your desires are many. What do you desire today?"

"Great father," Simon replied, "I need your counsel. This foreigner has proven difficult to unseat. My men have been unable to capture him."

"I foresaw that. You should have foreseen it as well. Have I not shown you what manner of man you fight? Use your strengths, Simon. He is powerful, to be sure, but he does not have what you have. You possess a great gift. Use it."

"I had a suspicion that you would give me that answer."

"I wonder then that you still thought to ask me."

Simon weighed the tone and decided that he had not displeased the amulé too much. "I have one thought that may work. He has taken a new wife in the city— old Mata-son's daughter Ivy. She's old for bearing him sons, and her capacity for thought is limited, but she does provide him an entry into the better houses. Once she is in my hands…"

"Why seize upon her at all? She would be more useful left where she is."

"I don't see how that is possible."

"I have begun to take hold of her mind and have seen much there that can be of use to us, but I am a stranger to her yet. You do not understand the strength of the love between a brother and a sister, Simon. That is how she will be most useful. Do you not already have the upper hand over her brother? I have searched him and found that strong affection binds those two together. She will listen to him as she will not yet listen to me. Through him, you may influence her so that she will betray a mere husband willingly. The seeds have already begun to grow."

Simon nodded as his course of action took shape in his thoughts. "Yes. Denei-son will do as I bid him, whether he likes it or not. He must, or risk exposure. Then, with her under *your* control, we will make her give us free admittance to Orlan in his most vulnerable moments. Yes. I see it in its entirety. It *must* work."

"There is no harm in a second plan."

"What do you suggest?"

"Orlan controls the royal guard, does he not? It would be to your advantage to lessen his control over this house. I have measured every mortal living within these walls. If you approach the matriarch, Lucinda, I believe she will heed your words. Her desires will work for you if you indulge her properly. Play upon her dislike of this house. Feed her dissatisfaction with the situation in which she finds herself. Promise her better things, and she will gladly undermine Orlan's orders for you."

"What do I gain by unruly servants?"

"Hand him ever-increasing concerns. Eventually he will make a vital mistake."

Simon brooded on these thoughts. When someone knocked at the door, he swept the cloth around the stone and replaced the entire bundle in its cabinet. It was the work of a moment to yank the window covering down as he rounded his desk to unlock the door. "What is it?" he demanded, staring at the Caretaker until the child lowered his eyes.

"Lady Maia wishes to speak with you. She waits outside in the park."

Exultation surged through Simon, but he refused to make a display of it. "Very well. I will come presently." He shut the door in the boy's wake. A square of mirror hung on a nail in the corner. Simon took a moment to inspect his appearance. His boots tapped lightly on his way down the stairs and out through the empty, dim ballroom. From the doorway, he saw her distinctive slim figure leaning against the trunk of the Prince's Tree. Simon threw back his shoulders and held his head high as he crossed the shorn grass. "I am at your service, my lady. How may I serve you?" *Lovely. Perfectly fashioned and exquisite. An unsurpassable beauty. Together, we will transform this kingdom.*

The girl did not turn her head to look at him, providing Simon with a rare opportunity to admire her profile at rest. "There is one thing you can do for me." These cool, unhurried syllables dropped from her lips with no emotion to tint them one way or another. For a moment, the princess did not continue. She let the words linger. Then she turned her head, only her head, and fixed dark eyes upon Simon's face. Caught in her gaze, Simon lost all sense of self and drowned in her presence. Every vestige of a plan that resided in his brain paled into nothingness, leaving him with nothing but a giddy image of the future, *his* future, with her.

"Name the task, my lady."

"Repent of the course you have chosen. It will destroy you, otherwise."

As the words permeated his reverie, Simon fought against them. She couldn't mean what she said. It was not possible. She must not understand what was at stake. Words bubbled up and spilled out of his mouth: "My lady, I don't know what deceit has clouded your eyes, but you do not know what you ask. You can't understand what you would have me do. These words were forced upon you by that foreigner. Listen to *me*, my lady. If you only knew the great plans that I have composed—a reawakening, Princess, glory like this kingdom hasn't seen in a hundred generations! Never again would we fear any other kingdom or principality. We would shine as the pinnacle of civilization. Wise and learned men would make pilgrimage to take counsel with us. If I could only make you see the greatness that lies within your grasp!" He was halfway into a great speech before he realized that she wasn't giving him the proper attention for it.

She looked away from him to gaze into the distance. "I am familiar with your great plans. But if you would befriend me, then forsake my enemies."

"What are you talking about, my lady?"

"I know about the secret you keep in your office. You're an ally of my enemies. I asked you here because I...because it seemed to me that you held me in some esteem. I had to try to persuade you. If you truly want greatness for my people, then prove that you *are* my friend."

"I've tried every conceivable means to prove that, my lady. It is you that are deaf to my voice. You don't understand what is good."

She sighed. "As I said, I had to try. I didn't expect that you would listen, but...remember what I said. Someday, maybe, you'll change your mind. He was right. I feel it. Now the dreams and the emptiness make sense. This should have been. Now it can't ever happen. It is strange to think—but I'm sorry for us both." Her sad, piercing eyes entrapped him again. "It's ruined before it had the chance to begin. Good day, Third Marshal. Goodbye." She walked past him without a backwards glance.

Simon watched her go. High above, a cloud drifted across the sun and cast the land into shadow before the sun blazed through against Simon's scalp again. When he could no longer see the princess, Simon let himself out through the wicket gate. Instead of walking in the orchard, he strolled in the opposite direction to the vegetable garden. A green-striped awning glowed under the renewed sunlight. Simon angled toward it.

The Caretaker matriarch Lucinda sat enthroned like a swollen frog beneath the canopy. At her right hand, a young woman fanned insects away from the matriarch. Ducking beneath the canvas roof, Simon made obeisance to the old woman. "Lady Caretaker! I hope I'm not distracting you from one of your many valuable duties?"

"Not at the moment." She looked him over shrewdly. "How can I advise you?"

"I have just spoken with the princess."

"Have you?"

"Yes, and if I had cause for concern before, I'm doubly concerned now. Surely you have some influence over her. You have served the Keeper house so well for your many years—surely she would have greater respect for your counsel than she appears to have for mine. After all, who am I? But you as a clan matriarch and her mother's right hand…" He let the suggestion hang in the air for a few seconds.

"Please sit," the matriarch replied. "Perhaps you'd like a cup of chilled wine?"

"Thank you, Lady Caretaker. You're very gracious to make the offer." Simon sat beside her, accepted the cup, and tasted its contents. His eyes followed the serving girl as she retreated a few steps for privacy. "Lady Caretaker, I feel sure that you will understand me. This new fellow…I've heard of him. I won't burden you with what I've heard about his past. Such stories are unfit for a civilized woman's ears. He's a savage. I don't know what passed between him and the king, but surely you've already seen how inappropriate it is for such a man to be near the princess without her father to stand between them. I don't like it at all."

"The princess depends upon him greatly."

Simon weighed her tone before making his next remark. "He is a bit high-handed."

"Tell me a thing I haven't learned already," Lucinda retorted. "He had the audacity to tell me how to organize this house—as if I hadn't known my duties before he drew his first breath! All of a sudden, for no reason at all, he insists that nobody can walk alone, not even in the house! I have to pair the maids for work that one of them alone can do perfectly well! If he had his way, I would get half as much done. The house would be a shambles."

"Since he's the princess' favorite, you'll have to obey, of course."

The matriarch snorted. "We shall see."

"You show great spirit, Lady Caretaker. I'm glad that you haven't been cowed…not like some others. I think it's shameful that any loyal subject submits to the rule of a foreigner. I shudder when I think what he would make of this kingdom. Uncivil brute. Between us, Lady Caretaker, it doesn't bode well that he refuses to adapt himself to our customs. Do you know he entered the Council Chamber armed? No civilized man would do that. Before long, he'll be forcing his barbaric customs on us. You wait and see. And the princess is so young. She doesn't have the judgment that someone of your experience would have."

"Royalty will do as it pleases." Lucinda chose to be noncommittal.

"I daresay you're right, but it's our duty to give her the benefit of our greater knowledge. We owe it to her."

The interview was over. Simon rose, handed his cup to the serving girl, and bowed again to the matriarch. "I feel better knowing that you will keep an independent judgment, Lady Caretaker. Sooner or later, the princess will be glad of it, once she tires of this foreigner's arrogance. I bid you good day, Lady Caretaker."

As he crossed the grounds, Simon flagged down a messenger. "Go to Nässey Denei-son and bid him come to my office without delay."

YESTERDAY: FIRST DEATH

A late afternoon sun of astonishing magnitude slanted down upon the lake. Such a brilliant light should have burned, but the lake's altitude stole the heat before it could ease the waters' chill. Just as the waters felt none of the sun's warmth, the young man on the shore felt as if he himself was beyond the reach of the light. In his mind, he cast a pall over everything around him. He stripped his clothes off, folded them, and dove into the numbing lake, but the pristine waters could not cleanse him of himself. In time, he gave up the subterfuge as useless. While he rubbed his shirt like a towel over his cold flesh to dry himself, he prepared for the moment when he would at last be completely truthful with himself.

As gruesome as the act itself had been, the thought that pursued Jarod most relentlessly of all was that he did not know who she was. The violence was nothing to him. For nearly three years now, he had lived with violence. Violence was his bread, the staple of his days. Blood meant little to him now, too. He had seen his own often enough that he no longer feared spilling it, and he had seen the blood of others often enough that it had lost its power to appall him, even if shed by his own hands. Every day, for hours at a stretch, he learned to fight with every weapon created, from his two bare hands to the two-fisted great sword that he alone was strong enough to wield as lightly as another man might wield a foil. In mock battles, in duels, in raids and open combat, he had been forced to prove himself day after day. Blood meant little to him now.

He was eighteen years old. Of all the cruelties in which he was pushed to distinguish himself, he had managed to avoid one until four nights previous. By eighteen, many of his peers had fathered brats by so many different women that the children were treated almost like a farmer's kittens. Women had only slightly more value to them. Captive women had only one value, unless they were clever as well as fortunate enough to win the right sort of attention. Those who would not submit fell into the broadening category of "sport" by which the raiders passed their idle hours. Malin encouraged them, understanding that warriors who turned their boredom against helpless captives were far less likely to turn against his leadership. Jarod knew well enough from Audune that the potential was in him to join his companions. The lust for brute power, for power at any cost, was always there, scantily buried by his waning sense of horror and shame. Audune's coaxing was relentless. Alone in his reluctance, for almost three years Jarod had resisted all of Audune's proddings and the raiders' bullying by increasingly narrow margins…until four nights previous.

She was no one to me. Never caused me loss or harm—Still unable to bring himself around head-on to the thought, he dressed slowly. Once he was stretched out on the sand, he shut his eyes to find the grisly image still painted there in all its lurid colors. It seemed strange to him that he should remember her in that final moment, long after he had retreated from the so-called sport nauseated in spirit. He had no longer been anywhere near, but from across the longhouse, he had seen her face—could still see her face—turn toward him with unseeing eyes that seemed to brighten with relief as death snatched her from her tormentors. *I cannot live like this anymore.*

You must, whispered Audune with a complaisant snigger. *Do you imagine that I would let you give up now? I have use for you yet. Go ahead, though—I give you leave to surrender your name. Give up who you are. It will ease your path. It could even be called an act of mercy. Let Jarod die. You have no use for him any longer. You are that foolish boy no more. Why should his queasy conscience continue to trouble you? Release him. Let him die.*

That suggestion provoked both grief and a sense of liberation in the young man—to lose himself, yes, was wrenching, but never again to carry on this solitary, futile struggle? After three years, the young man at last found the relief outweighing the loss. *Yes. Let him die.* He sat up on the sand. Suddenly he wanted to see his reflection in the water. The eyes that stared back at him were cold, expressionless, revealing nothing of the turmoil he felt. The eyes convinced him. He was lost already; why cling to what could never be? *Let Jarod die.* Aloud, he said the name once more, as if releasing the name from his lips ensured that it would vacate his soul permanently.

"Orlan!" A man poked his head up at the top of the steep path. It was Malin, seeking his protégé. "There you are. Come, we have a chance at Madoc at last— he's left himself open on the south pastures, the idiot. Could be he doesn't know of the landslide yet. Now's the chance we've waited on these months. Come on!" Drawing near, he gave the young man a shrewd look. "Brooding again, are you?"

"No, keiri." Orlan rose with leisurely agility to tower over his master. "I am ready."

∗   ∗   ∗   ∗

The assault on the rahgat of Madoc Alloradim, an old enemy of Malin, went as easily as they could have wished. By the time the household bells clamored their alarm, it was already too late for the rahg to gather his warriors. His mansion was awash with marauders. All that remained was to wait for the rahg's warriors to rush into Malin's hands like so many field mice flushed out of their holes by a deluge. Then an unwelcome fact surfaced: contrary to all information and Malin's hopes, old Madoc had removed his treasury from the house and secreted it somewhere else. Where it hid, he would not say, not even under threat. In response, Malin withdrew in company with his chief warriors to consult as to what was best to be done.

Consult, Orlan realized, was merely a euphemism. Once they had gone out of earshot of the imprisoned rahg and his warriors, Malin outlined a heavy-handed, inelegant plan. In it, he cast Orlan in the role of executioner. One by one, Madoc's warriors would be brought outside and asked the location of their master's treasury. Each man who could not or would not answer the question would then lose his head at Orlan's hand, until either Malin had possession of the treasury or Madoc was utterly bereft of warriors. "I hope," said Malin irritably, "I *hope* it won't become necessary to raze the house in a search. I wanted to keep this house."

Orlan had little to say in response to any of this. He could have told Malin where the treasury was. The paving stones still bore scrapes where narrow chests full of something solid had been dragged out of the house, as if someone had sacrificed stealth for haste. Malin had overlooked this, as he often overlooked the subtler things around him. Orlan could have pointed all this out to Malin. He had two reasons for refraining. First, he knew Malin well enough by now to understand that the man hated being shown a thing he should have noticed on his own, nearly as much as he loved making a show of his *fohral'aku*, the light-ning-vengeance that he had taken as his surname. The other reason had nothing to do with Malin. Orlan was preoccupied by an inward discussion with Audune.

They are no better than cattle. There is not a worthwhile servant among them.

But does that merit death? Orlan asked as a matter of form.

If you are the greatest among them, that is for you to decide. You must begin to make your name great sometime or other. Why not begin now?

As you said, they are no better than cattle. How would that make my name great?

You must begin small. You do not yet have the strength to challenge Malin. Once you have shown your merit as a warrior, worthy servants will come to you. You will build an army of your own, and when you have strength enough, you can seize control of the Thousand Companies. Malin is a fool anyway.

He is, replied the young man noncommittally. Deeper than even this silent conversation, he became aware of a thought. It grew upon him slowly, subtly, without provoking comment from his shepherd. Even as he realized that a deeper level existed within him, he sealed it hastily even from his own knowledge. The shadows of late afternoon were lengthening already. By nightfall, Audune would be at his strongest. If—and it was doubtful that such a thing could happen—*if* Orlan had found a way to conceal something from the persistent giant, noontide was the hour to explore the possibilities of such a discovery. At noontide, particu-larly a sunny noontide, Audune seemed to recede a little from the mortal world that Orlan inhabited. As of yet, Orlan had found no Prince's Tree anywhere in his travels, so he had long had to content himself with the brilliant midday hours to give him any respite from his tiresome immortal tormentor.

"Come, let's put it to practice," Malin was saying with callous enjoyment.

While lesser marauders started the ordeal of corralling their prisoners in ascending order of rank, Orlan wandered off alone. He had a particular prize in mind, and he found it without much trouble. In the armory, there stood a wooden case as wide across as Orlan's forearm, as long as a normal-sized man's height, and a hand's-breadth deep. This case stood against the far wall, as far as possible from the rest of Madoc's collection of weapons and armor, thus marked by the superstitious warriors as special. Orlan opened the case, took out the axe it contained, and studied it briefly. On the broad, heavy blade were inscribed mon-sters with long, scythe-like claws. They were called the Lethek by his own people, and unlike other giants who shepherded individuals for the duration of life, these Lethek shepherded the dead on their way to farther lands. By the inscriptions Orlan knew that he had found his prize. He turned to the case again and opened a small, hard leather pouch that hung above the axe. The mask inside the pouch was known in every land he had visited in the past three years. In Kavahran, for instance, instead of "executioner", the word for a man who wore this mask was called *bringer of death*. Death-bringers wore masks to keep the immortal Lethek from becoming too familiar with their faces. They feared that these ultimate bringers of death might begin to associate the mortal executioner with death so much that they would fail to distinguish between executioner and victim one day.

Orlan knew better than to subscribe to this superstition, but he took the mask anyway. The Lethek were not his concern, but rather the mortals who might see him and know him for who he had been. If Jarod was dead, he reasoned, then let his face die from mortal memory too.

What foolishness are you pondering now? Audune demanded in vexation.

I have made my choice. Content yourself with that and leave me this one small gesture. The world will never see my face again. I have decided.

To his surprise, the malicious shepherd-giant did not quarrel.

LIKE A WAVE TOSSED

Ivy inspected the sitting room absently, unable to recall what the messenger had interrupted. Her gaze fell upon a pair of her husband's boots, which reminded her. "Guenna! Guenna, come here, please."

A young woman came trotting from the kitchen. "Aye, zahn? What can I do for you?"

"Do you remember that I told you we can't leave these here in the middle of the room? If they were even clean, that wouldn't be so bad, but look at the dirt on them." Ivy reached down to pick up the boots, only to have them snatched away by the young maid.

"No, zahn, they're not fit for you to pick up. I shall tidy them. Forgive me."

Ivy watched her go. In any other circumstances, it would have been a pleasure to have such assiduous house help, but Guenna and her accomplice Ilan went at their work with such zeal that it was quite exhausting. They did not know where anything belonged, but as soon as she pointed out a need, they nearly fought over the right to correct the oversight. Above all, they would not suffer her to do any work. Ivy had had to scold Guenna once already in order to gain access to her own kitchen. Guenna seemed to believe that Ivy was too grand a lady to set foot in a room dedicated to labor. Ivy sighed. *And I thought house help made things easier...* She didn't truly believe that her husband had given her these servants out of generosity. They watched her so closely that she could hardly cross from one end of the apartment to another without their knowledge. Ivy felt fairly sure that they reported her actions to him.

Still, there were advantages to the extra help. One of the benefits was an increased amount of time spent with her mother. Riana still mourned, but slowly she was growing calmer about her outpourings of grief. Ivy had never seen her mother so emotional. It came as a mild shock to find she had been wrong about her mother and Denei. All her life, Ivy had believed that her mother had married Denei to provide for Brigid, Perrin, and Ivy after their natural father had died in battle. She never dreamed that such a passionate attachment existed between the two. Everyone knew they had been fond of each other, but somehow, Ivy had always assumed the attachment was stronger on Denei's side. Riana's collapse corrected her harshly in this assumption. For days, Riana had kept to her bed and wept to see anyone who reminded her of her late husband. But in the last few days, she had finally reached a point where she spoke of him freely. Ivy had broached the subject of this misconception gently. "It's silly, I know, but…I never knew you loved him this entirely."

Her mother's face had saddened, but she laughed at the same time. "No. It made him ill at ease whenever I showed it publicly. He wasn't that sort of man. Every morning before I left this room, I had to remind myself that I couldn't go about flaunting my feelings. It was my secret, and I treasured it. Oh, Ivy, I love him so." They cried together a little while. When it came time for Ivy to go to her own home, however, she was thoughtful. *How little we know each other,* she kept thinking. For instance, nobody knew that, if she kept herself very busy, Ivy could ignore certain things. If she busied herself with the housekeeping or Riana's care, she could almost forget that she had a husband. Every time her mother broke down weeping, Ivy had to leave the room before the guilt overwhelmed her. The only way to function was to forget that she was married at all. It did little good. Nothing helped her escape the knowledge that the elderly seer had shared with her.

Even now, as she prepared to leave for Takra to keep her appointment with Nässey, Ivy was still thinking more of her husband than anyone else. Ivy knew why Nässey wanted to see her. He wanted to try to persuade her again. He thought she would be safer if she broke from her husband altogether. Nässey did not understand. He thought it a simple, clear-cut decision to make, but Ivy knew better. The elderly seer had made it quite clear that, if Ivy didn't gather intelligence against the foreigner, then there was no way they could be rid of him. Three times now, Nekhral had called for her in the night, in dreams, summoning her to meet with him in Nässey's office at Takra House. Once, Nässey had been away; once, he had come in to find her there, and the seer had mysteriously disappeared; the third time, Nässey had been there when she arrived. Ivy and her brother had quarreled, so Ivy had gone home without meeting with the seer.

Nässey had become very strange of late. He seemed moody and displeased whenever he saw her. His argument was always the same: her husband was dangerous, and Ivy should leave him. In fact, it seemed almost superfluous to think of leaving a man who turned up so rarely at home. Ivy began to think he wanted nothing to do with her anymore. She sometimes caught herself wavering on the edge of absurd jealousy, wondering if he were keeping company with some other woman after all the trouble she was expending for his contentment. Then she would see him again, just at a distance. One sighting was enough to draw out memories of his vile secret, putting Ivy back where she had started, fighting to keep her hatred of the man hidden.

Outside, she looked up at the brazen sky and wished it would rain. Every passing carriage kicked up clouds of dust, until she had to cover her mouth and nose with a handkerchief so she could breathe. She saw a number of people she knew. Most of them greeted her politely, but some gave her odd looks and then pretended they had not seen her. She knew why. News of her marriage had spread. Those who felt that her husband had no right to be there accorded her the same treatment. Ivy lifted her head a little higher, but inside she knew that they were justified. Since she had backed him socially, she now bore a measure of his stigma. Ivy tried not to acknowledge her fear that others might be aware of his true nature and believe that she approved of it because she had married him.

It had been several days since her last visit to Selena. At the door of Takra House, Ivy greeted the guard she knew by sight. "Good afternoon to you, Danyel. How is your sister?"

"She's inside, ma'am," the man said. "Off duty today. She's got all the luck."

Ivy returned his smile. "While you drew the short straw and landed with door duty?"

"Somebody has to, I suppose."

To the other guard, Ivy said, "I don't know *you* yet. Are you one of Maia's new guards?"

"Yes, ma'am. My name is Ian. Pleased to make your acquaintance."

"What does your father's name happen to be? I think I could almost guess. Marius?"

"Yes, ma'am," the young man said, impressed. "How did you know?"

"I grew up in the corner of my father's office, Ian. Your father used to come by quite often when he was still active. You have his nose." She smiled at him.

"Well, Ian, I'm pleased to make your acquaintance as well. Good day to you both."

They bid her a good day and let her pass. Ivy entered the lofty front hall, climbed the steps, and then hesitated. She wanted very much to turn left and visit Selena in the private quarters, since they had not had one of their chats for so long. On the other hand, she knew that her brother measured his time very precisely, and she had promised to meet with him within the hour. That hour was halfway used up already. If she tarried at all, Nässey might assume that she changed her mind and go off on his own business. Even though she knew it would probably lead to nothing more than another fruitless argument, she did not want to give up this chance to spend time with her brother. Ivy gave up the left-hand door with a small, regretful sigh and turned right, heading into the public wing of Takra House.

When she arrived, the door was ajar. Nässey reclined in his chair with his feet stretched out in front of him and his head tipped back against the wall. He did not move when she entered. "Shut the door, Ivy, please?"

That surprised her. He normally paid no heed to the state of the door. She obliged him in his request and sat down, waiting for him to begin.

"Do you ever think of Jarod anymore?" he asked abruptly.

Ivy's eyes flew open. She stared in wonderment. "Why?"

"I was thinking of him earlier. Remember the time he and I got into that argument over Father?" He breathed a weary sigh. "I was a young imbecile back then, thinking I knew it all."

"I don't remember. Why did you argue?"

"Oh, it was a foolish academic debate…like so many I've embroiled myself in these past few years," Nässey added bitterly. "I was convinced that a warrior had to be something more than a good fighter. I was convinced he had no worth unless he contributed something positive to the world in the form of scholarship or wise laws, or even something tangible like prosperity. Colin was the one who first brought Father's name into the argument. He said I couldn't apply my reasoning to Father because Father was the quintessential old-fashioned warrior and yet he was still considered a model citizen and a hero. I belittled Father's accomplishments because they didn't suit my notions of 'contributing something positive.' Jarod…Jarod got so angry with me. That's when it turned into a real quarrel and not just an academic debate. I could never get the best of him in a fight anyway. I should have known better than to try. What got me then, and what got me thinking about it again today, was the ending, when Jarod went all quiet for a moment. I thought I'd finally won, but he waited until he was almost out the door when he fired his parting shot: 'He contributed *you* to the world and made space for you to grow up and learn in peace, until you could come to this moment in time and scoff at him and say he's done nothing of merit. I suppose *that* doesn't count.' I can hear the words almost perfectly in my head. I've never been able to forget them, not after all these years." He shut his eyes and rubbed his face with the back of his wrist. "Goodness knows I've tried."

Troubled by her brother's lackluster voice, Ivy asked, "What's wrong?"

"Ivy, I want you to know that, no matter what else may be true about me, I always was very fond of you. You're the dearest friend I've ever had."

"Don't frighten me like this."

His smile turned bitter. "I promise I will never try to frighten you again, Ivy. But you must promise me one thing in return."

"Anything, Nässey."

"You must never come here again to seek me out. You must stay as far from this place as you can. Even if your best friend herself says I've asked to see you, you mustn't come back. Leave me to myself."

"Nässey, you can't say that! Why did you say that?"

"Go, Ivy. Go home to your husband. Do what you can for him. He'll need you." When it became clear that Ivy meant to stay, Nässey rose from his desk and firmly escorted her to the hall. "Remember, Ivy—go. Stay as far from here as possible." With that, he shut the door.

Ivy was too shocked to give way to tears immediately. As she was leaving the office, she heard a soft, dull sound. The entire palace seemed deserted around her. Everything was silent except for that sound that repeated itself as she listened. Ivy could not identify it. She held her breath to listen more intently, but she only heard her own pulse throbbing in her head. At the end of the cross-corridor, a soft buttery light emerged from the door of the third marshal's office. Someone had left the door ajar. It was nothing like candlelight or lamplight; rather, it seemed alive in its own right. She crept nearer to see what it was.

This office too was empty. On the edge of the desk sat Nekhral's magical pendant. Ivy looked around to see if the old man was somewhere nearby, but the silence held true. She was alone. A few more steps carried her to the desk, where she gazed down at the magical stone with bated breath, making sure to keep her hands firmly clasped behind her back. The light sprang from the depths of the stone, dancing in curious patterns on the furniture and walls all around it. It was amazing, like nothing Ivy had ever seen before. Drawn to the beautiful show of light, she bent closer and peered into it. There was meaning in the patterns that the light cast everywhere—of that, Ivy was sure. *If I could only make sense of it,* she found herself thinking. Longings surged to the forefront of her thoughts as if enticed by the light. An image came to mind: her stepfather Denei, the person she most longed to see again. Ivy gasped, hardly able to believe what she saw next.

The magical stone began to change shape. First it rounded into a ball, which elongated into a squarish lump. Features emerged from the oval. When the process was done, Ivy gazed upon a perfect replica of her stepfather's face. The image opened its eyes. "Who called to me?" It was Denei's own voice. He looked around and saw Ivy. "Oh. Ivy, what's wrong? Why do you look so downcast? I'm listening."

The sound of those familiar words brought tears to Ivy's eyes. Before she realized it, she was pouring out everything to her stepfather. She told him of the uncertainties she suffered, of the things Nässey and the seer had told her about her husband, of the things she had witnessed with her own eyes that had proven the evidence against her husband. Then she talked of missing Denei, and of mundane family things: Momma's grief, Brigid's steadfast help, Nässey's inexplicable rejection, and Perrin's refusal to speak with them because Giles had taken the king's part and gone away to exile with him. As she spoke, she felt the burden lessening steadily.

"Now, now," said Poppa Denei gruffly, "don't worry. I'm sorry I got you into this trouble, but take heart. Things have a way of straightening on their own."

"But Poppa, he...he's the reason you're dead. I saw it! The seer told me so."

"I can't say one way or another. I don't know if he did or not. It happened too quickly. If he did—all the same, it was a mercy, Ivy. I would have sickened and died soon enough. Better to go in battle than to linger on, a useless wreck of a man. You must try to get past that, Ivy. It's not important. It's true that I didn't know everything about Orlan's past, but as long as you keep an eye on him, this seer you spoke of will help put things right again. If you're ever troubled by anything he does, you should tell him. You know, I was looking for a seer to help Colin. It's too bad I didn't come across this Nekhral in time."

Ivy found a little smile that she could give. "Thanks, Poppa. I really have missed you so."

"How is Owen these days?"

"I haven't seen him for a while. He went into seclusion for you, Poppa."

"You ought to go visit him. This mourning business is all well in its place, but he mustn't let it get in the way of his duties. He belongs here, in Takra House." The image yawned. "I grow weary, my dear. I had forgotten what a burden time can be. I must go now, and so must you. Look after your mother and Owen for me."

"I will. I love you, Poppa."

"There now," he said, flustered. "Go on with you." Slowly, the stone lost its shape and returned to the flat disc that it had been when Ivy had first entered. Its light dimmed slowly until all that remained was a pinpoint of yellow at the center of the stone.

Ivy left the office in pensive silence. In her preoccupation, she wandered all the way down to the dining hall by force of habit. Two women's voices recalled her from her thoughts.

"I know it makes work a little more difficult, but there's reason for caution," Selena said.

"With all due respect, my lady, it makes work well nigh impossible."

"Lady Caretaker, I beg to differ. It hasn't made your work more difficult because you haven't begun to obey the rule. You don't know what changes it might make until you try first!"

"I have no wish to offend," replied Lucinda in the tone of voice that usually indicates the opposite of what is said, "but I know my own business a good deal better than you possibly could, Lady Selena. I've been running the king's household twice as long as you've been alive. I will be the one to say what rules the servants shall follow. Now, if you'll pardon me, I have work to do. Good day." She heaved herself up from her chair and toddled toward Ivy. "Good day, Miss Ivy."

Ivy had to step aside to give the Caretaker woman room to pass. "Good day," she echoed as a formality. Her sympathy had already gone out to Selena, who had not bothered to wait for the older woman to leave before she nested her head on her folded arms. Ivy went to her best friend at once. "Oh, Selena, what's going on? I've never heard her so rude before."

"Colin isn't here to support me," Selena said in a tiny voice, "so she doesn't feel she needs to listen to a word I say."

One arm around Selena's shoulders, Ivy tried to give her some comfort. "But Colin should be coming back soon, shouldn't he?"

"I don't know. He never said. Have you heard anything about his return?"

"Me? I've heard nothing. Why? Did you expect him to send word to me and not to you?"

Selena sat up a little straighter, wiping at her eyes. "No, but I'd hoped that maybe—maybe your husband might have said something to you. I only see him sometimes when he comes to talk with Maia. Since you see him more often...but I suppose he wouldn't. Not unless things had improved."

"What do you mean by that?"

"Colin had to leave because his life was in danger, Ivy. Someone tried to kill him."

Ivy's heart leaped in fear, connecting these words automatically with her husband. She squeezed her eyes tightly shut to block out the images that the stone had shown her as they rose up to remind her. To cover the moment, she said, "I'm sure he'll come back soon. In the meanwhile, if Nana Lucinda *has* decided to be difficult, why don't you have Maia talk to her? She can't brush Maia off so easily."

"I hate to trouble poor Maia with something as lowly as housekeeping affairs, Ivy. She has more than enough to keep her occupied. You haven't heard yet? The Pamirsi want to appoint a regent. They say that Maia is too young and inexperienced. The worst of it is, they're putting forward that horrid woman Mearah, Berhus' sister, as the regent!"

Ivy made a face. "Not Mearah."

"None other. She's waited a long time to get into the palace. If she couldn't snare Colin for herself, I suppose she thinks it's second best if she takes my place as Maia's mother! She has done her best to humiliate me all these years, always doing it so that no one but I knew about it, over and over again. Now she's found the perfect way. With Colin gone, no one will listen to me. I cannot bear to think of that woman here in this house, triumphing over me day after day!"

"You're Maia's mother! They can't just appoint someone without consulting you first."

"Legally," Selena answered with a turbulent laugh, "since it concerns the crown, they can do as they please. I have no say in the matter at all because I'm not of the ancient blood."

Ivy grasped her best friend's hands between her own and shook her lightly. "See here, this will never do. I tell you what: I'll go talk to Uncle Owen for you, and he'll talk with the patriarchs about this. Maia doesn't need a guardian or a regent or whatever they call it, not so long as she has you to counsel her. It's just that old Pamirsi-Massifi mess stirring itself up again, nothing more. Uncle Owen will put them to rights. You'll see."

With brighter eyes, Selena tightened her hold on Ivy's hands. Her voice trembled with hope. "Yes, *you* can go see him! I hadn't thought of that. Please talk with him. I don't even know if he knows what's going on yet."

There seemed no further reason to stay, not when Selena needed the message sent as soon as possible. Ivy kissed her friend on the cheek and left her with a few more encouraging words. The sky outside was still as cloudless and unforgiving as before, but with the sun at a lower angle, there were more shadows to offer relief from the heat. Her husband's carriage sat conspicuously outside the palace door, the horses stomping their hooves impatiently. Ilan hopped down from his seat to help Ivy into the carriage. "Where do you wish to go, my lady?"

"Doran and Phoebe's cottage." She saw his look of incomprehension and said, "The first marshal's house." He understood that direction, to her relief. The carriage rolled off with Ivy leaning her head against the cushions while she rested one hand on the open window sill to catch the breeze caused by their brisk progress.

Ilan deposited Ivy just at the cottage fence, where one of the guards halted her with a kindly salute. "Afternoon, Miss. Haven't seen you for a time, have we?"

"I've been very busy, I'm sorry to say," she replied. "How are you, Wren?"

"Keeping busy myself. Who did you come to see today?"

"Uncle Owen, if he's taking visitors. I have a message to give him from Selena."

"I haven't heard that he's turning folk away. Mundy?" the lean guard called out, turning his head slightly toward the house. "Mundy, do you know, is Lord Sakiry taking visitors today? Miss Ivy wants to see him."

"Far as I know. Afternoon, Miss Ivy."

Ivy couldn't help a little frown of confusion. "What are you doing all the way out here, Mundy? I don't understand."

"Reassigned to his lordship's guard. 'Tisn't all bad, Miss Ivy. I get more fresh air these days. Too bad the weather's turned scorching on us, isn't it?"

"Yes," she said absently. "Isn't it? Thank you, Wren." She passed him without taking much note of his polite bow. The other man, Mundy, opened the door for her as she climbed the front steps of the cottage.

Inside, the air was stuffy but bearable. No one was in the sitting room, so Ivy wandered to the kitchen in search of Phoebe. What she found was quite unexpected. She had hardly set foot in the doorway when Phoebe appeared at her side, pulling her into a corner and hushing her. "Just watch first. Poor Laena! She doesn't know what to do." When Ivy turned around, she understood a little better. There stood her uncle Owen, patriarch of the Sakiry clan, prince of the ancient royal blood, doggedly scrubbing a heavy ceramic baking dish. To one side, the Caretaker woman who helped Phoebe with housekeeping hovered at his elbow with an expression of mingled dismay and bewilderment. "Why is he doing that?" Ivy whispered to Phoebe.

"I haven't the least idea, but he's bound to do it. He isn't very good at it yet, but then, he's only been at it for three days. He's sure to improve with a little practice. It *is* rather funny, watching Laena try to persuade him to stop. I'm not sure if she's worried for his dignity, or if she thinks he'll break too many dishes."

"Phoebe," said Owen with a laugh, "how you do go on as if I were deaf! How are you, Ivy? Getting along nicely?" He dried his hands. "There you go, Laena. I'll keep out of your hair for the rest of the day, just to make it up to you. Thank you for being so patient with a daft old man. Is there any ice left? It's perfect weather for your wonderful fruit ices. Don't you agree, Ivy? We'll get out of your way and let you get on with it, then. Will you take my arm, Ivy? We'll sit down and have our chat. Can I assume that's why you've come?"

Once they were seated and Owen gave out a hearty sigh of relief, Ivy explained, "I was just up at Takra talking to Selena, and she tells me that the Council has some stupid notion of appointing a regent for Maia. Worse than that, Mearah Pamirsi has put herself up for the job. You know she's always hated Selena for stealing Colin away from her—as if Colin would have married such a horrid girl. She was horrid then, and she's worse now."

"Ah, I remember Mearah back then. She was a lot closer to winning Colin in her own mind than she was in reality. Poor Kohanan. I remember the day old Carthus Pamirsi came around with the idea. The last thing Kohanan wanted was to further annoy Carthus, so he said very little about the matter, just nodded and promised to discuss it with Colin. Just to be fair, you see. But Colin had been to his father's office the night before, seeking his blessing for a match with your friend. The timing was more than a bit awkward, I'll tell you. Rumor had it that Mearah had a terrible fit, which gave old Carthus a terrible bout of indigestion. Some said he died just to get away from her yowling."

Ivy hid a giggle behind her hand. "I heard that, too. But you can see how it would never work, her acting as Maia's guardian. Even if she were bearable, she doesn't know anything more about ruling than Selena does. She couldn't advise Maia any better than Selena could."

"It has nothing to do with advising and everything to do with controlling, my dear Ivy. Berhus is probably so nervous with all the changes that he wants to see that someone in the palace will look after his interests. Who better than his own sister? Besides, it would get her out of his house at long last. Can't say that I entirely blame him for wanting to be rid of her, but you're right. It just won't do. Not for an instant. I won't countenance it."

"If you talk to them, they can't go through with it."

Owen looked strangely discomfited at that. He fidgeted a while with his fingers on his knees before he would answer. "It isn't so easy, Ivy. If they won't come see me, then there's very little I can do about it. Oh, I can send messengers, but it's easy enough for them to pretend not to be at home, isn't it?"

"But why can't you see them yourself?"

"Didn't he tell you?" Owen said. "I'm confined to quarters. I *can't* go visiting."

Quietly, in her most composed voice, Ivy asked, "But why, Uncle?"

Owen gave her a disheartened look. "I made a rather bad mistake, my dear girl. This is my penalty, you might say." Then he brightened. "Here's a thought, though: when you see your husband, ask him if he has an hour to spare for me. Sometime tonight would be best, but tomorrow morning would do in a pinch. I only just had an idea that might do, but I need his cooperation for it to work. Will you do that for me?"

It took all of Ivy's self-control to speak evenly, but she did. "Yes, Uncle, of course I will if you want me to, but isn't there something *I* can do to help? I hate to bother him when he has so many duties already." The interruption that Laena provided by bringing in the ices came at an opportune moment for Ivy. While she waited for the stir to die down again, she had time to collect herself. "I think I'll take an hour this afternoon to see if Russa is home. She may listen to me herself if I tell her how unsuitable this would be. If I can reach her, she might talk to Berhus about what you said, and then maybe we won't need to trouble with— with my h-husband."

"Perhaps." Oblivious to the slight stutter, Owen smiled in satisfaction. "I hope so. There's not much time to spare. Berhus will try to push this regent nonsense through quickly so no one has time to quarrel with him over it. How is your ice, Ivy? I do like Laena's lemon ices best, but the berries are a nice touch, too. With this weather, we won't have these luxuries for much longer. I don't understand it. Something has definitely gone awry with the weather. I don't remember the heat getting this bad before midsummer in, oh, I don't know how many years. Perhaps as far back as the year of the fires. I hope we get some rain soon. The last thing we need is another round of wildfires."

"Yes." Ivy dallied with the last blob of rosy red ice, watching it melt. "Well— the day is getting on. I need to be on my way. It was good to talk with you, Uncle."

"You didn't come by yourself, did you?"

"I took the carriage here," she said again, slowly. "It's perfectly all right, Uncle. Ilan, our manservant, he follows me everywhere." When she put the empty cup down, it rattled against the table because her hand was so unsteady. "It was good to talk with you. You aren't too downcast these days, are you?"

"I'm managing fairly well. If anyone asks, you may say so. The question is, are *you?* You don't look quite yourself today. Perhaps you should stop and see Doran."

That's the second time, Ivy thought with a trace of irritation. *Why do they think Doran can do anything to help me?* But she knew better than to loose her irritation. She gave her uncle a polite smile. "That's all right, Uncle. I'm sure it's nothing more than this awful heat. It throws everyone just a little off, I'm sure. Good day, Uncle."

In the attempt to be positive, Ivy thought to herself, *Well, it is nice to have this carriage at my disposal. It would have taken some time to walk there and back in this heat.* She gazed outside at the many pedestrians trudging alongside the road to Carthae. Business continued despite the unrest. Most of those afoot carried heavy loads to market in the Pamirsi sister city. Ivy felt sorry for them. When she arrived at the Pamirsi patriarchal mansion, Ivy was dismayed to find Berhus' sister Mearah also in attendance upon Russa. Given the choice, she would have preferred to carry produce on the road to Carthae than hold a conversation of half a dozen words with Mearah, but there was nothing to do but smile and make the best of it.

Russa gave Ivy a brief look of apology, but said nothing one way or the other. Instead, she gestured toward the window overlooking the garden. "This wretched heat is doing terrible things to my garden. If it keeps up like this, I won't have a single plant left alive."

"I do so look forward to the rain," Ivy replied. "I don't remember when it last rained."

An awkward moment interposed itself. Mearah had a poisonous gleam in her eye when she looked at Ivy, and Russa seemed downright eager to keep the two from conversing together. She said to Ivy, "So! You're doing well in an awkward spot, aren't you, you poor thing. I can't imagine why you should go to so much trouble for that absolutely bizarre man. I should think having to marry him would be more than enough. I declare, that mask gives me a cold chill. I don't know how you stand it."

"You get used to things, Russa."

"Yes, but aren't you terrified of him? His reputation, my dear!" Russa fanned herself.

Mearah interjected, "I'm sure that's the very thing that makes it bearable, dear sister. Surely you know our Ivy has always had a taste for the seamy underside of society."

Caught, Russa said only, "I'm sure I know nothing of the sort. Well, Ivy, if you say he isn't so bad, I have to believe you. Believe me," she said in a tone meant to elicit confidences, "I still pity you. He can't be at all easy to live with."

"Actually, I rarely see him. He's very busy."

"And so are you," Russa finished for her. "I see! I suppose that makes it easier. Of course, there's no comparing him with my dear Berhus, but I do know what you mean by that. If my dear Berhus is in one of his tempers, there's simply nothing I can do but pursue my own schedule and let him follow his, and hope that he improves on his own. I suppose men are like that. You do keep busy, I suppose?" Russa added desperately, trying to change the subject.

Ivy could see why: Mearah, always a spinster, was growing red-faced at this talk of husbands and how they must be handled. *That must be a touchy subject indeed,* she thought, *at least in this household.* "Yes. I have all my former pursuits, and now I have a small household to run. If my sister Brigid weren't here looking after Mother, I don't know what I would do."

"Let's not forget—you must be quite indispensable to your husband," Mearah purred. "It was a smart match for him, no doubt. I'm sure he couldn't have found anyone with more experience at introducing questionable people into the royal court. You're quite proficient at it after all these years…no doubt."

Russa interrupted almost passionately, "There's no one quite like our Ivy at soothing ruffled personalities. He's most fortunate to have you, dear Ivy, and I hope he realizes it."

"I'm sure a man of his sort was also glad to get a woman of your…experience," Mearah added like a shot. "Tell me, Ivy, for I've always been curious to know: how long did you spend under the whores' tutelage before you felt confident in taking your newfound skills to Takra?"

Ivy felt the blood drain from her face. She did not bother to look at Russa. The vengeful glee in Mearah's eyes was too plain to be smoothed over by any means. Ivy summoned her self-control. "Perhaps it would be just as wise to just say what I came to say, if that is all the civility I have to expect here. I have just been to visit my uncle Lord Sakiry, and he will be sending a messenger to the Council tomorrow at their next meeting. He will not have anyone as regent, but least of all you, Mearah. He will see you blocked at all costs. I thought I would put you on your guard, Russa," she said to the patriarch's wife, "to warn Berhus not to make a public spectacle of himself by offering up such an absurd suggestion ever again." She left the two women there in the salon without waiting for anyone to escort her to the door.

Outside in the carriage, she put her head in her hands to cry, but found no tears within herself. By the time she crossed the threshold of King's City, Ivy had had a peculiar idea. *I am free now.* For too many years, she had sought diligently to establish herself as immaculately, irreproachably respectable in the eyes of the high society around her. At first she had done it for her best friend Selie's sake, to facilitate her acceptance as the crown prince's bride. But now, hearing the accusation openly on the Pamirsi woman's lips, Ivy realized that quest for supreme decorum was over. If she were rumored to be spending time in disreputable quarters, it would hurt no one. Certainly it would do no extra damage to her husband, whose disregard for his own reputation was already established. She opened the grate to speak to Ilan. "Please turn at the next street." She gave him directions to Eva's old haunts. Then she settled back in her seat with a pleasant and rare sensation of freedom. *I will at last know what happened to my friend. Maybe I can find out what became of Alanah and find a way to help her too.*

They arrived at the abandoned tailor's shop and its rickety stairs. Ivy climbed up and tapped at the door with more confidence this time. The same abrupt voice answered. "Who's there? What do you want?"

"Maybe you'll remember me," Ivy said. "I came by some time ago looking for Eva, and you told me that she…she died. I had wondered if you could tell me what became of the little girl who lived here, too—her name was Alanah. Do you know where she is?"

"Why do you want to know?"

Ivy persevered. "Because I was very fond of her aunt, and if she's in need of help, I'm in a position to help her again. Please, won't you tell me where she is?" She was relieved to see the door come open a hand's-breadth. "I would take it as a kindness."

"I recall you." The woman who looked out at Ivy was younger than she sounded. She was probably even younger than she looked, but the hardships of her life had left indelible marks on her features, making her look at least thirty. "You're the lady who used to come calling. You gave us the money. Then you never came back." Her suspicion was slow to fade away. "What brings you around after all this time, then? Why should you want anything to do with me?"

"You—*you're* Alanah!" Ivy took a closer look. "Yes…I suppose…I can see it now that you've come into the light a little more. I knew you'd be grown. I just didn't expect…"

"Didn't expect I'd grown this much? That I'd look like a hag before I was twenty?" Alanah laughed with surprising little bitterness. "That's the way of women on this street, milady. Younglings, they don't last long here. One way or t'other, they don't last long."

"May I come in?"

"I don't recommend it, but you're free to come if you like."

It looked nothing like Ivy remembered it. There were still two rooms, neither one more than four paces across. All the furniture, what little there had been, was gone. All that remained was a battered copper brazier in the first room for cooking and heat, and two pallets against the near wall of the second room. One of these pallets was occupied by a frail, withered old woman. She lay still until she heard their voices. Then she burst into a fit of cursing.

"Shut up," Alanah said without venom. "We've company. Mind your tongue."

"Company, you say?"

When Ivy came near enough to see the old woman's face, she got a pair of unpleasant shocks. The first was the mere sight of her—the front teeth missing, the pus sealing one of her eyes shut, and the crabbed hands scratching at flea bites incessantly. Then came the second shock: Ivy knew the woman's name. "Silla!" she exclaimed.

"Oh, 'tis you? Aye, I recall you, general's daughter." Silla flopped back onto her pallet with a peal of hysterical laughter. "I recall, I recall, I recall—" The invalid, between fits of coughing, lapsed back into her barely intelligible swearing.

Alanah took Ivy by the wrist and led her into the other room. Once she had pulled the door shut on its one remaining hinge, she said, "I'm sorry about that, milady. I'm sorry you had to see that. I did warn you, didn't I? She's like that all the time these days. Just keeps sinking lower and lower."

The two sat down on the floor together. Ivy looked around the room. Despite its obvious poverty, the room was clean. "Eva was always particular about having the floor swept."

"That she was, milady. I suppose you want to know what happened."

"If it doesn't hurt you too badly to tell me, yes."

"Doesn't hurt. Not so much anymore. See, it was the money you gave her. She took good care of it, like she always did. She always told me she meant to see me put in school like a decent girl, so I could learn my letters and then a respectable trade. That was what did her, though. The money. I started school like she wanted, but Silla came to hear of it after not very long, and she knew school meant extra money. I figure she was drunk one night and told some of her friends, and they followed Eva home from her job one night." Alanah drew a deep breath and looked around the room. "I was there, in the corner, with my supper. Aunt Eva just finished listening to me prattle on about my school work when they came beating on the door. She said not to talk to them, that she'd handle them herself. Two men there was, I didn't know their names, and they pushed the door open soon as she answered it. They…They forced her to tell them where the money was hid, and they took it. Took it all. On their way out, Eva was following them, begging that they leave just a little of it for my suppers, and out on the stairs, one of them pushed her over. She was gone before I got to the bottom of the steps."

"Oh, Alanah, dear girl," Ivy breathed, "I'm terribly, terribly sorry."

"So'm I. I didn't have anything to do but look out Silla and stay with her. Except now she's staying with me, now she's sickly."

"You're a good daughter—better than she deserves. I admire you. Even with all you've been through, you still haven't given up. I know people with money to spare who wouldn't have shown such kindness to someone who deserves it so little."

Alanah gave her an encouraging smile. "You've only yourself to thank for that, milady. I never forgot the way you came down to visit us, and you the general's daughter and all. I never forgot what you were like. I thought, well, Allie, you couldn't do better than imitate such a fine lady!" She laughed as Ivy blushed. "I tell you, it kept me when nothing seemed better than giving up, that's for certain. I'd just remember you, and how Aunt Eva always said, 'You look at Miss Ivy, little thing. You look at her real good. Someday, if you work hard enough, maybe you'll spend your days among ladies like her, 'stead of down here in the gutters.' I never forgot."

"I'm glad I came back, Alanah. Truly, you can't imagine. Tell me what you need."

"I don't want to beg anything off you, milady. Really. We're doing all right."

"There will be no more of that. You must call me Ivy like Eva always used to, and tell me truly what I can do to help. Everybody needs help now and then. Even I do."

"Do you really?"

Ivy nodded. She began to recount, in a vague way, her newest conundrum about the generalship controversy and Mearah Pamirsi's bid for the regency. Alanah followed the tale with an avidness that betrayed her lack of entertainment in everyday life. "No, did she?" the young woman gasped when she heard of Mearah's rudeness. "I tell you what, if I had her money and fine clothes, I could find a better way to use my tongue than spittin' in folks' eyes."

"I know you'd make the best use of her good fortune," Ivy laughed. "I only wish *she* would. Now tell me, what can I do to help out?"

Alanah gave in with a rueful smile. "Truth is, I had to give out the last of this week's pay for powders to get rid of Silla's fleas. There's not a morsel in the house, not even tea. If I'd had more money, that would've gone to medicines. You saw how she's picked up some infection somewhere again." Despite her protests, Alanah looked greatly relieved to be confiding this to another soul. "I don't know where I'd get enough money to get her a healer. She can't walk upright anymore without falling headlong. She creeps out on her hands and knees, and I'm forever having to catch and stop her before she falls to her death on the steps."

"Let's make a list," Ivy suggested. "What do you need from the market? Tea, you said; I know that fresh produce is getting a little harder to come by, but I'll see what I can scrounge up." She coaxed a few more items from the girl. Then she said, "On my way back, I'll stop and see a healer I know. We'll see if we can't persuade someone to come here and look at your mother instead of taking her out. If we can't, then you'll just have to take her in my carriage. There, now!" She reached out a hand to wipe away the huge tear that rolled down Alanah's cheek. "I'm only sorry I didn't come sooner."

"It's like a good dream," the girl whispered. "I'm scared I'll wake up."

"I'll be back soon. You just rest easy for a bit."

Ivy headed directly for the market square to buy food. Once she had loaded her purchases into the carriage, she went to the main infirmary in search of Doran, reasoning that he could suggest a suitable healer to send to Alanah's mother. She arrived at the infirmary during a busy hour, however. The main room with its twenty cubicles was almost full, and there was no one at the door to direct newcomers; every staff member appeared to be occupied with some patient or other. Ivy came a little farther into the main room and saw at once the reason for the greater-than-average chaos. Most of the cubicles' occupants were soldiers, and the man from the front desk was one of several trying to hold two of the injured soldiers apart from each other. Doran himself was in the midst of the skirmish, shouting down the two combatants. "You will *not* behave in this manner in my infirmary," he bellowed. Ivy had never heard him so upset. "If you cannot control your tempers, I'll have you both tossed out without treatment. Now sit back down if you know what's good for you!"

One of them wiped a hand under his bleeding nose, panting for breath but visibly trying to calm himself. "As you say, Chief Healer. I'll do my best so long as *he* doesn't start anything again." When he sat down, he braced his side with his arm as if it pained him to breathe deeply.

"I can wait," the other panted also, "until we're outside, I guess."

As orderlies led the combatant patients into their cubicles again, Doran caught sight of Ivy in the doorway. He ran his hands over his unruly sandy hair. "Afternoon, Miss Ivy. I'm sorry you had to come in just then. Did you want to see someone in particular?"

"You, of course. But if you're busy—"

"No, no, it'll do me good to get away from this for a bit. Why don't we go up to my office?" Without waiting for her response, he led her up the stairs to his office and seated her in a comfortable leather and wood chair opposite his desk. He sank down into his own chair and ran his hands over his hair again, clearly still distraught. "I hate scenes like that one. They *will* fight, and there's precious little we can do to stop them. But enough of that. What did you need, Ivy?"

She explained her mission to him and asked his advice. While she waited for him to consider Silla's case, she looked around at his office. The only jarring note among all the medical writings and sketched diagrams was a rack of armor that reminded her suddenly of his other roles as first marshal and chief field healer. She looked long at the armor. *Doran was there. He must have seen something.*

"It's hard to say," Doran said abruptly, "not having seen the patient myself." His eyes brightened at his next thought. "Why don't I come back with you? I'll have a look at her, and then I can give the girl specific directions on the treatment. Yes, I think that'll be the best way to go about it."

"I didn't mean for you to interrupt your schedule and come in person, Doran."

"Believe me, it's for the best. I need to get out of here before the next skirmish. I don't know if I could take another scene like that last one—not today. We've had a total of four so far, and the afternoon isn't half done."

"But what are they fighting over?"

He fixed a shrewd look on her face. "Your husband, of course. He has already developed quite the following, you know, and I can't blame them. I can't help but admire him myself. Did you know he's a fully trained field healer as well? I confess that surprised me too. I hadn't expected it of him. It made me think all the harder about how I was taking these rumors, believe me. I wonder how many people know this side of him. I suppose that's what pushed me over the brink: a man can't become fully trained as a healer, not even as a field healer, without accepting the healer's vows. I told my entire staff this morning at the change of shifts." He beamed at her, expecting to see appreciation for this measure of support.

Ivy smiled as best she could. "That ought to help him a good deal."

They took her carriage back to Alanah's rooms, where the manservant Ilan unloaded provisions while Ivy introduced Doran to the girl. Alanah dropped an awkward curtsy. "Chief Healer," she said faintly, her eyes wide with surprise. "That's a…an honor, to be sure." She led him into the other room.

Doran knelt down beside Silla's pallet and for the first few moments gazed down at her intently. Then he opened his large satchel. Despite Silla's feeble muttering, he poured a tiny cup full of some cloudy medicinal infusion and slipped his arm under the woman's head. "This won't taste very good," he said kindly, "but you need to drink as much as you can of it." His glance at Alanah was eloquent, but he withheld any words until they left the sick woman's presence. "It can't have escaped your notice that she's failing at a pretty steady rate," he began. "I can treat this newest sickness of hers, but it will only delay the end for a matter of perhaps a few weeks at most." Then he began to measure out powders and explain their purposes to Alanah, telling her the proper size of dosage and the proper times for dosing the dying woman. At the end, he asked her gently, "Do you think you'll remember all that?"

"Yes, sir, I'll remember." Alanah shot a rapid glance at Ivy. "I'm sorry I haven't money to offer, but Miss Ivy said—"

"Don't give it another thought," Doran replied. "All is taken care of in that respect. You just give your mother the best care you can for these next few weeks. She ought to sleep a while now. I hope the sleeping draught I gave her will make it a healing sort of sleep, so she can wake up a little more lucid than she has been."

"It's all right, Chief Healer. She hasn't been—what d'you call it, *lucid*—since I was old enough to know of it. The best thing this sickness did was to make it impossible for her to go on with her drinking."

"As you say. Take care, then." Doran went to the door and turned back to wait for Ivy.

Ivy gave Alanah a warm hug and whispered to her, "If you ever need me, just send word. I live in a new set of rooms now, but if you send word to my father's house, they'll know where to find me. All right?" She leaned back to look into the girl's shiny damp eyes. "Oh, my dear Alanah, it is good to see you again. I'll come back in a few days or so to visit, shall I?"

"Please do," was all the girl could say.

In the carriage on the way back to the infirmary, Doran said, "She seems a good girl, in spite of it all."

"She was raised by a friend of mine who's dead now."

"Mm." Doran stretched out his feet comfortably. "You know, it strikes me I don't remember if I ever offered you my sympathy regarding your father. Did I? I don't recall. Probably not. I don't have a really good head for the…the social protocol and all that, and Phoebe is no use. She just assumes I've taken care of things like I ought," he said with a light laugh. "I've no idea why, after all these years, she doesn't know better. She should know I'm hopeless at such things."

Ivy shook her head. "That's all right." Then, gathering her courage, she asked, "You were with him, weren't you?"

"Up until the last, yes."

"This will sound…peculiar, but did you see…who killed him?"

The healer sighed heavily as he settled deeper into his cushion. "I have given this a lot of thought, make no mistake about it. Everything was so chaotic, with the giant cats and all."

"Giant cats?" Ivy exclaimed.

"Oh, yes, didn't they tell you? Another near-miraculous facet of your husband's character," Doran said, smiling. "He apparently has some manner of treaty with a pride of pardeléi, and they came to the battle on our behalf that day. I'll always remember the sight of him on that hilltop, standing beside the biggest cat of them all with his hand resting on its head, that blood-red tabard of his glowing in the sunshine like he was a walking flag. He stood up on that hilltop for the entire battle, just watching. It was chaotic, as I said, and we were getting pushed back in spite of ourselves." A shadow crossed his face. "I wish I'd been closer to your father, but there was nothing I can think of now that I might have done differently. I just happened to be looking in the right direction when he fell. Often I've brought back that memory to my thoughts to see if I could pick out which of the soldiers—*our* soldiers—struck him down. There wasn't anyone else near him at that point; we had just started to drive back the raiders with some success. In fact, that was the first I was able to see him through the press of bodies, and I noticed he was looking tired. I ran to him when I saw him fall, but your husband and his pardelé friend got there first." Pensive now, Doran spoke as if he watched the scene in thought all over again. "It was unaccountable for two men who were nearly strangers. If I didn't know better, I'd say they knew each other better than they did, especially when your husband pulled up his mask to let Denei get a look at his face, and then he gave your father a son's kiss on the forehead. You know how rare it was to see expression of any sort on your father's face, but I could've sworn he was happy."

"Poppa...he saw his face?"

Doran nodded. "I heard Denei's last words: 'It's time. Now I can die in peace.'"

Ivy drew back into her thoughts without responding. Doran, misunderstanding her silence, turned his face to the window out of kindness, to let Ivy have a moment with her grief.

RULE OF ONE

Why will you not tell her, little brother? If she knew you for yourself, she would not doubt you so. She would not heed these deceptions so readily.

Jarod did not answer.

You must not lose heart yet. I examined Ianthe very closely and could find no taint in her. She was very troubled at the experience and insists that the child does not know better yet. You must not lose heart. There is still hope.

Even at that, Jarod said nothing. He gazed up at the darkening sky. Filling his lungs deeply with air kept him from remembering the stench of the Unclean that he had scented near his wife. "I don't wish to deal with the guards at present, Chike. Deposit me in Owen's room, and then command Emre to prompt his charge to find me."

I do not understand you, little brother. Chike encompassed Jarod with all four limbs and bore him to a small, dark bedroom.

A single window looked westward to the last traces of daylight. Jarod sat on the floor in the corner, wedging his body between the foot of the bed and the south wall. His wait was of almost no duration at all. Soon a second voice joined Chike's. *Little brother! Have you come to tell Owen the good news? Am I permitted to acknowledge you for who you are?*

Not yet, Emre. Be patient.

Chike spoke with a decided edge to his words. *Time does not have the same meaning to us as it does to you, as you know. It is not our patience that is in question, but your honesty.*

If he did not so completely believe in my demise, Jarod returned, *perhaps I would not hesitate to make myself known. All my life, he has had no faith in me. What has changed in* him *that should give* me *cause to have faith in him? Until he has proven himself to me, I will continue as I began. Now keep quiet and let me deal with him.*

The door opened to admit the Sakiry patriarch. In the darkness of the room, he left the door ajar to give him light enough to find and light his own lamp. He turned the opposite way, with his back to Jarod, when he reached out a hand to push the door shut. Then the moment came: Owen took two steps forward on his way to the bed when his eyes fell on Jarod's motionless form in the corner. He stiffened for an instant before his poise reasserted itself. "Do you have an aversion to using the front door like everyone else?"

"I am not in a sociable mood this evening, Lord Sakiry."

"I apologize for my flippancy." Owen sat gingerly on the edge of the mattress, as if he hesitated to come any closer. "I suppose Ivy told you that I wanted to speak with you?"

"She did." *After she had tried every alternative to keep from speaking to me.*

*Little brother…*Chike's tone was a warning. *Be civil. He is your elder and kinsman.*

Jarod unbent a little. "She did not tell me what it was that troubled you, however. How may I be of service to you?"

"Did you know that Berhus Pamirsi is pushing the Council to elect a regent for Maia, saying she's too young to handle Colin's duties? He is, and what's more, as a candidate for regent, he put forward his youngest sister Mearah, an insufferable woman whose hostility to Selena is legendary. If for no other reason than that, we have to block this motion before Berhus bullies the Council into agreeing with him."

"It is certainly in our interests to see that the Pamirsi do not seize further control in the king's absence. What is your plan?"

"I have enough authority to prevent this, but only if I can make my position known. Since I am not free to do this in person, it is imperative that I find a suitable spokesman."

Jarod smiled without humor. "That certainly cannot refer to me. They will not hear me."

"No, I had thought of that, and you're right. You're too controversial at the moment. Doran, too, because he has already spoken out in your defense, is tied to you. No, we need to find someone whose impartiality can't be doubted. I have turned this over in my thoughts ever since the idea first occurred to me. Virlane son of Berhus is the only one that will do."

"Send for him."

With an apologetic lift of his hands, Owen said, "It isn't so simple. Lane isn't a sociable man. He doesn't see visitors unless they come on business—*his* business. He is a lore master of some repute. If I had any of my libraries at hand, I would lend him a book, but I have nothing to send to him. He doesn't call on other houses, either. He has a short list of acquaintances who may call on him without cause. Not even I qualify for that list, though Colin did."

"In short," Jarod said, "I must pay him a visit in my own way, and I must have a valid reason for this call, or he will pay no attention to me."

Owen nodded reluctantly. "Yes."

"Very well. When does the Council meet next?"

"If they hold to habit, they'll gather at midmorning."

Little brother, he is discouraged. Your rebuke has given him great pain these many days. Give him some small mark of your pardon, please, Emre asked him. *If you will not tell him who you are, at least offer him this one minor comfort.*

"I will see him tonight, then." Jarod cast about for something else to say. He felt the pressure of the shepherd-giants' attention as they waited for him to speak. Because he could find no compelling reason to deny this latest plea, he said, "You appear to be weathering captivity well. You are free to send for anything you lack, you know."

"Lack?" The word seemed to amuse Owen. "I've led a varied life, General, but nothing has ever fitted me for this. For once, I am reduced to the contents of this room. I keep little company, I own next to nothing, and I cannot even call this home my own. Would it surprise you to find that, given all this, I have never felt so free before in my whole life? It is the strangest thing to me. At my age, novelty is rare. I thank you for imposing this captivity, as you call it."

"You are welcome."

No, little brother, Chike admonished him when he thought to rise. *There is no demand on your time right now. You have no reason to leave. Speak with him. He is lonely.*

"You...perhaps have a little extra time?" Owen asked, as if he was able to hear the giant's words. "I know I have no right to ask you to stay, but I have often wished to talk with you these past few days. Please stay. I have so many questions to ask you."

"What sort of questions?"

"All sorts, I'm afraid. It's my nature to ask questions. I...I know now what I saw on the night of the assassination attempt. I've spent hours thinking about it. But what I don't understand is...how did you move Colin from his office all the way down the hallway to the sitting room like that? And what was that creature I saw?"

"That *creature* is named Chike. He served as Kohanan's shepherd until the king departed this world. He then transferred his ministrations to me. It is through his power that I was able to move the king as I did."

"But…" Owen frowned in thought. "But didn't you already have a shepherd of your own? And how is he able to…to *touch* you? I thought all contact between the Upper World and ours was forbidden by strict law."

"It is." *Chike, if you do not let me concentrate, I will leave. Let me do this in my own way.* "By merely existing, I break more than one of these laws. I make use of what I am, since I am unable to escape what I am."

"I don't understand."

"Nor do I, not completely. That has not hindered me yet. You place great faith in your understanding, Lord Sakiry. I wonder why."

The older man's forehead wrinkled with perplexity. "That's a curious thing to say."

"I often say curious things. It's a harmless pastime, and occasionally it turns out to be useful. You have known the king's family for many years, have you not?" *I will bring up the subject, Chike. What he chooses to do with it will determine the course of our discussion. Will that satisfy you?*

"Well, of course," Owen replied cautiously. "Why?"

"The king had a brother."

"Yes. His name was Jarod. He died years ago. What interest could he hold for you?"

Do you see now? He will not believe otherwise. "I knew him. It was, as you said, a good many years ago." Jarod watched the older man's face closely and saw only surprise.

"You…knew…Jarod?" The surprise was slow to fade. When it did, Owen said, "But that would mean—" He frowned again. "It means either you were…were born a subject of the crown, or that the fires didn't kill him. I'm not sure which of the two I find harder to believe." Then, flustered by the sound of his own words, Owen apologized. "That was an unpardonable thing to say. You took me by surprise."

"Another harmless pastime. I find it easier to get honest responses from people when they are surprised."

Owen reddened. "I am sorry. In all honesty, I did *not* mean it as it sounded. Once the initial surprise wears away, the imagination doesn't have to stretch far to believe it. You know too many customs to be a true foreigner. That business with Colin's seal ring, for instance—you surprised him with that. What clan did you spring from, if you don't mind my asking?"

"Sakiry."

Owen's eyebrows flew upward. "Did you? That's interesting. How did you come to live so far away, then?"

"I ran away from home when I was very young."

"Did we ever meet before? When you were a youngling, that is."

"It's likely. You circulate widely among the people."

Little brother! This time, Chike's reproof was accompanied by a sharp nudge.

Provoked, Jarod said aloud, *"I will do this in my own way, in my own time, Chike!"* When he drew a calming breath, he saw Lord Sakiry staring at him in wonder.

"I don't believe it." Owen leaned forward with wide silver-tinged eyes. "In my boyhood, I studied the ancient Hepuran tongue at the feet of my king, Amal. It is called a dead language, one to be read but never again spoken. I did never expect to hear any man speak it fluently. You constantly find ways to amaze me! Have you studied? I didn't take you for a man of letters."

"I have not and I am not. I have always had this knowledge. It is part of what I am." He saw that Owen wanted nothing more than to ask him exactly what that was. "I have no intention of discussing the nature of my existence with you, Sakiry; save your questions. I endure provocation enough from *him.*" At the older man's look of incomprehension, Jarod clarified, "Chike meddles in my affairs a good deal. I sometimes find it difficult to concentrate when he will not stop distracting me with his *advice.*"

"He was…speaking to you?" The forbidden curiosity practically had Owen holding his breath with the effort it cost him to restrain himself.

"Yes. He frequently does so, whether I want to hear him or not." Jarod's will to continue had dissipated. He leaned his head back against the wall. "Is there anything else you wished to say to me? If not, I have a request to make of you. I would appreciate it if you would search out the meaning of a phrase that I have uncovered. Have you any knowledge of the 'rule of one'?"

Owen shook his head. "I've never heard the term before."

"I will ask Virlane Berhus-son this same question. It may be that he will consider it enough a challenge to come here and consult you. Then you can attempt to engage him as a messenger to the Council. Good evening to you, Lord Sakiry." This time, Jarod left by the door. It was not yet so late that the healer and his wife had retired yet, and they stared at him as he passed the sitting room door on his way out the front.

Jarod was glad to turn away from the house at last. *That was a costly conversation. I hope you took pleasure in it,* he said to his unseen companion. *I certainly did not.*

How is he to see if you do not open his eyes? Yet you began to mislead him at the end.

If I did mislead him, Jarod allowed, *it was because I am not yet ready. You fail to take that into account, Chike. I am not yet sure that I wish to return to this place permanently. I have other responsibilities. My people, as few as they are, look to me for guidance.*

You are their lord and master. You may remove your servants wherever you choose. It is not a matter of choosing between here and there…least of all for one like you.

I am not yet ready. Where does this son of Berhus live? Jarod shut his eyes as the world disappeared around him. When he looked again, he stood in a brightly lit library. The centerpiece of the room was an enormous dining table cluttered with papers and books. At the table sat a man not quite thirty years of age, red-haired and husky. He stared blankly at Jarod's intrusion.

"What do you mean by breaking in on me in such a manner?"

"I had business that would not wait. I have just lately come from Lord Sakiry's presence. He has need of your assistance."

"What sort of assistance?" asked Virlane warily.

"He has come across a peculiar term whose origins he cannot trace. It was a question of mine. I have been made to understand that you have access to every significant collection of lore within a hundred leagues. Is that true?"

"As far as it goes, yes, it is true. That still doesn't explain what you're doing here."

"You do not grant entrance to many people."

"No. That is how I prefer to order my life, and for good reason. I am a lore master. I do not take an active role in political strivings, yet I happen to find myself planted in the midst of more political tangles than I care to admit. There is one way to keep it at bay, and that is to limit my circle of intimate acquaintance."

"You are a friend of the king, are you not?"

"Yes. Are you?"

Jarod could not help but respect this weak-eyed man's tenacity. "For my part, I am his friend. Whether he considers me in the same light, I cannot say."

"Then you won't mind explaining to me where you came by that ring on your left hand. Last finger. The ring with the royal symbol on it."

Raising the aforementioned hand, Jarod glanced at the ring in some surprise. It was the last thing he had expected the man to seize upon. "It was a gift," he said flatly.

"I find that unlikely, since it was a reminder of his dead brother that Colin kept always on his person," Virlane fired back. "He would not give it away. Not willingly."

"You will need to take that up with him when he comes back. Will you call upon Lord Sakiry tomorrow morning? He would be pleased to admit you immediately after breakfast." Jarod pinned the smaller man with a look and did not relent until he saw the acquiescence he desired. "Good. I bid you good evening, Loremaster. I will see myself out." *Get me away from here, Chike.*

The next time he opened his eyes, Jarod found himself in the monument grove at Takra House. "Thank you, Chike," he breathed, leaning against the nearest cenotaph. The calm and quiet felt like a cool breeze to his spirit. "Truly, I did not know that this would be so difficult. I did not." In the meager moonlight, he lifted his left hand and stared at the ring that had caught the lore master's eye. Its intaglio design mirrored the cameo of another ring, both of them wrought at the same time long before. "I had almost forgotten. Strange that he still wears his."

Strange? He does it to remember you. He has never let go of you. Do you know what nightmares he suffers even now because of you?

"I can imagine. Even in my worst days, every good dream I had was rightfully his. It is no wonder if his nightmares come because of me." Jarod got up from the ground and brushed the dead grass from his trouser legs. He met no one as he left the grove. Looking up at the multitude of blank windows, Jarod gave thanks that the household had gone to bed. *Dare I enter?*

Keep to the residential wing. I can protect you.

"He grows restless. Even I can feel it. He must move soon, before the advantage shifts to me." Jarod spoke in an undertone. "I can weather it, but...the danger to the others...I must warn the girl." He set his hand to the latch of the door. On the other side, he neither saw nor sensed movement in the darkness, so he let himself inside noiselessly. He went no farther for a moment. *Do you wish to know why I am not ready? I will show you.* Jarod shut his eyes and drew upon a memory of that very room. In his thoughts, the memory held all the pristine brilliance of the original experience.

"What are you doing up here?" The girl stood before him, her back to the railing and the ballroom view that it afforded. "I've been looking everywhere for you."

"Watching them." Even the memory of Jarod's voice, boyishly clear and uncertain, perfectly matched the original. He stepped aside and leaned his forearms on the railing to give himself a reason for not looking at the girl.

"You can't just stand up here all night, watching," the girl insisted.

The man Jarod flinched at the memory of that third voice, sly and conceited, baiting the naïve boy that he had been. *It is too late for her, boy. She deserves everything you could do to her. She asks to be dragged down along with you. There is no hope for either of you. Just give her what she desires. You cannot stop what is inevitable.*

"Yes, I can," the boy snapped aloud, realizing too late that he had spoken and not merely thought the angry response.

To his surprise, the girl had not fled in tears. Instead, she too leaned against the railing beside him in temporary silence. "All right. If you want to stay up here, that's all right with me. I don't care for dancing that much myself." Her lie was so transparent that the boy turned his head slightly to see her out of the corner of his eye. She was not finished. "You know, my birthday is coming. I'm supposed to have a dance just like this one. I don't really want to."

The boy Jarod had not known the truth behind those words. He had taken them for another little lie, but now, knowing what was to come soon after this moment, Jarod shook his head. *I never saw it coming.* Before he ended the memory, he watched as the girl Ivy crept her hand along the railing until she could wrap her fingers around the hand of the boy Jarod had been. *I could have destroyed her so easily then...and would have, whether I willed it or not. I was too weak to deny either of us.*

Little brother, the past is finished. Now you have reversed your role. You can save her.

"No," Jarod whispered, opening his eyes upon the vacant ballroom again. "No, Chike, I cannot. This one thing I do understand too well: I cannot save her from this. There is only one who can, and he is not welcome here." With overcast heart, he followed the path of his memories up the steps and into the residential wing. He had not taken three steps before his gaze turned to the open door of Colin's deserted office. Again, he shut his eyes to draw forth the past.

"Look me in the eye, Jarod, and tell me the truth this time! What did you think you were doing?" Owen's voice held an edge no less cutting than when it had first lacerated Jarod's spirits over twenty years ago. "I said look at me! This is the last time, Jarod, I swear—if I have to go to your father and insist that he keep you shut away in your rooms every hour of every day, I will, so help me! If that's what it takes to make you consider what you put your family through, it's a small price to pay. How could you, Jarod? Just tell me that one thing—how *could* you?"

A deathlike silence was the boy's only response. Then, with a tearful voice that still sent a pang of regret through Jarod, his mother Camille spoke. "Owen, that's enough." She reached out a hesitant hand that the boy suffered for only a few moments before he felt compelled to withdraw. "Please, Jarod, won't you just tell me what happened? I can't help what made you unhappy unless you tell me about it."

Why did you not let her comfort you, little brother?

I believed that she was afraid to touch me because of what I was. Audune made me believe it. I couldn't inflict that fear on her. Jarod shook off the memory. Shunning the darkened office doorway, he made his way down the corridor.

Maia is awake and anxious. She wishes to speak with you.

Very well. He headed for her bedchamber slowly, making no sound as he passed doorway after unlit doorway. This unearthing of memories unsettled him. Once before, he had gone to her door and come away again undisturbed, but only because he had not permitted himself to remember. This time, with the depths of his memories freshly stirred, he hesitated at the door to the room that once had been his and his brother's, many years ago. A weak light glowed beneath it. He opened the door quietly and leaned inside far enough to see and be seen. "You do not sleep?" he whispered. "What troubles you?"

The girl did not take fright at his sudden intrusion as he had half-expected she would. "Teacher!" She scrambled from her bed and ran barefooted to the door. "You know, it's funny you came—I've wanted to talk to you. I didn't think you would come 'til tomorrow. I'm glad you came now. I can't sleep."

"Why not?"

She looked past him into the murky sitting room. "Come inside." To emphasize her words, she tugged him by the sleeve until he was safely inside the half-lit chamber. She shut the door behind him as her words flooded out. "I can't stop thinking about the council meeting tomorrow. What if they try to force this regency matter? They won't listen to me, and now they won't listen to Mother or to you, or even to Doran. I won't have that Mearah woman here. It'll make Mother miserable, for one thing, and Mearah's no good as an advisor anyhow. She doesn't know the first thing about Father's work. It just isn't right."

"I've spoken with Lord Sakiry. Between the two of us, we will manage Berhus Pamirsi for you. Have no fear on that count."

"But that isn't everything." The girl threw herself onto the huge bed and curled up into a knot with her chin propped on her knees. Huge, unblinking eyes gazed at him with fear in their depths. "You said something the day Uncle Denei died. I didn't think much about it then, but I'm thinking about it now. Especially after I talked to Simon. You said the Unclean is here in my house." She shuddered. "Is that true?"

Jarod seated himself on the end of the divan across the room. Even if it were in his nature to lie to the girl, he could not. Her fear reached out to him and awoke his pity. "It is true. Simon has loosed this threat within Takra House. Even if you had persuaded him, he would not be able to undo what he has done."

"Can't we just…leave?" the girl whispered.

"It would spare you and your household," Jarod allowed with a nod, "but he would remain here, dormant, waiting to awaken as soon as another mortal being came near him. Given time, he would turn this house into another Garden of the Forbidden."

"What can I do?"

"For now, keep watch over those who look to you as their mistress. Try to protect them and instruct them. Above all, guard yourself. He will try to deceive you." Jarod held her gaze evenly. "You must be on your guard against the third marshal. You are drawn to him, are you not? Despite what you know to be true about him, you feel compassion for him. You wish to save him from himself. Is this not true?" He waited for her slight nod before he went on, "As admirable as this is, you must guard yourself all the more because of it. It is one thing to desire his salvation. It is another thing to grow fond of him, to make excuses for what he has done. It is true: he may not comprehend the truth of what he has done. It does not change the fact that he has done it. If you allow yourself to sympathize with his failings too much, he may easily draw you into them. Not only will you fail to save him, but you yourself will be changed to become like him. It is the nature of the destiny between you."

"At first," she said in a tiny voice, "I didn't know if I believed you when you told me about…about what should have been. After I talked with him—I'd never really talked to him face to face before—everyone always tried to keep him from bothering me, you know, but now that I've talked with him, I *do* see it. He has such wondrous dreams of what could be. For a second, while he talked, I could picture it, too. A golden age, he said."

"Yes, Princess, it is very sad that such a thing should have withered before it had the opportunity to grow." Jarod knew that his tone was more abrasive than he meant. He tried to gentle it. "There is no good to be had in it any longer. This is why you must guard yourself, Princess. Trust my counsel if you cannot trust your own good sense."

She sighed and uncoiled herself to her full length. "Yes, Teacher. I know." With her head resting on her pillow, she looked very young. "I wish Father were here."

"I understand." A smile came to Jarod before he realized it. He spoke the thought that had amused him. "You have much of him in you. Your father is fond of relying on the advice of others rather than trusting his good judgment. He questions himself too often. So do you, it would appear. This is *your* fight, not his."

The girl smothered a yawn forcibly with her hands. "Yes, Teacher."

He stood. "I will leave so you can sleep. You will need to be well rested for tomorrow."

"No," Maia protested tiredly, "don't. I'm awfully weary, but I just can't sleep. If you go, I'll just lie here yawning and thinking too much. Please?"

For an instant, she reminded him of his son Lucien. Jarod smiled. "As you will. I'll keep watch for you." He softened his voice a little more. "Nothing will come near to harm you this night. Rest. You are safe in my care." When Jarod saw her eyelids sink, he had a curious feeling of repetition, as if he had been there before. The last time—he corrected himself, realizing what the sensation meant—when *Colin* had last done this, he had knelt down beside the bed and stroked the girl's hair back from her forehead. Jarod obeyed the impulse. He rubbed her forehead lightly with the flat of his thumb, smoothing away the furrows of worry that marred her smooth skin. In a barely audible voice, he spoke Old Hepuran over her. *"Child of my brother, tonight I will bear your fears for you."* He knelt by the bed for some time after he was sure that Maia had achieved a sound sleep. With his eyes shut, he beckoned for Chike to witness another memory. *She is very like him. He too slept in my presence without a qualm, though he had far less cause.*

The scene in his memory changed to a night of gleaming moonlight. Instead of one large bed, the room held two. One held a sleeping youth, hardly more than fourteen years. The other bed was empty, rumpled as if a wild boar had rooted through the covers. Its occupant huddled in a far corner of the room with his hands clamped over his ears.

Kill him. He serves no purpose. You are smarter, stronger, quicker, and in every way better than he could ever be. Kill him now. There are ways, boy. No one would know. Kill him and recover what he stole from you. Have you not always known that your father loves him more? Kill him, and your father's attention will fall on you, as it always should have. I have taught you about the subtle poisons, have I not? A touch of the draught on his lips, and he will sicken. No one will know it for anything but disease. You will never have what you most desire until he is dead.

The boy Jarod shook his head until he was dizzy. His fear held him hostage in the corner. Too often he had somehow been duped into doing just as Audune bid him, led like a dog on a leash to the very evil he had no intention of committing, but not this time. If he refused to budge from his corner, Audune could not make him act on this heinous suggestion. *No. No. Even if Colin did die—Even if I did what you said, it wouldn't make any difference. You'd still be here. Father would know. Murder can't hide from a seer.*

Jarod opened his eyes to calm himself by gazing upon the sleeping girl. The sight of her repose made the memory ebb. *That was the longest night of my life. I was terrified that somehow, even if I meant not to do it, I would kill him. I don't know how I made it through that night.*

Gently, Chike whispered, *Close your eyes again.*

As Jarod meditated unwillingly upon his past, he felt his senses expanding as Chike poured his own memory into Jarod's. Now the walls melted to reveal an assortment of giants gathered around the periphery, their wills bent upon the boy Jarod in silent support: *Be strong, little brother. Do not give in. We are with you.* He felt the tears slide down his face beneath the mask and had to ask, *How were you near me, and I didn't know?*

The memory expanded yet again, engulfing the sitting room and dissolving the wall to the royal suite. Jarod saw his parents lying asleep—but suddenly he realized that, though his mother slept, his father was in the grasp of a vision. *What did he see?*

He saw that your shepherd was evil, and that you fought bravely against him. Your father requested that I stay near you through the night.

So when he sought me out the next morning, he truly did *know. I tried to hide from him…I could not bear the shame. But he knew even then.* Jarod opened his eyes.

Yes. He knew even then. He tried to breach your solitude, but you have never confided in anyone willingly. You hold yourself too separate from everyone. Tonight, little brother, you have honored me greatly. I thank you for what you have shown me. Chike paused abruptly. *I see I am to be doubly honored. Yes, O splendor of light, great master and king, come. I yield myself to you. Welcome.*

Jarod turned his back on the sleeping girl, his heart battering itself against his ribs. He felt the overwhelming presence begin to crush him inexorably for an instant before the greatest of immortals took up residence within Chike, thus shielding Jarod and the girl from his presence. Even so, Emunya's voice drove

Jarod onto his face on the floor. *Your enemy stirs this night, little brother. If you do not bar his path, he will prey upon the unwary again and build his strength. You and only you can do this tonight. Will you entrust yourself to me?*

If you pronounce me able, I will do as you bid me.

Do not fear. You are not yet ready to welcome me as Chike has, but I can support you through him. Your enemy will not feel my presence. He will suspect it, but I will not reveal myself to him in my true power this night. This night, he is yours to battle.

Trembling in spite of himself, Jarod rose from the floor and headed swiftly to the top of the stairs that served as crossroad between the eastern and western wings of Takra House, and between Takra House and the palace grounds. Already, the much-hated figure had appeared and would have descended to the entry hall if Jarod had not commanded, "Go no farther."

The stench itself was almost too much to bear, but then the figure spoke to him. "Ah. We meet again, Orlan? Always in the most unlikely places. You are sure of your paltry strength."

"Yours is greatly lessened. It must have cost you to cower in that tiny office day after day while so much unsuspecting prey wandered past. Did you venture out now, thinking that no one stood in your way to stop you?"

"No one stands in my way." The withered figure folded his arms. "You have mistaken yourself for someone, Orlan. How sad to see you fall this low—faithful lackey to a Keeper! I do wonder if you chose this fate to spite me. It cannot suit one of your temperament and talent."

Jarod felt the pressure of the old man's opposing will as it probed his resistance for a place of weakness. He refused to be moved. "My choice was and is my own."

"Ah, yes! So confident now that we have our new counselor, the king's fearsome warrior-giant, to prompt us? I have seen him at your shoulder. How asinine to think that you have choice! Choice is power. You *had* power. You chose death instead. Now you have nothing left to you but slavery. You are nothing."

"Better an honest death than the death that you chose, Phelan *hé nekhral,*" Jarod spat. "I know the truth of your 'power' as well as you do." When he felt the old man summon his will to push against him, Jarod countered. "If I had not uncovered the truth before, I know it now. You are weak here, so weak that even I can thwart your hunt. You can go nowhere but where your master rules. If you do not provide him with food, he will feed on *you* until you are no more."

They faced each other in the darkness, neither moving. The false seer replied, "You may be able to stop me from hunting…for now. You cannot stop them from coming to me. Whether you know it or not, my lord Laistes does rule here.

Already it begins: the discord, the shaking off of their age-old bondage to the Keepers. They will come to me, and my master will grow strong off of them. Then he will come in power to destroy the Keepers forever. The Keeper house will end; the rightful king of the earth will rise from prison at last. Your own master has foretold it."

Is this true, keiri?

The whisper of the immortal's response caressed his spirit. *Yes. Be strong, little brother. This night, you must do battle for your people.*

"I will always stand between you and the world," Jarod said to the false seer, "and I cannot die, so you will never win."

"Whoever told you that, Orlan?" Phelan laughed. "Just because you died once, that does not exempt you from death forever. You were spared once. Count yourself fortunate, by all means, but do not imagine yourself a great immortal now. You *can* be destroyed. I will prove it to you." His face split into a hideous death's-head grin. "How do you suppose I will do it? Oh, I have spent many a dreary hour devoting all my thought to the question. I have found the most delicious answer." The false seer held up his medallion. It shone dull yellow in the darkness. On the palm of his hand, the disc transformed into a familiar shape: Ivy. "It was really too bad. Before I took hold of her mind, I believe she was becoming *fond* of you. Can you imagine it? How could anybody be fond of a creature like you, who is neither flesh nor fowl? But then, the lady has always had questionable tastes in her company. She'll make you a proper wife now, I promise you. Just as treacherous, just as deceitful as you—but oh, so much easier to manage. She is quite...*delicious.*"

"You cannot have her."

"No? You forget who I am, Orlan. I have a right to any who welcome me. She is my prey now. I would have had her that first night when young Simon brought me here, had you not exerted your brutality to keep her from me. It was all for nothing. I have her now."

"You deceived her. She will see you for what you are eventually. She'll turn from you."

The false seer laughed again. "You do not know your own wife very well. I cannot tell which is more foolish: the woman for being weak, or you for believing her stronger than she is. She is blind and stupid. Once she has helped me destroy you, it will be my pleasure to drink the life from her and rid the earth of the burden of her useless presence."

"I claimed her as mine and my master's also. You cannot have her."

Throughout the night, they strove against each other, neither yielding a step for the other. Sometimes they were silent as they tested each other for weakness. Often the false seer would taunt Jarod. He delighted in weaving scenarios of Ivy's destruction, each more unspeakable than the last, but Jarod was unmoved. *For once,* he remarked to his master, *I can give thanks for the torment I suffered before. Compared to that, the false seer's gibes hold no power over me.*

You have undergone strict training already, preparing for your destiny. You have far to go yet. Take comfort in this: you are already able to endure much hardship.

And I am not alone, Jarod added grimly. He was able to resurrect the memory that Chike had given him earlier in the night, and it gave him the determination to fight the weariness of his own flesh as well as the relentless barrage of his foe. *I do not stand alone.* Even so, when dawn began to nibble at the edges of the shadows, Jarod was thankful to see the false seer shy away from the threat of light.

"Do not imagine that you have won. You were able to stand against me for a night, but your strength will not last. One night, you will falter. Then I will finish what we began three years ago. This I do promise you." As the light gained strength, the old man faded. The sun's first rays burst upon the house in glory, tinted green by the foliage through which they shone.

As soon as he could no longer detect Phelan's presence, Jarod reached up under his mask to rub his face wearily. "Is it over?"

The battle is yours. I will return to aid you when night falls once more.

Jarod trudged back toward the eastern wing, thinking to climb to the attic and steal a few hours' sleep before the midmorning council meeting. He was caught at the stairs by young Hollister, who said, "General! Good morning to you. The queen was just saying how she wanted to see you as soon as you came. Will you come with me to see her, sir?"

Down in the kitchen, Jarod found Selena in conference with a handful of Caretaker servants. When she saw him, the queen stood. "Are you here already? I hadn't thought to see you this early."

"I keep peculiar hours," he answered evasively. "How may I serve, lady?"

"Do sit down. I spoke with Ivy yesterday. She said she would go to Owen about this regency business, but I never heard anything about it afterward. The meeting is this morning—"

"Lord Sakiry has taken measures. If he was successful, then a messenger will arrive at the meeting to give his views, which are decidedly not in agreement with Lord Pamirsi's proposal. If not, then we will delay the vote until a suitable regent can be found. I have a candidate in mind, but it would take time to summon him." In truth, this solution had only just leaped to his thoughts as he was speaking the words *if not*, but Jarod was accustomed to the workings of his own mind and was not surprised to find the answer present itself like a soldier at muster.

"Really? Who do you mean?"

"Byram Solam-son. He is a Pamirsi clansman, but he is also Lord Sakiry's kinsman by marriage and served as the late king's last companion. They cannot quarrel against such a one."

"Byram Solam-son," Selena repeated thoughtfully. "Did you hear that, Isaac? Your uncle Byram. Rowan should be pleased to hear that."

The commander of the royal guard corps looked up from where he sat against a far wall, reading from a portion of the Book of the Kings. "I hadn't known he was still alive, sir. That's good news to hear. Is he coming home at last?"

"He is. At present, he abides in my house, but he would be pleased to finally return to his homeland. His qualifications suit the need here, in more ways than one. You may rest easy, Lady Selena. One way or another, this matter will resolve itself satisfactorily." Jarod glanced at the door when the princess entered. "Good morning, princess."

"Are you here still?"

"Still?" Selena looked closely at Jarod. "You mean you never left?"

Maia had a faraway look in her eyes for an instant. "So it did really happen. He was coming, but you…you stopped him."

"One day, Princess, you will make a fine seer. Already the seeds begin to grow."

She blushed. "I don't know about that."

"Give it time. It does not serve anyone's purpose to rush such things."

"Then why did you order Uncle Owen to stay in his house until he was ready?"

Jarod inclined his head, acknowledging the justice of her retort. "So that he may find time. He rushed. He needed time; now he has it. It may interest you to know that he finds his confinement 'a novelty,' to use his word. He is enjoying himself more than he had ever expected. I only hope that he is also using the time well." He swallowed a yawn. "As should I. A few hours remain before the meeting. If you need me, you will find me beneath the Prince's Tree."

Outside, the dew had already evaporated under the hot early sunshine. Jarod settled himself on the western side of the large tree, where two knobbed roots made a hollow. With his head bowed, he listened to the echoes of a sound that never failed to enthrall him, a complex melody resonating through the tree from its progenitor in another world. Vitality seeped through the bark into Jarod, reviving his spirits.

TRIALS

Giles glanced around before he dared set down the pestle and stretch out his cramped right hand. He wanted to massage it, but he knew that he would only make things worse if he went anywhere near the large weal that swelled the back of his hand. The red mark was as wide as two of his fingers. Four days had only just begun to ease the puffiness.

"Finished yet?"

He jumped at the question. "Um, no, not quite, ma'am."

Vienna, the master healer of Chamika, stood over him with her fists on her hips. She was a big, powerful woman with muscular arms and the most piercing brown eyes Giles had ever seen. When he hastily snatched up the pestle to resume his task, however, she held out her hand. "Let me see your hand." She examined the welt. "Come inside and I'll wrap that in a poultice."

The poultice felt cool against his swollen hand. Giles bobbed his head in polite thanks and said, "That feels good."

"She really did clout you a good one, didn't she? Rona has a wicked temper. She doesn't take provocation too well, either." Vienna's eyes danced with sudden laughter. "Back to work now, lad. I need those herbs."

Giles went back outside to his three-legged stool, took up the pestle from the table, and resumed his task: grinding herbs for the master healer. He had no real liking for this work, but even he had to admit it was better than his previous job, where he cleaned house for Rona, a young housewife with five children and a temper. Vienna was strict, but kinder and more generous with Giles than Rona had been. A woman of her physique could easily have snapped Giles in half with only her hands. Giles had so far been in such awe of her that he obeyed her exacting orders with uncharacteristic diligence and promptitude.

The work was tedious. Vienna measured out the herbs for him, not trusting an ignorant boy to get the proportions right on his own. Then she left him to the monotonous work of crushing the herbs into a fine powder. While he worked, Giles had plenty of time to take in his surroundings. He had never seen a mountain before, let alone ascended this high among them. Chamika was a plain little town, but its surroundings were so breathtaking that some of the glory seemed to soak into even the rough-finished cottages and dirt streets. The master healer's house sat near the edge of the high terrace. Only an unpaved lane separated it from the edge, affording Giles a broad view of the two lower terraces and all their cottages and traffic. The middle terrace was occupied mainly by homes, with one notable exception. In the midst of the cottages was the village square, now noisy with dogs, sheep and men as the village shepherds tried to sort out their flocks. Giles let his attention wander as he watched the dogs harassing the sheep.

"I hear no sound of pestle grinding herbs," Vienna called from within the house.

Giles decided it might be safe to engage her in conversation. "Ma'am, what are they doing with those sheep down there?"

She came to the window and looked out over his shoulder at the flocks. "Oh, them? They're taking the midsummer count. If there are lambs enough, we'll be eating really well this year. If not, we'll have to limit ourselves a little more. Menfolk have been out so often this spring, it's a wonder we have any sheep left at all."

"Why's that?"

"Nobody around to watch them but boys. Grind, grind, grind, my lad. Those herbs won't turn to good powder on their own."

Giles resumed his task, but he wasn't giving up on the conversation. "Why have the men been out so often? Has there been trouble?"

"Has there been—Where have you been keeping your head these past months, lad? In a pretty wooden case? Of course there's been trouble, more than our fair share. If something don't give one way or the other, this is bound to be a hard winter for all of us. I only wish Ammun would make up his mind one way or the other. If he chose his path, he'd put an end to all this trouble, but then," she added with compassion, "it isn't easy for him, going back into all of that. I don't blame him for wanting to stay away from his old ghosts, even if it is for a good cause."

"Old ghosts?"

"He's seen troubles to top anything you or I could boast. If he put his mind to it, he could quash old Malin properly, and then we'd have more time to mind our day-to-day business. Malin, now, he's a bit more than a thorn to Ammun. That's not to say they were ever close, though some say they were. No, lad, I saw it myself and know the truth of it. 'Tis no lingering fondness for old Malin that holds Ammun back. Do you want to know what it is?" Vienna only added that question as a mild jibe, because Giles was already leaning closer to hear her better. "It's my guess that Ammun knows it would mean a lot of killing, and he doesn't want to go there again. They say Ammun is the most dangerous man alive today." The healer chuckled warmly. "I don't doubt that he could be, but at the same time I say he doesn't have it in him anymore. He doesn't have the will for it. Gentle as a new pup, is Ammun. I've never seen anyone to match him for kindness toward the weak or generosity toward the needy—but if you're of a lazy or a too-proud turn, you'd best mind yourself."

Vienna's glance toward the pestle reminded Giles of his dereliction. He went back to his task, having lost interest in the sheep-counting below. Soon bored, Giles looked around for something else to hold his attention. He found a moment's distraction when a troop of young warriors-in-training came jogging past in strict formation. Giles watched them until, at the far end of the lane, they halted to wait for their trainer to dismiss them. As they dispersed, a few of them came back along the lane past Giles. There were three of them, one girl and two boys. They stopped and stared at him.

The girl laughed. "Look at him, there!"

One of the boys folded his arms and showed every sign of wanting to keep back from the conversation his friend had started. The other smiled with reluctance. "You see, Taima? It don't even help to be marriage kin to Ammun himself—you start at the bottom regardless."

"How old are you?" Taima demanded of Giles.

"Seventeen."

She laughed again. "Seventeen? And this is all you're good for?"

"Are you making fun of a healer's work, little girl?" a languid voice asked from off to Giles' right. When Giles looked around, he found a young man leaning against the corner of the house, his flat gaze directed at Taima. "Like to find another way to say that?" He pushed away from the wall and sauntered past Giles as if he wasn't there. When he came to a stop, however, the newcomer planted himself squarely between Giles and Taima. "I'm waiting."

"Tisn't what he's doing," the girl backpedaled. "I heard he was a house helper before this, too. He's as old as you, but this is all he's good for. Tell me you don't think that's funny, Ingram!"

The young warrior said something that Giles didn't understand. Its effect was immediate: the girl looked as if she had been properly scolded. The look she gave him was pitying instead of resentful. Giles couldn't account for it unless the fellow called Ingram had said something to make her feel sorry for him. He kept quiet while the three youths retreated from Ingram's gaze. Once the young warrior turned around to face him, Giles was ready. "I can take being mocked by the fledgling chicks, but I have a hard time swallowing the pity of a full-grown bird."

Ingram raised his eyebrows in surprise. "You speak Kavahran?"

"I don't have to. I'm good enough with faces."

"You haven't spent much time around Ammun, then," Ingram retorted. "What you get from watching his face might just get you from here," he pointed at the ground, "to here," and he stepped backward half the length of his own foot. "Note how the movement is not in a forward direction. Mind if I sit?"

"Should I mind?"

Vienna yelled from inside the house, "Don't distract him, or he'll never finish."

"All right, Mother. I won't." Catching Giles' glance, the young man lowered his voice. "She hears like a pardelé. Nothing's a secret from her for long. Aye, she's my mother. No need to hide that from anybody." For a time, Ingram leaned against the wall and said nothing more. Then he looked at Giles, and his glance was like a measuring rod set against Giles' uselessness. "That what you want to do?"

"I wasn't offered the choice."

"Everybody has a choice," Ingram countered without much inflection in his voice. "My mother's the village healer; my father's Ammun's personal field healer. Still, when it came time, they asked me whether I wanted to learn the craft myself. I thought it a handy thing to know and an honorable choice even for a warrior. Someone has to mend what the others break."

Giles offered, "I know a man who's a fully trained practicing public healer. He's sort of…well, not really, I guess…no, I suppose he's no kin of mine after all."

"Is he or isn't he? Don't you know?" The young warrior was amused.

"He's my adoptive grandfather's half-brother's son-in-law."

Ingram laughed at that. "A mouthful of a title. But he's a practicing healer, you say?"

"He's the chief healer of King's City. They say he's the best healer, male or female, to ever practice the craft. He's a good fellow, from what I've seen. A fellow could do worse than follow him…but I've never been inclined that way," he added almost mournfully.

"What way do you incline?"

"No way, so far."

"What an upright fellow you must be. You must have something you want out of life. What did your father do?"

"He's a journeyman typesetter at a printer's shop."

Warned by Giles' bleak tone, Ingram passed over that subject in favor of another tangent. "So you're saying there's never been a single thing that made you sit up and say, 'I'd like to share in that'? Nothing at all?" His eyes were sharp enough to catch the hesitation that kept Giles from answering at once. Ingram started to smile a little. "Ah! Now we come to it. Out with it, friend, and we'll see what we can do to start you on the road to getting there. What is it?"

Giles shook his head. "It isn't an occupation. Matter of fact, unless I find myself an occupation, it'll never even—but then again, it's so unlikely from the off—it's not possible," he finished in an unequivocal way. "Never mind. Forget I said anything."

"That's a hard thing to ask," Ingram complained. "Have it your own way. Here, give that over for a moment. You'll only hurt yourself doing it that way." He took the pestle and showed Giles the proper way to hold it. "I'd best get back before Bayne comes after me with a stick and herds me like one of those idiot sheep down there. 'Twas a pleasure making your acquaintance."

∗ ∗ ∗ ∗

Early the next morning, Colin lay back in the worn and sheltered hollow of the tree and watched as the southeastern trees began to glow with color. For once, he found himself occupying a moment in time that demanded nothing from him. It was good to sit in the hollow of the enormous old tree and simply watch the sunrise. He drew his cloak more tightly around himself to fend off the morning's chill.

When he saw human movement near the house, he nearly groaned, thinking that someone sought him for the start of the new day's rigors. However, as soon as the figure bounded over a low rise, Colin saw that it was only Lucien. The boy sprinted until he was close enough to see Colin's face. Then he slowed. By the time he reached Colin, he was walking.

"Morning, Lucky."

"Morning, sir. Sorry about disturbing you. I saw somebody from the window and I thought maybe Ta was home."

Colin shifted to let the boy sit beside him. "You miss him, don't you? Does he go away like this very often?"

"Lots of times he goes away, but not for this long."

"Ah, Lucky, I'm afraid that's my fault. I gave him a job to do, a really hard job, and it's taking a lot of his time." With an arm around the boy's lean shoulders, Colin gave him a hug. "I bet he misses you a lot, too, just like I miss my little girl."

"You have a little girl?"

Colin had to laugh at himself, admitting, "Well, she isn't so little anymore. She's sixteen years old and almost as tall as I am. How old are you?"

"I was nine in the spring."

"Nine? That's a good age to be. I remember when I was nine. Life was much easier back then. Everything was new, like an adventure. I helped build a city when I was nine."

"Really?"

"Really. Me and my brother, we got put to work just like anybody else, helping build the new King's City. Made me feel like I was a man already."

"Ta says sometimes a man's work won't wait for him to grow up."

"Is that why you carry that?" Colin pointed to the dagger that Lucien wore at his belt.

"Yes, sir. I already know how to use it some. I don't really like to, but maybe someday I'll have to, and then it don't—doesn't matter if I like it or not. I gotta know how." The boy slipped the dagger, sheath and all, from his belt and held it up so Colin could see it better. "It was my grandfather's before it was mine."

Colin took the blade and examined it. It was a plain dagger, the sort any hunter or traveler might carry in uncivilized territory. Colin returned it. "What sort of man was your grandfather?"

"Dunno. He died. I never met him. Who do you work with today?"

"Farris is my natai this morning."

"I like Farris. He lets me help him sometimes, when he's working."

"What sort of work does he do? I haven't gotten to know him yet."

"Stone work. Yesterday, he let me help build a retaining wall, to keep a hill where it belongs. He said I did good at it." Distantly, a feminine voice began calling Lucien's name. The boy got up, dusted the grass from his trouser legs, and said, "That's Aurelia, looking out for me. I better go now. Bye."

"Bye, Luck. See you later." Colin smiled as he watched the boy trot obediently to the house. After the boy was gone, though, his smile faded. "Now to business." With a slight groan, he rose from the ground to lean against the tree trunk for a few minutes before his conscience provoked him to start toward the village. He avoided the house, where he knew Byram would be on the lookout for him. There was a small side gate on the east wall of the property. It had only one guard. This morning, young Ingram held the post. "Morning, Ingram," Colin said. "Fine sunrise, isn't it?"

The young man yawned. "S'pose so. I'm partial to a good sunset, myself."

"You're young. Give yourself a few years."

"Who's your natai today?"

"Farris."

"You're lucky. He's a good'un."

"Yes. I'm no good at hand-fighting, but he doesn't seem to hold it against me." Colin ducked through the small gate and headed for the training field.

Despite the chilled morning air, Farris wore only a loincloth. He was a massive man, not tall but thick in body and limb. His head was shaved smooth, but a carpet of dark wooly hair covered his chest like moss on a boulder. The only bare patches were scars, and Farris had many. "Gather, my children," he intoned, his eyes twinkling. "You have much to learn ere you can beat old Farris at his tricks. Who believes he can throw me today? None of you? Perhaps the hour's too early for a challenge. Let us begin with sparring to stir your blood and awaken your brains."

Colin belonged to a group of fifty men occupying a narrow training field in the shelter of a ridge of bare rock. The dawn stillness carried every sound from the awakening village. Colin strained to catch Farris' instructions as the group paired off for sparring. He saw a glint in the natai's eye when the burly man came to him. Farris beckoned a young man forward. "Are you ready to turn teacher yet, Loren? If you can be parted from my cousin so long, that is?"

Loren grinned. "Aye, natai. Druze grows too predictable." The russet-haired warrior squared off before Colin and bowed slightly. "Welcome. I am Loren, son of Avven, of the Waller province in Nikobia."

Colin returned the bow. "Colin, son of Kohanan, of the clan Sakiry, Second Kingdom."

The natai had moved on down the line already, until all the participants were matched and their master-at-arms had climbed to the middle of the ridge overlooking them. "We begin, as always, at rest, arms extended but a little—find your balance. When you have found it, calm yourselves with a breath. Never let me

The King's Brother

hear that a student of mine rushed into a contest of strength without achieving balance. Battle, now, that's another matter, but not our concern at present. Man against man—that is our business. Look closely at your partner."

Colin obeyed this injunction. He saw a man several years his junior, lean and nimble. Colin outdid him in weight, but that gave him no comfort. Though his exile had stretched only a few weeks, he had managed to shed a noticeable amount of the excess that he had accumulated over a decade or more of sedentary life, yet Colin knew that he was slow, both in body and in wit. He watched Loren warily as the younger man measured him with quick brown eyes.

"What is your advantage? What is his? Without this knowledge, you cannot hope to win."

My advantage? Colin saw how the smaller fellow kept at a distance. *I have reach and size, but this one looks well-skilled. He's quick, too. I'll have a time of it, laying hands on him.*

"Begin!"

In the first few moments, Colin and Loren stood still. To Colin's surprise, the younger man ran at him boldly and tackled him around the chest in a seemingly futile show of strength. Colin pried at the fellow's shoulders to free himself. Then, without realizing how it happened, he found himself flying headlong to the ground. He rolled over and lay on his back, winded, with a taste of blood in his mouth and a nauseated ache in the pit of his stomach. He saw a hand extended to him and grasped it. "How?" he gasped.

A quick grin parted Loren's lips. "I didn't know it would work so well."

Spitting blood onto the grass, Colin got up. "What did you do?"

"Distract your opponent with a foolish attack, and when he tries to pry you off, use the force of his grip to plant a foot into his gut and catapult him over nice and quick onto his head."

Colin spat again. "Worked beautifully," he groaned. "Show me how."

"Can't. You need somebody bigger than you for that move. Care to try something else?"

Although his instinctive answer was *no, thank you,* Colin squared off again. As the dawn matured into rarified midday, Colin ended up on the ground more often than not. No matter what he tried, he was consistently unable to get the better of his partner, a failing that would have discouraged him if Loren were less cheerful and encouraging as a tutor. Every time he knocked Colin to the ground, he was there at once, offering a hand to help him back to his feet, telling him what it was that had felled him, and advising him how to guard against his short-comings.

Then it came to noontide at last. Loren helped Colin up once more. "I haven't worked this hard in many a week, Colin. My thanks for the exercise."

"Oh, aye," he replied in mimicry of the other warriors, "it can't have been easy, hefting my big, clumsy self around like a straw man all morning. You're very welcome."

Loren grinned. "Come to noontide with us, won't you? It's not as fine as what you'd get at the house, but we'll try to make it up to you with good company." His smile faded at the sight of Colin's hesitation, but Loren was gracious about it. "Ah, well, maybe someday soon."

"It isn't that I don't want to," Colin protested, "but I told Lucky I would eat with him."

An impish light came to the younger man's eyes. "I say we bring him with us. He's a good lad, and surprising good company, too, for his age. If we catch him before he heads back to the house and his nanny, nobody'll ever guess."

"Where is he now?"

"My guess? Up with natai Rafe in Bayne's group, learning how to use his dagger."

"Training?" Colin was dumbfounded. "Training with grown men? At nine years old?"

"Ammun says it won't do him any harm. He's a quick lad, too, picks up whatever you teach him as if it came natural to him. Runs in his blood, I guess. Natai!" Loren hailed Farris with a small gesture. He explained the idea to the natai, who nodded as he flung a robe around his shoulders and belted it securely. "Can't see any harm in it. You held up well today, Colin."

"Thank you, natai," said Colin with a bow. "Even if I spent most of my time sprawled out on the ground?"

Farris smiled a little. His small black eyes crinkled. "You are a peaceable man, not a warrior. To let one beat on you for an entire morning—that is the face of courage. Let us fetch the boy and be on our way to the table. I am most hungry."

They found Lucien hard at work on another training field. As Loren had predicted, the boy had his dagger unsheathed as he listened carefully to Rafe. Rafe reached down and corrected something in the boy's grip, explaining rapidly in a foreign tongue. Colin marveled at the boy once again, this time because the boy obviously comprehended this second language well enough to respond with brief phrases in it. In an undertone, he asked, "What language does Rafe speak? Where does he come from?"

Farris replied, "None but Ammun and Rafe can answer your second question, but the tongue is Kavahran. Most of us claim it for our mother tongue. Ammun insists that we hold to your language when in mixed company, however. It is less politically irritating than, shall we say, speaking to a Nikobian in the tongue of Galitaea. Is that not so, Loren?"

Colin had to smile a little, because that tag-end of a question was more than unnecessary—it was absurd. At the mere mention of the name 'Galitaea,' Loren had bristled instinctively, with his lips drawn back as if he were about to spit a foul taste from his mouth. Colin set a hand on Loren's shoulder. "I promise never to make *that* mistake. I had never heard of either land until I came here. Your home must be far from mine."

"Nikobia is a sea-isle. Ashore, there is nothing but wilderness and savages. And Galitaea," he said and wrinkled his nose in disgust. "To reach my land, you would have to sail a fortnight east-northeastward from Palas-by-the-Sea."

Since it seemed to calm the young man to speak of his homeland, Colin responded, "I'm curious to know how you ended up so far inland. Do your people trade with any land near here?"

"No. It was the renown of Ammun that drew me here. I fought for the right to come as hostage here, to learn from him and his elite." Loren expanded his chest with great satisfaction. "My brother and I won this honor out of a hundred peers. Ammun promised that we may serve as emissaries when we have completed our training here. He has many treaties and pacts in many lands. Nikobia is but the most recent to be so favored."

The boy Lucien saw them and spoke eagerly to Rafe, who nodded permission for the boy to sheathe the dagger and join Colin's party. "Good noontide, sir. Is it time to eat?"

"That it is. I was invited to eat with Loren and his bunkmates, so I thought I'd see if you might want to join us, too. What do you say?"

"May I, Farris?"

"Yes, Master Lucky. I have already approved the plan."

Colin soon deduced that Lucien was often present at Farris' table in company with the political residents of Chamika. The men, so diverse in accent and habits, all united in celebrating Lucien's appearance in the doorway. Lucien was passed along from hand to hand, his hair tousled and his back patted vigorously as he made his way to the head of the table. By contrast, Colin took the lowest seat at the farthest end of the table. His nearest tablemates were all strangers to him. Loren sat four places removed from Farris at the other end, but he called out a phrase in Kavahran, to which those at the far end of the table responded with cheerful alacrity.

"You are named Colin, are you not?" inquired one of the young men.

"I am. What might you be called?"

"Burr Duladi."

"And from whence do you hail?"

"Vedele."

Surprised, Colin said, "Indeed! All the way from there? How do you like it here?"

"'Tis too cold." The Kavahri hostage glanced down the table at Lucien and gave a nod. "A good lad, that 'un. I do envy him sometimes. To have such a father, such a place as this to grow up in—he's sure to make something especial of himself before long, with his advantages. If not a great warrior, then some manner of rahg with great influence, no doubt."

"He seems to be making good use of his childhood. I was surprised to see him out among the men, training."

"He won't ever come to harm at it," said another of the men shrewdly.

Colin ate in the midst of lively conversations. Sitting with the foreign warriors was for him an enlightening experience. He heard more trivial gossip there than he ever heard out on the fields or in the streets of the village. Some of it was amusing, as when he listened to speculation on which longhouse of bachelors was responsible for the minor flooding of another longhouse. From the sound of it, there had been little damage but much discomfort for the waterlogged bachelors, who had to sleep on damp pallets for more than one night. Colin developed a suspicion that some around Farris' table knew more about the prank than they were admitting.

The most interesting event, however, came not during the meal but afterward. At the close of the meal, Colin left along with the young men. He saw a peculiar look pass over Loren's face for an instant before the Nikobian hostage veered aside to the left. Colin looked after him, and then turned to see Farris gazing after Loren with compassion in his small black eyes. The tide of warriors washed down the slope and scattered among the buildings, leaving Colin and Farris by themselves. "What was that, natai?"

"It was a very sad thing," answered Farris heavily, "made all the sadder because there's a remedy for it, but Loren will not adopt it." This was the extent of the natai's gossip. As Farris trudged away, Colin lingered. A young voice interrupted his reverie by saying, "Are you heading back to the house, sir? I'll go with you." Lucien stood at his side, waiting with commendable patience for Colin's response.

"Of course." Colin turned from the scene, but his thoughts remained with the troubled young hostage from Nikobia.

∗   ∗   ∗   ∗

Things went from bad to worse on the day after Giles met Ingram. Instead of Vienna coming to fetch him from the house first thing in the morning, a new woman came to fetch him. Her name was Merta. At first Giles thought that this change might be for the better. Merta was young, chatty, and cheerful. She told him his new duty was running errands. Merta was still chatting when she led him to a house not far from the manor house walls. Giles' first impression was a house in total uproar. Before Merta could open the front door herself, the door flung open of its own accord and out of it stampeded half a dozen children, none of them older than eleven years. The last of them courteously left the door agape for Merta and Giles, allowing the noise of quarreling women to dash against Giles' ears without mercy. He couldn't understand what they said, but the argument didn't slow Merta down. She, not being content to merely thrust herself head-long into this storm of forceful verbiage, began to shout just as loudly as any of them as soon as she walked through the doorway. Giles followed more timidly. Once inside, he sidestepped the main fray and found himself a relatively safe place on the far side of a wooden cabinet full of knickknacks.

The house itself was somewhat finer than others he had seen. It had two full stories to its main body as well as a passage leading off to the side. From where he stood, Giles had a good view through that doorway and saw that it led into another wing of the house. The hearth on the opposite side of the room was massive, big enough to roast an entire pig without trouble. With his fingers in his ears, Giles shifted his attention from the house to its occupants. His first thought was that no house could possibly hold this many women. He counted nine, their ages ranging from young teen to elderly matron. For a while, he tried to sort them out: one was clearly in a position of authority in the group, although she was not the eldest of them; two others nearer to Merta's age seemed to be arguing for cessation of hostilities; another older woman seemed to be trying to communicate with the dominant woman over the noise of the argument. Then the stampede of children came back again, but Giles could distinguish between child and child this time. Most of them were boys, but the two girls in their number ran just as heedlessly and made just as much noise as their male companions. No sooner had the children entered than the dominant woman grabbed the eldest of the stampeding children by his arm and shook him lightly. She spoke to him in a voice of command, still speaking a language Giles didn't know. The boy responded in kind, keeping his eyes respectfully on the woman's face. The other children, knowing themselves caught in the act, stood still and fidgeted until the woman finished speaking. Then the children dispersed with a chastened air, leaving the room only moderately quieter than it had been.

This disruption was just enough to rein in the argument slightly. Even so, no one paid any attention to Giles. Even Merta seemed to have deserted him. She was busy trying to separate the oldest woman and a younger woman. Giles sensed that the argument had begun with them and that Merta was doing her best to calm the elder woman. The other older woman smiled tiredly at Merta when she saw what Merta was doing, as if (Giles speculated) she approved of the young woman herself and not just her present course of action. Another pair of young women reasoned with the younger of the two quarreling women and showed signs of success. The eldest woman then shook off Merta's attentions and stormed out of the sitting room, while her opponent put her face in her hands for a moment. Despite the other young women's protests, she retreated into the adjoining wing of the house. Only then did Giles notice the clutter of fabric all over the floor and the furniture. As a young man with two sisters, he knew perfectly well what was going on: they were making a dress.

With the exit of the contentious older lady, the room quieted. The dominant woman and her older companion retired to a corner desk and immersed themselves in conversation. Merta and her two peers shifted around to take up the sewing project again, while the two youngest girls took up embroidery samples of their own. Merta beckoned to Giles. "All is safe now. You can come out."

The other two young women smiled. One of them laughed softly. "You're Giles, are you not? Sit down. My name is Evany, and this is Niesha."

Giles bowed slightly. "Pleased to meet you."

All three of them giggled at this formality. Merta insisted, "No, sit down. We don't have any errands for you just yet." That said, she turned to Evany again. "Why did she say that?"

"Why does Mother do half the things she does?" Evany answered a little sadly. "I understand that it is hard on her, but she must reconcile herself one day to her lot, and part of that means she must get used to not being the mistress of her own house."

"If six years isn't enough time to reconcile herself," said Niesha, "then I don't really know how much time *is* enough. But poor Panya!"

"Nobody blames Panya." Merta was emphatic. "She has her rights, same as my sister does. It isn't as if she goes above her station, but—"

"—but she is young and it offends my mother to submit to her," Evany finished. "Yes."

Giles leaned back in his chair and listened, learning more about the politics of this chaotic household by listening than any amount of questioning could have taught him. When Evany said, "Oh! Where have I put my tape?" Giles spotted it and gave it to her, surprising her.

"Have you worked for a tailor?" she asked him.

Giles shook his head. "Two elder sisters." His impression of the household was turning more hopeful. For the whole morning, he did nothing more strenuous than hold up lengths of cloth for the women to compare. Their company was loquacious enough to suit Giles without being too gossipy or the least bit malicious. Then noontide came. Niesha looked at the window and became very somber. Her two friends noticed at once, but said nothing until someone knocked firmly at the door. Then Merta said, "Don't do it, dear heart. You'll only cause more hurt for both of you. You know you will."

Niesha stood up and set aside her portion of the sewing project. "I just want to see him." She went to answer the door. For a few moments, she exchanged greetings with a man, but Giles couldn't see the newcomer from where he sat. Then, with a backward glance at her friends, Niesha left with the man.

Giles ventured to ask, "What was that about?"

Merta deferred to Evany with an expressive look. Evany took up the tale. "I don't see any harm in telling you. Everyone else knows about Niesha. She was betrothed to a young warrior, one of Ammun's hostages, but now she is betrothed to Druze, the cousin of one of our natai—do you know Farris?" When Giles shook his head, she continued, "Though she is promised to Druze, Niesha does not love him. He knows this. The hostage that claimed Niesha's heart—his name is Loren—is best of friends to Druze. It was Loren who chose Druze as a husband for Niesha when Lachunn forbid the marriage. Every day at noontide, Niesha goes out to walk with Druze, as is proper between a man and his future wife, but every time, she persuades him to walk where she knows she will be able to look upon Loren."

"And he lets her do this?"

"Druze is sorry for her," Merta said. Her voice was thick, as if she was trying not to cry. "I feel sorry for him, myself, because he must stand between them when he doesn't wish to. He does not love Niesha as Loren does, but more as a brother loves his sister. He agreed to the betrothal because he knew that it would give his friend a measure of comfort."

"Awkward for him, though," Giles finished in comprehension. "That's too bad. Why won't her father let her marry the fellow she likes?"

"Because Lachunn and Loren's grandfather were bitter enemies, and Loren has made it very clear that he means to return to his homeland once he has finished his time here. Lachunn will not see his daughter return to Nikobia, so he will not let Loren marry her."

Someone else knocked at the door a few minutes after this revelation. Giles went to answer and discovered Ingram, the young warrior, standing on the threshold. "Hello."

"Here you are!" Ingram replied. "I wondered when I didn't see you at Mother's. You'll truly earn your keep here. I just came to ask," he continued, stepping inside to address Merta and Evany impartially, "whether my friend Druze has been here yet."

"Been and gone again not long ago," Merta said. "You can wait here. I'm sure he'll come back with Niesha." A female voice echoed from the depths of the house, and Merta added, "Giles, you're wanted in the kitchen. Faydra has work for you at last."

Disappointed not to continue with his comfortable chat, Giles nonetheless obeyed the summons. The kitchen was easy enough to find; in it, the two older women waited expectantly for his appearance. One of them was the dominant woman from earlier. Giles assumed that this was the Faydra to whom Merta had referred. "There you are, lad. Take these baskets and fill them to the brim with firewood. Don't dawdle at it. I need them for this afternoon yet. You can start with the groves on the second terrace. If you don't find enough, you can try the third terrace, but don't go farther than that. I don't want you getting yourself lost and eaten by beasts. Go on with you." She shooed him out of the kitchen as quickly as he had come.

With one basket slung over his shoulder and the other in his hands, Giles didn't return through the front of the house. It irked him to think of Ingram seeing him at this menial task. Giles didn't examine this thought, but it rankled. Once he was alone in the groves of the middle terrace, he vented his frustration aloud. "It isn't my fault I don't have a trade. Nobody cared to give me one, not until Uncle Owen tried me out as an errand-runner, and even *that* doesn't count. If they mean to help the situation here, I don't see how children's tasks will do the trick—"

"What's amiss with you today?"

Giles turned sharply, but relaxed when he saw who it was. "Afternoon, my lord. I didn't see you there. Sorry."

"No, you were busy," was the king's droll reply. "Who, may I ask, was the recipient of your scathing wit? I don't see anyone standing within earshot."

That question made Giles redden. He hesitated, unsure whether he ought to bother the king with this petty matter when the king obviously had something on his mind already. "Just talking to myself, sir. It wasn't anything."

"It was enough to upset you. If you've started arguing with yourself, I feel obliged to worry about you." Colin smiled. "What's the matter?"

"I oughtn't complain, I suppose, since I never deserved to come as your squire in the first place, but it isn't my fault. They won't even let have that much dignity."

"Nobody around here has a squire, Giles, and I hardly qualify as a warrior anyway."

"You get to train with them, at least."

Colin wrenched a dead branch off of a nearby tree, broke it in half and put it in Giles' basket. "Who makes sport of you?"

"Some of the young fellows say I'm here just because—" Giles blushed hotly. "I'm marriage kin to Ammun and he had to do *something* with me. Makes it sound like I'm stupid on purpose, like I don't *want* to know anything."

"So far, you've gone at your life as if you didn't really want to be or do anything."

"All right, aye, but that was before—" *Idiot,* Giles chastised himself over the mistake. *Do you really want to blurt out that the only reason you feel the need for a trade is because you think it might help your chances with his daughter?*

In the awkward silence, the king went on helping Giles fill his baskets. Casually, he remarked, "A man can change if he wants it badly enough, Giles, but ambition by itself won't take you far. You've found your ambition; that's clear. You need something more to get you anywhere, however. Do you know what that is?"

"If I knew, do you suppose I'd be out here picking up sticks?"

Colin laughed. "Yes. If that was what you were told to do, you would. I'm talking about perseverance. It doesn't matter how great your ambitions are, Giles, if you don't have courage to persevere at even the most menial tasks. Do *you* believe Ammun brought you out here simply to keep you out of the way? Neither do I. If he sent you here and instructed you to pick up sticks, does it not make sense to at least wonder how you can use this to further your ambitions?"

Grudgingly, Giles nodded his affirmation. He vividly remembered what the towering warrior had said to him on the night he rescued Giles from the Pamirsi jail: *I have use for you.* Ammun had believed that Giles was good for something, and it didn't seem likely that he had had menial tasks in mind. Another thought crossed Giles' mind for the first time: *At least you can do well at the menial work and make the king think better of you by it.*

"While you're thinking, how much wood are you supposed to gather?" the king asked.

"These two baskets full."

"You'll never finish by dark. I'll help you."

Surprised but grateful, Giles surrendered his second basket. They began to work side by side, until it turned into a bit of a competition. Despite his head start, Giles had trouble keeping up with the king's buoyant energy. They were both over halfway done with their baskets when they heard the sound of a wood-cutter hard at work. The king nodded in that direction. "Let's see if we can wheedle some chips out of him."

When they reached the source of the chopping noises, they found a warrior wielding a double-handed great sword. Sweat streamed down the warrior's face and chest. His shirt, completely saturated with sweat, lay draped over a low branch nearby. As soon as he saw Colin, he lowered his blade tip-downward and leaned on it. "Strange occupation you've chosen."

"My young friend is somewhat behind in his work. I thought I'd help him along."

As if Giles wasn't listening, the fellow said, "Too bad about that. At his age, he ought to be taking on a man's duties."

"He got to a slow start in life, aye, but I have hopes for him." Colin surveyed the cluttered ground. "We'll get some of this out of your way. You've been working hard. I didn't know that the woodcutters of Chamika used swords instead of axes, Loren."

Ah, Giles thought, drifting away from the other two for his own peace of mind. *So that's who Merta and Evany were talking about earlier. Niesha's true love.*

Loren chuckled. "They don't. This is meant to focus the mind. When you hit with all your might without fearing damage to your opponent, you learn better what your true strength is. You learn to strike true, to breathe without hindrance even when in motion—so says Ammun. I used to have great trouble focusing. In battle, I often nearly got myself killed, so he set me this exercise for when I…need control." He shifted his gaze to the trees around him and fell silent.

"I've never lived so far out in the wilderness before. It's very quiet, once you get away from the village," said the king. "Are there great cities on Nikobia?"

"There is one city of great beauty, the city of my birth. Wallema is its name. Twenty thousand souls live within its bounds."

"Ah! It's very nearly the size of my own city. We boast twenty-four thousand, which gets rather crowded sometimes. Of course, there are bigger cities in the kingdom. Chliaros is the greatest of all. The last census put it at past a million living in and around the walls."

"A million?" Loren scratched his head idly. "I cannot conceive of such a number."

"On the plains, there is space to stretch out if need be. I don't suppose you've ever seen the plains country? You should. It's a humbling sight. When you stand in the middle of the tall grass and look around at the big upturned bowl of sky, with not a building in sight, you know yourself for the tiny mortal creature you are."

"I would like to see this someday," Loren admitted.

"If you ever have the chance, you should ask to accompany Ammun there. You would find a welcome in my daughter's court, I'm sure."

"Perhaps one day I shall."

Too late for you, poor worm, Giles thought to himself as he scooped handfuls of wood chips into his basket. *The king already has a favorite. Sounds like he's already got plans. This Loren…* He glanced at the warrior and his heart sank. *He's everything I'm not, and a free man, too, thanks to Niesha's father.* He saw the young warrior knelt down and, despite the cost to his dignity, began to help the king gather woodchips.

The king was grateful. "Thank you, Loren. It's very kind of you."

"If you like," the warrior said, lowering his voice slightly, "I'll talk to your young friend. Perhaps he only wants encouragement."

"I'd take that very kindly. If there's ever anything I can do for you in return, tell me."

They struck hands on the bargain. "I'll remember that," said Loren.

Giles was far enough away by this time that his retreat went unnoticed. *I don't want the pity of that one, either. Especially not that one.* Even though his basket wasn't heaped full, he retreated to Faydra's house.

YESTERDAY: FRIEND
FOR THE FRIENDLESS

The raid was finished. Everything had followed plans. All that remained was to divide the spoils in a way that reflected each man's contribution to the raid's success. Orlan smiled inwardly when he saw the men tremble more before this ordeal than before a battle. *They know.*

Of course they know, and as well they should tremble. They are witnessing the rise of a greater and deadlier master—

Keep silent, Audune. It pleased him to thus nettle the giant. Both he and Audune knew that the giant could not disobey that command, and the limitation infuriated Audune. Orlan took every opportunity to use it against him. He paced along the edges of the rope corral and studied the livestock, both human and nonhuman creatures bound for slavery to either him or his so-called master Malin. Malin would descend upon the temporary prison camp within the hour. Orlan had arranged a series of diversions: a horse lamed, a tree fallen at a narrow point of the road, and any of a half dozen other minor hindrances to slow the raider prince's progress along the way. Every moment of delay gave Orlan another moment to make his selections. *If he were wise, he would give me my head and be done with it. Every man in the Thousand Companies knows that I made the greatest contributions to this raid, as I have all year. By rights, I should take fully half of the spoils as my reward. I could kill him so easily.*

Then do it, Audune hissed.

Why? When the warriors are discontented, they complain to him, not to me. When they cry for sport, they cry to him and make him give of his own treasury when they bear grievances against his leadership. Why should I take that onto myself?

But as long as he is named prince of the Thousand, the glory of his victories eludes you.

I told you to keep silent, he returned idly. *When the Thousand sweep through the land, it is not the name of Malin that the people wail in fear. They do not beg clemency of Malin.* Arrested by a face among the corralled prisoners, Orlan stopped to look more closely.

It was no one he had ever met. Of that, he was sure. Somehow, the air of familiarity went deeper than mere memory. For a moment, he imagined that it rose from his very blood. Orlan swung a leg over the rope enclosure, ignoring the shudders and moans of the captives nearest to him. He pushed through the common herd until he stood over the young man, who looked no older than fifteen or sixteen years. *Do I know you?* he demanded of the boy's shepherd.

At first, the only response was a shocked exclamation. Then, in a tearful, childlike voice, the giant whispered, *Little brother?*

Then he knew, more swiftly than thought could have told him. Orlan bent to grasp the young captive by his shoulder and hauled him to his feet. He approved of the boy's manner. He saw by the trembling knees that the boy was terrified. Others faced with the masked raider's scrutiny had wet themselves, wept, or babbled. Not the boy. He trembled, but he stood upright and silent. In the native language he had not used for some time, Orlan bid the boy speak. "Tell me your name, the name of your father, your homeland, and your business in this region, boy."

The boy found his voice. "My name is Damon Kyte-son, s-sir. I was born in the king's city, clan Sakiry of the Second Kingdom, sir." Suddenly he remembered the fourth question and blurted, "I ran away from home. I want to be an adventurer."

So I do know you, mused Orlan as he stared at the tremulous youth. *I remember your father…and my father…* He shook the connection from his mind as the noise of approaching horses interrupted him. Lifting his eyes, he saw Malin throw himself down from the back of a magnificent warhorse and stalk toward the corral.

"What meaning do I read into this, Orlan? The division of spoils doesn't begin until I give the word."

"The division of spoils has not begun. Give the word already. Some of us tire of waiting."

Orlan made no further move. The silence around them was absolute, as if the lesser warriors scarcely dared to draw breath until the outcome of the clash had been decided. "Why do you continue to waste our time like this? Give the word." Inwardly, he laughed at the raider prince's quandary. *Now, however he chooses, he cannot help but act in deference to me.*

Yes, you have been very clever, Audune grumbled. *You will not choose that boy as part of your portion, though.*

Orlan envisaged the voice as coming from Malin. *I think I will. He does not lack courage. If he wants the life of an adventurer, I will teach him myself.* He saw the moment Malin backed down; resentment was written in every line of his features.

"Is *that* your first choice?" the older man said snidely. "Doesn't look like much."

"All the more renown for me when I make a warrior of him." He switched languages and said to the boy, "You will follow me. Two steps behind me at all times, until I say otherwise. Speak to no one, acknowledge no one—don't meet the eyes of anyone we pass. Do this, and perhaps you'll live the night out." If he spoke more harshly than he meant, it was for the benefit of the few raiders who might understand the Keepers' tongue. The boy looked twice as frightened as before, more than enough to need none of Orlan's usual methods to keep him in line. He didn't seem to have understood any of the previous exchange. Orlan knew what had intensified the boy's fright. It was a common enough occurrence: the same happened with every captive who heard the name of Orlan spoken.

Orlan made his selections from among the herd, often choosing them from under Malin's nose as the raider prince was about to choose. He knew that Malin was unlikely to choose the same prisoners; he and his alleged master sought wildly different qualities in their slaves. Still, it gave the impression that he was taking something from Malin. That was all he wanted—that impression. It bothered Malin no end, so Orlan delighted in it.

Finally, with the spoils divided at last, Orlan returned his attention to the boy. Young Damon had followed obediently at his heels the whole day, eyes downcast, mouth tightly shut. He was quick enough to look up, however, when his new master addressed him. "Can you ride?"

"A horse, sir?"

Orlan had to stifle an unexpected snort of laughter. "Yes, a horse. I'll take that as a no. Come." He led the boy to the horses, which had remained saddled and ready through the division process, in case they were needed in a moment of tension. One of them stood unattended; its rider had not returned from the raid with them, but Orlan had a better use for his time than in mourning the unfortunate Tollewen. He planted the boy beside the riderless horse. "Left foot in the stirrup. Grasp the saddle and lift yourself up." Pleased that the boy required only two tries to make it atop the colossal war horse, Orlan proceeded to instruct him briefly in the use of reins. He then mounted up and led his mixed collection of belongings away toward the mountains.

Halfway there, an outrider caught up with him. "Still following us, keiri."

Orlan nodded. "Take the horses. Send the slaves with Niall. Whoever falls behind stays behind." He glanced at the boy. "Hang on. We'll make a fast run." With that as his only warning, he spurred his steed lightly into a run that carried them far from the road, through rough foothills covered in brambles. No one else came with them. At a certain place, Orlan dismounted. "Down. The horses are no more use to us." He grabbed his horse by its nose and said to its shepherd, *"Home. Now."* He did the same with the other horse before turning to the boy.

The boy gazed at him warily. Orlan could read his thought easily enough: he feared being left alone and afoot with his new master. He shifted from one foot to the other. "What do you want fr-from me, sir?"

"Keep quiet and make no rash moves. Above all, do not run." Orlan placed two fingers in his mouth and whistled three shrill notes into the calm air.

A bird called in the interval while they waited. Apart from the bird, nothing made a sound around them. The boy shifted feet again, growing impatient. When he started to speak, Orlan rebuked him in a low voice. "I said keep quiet. You must appear confident, even if you feel anything but confident. This lesson you must learn if you are to live among warriors, but especially if you are to have dealings with my...*other* companions. Stand firm and keep quiet. I will not tell you again." Distantly, he heard a light drumming of feet on sod. "Here they come."

To the boy's credit, he did not make any sound when the trio of great pardeléi loped into view. They were magnificence embodied, one golden female with black spots and two black with gold spots. Without pausing in their stride, they circled around the two humans twice before they settled on their haunches in front of Orlan. One sniffed the boy inquiringly, turning her luminous golden eyes to Orlan for explanation.

He fixed in his mind an image they would understand: a cub with its mother. The pardeléi did not accept the image, casting one back to him of a cuckoo laying eggs in another bird's nest. He altered his image to show the cub and its mother again, but this time he had a strange cub wander toward the imaginary pair, lost and mewling in fright. This they comprehended easily; in their own clans, any cub could approach any mother if it had lost its own. They sniffed Orlan's new "cub" approvingly.

That was the easy part. He knelt down before the golden cat and searched her eyes. In turn, he submitted to the same search, but deeper. The pardelé saw more keenly than even he could. She saw his very memories, the past few days of which he opened for her perusal so she could ascertain if he deserved to have his favor granted. Pardeléi had their own sense of honor, a very strict code of behavior, and little concept of mercy. They were the only living creatures Orlan had ever discovered who had no immortal shepherds accompanying them. Rather, the shepherds of all beasts consulted with them. The deeply intelligent pardeléi served as the judges of the wilderness. Any mortal creature—the pardeléi no longer distinguished between mute beasts and mankind as they once had—must submit to their code while in their domain.

Occasionally, he felt compelled to seek the great cats' company, and because of a service he had once rendered their matriarch, the pardeléi suffered him willingly. Orlan did not examine his compulsion. He only knew that he respected these powerful, rational, nearly fanatical beasts. Though he could not wholly share their stern code, he submitted to this examination of memory time and again, intentionally displaying how unequal he was to their standards. To his surprise, they never dealt with him accordingly. The display itself seemed to please them enough that they accepted him without violence and even suffered the indignity of letting him ride them once in a while. This was his hope now. He felt the pressure of time bearing down on him and risked a show of superiority by framing his request in words: "I have need of your swiftness."

The golden pardelé gave him a tolerant nudge with one of her massive paws. She touched her nose to his forehead in a gesture remarkably like a kiss of blessing. Then she turned from him and loped away into the underbrush. Her two sisters, the pair of spotted black pardeléi, prostrated themselves on the ground for the humans to climb onto their backs. From atop the cat, Orlan looked at the boy and found him still frozen in awe. "Climb up, boy. We don't have time for dawdling."

The boy rose a little higher in his estimation by obeying despite his fear. Pale and timorous, he laid a hand on the other cat's fur. He flinched when the cat sniffed at him again. Then, in a daring rush, he swung a leg over and clung tightly to the cat's neck fur.

"Not so tight, boy," Orlan said in a droll voice, astutely interpreting the cat's startled, pained yelp. "She won't let you fall, so long as you keep still." Then there was no further chance for speech, because both cats launched themselves from the ground in an initial bound calculated to impress their riders. This also Orlan had had to learn the hard way: the cats delighted in their great power and liked nothing better than to display it at every turn. He never tired of the thrill he felt every time he looked down to see the ground blurring past them.

Before long, they were at the base of the flat-topped peak where sat his found-ling village, Chamika. He dismounted and touched his nose to that of his oblig-ing steed in farewell. Out of the corner of his eye, he saw the other cat rub itself along the boy's side, nearly knocking him onto the ground. Again he had to stifle a laugh. "Come along, boy. Stop playing."

"Playing!" young Damon gasped, still recovering from the ride. He caught himself on the verge of uttering a retort when he remembered to whom he spoke.

Orlan led him up the switchback horse trail to the summit where a small hunting lodge overlooked a neat grid of cottages and lanes. At his approach, someone cried out to the rest of the village. One woman came running immedi-ately. Orlan gave the boy over to her. "Take him away and scrub him, Vienna. I'll dispose of him later. We're about to have unwanted guests." To a large, husky man standing not much farther up the trail, he said, "Gather every able body, Farris. Rafe and Niall come soon after me with the spoils. Malin followed us, thinking he'd catch me unawares at home."

The battle that followed had little meaning, except to prove once again that Orlan on his own ground was even more fearsome than he was abroad in the world, and that he was well able to defend his own belongings, human and other-wise. He hardly exerted himself, in all honesty. While he directed the brief skir-mish, he was otherwise occupied in mind.

You have no say in my choice of companions. You cannot stop me.

Audune skirted the issue. *He will slow you down. You know your weakness. Once you show the least affection for him, your warriors will begin to despise you. One such as you cannot afford to take friends for himself. You know this perfectly well.*

Who said anything about taking him as a friend? I will teach him. He has the makings of a good warrior. Then, once he has completed his training, we will see if he stays or goes.

*   *   *   *

From the edge of the upper terrace, Orlan watched the boy. Today's task was by no means the most menial of the duties that Damon had been assigned; it was, however, by far the most challenging. Today, Damon was given the task of exer-cising the horses that had not gone out on the last foray. He stood in the middle of the pasture down below, clinging to the tether of a restive black mare that circled around him at a barely restrained canter. Hand over hand, the boy shortened the tether until the tightening circumference of the horse's path forced her to slow down. Once he had brought the mare to a halt, he laid a hand on her sweat-flecked side to calm her as he spoke in too soft a voice to be overheard. So far, this was all according to the instructions that the boy received that morning. Orlan waited, watching for something more.

He did not have to wait long. No sooner had the boy gotten the mare calmed sufficiently than he hoisted himself up astride the mare's back. Disliking this sudden change in routine, she danced sideways in a series of violent little jumps meant to unseat an inexperienced rider. Damon very nearly was thrown to the ground, but he wrapped his arms around her neck and pressed his face against her. His lips moved frantically, to little avail. Now the mare had her temper up, and she meant to rid herself of this large burr at all costs. She bucked in earnest, and before long the boy went hurtling through the air. Damon picked himself up unsteadily. When he ran to catch hold of the dragging tether again, he couldn't. The mare was too quick.

Orlan watched this game for only a little longer before he descended to the pasture to put a halt to it. Crooning a low, nonsensical series of comfort words to the nervous mare, he strode closer and closer until he could lay hold of her bridle. Then he took time to stroke her and condole with her over the ordeal that Damon had inflicted upon her. Soon she was docile again, responding to the touch of her master willingly. He led her to the hitching rail, where he tied her safely. Then he turned to the boy.

Damon stood at attention, shoulders straight and head lifted. His eyes held no expression as he stared ahead stolidly.

"She is blind on her off-side," Orlan commented mildly. "Next time you'll know better."

The boy risked a startled glance. "Sir?"

"Never approach her from that side again, or she might well kill you. She has an unsteady temper. This time, you were fortunate. There is a reason for the instructions I give you."

"Yes, sir."

Orlan found within himself the stirrings of talkativeness. The sensation was so novel to him that he decided to pursue it and see where it led. "Do you know how she became blind on the one side? I once rode her on a raid into the southlands, not far from the Eternal Desert of the Kavahri." At once, he saw that he held the boy's rapt attention. "We rode against a rahg whose taunt was that none dared strike at him in his own lands, because he was too powerful there. I knew better; his own people loathed him and would have done any service in their power to aid the man who overthrew their master. Even so, it was a hard battle." As he spoke, momentarily reliving the memory, he felt another sensation, not new but so rarely experienced that it took him by surprise: reluctance. *I would not have him follow in my ways,* he realized.

Then you must give him up, Audune retorted triumphantly.

For a year, Orlan put this off. He had watched the boy's progress with a mixture of pride and dread that made him an uneasy companion, but the boy no longer flinched at his tempers. In truth, Orlan rarely thought of him as "the boy" any more. Damon had proven himself well able to carry the burdens of a young man, and so he was accorded that standing among Orlan's warriors. A few persisted in calling him "tame dog," however, a teasing acknowledgment of Damon's unique standing as Orlan's only constant companion.

"Do you know," Damon said idly as they flicked stones into a pond at the rear of the property, "my date of borning comes in two days?" His Kavahran was improving greatly as well, although a good deal less speedily than his swordsmanship.

"Which *birthday?*" Orlan replied, stressing the correct word for Damon's instruction.

"Seventeenth. In another year at home, I would've been declared a man."

Orlan laughed softly. "In another year, you would've been ruined for it, sitting idle as you were. You've more than earned your way already." He cast a stone so briskly that it skittered across the water's surface and hit the opposite shore with a distant click. "Should you return now, they couldn't deny you the title of man."

The look Damon gave him was too acute for his liking. "Who talks of returning?"

"Do you not miss your people?"

"I miss Ta, and sometimes my mother, but they'll keep a while longer yet. I still have lessons aplenty, do I not? Surely I cannot know everything already?"

"You know enough to make a respectable showing, should anyone press you. You should consider returning home."

"Trying to get rid of me?"

"For your good, Damon. This is no life for you."

The young man was silent for a time before he dared speak his thought. "Nor for you, sir. If you were what they say you are, you wouldn't be so concerned for my—" He caught Orlan's flat gaze and fell silent again, but not for long. "I would apologize, but I can't be sorry, sir, not for speaking my honest thought. If

you are concerned for me, then...then grant me the freedom to be just as concerned for you."

"You are wasting your time. You should go home."

"I won't go and leave my friend behind."

They often quarreled on this front, sometimes loudly enough to send the vil-
lagers running for shelter ahead of them. The other warriors began to offer
Damon subtle deference. He was the only living man who had quarreled with
Orlan and remained a living man. Thus his stature increased in the village, while
Orlan's reputation for unpredictable violence grew.

It had been years since Orlan had wrestled so fiercely with Audune. The introduction of this friendship with Damon reawakened all the old discord that he
thought he had shed with the death of his identity. Once again he sat up nights as
in his former life, held immobile by his own unwillingness to heed Audune's
command to kill Damon in his sleep. He became agonizingly attuned to every
opportunity to betray Damon to his death, whether in battle or in the hazards of
everyday activities. Others bore the brunt of his uneasy tempers. Whenever
Damon tried to intercede for his fellow warriors or for the hapless residents of
Chamika, Orlan fled the village for weeks at a time rather than risk harm to his
only friend. He may have been unable to do more than that, but he certainly
could do no less.

KITCHEN TALK

The kitchen was a much happier place when Lucinda was not in it, Maia noted. She smiled as Ardith, Lucinda's daughter-in-law, set a bowl of spiced milk on the table before her. "Thanks, Ardith." Over the rim of the bowl, Maia looked at her mother.

It had been decided that a different solution must be found in answer to the regent question, thanks to the astonishing appearance of Virlane, her father's friend, in the midst of the Council meeting three days previous. Virlane never set foot in the western wing of the palace. Everybody knew that, so everybody was surprised to see him. Maia's teacher alone did not gape at Virlane when he marched crossly to the dais. "Your highness, may I speak? I have rather limited time to waste—to *spend* here."

Maia had been hard pressed not to giggle. She was used to his abrupt ways and took them as a matter of course. "Go ahead. What is it you came to say?"

"I have this very morning been to see Owen, Lord Sakiry. He bid me come here to say that he opposes the proposed regency. As the princess' nearest and eldest kinsman, he invokes his rights to forbid such a measure from being raised ever again, unless he or a nearer kinsman should bring it up." The sardonic expression that had crossed Virlane's face was almost too much for Maia to bear in dignified silence. He turned and bowed toward his father and his father's sister Mearah. "Sorry, Aunt Mearah. It looks as if you lose this time, too."

Selena's relief over Owen's very public message was unmistakable. She hummed softly to herself now as they sat opposite each other in the quiet kitchen. Midmorning brought with it the same relentless heat, driving the servants out into the yard to do their work beneath the shade of the orchards if at all possible. Only Ardith stayed in the kitchen to meet with Selena over the details of house-keeping that were beneath Lucinda as matriarch. Part of that included plans for the upcoming midsummer festival.

"Where do you suppose Miss Ivy has got to?" Ardith asked. "Tisn't like her to not come when she's due for a visit. I hope she's all right."

"I'm sure something came up. She's a married lady now, you know."

What is going on? Maia's curiosity rose. She could tell that her mother knew more about the matter than she would admit. Maia did not pursue the matter, though. "I wasn't sure that holding the festival would be the right thing to do, but Teacher liked the idea. Do you think this is right, going on as if nothing happened?"

"If we don't go on, dear, where can we go? Life doesn't stop when bad things happen."

Selena's gentle sigh told Maia more than the words preceding it did. It told Maia that her mother deliberately meant not to reveal just how deeply the absence of her father grieved her. It told her that her mother was trying to be strong, most likely for her sake. Maia's pity grew. *Poor Mother. I wish I could do something to help her.* "That makes good sense, Mother. Do you think Ivy will come today? If we're to have everything ready, we need to start preparing."

Before her mother could answer, quick footsteps sounded just outside the door. Ivy came hurrying in as if fleeing something. "Good morning, Selie. Good morning Maia, Ardith." She slipped onto the bench beside Maia's mother and added in an undertone, "You got my note?"

"Yes." Selena touched the fabric of Ivy's robe. "My! This is new, isn't it? How lovely!" A sparkle of humor returned to her eyes. "A gift?"

Ivy blushed. "Yes."

"I like it. It suits you."

The praise seemed to unsettle Ivy, who changed the subject. "You're still planning the midsummer festival, are you? It might strike some as inappropriate, considering…"

"Well, then, those who see it in that light need not come. If their consciences do not permit it, then I cannot say otherwise to them. We, however, will go on as always. I do need your help with the planning. You have such a talent for arranging these things."

Maia's attention drifted away as the two older women fell into practical talk pertaining to the festival. In another few moments, however, she had something new to occupy her mind. Her personal maid Kenda entered along with another girl. Between them, they carried a basket of laundry for mending. When Kenda passed Maia, she gave such an expressive look that Maia had to follow them. She stood apart until Kenda had given the other girl her instructions. Then she and Kenda went to another corner of the room for privacy. "How on earth did you get stuck working with Rhendi?" Maia whispered, snickering.

"Better her than her friend," was Kenda's longsuffering reply. "Uncle Mattieu got *her* as his helper—Nana wouldn't hear otherwise—and do you know what? I just happened past the door of the library while he was trying to catalog the books. As I passed, do you know what Liande said to him? 'Falco, Falco, Falco—why does this person have to keep having the same name? I'm bored!' Poor Mattieu!" When Maia looked at her blankly, Kenda explained, "He was reading off the different titles and their authors for Liande to write down."

With sudden comprehension, Maia finished for her, "And Falco wrote a lot of books."

"Yes, so it would seem. At least with this one, I only have to remind her to keep working. She does tend to forget what she's doing. The smallest thing distracts her. If one guard happens past, all hope is lost. She's useless when there's a young man present. Any young man at all," Kenda sighed. "The two of them together are worse than useless."

"Nana Lucinda likes them well enough to keep them."

"Oh, yes, that she does. She likes their flattery so well that she foists them off on the rest of us to show us how we ought to behave toward her. She assigned me Rhendi on purpose, you know." Kenda stabbed her needle through the linen she was embroidering. "She ought to have retired years ago. Grandfather is much fitter for the work. Oh, no!"

Maia turned to locate the cause of that last outburst. Her teacher had just entered the kitchen, accompanied by Hollister and two of his friends, Eraste and Raven. Exactly as Kenda had warned, as soon as the girl Rhendi took note of the newcomers, she let fall the sock that she had been darning and began to fuss with her braids. "Well, so much for the mending," Maia whispered. She stood to greet her teacher. "Good morning!"

"Good morning to you, Princess."

"What brings you down here?"

"For the moment, merely the present company." Her teacher took up a wooden chair and carried it to the corner where Maia and Kenda had been in conference. The three young guards followed suit. Soon they had formed a comfortable circle of conversation. Her teacher began a topic that surprised her. "Do they plan midsummer over there?" he asked, gesturing toward the table across the way. "Good. In my village, they would have begun the planning many days ago. Our festival lasts two weeks instead of just one." He smiled a little ruefully. "I must confess that I do not like the thought of missing it. My people make much of it—all the more because they do not often have cause for much celebration. We are much at war."

"Why is that?" Hollister asked.

"Because we have many enemies. Rather, I should say, *I* have many enemies, and my village fights them for my sake."

A walnut-sized wooden ball came skittering across the floor, passing through their midst and halting only when it ran into Hollister's feet. He picked it up and looked at it curiously. All of a sudden, the girl Rhendi was at his shoulder. "Oh, thank you. I must have dropped that. How clumsy of me!" She took it from his fingers, in the process leaning a good deal closer to him than was necessary.

Maia looked at Kenda and saw that the incident had nettled her badly. *Clumsy, aye,* Maia thought with a hint of her own exasperation. *Anyone could see through that maneuver!* When she looked at Hollister again, she saw no such knowledge reflected in his reply to Rhendi.

Hollister winked at the girl. "Off to your work, now."

After an awkward interval, Maia's teacher said, "I am thankful to you for continuing with your own midsummer traditions, Princess. Since I cannot be present at my village, at least I will have some chance to celebrate here." He leaned back in his chair, as if the mere thought of a festival put him more at ease. His eyes sought the area around table again briefly.

Rhendi came back. She leaned into the circle to sift through the basket of mending, but her eyes were on Hollister. "Finished that sock," she said brightly. "What shall I do next?"

"Sewed it shut, as like as not," Kenda murmured just loudly enough for Maia to hear. She snatched at the blouse that Rhendi chose from the basket. "No, I think not. Here." She took out a neatly folded square of cloth. "The bottom hem is coming loose on this bed sheet. You might be able to manage that much."

To all outward appearances, Rhendi had not heard a word of it. She was still smiling at Hollister. "Bed sheets are so important."

"I suppose they are." His expression made it plain that he could have said anything to the flirting girl—*not that there's a proper response to make to such an inane remark,* Maia noted. Hollister returned the girl's smile pleasantly, but she was far from finished.

"Rather like you! You're *very* important, aren't you?"

Embarrassed by this display of vacancy, Maia said, "Go on, Rhendi. You have mending to do." She hardly dared look at Kenda, whose slow smolder she could sense beside her.

Her teacher only waited until the girl had retreated a few steps before he said to Hollister, "You could do better."

"What do you mean, sir? She does that to all of us. It means nothing. It's just her game."

"But you could do better." Amused, the general leaned forward and flicked his gaze toward Kenda with a meaningful air. "Unless you're satisfied with that type of...*game*, that is."

The thought had not occurred to Maia, but she saw a ruddy flush creep up Hollister's neck. She looked at Kenda again. Kenda had not looked up from her mending. The Caretaker girl was clearly annoyed, but it was not so easy to ascertain the reason for her annoyance. She might have been jealous. Then again, she might have been thinking of all the extra work she would have to do if Rhendi failed to carry her rightful share of the load. Maia turned back to find Hollister extremely disconcerted.

"I'll...I'll think on it, sir, if you say so."

Something else interested Maia about the exchange. She happened to look over toward the table where Ivy, Selena and Ardith sat in conference, only to find Ivy inattentive. The older woman gazed across the room at her husband with a peculiar uncertainty in her eyes, as if she had heard but did not know what to make of his advice to Hollister. Then, swiftly, Ivy reddened and turned back to her own conversation with alacrity. When Maia looked away from the table, she found her teacher gazing toward the table also. She was surprised by his melancholy.

The conversation shifted, thanks to the other two guards. Soon they were in the midst of arguing the merits of different midsummer customs, laughing as often as they argued. Kenda shook off her ire and joined the conversation freely, and thus they passed well over an hour. By the end of the hour, Kenda had completed most of the mending in her basket. Maia had to bite her lip when Hollister offered to carry the basket for her. Rhendi still wrestled with that one bed sheet, apparently unable to locate its loosening bottom seam for more than a few moments at a time. When Hollister was gone, Eraste and Raven decided to go out into the city for a while before Eraste's noontide shift began. Rhendi, noticing the exit of the young men, wadded her bed sheet under her arm and set off after them alone. Maia recalled her with a sharp tone. "Where do you think you're going by yourself?"

"About my work, miss," Rhendi said with a haphazard curtsy. Her eyes still held to the empty doorway as she shifted from one foot to the other in impatience.

"What is the rule, Rhendi? No one goes about the house alone."

"Oh, *that* rule. Lady Caretaker lets us go by ourselves. She says it's all right."

"Does she? We'll see about that. You stay here until someone else comes to accompany you." Maia drew herself up to her tallest and folded her arms. "Do you understand?" She watched the pouting young woman flounce back to her chair and throw herself down in it. Sitting also, Maia breathed an exasperated sigh. "I don't know about that girl."

"She and her friend cause me great alarm," her teacher said in agreement.

"If they weren't so stupid, it wouldn't be so hard to deal with them."

Her teacher smiled. "It goes the same with intelligence as it does with every other sort of good fortune, Princess. Those with much good fortune have obligations toward those who have little. The burden laid upon the fortunate is a tedious one at times. The rich are charged with care for the poor, deserving or not; so must the intelligent look after the ignorant and even the stupid. If we do not teach them and help them along the way, what would become of them? How can they improve if no one took the time to instruct them?"

"I could look after them much easier if Nana Lucinda didn't turn around and undo everything I did."

"Yes," he said slowly, thoughtfully. "*She* must certainly be dealt with according to her actions. It is bad enough that she forsakes her own vows, but to incite the foolish to that same faithlessness is unpardonable."

"I doubt she would even listen to Father now. She goes on about how she's been doing her work since before any of us were born, as if that has anything to do with the real problem. Anyway, she hasn't been 'doing her work' for as long as I can recall. Chessy and poor Ardith do the real work." Maia looked up in time to see Rhendi get up again from her chair.

This time, however, Ardith saw her also and said loudly, "It's time I went back to my other duties, my lady. Do excuse me. Come along, Rhendi. You can go with me."

"Of course, Ardith. Do what you need to do," Selena replied. Shifting her attention, she asked Maia's teacher, "May I borrow Maia for a few minutes? There are some details that I'd like her opinion on before we can proceed."

"Certainly, Lady Selena." Rather than leave when Maia exchanged his company for the women's, her teacher stretched out his legs and appeared to doze off quite comfortably.

*   *   *   *

Nässey's unaccountable advice remained at the forefront of Ivy's mind, no matter how hard she tried to banish it. Doran's account of her father's last moments only intensified the struggle within her. One part of her still could not dismiss the aged seer's revelations. The other part was beginning to yield to the respect she had always felt for her brother's knowledge and Doran's honesty. Her intuition prompted her to listen to the men she had known so long. *Either way,* she reasoned, *it won't hurt to stay away for a little while, like Nässey asked me to.*

It did not escape Ivy's notice that, for whatever reason, her husband stayed as far from her as the bounds of courtesy permitted. Now that she had reason to seek the truth of his character, she had no opportunity to approach him. She lacked for nothing that he could provide. Sometimes he presented these gifts in person, but more often than not, small luxuries would appear on his empty pillow in the morning. When he offered anything himself, he did so with an air of detachment, rendering the gift impersonal and any attempts at conversation impertinent. There had been one day—yesterday—that was different from the others. As always, he had come silently, startling her while she stood at the window watching for his approach. He had put his hands on her shoulders and kissed the side of her neck. "Good evening." But he would not let her turn to face him. Instead, he wrapped his arms around her, rested his chin atop her head, and looked out the window along with her. She began to grow comfortable in his arms. When the vista outside had grown too dark to be seen any longer, her husband finally turned her around and kissed her forehead in a light, almost brotherly way. "What a day I've had! Did you find Selena well? I know she has missed your company. She's very lonely without her husband."

Ivy had summoned her courage and asked the question that had begun to weigh on her heart so heavily. "Why did Colin have to...to go away?"

"You have already been told the greatest reason: because his life was in danger as long as he stayed. Any other reasons, he will find day by day until he returns."

That cryptic response stirred guilt in Ivy. She had not expected to hear him speak of Colin's return. In fact, she examined herself and found that she had taken for granted that her husband had already killed Colin for his crown. Ivy had long wanted to ask her husband about Colin, but something in her kept her from pursuing the old seer's orders this time. Standing so close to him, Ivy sensed nothing from him—no response, no desire, no emotion at all. *You haven't always been like this,* she suddenly wanted to say. It was strange to think that she could wish for the first uneasy days of their marriage, but that was the truth. Then, he had been unreadable as well, but Ivy had always felt that there was something there to be read, if he would only stop hiding it from her. Now, he had withdrawn so far that even the possibility of understanding him was gone. Ivy stared up into the depths of his eyes. It seemed as if no one was inside looking back at her.

All at once, Ivy knew she had seen that kind of look before. Growing up in the corner of her father's office, she had watched all sorts of interviews between her father and others involved in military affairs. She had unwittingly learned much in this way. Some of it, she had forgotten; some of it returned to her now and then, usually when triggered by similar experiences. As she gazed into her husband's eyes, Ivy was certain that he distrusted her, and not only that—he felt wronged by her. That was why she was refused entry into his life and thoughts. He considered her a traitor. She remembered what he had said only moments before: *What a day I've had.* Ivy knew the gossip that circulated these days. She knew that her husband stood almost entirely alone against everyone, without the sympathy or support of anyone save Doran and a few soldiers. *Without so much as the comfort of a loving wife to come home to,* her unruly conscience added acutely. *You promised your father to help this man, to stand beside him, remember?*

Yes, Ivy said to herself, *but remember what the seer showed me?*

What about what Doran told you he saw? the other side of her countered. *He doesn't lie.*

Yes, but the seer's stone is magic. Ivy thought back to the conversation that she had had with her deceased father. It seemed to her that any item with so great a power at its disposal could no more lie than Doran could—yet they told opposite tales. She had known Doran for so many years that she couldn't discount his tale. His testimony, combined with the request that Nässey had made, exerted a powerful influence over the way Ivy looked at her husband.

Out of nowhere, a sentence surfaced to trouble her: *The dead do not speak.*

Ivy could not recall where she had heard it before, but it made her pause. Then, with a start of embarrassment, she remembered that she was still staring absently at her husband's face. His expression—or, rather, his *lack* of expression had not changed. Ivy averted her eyes. When he pulled away from her, he left her standing beside the window. She felt guilty but did not understand why.

"I have something for you." He brought a parcel out of the corner and handed it to her.

Inside the paper wrappings, Ivy found a gorgeous robe. The fabric was like nothing she had seen before, a beautiful velvety cloth. From different angles, the fabric took on a slightly different hue: indigo, deep sapphire, black. Ivy ran her hand across it in admiration. "It's lovely. Thank you." Only that morning, she had gone through her mourning clothes with dissatisfaction, wishing that dark colors did not have to be so drab. This new robe had such a luster to it that Ivy could scarcely take her eyes from it. She touched it briefly to her cheek. When she tore herself from her examination of the gown, she meant to thank her husband, but he had gone without a word. All while Guenna fitted the gown for her, Ivy kept thinking of the chief healer's testimony. Her husband was a healer as well as a warrior. He held communion with pardeléi, and didn't every story say that pardeléi were incorruptible and noble? Ivy had stood before the mirror for some time after the alterations were complete. *I will thank him when he comes back.* But again he had not returned at all during the night. Ivy lay awake for several hours, one hand stretched out to lie where his head should have lain on the pillow beside hers, before she fell asleep. He was not there when she awoke, either. She decided to wear the new gown to her meeting with Selena, but felt a measure of guilt as well as pride over the garment. *Maybe he isn't what I thought he was...*

Any remaining doubts about her husband's character evaporated like the dew, thanks to an episode that occurred there in the kitchen while she worked out the details of the midsummer festivities with Selena and Maia. They were at the table in conversation when Ivy thought she saw a small blur of motion come through the kitchen door. Selena was in the midst of describing her expectations for the entertainment; she didn't pause, so Ivy knew that she must not have seen the child skid to a halt a few steps from the table. *Oh, Dara,* Ivy thought as her eyes met the child's. *What's the matter?* In this one thing, the little girl had been trained exceedingly well. She knew she was never to interrupt anyone who was in conference with the queen or her daughter, so little Dara ran to the broom cupboard instead and shut herself inside it. Ivy sighed. *Poor dear. Lucinda's been nagging her again, I expect.* Quite unexpectedly, Ivy saw her husband get up from his nap and go to the broom cupboard. For a moment, he knelt without opening its door, as if listening. Then he pulled the door open just a crack. Ivy heard him say, "May I come in?" From inside the cupboard emerged a teary giggle. "Well?" he persisted.

"You're too big."

"That I am." He put his head into the small space and withdrew it. "You shall have to come *out*, then." He lifted Dara out of the cupboard and into his arms, returning to his chair. "Why were you in with the brooms, child? And crying, too?"

"Gran'ma Ardit says I'm not s'poseda innerupt. I gotta wait."

"In with the brooms?" Ivy's husband sounded amused. "Do they make good company?"

Little Dara rubbed her face against his shirt front with another watery giggle. "Nuh-uh."

"They must not talk much. Who aren't you to interrupt?"

The child nodded toward the table. Ivy pretended not to be eavesdropping, but she strained to hear what passed next.

"Well, now, I cannot help you with that, but if you wish to sit and wait with somebody who isn't a broom, I am available. What is it you wanted to tell them?"

Just then, Selena asked Ivy's opinion on some detail, forcing her to recall her attention to the conversation nearer at hand. She knew what was most likely to trouble the little girl. Dara was the youngest sister of three; her elder sisters, Meghala and Kenda, were both full grown. Their mother had died giving birth to Dara late in life. Since their father Gian felt unequal to the task of being both father and mother to the littlest of his daughters, he had asked his own mother, Ardith, to fill the position. In reality, it was Kenda who spent the most time and affection on Dara, but Kenda had duties of her own to perform, so Dara often ran unchecked through the corridors of Takra House. She was an amiable and obedient child for the most part, but her curiosity was legendary. She liked to play imaginative games in the most unsuitable places. Dara also provided one more item of contention between her grandmother and great-grandmother. Lucinda saw the child's unfettered behavior as a smear on her reputation, not as a mark of creativity, as Ardith (and Ivy herself) tended to view it. Lucinda often berated the child if she caught her doing anything but her assigned chores. Each time she suffered such stinging reprimands, Dara took refuge in the kitchen, knowing her great-grandmother rarely went there.

The next time she picked up the thread of the unlikely conversation between Dara and the general, Ivy heard her husband say, "Some people are not very kind people, Dara. They may not intend unkindness, but that is what they show all the same. It does not mean that you have done something wrong to make them act unkindly. Some people *are* kind, but the ways they choose to show their kindness are easily misunderstood. Can you understand that, Dara? Maybe Nana thinks that she is doing what is right when she stops you from singing in the gallery. As for me, I do not mind a little music while I work. I cannot imagine why the marshals should mind, either."

Ivy chanced a look and found little Dara snuggled against the general's chest, her tears already dried away as she listened to him. "Mister Doran smiled at me."

"See? I told you so. One of these times, you must sing for me. I would like to hear you sing. Here's an idea—why don't we go out to the park? I will teach you a new song. Then, maybe, we could play seek. How do you like that idea, hmm?"

"Can we?"

"I don't see why not. We have a little time before noontide. You can ride on my shoulder—just mind you don't bump your head," he warned as he swung her up. "You've never been up this high, I wager." When he stood up, steadying the child with a hand, he grinned at her squeal. "Hang on tightly."

Ivy watched them leave together. Warmth pooled inside of her at the sight of that great warrior carrying little Dara on his shoulder while the child clung delightedly to his head. When the unlikely pair had disappeared, she returned her gaze to her best friend. Ivy had to blush a little when she saw the smile in Selena's eyes. It was not very difficult to see where Selena's thoughts led; Ivy's were there already. *He would make a fine father.* That, if nothing else, moved her heart to believe better of him.

After another half an hour of planning, their meeting ended. "I think we're finished for today," the queen said gently. "Will you stay for noontide, Ivy, or do you mean to get started immediately?"

Dragging her thoughts back to the business before her, Ivy answered, "We've little enough time to get everything done, especially now that we can't count on the Pamirsi offerings. I'm afraid I ought to get started at once if we're to stay on schedule. Let me know if you think of anything else that needs doing." She got up from the table and left, but she did not begin her appointed tasks at once. Instead, she crossed to the western wing of the house in search of her brother. She was certain now that he had been right to ask her to trust her husband. If she could talk with him, Ivy was sure she could ask him to explain how he suddenly began to believe in her husband. *What did Nässey see in him that I didn't?* Any report of her husband's goodness seemed desirable to Ivy now, but Nässey' office stood open and empty. She sat in his chair for several minutes, hoping that he might come while she waited, but he did not arrive. Ivy studied the walls and shelves of the office. Nässey owned so many books that he had a small library in each of his three offices: one in Takra House, one in the central building of the Academy, and one private office in his house on the west side of the city. Books always reminded Ivy of her younger brother. The books in the office, she saw, wore a thin coating of dust, as if they had not been handled for some time. The desk was clean. It held none of its customary stacks of paperwork. If Ivy had been able to entertain the thought long enough to speak it, she would have been forced to say it had been cleaned in preparation for a new occupant. Disheartened and repulsed by this startling impression, Ivy retreated from the marshals' offices. She decided to go back to her apartment and take a quick nap through the noonday heat before going on to deal with her list of midsummer preparations.

Out in the courtyard, she was so preoccupied by worries for Nässey that she failed to see her husband's approach until he seemingly appeared at her elbow. This time it startled but did not frighten her to find him looming over her. He still held little Dara on his shoulder. "Where are you off to now, my lady?" he said in a peculiar, tense voice.

"I thought I would go home and check on the baking, and maybe take a nap. There's no telling what Guenna will do if I leave her on her own too long." Ivy smiled, but her smile died when she saw the intensity of her husband's gaze. "Is something wrong?" She waited, but he only turned away to watch the approach of their carriage. Ivy altered her question: "What's wrong?" This received no more of an answer than its precursor. Instead, as the carriage rolled to a halt in front of them, Ivy's husband opened her door and assisted her with a hand at her elbow. He let go of her almost before she had caught her balance, though, and deposited the child into the carriage beside her. "I have an errand that will take me from this place for perhaps a fortnight or more. I asked Ardith, and she says you may keep my new little friend with you as your companion while I am away."

"Certainly," Ivy said, dumbfounded. "I would be glad to spend the time with Dara. Where are you going?"

"The first of the messengers has returned to report that the Pamirsi definitely mean to withhold at least half their tithe for the midsummer festival. Any wagons they might still offer for our use are useless without beasts to pull them, as they well know. I will provide the horses myself from my own herds as part of my personal offering to the crown, but it requires me to be away for a time. The queen will accompany me. She has endured without her husband for long enough." His eyes homed in on her face. "I hope to see you when I return."

"Certainly," she repeated. "I hope it won't take you as long as you expect. A fortnight is such a long time." As her reward, she saw the inexplicable anger recede from his eyes. A hope rose within her that she might this time be able to draw a smile from this troubled man. Suddenly shy, Ivy reached her hand out to press it against his where it gripped the carriage's door frame. Her hand looked small against his. "I will watch for your return." She pulled little Dara onto her lap and held her as her husband shut the door and bid Ilan to tend them with all diligence.

VOCATION

With Merta's wedding on its way, no one thought it necessary to remove Giles from his post as errand boy to the *natai* Rafe's wife and her female kin. Giles didn't complain. He was too fascinated by the family structure of this small village-within-a-village that was Rafe's family.

Faydra, Rafe's wife, ruled the house. Merta was her younger sister. Then there was Evany, who was a cousin to Faydra and Merta. Evany had a widowed mother, Hesteah, and two younger sisters (Emelie and Jacenda) and a young brother (Shad). Faydra and Rafe also had four children of their own: Rigel, who was already betrothed to marry Emelie although he was fourteen and she was thirteen; Romeny, who was ten years old and restless to start training as a warrior; Pari, who was a boyish little girl of nine years old and delighted in copying Romeny, much to his annoyance; and Rune, a boisterous six-year-old boy. As if this weren't enough, Rafe had a brother, Remi, who had a wife (Panya), who also had a sister (Sacha) who lived with them. Remi and Panya had two sons, Arsenio and Didi. This made a house of eighteen residents, of which only two were adult males. This by itself was enough to keep Giles wracking his memory for names, but the doors to Rafe's house were open to anyone, particularly anyone belonging to another natai's house. Merta was to marry Randal, son of the natai Lachunn, so Randal was a frequent visitor; Lachunn's daughter Niesha was fast friends with Merta and Evany alike, so she came even more often than did her brother Randal. Since Druze, the young cousin of natai Farris, was betrothed to Niesha, he often came to sit with her at Rafe's house instead of her father's house. Giles gathered that Niesha's preference for Rafe's house had much to do with her father's decision to forbid her marriage to her favorite, Loren, who came often to Rafe's house—but never at the same time as Niesha.

With so many women around the house, Giles found more acute pleasure in the times when Rafe and Remi came home for the evening, invariably bringing with them an assortment of warriors as company. Giles had to sit on the outer edge of this masculine circle, since he had so little in common with the warriors. He wished it were otherwise, but what could he do? He wasn't alone in hovering at the edges, however. Rafe's two elder sons, Rigel and Romeny, often sat with him in the same corner, eavesdropping on the men's conversation with equal longing. At first, Giles thought that his presence in the corner went unnoticed. Soon, little hints to the contrary began to reach him. One evening, when Niesha was absent and Loren present, Loren tried to stop Giles for conversation. Still mildly resentful of the king's favorite, Giles made brief replies and dodged away as soon as the opportunity came. He later saw Loren engaged in quiet conversation with Rafe and one of the other natai, a slender Alti man of less than average stature.

On the following day, one of Giles' first tasks of the day was to walk Merta down to the third terrace. Giles offered to carry her basket. "What's in it?" he asked.

"Seared beef for the mushroom man," was her reply.

"Mushroom man?"

"That's what the children call him. He's a simple—you know, he's not quite right in the head? He lives down on the edge of town in a cave. He tends the mushrooms; it's all he knows how to do, except to play his harpett on warm days. You must have heard it: a sort of buzzing sound. Mother needs mushrooms for the stew, so we must take this gift to the mushroom man, or else he won't let us gather any mushrooms."

Giles had never had much to do with simples and was slightly unnerved by this one. The mushroom man had a vacant stare. He seemed not to notice either of them once they had given him the seared beef to gobble down. Holding the basket for Merta to fill with mushrooms, Giles felt compelled to glance back toward the mushroom man. He was rather put off by the manner of the fellow's eating and could well imagine why Faydra wouldn't want her sister venturing into this cave without a little masculine company. All in all, Giles was glad to see the daylight again.

He was even more pleased to find that no one required his services that afternoon. Evany suggested that he take himself out to the rear courtyard, where he found Rafe tutoring his second son Romeny in the fundamentals of knife-work.

Giles was able to nestle himself at the base of a tree and eat roasted pai kernels while he watched father and son work painstakingly through their lesson. He listened and learned more than he expected. Romeny was a rather timid boy. Often, Rafe had to explain the same principle over and over until even Giles could have mastered it, but Romeny was still uncertain and fumbled because he had no confidence. The boy held his father in great awe as well as natural affection, thus disarming any frustration that Rafe might have felt over his timidity.

At one point, Rafe came up against an insurmountable difficulty. Romeny simply did not understand him, whatever he tried. Casting about for another way to explain his meaning, Rafe fairly pounced on Giles. "Here, lad," he said in that thick accent that Giles still had trouble deciphering at times. "Up." Rafe latched onto Giles' wrist, dragged him to stand in front of Romeny, and shoved the hilt of a blunted dagger into Giles' grasp. He then made corrections in Giles' way of holding the knife. "Eh?" he said, looking Giles in the face to make sure he knew what he was to do. "Show'm."

The solidity of the hilt in his hand made the things he had seen more real. It felt natural. Giles rotated his wrist, clumsily shifting the knife from point-upwards to point-downwards with only his fingers. He looked to Rafe for affirmation.

"'Gain," the laconic little man said.

Giles repeated the move half a dozen times before he could execute it without fearing that the dagger would slip from his grasp. The next half a dozen repetitions served to give him greater confidence. By the time he had finished his twentieth repetition, Giles saw young Romeny nodding with comprehension. Giles gave the blunted practice dagger to Romeny and would have returned to the tree's shade, but Rafe snagged him by the arm and wouldn't let him leave until Romeny was done with his lesson. Then Rafe bid Giles walk with him. Neither of them spoke to the other all the way from Rafe's family compound to the corrals at the back of the first terrace. There they met Rafe's brother Remi. Rafe asked a question in Kavahran; Remi answered likewise, leaving Giles no better informed than he had been. Remi strode off toward the stables while Rafe and Giles waited in the stable yard.

When Remi returned, he was accompanied by the Alti natai. Rafe addressed a few comments to the Alti and departed, leaving Giles there in the stable yard. "So," said the Alti, "you're the general's grandson, are you?"

"Yes, sir."

"My name is Greysin. I once belonged to the king's corps before I was taken captive in battle and Ammun saved me. Now I teach the young hostages to ride as if they were another of the horse's limbs. How many times have you ridden a horse?"

"Counting the trip here?" Giles said. "Once."

"I'm here to remedy that. Come along." The Alti man maintained a surprisingly rapid pace, talking over his shoulder as he went. "You'll spend the mornings with Rafe, learning to defend yourself. In the afternoons, you'll come to me and learn the ways of a horseman. For the evenings, you're on your own. Try not to get into trouble."

*　　　*　　　*　　　*

Colin descended to the main floor to find Byram and Lucien in the morning room with a copy of the Book of the Kings between them. He checked himself before interrupting them. He heard Byram say, "That's why your father wants you to learn these by heart. What's tucked away in your head is easily retrieved later. You're more fortunate than most. You have a prodigious memory, Lucky. I've never quite seen its equal in a boy of your age."

"How much for tomorrow?"

Byram flipped a page or two. "Well, with midsummer coming up, I think you can take a respite. Why don't you just work on these five pages? Then, once you have those done, just review what you've already memorized. Your father will be very proud of your progress."

"He's not going to make me recite, is he?"

"Well, if he doesn't come back before the festival, then I think you're safe," Byram teased. He chucked Lucien under the chin. "So you see—there's good in every misfortune."

The small boy grinned reluctantly, but he shut the book and hefted it under his thin arm all the same. "May I go out to the tree while I work?"

"Do that."

As Lucien passed Colin at the doorway, Colin was troubled to see the boy's downcast expression. He waited until Lucien was out of earshot. "He still misses his father badly, I see."

"They haven't been apart this long since the boy came to live here."

"When was that?"

"The same time I came, or shortly thereafter, I should say," Byram replied in a distracted way. He stacked the remaining books and tried to lift them. "Would you help me return these to the library? I'm feeling my age this morning, I'm afraid." He divided the stack in half, handed the top books to Colin and picked up the rest himself. "It doesn't come often, but when it does…I swear I can feel every joint twinge at once on such days. I miss the weather of the plains."

"What does Vienna say about it?"

"That I'm getting old," was Byram's tart reply. "As if I didn't know that myself."

They took their time replacing the books. It turned into an impromptu tour, with Byram pointing out various titles of interest and Colin leafing through them in curiosity. After some time at this, however, both of them perked their ears at the sound of the front door slamming. Heavy treads made the entryway floor creak. At first, only Lucien's boyish voice rose up softly to accompany the foot-falls. Then all fell silent for an instant. Colin's heart thumped when he heard the nameless warrior's voice echo through the house: "Where has he gone, Luck?"

The two men looked at each other. Byram patted Colin on the arm. "It's about time!"

Colin descended to find the nameless one approaching the stairs with Lucien clinging to his back. The boy peered over his father's shoulder with a sunny grin. "There he is, Ta."

They beheld each other without speaking at first. Then the nameless one said merely, "Better…much better." He bowed his head briefly in Colin's direction. Colin returned the gesture, but said nothing in return. The warrior's gaze made him want to shift from foot to foot in discomfort; there was something in it that suggested Colin was being weighed. "I can see you have been spending your time well. Will you come to the morning room with me, your majesty? There is a matter awaiting your attention."

Colin nodded, unable to make sense of the man's tone, which hinted of mischief. "If you wish." He fell into step behind the master of the house. Upon entering the morning room, Colin immediately understood the tone of mischief; the *matter* that awaited him stood immobile in the center of the room, looking at him in hopeful apprehension. Too amazed to move, Colin did little more than stare at his wife for several heartbeats. Then he crossed the intervening space in three strides and swept her into a fervent hug. He whispered into her ear while she wept against his shoulder. Colin felt none too steady, holding her again at last. When Selena lifted her head to look into his face, he found no reproach in her eyes. "Selena," he began, "I'm so very sorry—"

She put her hand over his mouth. "No. We need not go back over that. It's forgotten."

"You're better than I deserve," he said with a tightening throat. "I love you."

"I've missed you so much. Oh! You look so hearty—you've been out in the sun, haven't you? Have you been happy, my dear?"

Rather than answer immediately, he kissed her. "I couldn't call it happy, my love, not without you and Maia, but…I've found more than enough to keep me occupied. How have you been? How is Maia? I've thought of you both every day, without fail. What have *you* been doing?" Colin spoke the thought that crossed his mind without considering it first. "You look pale—maybe *you* ought to have been put out to pasture with me."

A wry voice from the doorway made answer to that: "Had everything gone as I planned, she would have."

Colin turned to find the master of the house watching them. "What do you mean?"

At almost the same moment, Selena started to say, "But I thought you said—" and stopped herself without finishing. She looked at Colin in apprehension.

"Go ahead," the nameless one prompted. "You are free to speak what's in your heart."

"I thought you said you were going to…to ask me to give him up, to save him."

"No," the nameless warrior replied, "I told you I would have to ask you to do something difficult if it was the only way. When I said that, it was not yet certain that he had to leave. If that did become necessary, I had in mind that you should both leave your daughter behind in my care, not that you two should be separated. But when I saw his mood, I could not in good conscience send you both together until he had time to repent of his words."

Colin blushed, but he could not deny the truth of the remark.

"You may stay now, my lady, if that is your choice." With a bow, the nameless one excused himself and left the morning room.

In his absence, Selena kissed her husband. "You do look as if this has done you good. I like this beard," she added with a twinkle of laughter in her eyes, stroking his jaw. "It makes you look very robust. And you've lost some around the middle. I can feel it." She tightened her hold around his waist. "Have you been working very hard all this long time? Tell me all about what you've been up to, my dear. Tell me everything. I've missed the sound of your voice!"

He smiled. "What if I showed you around the village, hmm? Would you like that?" So Colin walked arm in arm with his wife through nearly all the narrow lanes of Chamika for the rest of the morning. He introduced her to some of the hostages, all of whom were curious to meet her. Loren even made so bold as to quip, "High time he brought you around to show us what he's been nattering on about all this time. He didn't exaggerate. You're just as fair as he said."

Colin firmly removed his wife's hand from Loren's grasp. "After that, I'm inclined to take back the introduction, thank you. What sort of speech is that, I ask you? I don't *natter*."

"Of course not." Loren winked at Selena. "I'd do better to call it maundering."

Colin said, "I don't know why I bother with you."

"Neither do I, but that's your quandary, not mine." With an unrepentant grin, Loren whisked Selena out from under her husband's arm and began strolling down the lane with her, pointing out some bit of scenery. When Colin tried to insert himself between them, Loren said, "If you keep on pushing yourself in where you're not wanted, I'll have to take measures." The past few weeks had not been wasted on Colin, however. He put his friend in a stout headlock, against which the smaller man struggled vainly for several moments before sighing in amiable resignation. "I always wondered how it felt to be put in the stocks," Loren said, his voice muffled against Colin's forearm.

"I'm amazed you've ever had to wonder. Will you behave yourself if I let you go?"

Once released, Loren massaged his neck. "I should never have taught you that one."

"True, but that's your quandary, not mine," Colin mocked as he resumed walking with his arm around Selena's shoulders. "Be off with you."

She smiled up at him when they were alone again. "I'm glad you've found companions to suit you, Colin. He seems nice."

"You'll like his story. It's very sad and romantic." In a low voice Colin recounted to her the story of Loren, Niesha and Druze, and he was not disappointed in her reaction. When she asked him what he thought they could do for the ill-fated lovers, he asked her a question in return. "You've had more chance to watch our new general than I have. Do you suppose he would agree to any suggestion I might make on the subject?"

"I think he's very likely to agree."

"Then I'll ask him if he'll take Loren back to King's City with him."

When they arrived at the house again, the great room resonated with male voices. Lucien sat on the stairs with a book on his knees. He looked up from his reading when Colin and Selena entered. "Almost noontide, sir, lady," he said pleasantly. "Manon's working real hard in the kitchen, making all Ta's favorites."

"You must be glad to have him back home again," Selena said kindly.

"Oh, aye," replied the boy, sounding much like the warriors he trained with. Under Selena's gaze, he reddened. "Even if it's just for a day."

Colin asked, "He isn't staying longer than that?"

"Nope, but he says I get to ride along when they take the horses out, so I'm content. I never got to go to King's City before."

"You're going with him, are you?"

"Not exactly. There's more horses to fetch, so he's off to the farm to bring them, too."

There were too many questions to pose in response to that remark, but Colin was spared the effort. His return to the house had not gone unnoticed. The door to the great room opened and the nameless warrior emerged. Behind him, the council of natai was in the midst of disbanding. As the natai filed out of the great room, Colin approached the general. "There was something I wanted to ask of you, if you have a moment."

"Ask."

"When you return to King's City, will you take Loren with you?"

"Why?"

"So he can see that civilization exists in other places besides his beloved Nikobia."

Unnervingly fast, the nameless warrior picked up his train of thought. "So he can give Lachunn a different answer than the last one—a better answer. I see. Consider your request granted." After an awkward pause, he added, "I'm glad to find you've taken a liking to him. He is one of my more exceptional students."

"So I gathered while I let him toss me on my head for hours at a time as my sparring partner," Colin replied lightly.

Another pause ensued. "I was also pleased to hear of your choice to train with them. I had worried that you might spend too much time in the library, brooding."

This concern both puzzled and flattered Colin, who said, "You know me better than I expected." To this, he received no answer. "I expect Manon has just about finished readying the noontide meal. Lucky promised me it would be a true banquet, in honor of your homecoming. Not a day has gone by but he's spent at least a part of it watching the road for you to come back. He's a good boy. Good company, too, for one his age, as the hostages willingly attest."

"He is the only real good to come out of my life thus far."

They headed for the dining room, where Byram and Lucien sat opposite one another at the end of the table, chatting amiably. Lucien giggled for no apparent reason when he saw the trio enter. "What's tickling you now?" his father asked him.

"You look funny in that mask."

"You're jealous because I have one and you don't," his father teased. "I have a surprise for you. Do you want to guess at it?"

The boy clutched at the back of his chair in excitement. "My own horse?"

"Not yet. Guess again. Something better."

"Are we getting another house?"

Dropping into the chair at the table's head, Ammun gave his son an amused look. "Where did you come upon that idea?"

Lucien shrugged. "Something Damon said."

"I see I need to speak with him. No, that's not it. Guess once more. Something better."

With his thin face tensed in anticipation, the boy blurted, "A mother?"

His father merely grinned a little more broadly.

"Oh, Ta, really, really, really?"

"You know I wouldn't joke about something as momentous as that. Yes, really, I've found you a mother. A very good mother, I daresay, though you'll have to judge that for yourself once you meet her. Somehow, I think you'll approve."

"When, Ta? Is she coming here?"

"No, you're going to see her in King's City. There—is that a good enough surprise?"

Colin helped seat his wife at the other end of the table, but his mind was otherwise occupied. *He doesn't wear that mask all the time. Not a surprise; it must be inconvenient. But why did he want to draw our attention away from that detail? I'd take it on oath that he didn't plan on telling Lucky about Ivy just now. He did it to change the subject.* He said nothing along that line. He seated himself at Selena's right just as Manon and her daughter began to serve food.

During the meal, Lucien and his father fell easily into conversation that Colin found engrossing. The two clearly shared a rapport beyond what might be attributed to the natural affection between a father and son. In fact, the nameless one treated his son almost as if he were a companion, even a friend, rather than a child of nine years. In return, Lucien behaved toward his father with a measure of blithe trust that told Colin more about the nameless warrior in that single hour than he had learned of him in all of their previous encounters combined.

Selena was beginning to nod a little by the end of the meal. She apologized and said, "I'm so tired, Colin. The journey was rather long. Do you mind if I rest for an hour or two?"

"Not at all. If I'm not around when you wake, just send for me." With a light kiss, he escorted her up to his room and tucked her into his bed for a nap. By the time he returned to the ground floor, the master of the house had left. Colin asked Lucien where he had gone.

"He didn't say. I expect he's taking a tour of the village. Do you want me to go after him for you, sir?"

"That's all right, Lucky. I'll just wander around and hope for the best." First he headed for Farris' longhouse, but it stood empty. His next thought took him toward the main corral. There he found plenty of warriors milling around, getting in the way of those who had business there. None of them had seen Ammun since before noontide, so Colin wandered again. He saw Giles exercising horses in a smaller corral. The boy waved to him without hesitation, and Colin waved back, smiling over the improvement he could already see in the youth's bearing. Up and down the even dirt lanes, Colin went on searching for his general. When he came almost to the edge of the second terrace, an odd sight greeted him: the lord of Chamika reclining against a tree, cradling an infant in his hands—and making *faces* at the child. Colin hesitated. A look at the child's mother showed that Colin was not the only one unable to account for this scene. The mother looked absolutely bewildered. Colin decided to risk a comment. He crouched down beside the nameless one and cleared his throat. "What are you doing, if you don't mind?"

The general responded only after a few moments. "I should think it obvious enough. I'm making faces at a baby." He crossed his eyes and pursed his mouth, to the infant's noisy delight.

"Why?"

"You seek my permission to ask ridiculously obvious questions, but when the questions turn personal, you take my permission for granted. Curious."

Colin opened his mouth to correct the omission, but was not given the chance.

"Have you ever tried this yourself?"

"Ah…no. Not since my daughter was that size."

"I defy any man to find a way to amuse a child of this size for a quarter of an hour together *and* remain conscious of his dignity. It can't be done. One or the other must be abandoned. It's good to forget yourself now and then. Willa thinks

I'm mad, obviously. I cannot deny that that is part of the appeal, in its own way. People too easily believe that they know one another so well."

Colin smiled at the way that Willa's baby stared up at the masked face. One delicate fist waved spasmodically toward the mask, as if the child wanted to reach up and pull the fabric away. "Why do you wear the mask?" Colin asked before he could think better of it.

"Again taking my permission for granted…"

"It's a natural enough thing to wonder about, isn't it? Lucky gave the secret away. You don't usually wear it."

"Not anymore. There was a time when I wore it day and night. I never took it off unless I knew for certain I was alone." Ammun handed the baby back to its mother and walked slowly up the lane. Now that his hands were free, he lifted one to stroke the hem of the mask. "I had hoped I would never have to put it on again once I put it off the last time."

Puzzled, Colin asked the obvious: "Then why do you wear it?"

"For much the same reason that I donned it to begin with. I…"

Colin waited for him to go on, but the man would not. Finally, Colin felt brave enough to prompt him. "Why *did* you start wearing it to begin with?"

"To spare my people the shame of knowing what I had become."

"Someday," Colin remarked in as indifferent a voice as he could summon, "someday, you and I must sit down somewhere comfortable and take a full day to discuss things."

"What things?"

"All the things I know I'm not allowed to ask you right now, things that I'm in agony to ask." He ventured a sidelong glance and saw that he had not angered the man, so he hazarded a smile as well. "If I'm curious, I imagine Owen must be simply writhing with questions—unless you've unbent so far as to satisfy his curiosity already?"

"I have said very little to Lord Sakiry, one way or the other."

Colin felt a chill beneath the words that he could not account for. "I get the feeling you don't like him very well."

"I do not dislike him." The nameless warrior yielded slightly, adding, "It is not my first choice, to become a mere object of curiosity. Lord Sakiry collects curiosities in more than one sense of the word. He has no great interest in me personally…and I will be part of no one's collection. Walk with me a while, if you will." Having made this abrupt change of subjects, the man said not another word to Colin. The village traffic parted for the nameless one and, by proximity, for Colin as he followed Ammun up through the village to the manor house. It appeared that the entire household had congregated in front of the house. The steward held the reins of the most handsome steed Colin had yet laid eyes on, a roan of exceptional size. It was saddled for travel, and a light pack rested securely behind the saddle. Colin asked, "You aren't leaving this soon?"

"I have business at one of my other estates." The nameless one mounted his horse and gathered the reins. "Byram will escort Lucky back to King's City. I trust I do not impose any great hardship on you if I give over the run of the house to you? You may go wherever you please, without regard for any restrictions that may have previously been held over you." Having disposed of his farewell to Colin in that brusque manner, he bent low and lifted Lucien easily to the saddle. "We shall see each other again in King's City in a week or so, so I won't say good-bye to *you*. Do your best to look after yourself until then, Luck." He squeezed the boy and kissed his forehead with unmistakable affection, and briefly he welcomed Lucien's answering embrace before he dropped the boy lightly to the ground again.

The line of servants bowed low in unison. Acknowledging this obeisance with a nod, Ammun spurred his horse into an energetic trot that became a canter once the gate was cleared. Everyone stayed as long as they could see him on the road. In a manner of minutes, however, he dropped below the level of the terrace and out of view. The servants returned to their duties at once, but Lucien suddenly ran down the road and through the gate, stopping only at the lip of the terrace. Colin followed him. He stood behind the boy silently out of respect for this temporary bereavement that the boy endured with only a wistful gaze directed at the receding horseman. Before long, Lucien lost sight of his father and turned from the vista. Colin said gently, "When do you leave for King's City?"

"I'm not sure of the hour, but Byram says we'll go as soon as the horses are all rounded up and the provisions loaded. Probably tomorrow early." He looked up at Colin with clear, innocent eyes. "I wish you were coming with us, too."

"So do I, but that can't be helped. I'm sure we'll meet again soon enough. You must give my regards to your new mother when you see her."

"Do you know the lady, sir?"

"Yes, I know her quite well. I'm sure you'll like her very much, and I'm even surer that she'll be very taken with you as soon as she meets you. She's a gentle-hearted lady who loves to meet new friends and loves to hold parties for them. She loves to give presents, and nothing makes her happier than to see others enjoying themselves. With midsummer coming up, she'll be in the thick of everything." Colin looked up to see Byram observing their approach with an indulgent smile.

The older man patted Lucien on the back. "Is Colin telling you all about your mother? Well, tomorrow we'll start off, and if the weather holds, we'll be introducing the two of you within five days. In the meanwhile, I suggest you run up to your room and start packing your clothes. Aurelia will help you."

Letting his eyes follow the boy up the stairs, Colin said, "He's a good boy. I wish I could see their meeting. Ivy will fall in love with him immediately."

"I'm glad that you're...you're taking this better now."

That arrested Colin's attention. He turned his mind to the subject, examining it minutely. "It's easier, I think," he began slowly, "now that I know what sort of future she can look forward to. I've started to think of Lucien almost as—not as a son, but maybe nephew wouldn't be too far from the mark. He deserves a good mother, and Ivy will be one."

"Is that all?" Byram asked in a shrewd tone.

"That's the bulk of it, yes. I've scarcely had time to get to know Ammun better, as you well know." Provoked by an impulse he did not understand, Colin added, "Though, just from my dealings with him today, I can't summon the will to resent him for marrying her. Not anymore." He excused himself, went up to check on Selena, and found her still asleep. He thought of the great pleasure it would give her to see her best friend gifted with such a wonderful son as Lucien after her years of fruitless longings. To this image, some rebellious spark of imagination added the nameless one to complete the family scene. Colin thought for an instant he could see himself out in company with the nameless one, but this tenuous image of friendship was so incredible that Colin could not sustain it long. *He would never open his mind to me long enough for such a miracle to take place,* Colin told himself. He was at once both surprised and disappointed.

*　　　*　　　*　　　*

After talking long into the night, Colin and Selena agreed that it would be best for Maia if Selena returned to King's City in company with Byram and Lucien. As Selena said hopefully, "At least, she needs one of us there to see her through this present time. Once that is all settled, if you still need to stay here, I'll come back at once." To this logic, Colin agreed sincerely, if not with great enthusiasm. His own wish was to return and stand alongside his daughter in the present trouble, but he refrained from expressing this vain wish to his wife, to whom he knew it could give nothing but sadness. Instead, he encouraged her as best he knew how.

"I'll write a letter for you to carry back to her. That should give proof enough that I live and have some liberty—even if it is only liberty of will," he added as an afterthought.

Accordingly, as the rest of the household bustled to prepare the travelers for their departure, Colin invaded the silence of his absent host's personal office to take advantage of pen, ink, and paper there undisturbed. He sat for a moment with the dry pen in his hand, poised but not ready to ink the tip and begin his letter. *What shall I say to her?* Colin took a breath, stirred the surface of the ink with his pen, and began.

Colin son of Kohanan,
To my beloved Maia:
Peace rest upon you, my dear.

I cannot express how I have missed you, dearest. The great joy I took in receiving your mother was only half of what I would have felt, could you have accompanied her. If all goes well, I trust it will not be long before we meet again. In the meanwhile I have instructed your mother to give you every proof of my great affection for you when she returns home. As pale as this alternative seems, it is the best that I can offer. I assure you that I am well—indeed, I am in excellent spirits (but for missing you) and very pleasantly occupied with my present concerns and companions.

I trust that this letter finds you as lively as ever, and probably lovelier than even a father's fond imagination can conceive. From what I have been told, you have already weathered as much as should be expected of one so young, with prospects of more difficulty immediately ahead. I do not doubt but that you will meet these difficulties head-on, with such assistance as your mother and the new general can offer you. My pride in you knows no limits, but rejoices all the more to hear that you stand firm.

Besides my love and my encouragement, I send you your mother again. We have agreed that you would benefit more from her company now than I would, as hard as that is for me to imagine. She will stand by you and offer you the advice and support that I wish I could give you myself, but cannot. You already have a strong ally in the new general, and I can recommend nothing better than for you to give careful attention to any advice he gives you. He is a shrewd and sensible man, if somewhat eccentric in behavior. I have every confidence in his ability to see you through your difficulties.

In closing, I would like to recommend to you certain members of the company that escorts your mother back to you. Byram son of Solam is an old and valued friend of our family; you may not remember him from the days before he attended my father on his final journey, but he is to be trusted implicitly. If I may suggest it, he could easily take some of the burden from Doran's shoulders with regards to the Cabinet. He has for the past few years served as tutor to the boy Lucien, who also accompanies your mother. Lucien is the general's son and as fine a lad as I've ever been privileged to meet. My own recommendations can add nothing to his appeal, but I include them anyway. Welcome him as you would a younger brother. The final recommendation I must make is in regards to one of the warriors in the party, a young man named Loren son of Avven, of the Waller province on the sea-isle of Nikobia. He is a particular friend of mine. I would take it as a kindness if you would offer him every opportunity of acquainting himself with the society and customs of the kingdom. Your mother can acquaint you with my motives in asking this of you, should your curiosity get the better of you.

Again, let me say how greatly I love and miss you, my dear girl. I am hopeful that we shall soon have the pleasure of meeting again. I keep myself busy with that hope. Be careful, so that nothing should befall on your side of the matter to keep such a hope from being realized. I will do the same here and remain ever your affectionate father.

*   *   *   *

The house, though not very large, felt much bigger with the departure of its two chief residents. Bereft of the company of Byram and Lucien, not to mention Selena, Colin found himself drawn increasingly to the company of the villagers. He trained all the more frequently with all of the village natai, often from dawn to sundown. He even took many of his meals with the hostages. Their company helped him stave off his renewed loneliness.

To be just, many of them were feeling the lack of certain companions who had gone as part of the convoy that took Selena back to King's City. Druze in particular seemed to turn to Colin for companionship in Loren's absence. There was only one who seemed unhappy with Colin's presence. It was just Colin's ill luck that this one was a natai of the village, an ex-raider named Bayne who headed another longhouse of bachelors. Bayne alone seemed to resent the inclusion of an unskilled, clumsy pupil in his training sessions. He made no allowances for Colin and permitted none of his students to do so either, so Colin often found Bayne's swordplay tutorial a traumatic experience. Every other natai would pair him with an advanced warrior with patience enough to give explanations. Bayne insisted on taking Colin on himself. Under this hard tutelage, Colin was forced to recall everything he had learned of the sword in his early manhood, merely to keep himself whole and unbruised. Often he failed. Before long he found himself far better acquainted with Vienna, the village's skilled master healer and adoptive mother to all the warriors living in Chamika.

"What has he done to you this time?" she asked him when he limped across the threshold of her cottage one day. "Let old Vienna see the damage."

Colin pulled up his pant leg to reveal a huge contusion that ran the length of his calf. "It's not so bad now, but I know it'll stiffen so I'll hardly be able to walk by nightfall." He sank down onto the floor to give her better access to his injury.

"Don't say it—let me guess," Vienna sighed. "He said you needn't see me about it, since it wasn't bleeding outright, and you waited all the afternoon until it hurt too badly to be ignored. Then you came to me. You mustn't let him bully you into such foolishness. If it hurts, bring it to me. There's no increase of manhood to be found in bearing unnecessary pain, as I'm telling these younglings all the time. Admit that you hurt and bear the remedy instead. I should think a man of your age should know that by now."

Too pained to blush at the critique, Colin said, "Why does he resent me so much? What did I do to offend him? Come on, Vienna, you hear everything that passes in the village. Niall must have said something to you by now."

"It's the only thing the natai talk about amongst themselves these days," she admitted. "Niall is greatly concerned for you."

"But why?"

"Bayne's a rough sort. Good man, but rough. Devoted to Ammun, too. Rumor says he thinks you've been setting yourself up to replace Ammun here. I told Niall to tell him that's nonsense, but he won't be reasoned with."

Colin groaned. "Don't I know it? What makes him think I'm trying to replace Ammun?"

"Oh, little petty things." The older woman shook her head as she worked over his bruises with a smelly ointment. "You, living up in the manor house by yourself; you, just being who you are. It doesn't take much to set Bayne off, or so it seems."

It took him longer to reach the house, thanks to his stiff leg, but Colin put the time to good use in thinking. Vienna's words followed him. He went to his room, gathered a couple of blankets from his bed, and rolled his few personal belongings up in them. With this bundle tucked under his arm, he limped back out to the longhouses, where nearly everyone had returned in preparation for their supper. In full view of more than fifty witnesses, Colin approached Farris with a question. "With Loren gone, may I have use of his bed-place?"

"Why do you want it?" Farris asked.

"To sleep in it."

A swift, knowing look flickered in the stocky warrior's eyes. He nodded. "Be glad to have you."

Life in the hostages' longhouse, as Colin soon discovered, was communal to a surprising degree. There were no walls to separate neighbor from neighbor. The longhouse consisted of one large, multipurpose chamber. In the morning, Farris was invariably first to rise. Everyone else awoke when he returned from his pre-dawn meditations and slammed the door. At that signal, the hostages rose promptly, rolled their pallets up into tidy bundles, and pulled on whatever assortment of garments they had removed the night before. This was all in preparation for their dawn run, led by Rafe. On the first day of this closer fellowship with them, Colin found out why the hostages were always so tame by the time they rejoined Farris on the training field for hand-to-hand practice. Rafe seemed never to tire. The wiry ex-raider could maintain the most punishing pace indefinitely, until the entire company was near collapse. Somehow, though, he always sensed how far he could push them, and he would stop just short of that point to permit them a moment of rest. If Colin thought himself hard-pressed to keep up before, he now found himself always at the tail of the line. His new bunkmates rallied around him in the subtlest of ways, often in the form of offhanded advice that helped him adapt.

He was also drawn closer to the rivalries that existed between the longhouses. No one dared pick on him directly yet; the aura of Ammun's protection deterred the warriors from taking too many liberties, but Colin had the chance to witness their antics firsthand. Farris' cousin Druze, a permanent resident of Chamika, lived in the longhouse over which Colin's antagonist Bayne presided. Druze's familiarity with Farris made him the boldest of the pranksters. If anything unusual occurred—if a man found a family of grass snakes rolled up in his bed-roll, say, or was doused rudely with cold water through the high windows late at night—it was Druze who received the closest scrutiny. Druze welcomed all comers with a placid face. He was remarkably gifted with an ability to dissemble his way out of all suspicion. The driving ambition of most of Colin's bunkmates was to one day catch Druze in the act and so have firm grounds for their retributions, but Druze was never seen anywhere near the disasters. When appealed to for support, Farris would merely shrug and say, "If you haven't any proof, you haven't any proof."

Colin's nearest bunkmate, Burr, once gave him a hint about the tolerance given these childish pranks. "Oh, he got caught once," Burr said. "Damon caught him once. That was a rare laugh, no lie. He didn't let on he'd caught him, no. He just let him go free and merry back to his longhouse, thinking he'd got away with it again, but Damon had his turn next night, pulled the same gag as Druze had done the night before, the exact same way. How Ammun did laugh!"

"What," Colin exclaimed, "he knows that they do this to each other?"

"Knows? I haven't any proof, but I'm sure he's given the tip to a few of 'em, secret-like, as to improve their tactics. 'Tis all tactics. So long as it doesn't go too far and upset anyone, he's as bad as any. Worse yet, for he teaches, where the rest only learn. Rafe teaches us endurance; Bayne works with the blade; Farris teaches the wrestling and Greysin, he's our riding-master—they take us all, skilled or not, to give us their knowledge. Ammun only teaches tactics to a few."

This gave Colin much to consider over the following days, when he had time to consider anything. He had not realized how grueling the hostages' lives were until he became one of them. Some activities, like the dawn run, were daily. Others depended on the day. Some days he practiced wrestling in the morning and riding in the afternoon, with Giles given to him as a novice rider to mentor; other days, the morning was given over to swordplay and the afternoon to a trade. Every hostage served as an apprentice to one of the permanent residents of Chamika. Colin found himself taking Lucien's place, of all things, as Farris' apprentice. That meant he had to endure Bayne's hostile and brutal lessons all morning, eat a brief noontide around the common fire, and then haul stone blocks around all afternoon. By nightfall, he was more than ready to flop down in his place by the supper fire to swallow whatever was set before him. The remainder of the evening he endured in a stupor, too worn out to feel pain. He persevered only by virtue of a memory he held, in which he heard the nameless one say, *I was pleased to hear of your choice to train with them.* He thought that Ammun could not help but commend him for choosing the harder road, the road of stern discipline. It seemed the type of choice he himself would make.

HUMILITY

I, Owen son of Joced, have again the sorrow and the privilege of taking pen in hand to render an accounting to posterity. These days of trouble leave me much to explain that I would sooner lay to rest peacefully, were I not obligated by the claims of honor, not to mention duty, to record these events. I fear that the blame of future generations will rest heavily enough on us for our past shortcomings. Had we attended to our duty all this while, we would not face these troubles today.

In the second month of the new general's command, he found it necessary to absent himself from King's City for the space of a fortnight. I have not been informed of his real reason for abandoning us, but as his behavior has been in all other respects exactingly correct, I am unable to summon any doubt about his loyalty. The public reason is simple and unsurprising. After this latest fracas over the guardianship, the Pamirsi have chosen to withhold the greater part of their yearly midsummer offering to the crown. It was no more than I had expected. What I had not expected was the discovery that the general owns considerable herds of his own and out of his peculiar generosity has yielded control of them to the princess for the duration of the festival. Really, what this means is that Ivy controls them, since she is the true organizer and executor of all preparations. This is why the general left King's City to round up his offering, leaving us exposed to all manner of villainy.

The general left three days ago, without fanfare. Not even I received word of his departure, nor did Doran. In the first day of the general's absence, all remained calm; the second day, less calm as certain people began to realize that no one had seen the general. Somehow, through some carelessness, word slipped abroad that the general was gone from the city. At this word, Miklei-son rallied his men to carry out a plan that he had been developing ever since the discovery of his spies from among the royal guards. Even as I write this, they are ready to raid the king's jails.

The general was too wise to leave the jails controlled by men he did not trust absolutely, so the attack must come from the outside. One of the third marshal's Academy converts, a slender youth named Ehren, must climb the building and lower himself down through the main chimney. Once he is inside, he must find the cells in which the traitors are being kept for judgment—not a difficult task, but delicate, since he must do it without being detected by the jailors. If possible, he must find a way to free these allies. If this proves impossible, then he must secure a door for the attackers. Ehren locates the traitors' cells with relative ease and communicates to them Miklei-son's plan. Among them, they conclude that the risk of finding a key is too great. Ehren must focus his attention on opening one of the outside doors. Once this is accomplished, Ehren signals for his accomplices to enter the building by stealth, but they do not realize that their movements have been spotted by a guard up above, who alerts his captain to the threat. A battle ensues. Loyal men die and many more suffer hurt while thwarting this attack. Although this attempt has failed, we too have lost ground, for we are few enough as it is.

*   *   *   *

Owen found a use for himself not long after his unsettling conversation with the general. He was sitting beside a window, watching the street in front of the cottage, when he saw his son-in-law come through the small front gate. Since it was only an hour or so past noontide, Owen knew that something was amiss. Doran never came home until nearly dark most days. Even on an easy day, if hardly anyone came to the infirmary for treatment or on other business, Doran had other tasks in his role as first marshal to keep him busy at least until suppertime. Owen got up from his chair and headed for the door, only to collide with Doran in the entryway.

At once, the healer reached out to steady Owen, who had rebounded backwards wildly. "I'm sorry, Father; I didn't see you coming. Did I hurt you?"

"Not at all. What brings you home so soon?"

Doran suddenly appeared several years older than usual. "I'd just as soon not discuss it, Father, if you don't mind. I just need to be quiet for a while."

"I think we can manage that. The sitting room is yours. I'll even stand guard outside."

That drew a reluctant, fleeting smile from the younger man. "You don't need to do that." But he entered the sitting room and dropped down onto the sofa with a groan. With his feet on the arm of the sofa and his hands folded behind his head, Doran turned his face toward the wall and remained silent for a full three hours. In his comings and goings, Owen sometimes took it upon himself to check surreptitiously on his son-in-law, thinking that perhaps Doran was only tired and wanted to nap. Each time, he discovered Doran wide awake, staring at the wall with an unconscious frown rumpling his brow.

Owen had known Doran long enough to know when the younger man was upset. All the signs were present. Given time, Doran's carefully cultivated self-rule would smooth out his passionate temper enough that he could permit himself to rejoin human company. That was just Doran's way. Owen took this into account and, apart from his clandestine observations, kept his distance. Toward the end of the third hour of Doran's seclusion, Owen was relieved to find the slight frown relaxed into a blankness of expression that indicated something of the control Doran had finally achieved. Owen sat in his favored chair across the room, took up a book, and began to browse it in a leisurely fashion. He took further encouragement when Doran shifted slightly to lie flat on his back and direct his gaze at the ceiling instead of the wall. "I don't suppose there's anything I can get for you, is there? Are you hungry? Thirsty?"

Doran's eyes flickered from the ceiling to Owen and back to the ceiling. "Thank you, no. I don't need anything presently." While Owen went back to his desultory reading, Doran shifted again onto his side, this time facing into the room with his inscrutable regard fixed on Owen. "You've been patient, Father."

Owen moved his eyes without moving his head. He winked. "Someone has to try his hand at healing the healer."

"Indeed?" Rather than cheering Doran, the remark seemed to depress him. "I struck a man today." He sighed. "A wounded man. One of my own patients. I struck him with my fist. I was so angry, I didn't stop to think. I struck him."

"What did he do to provoke that?"

This drew an even greater sigh from the healer. "That's what I *cannot* wholly regret. It's a tedious, long story." Doran looked to his father-in-law, who nodded supportively. "Very early this morning, a young messenger came to summon me from bed to the infirmary to treat a sudden rush of wounded. Miklei-son decided he'd try to snatch his traitors out of the jail while no one was looking. Twenty dead on our side, nearly seventy wounded altogether in the series of resulting skirmishes in the neighborhood of the jail. As if that weren't bad enough, I had to stand before the Council still in my bloody smock, direct from surgery, to explain what caused the ruckus. While I was there, another fight broke out. Some of them refused to believe what I said, and those who did believe took offense at those who didn't. The fellow I struck, he came to the infirmary with me from the courtyard at Takra. He'd picked a fight with one of Maia's new young hotheads, and I'm glad to say he came out the worse of the two; that's why I took him to the infirmary—to treat him. I didn't have to do it."

"Of course not," said Owen soothingly.

"He'd got his head sufficiently addled during the fight, so he kept fairly quiet on the way there. I helped him to a cubicle, started treating him just as I would've treated anyone, and he repays me by…by announcing to everyone within earshot that the general killed Colin, and that he's been isolating Maia from her counselors to keep her from finding out the sort of man he is, and…and…" Doran blew his breath out harshly. "That you were keeping quiet about it because he must have found out something shameful about you and was holding it over your head. That's when I lost my temper and told him to quit talking like a simpleton and lie back down so I could finish with him. He said, 'You got plenty of reasons to keep things like they are, riding high as you are,' and I told him I didn't have to continue treating him if he wanted to go on abusing my character in public like that, and he said something else rude, and I hit him," Doran finished in a rush of embarrassment.

Owen nodded. His ear caught the slight note of dissembling in the last few words, but he understood its source. He never failed to regard Doran's finer sensibilities with fond amusement, since they were all directed at protecting him and his daughter from what Doran considered the impertinent or uncouth remarks of commoners. Doran himself knew plenty of salty remarks and, Owen had no doubt, used them on occasion when his temper finally got the better of him. He would not allow any such vulgarities to touch Owen and Phoebe, though. Owen smiled. "I see. If your account is complete, then he deserved a good deal more than what you gave him."

"Yes, that's as may be, but he deserved it at someone else's hand than mine."

Softly, Owen finished the thought for him. "That's not what yours are for, is it? No."

Doran went mute for a few minutes, dispirited by the topic. When he next opened his mouth, though, he did not change subjects. "That isn't the bulk of the problem—only the last and worst symptom of it. I've been busier these few weeks than I was when we were at open war with the raiders. We'll kill each other before Fohral'aku has the chance to do it himself."

That made them both gloomy. Neither one wished to speak the words 'civil war' aloud. To avoid that necessity, Owen and Doran both fell into brooding silence. Phoebe intruded upon this melancholy shortly thereafter with the announcement, "Father, Tyrell is here to see you."

Upon entering the room, the curiosity merchant thanked her in his precise, meticulous way. When bidden, he sat down, but only after offering Owen the formal greeting due his rank. To the chief healer, he gave a more general but still respectful, "Good afternoon." Tyrell composed himself in his chair, his brown eyes solemn. He started off without delay. "My lord, I am troubled in my mind. Something has come to my attention that troubles me. Of this, I have not yet even spoken to my good lord the general. As I meditated upon it, I concluded that you are the most suitable recipient of my concerns, for they relate to your own kinsman."

"Certainly, if you think it best," Owen said, bewildered. "What troubles you?"

"Perhaps it is known to you that I have offered my services in the settlement of your late brother's estate. His affairs, while not essentially untidy, are most complex. He had many concerns, none of which appear to be related at all. It is as if I had to reconcile the estates of three or four men, so widespread are these ventures. The late general was far from methodical in gathering his income. But I will not tire you with details that bear upon the tale only insofar as they led me to consult your nephew, the second marshal, who stands as heir to your brother's estate. I found it necessary to ask him his wishes before I could proceed in my tasks." Here Tyrell pursed his lips in a momentary reverie. He stirred himself only at length, with visible reluctance. "I have no desire to bear tales against any man. I have in past days held nothing but the most profound respect for the second marshal and his great trove of knowledge. I sent him a message outlining my predicament and requesting but a few minutes of his time. He was unwilling to meet with me and put me off for three full days. I persisted and sent him a brief letter that summarized my reasons for requesting my appointment, in the possible case that he assumed I came under pretense, to see him on some personal business of my own. He consented at last to meet with me for a few minutes this morning at his Academy office, but when I finally met with the second marshal, I was alarmed by his countenance. He has the look of a man in the latter days of a deadly plague, gaunt of face and with eyes like glass. His manner was anxious; fretful, at least. I quickly found that I must speak with great care, lest he take my words as some manner of accusation. He first demanded to know if his sister Ivy had sent me. When he learned that he must make certain decisions as his father's heir, he told me in the most abrupt manner that he laid no claim to his father's estate—indeed, he bid me go to his sister Ivy for answers. He gave me to understand that the estate would somehow devolve to her and not to him."

Of this, Owen could make little sense. He mused over it for a few minutes while Tyrell waited for him to respond. "I bore witness to Denei's will some years ago—too long ago to recall all the minutiae of it, Ty. I'm sorry I can't be of more help to you on this."

"It is not this point on which I seek your counsel, my lord. I wish it were. I have spent much of my time poring over the document of which you speak. I am tolerably versed in all its provisions. Priority of inheritance was given to the second marshal, with sizeable gifts set apart for the late general's three stepchildren. To Miss Brigid, the eldest, he granted the possession of a small manor near the Great River in the southern lake country; to his stepson Perrin he bequeathed a respectable annual stipend and the ownership of a carriage with its team of horses. Miss Ivy—the new general's good lady, as it were—receives a generous sum in accordance with her standing as the keeper of the late general's household for so many years. The house in which she grew up now belongs to her as well, with the stipulation that she continue to keep her mother in the same manner to which her mother is accustomed. The terms of the will suggest that the late general added this for the benefit of the notary, not because he doubted that Mistress Ivy would look after her mother properly." Tyrell pursed his lips again, but only for a moment. "If any misfortune were to befall the heir, prior consideration goes to Mistress Ivy in the case of the heir's failure to sire children."

"So Nässey thinks that some misfortune may befall him?" Owen asked.

"That was my impression of him, my lord. But that is not all. As I left, I chanced to pass an elderly man on his way to meet with the second marshal. My business is in rarities and imported treasures, my lord, but I have also found it necessary to trade in information from time to time. It is rarely my intention to eavesdrop, but unfortunately for me, I have trained my ears too well in that activity. Before the door closed on the pair of them, I heard the elderly visitor say to Marshal Denei-son, 'Baring your soul while you wait for the ax to drop? It is rather too late for that, don't you think?' Those were his words, my lord, and even they convey comparatively little to one who did not hear the tone of them. They were spoken by a hunter sure of his prey."

Troubled in spirit, Owen sank back against his chair to think. He liked Nässey. Of that generation, Nässey had been the one whose character traits came nearest to Owen's—peaceable, scholarly, urbane, and broadminded. To hear that Nässey was in trouble, most likely in danger as well, goaded Owen to action. He still felt the sting of the new general's reproof far too keenly to obey the impulse that surged through him. *What can I do? First Kohanan's son...now Denei's. And I can't help either one of them.* He thought suddenly of the solution that had presented itself in Colin's case. "What of the general?"

"He is away from home. Perhaps I should say, he has *returned* home temporarily."

"He hasn't," Owen exclaimed in dismay. "Why?"

"Due to the recent difference of opinions between the royal family and Lord Pamirsi, the Pamirsi clan has declined to supply horses along with their usual donation of wagons and carriages for the midsummer festivities. My lord the general has graciously offered to supply the lack out of his own herds. To do this, he requested a fortnight's leave from King's City."

A glance at Doran told Owen that his son-in-law was as uneasy about that prospect as he was. "He thinks this wise?"

"I only know that he thought it necessary. He came to me briefly before leaving. I did not think he seemed content with his lot. I doubt he will stay away any longer than he can avoid."

"How long has he been gone?" Doran asked. His voice rose on a note of comprehension.

"The general left in the early morning three days ago."

Doran shot upright on the sofa, energized by a sudden inspiration. "That's how long we've had this latest increase in patients at the infirmary—not quite three days. So that's it!" He went to the window and made a careful examination of the area. "We have more guards than we used to. Father, come and tell me if you know those fellows across the way."

Rising to join Doran at the window, Owen studied the faces. He uttered a sharp, inadvertent laugh. "I should. Those are old friends of mine. Retired soldiers, Doran. Look at them, sitting on the bench like so many dotty old men, telling tales." Owen grinned at the sight. "But you're right. We're being watched much more closely than before." Once he had returned to his seat, Owen thanked the curiosity merchant. "I'm glad you're keeping an ear open, Ty. You hear things we wouldn't. If it isn't too great an imposition, please keep it up. Let me know if you hear anything new. Oh," he said dryly, "and while you're out and about, if you happen to see Ivy, let her know I'd be glad to see her any time of the day, any day of the week. My schedule isn't as busy as it once was."

"I will see to the delivery of your message, my lord."

Owen saw Tyrell to the door. He waved a hand toward the retired guards across the street, all of whom returned the salute, each in his own fashion. "Wren," Owen said to the guard at the door, "tell Rowan I have a task for him."

"Yes, my lord."

Rowan, Sylva's younger brother, presented himself to Owen in the sitting room a few minutes later. "What was it you wanted, Owen?"

"I need someone to bring Nässey to me. I need to talk to him."

"I'll get right on it," Rowan promised.

While he waited on the results of Rowan's venture, Owen occupied himself by watching his daughter exert her particular brand of silliness to coax Doran further out of his doldrums. It always astonished Owen a little that a gifted, intelligent man such as Doran would have chosen Phoebe for his wife. If Doran had held political pretensions, at least that would have made sense of the attraction between the two, but Doran had always entered politics with reluctance and left the arena soon after with great relief. Owen knew his daughter well enough to see beneath the empty-headed manner to the steady, indomitable spirit within, but it still astonished him a little that Doran had recognized her real worth as well. Young men, Owen reflected, had no great reputation for exercising judgment in their love affairs. Luckily for them all, Doran was no ordinary young man. These meditations held Owen's mind until Rowan came back to report.

When he came, Rowan brought with him the guard Mundy and a pair of riding boots. "I went to Nässey," he said shortly, "and told him what you said. For his answer, he shied his left boot at my head and told me that was all the answer you needed. When I turned my back to go, he hefted the other boot at my back for good measure."

Owen was so dumbfounded by this turn of events that he dismissed the two soldiers to their duties at once. He tipped the boots slightly in his hands, letting the light reflect on their glossy, immaculate leather. "I don't understand," he murmured. "Nässey wouldn't do such a thing."

"He hasn't been himself for a while," Phoebe offered.

Her remark made little impact on Owen. He carried the boots to his own room and set them down in the corner. Then he perched on the edge of his bed to stare at the boots. The light grew uncertain with the coming of dusk, but Owen had a puzzle to worry his mind, so he gave no thought to the failing light. *What did Nässey mean by it? It's not like him, not at all.* He tried to think of some hidden meaning, some clue that his nephew might have meant by such an atypical gesture. When Phoebe came to the door later on to tell him that supper was laid out on the table, he refused the invitation with a distracted, "I'm not very hungry just now, child. Let me think."

In time, Owen fell asleep without having come to a satisfactory conclusion. His mind wandered among erratic images and words as it teetered on the brink of unconsciousness, dropping Owen into a peculiar dream: he found himself holding a pair of house slippers, irate and bewildered at having discovered them full of mashed grapes. In his sleep, it made perfect sense, although he found it unaccountable, even laughable, when he awoke the next morning.

*   *   *   *

Instability grows within the crown city even as I write. Factions have sprung up like weeds, nurtured by our neglect. It is only a slight credit to those of us who have taken the general's part in this quarrel; we do no more than our sworn duty, yet in these perilous times, even that may appear a credit, for there are many who have failed even to recognize their duty. The faction of the third marshal, Simon son of Miklei, who has conspired with the Unclean to destroy the royal house, grows in boldness. They have seen how few we are, we who oppose them on the general's behalf, and their confidence moves them to commit crimes openly under the guise of loyalty to the crown. "True loyalty," they call it, attributing to their cause the best interests of the king, but they have slain already three dozen of the king's loyal subjects in fewer than four days. They have ransacked house after house, purporting to search for the general in order that they might arrest him, but it is a sorry mask for their real aim: looting, vandalism, the infliction of fear upon those who might support the nameless general.

Tonight, they move with fresh purpose. Their leader has been informed by Phelan, that unspeakable traitor to his calling, that false seer who sold himself to the Unclean for a perverted form of immortality and a base form of wisdom—in short, that foul and wholly unnatural traitor has informed Miklei-son that the curiosity merchant Tyrell, my own friend, must be silenced by any means. Tonight, then, Miklei-son has commanded his followers to set an ambush for Tyrell. They mean to kill him. Whether or not they will succeed, I do not know yet. This knowledge has been withheld from me by my master.

*   *   *   *

Awakened in the dark of night by a sound that was gone by the time consciousness came to him, Owen lay in bed a while in hopes of returning to sleep. He listened attentively to the night at first. Apart from the infrequent calls of an owl, hardly a sound reached him. Owen began to wonder what could have awakened him in the first place. It seemed like such a quiet night. *My nerves aren't what they were,* he began to think. *It must be old age.*

He gave up the attempt at sleep and got up to light his lamp. As had become his habit, he took up his abridged version of the Book of the Kings from the small bedside table and turned to an early chapter to help soothe his uneasy mind. It was insufficient to distract him from the unexpected hammering of a fist against the cottage's front door, or from the scuffling of footsteps in the corridor. Owen went out to investigate.

"Lay him here," Doran was just commanding. He had his trousers pulled on, but no shirt beneath his suspenders. His sandy hair stood on end in the back, evidence of a sound night's sleep interrupted.

Two soldiers hurried to obey the healer, depositing their burden on the floor after a third soldier had pushed the furniture out of the way. Owen, not wanting to get in the way, peered through the doorway to see what was going on and was dismayed at what he saw. His dismay was all the greater when the two soldiers backed away from the man they had brought to Doran. It was Tyrell, the curiosity merchant. Owen had not seen so much blood on a man since the last time he had ridden to battle. A gentle hand tightened around Owen's arm. He pried his gaze from the direly wounded man to find Phoebe in her dressing gown beside him, trying to offer him some solace through her presence.

Doran knelt down beside Tyrell. "A knife. Knife—don't any of you have a knife?" he demanded without looking up. When one of the guards gave him a dagger, Doran took it without thanks and began at once to cut away Tyrell's tattered, blood-soaked clothes. He put the knife down in order to work on his patient, but Owen had to turn his eyes away when he realized that Doran was trying to scoop the wounded man's entrails back into his belly. A sick feeling rattled Owen. *Please,* he begged inwardly, hoping that the immortal master who had visited him once for such a brief time would heed him this time. *Please, take a hand here. Don't let Tyrell die on my account.* When he dared look again, it was because Doran spoke.

"You—kneel down here." The chief healer had seized one of the guards by the wrists, positioning his hands to either side of the monstrous wound so that poor Narayn had to hold the wound shut while Doran stitched it. Soon both men's hands were slick with blood. Phoebe darted in briefly to give her husband one of the kitchen towels, and then she returned to Owen's side so as to keep out of the way. Over his shoulder, Doran ordered, "Ready some wine. Warm it a little—and some broth too, if there's any to be had. We have to put some of this liquid back into him somehow. Ready the bed. He shouldn't move for at least three days, if he lasts so long."

While Phoebe went to the kitchen, Owen went to his own room, stripped his bed of its linens, and fetched new sheets from the cupboard. It had been some time since he had last made up his own bed, and never in such a hurry. By the

time he finished, Doran was just wiping his hands again. By the slump of the
healer's shoulders, Owen knew that Doran had done as much as could presently
be done. Owen caught the guards' eyes and motioned for them to take up their
fragile burden and follow him. Softly, he said, "Put him here. Gently...that's
fine. Thank you." he dismissed the soldiers, who filed through the door past
Doran. Owen asked, "What can I do? Should he be covered at all?"

"Just the sheet. He may catch chill in his weakened state, even in this infernal
heat." Doran kept wiping his hands on the towel—a fresh towel, Owen noted—
until he could see no more stains on them. The transferred stains showed as dark,
wild patterns on Phoebe's white kitchen towel. Doran groaned softly. "It didn't
take them long to go after him."

"No."

"I'll send for one of my orderlies. I'm afraid you've lost the use of your bed for
this night, Father. In the morning, if he's stable, I'll have him moved into our
room so you can have somewhere to sleep."

"No, you won't," Owen replied quietly. "You'll leave him here, and I'll look
after him, if you tell me how to go about it."

"You're sure you don't mind?"

"Not at all. Just show me how."

Doran brought in his traveling kit and showed Owen which ointments were
good for applying directly to the wound, should it show signs of putrefaction. He
showed Owen which was the powder that ought to be dissolved in water, and
how much to dissolve, and how often, if Tyrell should awaken in pain. Apart
from these, his instructions were simple. "Take a clean cloth and dribble water
against his lips," Doran said. "If you try to give him water from a cup before he
awakes, you might drown him. Just a dribble against the lips. He'll swallow it by
instinct if we're lucky. If he wakes, give him warm wine mixed with broth. Just a
spoonful at a time. We have to get him to take some form of nourishment. He
lost a lot of blood tonight." Doran's face turned harsh. "That belly wound was
only the last of the things they did to him. He's been beaten severely. I wonder
how long they worked on him before they left him to die in the street."

They stood silently together, regarding the fallen man. Then Owen propelled
his son-in-law out of the room. "You need your sleep. You can look in on him
again in the morning and see what sort of orderly I make when left to myself. I'll
call for you if he worsens."

Each second of the remaining night hours ticked separately by with horrible
slowness. For their passage, Owen was both thankful and impatient. He was glad
for each second that left his friend yet alive, but he knew that he would prefer

every second of the night safely past. Dawn could not come soon enough. Although it took its time, the sun at last peeked shamefacedly over Owen's windowsill, as if it apologized for its tardiness. Owen stood, stretched, and yawned. He looked out the window at the ruddy sky, savoring the feel of sunlight against his face. Tyrell had lived the night; with good fortune, he would survive many more.

✳   ✳   ✳   ✳

The injured man opened his bruised eyelids late that afternoon. His moan brought Owen upright immediately. "Ty?"

"What place is this?" Tyrell whispered.

"They brought you to the chief healer's house. You were too badly hurt to go as far as the infirmary, so we're keeping you here for the time being. Are you thirsty?" As gently as he knew how, Owen lifted Tyrell's head and let him sip water from a small, shallow bowl. Then he set the bowl aside. "Rest now. When you're ready, we'll try something a little more substantial."

"Thank you, my lord."

When it became clear that Tyrell did not mean to return to sleep, Owen said, "You probably shouldn't talk very much, and you certainly shouldn't upset yourself at all, but I would like to know who did this to you?"

"As would I, my lord."

Owen sighed. "I was afraid of that. You didn't see their faces at all?" Leaning back in his wooden chair, he sighed again. "We will have to leave it to the general to sort all this out, then. I do wish he would come back sooner than later." The door hinges squeaked behind him, making Owen turn his head. He found his daughter peering between door and doorpost. "He's awake. Let's try the broth and wine now." Once he had sent her off on that errand, he went back to his previous train of thought. "They would never dare such things if he were around. I hate to think of what other evils they might be committing. I don't doubt that they attacked you because of what you told me about Nässey. He refused to come and see me."

"They asked," Tyrell began weakly. "They wished me to tell…what you knew. They wished to know of the…the general's plans, of when he means to return, where he went." He winced and fell silent.

"You must be in a lot of pain," Owen said, berating himself inwardly for not thinking of it sooner. "Here, let me get you something to help with that." He went to the kit that Doran had left with him and began mixing the powders carefully in Tyrell's water.

"My lord…"

Something in the man's weak voice made Owen look back to the bed. "Yes?"

"You should not…trouble yourself so. It is beneath you."

"Right now, that's none of your concern. Your task now is to rest and let nothing disturb your mind. Understood? Here now," he said, carrying the shallow bowl to Tyrell and lifting the man's head again to let him drink. "I hope that doesn't take too long in taking effect. You needn't think I'm doing this for especially noble reasons. The truth is that I'm bored to tears cooped up in here. I'd do nearly anything for a little busyness, a little conversation," he said blithely. "I wouldn't give up my only source of occupation, not for all the coin in the kingdom. I'm afraid you're stuck here with me until you're able to walk out under your own power."

Tyrell held out until he had swallowed nearly half a bowl of mixed wine and broth, spoonful by painstaking spoonful. Then he drifted into a health-restoring sleep. Owen felt secure enough in Tyrell's condition to leave him there and join the assortment of company in the kitchen. His brother-in-law Rowan sat there in conversation with Phoebe, while Laena dished up cold cucumber soup from a tureen. Everyone looked to Owen at his entrance.

"How did he manage the broth?" Phoebe asked. "Doran will want to know."

"About half. He's sleeping now."

"Lucky for him we found him when we did."

Owen sat at the table. "Yes, Rowan, tell me about that. What happened?"

"That was all Dai's doing. You know how they've kept to the bench out front, minding things from that angle for us. They were on their way home when he had a funny feeling. I've never understood how he gets those feelings, but it's good for the merchant that he did. Old Dai didn't see anything to account for the feeling, so he went on his way, but it wouldn't leave him in peace all night. He finally got up from his bed in the middle of the night and sent two of his kinsmen to retrace the path he'd taken home; they were to poke their noses into all the crannies until they found out what had troubled him. Halfway here, they heard something fall heavy on the street. From what they said, the merchant's attackers had dumped him like a bird in a trap—those were their words exactly," Rowan added grimly, "like a bird in a trap, bloodied enough to lure something hungry."

"What does it mean?" Owen mused. No one answered the question for him.

*   *   *   *

The city lies in uneasy silence tonight. Even those whose awareness of the Upper World is at best second-hand sense that terror looms over us. I can scarce write for the shaking of my hand. Evil is loosed among us. I will write what I have witnessed by the grace of my master, so that there shall be some record remaining even if every living soul in this city perishes in our wretched helplessness. No one stands to fight, some because they do not know the fight lies before them and others because they do not believe it to be their responsibility. Both sides will perish together if our defender does not return to us.

It began this afternoon. I was taken to the halls of Takra House to walk unseen among those dear folk whose presence I have so greatly missed during my seclusion. In my vision, the time was mid-afternoon. I saw Maia and her maid sitting together in the family salon, one darning socks and the other mending relations with Lady Pamirsi. I saw a great commotion as the household prepared to remove from Takra to the festival site at my own beautiful house beside the Great River: Eleusia, fairest of river houses. It is my sincerest hope that Maia and those nearest to her may be safe there. As for those of us who remain behind, I have no such hopes for us. After what I saw in this latest vision, I am especially glad that Maia has chosen to leave immediately.

In the bustle of packing and departing, I am ashamed to mention that Lady Caretaker, Lucinda daughter of Shara, has allowed discipline among the staff to grow even more lax than it had been heretofore. Indeed, she has encouraged it deliberately out of resistance to the general's commands. I watched as one of the maidservants went alone to the archive rooms. She had not gone there to retrieve any documents, for none were required. Her motive in seeking the seclusion of the archive room was something far less honorable than her duty, though perhaps not so unsympathetic to those who yet remember what it was to be a foolish youth. This girl, Rhendi daughter of Amelina, came to tryst with a handsome young guard named Najhid, but in her eagerness she arrived too early. She waited alone in the archive room for several minutes, combing her fingers through the locks of hair that she had carefully arranged while she should have been packing hampers of food in the kitchen. While she prepared herself to charm young Najhid, the figure of another person appeared at the far end of the room. At first, I was unable to discern more than the vague silhouette because the room was very dark, darker than it normally is. A thought was pressed upon my mind: why so dark? By the time I understood that the room was growing steadily darker, the figure began to gleam a sickly yellow hue. It took the shape of a feeble old man, bald-headed and withered almost beyond recognition. I looked to the girl. She turned with a giggle, just like any young girl might when she thought her sweetheart had finally come to meet her. The sight of an old man stopped her short. "Wait," she said in confusion. "Wait. I don't know you."

"I think you do." The sound of that voice was familiar to me as the guise was not. This, then, is what had become of my childhood acquaintance Phelan, that traitor to his lineage and his calling. He stood within reach of the young maidservant but did not touch her. His eyes were as jaundiced as the rest of his appearance; they stared into the girl's eyes with a blood-hunger that could not be disguised. Smoothly he continued, "You know me as well as you know all the myriad ways in which you have knowingly disobeyed those in authority over you. I have lingered beneath every instance of trickery and betrayal that you have wreaked on your little friend: telling her to go one way while you reap the rewards in the opposite direction; planting tiny lies about her in the thoughts of every young man she coveted. Yes, child, you do know me. You know me very well indeed. I am you yourself." Upon that statement, the figure achieved a miraculous transmutation and took the shape of the girl in every particular. Even the voice matched perfectly. "Since we are one, you cannot deny me what I want. When have you ever denied yourself anything?"

In fear, Rhendi whimpered but made no move to flee. She trembled until the false image stretched out a hand against her face. Then Rhendi, silent even now, bowed backward in agony. She clutched at the hand that was clamped over her face, desperately trying to dislodge it and free herself, but her strength was woefully inadequate. In another moment, she was dead in the talons of the Lethek monster, which bore her away to whatever fate awaits those like her.

As bad as that was, the vision did not end with the poor girl's death. The false seer had been able through his arts to alter his appearance so that Rhendi's own mother could not have known that this young woman standing in the archive room was not her daughter, nor even a mortal woman at all. When the girl was dead, he did not return to his own guise. I wondered why. Then I remembered the tryst. Sure enough, it happened as I feared. Not five minutes after Rhendi was dead, the young guard Najhid arrived in the appointed place, full of rueful excitement over this rendezvous. He had even less warning than Rhendi. No sooner had he crossed the threshold than the false image came to meet him, finger against lips, and threw itself into his arms. That first kiss was Najhid's last moment. In the next, he too was dead in the Lethek's talons. The room stood empty; light again poured through the single narrow window at the far end of the room.

The false seer is strong enough now to roam the city freely, seeking new prey. We shall all long for mercy in the coming days, I fear, unless the general returns to us soon.

*   *   *   *

"How long have you been awake?" Owen asked in astonishment. He paused on the threshold of the temporary sickroom with a tray in his hands. "I thought you were still sleeping."

Tyrell smiled weakly. "I was asleep, my lord, until the door closed so sharply behind you. I have spent the time wondering how I may approach you on a subject that I fear may be of some delicacy. No solution has come to me, so…may I speak candidly with you, my lord?"

"I wouldn't have anything else. What did you want to discuss?"

"I know that I am nobody at all, my lord, particularly compared to your august self. Your friendship has been such an unexpected blessing to me that I am…I am reluctant to endanger it, even for such a cause." When he tried to elevate his head, he winced and fell back to the pillow. "It is unavoidable. If I remain silent—"

Owen set down his tray and crossed to the bedside, where he gingerly adjusted the pillows to support Tyrell in a more upright pose. "If you don't get to the point presently, I'm going to start worrying that you have bad news for me, Ty."

"That is what I myself wonder. You may well think it bad news, even though I cannot. To be candid, then—I have grown very—that is to say, my lord, I have a very high admiration for—since we have perforce worked closely together in the matter of your late brother's estate, and I have hopes that she may possibly share—that is, once sufficient mourning time has passed—I know it is the worst of times to advance a suit of marriage," Tyrell said in visible turmoil, "but I will not speak of it until the proper time comes—if only I knew it would not offend you. I would never offend you willingly, my lord."

Eyebrows aloft, Owen took his seat beside the bed. "Let's be a little clearer than that. Brigid?" He watched the merchant avert his eyes. "Why should it offend me? You're my friend, Ty. Moreover, you're a good man. I couldn't be happier to know that such a man admires her."

"I cannot see how any man could not. She is a rare, wise, and peaceful lady of character and strength. There is not another like her in the five kingdoms."

Owen smiled to himself. He knew that Tyrell would never notice; the younger man's gaze was vacantly aimed at the window, seeing something other than curtains there. In the course of a day, some of the brightness had returned to Tyrell's eyes. The wounded man still slept more often than not, but every time he awoke he downed a little more of the broth mixture. His wound showed no hints of putrefying, although it still caused him excruciating pain. He could only speak at a murmur and breathe shallowly, or else the pain worsened. Doran had come twice to examine him and had declared that the chances for complete recovery were good. In an aside to Owen, however, Doran had predicted a slow recuperation. The merchant would not be leaving his bed for more than a fortnight, and even then he would need an attendant to see that he did not overexert himself in his residual weakness. *After a year or so,* was Doran's reply to the question Owen posed. *After a year or so, he'll be back to normal, barring incidents.* This was the thought foremost in Owen's mind as he absorbed the revelation that Tyrell had offered him.

"My lord?"

Startled from his thoughts, Owen sat up from his slouch. "Yes?"

"You have eased my mind on that matter. It is good to know that I have not offended you. I will risk candor again. What were you writing so late last night? I asked you once while you were writing, but you would not stop to speak to me. I thought it best not to interrupt again. What is it that troubled you so?"

"Writing? I don't know what you mean."

Tyrell nodded weakly toward the small bedside table. "There. You were writing in that volume there. Your hand trembled so much that I wondered how you could write at all. Do you not remember it?"

Owen's hands were trembling now as they reached for the Book of the Kings. His heart clamored in sudden exhilaration. He held the book with its spine against his knee and his fingers ready to part the pages, but he hesitated for several seconds before he had the courage to see if his riotous hopes were true. With a deep, unsteady breath, he opened the book to a page close to the back. Slowly, page by page he turned through Kohanan's scrawl until his own familiar script sprang out at him. He had not looked again at that first and only entry after discovering the proof of his own ignorant presumption. Now he let his eyes rake over the page until they found the beginning of a new entry, one he had never seen before, at the bottom of his first entry. Hungrily he read through the subsequent four pages of recorded visions. His thoughts were practically incoherent. Again, he turned back and began reading anew, hardly aware of the tears that streaked down his face. Through the first reading, he was only aware of his joy at the gift's unheralded return. On the second time through, however, he realized what he had written. He had to read it a third time before he fully grasped the horrific importance of the words.

"My lord?"

"I must have time alone to think," Owen said distractedly. "Yes. I must think. Call for me or for Phoebe, or Laena," he added with a thought to Tyrell's condition, "if you need something. I won't be far." He took the tome with him out to the sitting room, where he spent more than three hours in undisturbed contemplation.

YESTERDAY: THE BLOOD-PRICE OF BELDENE

News of Orlan's approach blew ahead of him, shaking loose several townsfolk like so many dead leaves on a swift, chaotic flight before the wind. Only old men—they were few enough, but more numerous than the able-bodied younger men—noted these scattering souls with anything like perspective. "Treaty or no," said one, "some'll smart for it when he gets here."

Beldene was small enough that the infamous, faceless raider couldn't escape prominence wherever he went. Few had escaped the effects of his antagonism, but while their uneasy truce continued, none was willing to stir up the past. In fact, it had become something of a civic duty to pacify him. If those involved in this placation resented their duties, they didn't say anything. Flight was their only resort, and many took the chance when they heard that Orlan was passing through again after an absence of many months.

Those who remained began to avoid the neighborhood of one certain house, recently deserted. It stood near the edge of Beldene, perilously close to the dim forests that crept up the slopes of the mountains surrounding the town. Even those townspeople who didn't know the house's inhabitants personally knew that it was one of Orlan's most frequent stops when he came to the town. It was widely considered the means of obtaining his goodwill, for reasons that only a few knew. To see it standing empty on the eve of Orlan's arrival set people on edge, so they avoided the place and kept close to their own homes when they knew he was due in town.

They expected him near sundown; he came at noon, surprising them unpleasantly. Only a fool could miss noticing such a big man wherever he might go. When they first saw him, however, he was coming from the abandoned house with a sack under his arm and wrath in his cold eyes. "I want my answers first," he said, his voice as deadly calm as ever. "Then I shall decide what to do with you."

The town elder, Eckule, received the shock of this ultimatum in the shade of his own front porch, where he had sat down to rest from the midday sun. He didn't move. Those who witnessed the meeting doubted he was able to move while helpless under the towering glare of the raider. Eckule finally spoke as though dazed. "Ask, keiri, ask your questions. We deny you nothing."

"Where has she gone?" Orlan stared as if he knew that Eckule would not send around for tidings—that he did not need to send.

"Live forever, keiri, and never lack what your heart desires," the village elder said, straining his voice through his fear, "but nobody knows. As soon as we knew her to have fled, we made search for her, but..." He swallowed. "She is gone."

"Alone, or in company?"

"In...in company," Eckule admitted warily. "To my best knowledge, she took up with a stranger some weeks ago, in secret. None of us knew until only days ago, and only then to hear she'd taken in a stranger." When expected to describe the stranger, Eckule hesitated. "I have only hearsay on this; I never saw the man myself. He's said to be older, maybe as old as I am. Hale and stout, he was, but shrewd enough to keep himself hid from the whole town long enough to make any discovery too late. Few saw him near enough to note him as it was, keiri."

The town elder and all within earshot weighed their fate in the raider's silence. He stood for so long in thought that they knew some hideous new punishment had occurred to him, but Eckule held still and strangely submissive under the deadly stare. Orlan's next words gave them all a jolt. "Your daughter, she has a suckling child yet, doesn't she?"

Eckule blenched. All he managed was a faint nod.

Orlan took the wad of sacking from the crook of his arm and held it out. "Katiiya," he said flatly, "left this behind her."

With shaking hands, Eckule accepted the bundle. He recoiled when he looked at its contents. "What!" He turned his gaze upwards again, confused and relieved at once. "What sort of turning is this?"

"This, Eckule, is how you are going to spare your little village from an unspeakable fate," Orlan said. His voice never shifted from its quiet, almost indifferent timbre. "You are going to see that this child lives, has all he needs, and grows to be a healthy boy. His life is the blood-price of this town." With that, as if he cared nothing for the infant, Orlan turned from the conversation and left Beldene.

∗   ∗   ∗   ∗

The infant waited six months without a name. He was a silent baby. Few heard him cry in those first six months. To everyone's surprise and relief, however, he showed a tenacity that belied his fragile frame; it appeared that he refused to die. No child in Eckule's house had ever been watched as closely, or had given as little reason for close watching. They resolved finally that he would probably survive his hostile beginnings.

Then Orlan returned unexpectedly. He brought with him a money bag and a woman, depositing both in Eckule's care. At first, he seemed unconcerned with seeing the child. He asked Eckule, "Does he flourish?" and listened stolidly to the report that tumbled out so enthusiastically. Having debriefed Eckule, Orlan seemed satisfied. He gave the purse to the village elder: "For his keeping." He flicked his gaze toward the woman. "His own nurse." Then he elaborated. "She will keep accounts of what you spend on him from my money and how he is treated when I am not nearby. She will look after him every moment, apart from his feedings. That remains your daughter's duty."

"And when she goes dry?" Eckule asked tentatively. "Her child is to be weaned soon."

"You shall make other arrangements."

It may have been mere instinct. Eckule's daughter had much of her father in her, and he had come into the position of chief elder through good instinct as well as good luck, so it would be no real stretch to impute some of the same instinct and luck to her. She was a fat, comfortable woman, and she had been lingering outside the door with the child in her arms throughout this exchange. When it appeared that Orlan meant to leave, she came inside with her eyes lowered. "Keiri," she ventured in a voice that sounded stronger than she looked, "will you not look on the child once before you leave?"

For the first time that any of them could recall, Orlan's expression—as much of it as they could see, at least—changed. His mouth relaxed and his eyes opened a little wider as he wordlessly extended his hands to her. With the baby in his hands, he seemed absentminded. He murmured something foreign, staring into the wide sapphire eyes that stared back at his face. This went on for only a few moments. Then Orlan returned the child to its wet nurse and turned to leave.

"Keiri," she said quickly, "what are we to call him?"

"Lucien," he replied without turning back.

The pattern was soon established: roughly every four or five months, Orlan would descend upon the house to check on the child, would ask merely, "Does he flourish?" and then would leave without asking to see the boy. By the time Lucien was tottering on his own feet at eighteen months, Orlan came unexpectedly during the day. He had just opened the door when the little boy came toddling out in high spirits, only to rebound from Orlan's shins. Plopped down onto his backside in such an unceremonious fashion, the child tipped his head back and stared upwards in awe. He let out a small, uncertain, hiccupping cry.

Aside from that brief sound, the scene was mute. Orlan said nothing. He did not move to pick the little boy up, or even to touch him. Neither did he step around the child to enter the house. It was as if the boy blocked his way so that he could not proceed. After a moment, the boy's nurse came and scooped Lucien up with a quick apology, clearing the way for Orlan to enter. If the family thought anything of this odd meeting, they knew enough to say nothing of it.

In the periods of Orlan's absence, the boy did indeed flourish. He never grew physically as well as they would have liked; his mother's abandonment left that much of a mark on him. But his eyes were keen and quick to absorb his surroundings. Since he was such a silent child, the family worried that he might have been otherwise stunted—that is, until the morning his nurse overslept. That morning, Eckule came to his breakfast to find the toddler sitting in an empty chair, watching the doorway. As soon as the head of the household entered, the boy asked, "Where's my food, please," and he only two years at the time, as they liked to say.

Eckule watched the boy grow. In the back of his mind, Eckule knew that he would one day have to explain to the boy something of his parentage; the whole household treated the child like a young prince out of respect for Orlan. Yet Eckule also watched the raider's treatment of the child—his son, they assumed, but they never said the words aloud. Orlan treated the boy with a mixture of indifference and vigilance that puzzled Eckule exceedingly. He couldn't make up his mind whether Orlan would wish the boy to know of him or not. He wondered if the raider planned to put the boy into some kind of servitude, to keep him out of the way and see him provided for elsewhere when he came of an age to be useful.

Thus Eckule continued to put off the matter indefinitely, hoping that it would eventually be taken from his hands one way or another.

Then one day, a young fair-haired man arrived with a sack of coin and took the child away. No one in the village of Beldene heard another word about young Lucien until well over a year later, when that same blond warrior returned with a message sealed with a peculiar seal: the silhouette of a feline head frozen in a snarl beneath what might have been a sickle moon or a closed eye. From that day forward, Eckule's village maintained close bonds with another town farther west in the mountains, a town named after a foreign queen and ruled by a great warrior with no name.

HUSBAND, FATHER, KINSMAN

Preparations would not wait for the general's return. Ivy made use of her own carriage horses, borrowed two of the three teams that belonged to Takra House, and persuaded one or two of her father's old friends to pitch in and help transport provisions to Owen's gracious river-house, Eleusia. The festival was due to start in less than a fortnight. That was why Ivy was on her way to the festival site with the first load of supplies, a wagon with the silk canopy and its frame to make the royal pavilion. Even though there was a house at the site of the festival, it was midsummer tradition that no one dwell within four solid walls for the duration of the festival.

The festival preparations gave Ivy a convenient public reason to absent herself from Takra House, but her personal reason was more truthful. In the days since her husband's abrupt departure, Ivy had begun to feel uneasy. She could not put a name to her feeling. She only knew that she wanted to get away. Eleusia was conveniently placed at the eastern border, and though Ivy had no conception of what road her husband had taken, she suspected that he had gone to his home in the northlands and might easily bring his horses along to the festival site directly. It did not strike her as inconsistent, this new longing to have him home and close at hand. In all honesty, it did not strike her at all. Ivy never held a grudge or remembered a slight any longer than she could help, and the memory of her husband's parting look had overtaken every lingering slander against his character.

Eleusia buzzed with workers' voices when Ivy arrived. The Caretaker steward who minded the property in Owen's absence had already cleared the largest pasture, and several early revelers had already put up their tents. Ivy took charge of the chaos and directed the workers as to the location for the royal pavilion and the makeshift kitchen. A strong breeze blew off the river, driving clouds of mist through the festival site and obscuring the work at times. Its touch was deliciously cool against Ivy's cheek. She smiled. This would be a fine midsummer festival.

Ivy had arrived just after nine in the morning; noontide was haphazard, but not rushed. By two in the afternoon, the silken walls of the pavilion billowed in the wind like a ship's sails. As Ivy tried to communicate the layout of the kitchen to a team of inattentive youths, she heard a dull thunder. Her first thought was for rain, and she glanced apprehensively to the sky. It was pristine, completely cloudless—but the thunder came nearer, approaching at ground level. Ivy ducked out into the sunshine, shading her eyes as she searched out the noise's origins. From the other side of the river, a mass of bobbing figures pushed through the river mist. One blurred figure advanced alone, bravely, all the way into the water. The river gentled at once to reveal a man upon a horse in the knee-deep waters of the crossing; beyond him, a herd of horses began their nervous progress into the river, encouraged by other riders. Ivy's heart thudded forcefully. She headed toward the newcomers.

One of the foremost riders, apparently their spokesman, had dismounted while his fellows guided the herd onward to pasturage. The spokesman addressed one of the workers, who pointed him toward Ivy. He bowed slightly when they were within easy speaking distance of each other. "Lady, the lad there says you're in charge of the festival."

"I am." Ivy inclined her head slightly to acknowledge the bow.

"My lord bids me offer you this tithe of his herds for the Crown's use." The spokesman was young, possibly not yet midway through his twenties, and he spoke with the air of one who had memorized his role. "He follows in a few days with a herd of equal size from one of his other estates. Where do you want us to corral them, madam?"

"Half stay can stay pastured here, but the rest go to King's City. What's your name?"

The young man bowed again. "I am called Loren. And yours?"

"Ivy."

His eyes widened at the single word. A blush swept his face. "I beg pardon, my lady. I did not know. Forgive me." He bowed yet again, this time formally and deeply. "Your servant."

"That's quite all right," Ivy said, amused. "You did nothing wrong, Loren. Come. I hope we shall become good friends, if you belong to my husband's retinue. Did he say how many days longer he means to keep me waiting?" she teased. "I swear, if I see any less of him, I'll begin to doubt his existence altogether."

Young Loren admitted, "I've had much the same thought these two months. Were it not for his—" He checked himself. "That is to say, the king has been a constant reminder to me."

"You've seen Colin! Oh, you must tell me, how is he doing? Is he well?"

"As fine as fine, my lady. A very cheerful, good sort of man, and not at all proud," he said with a reminiscing look, "though he has every reason for it. Until I took up this journey, he was my daily companion. He was glad enough to see his lady. I was surprised that she chose to come back with us. They had their reasons, no doubt, but I wager he's missing her already."

Ivy gazed at him blankly. "She came away without him? Then she's with you?"

"Aye, somewhere in the procession," Loren said with a quick, craning glance around. He shook his head after another moment. "No good. You can't see anything in all this mist. Never mind. I'll hunt around a bit and see if I can find her for you. Where will I find you again?"

"That tent there." Ivy pointed to the kitchen. She went back to her work with as little heart for it now as the workmen, always alert for Loren's promised return with Selena. The youths had accomplished little in her absence. The sun's warmth mingled with the cool, wandering mist off the river and made them sluggish in mind and body. It was all Ivy could do to keep them on task, but she was too distracted to be annoyed. She herself had scarcely any desire to return to her work, not with Selena arriving back home so unexpectedly. *Maia will be glad to have her mother back,* Ivy thought, *but I wonder why she didn't stay with Colin a little longer.* She began to be convinced that her husband had curtailed the visit in some way; not, perhaps, out of unkind motives but—Ivy sighed in exasperation—he did seem unaware that husbands and wives were supposed to spend *time* together so they could enjoy one another's company.

"Ivy!"

Instantly forgetting the tasks at hand, Ivy greeted her best friend with a joyful hug. "Oh, Selie, I didn't think to see you this soon! How was the trip?"

"Long," Selena answered with rueful honesty. "Longer coming back than going out, of course, but that's only to be expected. The horses go slower. Have you been well? How is Maia managing all alone? Not that she's truly on her own, but you know what I mean. How is she?"

"Fine, fine. She had Russa over a couple of days ago for tea, just to patch things up."

"Good. Oh, Ivy, before I say anything else, there's someone you simply must meet." Selena glanced around the area. A puzzled look entered her eyes. "That's strange. Loren, where did Lucky go? I hope he hasn't gotten mixed up with the herd that's going on to King's City."

After some investigation, Loren returned to apologize for reporting that the person Selena sought had indeed continued on with the half of the herd destined for King's City. Loren volunteered to ride after them. "No, no," Selena said kindly, "that's all right. I wanted to get home before dinner anyway. Is there any chance of you coming with me, Ivy?"

"Why don't you have dinner with me at the apartment?" Ivy suggested. "The way Takra is all torn asunder with preparations, you'll be fortunate to get a mouthful in peace. Bring Maia and we'll have a quiet little party of our own."

"That sounds lovely. I'm eager to see all that you've done with your new rooms." So it was settled that Selena would ride ahead after the horses, while Ivy finished her present project and came afterward to prepare a light supper. Maia and Selena would then join her once Selena had had time to bathe and exchange her traveling clothes for something cleaner and cooler. The two women parted in cheery anticipation of the evening to come.

Ivy finally managed to organize the kitchen, almost in spite of her workers. It was with an eager heart that she climbed into her carriage and told Ilan to take her home straightaway. She began to ask herself what sort of provisions she had in the pantry. After some consideration, she opened the grate to tell Ilan that first he must take her through the market to pick up some last-minute items for dinner. The carriage rumbled agreeably along the road to King's City, lulling Ivy as she arranged the evening in her head. Soon the rumble changed to more of a clatter when they reached the cobbled road just outside the city gates. The shadow of the walls glided over them smoothly, and soon they were within earshot of the busy market. So many people were out purchasing supplies for the festival that Ivy's carriage slowed to a crawl in the traffic. She looked out the window, taking care to keep well back in the shadows to avoid drawing attention. Too many people were hostile to her husband these days and would take her presence amiss; that much she knew perfectly well. She saw many faces she knew, but many more she did not know. One in particular arrested her attention.

A dark-haired, sun-browned little boy stood with his back pressed against a shop wall to allow the crowds to pass him more easily. He was a slight boy to begin with, but he looked all the smaller because he was obviously alone in the crowd and did not know where to turn. He did not seem frightened, but his confusion was unmistakable: the boy was lost. Something about him seemed oddly familiar and caught at Ivy's heart. She rapped her knuckles firmly against the grate to signal for Ilan to stop. Once the carriage had ventured off to the side of the street, Ivy opened her little window and beckoned to the boy. "Hello," she called to him over the babble of voices. "Have you lost your way? You look as if you had."

He hesitated, looked around, and then finally nodded. "Yes, ma'am."

"Do you suppose your mother or father might be looking for you?"

He shook his head. "I haven't got a mother yet, and Ta won't be home for a while."

"All alone, are we?" Ivy's heart went out the boy even more. It seemed right to say, "Well, then, there's only one thing to be done." She pushed open the carriage door. "You must help me with my shopping, come home and have dinner with me, and I'll see you home before dark. How does that sound to you?"

He shook his head. "I don't want to be a bother, ma'am."

"Nothing could be farther from the truth. You're no bother. I was just saying to myself that I needed someone to help me carry my basket, and you look strong enough for it. If you do all that work for me, it's only fair that I should repay you with a little food, and I wouldn't think of putting you out on the street alone after dinner. Nonsense. I simply insist." Ivy wrinkled her nose at him comically. "Come on, then. The shops will be closing soon." When the boy climbed up into the carriage and took his seat politely across from her, she extended him a hand to shake. "My name is Ivy. What's yours?"

"Lucien, ma'am."

"I think I'll just call you Lucien, if you don't mind."

That drew a grin from him. "Yes, ma'am. Ma'am, I left my horse at a stable not far from here. I'll have to fetch it before long."

"Never mind that. I'll have my manservant fetch it for you after we're done with our errands. Tell me: what sort of desserts do you like?"

*   *   *   *

The uproar of Takra House only increased by the hour. Loren paced restlessly up and down the second-floor corridor, muttering to himself in some foreign tongue. His muttering only paused when he stopped pacing to receive more bad news: no one could find Ammun's boy. No one had seen the lad since the verbal skirmish at the gate, which had only resolved itself when the queen approached to vouch for the group of armed strangers. In the turmoil of horses and irritable pedestrians, somehow young Lucien had gotten separated from Byram and the rest of the men, and now nobody could find him. That much Selena understood. She communicated the whole tale to Maia after their first happy embrace.

"If he's truly my teacher's son," was Maia's calm answer, "he'll be able to find his way here, I'm sure. Why are you back so soon? I hope nothing's wrong with Father."

"No, nothing's wrong with him. Quite the opposite, in fact. It's been a long time since I've seen him so relaxed and at peace with the world. He and I had a long talk. We decided that you should have one of us at hand until this trouble resolves itself. Then," Selena said with a graceful shrug, "we will decide what should be done." She hugged her daughter once more. "Are you ready yet to be clear of this messy house?"

"Yes, please. May we go somewhere quiet? I can't think for all the noise, and there's no end to the people coming to ask me questions I can't answer. Where can we go?"

"Ivy has invited us to dine with her at her apartment tonight."

Maia brightened. "How soon can we leave?"

More reluctantly, Selena glanced at Loren (who was muttering again) before she answered, "I wouldn't feel right if we left before we knew anything. Let me bathe first, and if there's still no news by then..." She shook her head firmly. "Let's just wait and see. Ivy won't expect us until dinnertime."

When they reached the family sitting room, Maia rang for one of the Care-taker boys, who arrived soon after. "Yes, Miss Maia?" he said respectfully.

"Be a dear, Oliver, and have a bath drawn for Mother."

"Yes, miss." He hesitated on the threshold. "Not that I want to speak out of place, Miss Maia, Lady Selena, but maybe you should know there's a big to-do down in the dining hall. Lady Lucinda and Chessy are having it out, and it wasn't looking too good when I left."

Maia sighed. "Thanks for telling us, Oliver. I suppose we should look into it."

It may have been an argument, but the only voice that reverberated through the dining hall was Chessy's irate baritone. Lucinda reclined in a chair, faint-looking, fanning her face with a handkerchief. Beads of perspiration stood out on her forehead and rolled down her jowls. Once, she tried to interject her own defense: "If you think I'm to be held responsible for the actions of a young girl in love, then you're a greater fool than I thought."

Her son drowned her out. "You don't want to be held responsible for any-thing—not even your own actions! If she's come to harm at all, it's on your head, woman. 'Young girl in love,' indeed! I've spoken with the officers. The chances that that little fool eloped with the missing guard are so scant, they aren't worth considering. None of his comrades think it at all possible. *They're* treating his dis-appearance as a serious matter, worthy of investigation, but *you*! You won't trou-ble yourself to even *ask* after one of the children under your care and guidance—not that you've offered care and guidance, except to guide them into your own willful self-indulgence—you don't stop to think that her mother and father will want to know where she is, might even be *worried* about her welfare?" His voice crescendoed with fervor, ringing from the walls until it was fit to deafen the onlookers. "You—were—responsible—for—her! Does that not mean anything to you?" Chessy mopped his own forehead with a large white napkin. His own wrath seemed to overwhelm him until he could no longer find words for it. Pant-ing from the force of his tirade, he pressed the napkin to his mouth. When he lowered his hand, he spoke in a voice that was no less impressive for its lowered tone. "This is the last. I'm calling a gathering of elders. For the good of our clan, I will ask them to declare you unfit to continue as matriarch. You've gone too far this time."

Lucinda's ungainly bulk quivered. She hefted herself out of the chair. "You've been waiting for that excuse, haven't you?" she accused. "Just waiting to get me out of the way so you can take everything away from me!"

"If that's what it takes for our family to live up to the vows we swore," Chessy retorted. His pure Caretaker pallor was mottled red from the effort it took to contain his anger. Sweat stood out on his face and dripped from the end of his bulbous nose. He swiped at the perspiration with his napkin. "You're a disgrace to our bloodline. I will not risk anyone else. What of *her*?" he demanded con-temptuously, nodding toward a girl standing off to one side of the argument. "She's as foolish as her friend—maybe more so, although it's hard to imagine. What if she should happen to disappear as well? You'd probably just say she went after her friend and think nothing more on the subject."

The girl to whom he referred burst into tears. Only Ardith, Chessy's wife, stood at the girl's side, and she patted the girl's shoulder with more reluctance than sympathy. The girl, Liande, announced through her dramatic sobs, "I…I don't think it's fair…" She gave a violent sniffle. "It isn't! Why didn't somebody go after her and…and *punish* her? It isn't fair!"

"What are you talking about, girl?" Chessy demanded.

"Rhendi! She knew Najhid liked me better. She must've tricked him into going away with her! She must have! Why hasn't somebody gone after her and brought them both back? It isn't fair! It isn't *fair*!"

Chessy heaved an exasperated groan. "Somebody take her to the kitchen and find a use for her," he said, squeezing his eyes shut. "I'm tired of explaining things to her." Once Ardith had shepherded Liande from the dining hall, Chessy looked up and noticed Selena and her daughter standing just inside the doorway. "Oh." An indescribable expression crossed his face. "Your highness; Lady Selena. I'm sorry. I didn't see you come in. One moment, if you don't mind." He turned to his mother one more time. "Go to your chamber and stay there, Mother. I don't want to see your face until the elders' gathering. Stay out of our way." As Chessy approached, Selena saw him draw a deep breath to soothe his temper. His voice was almost hoarse when he asked, "What can I do for you, my lady?"

"What has happened?"

He glanced over his shoulder. "One of the girls, Rhendi, has disappeared. Since a guard has gone missing as well, my *mother* has dismissed the subject as a harmless elopement and feels we need pursue the matter no further. I've talked at length with young Rowan-son, as well as with his officers, and they all agree that their man never had serious enough interest in the girl to elope with her. They're very concerned."

"That's right," Maia added soberly. "Najhid wouldn't abandon his post. He might fool around a little, but nothing could make him leave without so much as a word."

Selena felt chilled despite the day's heat. She saw the fear in her daughter's face. It told her more than Maia's words did. Something had frightened Maia severely. "You haven't been sleeping well, have you? You look so tired. Has this been keeping you awake?"

The girl shuddered violently, as if racked by the same inward chill. "I think I know what happened to them." Her hand sought Selena's and gripped until Selena's fingers tingled. "I want to hope that I'm wrong, but I can't even hope. You remember what I told you? It's *here*." Maia glanced around nervously. She lowered her voice to a whisper. "It's here. That's what happened to Rhendi and Najhid. It took them...*ate* them. I know it did. I haven't slept the night through since you and Teacher left. I'm sure it knew he was gone. I wish he would come back."

All three of them jumped when a deep, rasping voice spoke. "Wish granted, Princess."

Selena pivoted to find Jarod standing on the other side of the threshold. Maia loosed her hold on her mother's hand and ran to give him an impulsive hug, which he accepted awkwardly. The surprise wore off sufficiently after a moment, and Selena asked, "How did you—? You said you would be three or four days behind us."

"I heard of what was happening here and came ahead without waiting for the herd to be gathered. They should arrive in a matter of days." He set his hands on Maia's shoulders and looked into her eyes. "You have shown enough courage for the time being. Tonight, you will be my guest. If you do not mind sharing a room with your mother, you will both stay in the spare bedroom of my lady's apartment. We have guards enough to secure the area, and it will keep you away from this place. Tomorrow, you and the rest of your household will go to the festival grounds to carry on your preparations for midsummer. I will go back and forth on your behalf."

The smile that brightened Maia's face offset the tears that gathered in her dark eyes. "Thank you, Teacher."

"Oliver must have seen to the drawing of my bath by now," Selena said. "Maybe Kenda could see to our packing?"

Chessy nodded. "I'll get her on it at once, my lady. You leave everything to me."

Selena, Maia, and Jarod ascended to the second floor, only to find Loren on the bottom step of the stairs leading to the third floor. He sat bowed double with his head in his hands, but he sprang upright when Jarod startled him from his muttering by saying, "What's wrong with you?" Loren composed himself, but not before Selena saw the stark terror in his eyes. "My lord Ammun!" Loren's bow was a trifle jerky. He kept his eyes lowered to the floor. "My lord, call my life forfeit if you so choose. It is no less than I deserve. Lucky is m-missing. I have every man out seeking him, but they cannot find him. I have failed you." The young man began to kneel down, and his hand went to the knife at his belt, but Jarod stopped him.

"There will be time for that later, Loren. When did you lose him?"

"We had difficulties at the gate. Once we were through, I assumed he was still with Byram, and Byram assumed he had chosen to ride with Lady Selena. Once we regrouped here, we found that none of us were correct."

Jarod shut his eyes. His lips moved, but the only sound that escaped was a low, anxious note or two. In another few seconds, he opened his eyes and tilted his head as if listening to someone or something that none of the rest could hear. A grin parted his lips. "Take heart, Loren. He isn't lost. The little imp somehow hunted up his new mother instead. He's with her now. Call off the search. He's perfectly well where he is."

Bowing, Loren withdrew. As he left, however, he cast over his shoulder a look of astonished reverence.

Selena was herself rather perplexed over what had just happened, but Maia seemed to take it as a matter of course. "I'm glad to hear he hasn't come to harm," the girl said. "I'm looking forward to meeting him. Mother, do hurry your bath. Ivy won't mind if we come earlier than dinnertime."

"If you will both pardon me," Jarod added, "I'll go ahead of you and warn her of the change in plans. By all means, come as soon as you're ready."

$$* \qquad * \qquad * \qquad *$$

One of his own horses stood tethered outside the chief healer's house, so Jarod knew that Byram had wasted no time in seeking out his kinsmen. He tethered his own horse, waved the guards aside, and entered the cottage without fanfare. Squeezing through the claustrophobic front entryway, he emerged into the sitting room to find Owen and Byram staring at him with their mouths open in identical expressions of surprise. "Good day, Lord Sakiry," he remarked. "Good day, Byram."

"What are *you* doing here?" Byram demanded. "By rights, you should be at the farm."

"I came ahead. He is found, by the way. You need not worry about him."

Byram breathed a thankful sigh. "That's good to hear."

Face to face with Owen, Jarod said only, "Are you well, Lord Sakiry?"

Owen's expression brightened. "Better than well, General. Better than I had hoped even three days ago. The gift returned to me. I have seen again." His blue eyes held a sort of eager pleading, begging Jarod to be pleased by this development.

"That is good news. I am happy for you."

"For me?"

Since the older man's bewilderment was genuine and childlike, Jarod could not help smiling a little at it. "Yes, *for you*. Such gifts may be given for the good of all, but they are also for the benefit of those who hold them. You stand at the start of a new road. I can only envy the life that you will now have."

"But—" Owen cut himself off sharply, reining in his curiosity.

Jarod gestured for him to continue.

"But you have spoken with immortals yourself. How is it that you envy me?"

"I have spoken with them, true," Jarod admitted, "but I have never seen them. I do not know why I am kept blind. I can feel them, speak with them, intermingle with them to an extent, but I cannot see these wonders. I have never even seen Chike, though I've spoken with him a thousand times and more. That, Lord Sakiry, is how I can envy you the experiences you will have as a seer." Refusing to look at Byram, he added, "I am pleased to say that you are now free to go wherever you please—as long as you take sensible precautions."

Owen blinked rapidly to keep the tears from welling up in his eyes. "I am?" His breath caught audibly in his throat.

"Yes. You will want to attend the midsummer festival at Eleusia, I imagine."

"Are you attending?"

"Does it matter?"

Turning suddenly intense, Owen nodded. "It matters. You deserve to take your ease. Let others worry about King's City for a few days. You must spend time with the family."

"Family?" Jarod echoed warily.

"You *are* a member of my family now, you know." Owen smiled a little. "Married to my brother's daughter—that makes you my nephew. You cannot escape the connection now."

The irony of the statement tickled Jarod's humor. He laughed. "So I am. It should please you, then, to hear that I mean to spend the entirety of the festival beside the river. For now, let us part in peace...Uncle." Examining himself, he discovered none of the old resentment lingering inside. That unexpected statement by which Owen had claimed him as kinsman warmed him more than he had thought possible. He gripped the older man's hand firmly. "My wife and son are waiting to be surprised as well. You two ought to come to dinner. The queen and her daughter will be our guests tonight."

"That sounds delightful. Thank you for the invitation. Let me leave a note with Laena so Doran and Phoebe will know what is going on." Turning to Byram, he said, "What do you say? Shall we walk together?"

Jarod shook his head. "Not as things stand. Byram has his horse; you must take mine."

"Then how will you travel?"

A playful thought made Jarod grin. *This should intrigue him.* "Chike will drop me off. I will see you when you arrive." *Do you mind it?* he added for the shepherd-giant's benefit.

I will never mind carrying you, came Chike's response, *but you must promise me to stay close to your kin for quite some time afterwards. You have still to recover from the journey here.* The giant's sturdy limbs encircled Jarod. Then the world disappeared for a heartbeat.

The chief healer's sitting room had been replaced by the courtyard outside Ivy's apartment in the interim moments. Jarod looked up at the open windows of the second floor. *Chike? Will she be glad of my early arrival?*

She has looked for you every day, even though she knew that you would not arrive.

Suddenly, Jarod could not proceed. His hands rose of their own accord to grasp the edges of his mask, but although he wanted nothing more than to be rid of it for good, he could not force himself to take it off. *Not so soon. Not without warning. I must find the right time and place. It must be private.* He sensed Chike's dissatisfaction with his choice. *Please...I made my peace with Owen in my own time. Let me do this the same way.*

As you wish, little brother. I do not see wisdom in it, but I will not argue with you.

Jarod climbed the stairs, dug the key out of his wallet, and let himself silently into the apartment. He heard snippets of conversation coming from some far corner of the apartment, so he followed the sound to the dining room. There, he stood unnoticed outside the door while Ivy chatted to young Lucien amiably.

"You do an admirable job with those napkins. If we had more time, I'd show you how to make swans out of them."

"Swans?" the boy asked, looking at the folded napkin he held. "Out of a napkin?"

Ivy nodded. She took up one of the napkins and deftly folded it into the shape of a swan for him to look at. "Of course, it's not as fun as making paper hats. Have you ever made a paper hat for midsummer? No? You poor thing. Imagine never making a paper hat. Before you go, I'll make one for you to take home with you, all right? Never made a paper hat—" Her gaze fell upon Jarod. Not a sound proceeded from her gently parted lips, but her eyes became very round.

Her silence alerted the boy, who perked up considerably. In Kavahran, he said, "Ta! You came early! I got lost coming through the gate, but then I met this lady. I like her. She's nice."

Responding in kind, Jarod said, "Do you, now? Is she?" He flicked his eyes to Ivy, to say, *Don't you think she deserves some explanation?*

Lucien turned to her and patted her hand. "It's all right. That's my Ta."

Ivy sat down abruptly in a chair. "*He's* your father?" Her expression was one of suddenly blossoming insight.

"You aren't upset that I wandered off, are you?" Lucien asked his father, reverting to the more private Kavahran again. "I didn't know where to go, or I would have found Byram and Loren again and told them I was all right. Then I met this lady, and she asked me to help her with her errands, and then we were going to have dinner. She said she'd drive me wherever I needed to go." A wistful look crossed his thin face, but he did not speak the thought that had caused it.

"Why go anywhere?" Jarod said gently. "Are you tired of your new mother already?"

At first, it seemed that the words had passed Lucien without registering in his mind. Two seconds later, however, the boy flung himself at Jarod. "Ta," the boy confided in his ear, "I hoped it was somebody like her!"

Jarod hugged the boy in return, grinning irrepressibly. At length, he set Lucien down and said, "Why don't you go ask Guenna if she needs help in the kitchen?" He watched the boy scamper away to the kitchen as bidden. Then he turned to Ivy, only to find her with her fingertips pressed over her mouth to contain some outburst of feeling. "You have made that boy very happy," Jarod said mildly. "I don't know how he knew to find you. His instincts are keener than I expected of him at his age."

"Oh, I can hardly believe it." The words came muffled through her fingertips. She stood up and crossed the room on unsteady legs. Her reaction was more restrained than Lucien's, but it was no less fervent. It was clear that she had come to some kind of decision. With both hands against Jarod's chest, she looked up at him in unguarded happiness. "I was just thinking to myself that I wished I didn't have to return him to whoever had lost him. He's such a sweet boy! I adore him already." Then, caught up in the emotion of the moment, she flung her arms around Jarod's neck and kissed him solidly. He expected her to back away once she realized what she was doing, but instead, when she stopped kissing him, she hung onto him. "And you! What are you doing back already? I'd convinced myself that you couldn't come back for another three days at the earliest!" She kissed him again. "Not that I'm objecting," she added, laughing gaily.

"Selena and Maia are coming here earlier than planned," Jarod said, "and they'll stay the night in the second bedroom. Lucky can camp out in the sitting room for tonight. He won't mind. Owen and Byram Solam-son are also coming, but just for dinner."

"Uncle Owen is coming? This *is* a good day!" Ivy dropped back to the floor and ran off to the kitchen to inform Guenna about the adjustments, leaving Jarod alone in the dining room.

What was that? he asked, feeling a little dizzy.

That is called 'acceptance,' little brother, despite your trepidation. I wish you ample time to learn the feel of it. After everything you have endured, I trust this shall be a more enjoyable lesson than most. This evening, you must not go out, the giant warned in a graver tone. *You will not act as defender tonight. Tonight, you will be husband, father, and kinsman only.*

But the risk—

Husband, father, and kinsman. Nothing more, little brother. You do not yet have sufficient strength to carry the world, though you may try.

MIDSUMMER

"Lieutenant," Selena exclaimed, "what are you doing?" She stood over a secluded bench near the river, where she had just discovered young Hollister holding hands with her daughter's maid Kenda. The girl blushed, but Hollister was unrepentant and amused.

"My lady," he said with dignity, "I'm securing a civilian."

That was the most peaceable occupation Selena had seen one of the soldiers doing since the start of the midsummer festival. There were entirely too many of them in the crowd. The factions that the city's terrain had half-concealed were exposed on the open plain amid the flimsy tents. It had become so tense that Loren and his comrades would not suffer their beloved Ammun or any of his kin to walk unaccompanied at any hour; the royal guards, sensitive following the king's disappearance, took this as a challenge to the quality of their guardianship. Thus provoked, they were equally attentive. It took a direct command from Jarod to settle them into any form of cooperation. Selena assumed that it was Jarod's wry humor prompting him to pair one of his own men with each of the guards for their rotation of duty. She ended up with Loren at one shoulder and Morio, one of the Alti lieutenants, at the other. Loren was slender and talkative; Morio was stout and silent. Selena tried to get the two to talk, but it was something of an ordeal until her discovery of Hollister's off-hours pastime.

"I can't blame the lad," Loren said with a grin. "She's a pretty girl. Unusual coloring."

"Caretakers are naturally pale, but Kenda is pure-blooded and, yes," Selena admitted, "prettier than most. Silver hair like hers is a mark of special beauty among them. Hollister was raised by his mother's Caretaker kin after his father died. His father was a royal guard, too." She remembered what Colin had told her about this young man. As artlessly as she could, she asked, "You're not far from Hollister's age, Loren. Why have you never found a girl of your own? I'm sure there are more than a few pretty girls around here for you to admire."

"My lady, it is a long and dreary story. I do not wish to tire you with it."

"Tire me," Selena commanded with an encouraging smile. "I have nothing better to do than be tired by your story. If it takes longer than an hour, then we'll have to curtail it in the middle. You don't want to miss the contests, I'm sure."

"That I do not. I wanted to ask, my lady, about a test of strength that is common to Chamika, but I doubt if it is practiced here. I hope it is." He began to describe it for them, caught a glimmer of interest in the silent Morio's eyes, and broke off to say, "This fellow here, for instance. I'd certainly want him on my team."

Selena was amused. "I have never understood why you would want to put something in a stump of wood, only to take it out again. Why put it in to begin with?"

"Why, to prove your strength—and Ammun's, while you're at it." Loren lowered his voice slightly. "That's my main reason for asking. Some of your people seem to think him nothing. I want to make certain that they know exactly what sort of man they belittle, calling him *savage*," he spat. "Him that's taken an honored seat at the courts of more princes and rahgs than they could name, him that speaks with immortals—*savage*? They'll soon learn to mind their tongues if they speak such words in my presence." Loren's face flushed, nostrils flaring, until the young Nikobian remembered himself and apologized.

"No," Selena assured him, "your loyalty to him is really very moving."

"He is a great man." Finally, Morio had spoken. He nodded to Loren. "We saw it at once, we in the corps. We swore our own loyalty to him when he became our commander. He has not disappointed us—far from it. A great warrior, but also a great man, I think. I mean no slight to the king your husband," he added hastily for Selena's benefit. "They are well-matched in strengths and weaknesses. It surprised me at first, how well they matched. I wish to ask, my lady—I remember a certain incident from many years ago, from my last tour before joining the corps. The king your husband, he had a brother once." When he saw a rapidly suppressed grin on Loren's face, Morio stopped short. "You've seen his face," he accused good-naturedly. "It was nothing for you to figure out what I have only begun to learn! You've no cause to laugh."

Selena laid her hand on Morio's wrist in warning. "Speak to no one of this."

"I won't, my lady, but others among us have begun along the same paths of thought that drew me to this conclusion." He shook his head in wonder. "I had not thought of him for such a long time, but I remember clearly the end of that year he spent among my kinsmen. Your own grandfather presented a gift to the brothers, a gift of matching rings—one cameo, the other intaglio. I have seen the cameo on the king's hand so often that I scarcely noted the intaglio on my lord the general's hand yesterday, but note it I did. That was what brought me to—"

Stopping for the same reason that Morio quit speaking so suddenly, Selena raised her head in alarm at the raised voices. She recognized her daughter's among them. There was no need to hasten her companions onward toward the ruckus; they were already hustling Selena onward, holding her behind them for safety. Loren stayed at her side with reluctance, as if to acknowledge Morio's greater privilege as a royal guard to defend the young princess. Selena could scarcely see Maia among the crowd, but she could hear her voice clearly.

"I'm not as easy a target as you'd like to think," Maia mocked. "Get away from me. There," she said, spitting on the ground loudly enough to do a full warrior proud, "that for the traitors to the crown. You thought it a simple thing, didn't you? Get rid of my uncles, get rid of my father, and I'd be an easy tool for your captain to manipulate! He's that much bigger a fool than I thought. I said go! Show him which way to go, Meg." As half the crowd began to retreat from the scene, Maia became easier to see. She stood tall and angry among a mixed assembly of guards and Jarod's foreign warriors, all of whom finally agreed on this one thing: they were not about to let anyone touch the princess. The Caretaker woman Meghala stood before Maia with her sword drawn. When it became clear that the rogue soldiers were unprepared to make an open fight of it, Maia set her hand on Meg's shoulder. "That's enough. Well done."

"Thank you, miss." Meg sheathed her blade. In a determinedly cheerful voice, she said, "Shall we go fetch you something to eat, miss?" After growing up close to the royal family, Meg still had not lost her habit of speaking like a Caretaker staff member rather than a soldier, but in that tense moment, her homelike choice of words calmed Maia as nothing else might have.

"Yes, thank you. Did you note them?" Maia asked Isaac in a less audible voice.

"We'll remember," he assured her. "Half a dozen of us saw their faces."

Maia came to meet her mother halfway. She tried to be nonchalant. "I didn't think it would take them so long to try. What an idiotic time to move. I've been swarmed by guards: my own, Uncle Owen's, even your friends," she said to Loren. "Idiotic to try anything just now."

"Just so, lady." Loren nodded. "They must be growing desperate."

"I think it must be the disorganization. Everything is so casual out here."

"Undoubtedly."

Selena caught a glimpse of Jarod approaching from the other side of a tent. "Look," she said mildly. "There comes the general, late for once." But to her surprise, he did not ask anything about the incident at all. He had come for Loren and spoke what Selena assumed to be Loren's native tongue. The upshot of the conversation was this: Loren nodded with enthusiasm, made a quick reply, and took off. "What did you say to him?" Selena asked Jarod.

"I only told him that we were beginning his favorite contest."

"Ah, the one with the stump? How can they begin without you?"

"They won't. With your permission, I'll escort you to the contest field."

The contest field, so called to distinguish it from the tent field and the pasture field, was not far away. Ivy was already there waiting in the royal enclosure. She smiled widely to include all three of them. "I really have no idea what this is all about," she admitted to Selena once Jarod strode off to the center of the field, "but his warriors are all very excited about it."

"I know," Selena replied. "Loren was just describing it."

Together, the three sat down to watch the preparations. Owen, Doran, and Byram brought Lucien with them after another few minutes and joined the ladies under the canopy. To one side of the field, the contestants waited. Jarod's men, Selena noted with amusement, were knotted together in conferences of three, having drawn in a few of the royal guards as well, and these watched Jarod very intently. The rest watched singly, speaking to no one, as Jarod lifted a great sword over his head and announced the contest. "The object is simple: remove this from the stump. Whoever succeeds will earn a horse from my herds." He waited for the hubbub caused by this declaration to abate before he approached the euphemistically-named stump, a massive block of hardwood that had been dragged in earlier by a team of horses. It stood as high as Jarod's waist. He laid the sword atop the "stump" while he stripped off his jacket, waistcoat and shirt. Unexpectedly, Lucien sprinted out of the enclosure to take the garments from his father, receiving a friendly rumpling of his hair in return. Lucien backed away a few steps with the garments draped over his arms. Now naked to the waist, Jarod took up the sword in both hands, poised motionless for an instant as he measured the center of the block with the blade. A profound breath expanded Jarod's chest, and then another. Then, with a loud cry, he drove the sword to the center of the stump.

Less interested by the exercise than by the man conducting it, Ivy fretted quietly beside her friend. "Look at him; he looks almost gaunt, doesn't he? He has lost weight even since he first came to us. The man wants feeding, that's what."

Selena was still looking at the hilt protruding from the block of wood. "It doesn't appear to have diminished his strength very much."

Maia shushed them both. "The first contestant is ready."

Indeed, one of the soldiers approached the stump rubbing his hands in preparation. A burst of disbelieving laughter rocked Jarod's men. When the indignant contestant stopped, Loren called out, "No, no, don't let us distract you. Go on and try it by yourself. See how far you get." That provoked a good deal more sniggering among his comrades. The Pamirsi contestant reddened. He turned his back on them, grasped the hilt of the great sword, and pulled with all his weight. He might as well have tried to pick up Cloudveil Mountain, for all the effect he had on the position of the sword. Shaken but undeterred, he tried a different angle of attack, with the same lack of results.

"Two tries is all you get!" Loren tapped Morio briskly on the shoulder. "Come, friend, let's show him what efforts we three can summon." He, the royal guard, and one of Jarod's other warriors came to the sword in the block and stood around it for a moment. Their voices did not carry far enough for Selena to hear them, but soon they took their positions, Loren atop the block, Morio with his hand on the hilt, and the third man with his arms clasped around Loren's waist. Loren counted three, and on three each man went into action. Loren and the third man tried to tip the block to counter Morio's attempt to lift the hilt upward and out. For a moment, it seemed they would succeed. Selena was sure that the sword hilt moved through the wood at least a finger-width. But that was as much as they could manage. They all fell away from the block panting, with Morio rubbing his sore hands. Jarod rose, nodding his approval.

"Good effort. The rest will have an easier time of it now," he said, pushing the blade down into its original position without exerting himself.

Eight other teams of three made similar attempts before the team comprised of Kintaro, his young brother Naokko, and one of Jarod's hostages, Hodge, came up with a successful strategy for attacking the sword. All three were sturdy men. Together they managed to tip the block twice in order to invert the sword so that Jarod's original cut pointed downward. From there it was a simple matter to wield their combined weight to force the sword to the ground. They tipped the block back in order to free the sword completely. Kintaro took it up in both hands to present it to Jarod with a ceremonial air. The Alti portion of the crowd cheered and stomped thunderously at the triumph of their two kinsmen. Hodge returned to his comrades to enjoy their more subtle accolades. After an interlude, Jarod beckoned for three horses to be brought into the center of the field. "Your prizes," he shouted to the winners over the cheering. The three men rejoined him, bowed, and walked around the horses to better admire them, pointing out the horses' merits to one another.

"Those are fine beasts," Owen remarked aloud to Byram. "What breed are they?"

"They are called Maransus horses. *Hé maransui* in the vernacular."

"Are they very rare? I don't remember ever seeing one before, except those belonging to the general."

Byram chuckled. "That's because they are *his* breed. He developed them for obvious reasons. Can you imagine any other horse able to carry a man of his size over distances? Rare? I should say so. He does not sell them often, and he gives them away as gifts even less often. Those three are fortunate men."

Other contests came and went. Jarod returned to the canopy to sit beside Ivy, while Lucien curled up at his father's feet contentedly and ran errands to the refreshment table when the occasion called for it. Then, in the late afternoon, the wind shifted again and drove the mist through the festive tent city, dampening everyone's taste for sport. The royal party withdrew into their pavilion, where the silk walls flapped lazily in the breeze and held off the mist. Others of the household joined them there. Hollister and Kenda came in from the riverbank drenched with the mist, to much laughter—their own as well as others'; Loren came and stretched himself out beside Lucien on the large patterned rugs that covered the grass; Phoebe came trotting up from wherever she had wandered, breathless with a child's delight in running through the mist and getting wet. "Can we have a story now?" she asked her father. "It's been a long time, hasn't it, since we've had a family story time. Do tell a good story, Father. You'll get rusty with lack of practice, otherwise."

Owen had a strange look on his face, inattentive to his surroundings but intensely focused on something else. He answered his daughter distractedly, "Yes, yes, a story. That's what's needed now. Family…story." Before he shut his eyes, they had a peculiar silvery glint. "I do have a story to tell you. It concerns a great man who lived among us. The ancient blood has produced many great men, but this one was special. Men of great power have walked the earth before in times of trouble, called forth to lead the kingdom, but never before had one been born of the ancient blood. This mingling of the two lines had a peculiar effect: instead of bearing only one son, against all natural law he fathered two. This natural law was in ancient times known as the Rule of One. Men of great power like this man could only father one son. If any other child came, a thing that happened only rarely, that child was a girl—but this man had two *sons*.

"The sons of great men are born with a burden that the rest of us do not share: the burden of their immense expectations. In the best of circumstances, these two boys would have at once fallen heir to this burden of expectation, with the eyes of all men upon them to see if they lived up to their father's greatness. In the best of circumstances, did I say? But these were not. When the boys were born, the second of them was claimed by a fallen shepherd. Not only did he have the burden of his father's greatness to bear; not only did he have the torments of his shepherd to bear; he also had the consequences of his unnatural birth to face. The Rule of One had been broken. The world has never seen this happen before, so it is no wonder that no one recognized what had happened."

Phoebe spoke suddenly. "What *had* happened?"

"The first boy inherited a measure of his father's greatness, enough to give him charisma to draw people to him. This often happens when a great man of power has a son. The second boy was unparalleled in human experience. He himself only knew at first that he was not like other children he knew. As he grew, he discovered that he was able to hear the voice of his immortal shepherd. More than that, the fallen giant would torture him in physical ways as well as in his thoughts, and torture the boy he did, more and more as the boy grew toward manhood. No one understood. They thought the boy morose without cause, moody, hostile. The boy had somewhat more than his share of wit and understanding. As part of his torment, his shepherd taught him things that he should not have known, both evil and good matters. The evil he used to corrupt the boy; the good he used merely to annoy, for the boy was of an independent nature and hated to have anything handed to him that he had not earned. In this way the boy sharpened his wits, hoping only to outmaneuver his unseen tormenter." For a while, Owen lapsed into silence. No one else made a sound. Then Owen began again in a thickened voice, "Had this all taken place in isolation—but it did not, and none can say what *might* have happened. The boy had family, a family he loved, and his tormentor used this against him. It was not long before the boy knew he had potential that was in its way greater than his father's, but he was second-born. His brother would inherit the kingdom. That much was settled: they expected this second son to take a supportive role, to act as his brother's right hand, and so he would have, had his tormentor not decided that it would suit *his* purposes better to supplant the first son with the second.

"The torture became more acute as the brothers verged on manhood. More and more, the boy understood what his giant wanted of him and refused it, but he was too young, and his tormentor too cunning. He received no support from anyone around him for the simple reason that he refused all support. He was, as I have said, particularly independent-minded and shied from revealing his nature, which he viewed as unstable and even murderous, to those who would have loved him. He had a slim hope. It was said that no man ever escaped his immortal shepherd, but it was also said that men of great power could sire only one son. If he had broken the Rule of One, then it dawned upon him that perhaps he could break the other law and free himself.

"The day this thought came to him was a tragic day. His shepherd knew the thought in his mind. This immortal, though fallen, knew the truth of the matter better than the boy did. He knew that not only was it possible—it was *ordained* that the boy should one day exchange places with his shepherd and become a shepherd himself. He knew that the boy was a whisper of things to come, and he decided upon desperate measures to ensure the boy's failure, hoping to destroy or at least corrupt the appointed order of things.

"The first act in this fallen giant's plan was to remove the boy from the reach of his family's love. This he accomplished through the most devious methods by arranging matters so that the family believed the boy dead. With this, he thought he had ensured that no one would come after the boy. Then he took the boy far away and planted him among the worst of men. In this setting, the giant embarked upon a campaign of relentless tortures until he had the boy ready to forget who he was and from what lineage he had sprung. He did his utmost to corrupt the boy, who in time became a young man—yet, for all that, he was not wholly successful. For every atrocity he committed, the young man also showed a kindness. He seemed like two men in one body to those who knew him. He used the name he had adopted, but deep inside he hid the name he had been given at birth, the name he no longer felt worthy to call himself even in secret. If someone had called him that name, he would not answer, but he could not forget it absolutely.

"He lived a criminal life for the most part, excelling as always. It was his nature to rise to the top of whatever he tried his hand at doing, and vice was no exception. Yet that unaccountable duality always plagued him. Even as he terrorized village after village, he somehow also drew a small but fiercely loyal following of those whose lives he had spared in one way or another. There was still goodness in him, no matter how hard his fallen giant tried to smother it. A more drastic step was required in order to destroy once and for all the young man's spirit. Once, when the torment drove this young man into the wilderness alone, his shepherd led him to a Garden of the Forbidden, from which no man returns alive." Owen's voice caught in his throat. As he sat, eyes closed, an unbidden tear slipped down his face. "He thought he had the young man in a trap. Day after day, in myriad ways the young man degraded himself under the tutelage of a false seer until he was sated with evil. He had tried everything and could loathe himself no more than he now did. In the midday sun, when his new master slept out of reach of the light, he stretched himself out on the ground and tried to sleep as well, but the moss was lumpy beneath his head. The longer he lay there, the wearier he became.

"A small voice addressed the moss, not him. 'Dear moss, am I not enough for you? Why do you try to drink this poor weary mortal as well?' The man sat bolt upright, startled at the sound of this unseen speaker so near to him. 'Who are you?' he demanded. 'Why are you here?' The little shepherd of the moss, though surprised, answered very politely, 'Ah! You speak the ancient tongue? How surprising. Pay me no mind. I am a simple shepherd and not worth speaking to. I fear my speech is fit only for conversing with my charge.' 'Who is your charge?' asked the man, much intrigued. 'Why, this moss that you tried to use for a pillow. I would advise you to avoid such mosses. They are insatiable. I give of myself to nourish it, but that is not enough for my little moss. It wants more and more. When I first had the honor of shepherding this moss, I made a very silly mistake and kept feeding it until I had very nearly emptied myself. Now I know better.'

"The man was bemused. 'I don't see why you speak with me. You seem very innocent.' To this, the moss-shepherd answered with a laugh, 'And you are not? I can smell death on you, but what of it? You mortals may choose one way or the other, whichever way your mood carries you.' The man asked, 'What does that mean?' So the little moss-shepherd began to teach him, saying, 'It means that today you may do evil things, while tomorrow you may choose good things, and yet you are not wholly evil or wholly good. Such is the curse and blessing of the mortal. You are free to choose between them and to repent of your choice if it seems right to you. If you were one of my kindred, you could choose only once, and then your very being and substance would change to match that choice forever.' This amused the man darkly. He told the moss-shepherd, 'Ah, but I *am* one of your kindred, and I fear I have made my choice already.' 'No. Now that I look more closely at you,' said the shepherd, 'I can see there is only half a truth in what you say. You are he of whom the wind sang to me long ago, the little brother born to bridge my kindred and the mortal world. Little brother, you still have the choice. How much longer you will *keep* the choice, I cannot say.'

"This conversation stayed with the man for days. He had learned long ago how to conceal his true mind from the immortals with whom he dealt until it had become his nature to do so. In secret, he mulled over what the innocent moss-shepherd had taught him. All the while, his fallen shepherd and the false seer believed that he still moved closer and closer to his irrevocable choice. When the final moment came, the false seer bid him lay his hand on a portion of the Unclean and voluntarily feed his blood to the stone. This would have sealed the man's fate, but he held aloof. He refused the command and declared that he had chosen otherwise. Life no longer was precious to him as it had been in the past. He felt the world would benefit from his removal, and if he could somehow thwart both his lifelong tormentor and the great enemy of his people in dying, he asked nothing better. He was then only twenty-seven years old."

After that, Owen was silent for so long that Phoebe asked, "He died?"

"Yes." In a choked voice, Owen said, "He died to the mortal world, but his sacrifice pleased that great prince of the immortals, he whom my cousin knew as Niyhaya. This great prince came himself to take him up in his arms. Rather than bear him across the threshold into his own lands, the prince Niyhaya carried the man to a secluded refuge that the man had built for himself far away in the wastelands of the north, where the sea is frozen ten months out of the year. Here he deposited his burden and breathed mortal life into the man's body again. 'Because you have chosen me,' said the immortal, 'he had no right to your life. I give it back to you, cleansed and ready for the new path I have set for you.'"

Selena looked around at the attentive listeners only to discover that Jarod and Ivy had stolen away at some point. Over Lucien's head, Loren met her gaze. To him, she mouthed the words, *Where did they go?* The young man shrugged. Selena got up quietly and went to the entrance of the pavilion. Not far away, two recognizable figures meandered together through the river mist. When Selena first saw them, they held hands and seemed to have no set purpose except to walk. *He still doesn't want her to know?* Selena thought to herself, puzzled. Then she saw Jarod turn and look back towards her. Ivy paused beside him, but when he lowered his head to speak, Ivy put her fingertips to his mouth. She shook her head and tugged at his arm until he gave up on the notion of returning to the royal enclosure. The last that Selena saw of them, Ivy had nestled closer to Jarod's side with her arm around his waist and his arm around her shoulders. No sound of their voices returned to Selena's ears.

*   *   *   *

Nothing went as it should. By rights, according to Simon's reckoning, he should have already won the support of every right-minded, loyal subject of the crown. Who was that foreigner compared to him? No one. Less than no one, in fact; barely more than a two-legged brute beast with the gift of speech. Simon had a great gift. Simon operated always within reason, under the auspices of his vast knowledge; that foreigner ruled by animal vitality alone.

Vitality...Simon was unacquainted with great emotions as a general rule, but he was beginning to learn fear. He recognized the weakness that leeched him dry bit by bit. He knew its cause. The seer had warned him that failure led to punishment. Even if the failure was not his own, he had to face the consequences himself. Others were to blame, but blame invariably came back to rest at the feet of the leader when all was said and done. This was no different. No different at all. It was simply part of the seer's bargain. Still, when Simon thought of what was happening to him, he felt as if a frigid set of talons encircled him bodily, never grasping, but waiting...waiting until the inevitable moment. He shuddered.

So occupied was he with this morbid train of thought that he jumped when addressed by a voice at his shoulder. "Third marshal?" Simon reared his head back to find the foreigner standing three paces distant. "The princess would have a word with you."

Simon loathed the wringing sensation that these syllables caused him. He knew now that it meant nothing, just as *she* meant nothing apart from a means to the outcome that every second slid farther from him. Fixing his gaze on the foreigner's eyes, Simon replied, "To what end?"

"She will explain that to you herself."

Even if it meant obeying a summons from his enemy, Simon still found himself unable to deny the girl her will in this small thing. "Very well." Restraint was all he could manage, to keep her from knowing that he still weakened when she came near him. The sight of her only intensified that idiotic streak of emotion in him. A tiny thought slipped through his control: *So lovely. Truly perfect.* Simon clamped his jaws tightly shut lest any hint of his recalcitrant thought-life slip through. "Yes, your highness?" he asked coldly. "What do you want from me?"

The girl did not bother to rise. She gazed up at him from the heap of cushions that propped her up. Her dark, wide eyes skewered him where he stood. "Do you remember what we spoke about last time, Simon?"

The sound of his name on her lips did nothing to loosen the vise-grip of unwanted sentiment. Simon had to carefully modulate his voice when he replied, "I remember."

"You remember that I warned you." Her tone was meditative; the look that accompanied the words turned to pity. "He's already starting to feed off of you, isn't he? I can sense it in you. You're growing weaker. It isn't too late yet. You can renounce your pact."

"I want none of your condescension," Simon snapped. "Why did you call me here?"

"Only to say what I said. It still isn't too late. It might not save your life, but what's left of your life could at least pass in—"

"Spare me, Princess. You, being a mere woman, can wallow in brainless senti-ment all you want. I choose to face the truth without such false colorations. Death is death. The manner of its coming makes no difference."

She drew an unsteady breath. "So you do know. You choose it knowingly."

"It is the consequence of my failure. Nothing more."

"No," the girl interrupted, standing to face him. "Even if you succeeded, you would've come to this sooner or later. He would've had you in the end no matter what. Don't you see? Sooner or later, he meant to eat you alive."

Simon laughed without amusement. "Eat me alive? I hadn't thought you were still such a little girl, your highness, believing in fireside tales concocted to frighten children into obedience. There are no monsters lurking outside in the dark, your highness. There is only a man's will to power and his will to turn that power to useful purposes."

"There *is* a monster outside in the dark," said the girl quietly. "It's you."

Unexpectedly, the remark stabbed. Simon snarled back at her, "If you want a monster to fear, then you ought to fear that brute beast you've chosen to back as your general."

"He was the one who told me I should try one last time to persuade you, Third Marshal. You should be flattered that *he* hasn't given up all hope for you, when of all people he should most want you dead."

"Flattered? I ought to be *flattered*," he said in undisguised derision. "He thought it worth his while to make one last attempt to divert me by means of a pretty face. How flattering—but more to me than to you, your highness. How does it feel to be made a tool of his intrigues? If he told you to seduce me, would you obey him in that, too? You follow a mercenary like him blindly and scorn the honest advice of loyal subjects. Oh, yes, Princess, the kingdom has every cause to be proud of *you*." Her fierce blow rocked his head back. Randomly, his mind said, *Strange—I thought women slapped with their palms, not their fists.* The metal-lic taste of blood washed across his tongue. He shook off the pain and spat blood on the luxurious carpets.

The girl glared at him. "I have nothing more to say, except this: when my father returns, he won't spare you from the judgment you deserve, if your filthy master hasn't killed you first."

"Your father is a coward. *If* he returns, he'll do nothing."

All that enabled Simon to keep his focus was the prospect of revenge. The girl had proven herself defective, without vision or intellect enough to deserve his attention. She would never be brought into submission to his will until he had severed her ties to the foreigner, as well as to all her weak kindred. Simon now readily acknowledged himself mistaken on one crucial point. He had gone into the business with the belief that there was substance behind the people's archaic reverence for the ancient royal bloodline. That foolishness had hobbled him. He was in every way superior to them, even without the pedigree. Whatever strength had originally inhabited that line was long since bred out of it, leaving the royal house weak-minded, good for nothing but producing handsome offspring. Now that his eyes were opened to the source of his failure, Simon felt sure that he could rectify it. He would keep his end of the bargain, and the seer would restore him and elevate him to the glory he deserved. It was as simple as that.

The shouts of muddy, naïve children intruded upon his thoughts. Simon looked up with a scowl, only to find the herd of brats ready to trample him. He had been so deep in thought that he had strayed into their silly game. Simon was not the only adult unfortunate enough to have mixed himself into this folly. That useless woman Ivy played with the children as if she had no dignity at all. One further thought amended this judgment: it was sense she lacked, not dignity. The absence of the one made the other impossible anyway. She could not hold to one course long enough to be of use to anyone. Simon had watched her cozying up to the foreigner when she should have still been terrified by him. But the woman was so weak-minded that she could not sustain even something as simple as an emotion for any length of time. Simon determined to first rid himself of her irritating presence. He suddenly could not bear the thought of breathing the same air as such a stupid person for one day more.

Inspiration lit his mind as he neared the river. *Drown her.* If Simon knew one thing with absolute certainty, it was that the river would not stop for such a woman. Her folly must be as offensive to the very earth itself as it was to every reasonable mind. The seer had even told Simon once that she had forfeited citizenship, but was too stupid to realize it. Simon cared little for the reasons behind this forfeit. It sufficed to know that the river would sweep her away as if she had never existed, as if the blot that was Ivy daughter of Riana had never blemished the ground she trod in that silly, helter-skelter manner. Simon considered his new plan and was pleased. The day would not be completely lost after all—*and*, Simon realized, he could strike a blow at the foreign mercenary at the same time. The brute seemed to enjoy her fawning over him. It wasn't difficult to conclude that the foreigner was fond of his idiotic wife. Simon had it in his power to take this one petty prize from his enemy. With careful planning, everything else would follow soon after.

Simon examined the herd of children and selected one with a particularly dopey grin on its face. He ambled toward the little red-headed boy and, when no one was looking, he whispered to the child, "Wouldn't it be funny to push Miss Ivy into the water? Imagine how surprised she'll be!" He had seen a number of the older Sakiry youths take it in turn to push one another into the river, knowing themselves perfectly safe in their play. As he had expected, the little boy had also witnessed these antics and wanted to take a hand in them himself. The chortling boy charged headlong at Ivy, who had positioned herself most obligingly on the riverbank with her back turned as she conversed with a dark-haired, runty little boy.

A number of things happened in swift progression. Simon's young dupe collided with Ivy, sending her tumbling into the river, which swept her downstream without pause. Horror-struck, the woman's undersized companion cried, "Ta! Help!" The words had hardly left his mouth when the foreigner appeared out of nowhere. He too shouted, but his tone was one of authority and his language one that Simon had never heard in his life. At the foreigner's sharp command, the river stilled. The foreigner dove into the water and disappeared for several long seconds, while a crowd gawked at the river's edge. Then, with a great splash, the foreigner surfaced, heaving his wife's inert body onto the bank and sliding out after her. Even from a distance, the fellow's skin looked bright pink, as if the water had scalded him. He picked up his wife by her waist and let her dangle until the water ceased to drain from her nose and mouth. She coughed, retched, coughed again, and gagged on the last of the river water. When the foreigner righted her, she trembled so fiercely that she could not support herself on her own strength. He carried her like a child, and together they disappeared into the royal pavilion.

All around, people murmured their astonishment. Simon heard nothing but awestruck praise: the foreigner had commanded the river to halt. Simon turned from the scene, feeling utterly cheated. *He turns everything to his advantage.*

EXACT TWINS

Midsummer festival was already halfway spent, as measured by the residents of Chamika. Colin had thought at first that two full weeks of festival would begin to pall, but to his great amazement, these villagers had developed ways to balance festival with daily duties. Every morning now, the dawn run became a race. Rafe no longer led them. Instead, he waited at the rally-point to greet each day's winner. The coveted prize was exemption from the dawn run for the duration of the festival—or an equal period of time for those who won later races. The sparring, whether wrestling or dueling, now turned to elimination tournaments, and it was rumored that the winner had the right of choosing any weapon from Ammun's own collection. Having seen the general's personal armory, Colin could easily appreciate the value of this prize.

The sword was today's weapon of tournament. Competition was open to anyone whose sufficiency had been established by Swordmaster Bayne. This automatically eliminated Colin. Bayne still despised him with such a passion that Colin wanted nothing to do with him or his tournament, so the prohibition did not chafe as much as it might have. He observed the drawing of lots with enthusiasm nonetheless, plunging into discussions about the paired opponents with as much zeal as any native villager. When they marked off the field of contest, Colin was at the front of the crowd, planted securely between Greysin and Farris as he cheered his favorites for all he was worth. Of more than fifty contestants passed by Bayne as especially creditable, Colin knew only four personally, so he had no trouble choosing favorites. Between the two of them, Greysin and Farris knew every contestant and pointed out to Colin those whom they favored. Their conjectures had to be carried out in a fragmentary manner at the top of their voices because of the noisy crowd at their backs. During a later round, when Rafe's brother Remi went up against Lorçan brother of Loren, Colin felt a jog at his elbow. He turned to find Farris gone and Niall standing at his side, beckoning for him to nudge Greysin. Colin did so at once. Speech was impossible with all the noise around them, so none of them attempted it. Because he was taller than most of the crowd, Colin saw Rafe and Bayne leaving their posts across the way. Farris was halfway to the house already.

Niall spoke when they were well beyond the reach of the crowd. "Natai council. You'll be needed, too. Damon sends word. Some of the news concerns you and yours."

They arrived last in the evening room, as Manon was pouring refreshments. Three others were there besides the chieftains, so Colin didn't feel quite so out of place. Giles was one of them, Ingram another, and Druze the third. As soon as Colin's party crossed the threshold, Rafe dismissed the housekeeper and shut the door. It was Niall who spoke, however. "Good news first: Damon sent word that he found what he went seeking. Ammun guessed it right. The old man kept his correspondence, most likely with an eye toward blackmail sometime in the future. What's more, he's been careless and kept them all in the same place. Once we get our hands on those papers, it won't be a moment's work to roust out your traitors," he added for Colin's benefit. "You'll have their names in black and white—their own hands testifying against them."

Bayne growled softly in his throat. Impatiently, he asked, "What's the bad news?"

"Word is out that Ammun won't be coming back for a while. Malin struck Beldene."

Every man present except for Colin made some sort of exclamation at that. Colin had no idea why this statement merited such spontaneous outrage, but he could see from Bayne's glare that the blame for it would fall at his own feet shortly. Niall held up both hands to still the outcry. "We'll get our own back, but not until we put our heads together and come up with a plan. Before I say what's in *my* mind, any ideas?"

In the silence, Bayne's acid voice spoke first. "Only one. As it's on *his* account that Ammun's gone," he said, nodding shortly toward Colin, "that means Beldene suffers on his account. That puts a burden on him to make things right."

Every trace of goodwill drained from Greysin's face as he stared hard at his fellow natai. "You and I will have a long talk about your attitude one of these days," Greysin said, "but one small kernel of truth lies buried in that steaming heap of dung you just spoke. It was in my mind, too. My lord, I know this lies outside the terms of your stay here, but you have the chance to help us avenge Beldene and recover the prisoners. They only struck because they thought Ammun was too far to punish them for it. If we can make them believe he came back, they'll back off quick enough and keep quiet. Here's the snag in that plan: he isn't here, and none of us are nearly tall enough to fit in his clothes. You, on the other hand, are tall enough."

"Not quite," Colin demurred. "He has half a head on me."

"But without him beside you for comparison, they won't know it. How about it?"

"I'm no warrior, either. I can't fight in his stead."

"Most times, he stands aloof and watches the battle. They won't know the difference."

Colin considered the possibility. He had fought among the hostages, had run and wrestled with them for two months. He knew that he had improved under their tutelage. *But is that going to be enough? Am I ready to do battle in Ammun's place?* A look into Greysin's intent gaze told him that the Alti believed inexplicably in his competence. He knew something; so did Niall, who wore a similar expression. Colin had no idea what knowledge gave them such faith in him. "You truly think this will work?"

"Think of it like this: it couldn't hurt. We shall do the hard work while you stand apart and frighten them. We do know how to look after ourselves out here, my lord. They're so superstitious about Ammun, the sight of the mask and red shirt will be enough to send them running with their tails tucked low."

Refusing to look at Bayne, Colin nodded. "If you're game, so am I."

"Fine," Niall said. "Damon says to send him a raiding party to help him fetch the papers. The question becomes trickier now that we've got prisoners to consider."

"We promised them our aid and protection. Our honor—worse still, Ammun's honor—depends on how swift we are to ride out to rescue their prisoners," Bayne stated flatly. "We can be in no doubt as to that."

"No one doubts it," replied Niall in an attempt to soothe the man's temper.

"No? From all I've heard, we're here to solve *his* problems nowadays."

Greysin's snarl was the only sound that lingered in the air following that sarcastic remark. Rafe imposed his presence on the discussion then, but in his native Kavahran so that Colin could make nothing of the words. It struck Colin as amazing that Rafe, smaller than any of them except perhaps Greysin, had authority enough to subdue this assemblage of powerful men with a few words and nothing more. Bayne sank back into his chair, rebuked, and Greysin no longer bristled with wrath. The rest breathed more easily as they turned their attention to planning retribution. This was where Colin understood Druze's presence. As soon as the maps were rolled out on the table, Druze was summoned to examine them and give his opinions as to the best way to accomplish both tasks that lay before them.

"How many men will he keep around the house?" Druze asked, studying the maps.

The older warriors exchanged a look. Bayne finally said, "He won't let most of them stay once they've split the plunder, but that's too late. We can't go chasing after every single prisoner. We don't have the numbers for that. We have to assume we're dealing with a full raiding force—say, upwards of four hundred."

Druze made a noncommittal sound through his nose. His lips were pressed firmly together in concentration. "Natai," he said, addressing Rafe, "what say you? How many should we call out? Damon wants a quick-raid party for the house, so the rest will have to be enough to draw attention away from the house." He listened to Rafe's reply deferentially. His next words were, "Then I'll give this to you, cousin," as he handed the blueprints of the raider prince's house to Farris. "You'll know it best, if you built it."

The assembly broke into two groups. Colin, being of no real use to either group, gravitated toward Farris in order to keep out of Bayne's path. Quietly he said to Farris, "You built Malin's house?"

"Ammun drew up the plans, but aye, the work is my own."

From the nearest window, Giles cleared his throat. "Has anybody looked at the sky outside recently? I wouldn't ask, except…it doesn't look promising, does it?"

Everyone stopped at once and went to a window as Giles had suggested. Outside, the sky had gone gray and the wind had whipped itself into a frenzy that presaged a storm. Colin was impressed. Beside him, Greysin said, "It happens sometimes that the weather turns a season early in these heights. If we're lucky, it will only drop rain on us."

"And if we're not…?"

"Snow."

Colin shook his head. "At midsummer? Madness."

"It won't last. Within a day or two, it will have melted and we'll have a month or more of summer left." Greysin led the rest of them in drifting away from the windows to their respective maps again. He crouched down beside the map of Malin's house and said, "Damon will tell us more when we rendezvous with him at the site. I've never been in the house myself." Greysin stared inquisitively from face to face, waiting for someone else to chime in on that point.

"I was in it," Farris said, "but years ago. Anyway, I don't have the right build for the job. This wants stealth. It'll have to be you. There's bound to be a window open this time of year."

Just then, Colin gasped. He had been studying the blueprints with a strange sense of familiarity that he suddenly understood. "That's Takra," he exclaimed.

"Pardon?"

Aware that Giles had come away from the window to look on in curiosity, Colin elaborated on his statement. "That's my home. That's Takra House...only it's backwards. That's north, right? This should be the residential wing, and this should be the official wing, but they're reversed in these plans." He raised his face to survey those around him, only to find Greysin's bright green eyes fixed intently on him. "Why?"

Farris answered instead. "The old man wanted a kingly house as befit his puffed-up notions of his own importance. So Ammun built him a king's house, but not the kind he wanted. It caused a rare scuffle between the two of them, Malin thinking that Ammun did it to mock him and Ammun insisting that it *was* a king's house. He said if Malin wanted more than that, he ought to have been clearer in his directions. He never said *which* king's house he wanted." Returning to his study of the blueprints, he said to Greysin, "That makes a difference. You were a king's guard. You know these halls better than you think."

"Aye, a little better, but it's been a long time."

"What if I went with him?" Colin asked.

Immediately, the warriors shook their heads. Greysin said, "No, my lord, we can't risk you as much as that. Besides, you're needed outside, to carry off the appearance of Ammun overseeing the battle for the prisoners. You can't be in two places at once."

"I know the house."

All of the men, Colin included, turned to stare at Giles as if he had spoken gibberish. Farris had already begun shaking his head, but Greysin had a speculative look in his eyes. "You think you're ready for this, lad?"

"It isn't as if I'd have to fight. You want someone to sneak into the house and sneak out again? I can do that...probably I can do it better than any of you. I've had a lot of practice for my years," the young man added dryly. "Yes. I can do it." His features were firm with this new resolve. Colin thought that he looked older than before. "Does he have lots of servants?"

"Slaves," Greysin answered with a touch of bitterness that came from memory. "I've seen them. They're kept under lock and key here, in these rooms." He pointed at the blueprint.

Colin nodded. "Caretaker quarters. If he follows true to form, then he'll keep his papers here, in this office. You know the place, don't you, Giles?"

"Yes, sir."

"You'd best tell me what's going through that head of yours," Druze interrupted, "so we're all together on this. Why do you want to know about servants?"

"If they're slaves, it's better still. They'll be wanting out of their rooms. I don't know what papers to look for, but I know how to make a diversion if needed."

*   *   *   *

The weather broke just before dark. True to Greysin's prediction, the dismal twilight sky dumped down a thick flurry of snowflakes at such a pace that within an hour, the ground was an unbroken slope of white all the way to the edge of the terrace. It was discovered that Giles had no suitable winter gear, but Rafe's household rallied to the young man and by the next morning had a fine sheepskin riding-coat to present to Giles. Giles was so pleased with his new garment that he wore it indoors and out all day. It was still snowing at dawn, but the wind had died down and the flurries became intermittent by noontide. A swarm of young boys appeared with spades to dig paths through the soggy drifts so that arrangements for the following day's sortie could go forward unhindered.

No one would let Colin take a hand in these preparations. Toward evening, Niall sent him upstairs. "We'll head out in the small hours, so you'd best go upstairs and get dressed now. Call if you need anything. Laszlo knows the routine. He'll help you along if you need it."

"All right." *What have I got myself into now?* He asked himself that all the way up the stairs, finding each step more difficult than the last. He passed the room that had been his before his removal to Farris' longhouse, passed the library, passed Lucky's empty room at the corner, and then in a few more steps he came to a room he had never seen, the master's bedchamber. Colin almost turned back at the door. With a push of determination, he forced himself to enter.

It was nothing like his expectations. Compared to the rest of the house, this room's walls were stark and empty, except for a rack of light armor in one corner; not a single weapon, ornamental or otherwise, adorned the paneling. Art likewise was absent. In fact, the entire room was starkly spartan. A bed, a large wooden chest, and a small table were all the furniture the nameless warrior kept for him-

self. The bed was sized to fit Ammun's build, thus taking up most of the floor. The chest sat snugly against the footboard. The table sat in a corner without even a chair to its credit, but it was so cluttered with oddments that adding a chair to it would have been superfluous. In his curiosity, Colin went to the table first. It was the first sign of personal memorabilia that he had found, and he wanted to know what sort of curios Ammun would collect for himself.

At first, his brain refused to acknowledge what his eyes showed him. The table held only pictures. He knelt beside the table and picked up the nearest of the exquisite miniature portraits. What shocked him most were the subjects: his own parents, Kohanan and Camille. Colin set down the miniature and picked up another, only to encounter his next shock. It was a picture of Colin himself, painted quite recently. Three other miniatures sat farther back: one of Selena, one of Maia (painted when she was a child of ten or eleven), and a more recent portrait of Colin, Selena, and Maia all together. A recent one of Lucien occupied the far edge of the table. Colin sat back on his haunches and stared at the collection until he recollected his reason for coming. Rising, he went to the trunk, since there was no wardrobe in the room to hold clothing.

The trunk itself was a curiosity. It was lavishly carved and painted black with accents of a beautiful deep red. Around the lid, some craftsman had painted gilt letters, phrases in several languages that Colin did not recognize—except for one, his own, which proclaimed in boldness, *Of the Keeper House Unending.* He put his hand to the latch without realizing that he did it. It felt so natural, swinging the lid up and propping it against the footboard of the enormous bed. Colin obeyed the feeling further when it led him to unbutton a stiff leather packet tacked into the underside of the lid. Inside was a soft pouch; inside the pouch, a thick sheet of paper, its edges worn and its creases soft from much folding and unfolding. Numbly, Colin read the following words: *I know my plea holds less weight than your father's, but I know too that I have always wished you could be my own son as well. In a way, perhaps you are, in ways you know even better than I. I wish I had room and time enough to tell you how I once suffered under the type of short-lived madness that an immortal's unguarded contact can cause. I know what it is to hate oneself unduly because of lost self-control and irretrievable mistakes. What I want to tell you more than anything else is this: you were and are loved, whatever you have or have not done. You may not believe this assurance from others, but I trust I have never given you reason to doubt my word. Come what may, you belong to us. If your father is unable to speak when he finds you—and I have no doubt that he will succeed—then let me say this on his behalf as well. Come home, Jarod. Please, come home to us.*

Colin knew the handwriting. Hardly cognizant of the tears on his face, he refolded the missive with reverence and returned it to its resting place. He began methodically to choose clothes from the trunk's depths. Everything was ready at hand, including a mask identical to the one he had seen so often on his general. He left that alone for the time being and dressed himself in the other man's clothes as if he had done it innumerable times, even down to the pieces of light armor that hid beneath the scarlet tabard. Someone else's habits guided Colin through the routine, until all that remained was to don the mask. An overwhelming sense of revulsion kept him away from it. Colin turned instead to the windows to look out at the courtyard.

Beneath the only east-facing window, someone had tacked down a kneeling pad. The fabric, originally a length of rich emerald damask, had faded with time and sunlight. Two marks had been worn into the texture of the fabric. Colin knelt and found that the marks corresponded perfectly to his knees. As he stared out into the darkness, he thought, *How do they fare? Are they well?* Then, with amazing timidity, one more question arose: *Am I missed even now, after all these years?* He nearly pushed the thought aside. Whatever habit of thought now guided him wanted him to submerge the question entirely, but Colin resisted the lure of this strange feeling. He examined the question frankly. *Do they think of me ever? Have they forgiven me?* The almost physical pain that accompanied this examination told him why the question was buried so deeply. Colin got up from the kneeling pad and turned back to the open chest.

He had to pick up the mask. In his own mind, he knew that the disguise would not be complete without it. Colin was not guided solely by his own mind any longer, though, and the aversion he felt for the mask was enough to nauseate him. He hated the mask, loathed it with all his being, and wanted nothing so much as to fling it from him and never pick it up again. It beckoned to him with a taunting echo of a voice: *Give up who you are.* Colin, out of breath without warning or explanation, clenched his fist around the coarse fabric. He struggled with himself, knowing that he had to wear the repellant garment for the sake of disguise. *Remember who you are,* he found himself thinking. *The mask is nothing but a tool, a passing need that will soon be gone. One way or another…all will be revealed.* This thought comforted him a little, but as Colin began to draw the mask over his head, he felt his heart accelerate. Flashes of imagery spun through his mind, pictures of a sickening past. Worst of all was the self-loathing that flooded him once he had the mask over his face. He hated himself with a passion that would not be wholly erased, not even years after the fact. Horrified, Colin ripped the mask off and threw it back into the trunk.

"How are you getting along, sir?" the steward Laszlo's tentative voice said from the door.

Startled at the interruption, Colin jerked his head upright. "Fine." His voice cracked.

"You've found everything, I trust?"

"Yes," Colin assured him. "I've found everything. Thank you." He waited until the steward closed the door. Then, refusing to take up the mask again, Colin stretched himself out on the bed to wait. The armor, light though it was, dug uncomfortably into his flesh at various points when he lay down, but the discomfort made no difference to him. He stared up at the ceiling of dark, polished beams separated by stretches of cream-white plaster and let his mind go completely still. The night would be hard and long, he knew. If they left at the small hours, that meant they would attack in the predawn hour—Colin dared not question how he knew this—when the marauders might be cold and stupid with sleep. Since they believed their uncanny foe too far away to retaliate, perhaps they had not put out more than a token watch. With luck, some of them would have begun a premature celebration and gotten drunk. Colin shut his eyes. In his head, he had images of how he wanted the battle to go. The marauders would keep the prisoners with the horses, tethered (much like the horses) in a corral off to one side of the courtyard...

In time, Colin fell asleep. He awoke to a dark room, and someone stood over him. In the space of time between waking and comprehending, he lashed out with a hard hand to grasp the intruder's wrist. "Ow," Greysin complained mildly, but he sounded more amused than hurt. Still, when he was released, he rubbed his wrist gingerly. "Are you ready to go, my lord?"

Colin rubbed his face, disoriented, unsure *who* he was, let alone where. "Sure. Just give me a little time, all right?" The other man left him, but before the door shut behind Greysin, Colin heard a second voice, Niall's, begin quietly, "Go ahead; say it. You were right. Gave me a start, the way he did that. Almost just like..." before it drifted into the distance as the two men headed for the stairs. Colin sat on the edge of the bed with his elbows on his knees. *Almost just like,* he mused. *They knew. They planned this. Probably,* he amended, *they were tired of waiting for me to figure it out myself. I wonder if I'm the last one to know.*

The corral outside thronged with activity when Colin finally arrived. He was quickly noticed and taken in hand by Greysin and Niall, his ever-present guardians. When they tried to converse with Colin, he answered in terse, disjointed sentences. Peripherally, he saw the pair exchange a knowing look. Colin ignored them and saddled the horse that had been set aside for him, a vibrant chestnut with a black-streaked brown mane. The largest of all the horses present, it was a well-muscled beast with sturdy legs and an arched neck. Its head looked almost too small for it, too finely chiseled for such a strong beast, but its eyes were large, dark and intelligent. Stroking the arched neck, Colin gave a covert glance around at the warriors. He felt a burden of responsibility for them that he knew was not his own, since he was far less capable than any of them in his own right. It made him withdraw inside himself—also not one of his natural responses. He thrust one hand in his pocket and closed his fingers around the mask, but he could not make himself put it on, not yet.

"Ammun never puts it on until we're ready to attack," Niall said in an undertone. He had led his horse abreast of Colin's like a wall between them and the others.

Colin twitched. "How did you know—?"

"He keeps it in that pocket, keeps his hand near it, just as you're doing now."

"How long have you known him?"

Pondering the abrupt question, Niall rocked back and forth on his heels. "From the beginning. I was there the night they brought him in. He was burnt up pretty bad on the one side, down his arm and up the side of his head. Didn't wake up for more than a day, but when he woke, seemed like nothing could down him again. Malin made him fight that first day, just to see if he was worth sparing and training. I took a liking to the lad. When he asked me to teach him how to treat his own wounds, I agreed, but he wasn't made to be a field healer. Wasn't long before he proved he could more than hold his own among the warriors, and I sort of followed him around as his personal healer. Nobody needed one more than he did, let me tell you. He pushed himself nigh to the point of collapse time and time again. Didn't care how bad he got hurt, only how fast I could patch him back up again so nobody knew how bad he was hurt. He would've wore me out, if it weren't for saving my Vienna—but that was back before she was mine. Once he picked her up, the two of us split the work between us, me abroad and her at home, so it was easier on us both. Maybe it was easier on him, too. Vienna took to him, sort of in a motherly way. We've been trailing around after him together ever since." Niall looked up as a shrill whistle sounded from the other end of the corral. He mounted his horse.

Colin did likewise, noting how Greysin had already come alongside to flank him closely on the right. Then all was thunder and darkness as the company of horsemen headed off into the night. They rode without pausing, so additional discussion was impossible. Colin did find time to wonder at their breakneck speed, given the darkness of the night. The horses seemed to know the route so well that they did not need to see where they were going. The wind of their passage whined in Colin's numb ears. After a long while, the whole procession slowed to a quick walk. Druze fell back to a position between Colin and Greysin.

"Damon will be up on that ridge," he pointed, indicating a dark wall that rose against the slowly brightening indigo sky ahead of them. "From there, you can get the best view of the grounds and the house."

"We go afoot from here," replied Colin on impulse.

"Aye."

DESTINY

The Second Kingdom's most eventful midsummer festival in half a century ended as notably as it had proceeded over the course of the week, culminating in a man's being thrown bodily from the dais. Ronán Heir Alti paced off the distance afterward and declared it a full sixteen strides from the dais to the landing-spot. That only added to the gossip that swirled around the enigmatic new general.

Speculation abounded. More than a hundred festival-goers had witnessed how this man, reviled as a foreigner, had summoned power enough in one word to stop the flow of the Great River. His physical prowess and stamina had already impressed them during the contests; this latest display overwhelmed them. The young gallants who had come from the outlands in the general's service were in great demand as the people clamored to know more about him. Thus new stories mingled with the phenomena that the people had already witnessed. Those who had stood out against the new general now found themselves in an uncomfortable place. Lord Pamirsi enjoyed nearly as much attention as the general—though his *enjoyment* of that attention was rather hindered by the fact that he was continually forced to answer the question, "How could the man be a bloodthirsty mercenary and yet command the Great River to obey his will?" It was rumored that his regrettable sister Mearah had confronted the general's wife, had pressed her to explain the matter, and for her troubles had been banned from the royal enclosures indefinitely. Shortly thereafter, Berhus Pamirsi and his household departed the festival a day before the closing feast. His departure was excruciatingly public as he bowed his head to Lord Sakiry and the princess. His parting words reached everyone near the royal pavilion. "Your highness…Lord Sakiry…I bid you good evening. I think it is time I went home." As he turned to go, however, he caused more of a stir by pausing reluctantly before the general, stiffly bowing to the man for the first time ever, and offering a civil "Good evening" to him as well.

This shift in Berhus' stance bore the speculation along with it. It seemed impossible that the Pamirsi patriarch should, after such vehement opposition, yield to the king's decision and accept this foreign general. The third marshal's partisans grouped closely together in the hours between Berhus' departure and the closing feast. They too sensed an unfavorable change in the political climate. Indeed, only a fool could have missed the thinning of their ranks. Once the influential Pamirsi/Nandevi party left the field, the vitality drained from the marshal's faction. They gathered in a sullen knot at one of the tables on the far left of the field and kept quiet.

Only the third marshal himself behaved as if nothing had changed, and that led to his amazing public downfall. When the feast was announced and the royal family took its place at the dais, one seat between the princess and the new general was left vacant to mark the absence of the fallen general and the missing king. The rest of the table's honored occupants took their places after the royal family had done so. To the indignation and scandal of many, Third Marshal Simon Miklei-son thoughtlessly appropriated that one empty seat for himself. What happened next was to pass from generation to generation at innumerable firesides for years to come.

No sooner had the third marshal taken the empty seat than the new general rose to tower over him. In a cold voice, the new general declared, "That chair does not belong to you. Get up!" He dragged the third marshal to his feet with one hand. Taking a grip with his other hand, he heaved the smaller man aloft. The third marshal soared through the air to land with a meaty thump sixteen paces away. Amid a buzz of astonishment, the general sat down, and his wife took his hand to calm him as the feast continued.

Many of the spectators tactfully avoided staring at the third marshal as he righted himself with a groan of pain. He had landed on soft turf and thus escaped injury in the physical sense. By the rigid set of his shoulders, however, it was plain to see that he had suffered injury of a kind—of the worst kind a warrior could suffer. Those whose curiosity overpowered their tact watched Miklei-son to see if this violent rebuke had humbled him; everyone was aware that, if Miklei-son retreated to sit with his faction, the general had won the battle. Miklei-son stood motionless at first, staring at the high table with expressionless eyes. Then he wheeled around and stalked away from the feast. No one dared to follow him.

He fetched his horse and rode back to King's City in the gloaming. Rather than continuing on to his home in Carthae, he went directly to Takra House. The palace stood vacant, but it was never locked, so Simon wrenched open the heavy front doors. Up the stairs he went, heading for his office. "What must I do to get rid of him?" he demanded, unable to stop his voice from wavering with a fresh surge of rage.

The stone that sat on his desk dazzled bright yellow at the sound of his voice. "Are you resolved at last?"

"I will not share the world with him another day, if only you'll say there's a way to be rid of him. What must I do?" Simon paced up and down the confined space of his office. "He is not immortal. He has a weakness."

"In that," replied the stone ominously, "you are incorrect. He is immortal, after a fashion, which you are not."

"What does *that* mean?"

"It means that you are facing a superior foe. You have a great gift, but he has something more. You do not know what he is." The voice rang out like a taunt. "With all your genius, you failed to ask that one simple question, and now he triumphs over you."

Simon leaned over the stone with his arms braced straight on either side and his head thrust forward. "What do you mean? What *is* he? And why did you never tell me of this? You knew all along, and yet you didn't bother to tell me! If he does triumph, it's thanks to *your* negligence. You made me a promise."

"Remind me, young Simon. What promise is that?"

"You said that I would one day reunite the five kingdoms and the masterless lands."

A soft, mocking laugh rose from the depths of the stone. "On the condition that you reconciled the secrets of the Gardens, was it not? And of that condition you have fallen short. Only by making that last step can you fulfill the nature of the promise *and* defeat your enemy."

Something in those words made Simon draw back a pace. He gazed at the unlovely, rough-hewn lump of stone with a calculating expression. "You yourself seem to have discovered these secrets," he began slowly. "Why then have you not fulfilled your own promise?"

"I do not have what you have. I was born perfectly ordinary and learned too late that the union of this fractured world requires one of your kindred—*kie sonhé Misomaoz*," added the voice of the elderly seer. "That is what you would be called, had the old language not fallen out of use: *Misomaoz*. The king's father, he was one, and I did my utmost to destroy him before he came of age. My fears turned out to be unfounded in that case. Despite his great power, he turned out to be a man of weak will, docile, ready to submit to the control of ancient tradition. His son is weaker still. Now I have found you. If you have the courage to take one great risk, you can accomplish all that your heart desires in this world."

Once again, Simon asked, "What must I do?"

"Only a simple thing. Do you remember the warning that I offered when first we met? I told you that you must never be tricked into touching a piece of the Forbidden. These few years now, you have adhered to this one rule. Now you must break it. You have progressed far enough to understand the dangers, but now you are also advanced enough to hear the possibilities. With the proper incantation, you may bend the will of the Forbidden, conform it to your own. It will be your armor; it will enable you to successfully battle the half-breed creature Orlan. Its power will, for a time, become your own, guided by your superior intelligence. Do you have courage enough to obey me in this?"

Simon breathed deep. The prospect of crushing the preternatural Orlan held a powerful attraction for him, but again he reminded himself to keep an independent judgment. "And if it doesn't work? I will not fall prey to its thirst."

"That is why you must learn the incantation perfectly. Stay here through the night. I will teach it to you. Tomorrow at sundown, you will make your choice."

"Very well." Simon seated himself at the desk and grasped the cloth that supported the powerful stone. Dragging the stone close by means of the cloth, he stared into it and absorbed the words that the seer repeated. Once he had the rhythm of the unintelligible syllables memorized, he began to repeat them. Time meant nothing to him. He might have sat there one hour or ten; he had no sense of time's passage. The chant moved him beyond hunger or thirst or weariness. He felt stronger, stronger, stronger by the minute. Dimly he realized that daylight finally glowed at the edges of the blackout cloth, but even this awareness meant nothing. Only the return of night brought him around from his trance-like state. He lifted his head and stared around at the room as if he had never seen it before.

"What do you choose? Will you risk everything on one last venture?"

Simon's hesitation had vanished under the heady power of the incantation. He began to chant again, closed his hands around the irregular surface of the stone, and gasped at the sudden shock of heat that engulfed him. Mindful of the need to continue the incantation, he persevered, although the stone seared the palms of his hands. Then it seemed to liquefy, but instead of pooling on the desk, the molten rock flowed up his arms, over his shoulders, down his back and chest to harden like a shell around him. The last sight his eyes beheld was the complete dissolution of the stone. Then it swept up over his head, blinding him.

Now hunger rumbled through him, a thirst unquenchable, fueled by a power so great it demanded a constant feast to maintain it. Simon rose to his feet. *Feed...I must feed. Give me...give...give, give, give...I must consume.* With a thrill of longing, he saw that a vast banquet lay before him as the city settled down to a night's sleep. They appeared to him like a field of roses, their tiny crimson flames blossoming in clusters as far as he could detect—unwary, waiting to be plucked and devoured. Although he couldn't see as he was accustomed to seeing, Simon knew the way to go. He abandoned Takra House on a hunt for vengeance.

THE WEAK AND THE
STRONG

Only Colin, Giles, and Greysin made the ascent up the slope to where Damon was supposed to meet them. The ground underfoot was dry and stony, fit to twist a man's ankle beneath him if he didn't take care in his climb. They proceeded quietly, not hurrying, preserving the advantage of surprise. Halfway up, Colin paused, gazing up at the ridge. He saw a teasing flicker of light beneath an apparently solid slope of greenery that still bore a melting crust of ice. Greysin nudged him onward toward this flicker. It wasn't until he was nearly upon the spot that Colin saw the lip of a hollow covered by a screen of vines and slender branches. From this hollow, a familiar face peeked out into the night: Damon, besmudged and weary. He motioned for the small company to follow him upward, so they kept climbing in silence until they arrived at the ridge.

Below, Colin saw his home, Takra House, sleeping peacefully in the shadow of the ridge. Closer inspection showed him a few of the differences. Someone had added a set of wholly unnecessary pillars to the front. The lower story windows were barred where the servants lived. There were no trees, no orchard, no monument grove to occupy the grounds. The grounds immediately around the house were bare; farther out, a ramshackle settlement housed Malin's warriors. Immediately underneath the ridge there were corrals that now stood empty. Colin surveyed the prospect and spotted another set of corrals nearly hidden on the other side of the house, between the house and the settlement.

Damon spoke in a whisper. "Pleased to see you again, my lord. Come to watch the fun? And what of you, little man? What are you doing here?"

"Breaking into a house," retorted Giles, also in a whisper. "I know the house. The rest of them don't." He pulled up his collar against the gentle chill of the breeze and looked defensive. When Damon grinned at him, Giles averted his gaze to the view below.

"House seems to be sleeping. The guards came out some hours ago, so the slaves must be safely locked in for the night. If he holds to his old habits, there won't be anyone else inside the walls to stand in your way. Good fortune is with us; they put up the prisoners in the main corral yonder. You should have a clear path back to us here once you've done what you planned."

Colin saw Giles nod soberly. Greysin was there at his shoulder with a steadying, heartening grip on the young man's arm. Then the two of them dropped over the ridge and out of sight temporarily. Colin drew a breath. *So it begins.*

Damon's whisper in his ear startled him. "You'd best come down the ridge a safe distance, so no one suspects their route. Then you can show yourself when you know they're in the house. The others won't start in until they see you." Moving in a low crouch, Damon led Colin along the ridge to a different vantage point, an outcropping of stone that rose up in a spike above the level of the ridge. Then he said to Colin, "You'd best put on the rest of the costume and get out there. Greysin and the boy are already inside."

Colin let his hand seek the pocket where he knew the mask awaited him. When he finally put it on, however, he discovered that the context had changed. Now that he stood on the verge of a clash with the marauders, when he put on the mask, he put on the persona *they* associated with it. It was something outside of him now, a useful weapon to wield—yet even so, it was enough to raise traces of loathing. Jaw clamped, Colin took up his post atop the ridge and folded his arms as the warriors swept forward in two silent waves, from left and right. Borrowing his brother's inerrant instinct, Colin sought out the sentries at either end of the grounds. He watched as both were silenced, one after the other, by his reconnaissance. Shortly afterward, the marauder's horses ran loose in an impromptu stampede straight through the camp. A wild battle cry rang out in the darkness; someone was alerting the raiders of their danger. The stampede signaled that Rafe's force had taken the prisoners successfully. Bayne's group attacked from the other side, but even now the marauders were regrouping amid chaos and put up a stout defense against the attack.

Colin listened closely. His hearing, unnaturally heightened beneath the mask, picked out a heavy footfall somewhere on the ridge to his left. He turned to find a pardelé loping toward him. Aside from a catch in his breath, Colin did not move. The cat did not slow until it was close enough to stretch out its neck and sniff him. Then, threateningly, it lifted its luminescent golden eyes to pierce his disguise with an accusatory stare, as much as to say, *You are not he. Who are you?* Into his mind it deposited an image of a serpent stealing eggs from a nest.

He shook his head. Aloud, he whispered, "It is not what you think," but at the same time, from deep within him a responding image came to the forefront of his mind. He was not sure where it had come from, but it showed him a bird with lovely gray and white plumage leaving its nest in search of food. A fox lay in wait under the brush, but as it sprang for the unprotected eggs, another of the gray and white birds sprang forward to peck at the fox's sensitive nose. With this image exchanged between them, Colin and the pardelé stared at each other in a tentative alliance. "Help me convince them I am my brother," Colin whispered. "Please."

The cat bobbed its head decisively. It shifted to sit beside him, its bulk radiating warmth in the cool predawn air. Thus settled, the pardelé screamed. In response to this unnerving summons, half a dozen other cats climbed the ridge just as the sun broke over the horizon behind them. Below, the combatants all paused at the scream. One of the marauders pointed and yelled to his comrades. Taking advantage of this distraction, Bayne led his portion of the company in a retreat. The marauders had to round up their horses before they could pursue. Colin was about to turn away when he saw an alarming sight: Giles was on the roof of the house, waving wildly to gain his footing. He bent to drag a strangely bloated figure out of the dormer window nearest him. It took a few moments for Colin to realize that it was two men, not one, whom Giles helped onto the rooftop. At the same time, thick smoke began to billow from the middle floor of the house, and slaves were running everywhere in the courtyard. Colin glanced at the pardelé. "I have to get them safely out of there," he said. "Can you help me?"

The gigantic cat sat immobile, unresponsive, but two of its younger kinfolk suddenly launched themselves from on high, gaining speed as they bounded down the almost vertical slope toward the house. At the base of the ridge, first one and then the other pardelé made a great leap and soared in an arc that spanned half the distance between the ridge and the house. A second bound carried the two cats easily to the rooftop. Giles' startled outcry carried all the way to Colin up on the ridge. The larger of the two cats took the inert figure in its jaws and started back to the ridge. The other cat lay on its belly for Greysin and Giles to climb astride. Then it too carried its human burdens back to the ridge. Windows were already shattering with the heat of the blaze inside the house. A timber cracked as the roof caught fire.

Once he knew that all his men were clear, Colin turned to the cat beside him. "I thank you," he said formally, bowing politely to the cat. When it stretched its neck to touch its nose to his, he smiled. Then, to his surprise, the cat lay on its belly as if to invite him to climb on its back. With more than a little trepidation, Colin accepted the invitation.

A few seconds later, he arrived down in the ravine where Damon and the others waited for him. The pardelé stopped in a spray of gravel and let Colin dismount on shaky legs. "Again, thank you," he said to the cat, who nodded before bounding away into the low shadows. Above, its kinfolk had already dispersed. Turning to Giles, Colin said, "Well! You made it back alive."

The young man was a little bloodied, but otherwise seemed more dazed than hurt. A gash on his forehead was trickling blood down the side of his face. Giles touched his hand to the blood, gazed at it blankly, and wiped the stain onto his trouser leg. "Yes, sir."

"Giles, Giles, what have you done?" Damon exclaimed, throwing an arm around the younger man's shoulders with enthusiasm.

"He only captured Malin," added Greysin, also grinning. He nudged an inert body with his foot. "Captured him and burned down his house. This is a story worth the telling."

*　　　*　　　*　　　*

The celebration of midsummer took on a new vibrancy and enthusiasm once the warriors returned triumphant from raiding the raiders. Colin found himself caught up in the midst of this jubilation, protesting all the while that he had done nothing but stand by and watch the battle from above. Giles became the instant hero of the village. Colin left him to his newfound fame.

Immediately upon returning to Chamika, Colin changed back into his own clothes without speaking to anyone else; once he escaped the thanks of the freed prisoners and the praise of the villagers, he nestled himself amid the roots of the ancient, gnarled Prince's Tree that grew in the corner of his brother's property. The tree's mute company was sufficient. Overhead, a gently nodding cluster of leaves brushed against his hair as if to soothe his turmoil. There was too much to absorb, too much to comprehend, and Colin felt unequal to the task of mingling with people for whom the revelation must have been quite commonplace by now.

Damon came to seek him late in the afternoon. "Thought I might find you here."

"Let me guess," said Colin, subdued. "This is one of his favorite thinking-places."

The younger man settled into an adjacent hollow of the roots. "During clement weather, he often stays out here through the night."

Taking a deep breath, Colin forced himself to say calmly, "I feel like an absolute idiot. You knew this would happen. At least, *Greysin* must have known that putting on the clothes and taking his place would do this to me. Did you tell him to do it, or was he tired of waiting on me?"

"If he knew that I was planning such a thing," Damon admitted, "Ammun would've cuffed me over the head and told me to mind my own affairs. But that never stopped me yet. Many a time I've gone ahead of my authority for his good, and maybe he'll admit it, if he's in an admitting mood. Maybe, just *maybe*, I was getting a trifle impatient. Exact twins being what they are, I had thought you would have figured it out long ago."

"I wasn't looking."

"That's what I figured. May I ask what you meant by 'putting on the clothes'? What did that have to with it?"

Colin sighed gently, leaning his head into the scarred bark of the tree. "It happened once before, when we were younger. Twelve years old, if I recall correctly. My brother was in one of his moods. He wouldn't tell anyone what it was about, and I got curious to know what was bothering him. I don't know where I got the idea from to start with, but I went into his hamper and pulled out the shirt he had worn the day before. I put it on and, all of a sudden..." His voice faded before the power of memory. He cleared his throat and went on hoarsely, "All of a sudden, I felt such self-hatred, such fear, that I peeled the shirt off as fast as I could and threw it into the hamper and ran. I didn't understand what had happened to me, so I went to my father in private and asked him. He said...he said I was feeling a trace of what Jarod felt. To this day, I don't know what had happened to Jarod the day before that. I never had the courage to ask him. Whatever it was, it was terrible, and he never confided it in anyone, to my knowledge." He turned on Damon abruptly. "You've known him how long?"

"More than ten years. It wasn't until after he disappeared and came back, after the king your father had died, that I knew him for who he truly was. I'd gone home to visit with my family, thinking to lie low until his latest mood passed. I found out when I came back that he had never returned the whole two months while I was gone. He didn't, either, until weeks after I came back looking for him. Anyway, while I was at my father's house, Ta pulled me aside for a chat. They were never too happy with the life I'd chosen for myself, and Ta tried to talk to me about it, but I wasn't about to budge. It wasn't the life *I* would have chosen for myself, not after I knew what sort of life it was, but I was the only friend he had for a long time. Nobody else could get close to him. I always wondered about that, until he broke down and told me a couple years ago that he recognized my father in me the first day we met. He says I was like a bit of his past come to remind him of where he'd come from, or something like that. Anyway, I was trying to explain why I was friends with him when Ta got this funny look on his face. I'd said something that made him curious, so he got me to describe Ammun the best I could. He didn't say anything else that day, but you and your family were in the neighborhood for your annual visit, and Ta finagled it so that I saw you from behind, without telling me who you were, and from the reaction I gave, he figured out who Ammun must be. He took me aside, told me the story, and sent me back to find out if it was true. And it was."

The two sat in mutual thought for long enough that the sun sank to the western horizon before either of them stirred. Damon said, "You coming down to the feast, or do you still need time to think?"

"I'll come down. I suppose they all knew about it from the first."

"Yes, sir."

"Is that why Bayne hates me so?"

Damon expelled a harsh, growling breath. "That's right—I still have to talk to him about that. He's apparently gotten some notion stuck in his head that you're trying to take Ammun's place or something."

"How paradoxical of him," Colin replied. Then he said, "Let me deal with it."

"You sure?"

"I need to do this. Let me try to smooth things over with him myself."

They descended to the village square to find that Bayne was nowhere in sight and the feast was already well underway. Instead of the perpetual feasting that Colin was used to in his homeland, the villagers reserved their best culinary efforts for the nightly meal. Even this was a sort of contest, he learned to his cost, as each cook tried to create the spiciest dish and each warrior tried to show how tough he was by sampling them all.

To Colin's amusement, Giles had to try this contest for himself. The lad held his own, although his face flushed and his nose ran as every course set before him came spicier than the last. At last, the challenge came down to a sort of duel between Giles and Niall's son Ingram. Colin had watched the two become fast friends over the course of Giles' stay in Chamika. More than once, Colin had found cause to wonder if Giles had ever had a best friend before. The experience certainly seemed novel to the boy. Whenever Ingram came around to summon Giles from his chores for some outing, Giles looked surprised, and then inordinately pleased, as if he had just received a present. Colin often had harbored a suspicion that the two were up to mischief together. Now, though, seated opposite one another at the board, the two youths might as well have been lifelong rivals. Each was intent on outlasting the other. All around them, other youths and even some of the full-grown men cheered one or the other onward. Many onlookers took Giles' side, including Druze, who called, "You show him he ain't as tough as he says!"

The pair finished their last mouthful at the same time. Ingram held out a hand and said, "Truce?" He sounded as if his lips had gone numb.

"Truce," Giles agreed. Sweat stood out on his flushed face He grinned. "Ouch."

Ingram burst into laughter, followed by most of the bystanders. "Ouch, he says! *Ouch* is for pricking yourself on your mother's pincushion! I know what you really want to say." The young warrior threw back his head and howled long and loud. "That," he declared, "is what such a meal really deserves."

Colin watched the two head off to the nearest well to cool their mouths, running and shoving each other all the way like pups, even loosing the occasional howl. "It's good to see him starting to settle in properly," he observed mildly to Niall, Ingram's father.

"It's high time we had the story from him. Greysin won't spill it."

"I know," Colin laughed. "He wouldn't even take a direct order from me. He says it's Giles' story to tell. Let's round the lad up and hear what he has to say for himself."

They found Giles and Ingram lapping up cool water from a pair of buckets at the well. Colin and Niall each seized Giles by an arm and marched him up to the house. A sizeable crowd of warriors fell into step with them. By the time they had all settled, the great room of Ammun's house was full to overflowing, with Giles in the place of honor beside the banked coals.

"All right," said Damon, "let's hear it. What happened out there? The truth, now."

Giles shrugged. "I didn't really *do* anything. Like Druze expected, there was a window open in the kitchen, so we let ourselves in from that side of the house. I saw how the servants' rooms were all locked and the keys hung on nails beside the doors, but there wasn't really time to look around much. We went up to the second floor, to where I knew the office would be. Greysin left me at the door to keep watch while he hunted for the papers we were supposed to get. Anyway, I heard somebody stirring at the end of the hall—the end of the hall where the royal suites are," he added with a significant look toward Colin. "I knew it wasn't a servant, but I couldn't really see anything. I knew Greysin needed time to search, so I figured I should decoy whoever it was. As it turned out, it was a woman. She didn't see me where I'd hid myself, so I let her go on past me toward the stairs. I was a little curious, though. I mean, why were all the other servants locked up, and she had the run of the house? From the way she was dressed, I figured out what sort of woman she was, but I still didn't know why she was running around loose in the house, so I followed her a little way, and it was a good thing I did, too. There was a warrior in the house."

Some of the audience nodded, grinning, but Damon said, "In the house? What was he doing in the house? Malin turns them all out at the end of the night."

"I know; that's what you said, so I knew there was something odd about it. He and that woman were pretty friendly. They weren't so friendly that they didn't hear the floor squeak in the office where Greysin was searching, though. The woman, she looked scared, like she'd been caught, but the warrior got suspicious. I backtracked up the stairs and made as if I'd come from the office, ran right past them so that the warrior would chase me instead of investigating the office like he meant to do. I've had better chases from the guards at home—"

Colin interrupted, "I could tell a story or two on that subject, come to think of it."

"Let him finish," said Greysin impatiently. "All this while, he never stopped to tell me what he was about. I found the papers and went out to fetch the boy, but he wasn't there. There was a mighty rumpus going on downstairs, fit to wake the dead. It certainly woke up Malin. I heard him call out a woman's name from the far end of the corridor, and when nobody answered him, he came down the hall with a candle to investigate. What *were* you doing downstairs?"

Giles resumed his narrative. "I was unlocking the servants' doors and setting them loose. I like to blend into a crowd when I can, so I loosed the servants and told them to run for it. If I'd been quicker, I could've got clean away, but I wasn't so lucky. That warrior spotted me as I dodged back up the stairs and he came after me, bellowing like a madman."

"So then," said Greysin, "the next thing I saw, Giles came bolting up the stairs and ran headlong into Malin. Malin got thrown back and struck his head against the doorpost of the office, and he dropped his candle and lit the carpet afire. I took care of the warrior that was after Giles. The lad asks me, 'Who's that?' and I told him who Malin was. It was his idea to take him prisoner; I was all for killing him there, myself. By that time, somebody had thrown the door shut at the bottom of the stairs. We could only go up, with the house aflame and a skirmish going on all around us outside. I was glad enough to see the pardeléi coming for us, because I certainly had no idea how we were to get off of that rooftop on our own."

*   *   *   *

Since it was the last day of the festival, no contests had been arranged. This was a rest day, where no one worked and everyone wandered freely in and out of each other's homes giving gifts. If they could afford it, they gave of their possessions. If not, they found something else to give. Among the young men, it seemed traditional to give kisses to females. More than one betrothal was announced in Colin's hearing as he roamed the village. He had nothing of his own to give except time and companionship. With these he was generous, lending an ear to the garrulous elderly folk who stayed at the doors of their cottages because they could not roam as easily as the younglings. He found the young mother Willa and made faces at her baby for no less than half an hour, thus freeing Willa to roam unhindered for a time.

On his way back for noontide, Colin met Bayne, who watched him with narrowed eyes from the other side of the road. Before he had a chance to talk himself out of it, Colin crossed to face him directly. "Has something upset you, natai?" he asked in a pointed tone.

The shorter man ground his teeth audibly. "No," he said eventually, although it cost him a good deal of self-control to give that answer. His eyes shifted to a point behind Colin, just enough to tell Colin that they were not alone.

"How strange," answered Colin. "I could have sworn you hated me. Well, then! If you aren't upset, then perhaps you'll accompany me to noontide?" He knew he was applying undue pressure to the man's self-restraint, but Colin felt reckless that day. "We can share a table and exchange our stories. Well? Will you come?" He took hold of Bayne's sleeve, only to be shaken off with vehemence. Refusing to back down, Colin took the offensive. "So you *are* upset. Come out with it, natai. What makes you so hateful to me? What have I done to provoke you? No," he said, seeing the shift in Bayne's gaze again, "no, you're free to say what you please. I promise you, none of the other natai will step in to intervene." He raised his voice to make sure their audience heard him.

"You've no right to say what I'm free to do," the natai growled.

Colin responded with a pleasant, "You're absolutely right in that." He saw the second glance that he had earned with that statement, so he pressed onward with it. "What I said had less to do with your freedom of action than it did with my choice to limit my own: I won't call on anyone to interfere. I don't need to. We can work this out between us, I'm sure."

To this, Bayne had nothing particular to say. He stared hard at Colin. "You want to make some kind of deal?"

"If that's how you want to look at it. What do I have to do to convince you that I have absolutely no intention of taking Ammun's place?"

"So the notion *did* come to you?"

Colin smiled. "Only when others pointed out that you were rather obsessed with it. Let me tell you about Ammun and me." He gestured for the warrior to walk along with him. Without regard for anyone else who might be listening, he said, "The first time I knew he was superior to me, I was five years old. Since I am presently in my thirty-fourth year, that means I've had nearly thirty years to get used to the idea that my brother has advantages on me that I can only distantly imagine. Thirty years, Bayne. From my childhood, I've known him to be smarter, faster, stronger—in short, better than me in nearly every way. A fluke of birth put me on the throne of the Second Kingdom. It should have gone to him. In a way, it has now. He has put me aside for safe-keeping and taken my place. So it's me you should worry about," he laughed easily. "I'm the one who got ousted."

"All the more reason," said Bayne, but without any conviction behind it.

"And why not? Perhaps it's more fitting that I take up the governing of a little mountain village while he takes control of a vast kingdom. If it doesn't trouble him, why should it trouble you? You never know, Bayne; he might come here and shift you from your place and set you up as natai of a whole clan, while one of my clan patriarchs comes here and takes up the duties you leave behind. Would you quarrel at that?"

Bayne walked along in meditative silence for a few minutes. When he looked at Colin again, he had no expression at all in his eyes, but neither did he summon any arguments against what he had been told. He retreated to the end of a trestle table where the bachelors of his longhouse had gathered to eat, and Colin took up a place among Farris' young hostages. From time to time, Bayne still glanced at Colin in a ruminative way. That was all.

Colin was not the only one relieved by this abatement of hostilities. The young men had been sensitive to these currents too. Without this worry to fetter them, they grew rowdier and more voluble as the afternoon passed. From one end of the village to the other, they roamed wherever their fancy took them, admiring the pretty girls, and when all other amusements palled, swimming in the pond behind the manor house. Declining the chilly waters without regret, Colin sunned himself lazily in the grass. These casual celebrations outlasted the villagers' by several hours. When Farris finally ordered his bachelors into their beds, an exhausted Colin flopped onto his pallet contentedly and fell at once into slumber. He dreamed of his wife and daughter at first, but as the night deepened into the speaking hours, his dreams turned uneasy. At the coldest hour, he started upright with a shout that woke all his companions: "Jarod!" He could not stop shaking.

"What is it?" Farris asked, sitting up. "What is wrong?"

Lorçan, Loren's brother, answered as he crossed the floor to grab Colin by the shoulders. "We know as much as you, natai. Colin!" He shook Colin firmly. "Wake up! What is it?"

Colin's breath came in harsh gulps. "I don't know. Something's wrong. He's hurt. I can feel it. So cold…" He pulled away, got up, and put on the rest of his clothes without regard for the stares of his companions. "Where's my horse? Saddle the horses. I have to go find him."

YESTERDAY: LOVE
REGARDLESS

It had been so many days since the world had intruded upon Kohanan that he scarcely recognized it when he saw it. *So close, so close,* he mused, stretching out his hand to touch the curtain-like barrier between him and his goal. *Another few steps and I'm there.*

You have one task to finish, the gentle voice of his master reminded him.

Do I? Kohanan blinked. Everything around him shone blindingly white. He lifted his eyes and squinted at the brilliant blue sky. Then it came to him: he was sprawled on his back on a field of snow and ice, with plumes of his breath hanging in the still, frigid air above him. He coughed. Breath tickled in his throat. His ears picked out sounds in both worlds now. Lifting one hand, he marveled at its transparency and weakness. Recognition of the physical world brought with it a return of pain in body and spirit. He remembered that Camille was gone—*but not far ahead,* he reminded himself—and that he had left home and family behind him. Beside him, Byram knelt and pled with him, almost in tears.

"Please," the man said raggedly, "please don't leave me out here alone. I don't know how to find my way back alone."

Kohanan searched for his voice and found it hoarse with disuse. "You won't be alone." Even as he spoke, he felt a tremor that made his spirit swell with anticipation. *He's near! At last!* "He's coming even now." Kohanan turned his gaze from his companion to see a gaunt, unkempt figure approaching. Chike rose in welcome and engulfed the figure in his wings for an instant, to Kohanan's surprise. *Chike touched him,* he thought, amazed. At that moment, Chike moved aside to leave the two men staring at each other.

Byram still had not seen the newcomer. He jumped and craned his neck back when the man's heavy hand clapped down upon his shoulder. Because his profile stood out clearly against the immaculate blue sky above, his expression of shocked aversion was as apparent to Kohanan as it was to the death-like gaze of the man who stared down at them both. Kohanan cleared his throat softly to disperse the moment.

"I have found you at last."

A pair of piercing, enigmatic eyes fixed upon him as if weighing his honesty. His voice was emotionless and surprisingly guttural when he rejoined, "Or one might say *I* have found *you*. It depends upon the perspective." Stooping, he lifted up Kohanan in his arms without regard for the stunning power that never left the dying king in these latter days. Kohanan had never felt such strength; he had not known the sensation of being borne in arms by one person alone since he was a child, but his emaciated frame seemed as nothing now. He gazed up, unable to take his eyes from the face above him. Something was wrong. Chike seemed to share this sense, because he kept his wings furled around them both. From time to time along the path to the hut ahead, Chike would breathe gently upon them also, instilling some of his life into Kohanan's son. Only after he realized what this meant did Kohanan see the excessive weakness underneath the physical strength. *So near…*he thought again, this time with another's death in mind.

The pull of otherness was too great for him to withstand. His knowledge of the world faded from him for a time, leaving him only an awareness of his son lingering nearby, just out of reach. When Kohanan next saw the world of men, he found himself in a single-room hut. One curtainless window gave him a glimpse of a pristine field of stars in the black sky outside, nothing more. A meager heap of banked coals glowed in the hearth. Otherwise the hut held no indications that anyone had lived there for some time. Its walls were carefully empty of personal effects. Byram slept against the far wall beneath the window, but Kohanan's son kept watch still. He stirred up the fire and added fuel to keep the coals alive. Kohanan watched him. His hangman's mask hid much, but it was still easy to see the ravages of life and of death's approach: the lips beneath the mask were bluish, thin, and drawn taut as if in pain; scars covered his jaw and neck all down the one side. His skin was wan and lusterless, his eyelids heavy. He took an unconscionable time in building up the fire. Kohanan looked to Chike, trying to communicate these words: *You can touch him. Can you speak to him as well?* It still amazed him, although he had seen it before, to see Chike reach out and prod his son with a wing.

The kneeling man jerked away from the touch irritably.

"Jarod," Kohanan said softly.

"That is not my name."

"That is the name I gave you," said his father, "and it's still the name I call you. Come and sit by me. You're avoiding me. You've always avoided me, but I don't have time to waste."

Without protest, his son came and sat cross-legged beside the pallet. "What is your will?"

Kohanan laid a hand on the nearest knee. "To speak with you. Nothing more." He felt the otherness pulling at him. "I don't...I don't have much time."

His son replied, "I can deal with that much." Bending forward, he touched his forehead to Kohanan's. "Just let go."

The world faded as it had so many times before, but his son remained in perfect focus. Since they were so close together, Kohanan stretched out a hand to pluck at the edge of the mask and felt a surge of tension seize hold of his son. "Why do you imagine your face should hide?" he asked gently. "I have looked at its exact copy—maybe not as exact a copy anymore—for so many years, wondering where you were and whether you were all right. There isn't any need to hide anymore, Jarod."

"Isn't there?" His son vanished suddenly, replaced by a monstrous beast, a creature of slime, darkness, and venom.

Kohanan snatched at the creature and found a human hand to grab. At the touch of his hand, the creature disappeared and Jarod came back, looking shaken. "No," Kohanan said as if nothing had occurred. "There isn't."

"I wonder."

"You've been wondering for a long time now, haven't you? Stop wondering, Jarod. Tell me what it is that you believe warrants this disguise."

In response to this slight encouragement, there came such a rush of confession—pictures and words all mingled and blurred together—that it would have been anarchy if Kohanan had not kept his eyes fixed on his son all the while. Jarod changed as he spoke, shifting his form to suit his confessions, and through these transformations he communicated more to Kohanan than he expected. Kohanan doubted that Jarod realized he was changing shapes. Every shape was that of a beast, always an unclean or despised beast. Listening attentively to these confessions, Kohanan grieved what he heard, but he never interrupted, never let go. The last transformation was the most encouraging to him. When the tumult of confession had stilled, he was left holding a boy of eight years. He lifted his son into his arms and hugged him close. "My boy," he said.

"But, Father—"

Kohanan shushed him with a finger against his lips. "You've done wrong things, I know, but do you think that makes the least difference to me now? Now listen. Do you remember what I asked you to do for me, back when we evacuated Halimeda?" When the boy nodded solemnly, he went on, "The need is still there. I'm leaving them in your hands. Will you do this for me?" Jarod looked back at him in ambivalence, plainly caught between his longing to go home at last and his fear of going back to face those whom he had abandoned. He stared desperately into his father's eyes. Kohanan guessed at his reason for hesitating. "I think I've never told you this before, but I know what it means to be feared for being what other folk call unnatural. Do you think I never saw how everyone took to your brother and feared you? Hear me: I know it's a hard path to follow, but you mustn't draw back because of that. Some will love you in spite of their fear. Your brother loves you still. He has been lost without you. It's those few that you have to gather close to you. Can you do this for me?" He watched the child rally his resolve.

"Yes. I'll look out for them."

Kohanan smiled. With one last affectionate hug, he said, "I knew you would."

VICTIMS

A more peaceful scene could not be imagined. The sitting room was illuminated by no fewer than nine large oil lamps, each trimmed for the long night hours and placed at the periphery of the room. In one chair, Riana sat mending the suit of clothes that Tyrell's attackers had ruined; the cloth was still good and would do for charity, once Riana had repaired the knife-gashes. To her left, the curiosity merchant himself lay half-awake in his makeshift bed, listening to the desultory conversation that passed between Brigid and Ivy. The only feature of the scene that couldn't be remotely perceived as peaceful was Ivy's husband, who stalked the perimeter of the room with measured treads from window to window, pulling back the edges of curtains to peer outside from time to time. As dusk deepened into night, his disquiet grew more marked. Ivy's conversation faltered. Calmly, Brigid reached out to take her sister's hand. No one spoke into the silence. Riana put down her mending, rose, and brushed the loose threads from her skirt. At Riana's approach, Brigid surrendered her chair to her mother and contented herself with kneeling on the floor at the other side of Ivy's chair.

Juxtaposed against the heat of the summer night and of the bright lamps, a trickle of cold like a winter draft crept across the floor. Jarod was first to sense it. He lifted his head swiftly, and a peculiar exultation burned in his eyes. Ivy, on the other hand, felt its touch and cried out softly. Her husband crossed the room to kneel at her feet. "No," he urged her, "do not fear it. This is a mark of your safety tonight. Let him envelop you."

"I don't know what you mean," she whispered.

"There is only one powerful enough to defend you through the night. He has come. Don't reject his presence. Let him have his will."

"What's his will?"

"He speaks to you, not to me. What do you hear?"

"I don't hear anything." Ivy was nearly sobbing by this time. "I can't hear him!"

Jarod hushed her gently as she leaned forward into his arms for shelter. He held her, but he did not let her flee the moment. "Be still. Just be still. He does not give impossible commands or speak to those without ears to hear him. Rest in stillness and trust what I say, if you cannot yet trust him." He stroked her hair as if she was a child. Gradually she calmed. When he released her, she leaned back into her chair with a curiously blank look on her face. Jarod watched her, but made no move to speak again.

The two older women held Ivy's hands just as before. Riana smoothed the wisps of loosened hair away from Ivy's pale, sweat-dampened face. A cry rose in Ivy's throat, strangled and fearful, but still her eyes seemed to see nothing of the room or the faces around her. She shook her head violently, almost in disbelief. Suddenly the tears began rolling down her cheeks. "No...no, you can't...no, no...*leave them alone!*"

Appalled by the anguished horror in her daughter's voice, Riana exclaimed, "Whatever's the matter, Ivy?"

"There's something outside," Ivy whispered. "Out in the city. A monster—I don't know what it is—*no!*" She fought for control over herself, but her tears continued to run freely. "It's hungry. There are so many, so many, and they won't go where it's safe. It...it follows them, and when nobody else is looking, it...it takes them. There was an old woman on her front steps; then a man who stepped outside for a breath of air; then a pair of tavern girls heading to work. It's still there, up and down the streets, hunting..." Her mouth worked silently for an instant. All at once her gaze sharpened with awareness as she looked into her husband's eyes. "No...I *do* know what it is. And it's my fault..."

He shook his head. "If there is blame here, you do not carry it alone. It is the fault of everyone who failed to remain true. Do not let it persuade you otherwise."

"Persuade me?"

"Do you suppose it hasn't yet noticed that you are watching? It means to strike at you. Your heart is soft, Ivy. That is where he will strike first."

It was a long night. Ivy's outbursts marked every time the Unclean claimed another victim. Long before the speaking hours of night, they gave up counting them. It was like a plague, but like no plague the women had ever experienced, because there seemed no cure. The worst came when Ivy cried out a name—*Alanah*—and could not speak again for a full quarter of an hour. By sunrise, the only one not exhausted was Tyrell, who had slept through most of the distress thanks to his weakened condition. Ivy had to be escorted up the stairs to her childhood bedroom. She responded to none of their solicitude, turning her face to the wall and falling into a deep slumber almost before they had shut the door on her.

While Riana and Brigid chose to lie down and sleep for a few hours themselves, Jarod left the house. The beclouded dawn sky burned a sullen orange-red in the east. There was no breeze to note. Few others were out at that early hour, leaving the streets bare enough for the hunter in Jarod to read the signs of his foe's passage easily enough. It had come close to the house at some point during the long, difficult night; a dead shrub marked where the Unclean had looked in through a sitting room window. Seeing all this, Jarod turned his steps toward Takra House in search of more allies.

*   *   *   *

Maia slept uneasily the first night back from the midsummer festival. Then her teacher came the next morning to request that Selena come to sit with Ivy through the second night. Ivy, he explained tersely, was not feeling well. Maia supposed that he would have been more forthcoming, had there not been an audience composed mainly of the third marshal's pupils passing through the entry hall just then. In fact, when he accompanied Selena and Maia to the family quarters to wait for Selena to pack a bag for the visit, he did speak briefly to Maia, but not about Ivy. What he said required some discernment because, as usual, he didn't bother to explain himself for her benefit. "If you begin to sense that you are endangered in any way, Maia, there is a place to hide here. They cannot find you there because it is my own place, a place that I made for myself long ago. Only four know where it is: me, Ivy, you, and Giles. You can find it again if you need to get away. See that you tell no one about it unless they too are endangered alongside you. Trust your intuition." He had a peculiar air about him. It took some time after he left before Maia figured out what it was: anxiety. She was sure she had never heard that in his voice before.

It had become habit for her to solve all of her teacher's riddles herself. For this reason, she said nothing to Owen as they spent the day receiving visitors and hearing petitions. Maia kept the questions fermenting beneath the surface courtesies she dealt out to each person who came to meet with her. *A place to hide...* That was the easiest part to solve. She had often pondered the memory of the last time she had spoken with Giles. Even now, Maia wasn't sure if she missed that young man. If the quantity of thoughts indicated anything, then she missed him. It was the feelings she had expected—the absence of these feelings made her doubt. She had never tried to return to that strange, makeshift chamber in the attic. Now she considered it, only to reject the notion. If she went now, when there was no need, she might only succeed in revealing it to someone else and ruining its usefulness. No, it was enough to know that it was there, should she need it.

That was the difficulty. Just by gauging her teacher's anxiety, Maia knew that it was less a question of *if* than of *when*. He sounded as if he knew that danger was approaching, but if he had certain knowledge of an attack of some sort, why would he not tell her so they could plan? Unless, Maia reflected, maybe he didn't yet know exactly what form the attack would take. She herself was familiar now with the sort of knowledge that had yet to grasp at specifics, the knowledge that was not true knowledge but rather a prelude to it. Her teacher had proven his awareness of her struggles, so she knew he understood what it was like to stumble along in the dark like this.

Slowly, these elements settled into a tentative answer. Maia was on her guard for the rest of the day, watching the visitors to Takra House. In a way, she was glad that her mother was well out of the way. If anything happened, it would happen here, not at the general's house. After the day's audiences were finished, Maia went down to the Caretakers' quarters in search of Chessy. She found him in the patriarch's office. "Chessy, I have something for you to do. You won't like it, and you won't understand it, but it's important." As plainly as she could, she outlined the idea that had come to her earlier that afternoon. Just as she had expected, she saw refusal rising in the Caretaker elder's face.

"How would the household function, miss?" he asked when she was done.

"Very simply. Really, Chessy, it *is* for the best. I want your kinfolk to be safe, or at least safer than they are now. How soon can you start?"

Grudgingly, he replied, "Well, miss, if it's truly your will, then we can start now."

"Don't make a show of it. Try to keep it as secret as possible, in twos or threes at first."

"As you will, miss."

Out in the corridor, Maia found Isaac waiting patiently against the near wall. He straightened as soon as she emerged. "Did you want to meet again today, my lady?"

"Yes. All your officers, in the kitchen, at once." Maia breathed deeply to steady herself. She had made a practice of meeting with Isaac, Kintaro, and at least three of the four lieutenants on a daily basis, usually just before supper. Now she went to the kitchen while Isaac summoned his officers. While she waited, she asked her ever-present personal maid Kenda, "How long do you think it'll take?"

"In twos and threes?" Kenda took out the most recent piece of darning from her work bag and began to mend. "Not more than a day. I'm leaving last."

"Kenda," Maia began to protest, but her friend only smiled.

"I know. Meg will stay with you, since she's better able to look after you now, but that doesn't mean I can't hold out until the last minute." In a softer voice, she added, "If I could fight, I wouldn't leave at all. Since I can't, I just have to trust you to Hollister and his friends."

"Has he spoken to Gian yet?"

"This morning."

"Congratulations."

Kenda glanced at her with an eloquent, questioning expression, but Maia was too embarrassed to chide her for it. She knew what Kenda wanted to say. They had only spoken of it once, after Kenda had come to Maia to ask for freedom to marry. It was a formality that Maia's father should have been there to handle, so it felt a little peculiar to do it herself when she was two years younger than Kenda and had looked to Hollister as an elder brother all her life. Maia gave them her consent with a glad heart. Afterward, however, Kenda had lingered on the subject long enough to ask, "What of you, miss? Hollister says your young man disappeared."

"He went with my father—and he *isn't* my 'young man,' Kenda," had been Maia's tart reply. After that, Kenda had never broached the subject again…not aloud, at least. Maia was relieved to have the present conversation interrupted by the arrival of the officers

"What did you have on your mind?" Hollister asked once they had all settled around Maia. He slung his arm around the back of Kenda's chair in a loosely possessive gesture.

"I've instructed Chessy to begin a slow evacuation of the household staff. This morning, the general informed me of a greater threat against this house. So far, nobody knows exactly what it is, but I don't want to take risks with civilian lives.

The Caretaker staff will leave at once, a few at a time. We aren't announcing anything."

Isaac leaned forward to rest his elbows on his knees. He had a pensive look. "Retaliation, you think? That was a harsh blow to the marshal's pride."

"It could be anything," Maia allowed, "but I expect the third marshal will be responsible for it. I've been having trouble sleeping lately; that doesn't comfort me any, considering what usually causes it." She had long since informed them of the unwanted resident of Takra House in order to convince them to obey her teacher's new household rules. That day seemed so far in the past that it might as well have belonged to the previous generation. Maia gathered herself to add, "The general cannot stay here with us, so it's our duty not to disappoint his faith in us."

"What do you want us to do?" asked Isaac.

"A little sleight of hand wouldn't hurt. Try to keep people from noticing that the staff is leaving. Whatever else you do, make no mention of it. If possible, fill in the gaps as best you can, so the household can remain running for as long as possible."

Kintaro, the massive Alti captain, lifted a hand to gain her attention. "My lady, if the danger is so great, why not evacuate the house altogether? I'll be the first to confess that I'd feel much better to see you safely out of the way. There must be a place we can go where there's at least the possibility of mounting an adequate defense. This place wasn't built with that in mind."

The idea held so much appeal for Maia that she had to steel herself to answer, "No. If we leave the house, it'll only turn into a Garden of the Forbidden. There hasn't been an abomination like that on our soil in over six hundred years. I won't be the one to let it happen."

"But how are we to fight?" Hollister argued. "No mere mortal can fight the Unclean and live to tell about it. There's no weapon we can wield that will destroy what the traitor brought in with him. If we stay, we face our own deaths, not in honorable battle as warriors but as the Unclean's dinner, as helpless prey. There's no way we can win this as things stand."

"Maybe we can't fight, but we can weaken him by taking away his easiest source of prey, Hollister. My teacher told me that he's weak here. The only way he can grow strong is by draining mortals of their lives, like he did to Rhendi and Najhid. We're wary now. We can resist him. I'm not so sure about the civilians. That's why I want them to evacuate until we can find a way to drive him out. We aren't totally helpless." Maia studied each face in turn, hoping for signs that they believed her. "My teacher will still be nearby. He stopped the Great River with a word. He can find a way to cleanse this house. I know he can."

Morio gave her a significant glance. "When are we allowed to recognize him, my lady?"

"When he says so."

By late afternoon, twenty-five of the forty Caretakers had filtered out through Takra's gates to disperse into the city or to other properties nearby—Eleusia House, for example. Chessy and his wife came to Maia's sitting room together, still mindful of the general's rules, to report on the evacuation. "Young families with children went first," Chessy said in a distracted way, "and the young maids next. I reckoned them as running the greatest risk."

"Good. What's wrong?" Maia asked. "You seem troubled."

"My mother…she's resisting this new order. She set herself up in her bedroom and won't come out for any inducement." Chessy fell silent in embarrassment.

His wife was too angry for delicacy of expression. "She claims it's all just a ruse cooked up to take away her privileges before the eldership meets on Chessy's dispute. She's making herself completely odious about it."

Maia sighed. Sympathetic to the clan elder, she said, "Well, just leave her for now. All those who are left will have to stay close to their rooms anyway until morning comes. Does everyone have a roommate? It's all the more important that no one is alone at night." *Even old Lucinda,* she added inwardly. It didn't surprise her to find that the old matriarch was making a fuss. Since the quarrel, Lucinda had become even more jealous of her position as matriarch, and the staff had been strictly enjoined to take no notice of her. "You've done very well, both of you. I'm glad I can rely on you like this."

"Our duty and our privilege," answered Chessy with an effort at a smile. "Is your mother spending just this night with the general's wife, or will she need more of her things tomorrow?"

"I'm not really sure. We'll just have to wait for her to send word, I guess." Maia dismissed the pair to accompany the next batch of refugees. In half an hour, supper came in the form of a basket of sandwiches and a jug of chilled wine, carried by two of the guards. "Here you go, my lady," said Raven, bearer of the sandwiches. "I'll tell you truly, it was hard duty to bring these straightaway without sampling any of them first."

His comrade Hardee, who had been one of the king's guards, smiled tolerantly at his young partner's confession. "I thought I'd have to slap his hand once or twice, my lady, but he made it in the end." He stood by to pour for Maia as Raven laid out the sandwiches with many a regretful gaze.

Taking pity, Maia handed him one and gave another to Hardee before she dismissed them. "Here. Every good table server deserves some kind of recognition, don't you think?" They thanked her and left.

"Are you still thinking of an early bedtime?" Kenda asked while they ate.

"I'm so tired, Kenda. I hardly shut my eyes all last night—or so it feels," she amended ruefully. "Worse yet, I get the feeling that tonight won't be any better. Whatever is going on, it's only bound to get worse from here onward. Maybe if I lie down before it's completely dark, I'll get enough sleep." Maia yawned. "I've never been so tired."

Consequently, shortly after eight that evening, Maia climbed into her bed and fell asleep at once. Her troublesome dreams didn't come to bother her until later, near midnight, when the sound of a child's shriek propelled her out of bed with a pounding heart.

*　　　*　　　*　　　*

The ground floor of Takra House's residential wing was primarily taken up with Caretaker quarters and work areas. Out of all the bed chambers on the ground floor, only one wasn't rectangular in shape. It had three walls and, because of the odd corner of the building that it occupied, was the most spacious chamber. Because of its longtime occupant, it was also the most lavishly adorned. The only good thing it couldn't boast was contentment. To Lucinda, Lady Caretaker, her stately bedroom had a distinct prison aura hanging around it. They had taken her maids away from her—even Liande, such a devoted girl—and were even now trying to oust her from her own bedroom and smuggle her into the countryside. Lucinda would not be moved, not until she had had her chance to air her grievances before a proper elders' council. She had long suspected that her son harbored designs against her, jealous of her office and all the honors that went with it. Her suspicions had only grown over the summer. Now she had proof.

Taken away her maids, taken away her freedom—or the next nearest thing to it, since Lucinda knew that to budge from her bedroom would be to walk directly into their hands—and now she could only sit and wonder what they were scheming to take from her now. The house had been so quiet. Not a soul had come to her—obviously, the staff had all been ordered to isolate her—not a soul had set foot inside her room after Chessy's conniving wife had quite unceremoniously left the child Dara there for Lucinda to mind. It wasn't as if the child had exhibited any of her appalling misbehaviors, not yet at any rate, but it was on *principal* that Lucinda objected. She was no nursemaid and would not have anyone believe that she could be so reduced in position that she would willingly play nanny. If the child needed constant vigilance—though Lucinda was sure that children in her day never needed watching once they were able to understand simple instructions—then it was the fault of Ardith, who was supposed to mother the child in place of her dead mother. If she couldn't manage it, then surely one of the child's sisters should have been given the responsibility. The elder sister had chosen a ridiculously unsuitable position as royal guard, and the other (Lucinda was sure) aspired to supplant her one day as Lady Caretaker. It was always there in the girl's superior, sneering looks, looks that proclaimed *I can do a better job than you*. That was a girl who needed to be taken down a peg or two.

Hours passed, and still nobody came to attend Lucinda. The sun went down, darkness crept from the corners of the room, and still nobody came. Lucinda had to get up and light her own candles for herself. She gave the child a glance. To her relief, Dara had fallen asleep on a cushion in the corner. Returning to her sofa, Lucinda took up a slim illustrated volume of poems, but the light from the lamps made her head ache with reading. She cast aside the poetry and heaved herself up from the sofa to look out at the windows. There she saw a small party setting off in a carriage. They appeared to be packed for more extensive traveling than a night of receptions in Carthae. No one had said anything to her about a tour of the countryside...Lucinda began to grow angry again. Certainly, if there was anything major to be arranged regarding the situation of the household, they had no right to begin it without consulting her first. She was still Lady Caretaker, dispute or no dispute.

She disrobed and put on her voluminous nightgown. Try as she might, she couldn't sleep at all. Across the room, the child Dara slept soundly enough for two. Lucinda felt a bubble of resentment at the greedy privilege of youth, which was too ignorant of insomnia to appreciate the soundest slumbers. Rising from her bed, Lucinda swathed herself in a warm robe and lumbered back to her sofa to think. *If no one will come to me*, she finally decided, *then I must seek out someone who will listen to me*. Only the silence of the sleeping house gave her the courage to take this step. *I will go to the third marshal. Oh, I doubt he is still here—although if he's that conscientious, perhaps he might still be at his desk with some business of state—but even if he isn't, I shall leave a message on his desk.* She found her slippers. Then she woke the child. It was the only thing to do; if the child had awakened in her absence, she might have raised a fuss that would alert the whole house to Lucinda's activities. Lucinda made the child drape a throw blanket around her small shoulders for warmth. It was not in Lucinda's nature to imagine that anyone could be comfortable when she herself was not, and it had been years since she had felt properly warm, even in the heat of summer. In addition to her robe, she wrapped a capacious shawl around her shoulders, seized the child's warm hand, and set off into the darkened house.

Everywhere she saw signs of poor management. Lamps had been left alight at every corner, at the end of every corridor, wasting oil and threatening a disastrous house fire. Closed doors kept air from moving through the house. Lucinda could smell a musty odor already. As soon as she set to rights this entire dispute with Chessy, she would have to order a thorough airing of the house before the mildew took hold. She tugged at the child's hand, though in reality the child was keeping pace well enough. Lucinda's impatience sprang from the certain knowledge that it was her reputation as Lady Caretaker that was suffering under Chessy's mismanagement, and she had no doubt that that was his intention. He *wanted* to make her appear incompetent. Lucinda fairly snorted with wrath as she clumped grimly down the corridor in the direction of the marshals' offices.

The stairs were a bit much for her. It was bad enough that the child Dara wouldn't go up the stairs at all until Lucinda smacked her sharply across the face and ordered her to ascend. Then the child wanted to hold Lucinda's hand on the way. That was impossible, as they wouldn't both fit in the narrow, twisting staircase together. Lucinda told the child, "You're far too old for this foolishness. Dark or no, you're going up the stairs. Now go!" Another sharp little slap was sufficient persuasion. The little one scampered upwards as if pursued, while Lucinda ascended with a rolling, painful gait, pausing to lean against the wall every few steps. It had been some time since Lucinda had attempted to climb a flight of stairs, but she remembered every detail of the upper floors with perfect clarity. It pained her to see how shabby everything had become in her absence. Worn carpets had remained long past the time when they should have been discarded. The marks of mending were clear in the light of the forgotten lamps at every corner. *For shame,* Lucinda thought, shaking her head and wheezing from her exertions. *For shame! Why, the carpets in my own room are finer than these! Chessy owes a good many explanations.*

Turning her attentions from the private wing, Lucinda had to drag the child along with her into the other side of Takra House. The child had suddenly taken to lagging behind and whining in the most irritating manner, loudly enough that someone was bound to hear. Lucinda shook the child. "Hush, child! Nobody's harming you. Stop making such an offensive noise!" Once she had diminished the child to a soft whimper, Lucinda continued on her way. This side of the building, she noticed, was scarcely lit at all. It encouraged her to see a solitary yellow light still glowing in the third marshal's office. *So he is still hard at work!* Relieved, Lucinda began to gather her thoughts so that she would waste none of the young marshal's valuable time once she arrived. *He will listen to me.*

When she knocked courteously at the door, she heard him bid her enter. She started back at the changes she found in his face. "You have been working too hard, Marshal," she chided with maternal warmth.

"I do what I must. What brings you to me so late in the evening?"

There wasn't a chair for sitting on, so Lucinda rested her weight against the edge of the desk. She started to tell him why she had sought him out, but then her attention was snared by a thing she had at first taken for a lamp on his desk. "That is a curious relic," she said, reaching out to trace it with a blunt forefinger. "What sort of light is this?"

"It is a light that burns without fire. You may well call it curious, Lady Caretaker." The young man stood, lifted it from the desk, and held it out to her. "Go ahead. It is warm, but not hot to the touch."

Lucinda took it. "Goodness." She turned it back and forth to examine it on all sides. It was a singularly unlovely object, yet somehow that made it all the more fascinating. As the marshal had said, it was warm. For once, Lucinda felt sweat beading on her upper lip. The room felt too stuffy. Suddenly, she wanted to put down the lamp, but her hands and arms no longer obeyed her will. Instead, they heeded only that low, dark voice that echoed dimly inside her head: *She is too old and foolish. There is hardly any life left in her worth the taking. The child. Give me the child as well.* Slumping to the floor, Lucinda turned her head with great effort. As she exerted her will, the dark voice grew more powerful, but she had to try. Her lips emitted gibberish rather than the warning she meant to call out. She wanted to tell the child, *Run! Run quickly!* She could see the child cowering against the doorpost, caught up in the sound of the dark voice just as Lucinda was. The child wept piteously, but still the voice beckoned for her to come nearer. The cold was returning now, coiling around Lucinda like the talons of a great bird of prey. Her eyes remained fixed on the child.

Dara was creeping away. Despite the attraction of the terrible voice, she was creeping around the doorpost, dragging her feet with the effort it cost her to move away. Lucinda could see her clearly through the open doorway, until the third marshal blocked her view as he went after the child. Lucinda heard a scuffle and the child's shriek. She shut her eyes, unwilling to watch the child's demise. Soon, it was no longer a choice. The talons tightened; Lucinda, Lady Caretaker was gone.

*   *   *   *

"Go out the solarium door," Maia demanded, still pulling a light robe around her body. "I'm sure it came from behind the house, out in the park."

Hollister nodded. His face showed none of the alarm it had displayed when she had first summoned him with such urgency. To his credit, he hadn't once questioned her story or her demand that he and his squad search the pleasure garden outside with torches, all on the strength of a half-heard sound. He mustered his squad and alerted the captain and the other on-duty lieutenant as to his actions. Then he and his six guards took themselves out into the impermeable darkness of the garden to make their search.

Leaning out of her bedroom window, Maia watched them make their painstaking progress, step by step, across the garden, rifling through the shrubs for signs of anything that might have disturbed Maia's sleep. Then the guard nearest the house shouted out, "Lieutenant!" The rest came running to gather around some pale blot among the flowering shrubs. Hollister's voice rang out in command. For a few terrible moments, they made so little movement that Maia was in an agony of curiosity and impatience to know what they were doing. At her side, Kenda grasped her by the arm, steadying her as well as keeping her from leaning any farther out the window. Then the guards rearranged themselves. Two of them stood with hands linked to form a makeshift stretcher, carrying a petite, limp figure swiftly back to the solarium door. The remaining five stood gazing up at the side of Takra House, pointing upward at something, then examined the ground more closely where the fallen figure had lain.

Maia had to restrain herself from running through the house to find out what was going on. For the longest time, no one came up to report to her. She could only sit with Kenda as her only comforter until Hollister returned. The first thing Maia noticed was his pallor. Something had severely shaken him. "What is it?" she demanded. "What did you find?"

He cast an apologetic look to Kenda. "You were right. When we got to the other end of the pleasure garden, we found...it was little Dara. From all the signs, she fell from a window. There was only one window open, that of the second-floor corridor outside of the third marshal's office. She's hurt," he admitted, but then hastened to add, "Nothing mortal, as far as we could ascertain. I want to send for the chief healer without delay, though."

"Let me go down to her," Kenda said unsteadily.

Hollister shook his head. "Not until a healer has been to see her first. She's unconscious. She wouldn't know you were there." He looked to Maia for support.

"Send for Doran," she instructed. "Make sure you're following the proper precautions, but see that he comes as soon as can be. We'll wait here until you get back, but as soon as you get back, I want Kenda to be able to stay with her sister at all times. I won't be sleeping anymore tonight anyway," she added as an afterthought. A shudder rolled down her back.

They brought Doran so swiftly that Maia had to wonder just how furiously they had driven the carriage through the narrow city streets. The healer's steadying company relieved some of Maia's fears. "Where's the child?" Doran asked as soon as he entered. Once Maia had led him to the table where they had installed little Dara's still form, Doran said nothing more except to make demands of the remaining Caretakers as he needed their assistance in setting the little girl's broken bones. Maia watched the healer's face. She saw how gravely he looked at Dara, and how sad his eyes became as he gingerly straightened the child's body limb by limb. At length, Doran breathed a sigh. "I've done all I can. Right now, all we can let her do is wake up of her own accord once her body has had time to recover from the shock of the injuries." With a glance at Kenda and Meghala, he gestured for Maia to step aside to confer. "What happened?"

Like the healer, Maia kept her voice to a whisper. "I don't know for sure. Hollister said it looked as if she'd fallen from the window of the corridor that runs past the marshals' offices. She was supposed to be in Lucinda's room for safe-keeping." Briefly, Maia explained about the evacuation of the civilian members of the household. "Ardith and Chessy took the last group out just at sundown, with orders not to stop for anything until they were well away from King's City. I haven't dared go down to disturb Lucinda; she's been fussing so badly that nobody wants to have anything to do with her now that Ardith isn't here to deal with her."

"Second floor window," Doran murmured with a frown. "That explains a good deal. It explains even more if it was the window near Miklei-son's office. It isn't safe for you here."

"Leaving here will only postpone the trouble," returned Maia. "I won't see this house turned into another Garden of the Forbidden. Someone has to stay and fight."

To her secret relief, the chief healer smiled. "I thought you'd say that. I admire your perseverance. Oh, and that leads me back to something I'd forgotten in all the commotion. I'm to tell you that tea brewed from the leaves of the Prince's

Tree should be administered to everyone who remains in Takra. The general says it's a good restorative. I myself must gather some leaves before I go, but you need some for this house as well. I'd suggest making three or four jugs per day, enough for everyone to have a cup at each meal...especially now." His backward glance at the small, stricken assembly of Caretakers was eloquent enough.

"Yes, of course." Maia scarcely had the heart to ask him to stay for the rest of the night, but she was relieved when Doran volunteered to tend the little girl until the sun rose. Then he himself strapped little Dara to a sturdy board, talking gently to reassure her all while he and one of her Caretaker kinsmen carried the board out to the wagons that held the rest of the civilians. Doran waved aside offers to drive him separately in the carriage, as befit his status as chief healer and first marshal of King's City. Instead, he sat on the floor of the crowded wagon beside Dara as the wagon rattled out through the gates on its way to safety at Eleusia House.

Maia watched them go. Part of her was glad to see them on their way; it marked one less concern for her to carry. With all of the servants absent, Maia felt the hollow lifelessness of the house all the more keenly. Her guards began to make adjustments—ground floor windows were shuttered, second floor watch was doubled to four guards per shift, and the third floor connection to the rest of the house had to be barricaded. Takra House was preparing for battle.

JONAS SON OF DENEI

Owen had an inexplicable dream. It was neither a vision nor a product of his overwrought mind, as had been the case for the duration of the festival. Instead, it was a memory of his past, resurrected from the depths of his mind and presented as clearly as if it were happening again. When he awoke, he suffered immense confusion. His mind was so entirely oriented to the memory that the present moment seemed too alien to be real. First he looked for Sylva, expecting to find her beside him. The truth of her absence stabbed deep. Then he realized that Kohanan too was gone, and Denei, and Camille as well. Then he remembered the true state of his world and understood that it had been a dream. Owen applied his mind to the dream again—in no small part because of the comfort it gave him to retreat so far into the certain and secure past.

Young Nässey was born not quite two years after Kohanan and Camille had produced their twins. Owen had been there to sit with Denei while Sylva attended Riana through the birthing. He had seen the grin of wild happiness on Denei's face when the first cry filled the air. Then, when Sylva had come to the door to announce that the child was a boy, Owen had been forced to hold Denei back from rushing into the birthing room before the healer's assistants were finished with their work. He had never seen his brother so excited before. Then the surprise: Owen had overheard Sylva ask in the ordinary way, "What name have you chosen?" He himself had been busily inspecting the red-faced, wrinkly infant, but he raised his head when Denei answered, "We chose to name him after someone I owe a great debt: Jonas Maury-son." When Owen had looked at his brother, he found Denei watching him. Owen knew that no great love had ever existed between Denei and Jonas son of Maury in life, but Jonas had died saving Owen's life in what had proven to be the last battle of the Kavahri wars. Before Denei's newborn son was a week old, however, it was the diminutive form of the name—Nässey—that had taken firm hold for everyday usage.

At length, Owen got out of bed and shook off the melancholy that the dream had left behind. He hunted around for his slippers, which were nowhere to be found that morning. After the upheaval of the festival, nothing was exactly where it belonged anymore. Owen found to his chagrin that he had no memory of leaving the slippers anywhere. In the midst of his hunt, he came across Nässey' riding boots again. He picked them up for a few seconds. Then he put them down and turned away. Until that morning, he had given no thought to Nässey since the day the younger man had refused to see him. Remorse pricked at Owen's heart. *He didn't come to the festival,* he thought for the first time. *I was so caught up in my own freedom that I gave no thought to him.* Absentminded now, Owen discovered his slippers protruding from underneath the bed, put them on, and went to the breakfast table in his pajamas.

"Good morning, Father," Phoebe said. "Laena, where has he put his robe this time?"

Owen looked around, momentarily confused, as the Caretaker housekeeper tucked the dressing gown around his shoulders. "Oh. Thank you, Laena."

"I'm starting to worry about him," continued Phoebe mildly.

"So am I," Owen echoed, still thinking of Nässey. He realized that the conversation had halted. That arrested his attention enough to make him raise his eyes from his bowl. "What?"

Phoebe and Doran stared at him as if torn between laughter and concern. Phoebe spoke first. "Who are *you* talking about, Father? I was talking about *you.* Your memory is simply shocking these days. Slippers, dressing gown, spoon…"

Owen followed her expressive downward glance and realized that he had let his spoon sink so deep into his bowl that it had disappeared beneath the surface of his porridge. He swirled a finger around in the porridge to fish out the spoon. "You distracted me," he protested.

"It wasn't difficult," his daughter retorted. "A buzzing fly could distract you."

"If you have something troubling you, Father, we're here to listen," Doran added. "Is it about Maia?"

Owen shook his head. "No. I was thinking of Nässey. Last night, I dreamed of the day he was born. Have you seen him—even in passing—since we came home?"

Doran shook his head. "He hasn't been at Takra at all. His office door was wide open all day yesterday, so I assumed he was somewhere around, but I never saw him. Byram asked me if I'd seen him. That was the first I knew of his absence. After what happened at Takra last night, it's something to consider. Do you believe him to be in some sort of trouble as well?"

"I was thinking of the day he wouldn't come to see me. Something is certainly wrong."

"Well, now that you don't have to wait for him," Phoebe said, "why worry about it?"

"You think I should track him down and confront him?"

"He's bound to be easier to find than your slippers."

It wasn't as simple as that, of course. Owen had to summon Rowan and Temora in order to give them time enough to scout the streets and ascertain which way was easiest to secure. That took up the remainder of the morning and ensured that Owen's departure, when he finally was able to depart, would be a circus of last-minute scouts' reports and debates between his guards and the retired soldiers who kept watch from the bench across the street. They brought the carriage from the stable around the corner and drew it up in front of the house in preparation for the outing. Then Phoebe popped her head into the sitting room and asked Rowan if, after all this bustle and commotion, anyone had thought to discover Nässey' precise location before they set off to meet with him. Even Doran, tired as he was, had to laugh at Rowan's consternation, but Owen was too preoccupied for more than a vague smile. Suddenly, he got up and went to his room to examine the riding boots once more, heedless of the way everyone turned to stare.

There was something about those boots. He turned them over and over, one at a time, waiting to see if the elusive thought would come back to him. *I must be getting old*, he thought grimly, *if I can't remember something this important.* It felt like a half-forgotten dream. Something about them—something known in a dream—came to mind when he ran his hands over the glossy leather boots. He shook them upside-down, but nothing came out. When he dropped them both, however, one made a slightly different sound than the other. Owen picked them up and held one on each palm. Their balance was off. The left boot tilted backwards, while the right was prone to tipping forward. Owen attacked the right-hand boot first. He thrust his hand down the boot as far as the toe and discovered something crammed into the toe of the boot. His fingers worried it out of position enough for him to pull it out.

It was paper, folded until it formed a wad too thick to fold one more time. One side was abraded, as if Nässey had worn the boots for some time with the paper shoved down into the toe. Owen unfolded the battered packet of paper and separated the two sheets with difficulty. Dark brown stains blotted some of the words and bonded the sheets of paper together at a number of points. Both pages started in the middle of a sentence, so Owen gently set them aside for a time. He attacked the other boot at the heel. Like most fashionable riding boots of the day, it had a sizeable square heel on it, useful for helping riders keep their feet from slipping unexpectedly forward in the stirrups. Caring nothing for the preservation of the boots, Owen wrenched the heel off more easily than he should have. He didn't have to wonder why; the inside of the heel had been made hollow, creating a natural repository for a small wad of paper like the one in the toe of the ,other boot.

Once straightened and smoothed out flat, this paper proved itself the first of the three. To Owen, this made sense. This sheet was written in a steadier hand, with fewer blots of ink and no bloodstains. Owen knew that Nässey must have taken more time over it, both in composition and in concealment. He began to read.

If I had only dissolved my pride at the very first and spoken of my doubts, this could never have come to pass. Poor Colin! I feel sorry for him as I cannot feel sorry for myself, because he was deceived—yes, even by my own cooperation. I should have spoken at the first. Who else suspected the treachery of which Simon was capable, if not me? I, his own teacher and mentor, stayed silent and let him insinuate himself into Colin's confidence. I hear the accusing words even now: you failed your king and kinsman. You betrayed your countrymen. The belated fact that I have also condemned myself to prison and, no doubt, to eventual death means so little to me that it seems an impertinence to even write it alongside the rest. I stayed silent then; it is only right that I stay silent now as well. My life is not worth saving. I have been a fool and worse. If I can only find a way to warn Colin to listen to my father this time instead of to me. I must. For now I see that Maia is the present object of my foul protégé's ambitions—that he means to obtain her as his wife—in short, that Father was right all along. That should please him. Yet it isn't the Academy that bears the blame for this intolerable situation. I'll swear to it that the fault lies entirely with its administrator and master. If not for my own foolishness, this state of anarchy would never have taken place. I wish Father could be made to see the truth of this. I was weak-minded. My creation failed because I failed. It is still a good idea in itself. Given a better master, it will prove its worth one day.

Owen bowed his head in sadness, unable to read further for the misting of his eyes. He had known that Nässey and Denei had been at odds for the past several years. Denei had always disagreed with Nässey's philosophy of training warriors as potential statesmen. Their feud had been unpleasantly public in nature, especially because they both were so closely involved with the Cabinet. Owen perceived how easily such a split could deepen at the hand of an unscrupulous outsider who was eager to play the one against the other for the sake of his own advancement. Rubbing the back of his hand against his eyes to clear them, Owen skimmed the rest of this first sheet, catching a name here, a date there.

Nässey had documented the traitor's actions with scrupulous care on the first page. The remaining sheets, those spotted with dried blood, were of a different tenor altogether. By the content Owen judged that these must have been written sometime shortly after Denei's death. Each paragraph was a brief letter of apology. In a disturbingly jagged script, Nässey had written to beg forgiveness first from his mother for bereaving her of her husband, then to Colin for abetting the traitor in his schemes, and then to his sister Ivy for both depriving her of a father and trying to turn her against her new husband. He concluded with a vehement apology to the new general. Owen had skimmed over the highly personal notes to Riana and Ivy, but this note he read closely, all the while aware of a churning mix of emotions.

Sir, I owe you all duty and loyalty. As kinsman by marriage, I owe you more than that, but I have given you none of these. My regrets are beyond expression. If you are reading these words now, however, that means that I have succeeded in my last and greatest ambition — to notify the world of the perfidy that lives within Simon son of Miklei. I have heard enough of your greatness to know that such news cannot be truly news to you. Indeed, I believe you must have known it longer than any of us. Please believe that I wish you nothing but success in this campaign and every campaign that will follow in the long and illustrious career that must come to one so accomplished. I have only the deepest respect for you, as did my father. You may have heard that I loved my father little. You certainly have seen me champion his most hateful enemy. The first is an unfortu-

nate lie; the second is unfortunate but true, and in this I cannot justify myself. In vain might I wish for the ability to set back the time and recover those first moments of my failure. Being incapable of that, I will do the next best thing: enclosed with these letters, I add a page from my own notes, naming the primary movers of this rebellion and enumerating the stages of their treason. Use this to cleanse the kingdom and to protect the king. It is the best that I can do.

Rowan, standing patiently at the door, cleared his throat to attract Owen's attention. "You'd best come out and hear the latest. I don't know what to make of it."

Owen followed him out to the sitting room. When he had settled himself in a chair, he said, "What is it?" Succinctly, one guard reported that Nässey's household servants had sworn he was at the Academy; the second guard then reported that, at the Academy, Nässey's assistant had insisted that Nässey was working at home that day. When these two reports were finished, Rowan added, "One of them is lying, or both of them. Which is it?"

Owen, someone whispered. Owen was not aware of an additional presence in the room. He glanced around to see who had spoken his name, but all he found were expectant looks. Then, softly, it came again: *Owen. Your brother's son remains a prisoner in his house. You must go to him. You must take Doran with you. He will help you to stand.* Owen blinked rapidly. He suffered a moment's doubt, wondering if he had somehow fallen asleep and dreamed all of this. The whispering voice was that of his immortal master, certainly, but it had never visited him while he was awake and in company. Owen spoke in spite of himself. "He is at home. They hold him against his will there. Doran, you're to come with me. We have to retrieve him. We'll take him to Denei's house. I'm sure he'll be safe there."

No one argued with him, but Owen saw how they exchanged dubious glances amongst themselves. "Yes, I'm going. I have to go to him myself. None of you can see what's truly happening to him."

"What does that mean?" Rowan demanded uneasily.

"It means that Nässey is in danger of his life, but not from anything that *you* can guard him against. Come, Doran. There isn't time to debate about it."

Four guards accompanied them, riding on the outside of the carriage. Inside, Owen stared at his son-in-law. "I'm sorry to have to drag you into this. I'm old. If anything happens, I've had my day. I hate to put you at risk."

"If you need me, that's all there is to be said." A protracted silence fell between them before Doran spoke again. "He's mixed up with Simon's treason, isn't he? That's what you meant back there. I wouldn't have expected it of him. Nässey?" Doran sighed heavily. "Poor fellow. He must have thought he hadn't any other choice. But it isn't too late yet?"

"I hope it isn't. You have to help me once we get there."

"How can *I* help? I'm no seer."

Owen quit fidgeting with his walking stick and tipped his head to regard the younger man closely. "I am, and I know that you can help. You've always been special, you know. No, Doran, it's more than just the fact that you're a talented healer. Sylva used to talk with me about you. She was talented in her own right, but she said you belonged in a class beyond her. I never did tell you what I found in my studies, did I? After Sylva told me about the things you could do—things none of the other healers could do, mind you—I did a little studying on the subject of healing. Did you know that healing is among the seven great gifts? They call it "hands of healing," or *iatrafa*. Next to bornsight, it's the most commonly held of these rare gifts...and you have it, Doran."

"How do you know for sure?"

Despite his concern over the coming confrontation, Owen laughed quietly. "Oh, Doran, you don't suppose it's possible to heal someone without their knowledge, do you? Every time I feel the slightest twinge, you're there in a heartbeat. It doesn't feel the same as when the power used to flow through Kohanan, but it's certainly of the same source. Since I knew you disobeyed me out of love, I never said anything about it—although I'm *sure* I made it clear that I didn't want treatment of any sort," he added dryly. "That's how I know, Doran. You have one of the great gifts. It's the very one that I need most right now. Nässey is in bad shape. He's been a prisoner for a long time."

The carriage halted in front of a tall house. As soon as one of the guards opened the carriage door, Owen descended. He ordered the guards to stay with the carriage. Keeping Doran close at his elbow, he approached the front steps of Nässey's house. A glance at the sky didn't reassure him. It was still mid-afternoon, but the sky was swiftly clouding over with such thick clouds that it looked like dusk. They had endured such a long stretch of scorching, cloudless days that Owen had almost forgotten what a storm looked like. It didn't look like rain, unfortunately. The wind tousled the dry grass with a forceful, reckless hand. Owen thought it looked like perfect weather for a cyclone, down to the tinge of green among the clouds. He tightened his grip on his walking stick and hammered at the front door until someone answered. As it turned out, a young fellow came to the door. He was about sixteen and had a look in his eye that Owen disliked at once. "What can I do for you, Lord Sakiry?"

"You can admit me to this fine house so that I can visit my nephew."

"You're welcome to come in and wait, my lord, but my master isn't at home just now. He's at the Academy."

"That," Owen said mildly, "is what the fellow at the Academy told us."

But the doorkeeper wasn't to be caught so easily. "Ah, well, the second marshal goes where he pleases. He may well be out visiting his sisters or one of his students' families."

"You may be right. I'll come in and wait for him." Owen brushed past the youth. He shrugged off the doorkeeper's efforts to relieve him of his walking stick. "I prefer to wait in the private salon. Please have refreshments sent up to us there."

"There's a project laid out in the private salon, my lord. It isn't fit for visitors. There isn't hardly any place to sit," protested the youth.

"I'm perfectly able to shift a few papers. It'll be interesting to see what Nässey has been working on these past few weeks." Pretending that he didn't feel the fingers plucking at his sleeve, Owen proceeded through the house to the stairs. He risked a glance over his shoulder and found only Doran following him upwards to the next floor. Owen kept his voice low. "Gone to fetch reinforcements, do you think?"

"Probably. We'd better make this quick."

They went to the private salon, but rather than stop there, Owen went through to the corridor behind it, the hallway that led to the master suite. He found the door at the end of the hall locked. The key hung on a nail to the right of the door. Owen used it to unlock Nässey's bedroom door and let himself and Doran inside.

The curtains were drawn and the room dark. "Why are you here?" came a wearied voice out of the darkness. "It isn't night already."

"No, it isn't. It's still daylight."

"Uncle Owen!"

By groping along the wall, Owen reached the source of the voice—a clammy, trembling, lean body. The tremors came from Nässey's weeping. "Come, come, my boy," Owen encouraged him. "You're coming with us. We'll take you home."

"No, no, no, you shouldn't be here." The younger man groaned. Then, suddenly, light filled the room as Doran yanked the curtains apart on one window. Nässey flinched from the light and shielded his eyes. "Please, go away. Now. You must."

Shocked, Owen couldn't tear his gaze from his nephew. He couldn't imagine what kind of torments Nässey must have suffered to change so greatly over the past few weeks. His hearty square face was gaunt now. Bruises showed clearly against his sickly pallor. A streak of dried blood darkened his unkempt beard and terminated in a splotch on his filthy shirt. What troubled Owen more than these was the dread in Nässey's eyes.

"You shouldn't be here. Where is the sun? How high is it yet? You might still have time to get away."

"What do you mean, 'get away'? We came to take you out of here."

"I'm grateful, Uncle, but you don't understand. Wherever you take me, he'll follow. It's better that you leave me here and go." The younger man's legs were shaky as he stood, but he insisted on staggering across the room to the window that Doran had uncovered. Nässey shut his eyes against the light again once it touched his face, but his look was one of stolen bliss that lasted only until he squinted at the sky. "The sun," he muttered. "Where is the sun?"

"There's a storm coming," Doran answered. He had his hands on Nässey's shoulders already; Owen knew why. "The day has been clouding over since mid-morning."

"It's too dark. He'll be coming soon."

"You won't be here when—" But Owen had to stop. He knew that there was no reassurance that he could offer his nephew. Already, he felt a sickening fear building in his own spirit, signaling the approach of that which he most dreaded. There would be no time, just as Nässey had predicted. With the sky abnormally darkened so early in the day, nothing stood between the Unclean and his prey.

Nässey seemed energized by the pending danger. Suddenly, he grabbed both Owen and Doran by an elbow, propelling them toward the door. Then they stopped. A deceptively ordinary figure blocked them: the third marshal, wrapped in a cloak despite the stifling heat. "Sakiry! What a twist of luck. I had planned on coming to call on you when I finished my business here." He stepped forward, gesturing over his shoulder for the servants to lock the door behind him. Then, once the door was shut, Simon shrugged out of his cloak. He wore a peculiar type of armor; Owen saw that it was made of stone, but he couldn't think why a man would wear armor at such a time. Then, to his horror, he saw the armor spreading upward to engulf the man's neck and head in a stone casing. "You see? I have overcome the final mystery. I have mastered the secrets of the Forbidden." His voice resonated eerily in the close room. "The world is mine, Sakiry. Not even your general can stop me."

"You are deluded," Owen replied. "He *will* bring an end to this."

"All endings belong to me, Sakiry. I am the end of all things." Simon reached out a blunted hand to grasp the front of Nässey's shirt. "Today, I will be *your* end. See? This one has held on for an amazing amount of time. Little by little, I have worn him down until he no longer has the will to resist. I admit that I have taken my time. It's surprising, how much one develops a taste for this type of work. I have never seen anyone hold on for so long. From him I learned why the speed of devouring varies so greatly. I look forward to seeing how long you hold on, Sakiry. Your spirit burns very strong…very steadfast. You could last probably six months, assuming I had time enough to devote to your leisurely destruction."

"You have no right to his life or to mine," Owen replied as calmly as he could. Inside, he seethed at the helpless situation into which he had trapped himself and Doran.

"I take what I want. I am lord of all the earth. In time, the whole earth will gather under my rule. All I must do is rid myself of a few hindrances—like you."

Nässey tried to pull away from his captor. Suddenly, he seized up from head to foot and began shuddering uncontrollably as Simon began to gleam with a sulfurous yellow light. The putrid reek of death wafted through the room. Then, as soon as it had come, the glow and the stench retreated. Nässey fell to the ground in a limp tangle of limbs, the occasional twitch still wracking his body. With effort, he turned onto his back. His face shocked Owen. It had been gaunt before; now, it was shriveled as with extreme old age. While Owen watched, Nässey's features slowly lost these hideous marks of premature age, but not entirely. Nässey gazed up at Owen in silent resignation.

Tell him, Owen.

Owen was not startled this time. He breathed deeply to calm himself, drawing upon this comforting, secretive presence. *What must I tell him, Great One?*

Tell him that all is forgiven him. He needs to hear the words from you plainly.

Kneeling, Owen took his nephew by the hand. "Nässey, all is forgiven you." He could tell by the astonishment in the younger man's suffering eyes that this was the last thing Nässey had expected to hear. Life returned like a spark to brighten the gaunt face, life that sprang from hope. Owen gripped the trembling hand even more tightly, ready to fight for his brother's son.

"Isn't that good to hear?" Simon mocked. "A man can even be forgiven for betraying his own father to his death. Aren't you glad to know that you can die in peace, son of Denei?"

"He will not die tonight."

"You are an old man and a weak seer, Sakiry. You haven't power enough to fight me."

"Be that as it may," Owen insisted, "he will not die tonight."

"Tonight, tomorrow night, or maybe the night after that—what difference does it make? He will belong to me in the end. Don't trust in your guards to rescue you, either. They have already been given the message that you have chosen to stay the night. Your nephew is stubborn, but you yet hope to persuade him. They will not look for you until tomorrow. By then, you will be dead. I will see to that myself."

Doran stepped forward and placed both hands on his father-in-law's shoulders. "He doesn't stand alone. You can't take all three of us."

Simon merely laughed at this. He knelt on Nässey's other side and took the prone man's other hand in his own. "Don't the children have a game they play? They take a rope and pull it between them to see which of them is the strongest? Let us play our own version of the game, Sakiry. Since you trust so greatly in your newfound power, challenge me for the life of your nephew! We'll test one another and prove which is the strongest." The sulfur-light burned dully again, emanating from the stone armor that encrusted Simon's entire body. Then the light flared high, filling the room, and with it returned the unbearable reek of death and decay. Under Simon's grasp, Nässey's other hand began to wither until it looked like nothing more than bones encased in dried leather. Nässey groaned.

Determined to stand his ground, Owen clasped his other hand around Nässey's clenched fist. He began to feel lightheaded; the power that drained Nässey's life away was leeching his own life as well. Then a flow of warmth cascaded down his shoulders, through his arms and into his hands—from Doran, who healed him so that he could stand firm. Owen bowed his head. *Great One,* he implored, *how am I to fight so great a force? I am insufficient to the task.* No answer came, though he waited for one with bated breath. He felt the ebb begin again as Doran slowly weakened. Owen suspected that the healer had never had his gift tested so brutally before. In spite of his desire to help, Doran would not be able to sustain him for very long. "Hold onto my hand, Nässey," Owen urged his nephew. "Don't surrender to him."

Both of the younger men seemed to rally at these words. Nässey ground his teeth audibly, refusing to relax under the approach of death even though the torment was fierce. Behind Owen, Doran dropped to one knee and wrapped his arms around Owen's shoulders. With this increased contact, Doran seemed to be redoubling his efforts. Owen could feel the healing warmth building again, driving back the death that sought to encroach upon Owen through Nässey. Time meant nothing any longer. The last of the daylight stole quietly away. In its wake came thick, stifling darkness that seemed nothing less than an extension of

Simon's power. The rough wind threw debris at the windows in waves, and the hissing of dirt cast against the side of the house sounded continuously in their ears.

Simon didn't speak to them again. Instead, he chuckled to himself occasionally, as if he knew something that amused him about this alleged game. As the evening deepened, the power of the Unclean never wavered. It seemed eternal, unshakable, inexorable. Owen choked on its fetid emanations. Deep within himself, he knew that this contest of strength could not endure even as long as the night lasted. They were nowhere near powerful enough, not even the three of them united in resistance, and Simon knew it, too. He was toying with them. Owen saw the glow deepening rather than brightening. From his years of study, Owen knew what was happening: the Unclean was beginning to show its true form through Simon. The jaundiced light went from yellow to orange, from orange to red, from red to blue. In the midst of the cold blue light, a pinpoint of darkness appeared and began to widen. The heat in the room was unspeakable and only got worse as the flames without light overtook everything. Soon only a halo of blue remained to outline Simon's encrusted body. Owen heard other voices from a distance. One was Ivy's. She was sobbing aloud. "Please, not Nässey," she wept. "Isn't there anything you can do? Please, don't let him die."

Just as the dark fire was on the brink of swallowing them all, Owen caught sight of a blinding green streak, flame of a different kind, arcing through the darkness. Words burned themselves into his vision, inscribed in symbols from the ancient Hepuran tongue: *Of the Keeper House Unending.* He found himself kneeling in a pool of jade-green light just in time to see a familiar blade sweep through the air. The blade cut easily through Nässey's wrist, severing his hand from the rest of his body. Simon fell back; the hand he held disappeared in a cloud of dust as he drained the last life from it. Then he too vanished.

Shocked into stillness, Owen could not react at first. A harsh, familiar voice roused him from his daze. "Bind his arm," Jarod commanded, sheathing his sword. The delicate green light shone through him as through clouded glass. "There's no time to waste." He kicked the door hard enough to crack it. A second kick made the wooden door burst asunder as if a team of horses had crashed into it. By this time, Doran had hastily bound the stump of Nässey's wrist. Nässey still had not made a sound, but his lackluster eyes were aware. Jarod came back to heft the second marshal into his arms. "Come on." He carried Nässey down through the silent house while Owen and Doran followed him as best they could. Outside, Owen's carriage still waited dutifully at the front steps. As the guards sprang to attention, Jarod commanded, "Wren, inside with Lord Sakiry and the chief healer. Help them however you can. The rest of you, hold on for your lives. I will not stop for you." The maimed second marshal had hardly been safely installed within the carriage with Owen, Doran, and the guard named Wren when Jarod climbed up onto the driver's box and took up the reins himself.

What followed was a reckless, terrifying flight through the narrow streets of King's City. Time and again, Owen was certain that he felt one or even two of the carriage's wheels lose contact with the ground as they careened around corners. He and the other passengers were hard-pressed not to let the momentum throw them around the carriage like so many beans in a hollow gourd. The only good thing about the ride was its brevity. It seemed hardly a minute before they had come to a breathless halt. The carriage swayed as Jarod sprang to the ground. He didn't wait for the rest of them, so Owen didn't wait either. He ran toward Denei's house after Jarod but couldn't catch him until they both came to the front parlor. Then Owen realized why the general had been so urgent.

Ivy lay on her side on the floor. In her face Owen saw the same horrific transformation that Nässey had undergone. Ivy was not alone in the room, but no one stood near her. Three paces away, Riana looked as if she urgently wanted to run to her younger daughter, yet even she stood at a distance, held there by Ivy's pleading. "No! Stay away!" Ivy sobbed. She had not yet seen her husband's entrance. "Don't take her too, please, please, don't—" She screamed.

Owen had never heard such a soul-piercing sound before. His heart lurched. Before he could do or say anything, however, he saw Jarod throw himself over Ivy's prostrate body as if to shield her. In another moment, both of them were gone. Shaken, disbelieving, Owen stared at the place where they had been. Then he raised his eyes to the room's other occupants. Every face bore the same heartsick look of denial: Riana with her hand still outstretched, Selena with her arms around a pallid Lucien, Tyrell on his sickbed, Brigid on her knees beside him. Lucien tried to pull free, to run to the place where he had last seen his parents, but Selena held him all the tighter against her bosom and would not let him go. Riana started to cry.

For his own part, Owen sank down into the nearest chair and held his head in his hands. *What can we do now?*

LITTLE SISTER

It's my fault, all my fault, was almost the last thought to surface in Ivy's mind as the frigid talons closed around her. She opened her eyes once more to make sure nobody else came near and suffered for her mistakes. As the enormous death-monster materialized before her dying eyes, Ivy gazed through its translucent body to see her mother coming. "No!" *Please, no, don't let her die because of me!* "Stay away!" As if drawn by her warning, the Lethek reached out another clawed limb toward Riana. Ivy pled with the monster to spare her mother. Then the talons pierced deep into her. Ivy was unable to stifle the scream of terror as the world began to dissolve before her eyes. Beyond the world she knew, some unspeakable horror waited for her in the night. Ivy stiffened one last time.

Unexpectedly, the death monster paused on the threshold. Ivy still dangled from its clawed foot, but she had gone limp, unable to struggle. The last of her life was trickling out when a warm, living body collided with her, pulling her back from the Lethek's grip. It was her husband. He clung to her cold, unresponsive form and anchored her to the world of the living with the force of his will. Ivy could see it. She had no time to question what she saw. She knew only that a flood of life returned to her body, pouring from him into her freely in such quantity that Ivy grew strong all in a rush. Then Jarod gasped aloud and sagged to the floor, completely spent from his rescue of Ivy. Simon's triumphant laughter rang in Ivy's ears, and she knew that this too was her fault. She knew the horror was still outside in the dark. Now, instead of seizing her, he would seize Jarod—a loss infinitely more severe than Ivy's death would have been, as she knew perfectly well.

She tried to scream again when something unseen scooped up both her and her husband, but the world disappeared and left her silent in an unfathomable void. In the next second, she felt the wind against her cheek. Compared to the darkness of the void, the night sky was luminous. Ivy sat up. Heart racing uncontrollably, she gazed around at unfamiliar surroundings and listened to the sound of wilderness. Another breeze stirred against her cheek. Part of her mind had grown unnaturally alert and noted that the breeze came from a different direction than at first. Ivy laid her hand on her husband's still chest. "Jarod? Jarod? Wake up." She shook him gently—and then not so gently—but in vain. He would not awaken. Ivy bent low with her ear to his chest and listened for his heart. After a very long wait, she heard one slow beat...and then nothing...and then another slow beat.

Then she heard something that she had never heard before. The night around her was emptied of human company, but Ivy heard a voice whisper, "For you, little brother," just as another of the breezes touched her face. That one voice became a choir as others joined in: *For you, little brother.* Ivy felt as if she sat in the middle of a windstorm. *The voices belong to the wind,* she thought. The notion frightened her so badly that she instinctively scrambled to her feet and tried to run away. Then, unexpectedly, she felt a cool, solid object—it felt like a silken sheet—drape across her back and begin to constrict around her.

"Do not fear," a tiny, timid voice said in her ear. "You are safe."

Ivy shrieked and scrambled away from the invisible creature, only to stumble into what felt like a pliable wall. This too began to close around her, but this time Ivy couldn't break free from it. It coiled around her until she could just barely move her head. This thing had a voice as well. It spoke in deep, resonant notes. "Child, stay still. There is nothing to harm you here, but you must not go outside of the light. Stay with our little brother. You will be safe with him."

Her heart quailed within her. "Please, let me go," she begged, still struggling to move. "Please! I've never done anything to harm you. Just let me go."

It sounded like the creature at her back sighed then. "It will not do, Ianthe. She may be able to hear, but she will not listen."

"I have come, Chike," a third voice said, joining the conversation abruptly. "You may release her."

Ivy staggered when she found herself suddenly free. At first, her relief was immeasurable when she saw Jarod sit upright. She ran to kneel beside him again, only to look into his eyes and realize that it was not him. Ivy herself could not say how she knew that he was still gone. The appearance was the same. Something about the voice, however, didn't match. "Who are you? What's going on? What have you done to Jarod?"

"Be at peace, Ivy. Your husband will return before the dawn. He has spent himself and must take time to renew himself now at the knees of Eshayl. While he takes refuge there, I must speak to you now."

"Who are you?" Ivy whispered it this time. She felt a relentless pressure bearing down on her, crushing her to the ground.

He didn't answer. When he got up, Ivy couldn't stand with him until he took her by the hand and lifted her to her feet. "Walk with me for a little while, and we will talk together. We have much to discuss. You and I did not finish our business during the festival." He supported Ivy with his arm, leading her into the darker shadows of the trees. Night under the canopy was impenetrable. Ivy snagged her foot on tree root after tree root, but her guide never faltered. By the time he stopped walking, they had reached a pond in another small glade. Her companion gestured toward the water, which appeared to be bubbling, almost boiling. "What are you willing to do for your husband's sake, Ivy?"

"What do you mean?"

"He needs you. His life has been lonely because he is the only one of his kind, and he believes that this will be true forever. I have another way. All that is required is your willingness. Are you willing?"

Whatever voices were on the wind had stilled, but Ivy sensed that they had in fact gathered closer to listen. It was unnerving, this certainty that she was being watched by creatures she couldn't see. Ivy wrapped her arms around herself. The sound of churning water reminded her unpleasantly of her accident during the festival. She couldn't think with that sound filling her ears. "I don't understand." Covering her ears did no good; the sound still pervaded the air all around her.

"The sound will stop when our business is concluded," her companion said, hardly louder than the water's babble. "Then, one of two things will happen. Either you will never hear the river speak again...or you will understand what it says to you. I have left this choice to you."

These words arrested Ivy's attention at once. So did the thought of the river speaking to *her*. She thought back to the incident at the riverside. Since then, she had not had much time for sleep, but she knew she had dreamed something like this recently. Ivy opened her mouth to speak, hesitating only because of the invisible listeners.

"Open your mind freely, Ivy. Tell me what it is you dreamed."

Eyes open wide, Ivy asked, "What do you know about my dreams?"

"Everything. Tell it to me anyway."

"It's true...I *did* dream, but the river wasn't speaking. It was singing. There weren't any words in it."

Her companion laughed. "Because you were so close to your husband, you heard that much on your own. He understands the river. It is as like him as anything in this world can be, because he and the river are both here and...*not* here, all at once."

"Is that how it stopped for him? Because he understands?"

"No. That is a far more complex matter, child. We do not speak of that tonight. Tonight, you must settle your future first." Her guide knelt down beside the pool. When he dipped his fingers in the roiling waters, the water rose up to spiral up his arm like a living creature. He stroked it with his other hand. With a whisper, he freed himself from its caress. The water then took form: first as a stately tree, then as a mountain, and lastly—lastly, it took Ivy's form for an instant before falling back into its natural basin as smooth as a mirror and mercifully silent.

Ivy knelt down, leaning anxiously over the water and looking at her own face in its silver surface. "It's quiet. What does that mean? Does it mean I've...I've missed my chance?" When she tore her gaze from the water's surface, however, Ivy found herself alone. She cried out, "Where have you gone?"

Come, little one. You must come to me. I am waiting for you here. It seemed as if the voice came from beneath the waters, which suddenly resumed their turbulent babble.

Knowing that it would only frighten her to think over the command, Ivy shut down her mind and, with her eyes squeezed tightly shut, tumbled forward into the water. As the liquid enclosed her, it turned to searing flame. Ivy wept at the fierce pain, but she could not stop her progress. Dizzying currents spun her until she had the bewildering sensation of rising, not sinking. All the while, the flames licked away flesh, blood, and bone, until all that Ivy had left was a self-consciousness she had never before known. She was. At first, that was all: she was. The awareness of existence had never stabbed so deeply before, but Ivy was not finished. As soon as she knew that she was, Ivy knew something else just as keenly: she was small. All around her, great and glorious creatures rose up to show her that she was the least of them, as fragile as a newborn infant, as light as a wisp of cobweb. None of them said a word to her. Their presence was sufficient to force the comparison. Ivy was small.

Then the current slowed and abandoned Ivy on a knobby tree root that protruded like a little island in the midst of a lake. When Ivy was able to control her trembling, she sat up to take in her surroundings. Before her, as far as she could see, there was only a measureless expanse of water rushing heedlessly past her perch, returning to its headwaters to begin the journey anew. A shadow stretched across the water for what seemed like several leagues. Ivy turned her head to discover the shadow's source: a tree of monumental stature whose limbs stretched so high above that they disappeared into the clouds. A streamer of gigantic red blossoms coiled around the tree trunk. From them wafted an intoxicating, tantalizing, delicately sweet aroma.

"Very good, little sister. The hardest battle is won."

Ivy raised her head. Towering above her, almost invisible in the shadow of the tree, a man stood smiling his approval. Although she had no memory of his face, she knew the voice.

"I want to show you something. Come." He strode toward the tree without waiting.

"But—"

He paused. "What is it?"

Looking from the water under his feet to his kindly, expectant eyes, Ivy said, "But I can't do that. I'm...I'm too small."

"Nothing that I command is outside of your grasp. Come."

Ivy watched him continue to walk away from her, leaving her behind. She touched the water and drew back at once from its heat. Desperately, she looked up to find her companion already so far distant that he looked half his rightful size. Ivy shut her eyes tight, gathered her courage, and started to run. She ran, always half-expecting the feel of scalding water to engulf her at any moment, until she ran headlong into solid flesh. Out of reflex, her eyes opened. "Oof!" She had run into her companion, who was laughing at her.

He bent and scooped her up in one arm, just as she remembered her stepfather doing so often when she was a child. The feel of his laughter rumbling inside his chest made Ivy smile, albeit rather tremulously. It felt right to snuggle close and let him bear her along toward the tree ahead of them. Ivy watched the massive tree trunk as it loomed closer and closer. All around it, the glorious creatures she had seen before were swirling and dipping like a flock of luminous birds of every conceivable shape, color, and size. Something about their aerial dance made Ivy take notice. She saw that they had purpose in their circling. Upon the knee-like islands formed by the tree's roots, small, limp figures lay huddled here and there, not moving. At first, Ivy thought the flying creatures were tearing at these helpless figures. Every time one of the fliers swooped down, it darted away almost at once, dripping a trail of what seemed like blood. "What are they doing?" she asked, prepared to get angry on behalf of the helpless, prone figures.

"You shall see."

As they drew nearer, Ivy saw that the nearest of the prone figures, the one on whom the graceful birdlike creatures focused most of their attention, was Jarod. He looked not more than fifteen years old. His skin was wan, almost translucent. Then a gigantic, wispy creature swooped low…and *breathed* on him. Something visible transferred from the flier to Jarod, but the creatures all moved so swiftly that this one hardly had time enough to finish its task before the next came hard on its tail, so it had to wing away with the last of its gift trailing away into the water behind it. These gifts had a tangible effect: with every one, Jarod seemed to grow more solid, even a little older, than he had been.

Ivy's companion set her down beside Jarod. "Do you see the rest of these?" he said, pointing to the other figures scattered around the base of the tree. "They are immortal shepherds, giants, those who have given deeply of themselves for their wards' sakes. They come here to renew under the shadow of Eshayl. For this reason your husband comes—to renew—but he has need of greater haste, so his brethren aid him in his recovery. He has one task yet to accomplish, one more great battle on behalf of his people, before he can rest."

Ivy stretched herself out against Jarod's chest. Compared to the other creatures, he too was small, but he was large enough that he could have picked Ivy up and carried her as easily as had his master. "When that one last battle is done…will he leave again? Will I lose him again?"

"Child, because you chose to come after me, I have made certain that you will never lose him again. You have become like him. Can you not see this? You are small, Ivy, but you will grow. With every choice, you will grow. I have so decreed it. Let me prove it to you. There is set before you now another choice. Look around you."

Ivy sat up and obeyed. She saw how all the flying creatures hovered now, watching, holding aloof from the moment. "What do I see?"

"You see what frightened you such a little while ago. When you tried to run from them before, Chike stopped you for your good." The man gestured, and one of the flying creatures descended. It was colossal, like a great winged deer with the neck of a swan and a smooth oval for its head. It stared at her with solemn blue eyes. "He guarded Kohanan until the day when Kohanan found his lost son. Now Chike guards and advises your husband." As Chike settled near Jarod's head, Ivy's companion gestured again. Another of the giants descended. This one was nearly as large as Chike, but was shaped like a stained-glass window, with its colors shifting to form exotic images of places, people, and even beasts. It draped itself over Jarod, lapping against Ivy's knees like a quilt. "Hello, little sister," it said in a faint, timid-sounding voice.

"I know your voice," Ivy answered in wonder.

"And so you ought," replied her companion. "She is Ianthe, your own shepherd. She has watched over you from the day of your birth. Here is your choice, Ivy. Your own husband has never seen these, not even his own shepherd, but they are his kin just as surely as his own brother is kin to him. Here in my own lands, you see them as easily as if they were mortals. In your own world, that will not be the case *unless* you so choose. These shepherd-giants do not always take pleasing forms, but not every hideous aspect marks a giant as evil. Some of them will frighten you. How will you choose? Keep in mind that the gift will not be taken from you, should you choose to welcome it."

"I will," Ivy answered immediately. "But how will I know the good from the bad?"

"That knowledge will come in time, as you grow stronger in this new life of yours. You can learn much from your husband in this. He has had his whole brief lifetime to learn such things." Her companion's face turned solemn. "You have been made equal to him, though, and he must learn from you as well. Are you brave enough for that, Ivy? It will not be easy. You must stand against him from time to time. He has lived his whole life as the only one of his kind, with no one to oppose his will. That will be your responsibility. You must hold him to what you both know is right and good, no matter what."

Ivy nodded. "I'll try my best."

"These elder siblings of yours will advise you."

Looking first at Ianthe and then at Chike, Ivy nodded again. "Good."

"Ianthe, show her what she must do next. The river was too subtle for her."

The shepherd-giant rose up to display the image of a mountain. A disembodied hand appeared and pointed to a pinpoint of light two-thirds of the way up the mountainside while Ianthe's voice explained, "Here the king wakes in fear even now. He will rally the servants of our little brother, and they will begin to search for you. Our little brother is not yet ready to return, but you are. You must speak on his behalf, have his body taken to shelter and cared for until he is ready. You must speak on his behalf to the king, who has only begun to understand."

"Do you see what you must do?" said Ivy's companion.

"I think so. Please," she said shyly, "will I see you again? What is your name?"

"You will know me by the same name that I have taught your husband: *Emunya*. We will meet again, Ivy. Depend upon it."

Ianthe wrapped herself around Ivy, saying, "Come along, little sister. It is time." For an instant, Ivy saw and felt nothing. Then, she opened her eyes to darkness. She blinked to be sure that her eyes were open, and gradually she realized that there were stars above her. It was night, but a line of dark blue was already growing at one horizon. Ivy felt around until she found her husband's body lying motionless beside her. She kept her hand on his chest until she felt it lift with a single breath. Thus reassured, she lay down against his side. The night air was cold. For the first time, she sensed the slope of the ground and understood that they were somewhere on the mountain that Ianthe had showed her. "Where have you gone, Ianthe?" she asked in a voice that hardly rose past a whisper.

I have gone nowhere.

"Good. There was light last time, but now it's dark. Why?"

You are safe, so you do not need us to light your way. There is evil nearby this place. Had you run away from us before, it might have taken you before our master could speak with you. Now that he has spoken with you, the evil has lost its power to harm. You are safe.

"I'm glad," Ivy yawned. "I'm so tired, and it's so cold out here."

Help is coming. Listen.

Straining her ears, Ivy listened to the whisper of the light, fitful wind that stirred the trees around her. The sound came as an echo first. Then, after a little while longer, it came again, this time distinguishable as a human voice: "Ammun!" Another voice, and yet another voice in rapid succession, cried out the same word. Ivy stood up. "Ianthe, Colin is coming, isn't he?"

He comes, yes.

"Doesn't he have a shepherd, too? Can you call to his shepherd?" Ivy waited, but rather than hearing a word, she heard a low, resonant note humming along the air, answered in time by a similar note from higher up the mountain.

Yana says that he is trying his best, but he fears that his ward is quite frantic and will not heed him. You must call, mortal voice to mortal ears, so that they will know where you are.

"Colin!" Ivy shouted, cupping her hands around her mouth. "Colin! Over here!" Within a few seconds, she saw a bobbing fleck of torchlight among the trees higher up the slope. She shouted again: "Colin!" She heard men's voices shouting, then the faint sound of horses' hooves. Then, only a few minutes later, she heard someone shout, "Where are you?" It was Colin's voice. Ivy's throat closed with tears. She had to cough before she could answer, "Colin! Down here! We're down here!"

Then it was only a matter of waiting for them to home in on the sound of her voice. As soon as one of the men was near enough for her to see his face in the light of his torch, Ivy began waving her arms to draw their attention. Soon Colin came bounding down the slope on horseback, guided by the men who were running afoot toward Ivy. Colin outpaced them easily and swung down from his horse to embrace Ivy. "What are you doing out here? Where's Jarod?"

She took Colin by the hand and showed him where his brother lay. "It's all right," she assured him quickly. "He isn't hurt. He needs somewhere warm and dry to rest, though, because he's completely spent."

"Farris!" Colin shouted. "He's here!"

By this time, men were running from all over the place, converging on the dark hollow to which Ivy had beckoned them. One, a stout warrior, knelt down immediately beside Jarod and laid a hand on his chest. "Why does he not breathe?" he demanded. "What is wrong?"

"Oh, he's breathing," Ivy answered, "but very slowly. He's very tired."

"Who is she?" the man asked Colin.

"Ammun's wife."

A murmur ran through the crowd of men. Another of them, a thin man with a powerful accent, asked her, "How came he to this?"

"Saving my life. Please, can we not take him to shelter before we sit down for a chat?"

Colin took charge. "Druze, Farris, lay him over my horse—" Then he stopped as if to listen. "No, wait." In the torchlight, Colin's expression was vague, almost absentminded, but he raised his fingers to his mouth and whistled sharply. After a pause, he whistled again.

The only warning was a last-minute thumping of paws in the underbrush. Then, startling the men, a huge cat loped into the clearing. It bent to sniff Jarod, nudged him with its nose, and then looked to Colin with a mild, quizzical expression in its eyes.

"He needs help," Colin said, kneeling down on his brother's other side. "Can you take him up the mountain? You won't let him fall." All alone, Colin lifted his brother to a sitting position while the cat lay on its side with its back to both men. Colin gave a great heave and managed to drape Jarod's inert body over the pardelé's back. Then the cat rose up. It stood for a moment with its head craned back, nudging at its burden as if to adjust its balance. Colin helped. Between the two of them, they finally had Jarod arranged suitably. The cat nodded to Colin and began to ascend the slope, sure-footed and swift.

Colin returned to Ivy. "You can ride with me. Come along. We don't want to fall too far behind." He lifted Ivy up onto his horse and mounted behind her. Leaving the others, they rode up a switchback dirt road until a few village lights were visible. Ivy gazed around at the terraced village that slept all around them, but she had little time to see much. Within minutes, they had arrived at a small manor house. The pardelé waited patiently for them on the doorstep. Colin barely remembered to help Ivy down before he ran ahead to meet the cat. "Thank you," he said respectfully, ducking under Jarod's limp arm and taking the burden of him from the cat.

The house door didn't open until the cat was gone. Then a small wave of people rushed out to help Colin carry Jarod into the house and up to the second floor. Ivy followed behind them, momentarily forgotten in all the excitement. One of them, a healer by the look of her, asked Colin, "What happened to him?" Then Colin seemed to remember Ivy at last. He took her by the hand and led her forward, while the people hushed around them.

"This is Ivy. She is Ammun's wife and friend to me and my wife. Ask her."

Suddenly the center of attention, Ivy was at a loss for answers. She sat down on the edge of the bed opposite the healer. She wasn't sure how much they knew about Jarod and what he really was, so she started out cautiously, saying, "He isn't injured. He's very, very tired. He...he saved me from a great evil, but it cost him, and he was tired already. If we just clean him up and cover him with warm blankets, he'll rest better." She heard him draw a deep breath. Something within her said, *It won't be long now.* Ivy smiled.

Unable to find any physical evidence to contradict this diagnosis, the healer shrugged eventually. "As you say. Laszlo, come and help me ready him for bed."

"Beg pardon, zahn," said another woman, drawing Ivy toward the door as the others set to work tending Jarod. "You need food? Drink?"

"That would be nice, thank you." Suddenly very tired in her own right, Ivy let Colin guide her out of the room and down the stairs to a room at the front of the house. There a warm fire crackled on the hearth. Colin deposited Ivy in a chair and tucked a blanket around her knees. "You've had a hard night, I can tell. What exactly happened? What's going on at home?"

Ivy sensed his restlessness, so she said, "A lot of trouble. Maia is holding up well. She was glad to see Selie again." She began her account with the midsummer festival and the upheaval surrounding it. From there, she told Colin as plainly and truly as she could the things that had happened in King's City: about how there was a monster wandering the streets at night, about how it had begun feeding off the unwary, about how she had watched all of this in a kind of vision-state until she had seen it go after her brother Nässey. "It was my fault," she said dully. "I begged him to do something, to save Nässey for my sake, and he did it. He left me to save my brother, and while he was gone, the monster came after me. I was very foolish. I never knew—that is, I'd heard all the old stories, but I thought they couldn't be true. Such strange, unnatural things happened in them, so I thought they were just stories, but they turned out true after all. I let it take hold of me without knowing what it was—unsuspecting, never asking any questions, just believing everything it told me. I remember now," she added, speaking even as she realized it, "how Uncle Owen always used to say, 'the dead can't speak.' I talked to the monster and told it all sorts of things it shouldn't have known, all because I never remembered that the dead don't talk to the living. I've been very foolish. Now I'm scared, Colin. So much depends on *him*." She glanced upwards, as if she could see her husband through the ceiling. "I've weakened him. He exhausted himself to save me. Now he has another battle to fight, and he's so tired; I don't know what will happen."

Colin looked sharply at her. "What battle?"

"I wasn't told, but I imagine he has to fight the Unclean."

He rose up and paced to the door, where he paused for a moment to listen to the noises filtering down the stairs from the second floor. Then he turned back, shut the door securely against the rest of the household, and demanded, "How long have you known who he is?"

Ivy smiled a little at that. "Since I got to know Lucky. Lucky has a habit of looking sidelong at you when he has something personal to say to you, just like Jarod used to do—back when he wasn't as sure of himself as he is now," she added with tired amusement. "It was always there, I think, waiting for me to take hold of it. I wasn't looking for it to happen, so I didn't see it until I couldn't help seeing it in Lucky. He's such a wonderful boy. Like his father."

"I didn't even see it then," Colin replied. His voice was almost bitter. "Why, Ivy?"

"If I knew what you were asking, maybe I could try answering."

"I talked to him. I *talked* to him, Ivy, and he talked to me, but I still didn't see it. He never said a word, never gave me a hint."

Ivy sighed, not eager to say what she knew she had to say, but it wouldn't wait. Her husband might wake up at any time, and Colin had to be ready. "He's been saying it all along, just in his own way. Do you know, I don't think he realizes that I know his name yet? I didn't tell him I knew. I was waiting for him to say something first…and, you know, I've had a lot to think about, too. Lucky, for one—he's a wonderful boy and I adore him, but…Jarod has been places and done things that I never thought he could…" She sighed again, remembering the sting of that first realization embodied in a child, the proof of his father's faithlessness. "And he never said anything when he *did* come back, and that hurt a little, but now that I've thought on it, he really *did* say something. He said to me a while ago that knowing his name wouldn't tell me any more about him than I already knew. You see, Colin? He isn't the Jarod we knew. As far as it goes, I don't think we knew him even then. All these years, I've lived with the memory of who I thought he was—who I wanted him to be. He's been telling us all this time that we don't know him, and we never knew him, but Colin, he *wants* to be known. He wants to be named. He's just waiting for us to do it. I think he's a little afraid of us."

"When did I ever give him reason to be afraid?" Colin asked, dumbfounded.

"Maybe it wasn't anything you did. Maybe it just comes from being what he is."

Colin gazed at her in blank surprise for a few moments before he gathered his wits and said, "Do *you* know what he is? I certainly don't."

Ivy thought, *How do I explain this to him? I don't really know it myself.*

Softly, Ianthe answered, *Speak, and I will instill the words in you.*

"He is…" Ivy paused. "He is something new…a—a whisper of things to come. He's a demigiant, partly man and partly giant, like a—a bridge from them to us." Even as she said the words, Ivy said to herself in wonder, *And so am I, now.* "What he is now, someday others will be. I don't know much more than that. As mortals go, he's very powerful, even more powerful than a seer. All this time, he's been learning how to use the immortal part of his nature." An inward image of a corrupted shepherd-giant solidified in her thoughts. Comprehension dawned. "Do you know how the old stories all say that every mortal has a shepherd-giant? Well, Jarod's first shepherd was evil. It tried to corrupt him, to make him hurt people. No wonder he tried to stay away from us. He has always tried to protect us, even from himself. Now he's free and he can come home again. He's only waiting to see if we'll have him. He's waiting on *us.*"

Colin slumped into a chair beside Ivy's. He put his head in his hands and said nothing for a while. The housekeeper came in with food and drink on a tray. Ivy thanked her, and the woman left them again. While Ivy ate, she watched Colin struggle with himself. A stirring swept through her spirit all of a sudden: *He comes.* She put aside her half-emptied tray. "He's coming back even now. I'll talk to him first. If you're ready, then I'll call for you to come." Ignoring Colin's amazed look, Ivy went back upstairs to her husband's room.

The healer held vigil at Jarod's bedside. Ivy stayed a few steps away from the bed and listened to the wind as it tossed the treetops violently. It sounded like a storm was sweeping through the mountain, gaining momentum by the minute. The walls of the house stood firm against the wind, muffling it, but Ivy felt a different sort of storm approaching. When she looked out the windows, she saw a legion of giants racing through the air towards the house. Their approach was terrifying. Ivy gripped the window sill to steady herself. She reminded herself that these creatures were now her brethren and meant her no harm. Soon the house was surrounded by them as by a wall. *A shield,* Ivy thought suddenly. *To protect him while he's weak.*

"Ivy!"

She turned at the sound of her name on his lips. He was awake, propped up on his elbows as he gazed around in confusion at these different surroundings. Ivy went to him. "I'm here. Don't worry." She nodded to dismiss the healer.

Her husband fell back into his pillows, relaxing, but his confusion was still evident. "What—? This is my own house…but how did we—?"

Smoothing the covers across his chest, Ivy said, "You exhausted yourself. You've only just come back. Don't worry. Everything will be all right." She leaned forward and kissed him. "I will look after you for a change."

"I have to get back to King's City. The danger—"

I have told you before, the shepherd-giant Chike said mildly, *you do not yet have the strength to carry the world. Do as she tells you.*

"Thank you," Ivy said, smiling. "There, you see? Even he agrees with me."

Jarod stared at her in open-mouthed astonishment. "You…heard…"

"Of course I heard him. He's sitting right there." Ivy pointed at the shepherd-giant. "I think he sounds highly sensible. You need your rest. The hardest is still ahead of you, after all."

"I don't understand."

"When you've rested, we'll talk all about it." Leaning forward to kiss him again, Ivy took advantage of his bewilderment to slide his mask off. "And I'm sure you'll rest much easier without *that* thing. At the least, I'll have to have someone wash it. It has Nässey's blood on it. By the way…thank you. You saved him." She kissed him again.

Staring back at her bare-faced, her husband seemed utterly lost. When she stroked the side of his face, he finally spoke. "How long have you known?"

"I have no idea how anyone could know Lucky and *not* know. Since you wouldn't say anything, though, I thought maybe it was time for me to speak. While I'm on the subject…Colin wants to see you. He's downstairs, waiting."

"He knows?"

Ivy nodded. It intrigued her to see how Jarod averted his eyes to the windows. "I'll bring him," she said.

Outside the bedroom, she didn't have to go far. Colin leaned against the opposite wall and sprang upright as soon as he saw her. "He's awake?"

"Yes. Try to keep it to only a few words. He's still very tired and very weak."

When they entered, the bed was empty. Jarod stood with his back to them while he gazed out the windows to the east. He was leaning his head against the window frame, and his hands were unsteady as they propped him up against the window sill. Ivy looked to Colin in silence, giving the moment over to him. Colin went to stand beside Jarod. "See here," he said clumsily, "you shouldn't be out of bed yet."

"I suppose not." The effort it took Jarod to take those few steps from the window to the bed seemed to drain him. He sank into his pillows and stared dully at the ceiling for a moment.

"You've missed a lot while you were away," Colin began with hesitation. "We have a new prisoner in the jail, thanks mainly to Giles. You see, Damon finally tracked down the letters and such that proved Malin and Simon were allies all along, so he sent word for us to give him a small raiding company to help him get hold of the proof. Then Malin hit Beldene and took prisoners, so Rafe had to put together a company to get them back. I...I went, because Niall and Greysin thought it would help their cause if somebody went dressed as you, and Giles went because he was the only one who knew the layout of Takra well enough to navigate the halls in the dark. He and Greysin went in for the papers while the rest of them snatched up the Beldene prisoners. While they were inside the house, Giles knocked into Malin—literally, knocked into him headlong and stunned him—so Giles and Greysin grabbed him along with the papers and brought him back in chains. And they burned his house to the ground."

"Giles?" Ivy exclaimed. "My Giles?"

The account had drawn a weary smile to Jarod's face. "So he's found his footing at last?"

"I'd say so," Colin said with a grin. "He and young Ingram are inseparable. I think he knows the entire village by name. Druze has been hinting that some of the more recent pranks were carried out largely under Giles' initiative. Apparently, the boy has a good head for tactics." Colin stood up. "Well, you need your rest, and I need to go tell everyone that you're well. I'll...I'll see you in the morning?" Without looking at Jarod, Colin strode hastily from the room.

An awkward silence followed his exit. Ivy shut the door and went to the bed, where she found her husband looking a little downcast. "He'll be more like himself in the morning. No doubt, so will you. Is there anything you need at the moment?"

Jarod rallied himself to meet her eyes. "Only you." A yawn overtook him, and when it was finished, he added ruefully, "And a few more hours of sleep."

DESCENDANTS OF KINGS

Maia fell asleep to the enticing aroma of tea brewed from the leaves of the Prince's Tree. A premonition had goaded her to order the brewing of several jugs, a task that Meghala and her squad carried out over the course of the afternoon. By nightfall, the scent permeated the entire eastern half of the house. Maia noticed that the soldiers who brewed the tea were more at ease than were the rest of their comrades. Everyone was tense. Everyone sensed that trouble was near at hand—but none more acutely than Maia.

She slept, but her sleep was troubled. In one of her dreams, she saw a mosaic come to life, its colors shifting so that all of the crimson fragments clotted together like spilled blood. In another dream, she thought she saw Takra House burning. Mountains had grown up around it to hedge it away from the world, and marauders encamped on all sides of the house. She thought she saw Giles riding a pardelé, fleeing the ravaged house. The burning of Takra House featured largely in several of her dreams; so did death, her own among others'. Sometimes she was older by several years, and sometimes there was an infant involved, but none of the dreams made sense. Maia awoke after each and fell back to sleep immediately, so the night seemed to pass in flashes of consciousness alternating with vague intimations of fear. At two o'clock in the morning, she awoke to the sound of a distant chime. Her heart was pounding so fast that she couldn't catch her breath. "Aliya," she said loudly, her tone one of command. "Aliya, wake up."

The female guard who slept on the couch across the room came upright like a puppet on strings. "Yes, milady, what is it?"

"Where did Meg put the tea?"

"I believe it's in the kitchen, milady."

"All of it?"

"The lieutenant sent up a jug to the sitting room, in case you needed any. Should I fetch some for you?"

"No. Come with me." Maia shoved her feet into her house slippers. Wrapping herself in a light dressing gown, she hurried out into the sitting room to startle another of her guards. "Raven! There isn't much time. Something is going to happen tonight, probably within the hour. Go downstairs and warn everyone else who's on duty tonight. I'm going upstairs to wake everyone who's on rest. Hurry!" She saw him to the stairs. When he descended, she ascended with the Alti woman Aliya close at her heels. Maia ran along the hall, pounding on doors to rouse her off-duty guards. As it turned out, only Meg's squad was at rest. Maia gathered all seven of the warriors around her. "Something is going to happen tonight. I'm afraid it'll be something really serious."

She had no time to say anything beyond that. From outside, a shrill Alti war cry rose in the night air, only to be cut off with disturbing swiftness. The sound, as brief as it was, electrified the guards around Maia. Meghala took Maia by the shoulders and drew her toward the wall while the others fanned out to place themselves between the princess and any paths of attack. Then, frozen in place, they listened for any indication of what was happening. Meg spoke softly. "Iniko—the window. Careful."

The weathered immigrant Iniko Raviv went to the window at the end of the corridor, keeping well out of sight as he peered out into the night. He squinted. "Third marshal's colors on the wall, lieutenant. If ours aren't dead, they're prisoners. Must be four of them for each of ours. P'raps more."

Rapid footsteps resounded in the stairwell. Four of Maia's guards formed a human wall at the top, ready to stop anyone who tried to break through, but then a voice commanded, "Stand down!" The soldiers fell back. That voice belonged to another of their lieutenants, Hollister, who shot out of the stairway. Skidding to a halt before Maia, he said, "Good. I went to your rooms first—you weren't there—" Far below, a dull, thunderous sound interrupted him. "They've broken through," Hollister breathed. The noise of combat rose up to confirm his statement. "There's no going down. We'll have to seal off the stairway and try to hold this floor."

"No."

Maia's sudden contradiction drew everyone's attention. She went to the trap door of the attic and pulled it open. "Do nothing. Don't make it look like anyone is defending anything up here. We'll go higher up. They won't find us there."

"What are you—" The Caretaker warrior Meghala gaped as the trap door swung down and a ladder descended. "In all the years I've lived and worked in this house...How did you know that was there? How long has it *been* there?"

"Later. Everybody up." Maia led them up the ladder into the attic. When the last guard had followed her, she pulled the trap door shut again. For good measure, she pulled the cord taut and tied it to a dusty chair. "Tread lightly," she warned the others. "Don't knock anything over. Here, that won't do. Come over to this side, where the window is." She herded them into the makeshift bedchamber that Giles and she had explored on that afternoon that now seemed a lifetime ago. Once she had them safely gathered together, she said, "This is my teacher's place. It's for when you need to get away. He made it for himself—don't ask me how—long ago."

"How can they not find us here?" Hollister asked. "Surely they'll search the house."

"Meg never knew this was here, and her kinfolk have been all over the house—haven't you, Meg? We'll be all right here."

Iniko added what they were all thinking: "For now. We've no supplies, no escape, so we have to go back down, soon or late."

∗   ∗   ∗   ∗

"Speak," demanded the third marshal.

"Sir, we have made a thorough search of the residential wing. There are no more guards left to resist, but we...we have not found the princess yet. The servants appear to have left, also. The men report a bad odor, not unlike the odor left after a plague."

Simon shook his head. "No. The princess is alive. The servants may have left, but I sense no such thing about her. She must be somewhere in the house. Keep looking. Pay no attention to the odor. How many prisoners do we hold now?"

"Six, sir, all wounded. The rest would not surrender."

"Are you certain that none escaped?"

"We cannot be completely certain, sir, but all the tallies suggest that we caught or killed all that were on duty."

"What of the off-duty guards?"

"I've dispatched men to seek them out, sir. I expect to hear the results before sunrise."

"Very well. You're dismissed for now." Simon saw how the young soldier couldn't help but hurry out of his presence. They all did it now that he had acquired such vast, unimaginable power. It was right that they should fear him. He was immortal now, wielding life and death among the lesser beings. As he paced back and forth on the dais in the empty petition hall, waiting for the next report to come, Simon examined his situation. He had seized Takra House with a minimum of cost to his own forces. The much-vaunted royal guard corps had fallen to his hand-picked elite with hardly a whimper, leaving Simon in a position of total command. All he lacked was the princess in his possession, and he would have unassailable control of the kingdom. Not even old Lord Sakiry could gainsay him, not when the princess publicly announced Simon as her consort, and she would, one way or another. Simon had given this a great deal of thought and had concluded that he had only as much use for her as he had control over her. To gain the control he needed, Simon knew he had to introduce her to his newfound power. He therefore had to find out where she was hiding before the sun rose.

He sensed her presence within the walls of Takra House. He knew she was there still, alive and in hiding. He could feel her. When he tried to home in on that sensation, however, it eluded him. Something was protecting her. The knowledge tantalized him by its persistence, but still he couldn't pin down its source. She was there, and time was in short supply. When morning came and the gates didn't open, which they couldn't if Simon wasn't yet in full control of the situation, people would take alarm. Without the princess' assurance that he had her consent, he would lose what support remained to him among the people. If he had to do it, he would conquer by force of arms, but that meant armies and vast expenditures and needless destruction, followed by more costs for rebuilding. It would be so much more efficient to avoid open warfare…if only he could find the princess.

*   *   *   *

It was an odd sort of council of war that gathered in Denei's house late into the night. As the highest-ranking participant, Owen sat enthroned in a deep, comfortable chair at their head. Byram Solam-son sat at his right hand, with Doran seated at *his* right hand, heartily glad to be able to step down in favor of a more experienced marshal for once. The hall clock chimed a quarter past two, instilling a moment of silence into the conversation. From his seat at Owen's left hand, Ronán Heir Alti exchanged inaudible comments with his Sea Folk associate Durrant son of Dermot. Neither of them looked especially pleased at the inclusion of the three foreigners at the opposite side of the room. Contrasted against their peevish ill-humor, Loren and his comrades showed nothing of their feelings about being ushered into conference with such exalted company. Those three knew how to keep their own counsel, Owen reflected. So far, he hadn't heard a sound from any of them, although they followed the discussion with keen attention. Owen was inclined to approve of them, Loren in particular.

"Everything points to trouble," Durrant said. "There's no doubt in my mind: Miklei-son is going to try something. If the general is missing, we have to handle it ourselves. I trust that you still believe us capable of taking care of our own, Lord Sakiry?"

Owen smiled politely, ignoring the tenor of the question. "I don't doubt that you and Ronán are capable of handling any mortal threat that Miklei-son poses. That is not what troubles me. The fact that the general is my kinsman is enough to give me cause for concern over his disappearance, along with my niece. What you seem to have missed, both of you, is that Miklei-son does not merely pose a mortal threat. He has allied himself with the Unclean, and that is a threat that surpasses all our ability. That, my dear fellows, is why we need the general."

Durrant looked just as obstinate as ever. Ronán, on the other hand, had a thoughtful look. "We cannot come to a conclusion tonight. The hour is late. I suggest we call an end to the day and reconvene in the morning, when we've had time to sleep on it."

"That's as good an idea as we've had yet," Owen admitted. "You must both stay here as our guests, gentlemen. Then we can resume our talks first thing in the morning."

The Sea Folk warrior and the heir to the Alti patriarchy offered suitable thanks and followed the housemaid to guest rooms upstairs, leaving the assembly freer for discussion in the stuffy front parlor. "What about it, Byram?" Owen said. "You know him better than any of us."

Byram paused for thought. At length, he admitted, "I don't know much, and that's the truth. Judging by what you said, it *looked* like death. Nothing else fits the description."

"Ta isn't dead," a defiant voice announced suddenly, startling them all. Owen turned to find young Lucien curled up on a pillow in the corner, watching them. "He isn't dead," the boy repeated. "I know he isn't. He'll be back."

The young boy's conviction touched Owen, but it didn't stop him from thinking, *If I were him, I wouldn't want to believe it either. Jarod is all the family he ever had.*

Loren intervened. "Even so, Luck, until he does come back, we're in a bad place."

"It's good of you to take this on yourself," Owen said to the young warrior. "I know these are not your people. I thank you for your assistance."

"Ammun's people *are* my people, Lord Sakiry. Besides," he added, "Colin's daughter is as brave as they come. I am sorry that she must go through this without her father. I know he would want me to do what he cannot presently do himself."

"Whatever the reason, I'm glad for it." Yawning, Owen turned to his son-in-law. "Doran, you ought to head home and get some sleep, too, while the night lasts."

"With your permission, Father, I'll just find a corner somewhere in the house here. The house is a little empty with Phoebe at Eleusia." Doran spoke distractedly, hardly paying attention to what he said while he gazed out the window instead of at Owen. "I don't like this night. It's a blood night."

Loren gave him a sidelong look. "What does that mean?"

Seeing that Doran seemed to have missed the question entirely, Owen said, "Doran has a powerful gift for healing. With it comes a certain set of instincts. He can smell blood, even in minute quantities—sickness, too. He knows when someone has died or is direly hurt, for example. If it only involves one or two people, it isn't usually enough to trouble him, but a battle or widespread contagion can leave him sleepless for days." Owen raised his voice. "Rowan!"

Rowan appeared at the door in moments. "Aye?"

"Doran is having one of his moments. Have the yard and the street searched thoroughly. There might be someone nearby who is injured and in need of a healer."

Rowan disappeared. From a distant part of the house, a subdued hubbub rose as the soldiers of Owen's guard corps were sent on their way. Owen knew that Rowan was sensible enough to look after his own men, that none of the guards would go out alone, but still he became uneasy. Doran remained vague and ill at ease, even after Rowan returned to say that the neighborhood rested peacefully. Because Doran was unable to sleep, Owen refused to sleep as well. He dismissed everyone who wanted to go. None of the outland warriors moved from their places. "There's no reason for you to stay up," Owen said to Loren.

"As sorry as I am to contradict you, Lord Sakiry, I disagree. If you'd been around Ammun long enough, you'd know. When he has forebodings like this, you learn to keep your boots on and wait for trouble to fall. The first marshal draws from the same source, I'd guess, so the same reasoning applies."

Silence held perfect sway in the house after that. Owen felt the sweat trickle down his back and ribs in the sultry night air. The air was close enough to suggest the coming of bad weather, which would have set him on edge by itself, had Doran's presentiments not already done so. Owen tried to calm himself with the thought that a vigorous rainstorm would be the best thing for all concerned—for the farmers, yes, but also for those who suffered in the sweltering cities. He tried to distract himself by reckoning the last time they had received measurable rainfall, but springtime seemed so far in the past that he was unable to remember it. Then he tried to discipline himself to recall the events of the season, everything that had led up to this present moment of awful waiting. He made it as far as the murderous attack on Tyrell before his ears perked at the sound of hooves approaching at a brisk pace.

Everyone else had stiffened at the noise. When the horse clattered to a halt in front of the house, Loren sprang up and ran to investigate. The rest of them followed as far as the entry hall in time to see Temora, a lieutenant of Owen's guard corps, charge through the doorway. She swept the assembly with a gaze and settled on Doran. "Chief Healer," she said, "you must come with me at once. There's no time to explain. Takra has been attacked. One of theirs made it clear to warn us, but he's badly hurt and hardly able to speak."

Already, Loren was speaking to his comrades in Kavahran, dispatching them in different directions. Owen spared them a glance before he turned to Doran. "Find out what you can. We'll summon all the help we can find. Send someone to us when you know what's going on. Rowan, you're well able to handle that job. Where are *you* going?" he demanded of Loren at last.

"To Takra House, my lord."

"And what do you think you'll accomplish there?"

Loren bowed, but his bearing was anything but subservient. "I have been trained far differently from your warriors, Lord Sakiry. I can but do what I have been taught."

*   *   *   *

By dawn, they knew the truth. Eraste, the only guard to have escaped the lightning siege of Takra House, lay on the threshold of death, having delivered his message despite wounds that made Owen's more experienced guards flinch to look at them. Jarod's outland allies, once they had left Owen in the night, seemed completely to have disappeared, but Owen had no time to wonder where they were. He welcomed an incessant stream of visitors at his late brother's house. Since he had no reassurance to offer the civilian leadership, he greeted them calmly and found them places to sit in the oppressively hot, overcrowded sitting room. From there, however, he kept them as quiet as politically inclined men could reasonably be expected to be.

In the middle of the afternoon, when tempers frayed by anxiety had reached their thinnest point, Owen saw Rowan gesturing for him to come out into the entry hall. Rowan looked grimly satisfied by something, so Owen got up immediately without so much as a word to anyone else in the room. "What is it? You!" he exclaimed in surprise. There beside Rowan stood Loren, grubby and slick with sweat. "What news do you bring?"

"If you'll come with us, your lordship, I wager you'll learn some news indeed."

They escorted Owen out the front door, where the general's carriage had drawn up close to the steps. Inside, Owen said, "I don't suppose I merit a hint, do I?"

"We've done what we could, and good came of it, your lordship. As for the rest, you'll have to hear it for yourself from the source." Though he smiled as he said it, Loren would add nothing to this answer. He leaned back with his hands clasped behind his head as if he had no cares. When the carriage stopped, he sprang out and held the door open for Owen. They were at the infirmary. Owen was intrigued to note that the guards standing outside stepped aside for Loren without either word or gesture required. "Through here, your lordship." He guided Owen through to the cubicles, where an inordinate number of soldiers kept watch.

A murmur heralded Owen's coming. Near the opposite end of the main aisle, Doran stuck his head out of a cubicle. He had a grin on his face that heartened Owen. "Down here, Father." Then he drew his head back into the cubicle like a bivalve into its shell.

Owen went expecting anything but what he found. Doran was working over the injuries of Morio, one of Maia's lieutenants. "What is this?"

"Four more snatched back from death," Doran answered. "Thanks to the general's friends. Loren, you tell him. I want Morio to keep still for a while yet."

"As I said, your lordship, we did as we have been trained to do. Our teachers, our *natai*, are nearly all ex-raiders, you see, so we have been taught their ways. When we left you, we went to the walls of Takra House and observed the move-

ments of the house. It was clear to me that the house had been overtaken by enemies, but they were too active for men who had secured their territory
completely. They searched the grounds more than once, and I saw them through
the windows, searching the house again and again. By sunup, they refused to
open the gates to the first visitors, and trouble started stirring on the south side of
the walls. We slipped over the north side and went inside to see what we could
see. There were lights in the western end, down on the ground floor. They were
keeping their prisoners there, four of them. Six of us were enough to dispatch the
enemies who remained, those who hadn't gone to see what was to be done at the
front of the house. We brought the prisoners back over the wall and to the infirmary for the good healer here to tend. They bring with them better news than
we'd hoped."

"What news?" Owen demanded.

Morio roused from his pain to answer, "They haven't found the princess yet."

Owen sank down onto his haunches beside the cot, weakened with relief.
"Why not? Where is she?"

"I don't know, my lord. It started out that Raven came through to warn us, on
his way to warn those on the walls. The princess knew something was hanging
over our heads. We were on alert, but even at that, we hardly stood a chance.
There were at least three of them for each one of us. We held out for not quite an
hour inside the house, without much hope. By the time they overwhelmed us,
there were six of us left, all of us hurt to some extent." Morio gestured carelessly
to his side and the gash there that curved around from navel to shoulderblade.
"They kept us in the kitchen at first, until they complained of a stench and
moved us to the petition hall. By then, I heard one of them say they couldn't find
the princess. There were six of us until they started questioning us one by one,
trying to force out of us information that we didn't possess. We didn't know
where she is any more than they did, but it didn't stop them from trying."

"Questioning you?" Doran said ominously.

"That's what they called it. It's a pretty word for torture, isn't it? They started
with Danya, but she spit in their faces and rebuked them up until the very last."
Morio blinked back a sudden rush of grief. "Brave woman, that one. Hanno was
hurt worst of us all, so they started on him next. He didn't last long. Then they
started on Isaac. He's a tough lad," he added specifically to Rowan. "They didn't
get the time of day from him, not even after the—" Morio winced as Doran
applied a cleansing medicine to a raw wound, "—the traitor joined the inquisi-
tion. I've never been so proud to call a younger man my commander, my lord.
Wounds and all, young Isaac stood face to face with the Unclean and told him

where he could stuff his questions. They would've done something irreparable to him then, but there was that uproar at the front gate that my friend here mentioned before. Don't let him fool you, my lord. The traitor went out to deal with it, but he left more than a dozen guards to continue with us while he was gone. Loren and his companions are men, my lord. I wouldn't regret knowing them better, if I'm spared so long."

"We'll do our best to see that you get your chance," Doran said. "Rest now and let others take up the fight for a while." He finished wrapping the last wound and took Owen out of the cubicle. "Four," he said in an undertone. "Morio, Isaac, Idreis, and Dai's young Sam."

"Those numbers are appalling. Five spared out of thirty? And all we know from them is that Maia isn't a prisoner yet. Where could she be?"

"Even negative knowledge is of use," Loren said out of the blue. "If she isn't held prisoner, then she's free. If she's free, then we still have a chance to help her. We just have to figure out where she might be before *they* figure it out. We'd best start now."

Owen nodded, already thinking it through. "Let's buy ourselves some time. Come. We need Durrant and Ronán for this."

*　　*　　*　　*

"Your highness?"

"Yes," Maia said, rousing herself from the stupor imposed by the heat of the day, "what is it, Isam?"

"We were talking over there, me, Iniko, and young Jules. It doesn't matter if they can't find us, not if we die of thirst up here. We were talking about what we might do to fix that."

"And...?"

"There's those jugs of tea that the healer had us brew up," the guard said, "one of 'em in your parlor and one in the picture gallery downstairs. Now, we don't stand much of a chance getting anything from as far away as the kitchen, but we thought we might get that jug in the gallery downstairs without too much trouble. That'll hold us over for a while, if we're careful."

"It sounds like a good idea. What have you heard lately?"

"Not much, not for a while. Now's the time, your highness."

Maia took a steadying breath and nodded her consent. "If you think you can do it, then do it. I won't deny that I'm getting plenty thirsty myself. A cup of cool tea would be good. Just don't take chances if you don't have to."

"Not to worry about that, your highness." Isam withdrew to relay the conversation to his fellow guards. The three of them whispered together a little. When they had settled the business between them, they went to the trap door. Iniko, an experienced ex-raider, untied the cord and began to inch the trap door open with his head at the opening. He was so slow in opening the door that Maia thought perhaps someone might be in the corridor below them, but eventually he let out the cord to its full length and shifted so Jules, the youngest of them, could drop down into the third floor hallway. Iniko watched for a few seconds before he shut the trap door to a slit again.

They waited an uncomfortably long time, all the while listening not only for Jules' return, but for indications of discovery and pursuit. An unpleasant realization occurred to Maia during this interim: if Jules was discovered, he couldn't come back to them or he would expose them all. He would have to flee for his life. For a few moments, Maia couldn't hear anything but the drum of her own heart in her ears. *Jules is taking so long; if he were only sneaking to the picture gallery, it wouldn't take him this long.* But she took heart when she saw how patiently Iniko waited at the trap door. He made no sign that he thought anything had gone wrong. Then he made a soft noise to Isam. The cord that held the trap door hissed between his fingers as he let the door drop. A jug soared up from the third floor corridor; Isam caught it and set it aside. Together he and Iniko hefted Jules back into the attic by his arms. Then the door shut, and Maia breathed again.

"What did you see?" Isam asked.

"They dumped the jug out on the gallery floor," Jules said, his breath short from the combination of nerves and exertion. "I had to go down to the princess' parlor for the other one. I guess, it being under the table and all, they didn't notice that one. Something's going on outside that's keeping them busy. I thought I heard a battering ram outside."

The two older warriors nodded with satisfaction. Iniko said, "General won't let us stay up here too much longer."

They woke the others from their "off-duty" nap, but when everyone was gathered, the guards glanced at each other in embarrassment, like a host who has underestimated the amount of food needed for his dinner guests. "Um," said Jules shamefacedly, "I didn't think to pick up cups or anything. Sorry."

"What," Maia retorted, mindful of the need to keep her voice down, "don't tell me none of you has ever shared a canteen with anyone before! Don't be silly. We'll be fine drinking straight from the jug."

Meghala hefted the jug in her arms and said, "Fair enough, miss. If it doesn't bother you, then all's well. You first." She steadied the jug so that Maia could drink from it. Then she passed it on to Osgood, a guard several years her elder, with a quip: "Age before beauty."

Maia leaned back against a dusty table leg. For a day-old brew, that tea had refreshed her far more than she had expected. Even the odor of it brought a sense of freshness to the stale, muggy air of the attic. It certainly enlivened the guards. Confinement suited none of them. Maia knew that if she couldn't keep her mind off of the certain death that had befallen their comrades below, then that contemplation must have been weighing on her guards a hundredfold. Although their situation had scarcely changed, they all seemed a little cheerier for drinking that tea. The jug made its way all around the circle. Meg kept warning them to save as much as possible and drink only a little. Will, one of the other young guards, made a droll face. "Yes, mother."

"If I were your mother," Meg replied with a dire expression, declining to finish the threat.

"She'd never admit such a homely hatchling ever tumbled from her nest," Hollister said. "Come to think of it, I don't know that I've ever seen your mother acknowledge you in public, Will. Isn't that odd?"

Will pulled another face, this time for Hollister's benefit. Jules, Will's best friend, spoke up then. "Oh, she acknowledges him at the top of her lungs often enough. That's how come he runs so fast. Pity we didn't think to send him after the jug." He glanced at Maia and, encouraged by her amusement, added, "Come to think of it, it's a real pity we don't have that friend of yours—Giles, was that his name? I never saw anyone scamper like him; put Will and me to shame. What became of him, your highness? If you don't mind my asking," he added belatedly.

"I don't know."

There was compassion in Hollister's look when he urged Jules, "Tell the rest of them your story. I don't think Iniko over there has heard it yet."

So Jules and Will began to recount how Giles had led the two of them on a full-out dash around King's City, "as if we were country bumpkins and he were giving us the tour," Will said with a laugh. Before long, they had brought the smile back to Maia's face. The jug of tea went around the circle again so that each of them could have another mouthful, and the hours slid onward toward dusk.

*   *   *   *

The call went out midway through the morning. For once, Berhus did nothing to obstruct the massing of other clans' soldiers on his land. He made room in his stables for their horses and let the riders sleep in the hay mow above the horses. He seemed more relieved to be of assistance than annoyed or even worried. Owen thought he knew the reason. As unpleasant as it must have been for Berhus at the time, his humiliating public abasement to Jarod at the midsummer festival had placed Berhus beyond suspicion now that his favored candidate had shown himself for the traitor he was. Everything Berhus was called upon to contribute to this campaign served only to further distance himself from Simon.

Loren or one of his companions stayed within sight of Owen at every moment, freeing Owen's guards to join in the assault on the grounds of Takra House. This would have surprised Owen, had he not heard fragments of conversation among his guards that explained it adequately. The rescue of Isaac and the other three surviving guards was on its way to becoming legend, and Owen's guards were setting the tone for the way other warriors treated these men. Giving Owen into their care was a mark of trust that no one could dismiss. Owen didn't mind. He had taken a liking to Loren and was perfectly content to have him nearby for advice and companionship during the long, stifling afternoon hours.

They had chosen a cautious approach. The goal, as Owen kept stressing to Durrant, was to harass the traitors, keep them distracted, and create confusion around the grounds of Takra House. For this, there was no need to risk any casualties on their own side than were absolutely unavoidable. Durrant made little comment about this. He had professed to admire what Loren and his friends had accomplished, but he made it subtly clear that he wasn't pleased to play decoy so that they could dart inside Takra House to make clandestine searches. Every time one of the outlanders came back to report a failed search, Durrant snorted. He never said a word, but the snort became more pronounced with each unsuccessful attempt. At one point, when Durrant snorted with particular vehemence, Rowan offered him a handkerchief so pointedly that the snorts subsided.

Just before true dark, they were in Denei's front room awaiting the next report when they heard the sound of a horse ridden hard. "Someone's coming," Loren said idly, raising his eyes from the knife he was sharpening. The steady rasp of the whetstone ceased. Loren handed the blade and the whetstone to young Lucien and bid him carry on the work while he went out to meet this newest turn of events. Owen followed.

"Well, I never," Loren muttered. He snapped to attention as the rider entered. "Natai."

Owen himself was without words as he gazed upon a face he had thought never to see again. "Greysin Alti," he breathed. "You live?"

"Yes, my lord. I bring advance word: the king is on his way."

"Colin's coming?"

"Yes, my lord. He, the general, and the general's lady, all together. They are all well, although—" Greysin paused. "I worry for Ammun, my lord. He is but partially recovered from whatever ordeal brought him to us so suddenly, and he means to engage the Unclean when he arrives. I would not say this to any but you, and I beg you not to let it spread beyond us, my lord, and not only because Ammun would be severely displeased if he knew I had spoken thus."

"No worries on that account. He'll never know from me. How long until they come?"

"I'm half a day ahead of them; they're riding that hard on my heels."

"Half a day," mused Owen, calculating the time. "Here by dawn?"

"They meant not to stop. My lord, I have something to say to you in private."

Loren bowed out and returned to the sitting room. Owen gestured for Greysin to join him in the study at the end of the house. "What now?"

Greysin went directly to the writing desk. From within his jacket, he withdrew a weatherproof packet full of papers. He spread the papers over the desk's surface. "First, I must explain that these documents were seized from the favorite stronghold of Malin Fohral'aku just before we burned it to the ground. Only Ammun, the king, and I have seen what's in them. I was instructed to give them to you in this manner, without notifying anyone else." He stepped back to give Owen unobstructed access to the papers.

They were letters, for the most part, sealed with a cheap form of wax common to students and impoverished teachers. There was no identifying mark on the seal, only an anonymous square indentation. The handwriting was legible, but not distinctive. It could have been the hand of any hired scribe or notary. Owen read the contents of the first and realized that they were business letters. The writer was offering to the reader something like a contract, the terms to be worked out in a subsequent exchange of correspondence. He leafed through the sheets until he found the one bearing the subsequent date. Sure enough, it bore witness to a treaty wherein the writer promised the reader weapons and other sundry military-related supplies in exchange for a set date and time of attacks. The dates corresponded to attacks by the raiders on Colin's forces, although the target of these attacks was never specified in the text of the letters. The crux of the agreement was that the attackers should pull back upon a predetermined signal, giving the victory to the writer of the letters after wreaking suitable amounts of damage upon their target. Owen exhaled. Further examination of the papers showed that there was no way to identify the writer conclusively. Each letter had been carefully composed to leave out key information. Then he found a pair of sheets that were different, not letters but bills of lading. Eagerly, he scanned through them, noting vaguely that they were authorizations for the shipment of a large quantity of arms and armor from a well-established Pamirsi armorer to an unspecified outland buyer. Owen knew the rules governing such transactions. That was why he skimmed over the main body of inventory in search of the signatures at the bottom. Every sizable export of any sort had to be signed by two members of the Council; exports of a military nature needed the signatures of two Cabinet members. Just as he suspected, the first signature was none other than that of Simon son of Miklei—proof of his collaboration with Malin Fohral'aku, an undeniably treasonous act by itself. Owen was still exultant over this discovery when his eyes fell upon the second signature, which stopped Owen cold. It belonged to his son, Lyndall. Owen met Greysin's eyes.

The Alti man was carefully expressionless. "I am instructed to leave this matter entirely in your hands, to do with it what you will. That is Ammun's will. The king has concurred."

"Thank you. I will…see to it. Loren can tell you anything you want to know about matters here." Owen waved the younger man away. He sent the housemaid out to tell the grooms that Lord Sakiry required the carriage immediately; the wait gave Owen time to sort himself out a little. He wasn't sure which struck him hardest—the fact that his son was complicit in treason or the fact that he had paid so little attention that this had escaped his notice altogether. *Perhaps he signed the papers without knowing what they were for,* he thought at first, but his sense of honesty wouldn't let him get by with that excuse. *True, he isn't the sharpest blade in the armory, but he does know his business. He would have had to know where those crates were going. He was the last to sign the lading documentation. That means he must have arranged transportation himself. He knew where they were going. He knew what Simon was doing. But why? Why would he do such a thing?* Only one course of action could resolve this question. As soon as the carriage drew up before the house, Owen went out in search of his son.

It had been some time since Owen had last visited the modest, narrow house where his son lived. It had been even longer since Owen had seen Lyndall's son Sandor, but he recognized the boy as soon as the boy opened the door to him. "Afternoon, Sandor. Is your father at home?"

"Yes, Grandfather. He's in his study." The boy stepped aside to let Owen pass. There was no welcome in his voice or bearing. Owen did quick calculations and reckoned that the boy must be eight years old by now. It became urgent that Owen remember the last time he had spent an evening in company with Lyndall and his family. *Last winter,* he realized. *Last winter, when the boy turned eight.* He remembered the occasion as an awkward one, where only Owen, his son and daughter-in-law, and the boy were present. Lyndall's wife Nadia was as dreary as Lyndall, making conversation a chore. The boy showed a sharper wit, but he was moody and had said as little as possible to Owen. It had been an altogether tedious evening. Owen had not returned since then.

Owen went upstairs as directed. He found his son at a desk stacked high with tidy bundles of paperwork. "Lyndall?"

"Father?" Owen's son looked up with an expression of bland surprise. "What brings you around here? Is something amiss?"

Is something amiss? Owen said aloud, "Yes. I have come to ask you some questions. Answer them for me, and perhaps we can straighten things out before you're called before the Council to answer charges of treason."

"Treason?" That bland expression never wavered. "I don't understand. What treason?"

"You cooperated with Simon Miklei-son in arming our enemies so they could attack us. That alone exposes you to severe penalties, Lyndall. Do you not see this?"

"That isn't treason, Father. That was just an exhibition. We had to show everyone the dangers that would come if Nässey wasn't allowed to expand his programs. It didn't hurt at all to show what the third marshal was capable of accomplishing. Uncle Denei was very stubborn and obstinate about him. I don't know why he had to be so unreasonable. He never gave the third marshal a fair chance. We had to show everyone what he could do, and show them the dangers so that Colin would authorize the expansion of the Academy."

"Our soldiers died," Owen retorted. "Killed by weapons *you* shipped to our enemies!"

"Nobody really noteworthy died, you know…well, not until Uncle Denei died, and I was sorry to hear about that, but he really should have known better than to exert himself as if he were as young as he once was. It was only to be expected."

Suddenly, Owen's wrath surged forward. "He was killed by Miklei-son's assassin."

"That isn't possible," Lyndall said slowly. "The foreigner must have done that."

"What foreigner?"

Lyndall looked at him as if he were stupid. "The one contesting Simon for the generalship, of course. What other foreigner would I be talking about but that one? What other foreigner, indeed." He chuckled at the thought.

"That," said Owen between clenched teeth, "that is no foreigner, and he would never have laid a violent hand on Denei, not for any inducement."

"Of course he's a foreigner; he comes from abroad. He's the one causing all the trouble. If Uncle Denei had just listened to Simon, none of this would ever have happened."

Try as he might, Owen could find no way to penetrate the web of perceived logic that Lyndall had woven around himself. At every turn he met the same slow, obstinate refusal to see the truth, so at length he gave up the fight. "Lyndall, I—" *I don't know how I could have fathered such a dim-witted son? I don't know how I could have made any difference? No,* Owen thought abruptly. *The blame will rest on you in the public eye, but I will bear it myself for as long as I live. I failed you. I tried to look after everyone's sons but my own, all because I can't bring myself to like you.* He tried to summon any trace of fatherly affection for his son, but it wasn't in him. "I'm sorry."

"That's all right," Lyndall said in his vague way. "Why?" he added a moment later.

"I didn't try hard enough. For your mother's sake, I'm sorry. She would be disappointed in me." *Sylva would have loved him despite his deficiencies. She would have kept an eye on him. Instead, she left him to my keeping, and a fine guardian of her trust I turned out to be.* Head bowed with these thoughts, Owen left his son's house. As he settled himself in the carriage, he looked back to see young Sandor standing in the open front doorway. The boy stared at him with hostility. *I will not fail him as well. I must find a way...* Then the carriage lurched forward. Owen reluctantly set aside his resolution and returned his attention to the urgency of Maia's situation, trying to figure out what avenue of action they had not yet explored.

SAPLING AND TREE

By the time they reached King's City, Giles was fully prepared to live the rest of his life without the sight, smell, or feel of a horse ever again. Despite this, he wasn't tired. He kept remembering the news Greysin had brought back in the middle of the night: Maia was trapped and in danger. That alone was enough to energize him. He hardly felt like a potential hero when he dismounted in front of his grandfather's house and had to cling to the stirrup or fall to the ground. Then someone grabbed the back of his collar.

"Up you go," rumbled a voice above his head.

Giles found himself being pivoted to face the man all of his companions called Ammun. He craned his neck back. "Uh, thanks." It was like looking at the king, except for the scars and the deadly cold, stern eyes. "Sir," he added tardily.

The general's face eased into a smile. "I knew I would find a use for you some-how." Keeping a supportive hand on Giles' elbow, the great Ammun helped him toward the house where Ivy and the king waited at the door.

"Hello, the house!" Colin called out.

A window opened higher up. Loren stuck his head out, rubbing one eye. "About time," he grumbled—but at the same time, he wore an irrepressible grin. Turning to someone inside the house, he made a remark that those below couldn't hear. Then he returned to the window. "Look out below."

Scarcely a moment later, the front door flew open and Lucien launched him-self from the threshold into his father's arms. Giles was impressed that such a lit-tle boy could jump so far. Ammun held the boy tightly. "Missed you, too," Giles heard him say. Then Ammun hefted Lucien under one arm and carried him to

Ivy, who bent down and kissed Lucien on the nose. The young boy blushed. "I'm glad you're all right, M-Momma Ivy."

They went inside while the men cared for all their horses. Giles saw his great-uncle waiting for them. When Owen saw Giles, he smiled. "It's good to have the whole family together at last." The smile faded from his face as he looked from Giles to the general. "I'm glad you came so soon. We've needed you greatly." Owen looked weary. He came to stand before the twin brothers, studying their faces as if he sought an answer in the differences. "Welcome home." He held out a hand.

By way of response, Ammun clasped the hand in one of his and set his other hand on Owen's shoulder. His words made little sense to Giles, though they had a profound effect on Owen: "He made his own choice. In that, you are not to blame."

"Perhaps you're right."

"He's always right," Ivy retorted with a wry face. "Haven't you noticed yet?"

"That's enough from you, woman."

Smiling again at the exchange between Ammun and his wife, Owen turned to the king. "You're very quiet, Colin. Don't lose heart. Nobody has found Maia yet, but it's only a matter of time. Loren has been directing hourly searches. I don't know what I would have done without him, even if he does annoy Durrant beyond all measure."

"You could search every hour for days and not find her," said Ammun. "Whatever I hide stays hidden."

"But if you hid her, then you can retrieve her, right?"

Ammun shook his head at his brother's question. "No. I have another task before me. Maia is safe where she is. Only three people know the way to her hiding place: me, Ivy, and Giles. That is why Giles will go after her in my stead."

"Me!" Giles blurted.

"I told you I had a use for you."

Gathering the few warriors who were resting in the house, Ammun prepared to depart for Takra House. He kissed Ivy goodbye before he left. They exchanged a long look full of meaning, but not the sort of meaning Giles had anticipated. Ivy nodded as though her husband had said something to her. "Until we meet again." She put an arm around Lucien and hugged him to her side. "And we will."

Ammun seemed more depressed to take leave of his son. He knelt before the boy, hugged him, and kissed his forehead. Then he murmured something barely audible over the boy, a blessing of some sort, Giles thought, judging by the cadence of the syllables. The boy clung to his father, but he didn't complain or cry.

"Are you sure?" Owen said. No one else dared address Ammun, who had a bleak, ruthless manner about him.

"I'm sure."

Colin cleared his throat. "What about me?"

"My battle will be a solitary one. No one can stand beside me. You can do as you choose, but you cannot come with me. It would destroy you."

"What about *you*?"

"Nothing can destroy me."

Giles looked at his great-uncle's worried frown and wasn't reassured, so he declared, "Let's get to this, right? My nerve won't stand this much longer. What do you want *me* to do?"

"By all means, little man, let's get down to what really matters," Damon said dryly as he hefted a pair of bags into the entry hall. "*You*. But be advised, you aren't going to like what's been planned for you. Rope and hooks, Druze. Off with your shirt, little man."

"I thought I told you to quit calling me that."

"Pull this off well and I'll think about it. Come on, *dielhro*, we haven't got all day."

When Giles started to sputter about this new nickname, Ammun said, "That's a compliment well-disguised, Giles. You'd be well off to take it as such. That was what they used to call him when I first took him on as my apprentice."

"What does it mean?"

"Tame dog."

Giles glared at Damon's grinning face. He stripped off his shirt anyway. "Now what?"

"Arms up." With Druze's help, Damon proceeded to wind a coil of rope snugly around Giles' chest. At the end of the rope, he tied a strangely-shaped piece of metal with two bent prongs like curling fingers at either side. Then, grinning, he tucked this cold metal into Giles' waistband. "Comfortable, are we?"

"Just terrific; thanks for inquiring." Giles had to grit his teeth. The rope chafed his skin from his armpits to his waist. "Who am I to be favored with such a lovely hemp shirt?"

"You have to get this rope up to Maia," replied Ammun. "You know the house and you're quick on your feet. Once you get up to her, the window will be your only route of escape. Unless you'd rather jump four stories…? I expected you wouldn't."

The sun was entirely up by the time they arrived at Takra House. It looked like a siege in miniature, complete with a small catapult loaded down with fist-sized rocks and hunks of scrap iron. Giles gazed at it and felt his throat go dry. He was vaguely conscious of the report being given to Ammun by the man in command of the siege, and of Ammun giving new orders. All Giles was able to think about was the idiocy he was about to commit. He had to run across the open courtyard, where all of those windows now hid hostile soldiers, get inside a house held by men who would rather kill him than not, make his way all the way to the top of the house without getting caught, and find Maia. It was this last thought that enabled him to steady himself. *For once in her life, she needs me—me, not somebody else. I have to do this.*

"Knock it down," Ammun commanded. "We end this today. The house doesn't matter."

Giles reminded himself to breathe as he followed Ammun straight to the battered front gates. A team of soldiers heaved a long battering ram up from the ground. The gates were not meant to withstand true force. Within four strokes, they fell with a resounding crash and a cloud of dust. Then Ammun started forward alone. Rousing from his shock, Giles hurried forward, a swarm of soldiers close behind him.

Ammun waded through the fray. Sheltered behind Ammun as he was, Giles felt marginally safer than the other soldiers, who were busily engaging Simon's elite in battle to draw them out from Takra House. Giles noticed a faint illumination surrounding the general. "I do not battle men," the towering warrior bellowed when a few of Simon's allies dared engage him. He batted them aside in wrath, one by one, as they rushed him. A few steps later, Ammun and Giles stood in the entry hall of Takra. Giles looked to his commander for a word or a sign, but Ammun may as well have been alone for all the attention he paid Giles. Shrugging, the young man dashed toward the east wing stairs.

If he had entertained hopes that all the soldiers had been lured outside into battle, Giles was disappointed. One of them saw him as soon as he rounded the banister on his way to the third floor. With a shout, the elite soldier took up the chase. *Can't lead them to her,* Giles thought frantically. He dodged into the portrait gallery and nearly came to catastrophe by running headlong into another of Simon's men. Only by vaulting a chair and swerving so that he nearly fell did he escape being trapped between them, but that was only the start. Soon he had four men after him, pressing his ingenuity to its limits as he beat his brains for a way to lose them long enough to get to the attic trap door. He downed one by breaking a chair across the man's back, but that slowed him down so that another almost snagged him by the shirt. Sweat ran down his body, making the rope feel itchier than ever. Giles was convinced that the rope was beginning to loosen with all the contortions and quasi-acrobatics that he was forced to adopt to keep his person out of their hands. He pushed another of them downstairs; that one didn't come back up again. On his way from the stairs to the other end of the corridor, Giles saw the trap door—it was ajar. He yelped and threw himself to the floor as one of his pursuers lunged for him. Not even pausing to see the man smash headlong into the wall, Giles scampered the length of the hall again with the last man still close behind him. The door leading into the rest of the house was nailed shut and barricaded, so there was no escape that way. Giles dodged into the portrait gallery again. There was another door there that led to a disused children's playroom. On his way through, Giles stooped, grabbed a handful of wooden building blocks and flung them at his pursuer. Then he passed through the nursery and back into the hallway, slamming the door behind him. The key was in the door, so he locked it just as his pursuer barreled into the door from the other side. Glancing about for inspiration, he found a vaguely familiar face hanging upside down from the trap door. Giles didn't hesitate. He grabbed the young guard's hands and let the fellow haul him up into the attic.

Below them, the pursuer's footsteps were muffled. They stopped for an uncomfortably long time and then slowly paced to the top of the stairs. Finding no Giles there, they tapped along swiftly in the other direction to begin a search of the third floor. Giles, panting, leaned back against his rescuer. "Thanks," he whispered. "That was a near thing."

"Good thing you still run like a rabbit."

Giles turned around. "Have we met?"

"Nearly, but you were too fast. The name is Jules, and I'm glad to finally meet you."

All around them, other forms rose up. Giles recognized one of them as Jules' friend, and in another moment the name came back to mind. "That makes you Will, then?"

"That it does."

"Giles!" The princess brushed past her guards. "What are you doing here?"

"Providing you with a way out. I didn't know there was going to be a whole party," he added, counting heads. "Ammun's back."

"Who?"

"The general. King's brother. Your uncle—and mine, come to think of it. Whatever you want to call him, he's back, and he sent me to hunt you up and see if you'd like to get out of here. Beg pardon, ladies." He stripped off his shirt and unwound the rope gratefully. "Itches like nobody's business," he complained, looping the rope in Will's arms. "Now that I've roused the whole household, the only way out is through that window. Are you up for a little climbing, my lady? Follow me." Giles went to the window and pushed it open. Hooking the metal fingers onto the sill, he fed the rope out the window slowly. Then he leaned out to see how near the ground it went. "No time to waste. When you get to the bottom, run for the monument grove. We've got friends there waiting for you." He held onto both of her hands while she backed out the window. Then he held one of her hands as she grasped the rope with her other hand. Finally, he had to let go of her while she slithered down the rope. He held his breath while she dashed across the pleasure garden, jumped the hedge, and sprinted for the door to the monument groves. Once she was safely out of view, he said, "All right—who's next?"

One by one, he saw each of the guards down the rope. Jules was last. "See you later," the young guard laughed. "Let's see if you can catch *me* this time."

Then there was nothing to do but descend the rope, blessing whatever good fortune had smiled upon him. Giles went out the window, and immediately his hands began to slip down the coarse rope. As he paused to adjust his grip, he saw that he staring through a window at the man who had been trying to catch him earlier. He was so startled that he slid the rest of the distance down the rope, burning his palms, but he didn't care about the pain. He was too busy sprinting toward the monument grove. The hedge was too high for him to jump. He nearly tore the wicket gate from its hinges as he wrenched it open. Voices shouted out behind him, bidding him to halt. Giles shouted back, "I certainly will *not!*" Free of the hedge at last, he took off running. Ahead of him, a small squad of warriors emerged from the monument grove to help him.

A powerful explosion shocked them all into stillness. Every window in the western wing of Takra House shattered, pelting them with a stinging shower of broken glass. Then all was silent. Even the battle at the front of the house ceased. A cool breath of air touched Giles' cheek. The sullen skies began to pour down on Takra House and all those who stood staring at its ravaged exterior. In the deluge, Giles saw how every face around him seemed to have tears streaming down it. That seemed to him the most fitting response. He stared at the broken windows of Takra. *Ammun was in there. What became of Ammun?*

*   *   *   *

Although the sun had risen and the windows had no coverings, all was dark within the petitioners' hall when Jarod strode through its doors. Jarod himself gave off just enough light to see the floor two steps ahead. When a voice addressed him from the darkness, he was prepared.

"I hadn't expected to see you so soon," it said. "You must be very shaky: terribly weak and terribly foolish. What stratagem have you devised to convince yourself that you can defeat me now? Even if you were at the pinnacle of your strength, you would still fall short."

Jarod held his tongue. He turned his thought inward to the inmost secret place of his mind. *He speaks truth when it serves him, keiri. He and I both know that I am not strong enough.*

What are you willing to do on behalf of your people?

Whatever I must. My Ivy will wait for me, even if everyone else has died in the interim. I welcome you, my lord, though it obliterates me. Enter into our world through me. Destroy him and wipe all trace of him from this ground.

Everything he had anticipated from such a moment, everything he had feared, was swept clean from him as the transfer took place. Suddenly, he was nothing but an empty skin that someone had washed and filled with strongest spirits. He saw as if he had never seen before. The darkness was no longer darkness to him; the hands he raised were no longer his hands, but a stranger's, scarred heavily with so many old scars that they ought to have been crippled and useless. They grasped and drew his sword with a greater skill than even he, a warrior his whole life, had ever exhibited. The sword that his father the seer had forged years ago gleamed with the overflowing power of those hands. The inscriptions burned with their own fire, but they no longer read *Of the Keeper House Unending.* No...now he read them anew, and they spelled out these words: *Upon this blade shall death die.*

That was not all he saw. Across the room he saw his enemy, encrusted with the manifestation that Laistes, oath breaker and king of rebels, had once taken as his visible form in this lower world. Jarod saw through the evil to the young man who rotted within even as he lived. Sores festered and wept pus freely all over his body, but Simon noticed nothing. The pity Jarod felt went deeper than emotion, permeating him through and through, pity commingled with hatred for the evil he saw now incorporated in the young man's flesh. He spoke with a voice not his own. "Simon. I will give you another chance if you ask it of me."

"You? What could *you* give me that I could not just as easily take from you?" Young Simon was still there, but only just. The essence of Laistes the Unclean had taken hold of him so entirely that the young man now believed that the power he felt was his own. "I will destroy you. Once I have killed you, everything you have will be mine. I will be immortal, knowing all things and ruling all peoples." He approached confidently, certain that the darkness still veiled him. He did not see the blazing symbols on the sword blade.

"I offer you the chance you need. Life is not yet beyond you."

"I need nothing from you!" Face contorted with fury, body riddled with evil, Simon lunged forward to attack.

Emunya waited until there was no possibility of turning back for either of them. Then he swept the Keeper's blade to hew his foe in half. The impact of immortal power upon immortal power in the physical realm generated a blast that shattered every pane of glass in that half of Takra House. Emunya breathed, and the shattered fragments of the Unclean dispersed as before a gale. "Let your rain fall," he said to the sky. "Wash the earth." He shed the bloodied body of his servant Jarod and gathered Jarod's spirit in his arms. "You have earned your rest, little brother. Sleep soundly until you are ready to return to your people."

EPILOGUE

▼

Awake, little brother.

Dark clouds met Jarod's gaze all around. "Why can I see nothing? Why am I blind?"

Walk with me.

Suddenly, a violent gust scuttled the clouds in all directions. Jarod stared hungrily. It felt like years since he had opened his eyes. When he sought the voice that had spoken, he found himself alone. "Where have you gone?" He listened for a response and received none. He saw the gleam of a house in the dusk ahead of him. Its windows emanated light, warmth, and mortal voices that attracted him to the house. The nearer he came, the more familiar it looked. By the time he stood in the doorway, he could put a name to it: *Eleusia*. Its graceful white architecture shone with jewels of river mist; its windows were glazed with intricate frost patterns. He entered.

The very walls seemed to hum with good cheer. Caretaker servants busied themselves with hanging brilliant festoons all around the entry hall. Their shepherd-giants turned to Jarod as he passed; they bowed to him and broke into a spontaneous, jubilant dance. He watched them for a while, smiling at their joy, but something drew him onward, deeper into the house.

Standing at the cross-section of the house's E-shaped layout, Jarod looked straight ahead, left, and right for anything that would prompt him to choose one direction over another. He saw movement outside at the colonnade. The wall yielded before him when he laid a hand on it. He took two steps outside and came to a halt beside a face he knew better than his own. "Colin."

Colin heard nothing. He stood alone in the cold river mist, arms folded across his chest. His eyes stared outward across the starkly beautiful, barren grounds of Eleusia, yet he seemed to see none of the beauty. He alone demonstrated no signs of the general good cheer that the rest enjoyed. He looked so downcast, so solitary, that Jarod reached out a hand to him.

Little brother, Chike's voice warned, *it is not permitted for us to touch mortals.*

Jarod turned to look upon his shepherd-giant for the first time. "You're bigger than I thought you'd be." He studied the long, powerful neck and the round blue eyes. "What are you talking about?"

You live among us now. You are bound by our laws, just as we are.

Glancing back to his brother, Jarod said, "Am I?" He sighed and returned to the interior of the house. "Where's Ivy?"

Upstairs.

He heard her voice before he saw her through the open door of a small office. Then he saw her. Ivy hummed cheerfully as she checked off the lists of provisions for each day of the festival. One hand rested on her rounded abdomen. "Feeling your mama's good humor, are you?" she laughed aloud. "And so you should. This will be a fine party."

"Without me?"

Ivy looked up from her lists. Her mouth rounded in a soundless gasp when she struggled up from her chair and waddled to meet him. "Jarod." She stretched up a hand to touch his face, but drew back in disappointment. "You haven't come back. You've only come to visit."

"I've received no command. I'm just wandering. Don't cry, Ivy."

"It isn't you. I was just…I was so happy, believing you had come home. I'll be fine. As long as I can see you…" She forced herself to smile. "It won't be so hard."

Jarod was taken aback by a new thought. "Why *can* you see me? Even if you've become like me, *I* never saw."

"I can see," she answered simply. "Yes. I didn't tell you because…it doesn't matter."

"This is the first time I've ever been whole, Ivy, so don't say that. It *does* matter."

Little brother, are you genuinely whole?

"Don't interfere in something you cannot understand."

"Wait," Ivy said. "What do you mean, Chike? Why say that?"

No, little sister. If he will not listen to me, then I cannot cross his will. Do not force me into a position of being at odds with you both.

"I'm sorry, Chike." Head reared in defiance, Ivy said, "I think I know what he meant to say anyway, Jarod. This is the first time you've ever been whole? How whole can you be if you're half mortal but you have no body? How whole can you be if you can see your family, but they'll never see you? Do you want to know what I've been thinking over and over again these six months? This baby that's coming may never know his father. Even if I can see you and you can see us, he'll never know you. Lucky has spent every night of the past six months sleeping beside your body, hoping every night that you'll wake up when he does. You were nearer to being whole when you were blinded than you are now!"

Her scalding reproof staggered him. "I want to come home," he said at last, but slowly.

"You'll see again, Jarod; you *will*. We'll find a way."

The words he had heard in the darkness returned: *walk with me*. Jarod heard them again as he regarded his wife. He bowed his head in acquiescence. "Where have you put me?"

"I'll show you. This way."

"What is this festival you're putting together?"

"Oh, that? It's called Ghibôran, the ancient feast of heroes. I've been talking with Uncle Owen, trying to think of anything I could do to help prevent what happened from happening again. I'm no teacher, nor a warrior...as a matter of fact, all I really know how to do is throw nice parties, but Owen showed me that I'm not quite as useless as I first thought. He found records of this festival. It hasn't been celebrated in several generations." As she talked, Ivy grew animated. "We're hosting three days of feasting. It's too cold for outside games, although Loren and his friends seem to think this nothing at all compared to winters in the mountains. I've found nearly forty storytellers. Owen drew up a list of stories for them to tell, all about ancient heroes of the kingdom. It's going to be wonderful. Oh." She gave Jarod a rueful look. "I've spent quite a lot of your money on this."

Jarod laughed aloud. "You cannot spend so much on one party that it would bother me. I have enough."

"Oh, and when you're back, Owen means to step down as patriarch in your favor, since you're Colin's eldest relative of the nearest degree now."

"That is the law," Jarod agreed blandly.

"But you'll see him later. He didn't think it proper to come to the festival while he's still officially in mourning after Lyndall's execution. The clan has nearly doubled, by the way, since they relocated Chamika."

"They did?"

"Damon and I talked about it. The village was in such a difficult place, and now with Malin beheaded and the raiders quarreling amongst themselves, we thought it best that the whole village should settle here. They're on the other side of the River, just opposite Eleusia, as an outpost to guard the crossing. That way, it's still neutral territory, or so Damon says. All of Chamika came, and most of another little village whose name I can't remember just now."

Jarod nodded approval. "A fine idea."

"And Druze wants to marry Mearah, but I'm not sure how I feel about that." Ivy stopped abruptly as a pair of Caretakers paused to stare at her. She smiled to them and passed them by, but when they were out of earshot, she said, "It's a good thing you're coming back. People will think I've lost my mind if I go around talking to empty air."

They came to a room on the third floor of the middle wing. The entire floor was hushed. Ivy entered the room. "Good evening, Damon. Are you coming down for the feast?"

"Not tonight, my lady. However good the tales may be, I'd sooner stay by my own hero."

The words passed Jarod without making much impact on his mind. He stared down at his own body, laid out on its back in bed, tucked in lovingly beneath a colorful quilt. Jarod took a deep breath and saw the body's chest rise accordingly.

"Hey," said Damon, brightening. "That's four times this evening."

"You'd best sit back down." Ivy shut the door against the rest of the house. She gazed eagerly at Jarod, waiting. "I expect this will be startling."

Jarod, still staring at his body, clenched his fists and saw the body do likewise. *How can I be whole?* The words floated to the surface of his mind. He averted his eyes only to seek out Chike one last time, fixing his appearance in memory. *Goodbye.*

When will you learn that we are bound now, little brother? We will never say goodbye.

With another deep, calming breath, Jarod went to the bedside and picked up his inert body, tightening his arms around the body until there was no longer any distinction between them. He opened his eyes to the disorienting sight of the physical world as he had originally known it, as he had not seen it for six whole months. He held out his arms as Ivy circled around the bed to snuggle into his embrace. Then he looked for Damon. "Where has he gone?"

Running footfalls echoed down the hall as Damon's voice drifted back in a wild, exultant ululation fit to summon the entire house, guests and all.

"You'd best change out of your pajamas," Ivy laughed. "I'll hold them off until you're dressed and ready for the festival. You *are* coming to the feast," she said peremptorily. "No hiding away from everyone this time."

"I owe you a dance or two, if I recall."

"If I *can* still dance in my condition."

"We'll find a way." He watched her slip out into the hall. *We'll find a way.* His clothes chest sat against the opposite wall, so he pulled out a suitable outfit and smoothed it flat on the bed to wait for him while he washed quickly at the basin.

Life is good, little brother, Chike whispered.

"Yes…" breathed Jarod. "Yes, it is." The enormity of it all suddenly broke over him like a wave. He had to stop moving altogether and swallow rapidly to prevent the tears from welling up in his eyes. "It most certainly is." Then he laughed at himself. He was, at last, exactly where he had always wanted to be. People were expecting him: old friends, family members—*family*—and he had yet to put on his trousers. Jarod began to hasten in earnest.

✳   ✳   ✳   ✳

So many people wanted to be officially introduced to the king's brother that, when Ivy and Selena came looking for their husbands two hours later, they found both men still occupying the dais in a hall adjoining the banqueting hall. Ivy exclaimed, "Are you insane, Colin? Look at him! Two hours? It's a miracle he's still able to see straight. Come along, come along," she ordered, pulling her husband by the elbow. "You need a bit of food and some music."

Jarod made no effort to hide his relief as he rose from his chair. "I like that plan."

"If you aren't sick of people altogether," Selena ventured, "Maia wanted to see you."

Raising his eyebrows, Jarod only inclined his head in the affirmative toward the queen. He lent Ivy his arm as they proceeded toward the music that flowed out of the banqueting hall, never pausing, although nearly everyone offered greetings as Jarod waded through the mingling crowd. Greysin Alti popped up at his side with a platter balanced on his shoulder. When he said, "This way, my lord, this way. We've reserved a place for you already," Jarod acquiesced readily and found that Greysin had led him to a table of familiar faces. As glad as he was to catch up with his natai again, though, Jarod excused himself from the table before long and sought a more secluded part of the house where he could catch his breath.

The rhythm of the music reached even to the quietest corner of the house, as if it were the house's pulse throbbing peacefully through the corridors. Jarod leaned his head against the wall. Away from the crowded banqueting hall, the air was chilly. The whole house overflowed with delicious aromas. Jarod savored these in solitude for some minutes before he realized that someone else had absconded from the feasting—two people, both young, arguing passionately as they drew nearer. "What is wrong with you two?" Jarod asked, startling them.

They stopped and stared at him. Maia recovered first. "Teacher!"

"Well?" he pressed.

Giles said, "Nothing's wrong, sir; at least, nothing *would* be wrong if she would just stop a minute and consider what I—"

"So I'm to blame?" Maia exclaimed.

"For never letting me finish what I've started to say, yes!"

"Enough." Turning to Maia, Jarod said, "Your mother said you wished to talk with me. I presume this has something to do with it? Then Giles will have to excuse us. The upper portico will offer sufficient privacy, I think." He led Maia to the front of the house, where a pillared gallery ran the entire breadth of the house above the gracious entrance. Every breath hung in the air before them, but Jarod felt little of the cold and Maia never complained of it. "Let me make a guess: the boy has made his intentions clear, but you have doubts."

"That's it, more or less."

"What are your reservations?"

"He says…he wants to marry me," she said with a blush, "but I don't know. That's why I wanted to talk to you. You know about…about the way things were supposed to be, and I thought that maybe…maybe…" Maia exhaled her frustration in a cloud of pale vapor. "I don't know. Before, when it was Simon involved in the question, I knew the answer had to be no. I don't have any *feelings* about this. No dreams, no premonitions. Nothing at all."

"What does your father say?"

"I haven't talked to him very much about Giles. He's been very busy putting everything back on a sound footing. I didn't like to bother him." Maia gazed away into the evening. Her face showed signs of conflict. "Everything I've seen in him makes me think he doesn't mind Giles in that respect, but I haven't talked to him specifically about it."

"Forgetting the idea of things as they are *supposed* to be, what do your feelings tell you? Not the feelings you get from your dreams," Jarod clarified, "but your everyday, ordinary feelings. You are still allowed those, you know. What do they tell you? Do you like him?"

"I don't *dis*like him."

"Princess…"

The remonstrance behind that single word elicited a rueful giggle from Maia. "I do like him. He's interesting. He's different now from what he was, too: more resolved. What bothers me is…well…he doesn't have a trade of any sort, first off, and he hasn't ever seemed to mind. I mean, he *is* different now. It's just hard to know if it's a real change or just temporary. On top of that, I keep thinking about what it was like to be in Father's place. I don't want to go through that alone again. If I do marry, I want to marry someone who's going to help matters. Do you know what I mean?"

"Perfectly." Jarod leaned his forearms on the icicle-adorned railing and gazed down into the courtyard. After a while, he said, "I am not acquainted with Giles as well as I could wish. You were right to note that he *had* no direction for his life. I believe he has found one now. A man can change, and this one has taken his life in hand at such an early age that he has time to make something of himself yet. You are in a position to help him along that road. As for whether or not he would make a suitable consort for you, as I said, he can make anything of himself. Right now, he is willing to make of himself whatever pleases you. Your father and I can help him, if you wish. I can promise you that, whatever may happen, Giles has your interests very much at heart. Even if he is unable to assist you in your duties directly, he will always be at your side to encourage you. He has that in his favor. He risked his life for your sake once already. He will do it again if the need arises."

"Does that mean you think I should marry him?"

Jarod laughed softly. "You cannot entrap me in my words so easily. All I will say is that Giles deserves to stand on an equal footing with other young men. He has earned that right. As for marriage, that decision rests on your shoulders alone."

They returned to the banqueting hall to find the musicians resting, supplanted by the first of Ivy's storytellers. Maia slipped away from Jarod's side. A few minutes later, he saw her turn up again at Giles' side. The two young people sat without touching or looking at each other, but Giles was smiling, whereas he had earlier worn a downcast expression. Jarod sought his wife from the periphery of the crowd, without success. *Chike, where has she gone?*

Upstairs in the balcony, awaiting you where she knows you will be more at ease.

He found her curled up on a sofa in an alcove overlooking the banqueting hall. As soon as Jarod entered, Ivy held out both hands to welcome him. He arranged himself at her back with his arms around her, and together they listened to the stories of heroes of old, content in each other and in the comfort of the present moment.

APPENDIX A

▼

CHARACTERS

[Names of primary characters in each group are in **bold** type.]

In The Royal Family—
Kohanan (*kwahn*-an): Keeper king and natural Seer
Camille: Keeper queen; married to Kohanan; mother of Colin and Jarod
Colin (*kah*-lin): elder twin son of Kohanan and Camille; Kohanan's heir
Selena: Colin's wife and queen
Maia (*my*-ah): Colin's daughter and heir
Jarod: younger twin son of Kohanan and Camille
Audune (aw-*dyoon*): Jarod's immortal shepherd-guardian
Chike (*shee*-kay): Kohanan's immortal shepherd-guardian

Owen: patriarch of the Sakiry clan
Sylva: Owen's wife, chief healer of the kingdom.
Phoebe: Owen's daughter and heir
Doran: husband of Phoebe; Sylva's successor as chief healer; First Marshal of King's City.
Lyndall: Owen's son; a prosperous merchant and Senior Counsel to the Cabinet

Denei (den-*nay*): aging Keeper general
Riana (ree-*an*-ah): Denei's wife, mother of Brigid, Perrin, Ivy, and Nässey

Brigid: Denei's eldest stepdaughter; twice widowed, lives in contemplation beside the River

Perrin: Denei's stepson; works as a typesetter; has three children: Tsarai, Jennin, and Giles

Ivy: Denei's youngest stepdaughter and favorite; keeps house for Denei and Riana.

Ianthe (Ee-anth-uh): Ivy's immortal shepherd-guardian

Nässey (*nah*-see): Denei's son; administrator of schools, Second Marshal of King's City

Giles: son of Perrin; Denei's step-grandson

In Takra House—
Royal Guards (Colin's):
Rowan Solam-son: Owen's brother-in-law; commander of the royal guards; Pamirsi clansman

Hobe Merrick-son: Second Captain of royal guards; Pamirsi clansman

Morio (*mor*-yoh) Jubilee-son: lieutenant of royal guards; Alti clansman

Meir (mare) Hassian-son: junior sergeant of royal guards

Alwen Dellim-son: senior sergeant of royal guards

Iniko Raviv: senior sergeant of royal guards; immigrant sent to the kingdom after he and his kinsmen were spared by Orlan

Royal Guards (Maia's):
Isaac Rowan-son: Owen's nephew by marriage, eldest son of Rowan; captain of royal guards; Pamirsi clansman

Meghala (meg-*ha*-lah) daughter of Tsiada (see-*ah*-dah): lieutenant of royal guards; Caretaker clanswoman

Hollister Yuri-son: lieutenant of royal guards; Nandevi/Caretaker mixed heritage
(For more information, see Appendix B: detailed chart of royal guard corps membership.)

Caretaker Servants:
Lucinda (loo-*sin*-dah): matriarch of the Caretaker clan

Chessy: Caretaker elder; heir to Nana Lucinda

Ardith: wife of Chessy

Kenda: Chessy's granddaughter; sister to Meghala; Maia's best friend and personal maid

Mattieu: son of Chessy and Ardith; uncle to Meghala, Kenda, and Dara

Dara: granddaughter of Chessy and Ardith; sister of Meghala

Liande (lee-*and*) & Rhendi (*ren*-dee): two housemaids; favorites of Lucinda

Berdina: Hollister's mother; head of kitchen staff at Takra House

In King's City—

Tyrell: a merchant in curiosities; an immigrant from the principality of Sulvisin; Owen's friend

Ronán (*row*-nahn) son of Greynán (*gray*-nahn): heir to the Alti patriarchy

Durrant (der-*ant*) son of Dermot (*der*-mt): the Sea Folk clan's candidate for the generalship

Alanah (ah-*lah*-nah): a poor young woman, raised by a former friend of Ivy.

Kyte (kite) Noah-son: best friend of Kohanan; clockmaker by trade; father of Damon

Damon Kyte-son: best friend and legal proxy of he who was once called Orlan.

Orlan (*oar*-lan): said to be the most fearsome warrior alive; once was the right hand of Malin Fohral'aku, prince of raiders; since quitting Malin's company, he repudiated his name and refused to take another; known by his closest followers and friends as "Ammun (*ah*-mun)," which means only "the man."

In Carthae, the Pamirsi sister city to King's City—

Berhus (*bear*-oos) son of Carthus: patriarch of the Pamirsi clan

Russa: wife of Berhus

Mearah: sister of Berhus

Verlane: younger son of Berhus; Colin's best friend; also called simply "Lane."

Simon son of Miklei (*mee*-klay): the Nandevi clan's candidate for the generalship; a teacher in Nässey's Academy with a widespread following among the young warriors

Phelan hé nekhral (fay-*lahn* hay *neck*-rahl): an aged seer from the outlands whom Simon brought back with him; derives his powers from his connection to the Gardens of the Forbidden.

In the mountain village of Chamika (shah-me-kah)—

Rafe (rayf): principal chieftain of Chamika; ex-raider

Farris: chieftain of Chamika, stonemason, ex-raider; teacher of hand-fighting

Bayne: chieftain of Chamika; ex-raider; teacher of swordplay

Lachunn (lah-*choon*): peace-time chieftain of Chamika

Niall (*nee*-ahl): chieftain of Chamika; ex-raider; field healer
Greysin (graissn): junior chieftain of Chamika; younger son of the Alti patriarch, former member of Colin's royal guard corps taken prisoner in battle and rescued by Ammun
Vienna: master healer of Chamika; wife of Niall
Ingram: son of Niall and Vienna; apprentice field healer and warrior
Byram: Owen's brother-in-law; private tutor of Lucien
Lucien: illegitimate son of Ammun
Druze (drooz): resident warrior of Chamika; cousin of the chieftain Farris
Loren: political hostage of Chamika; best friend of Druze

▼

ROYAL GUARD CORPS

Colin's Guards:

Commander:
Rowan Solam-son

First Captain: Noriem "Norrie" Clem-son		Second Captain: Hobe Merrick-son	
Lieutenant: Morio Jubilee-son	Lieutenant: Reyand Liron-son	Lieutenant: Lonya Odall-son	Lieutenant: Bodell Saben-son
Isam Halsin-son	Isam "Sam" Dai-son	Kintaro Kedem-son	Uriel Galt-son
Meir Hassian-son	Barden Mansa-son	Hanno Mekaa-son	Iniko Raviv
Danyel Dane-son	Arald Halsin-son	Darvon Levon-son	Numayr Kivva
Danya Janessa-daugh- ter	Diems Rylan-son	Stavres Niles-son	Osgud Lee-son
Josu Nikodim-son	Alwen Dellim-son	Falko Ivvandar-son	Gael Guryon-son
Hardee Virdune-son	Imra Noura-daugh- ter	Kibo Kibbe-son	Mundy Hobard-son

Owen's Guards:

Captain:
Temora Kalanna-daughter

Lieutenant:
Allayn Carolo-son

Gaillen Kal-son
Narayn Kivva
Wrennar "Wren" Amarde-son
Orwinn Dai-son
Cerel Pauly-son
Joji Hanlon-son

Maia's Guards:

Captain:
Isaac Rowan-son

Lieutenant: Lieutenant:
Hollister Yuri-son   Meghala Tsiada-daughter

Aliya Dinae-daughter   Jules Dai-son
Najhid Gregor-son   Eraste Eraste-son
Ian Marius-son   Olajide "Ola" Egil-son
Mikah Gisell-daughter   Keera Cerise-daughter
Idreis Jodhan-son   Naokko Kedem-son
Sulliaven "Raven" Walker-son   Will Tam-son

RECONFIGURED GUARD CORPS (after the assassination attempt):

Maia's (30) Guards:

Commander:
Isaac Rowan-son (Pamirsi)

Captain:
Kintaro Kedem-son (Alti)

Lieutenant:	Lieutenant:	Lieutenant:	Lieutenant:
Hollister Yuri-son	Meghala Alene-daughter	Morio Jubilee-son	Lonya Odall-son
Numayr Kivva	Iniko Raviv	Hanno Mekaa-son	Isam "Sam" Dai-son
Josu Nikodim-son	Isam Halsin-son	Danya Jan-essa-daughter	Kibo Kibbe-son
Hardee Vir-dune-son	Osgud Lee-son	Danyel Dane-son	Imra Noura-daughter
Aliya Dinae-daughter	*Jules Dai-son*	*Ian Marius-son*	*Najhid Gregor-son*
Idreis Jodhan-son	*Naokko Kedem-son*	*Olajide Egil-son*	*Keera Cerise-daughter*
Raven Walker-son	*Will Tam-son*	*Mikah Gisell-daughter*	*Eraste Eraste-son*

Owen's (17) Guards:

Captain:
Rowan Solam-son

Lieutenant:	Lieutenant:
Noriem "Norrie" Clem-son	Temora Kalanna-daughter
Barden Mansa-son	Allayn Carolo-son
Diems Rylan-son	Hanno Mekaa-son
Stavres Niles-son	Gaillen Kal-son
Narayn Kivva	Falko Ivvandar-son
Orwinn Dai-son	Wrennar "Wren" Amarde-son
Gael Guryon-son	Mundy Hobard-son
Cerel Pauly-son	Joji Hanlon-son

Personal details:

Siblings:

Isam Halsin-son, Arald Halsin-son—brothers

Danyel Dane-son, Danya Janessa-daughter—brother & sister

Kintaro Kedem-son, Naokko Kedem-son—brothers, eldest & youngest

Isam "Sam" Dai-son, Orwinn Dai-son, Jules Dai-son—brothers, cousins of Selena

Numayr Kivva, Narayn Kivva—brothers

Other Relationships:

Rowan Solam-son, Isaac Rowan-son—father & (eldest) son

Numayr Kivva, Narayn Kivva, & Iniko Raviv—cousins

Isam "Sam" Dai-son, Temora Kalanna-daughter—husband & wife

Kintaro Kedem-son, Naokko Kedem-son, & Kibo Kibbe-son—cousins

Other Notable Details:

Numayr Kivva, Narayn Kivva, & Iniko Raviv—immigrant warriors whom Orlan spared from marauding and sent to serve the Keeper royal house

978-0-595-36252-3
0-595-36252-4

Printed in the United States
37108LVS00004B/25-51